I0831849

BEYOND

by Jeremy Shorter

Sale of this book without a front cover may be unauthorized. If you purchase this book without a cover, it may have been reported to the publisher as "unsold or destroyed" and neither the author nor the publisher may have received payment for it.

Beyond is a work of fiction. No similarity between any of the names, characters, persons, and/or institutions in this book with those of any living or dead persons, entities, or institutions is intended, and any such similarities that may exist are entirely coincidental. The entire work is a product of the author's imagination, or is used fictitiously.

Published in the United States by Jeremy Shorter, through Lulu Publishing.

ISBN: 978-0-6151-5327-8

Printed in the United States of America

www.lulu.com
www.jsevoke.com

To my parents, family, and friends who believe in me. This is the fruit of your support, and a work of love. You all mean so much to me, and you know who you are…

Beyond

Table of Contents

Beyond

BEYOND

Written by Jeremy Shorter

Episode 1

The Night Sky Filled with Every Wonder

OPENING:

"...Beyond what we believe, beyond what we fear, beyond what science has taught us, lies fact. Things that were fact one hundred, fifty, and even twenty years ago become fable, and the fables of the past become truth. Who is to say what is true? Whether we believe it or not, truth is there. It is in the pictures. It is in the pages. It is in the moment. But moments fade; one after another; and pictures and pages become memory. Memory becomes lore. Lore is always the story of destruction. Destruction, after all, is what we believe, what we fear, what science eventually, inevitably brings..."

A vessel floats through space. No boosters are firing, but the ship seems to be floating in a forward motion. The blackness of space against the hull of the ship makes it look just as black as the nothingness. A not-too-far-off light glints slightly off the top left of the ship.

Sherise awakens inside the ship and sits up very quickly, and takes a deep breath as she does. She looks out the front of the ship in disbelief, her mouth barely open with eyes darting back and forth at one side of the window to the other, her heart beating hard in her chest.

She hears something to her left and looks over to see a man smiling and fiddling with something in his hands; both of which he seems to be doing almost nervously. He is leaned up against a wall of the cockpit with his legs up and away from him on the bed/table. One person lies between them, and three others on her right.

"Who are you?" he asks.

She pauses, remembering, and says slowly with a furrow in her brow, "Who are you?"

She does not wait long for an answer; "I don't know." He looks more nervous now.

She awaits more, and finally, "Neither do I." She pulls her legs around to the left to dangle off the bed/table she is on. "Do you remember anything?"

Never looking directly at her, he gives a silent laugh and says, "You know, it's funny you should ask that. I remember all kinds of things. It's just that none of the movies playing in my head have anything to do with me, or what brought me to this point in life. I remember what kind of ship this is, though. I can tell you everything about it except what I probably should know. I can sit down at the controls and fly us anywhere we want to go, but I don't know its current payload, or if it's carrying any weapons, or anything like that." He takes a long breath, pauses, and then asks, "How about you?"

She sits and thinks a while. "I can remember all kinds of weapons and defense systems; their inner workings, how they function and why. Just like you, though, I can't remember a cursed thing beyond that." Another pause, as she looks around the empty space behind the cockpit. "Have you tried flying this thing, yet?"

"Nah. Where would we go?"

"You could check for planets, or other vessels, or something…" she says slowly and deliberately as if to hunt for each word.

"I can tell you we're not near any planet."

"How do you know?"

"The sensors are working fine, it seems, and they're right there. We're quite alone here; no vessels within our ship's sensors range. I can see from here that we're seven light-years from the nearest inhabited planet."

She looks over, but the sensor he is speaking of is behind the pilot's chair.

"It says so, on the display…" he manages looking in her general direction, but not into her eyes.

"Have any of the others awakened?"

"Not yet, that I'm aware of… At least, not since I awoke about an hour ago…"

Both say nothing for a short time.

Sherise finally says, "I'm starving. Is there any food around here?"

"I would assume there's some in the mess, but I haven't been up from this spot."

"Maybe you can show me where the mess is. I'm not familiar with this vessel…" she pauses, waiting for him to look up, "…at all!"

"You won't hear me argue. I'm pretty hungry, too."

The two of them get up and walk back through the door toward the middle of the ship. As they walk, Sherise brings up the rear.

The man places his hands in his pockets and suddenly stops. He feels a sheet of paper in his right front pocket and pulls it out, turning to her.

"Um, do you have to stop without so much as a warning," after she almost knocks him down. "What's that?"

"It's a sheet of paper. It reads, 'Mathew.' I guess that's my name."

Sherise reaches down in her front right pocket and feels around. In it she feels her badge; behind it is a slip of paper. She pulls out the sheet of paper. As she does so, Mathew slips his back into his pocket.

Facing him, she mentally reads the sheet: 'Sherise, I know what you were up to. That's why you're on this ship. You won't get away with these peoples' murder. I have seen to it. You cannot control this ship, but one of them can. You'll need them all to get back where you belong, and by that time, I expect you won't be able to kill them since I'll be there to keep you from carrying out your orders. Thanks for volunteering…'

"What is it?"

"Uh, it's my name," she says. "Korsaume." She carefully folds the sheet and places it back in her pocket.

"That's all?"

"Yeah."

They look at each other, and Mathew is about to go through pleasantries when they hear a scream from the cockpit. Both run back to their waking place and find the woman on the right of Korsaume's bed/table sitting up with a look of sheer terror in her eyes, her heart noticeably racing, and her hands gripping the edges of the bed/table so tight her knuckles are white.

"Are you alright?"

"I…don't…think…I've…ever been on one of these…" she says with horror in her eyes. She looks like she is having trouble breathing.

"Do you remember anything?" She doesn't say anything. "Your name…? Anything…?" Mathew stands in front of her trying to look reassuring.

Korsaume stands on the woman's right side. "We both found sheets of paper in our pockets. Maybe you have one as well…"

She acts like she is doing something, but she cannot move her hands. She seems to realize this, looks up at Mathew and quickly averts her eyes to look at Korsaume. "Would you help me?"

"What would you like for me to do? Move your arm, or reach into your pocket?"

"Whichever."

Korsaume pulls the woman's fingers loose from her tight grip on the bed/table.

The woman pulls up her arm to look at her hand, badly shaking. She sits and stares at her shaking hand for a while, and then finally reaches down into her pocket. Nothing. She manages to free her own left hand and uses it to feel around in her left pocket. There, she finds a sheet. Pulling it out and opening it, she reads aloud, “Lacendu.” She takes a big gulp and realizes her throat is dry. “Um, I’m really thirsty. Do either of you have…”

She is interrupted by Mathew who says, “We were just on our way to the mess hall for something to eat. I’m sure that if there’s anything in there to eat, certainly there’s something to drink there as well.”

Mathew and Korsaume help Lacendu off the bed/table.

Lacendu looks around at the other three, asleep and blissfully unawares. “Why did I have to wake up?”

Mathew and Korsaume look at each other, and then help Lacendu along back toward the mess hall.

A short while later the three are seated in chairs around an eating table with food and drink. None of them talk to each other as they fill their mouths like they had not eaten or drunk in years. Lacendu finishes eating rather quickly, then looks at the other two with surprise, runs over to the sink and forces herself to throw up all of it. The other two look at her with some amount of shock. Mathew pushes his food away and holds his stomach as if trying to keep himself from doing the same. Korsaume continues to eat as if nothing happened.

*****

Meanwhile, back in the cockpit, another man wakes up. He instinctively begins checking everything, including his clothes. He finds a sheet of paper in his right pocket with his name; Allen. He then tries to wake up the other male, but is unsuccessful. He walks over to the female and grabs her hand to try and wake her. In a flash, she pulls his arm around, forces him to turn around, grabs his other arm, and holds a small sheet of paper to his neck.

“WHO ARE YOU?” she yells in his ear, startling him.

“I…um…my name is Allen.” He says feeling the sharpness of the paper against his throat.

“Who am I,” she says with clenched teeth.

He pauses. "I don't know. I couldn't remember my own name until I found it on a sheet of paper in my pocket."

"Likely story, my friend... Perhaps, if I wake up this other person here, they'll give me a different story."

"Unlikely, Madam… It looks like there were three others here as well, and they're probably walking about this ship without any knowledge about themselves, either. I," he gives a scared laugh, "think we're all in the same boat, er, memory-wise, that is…"

The woman releases him thrusting him forward against a bed/table. He pauses leaned over the bed/table, relaxes a bit, and turns to face the woman. She has the piece of paper in her hand, open, but is looking through the back door at three faces staring back at her.

"Is everything alright?" asks Mathew.

The woman looks at the piece of paper, reads the name aloud, "Vaskette," and turns her head back to them. "Who are you?"

"I'm Mathew, this is Korsaume," he gestures at Sherise, "and behind her is Lacy."

"I'm Allen, in case anyone wanted to know." He walks around the bed/tables to see the three coming in.

"We heard," Korsaume and Mathew say in unison.

Allen walks over to the other man, but he shows no signs of waking. Allen looks up at Vaskette. "Perhaps you should try to wake him. I don't want to take my chances with him…"

Vaskette beams a mean-hearted smirk at him and says matter-of-factly, "Well, I am a doctor. I guess it couldn't hurt." She steps over to the sleeping man and checks his pulse. In passing, she asks, "What are you, Allen?"

Allen is looking at the man on the table when she asks this and looks up at her with his mouth open to speak, but nothing comes out. He looks around the room at random, closes his mouth and looks at the other three who have gathered around Vaskette to watch.

Allen opens his mouth and shuts it again a few times. At last, he says, "I'm not sure. I might be a game-player. The only thing I can remember right off hand is a game of chess. I don't know if I actually play it, or if I just know how the game works."

"I'm a pilot," says Mathew.

Korsaume glances at Mathew as if taking her queue and says, "I think I'm a weapons' expert."

Lacendu looks at everyone in turn and thinks hard. "I guess I'm a mathematician. I like math problems..." and more to her self than the others, "I wish I had one right now to get my mind off this quack ship."

Vaskette continues checking the man for vital signs. "He seems alright, and since Allen and I woke up just fine, I'm going to assume this man," at this she reaches into the man's right pocket, and finding nothing pulls out a sheet of paper from his left pocket, "Agoparn, and in parentheses it reads 'Parn,'" she pauses again to remember where she was in the sentence, "will wake up soon enough."

"Well," says Korsaume, "there's food down the hall and to your left in the mess hall. You're all welcome to some. Mathew here says we're a good seven light-years from the nearest habitable planet, and..."

At this, Lacendu faints. Everyone glances at her body on the floor of the cockpit, then look back at each other.

Korsaume just looks down at her on the floor and continues, "...and so far there have been no ships on radar since we've been awake," she glances at Mathew for acknowledgement and receives it, "that we're aware of."

"Well," says Allen, "Where are the crew quarters. If we've got sheets of paper in our pockets telling us who we are, maybe we'll be lucky enough to have some belongings in a room somewhere."

"You're very intuitive," says Mathew. "On our way to the mess hall, we saw a crew quarter with my name on it. Yours is probably down-stairs."

"Great," Allen smiles at them all, "Excuse me. I'm famished." He steps over the fainted Lacendu and walks through the cockpit door.

Mathew looks at Vaskette and says, "Perhaps we should get him into his quarters, or an infirmary. Either one will do since he's actually lying on a cartographical and star-chart table."

Vaskette looks at him with a rather sarcastic smile and remarks, "Or perhaps we could just let the man lie until he wakes up, just like the rest of us."

Groggily, the man on the table says, "That won't be necessary. I'll be glad to go to my quarters, if you'll just show me the way." He brushes his eyes with the backs of his hands. "What happened to me? I can't remember a thing."

"Nothing at all?" asks Korsaume.

"Well, I wouldn't say 'nothing at all,'" he says as he pulls himself up and drops his forelegs off the right side of the table. He hops off the table and looks at Mathew. "There's your cart-whatch'a-ma-call-it and star-chart table. I don't remember why I was laying there. I can't imagine choosing to lie there. It's the least comfortable thing I may have ever slept on." Then turning to Vaskette he asks, "Am I going to be alright, doctor?"

"As far as I can tell, we all are, for now. There's food, drink, and a room for each of us on this vessel. As for your memories, it seems you're on an even keel with the rest of us. None of us seem to remember much either, but it's evident in my opinion that someone had plans for us. We each seem to have something important to contribute to an expedition. What that expedition is is anyone's guess. If you think of anything, please feel free to clue the rest of us in on it."

"Will do, Doc." Agoparn smiles. "Did I hear you right in saying my name is Parn?"

"Agoparn seems to be your full name, and I'm assuming that the shortened version, 'Parn,' is your nick-name." She hands the sheet of paper back to him.

He stuffs the sheet in his pocket and looks down at the fainted Lacendu. "Do you need some help with this one?"

"Sure. I think we should take her to the infirmary, if there is one, Mr. Pilot," Vaskette says eyeing Mathew.

"Um, yeah; down to the end of the hall. Take a right, go down the stairs, turn around the corner to the right and it's in the back."

The two pick up the fallen woman by hands and feet and carry her on to where Mathew stated.

As Mathew turns around toward the pilot's chair, Korsaume questions him, "What shall we do next? Since you're the only pilot here and you also seem to be the only one that knows how to understand this ship's read-outs, I'm going to recommend you to the others for captain. I see no reason for this ship not to be a democracy until some of us get our memory back."

"How nice of you," Mathew says without turning back to her.

Instead, he climbs into the chair and begins checking the ship's readings. "Korsaume, do you remember how to read those star-charts?"

"I seem to… Do you want me to check something?" She begins turning on the closest cartography & star-chart tables.

"Yes. Check for a fuel-station. Quadrant 91332, Latitude 964, Longitude 14 is our location. Check a 100-square thruster-burst."

"Checking…" she does some seemingly complicated calculations on one of them. "I've got something. It's a small station. It should be able to give us more information on our whereabouts, and if there's anyone out looking for us. Beyond that, I don't think we can dock. The station is for one-man vessels. It orbits a category-7 planet and services cargo-carriers. We'll be lucky if they offer us a hot meal."

"Understood… That's where we're headed. I need coordinates."

"Heading from stated location, Latitude 38, Longitude 1799, requires a maximum seventy-eight filtered burst for six hours."

"Fuel capacity is at ninety-six percent maximum; we should have no problem reaching our intended objective. Good job, Korsaume. I'll recommend you for Lieutenant." Mathew makes the suggested course adjustments and in a matter of minutes the vessel is speeding toward the station.

*****

All six people sit in the mess about an hour later, giving Lacendu time to recover and rest. She now seems lethargic, thanks to a drug Vaskette injected for space sickness. The other five try not to mention the fact that the ship is moving.

"I would like to make a recommendation for Mathew to be captain of the ship. He is a pilot, and knows a lot about other vessels. I believe he would make the best command decisions in a pinch." Korsaume has a very stoic face. The others are looking at her, except Mathew who continues to play with the object Korsaume saw him with only an hour and a half earlier. Lacendu has her eyes closed, and she is breathing heavy, but she seems quite perceptive.

"I will second that recommendation," comments Vaskette. "I know a sharp man when I see one."

"All in favor…?" Korsaume raises her hand at the question.

Everyone but Mathew raises his or her hands. Lacendu's hand goes up just above the table as she wipes her forehead of some sweat.

"You don't want to be captain?" asks Allen.

"Oh, I just figured it's unfair for me to vote for myself."

"It's unanimous," Allen says. "Mathew is our Captain."

"Does the captain have any recommendations? Say, in case you become disoriented…" Agoparn asks.

"You mean, decapitated?" Allen laughs, then realizes it's not very funny, and sobers up.

Lacendu does not seem to handle that very well, stands up and walks over to the sink, but just stands there.

"Sorry, Lacendu," Allen apologizes.

"I will recommend Korsaume as my second-in-command. She is…" but Mathew is interrupted by Agoparn.

"You don't have to justify your recommendation unless anyone questions your judgment, and between you and me, I don't see anyone questioning anything right now."

"Fine… I will just recommend Korsaume as Lieutenant. All in favor…?"

"I will second the recommendation," says Allen.

Everyone but Korsaume and Lacendu raise their hands.

Allen looks at Lacendu standing at the sink. "Lacy, do you want to vote," he asks.

"Not really. You all just do what's best for the ship. Just get me off the first chance you get."

"Alright; then it's settled. Mathew is our captain, Korsaume is our second-in-command. If anyone wants anything done on this thing, you go to them first. We don't question their command decisions unless we feel they are missing some information or decide they are incapable of making decisions," says Allen.

"Wow, Allen; you make this sound like we chose to be here…like maybe we want this. I personally don't believe any of us intended to be here." Vaskette seems irritated by his short speech.

"I'm not so sure," says Mathew. "I think we chose something. We have clothes in our quarters, which means we've been here for a while. We obviously had some sort of knowledge about the goings-on aboard this thing or we wouldn't have personalized name-plates on the doors of the cabins."

Agoparn interjects, "What do you suppose caused the memory loss?"

Lacendu speaks up, "Is it possible it was some kind of cosmic joke?"

Mathew and Agoparn both laugh lightly at this.

"I think she might be on the right track…" says Korsaume.

"…You remembering something, there, Lieutenant?" asks Mathew.

"No," she says quickly. Then she takes a moment to think, "I was just wondering if the cause of our memory loss was due to some kind of anomaly. You know, like an earthquake, or a volcano. …Something that just floats out in space doing God-knows-what to passers-by."

"I suppose that's a possibility…" Agoparn begins.

He is interrupted by Vaskette. "No. It's not a possibility. Memory loss this precise takes deliberate means... We remember what we are, but not who we are, how we got here, or why we are together on a..." She looks up at Lacendu.

"A vessel..." Korsaume finishes for her.

Lacendu dry-heaves... The others sit for a moment to give her time to recover. She breathes heavily for a moment, then stands up straight and tilts her head back.

"Are you saying someone brain-washed us, Miss?" Agoparn cocks his head to the right.

Vaskette takes a deep breath. "I'm saying someone doesn't want us to remember who we are, or what we're here for. However, they do want us to be together for some ominous purpose."

At this, Lacendu turns around and places her hands on the table to hold her self up.

"Maybe it's not that simple," says Korsaume. "I think maybe we saw something we shouldn't have, and in order to keep us from going back to whatever that place was we were brain-washed to keep us from going back there. Mathew, uh, Captain did say the ship showed a log of being tesseracted across the galaxy..."

"That I did," counts Mathew. He folds his arms, looks down at the table and says, "I wonder if it was an alien race or a verifiable document that says we have no purpose in the cosmos..." At the second recommendation, he laughs.

"Well," Korsaume clears her throat and continues, "whether our existence is a cosmic joke, or an intentional conundrum, one thing is infinitely clear. We all are missing our entire lives, and I believe our first goal should be to find out more about ourselves before we make any other moves."

Mathew says, "Going to this orbital station we are headed for should help us with finding clues to that motive. We'll be arriving in a few hours. I think we should all get some rest."

"Agreed," proclaims Allen.

Everyone goes his or her way.

*****

It is five hours later, and the orbital station around Straite-mogue is in view of the ship. Mathew sits down in the pilot's chair. Agoparn sits down at the engine controls on the left side of the cockpit in the chair closest to the star-chart tables. Korsaume takes the seat in front of the weapons/tactical terminal directly across from Agoparn's.

Mathew punches a button to call the orbital station. "This is Captain Mathew Arnold of the Vortex class Planetary Cruiser, designation 'Vibrant,' serial number 7 – 8 – 1 – 0 – A – 9 – 8 – 1 – 3 – X – 2 – 0 – 7 – 0 – 6. There are six people aboard; all systems functional … requesting permission to dock at lower port for fuel and info. Please respond."

A long moment passes and Mathew slows the ship down to a near stop about twenty kilometers from the orbital base.

Several cargo vessels are docked at the station from the top to the bottom, and one on the left is leaving aft.

Finally an answer comes through. "Captain Mathew, your ship is registered as a Solar Union vessel with full permissions. Please feel free to dock at your leisure. We will send an escort down to greet you and show you around. We hope you enjoy our humble hospitality."

Mathew turns off the communications display with a slight furrow in his brow as he glances back at his lieutenant.

"We're registered as a Solar Union vessel…? What did we do; steal this thing?" she responds.

"Parn, please prepare the docking shell for enclosure," says Mathew.

"Preparing, sir... All systems are ready. I'm showing no signs of problems with the shell. Enclosure should be cleared with no leaks. I will continue to monitor until we are docked."

"Thank you, Parn," is Mathew's rapid reply as he maneuvers the starship to the lowest docking shell.

It is only a matter of minutes before the ship is docked and the entire crew steps off their vessel and onto the orbital station. There is a compliment of two men and one woman, all dressed in formal attire.

"They think we're Solar Union officials…" whispers Korsaume to Mathew.

The others stand looking around. Lacendu still seems troubled, but less anxious than when on board the ship.

"I am Captain Mathew. Your designation," he asks looking directly into the eyes of the man standing in front.

"I am Master Sergeant of this station. The Colonel wishes his best, but was unable to greet you in person as he is dealing with some pressing matters."

"Well, Master Sergeant, this woman is my Lieutenant, Korsaume. The folks behind me are my crew. I don't need to speak with your Colonel. We need fuel, food and supplies. My Engineer, Agoparn, will be handling that. All of us need access to news terminals."

The Master Sergeant seems perplexed at the latter, but turns to the woman behind him on his left and says, "The Corporal will handle your fueling, food, and supplies needs. If you will all follow me, I will show you to the news terminals. My Sergeant will take a full cleaning crew through the ship."

"Thank you, Master Sergeant."

Agoparn heads off with the woman Corporal. Mathew and the crew follow the man to the elevator and board. Several minutes later, they step off onto the promenade where shops line all walls, and people big, small, short, tall, clean, and scruffy walk to their destinations.

The man continues to walk and takes a right. A few meters in this direction, he leads them to computer terminals that line three walls of a large room.

He turns to the crew and says, "Feel free to do what you need. I will have a man standing by in about ten minutes to accommodate your needs."

"You've been very helpful, Master Sergeant," says Mathew with a professional tone. The Master Sergeant smiles comfortably, turns, and walks away.

As soon as he is out of earshot, Korsaume leans in to Mathew and says, "They probably sent our arrival information off to the Solar Union headquarters. From the star-chart data I read, it's not very far away. Tesseracting the data should take about eight hours, and this station will most likely have a response within the day. We will probably want to be far away from here by that time…"

"Understood, Lieutenant…" Mathew turns to the others, "Let's get all the info we need, no more than is necessary, and get out of here. Everyone take a terminal and look for 'wanted' and 'missing' ads."

The five of them head for different terminals, two on one side of the room, three on the other, and intentionally sit in random pods.

Mathew begins typing in as many different words as he can to look for the latest news from the other side of the galaxy. He pulls up several news columns about missing persons over the past several months. He soon realizes he does not have anything to store the information on.

He looks over at Korsaume. "Did you bring some currency?"

She reaches into her pocket. "No currency, but the ship did have a card full of funds. Here…" Korsaume hands the card over to him.

"Do you know how much?"

"About eight-hundred thousand… There should be more than enough there to buy all of us separate ships just like the one we're running. I assume that whatever mission we're on, we're either REALLY good at what we do, or our boss has a BIG job for us."

"Great," he says, taking the card, "Let's just hope that if it's the latter, we figure out what that job is before our boss finds out we don't remember anything…"

Mathew leaves to find a data storage shop.

As he walks through the promenade he looks at all the different shops. Many of them are selling pleasure; some are selling specialized foods and drinks both for the station and for journeys. Still others are selling computers and parts.

He arrives finally at a computer file storage shop and looks up at the name; "Meager's."

Suddenly, he has a flash in his mind that carries through to his eyes. It is rather quick, and by the time he tries to remember what the memory is about, it is gone.

He wobbles a bit from the flash, and puts his hand to his head.

"Are you alright, sir," a voice comes from his right.

He glances over at the speaker and notices a pleasant-looking woman with a "sweet-pistol:" a very long sonic gun, holstered at her side. She is dressed in tight light-red clothes and her blondish hair is wavy and hangs down just over her shoulders. She is resting against a wall.

"I'll be fine, ma'am. I just had a momentary flashback at the name of this establishment; as if I'd been here before…" he quickly justifies, "I mean a very, very long time ago."

"Like, before you were born? You don't look old enough to have 'a very, very long time ago' under your belt."

"You could be right. I'm Mathew."

"I'm Rosetta. I'm a bounty hunter."

"Are you currently hunting bounty?"

"I am…"

"Should I be concerned?"

"Not unless your name is Strager Fortune and you make your career killing young women…"

"Well, then I guess I have nothing to fear, Rosetta." He sounds quite relieved, and she looks at him with some skepticism, but smiles anyway. "I'd love to continue this conversation, but my crew is waiting for me. You have two choices: give me your ship's portal-address, or follow me. Both would be a pleasure."

She stands away from the wall and walks with him toward the store. Smilingly, she says, “I’m certain you’re much too young for me, but there’s just something about you I can’t resist. You don’t seem like a ladies’ man. I like that.”

The two arrive at the counter of Meager’s and Mathew slaps the funds card down. “I need six high-memory chips for your Stat terminals.”

“I HAVE JUST THE THING FOR YOU, MY YOUNG MAN,” says the older, barrel-chested man behind the counter. His voice carries over the promenade, but it seems that the customers are used to his loud happy voice as Mathew looks around the promenade, keeping his hand over the card. “HOW ABOUT THE LATEST MODELS OF TEN ZETABYTES OF MEMORY…? ONLY ONE THOUSAND CURRENCY A PIECE, KIND SIR…”

“He’s only going to pay four-hundred for each of them so you might as well cut your loss now and take the funds,” Rosetta speaks up.

“MY DEAR LADY, FOUR HUNDRED CURRENCY IS A REDICULOUSLY LOW AMOUNT. HOW DO YOU EXPECT ME TO RECOVER MY COST OF DOING BUSINESS? NO LESS THAN NINE HUNDRED!!!

“You’ve got a deal, mister. Nine hundred currency for all six,” smiles Mathew.

The man looks at Mathew with his eyes wide open and prepares to denounce his offer outright. He is not fast enough.

Mathew continues, “I know you don’t pay anywhere near a hundred currency for any one of those cards. You’re doing some mighty big price gouging, and if you don’t want me to turn you in to the Solar Union’s Credit and Business Department, I suggest you take the seven hundred and stay in business.”

The man’s demeanor changes instantly. He speaks much softer, now, “Sir, I do believe you’re a man of the business persuasion. Please, though, I beg of you, please pay twelve-hundred, two-hundred for each of them. If I let you get away with less, I’ll have to do this for everyone.”

"Fine, one-thousand for seven, and if I come back and you're still taking your customers for a ride, I will see to it personally that you never work as a computer file storage salesman ever again." Mathew feels he is in his element and looks at Rosetta as if for approval.

Rosetta looks even more surprised than the man behind the counter, glancing back and forth between her new friend and the salesman.

The man is shocked, takes the funds card, runs it, and then hands Mathew seven 10-Zetabyte cards and the funds card back to him, his spirit completely defeated. However, it does not take the man long to recover and he raises his voice once again to gather more customers.

Mathew and Rosetta walk toward the computer terminals.

Rosetta starts, "You were quite amazing back there, Mathew."

"Thank you. I don't know where any of that came from, but…"

"What do you mean?"

"Oh; um … nothing…"

"You're not telling me something. Either you're scared of me, or you don't trust me."

"Neither, actually… My crew and I have nothing to hide, that we're aware of."

"Are you going to fill me in?"

"Well, perhaps later… Right now we have things we need to do. You're welcome to join us."

"Thank you. I guess I'll just watch you. I don't like those computers. I prefer the old clunking of my onboard systems to these fancy-schmancy super-computers."

Mathew just smiles.

Soon, the two of them walk through the open space of the computer terminals, and Mathew hands out discs to all of them, and keeps two in his hand.

He sits back down at the one he was working on and opens the file he set on temporary memory.

Rosetta stands next to him and looks over his shoulder as he plugs the file storage card in the computer and saves the data to it. When it is done, he does a search for more information regarding missing-persons reports and obscure death records with little information. He finds several good sources including some local planetary newspaper columns and some high-profile system papers.

"Are you looking for someone in-particular? I have some good resources for that kind of stuff, you know?"

"I'm certain you do, Rosetta. I may just ask you for some help at a later date. At this time, I would greatly appreciate your silence regarding what I'm downloading." Mathew looks up at her and smiles.

Their conversation is very quiet, and when Korsaume overhears the last sentence, she looks over at Mathew, and clears her throat. Mathew looks in her direction.

Korsaume glances at the woman standing behind him and asks, "Who's your new friend?"

"Korsaume, this is Rosetta. She's a bounty-hunter. Rosetta, this is my Lieutenant, Korsaume, aboard the 'Vibrant.'"

"Very good," says Rosetta giving her brightest smile and holding out her hand to the Lieutenant.

Korsaume gives Rosetta a cold smile, as if she does not trust the bounty hunter, but tries to sound warm, "A pleasure to meet you, Rosetta. Do you know the Captain?"

"We just met," and as she says this, a person walks up behind Rosetta and taps her on the shoulder. Rosetta puts her hand down and turns around.

"Are you using this one," asks the man.

"Oh, no… I'm just speaking with a friend."

"May I," he adds gesturing with an open hand away from the terminal.

Rosetta looks unpleasantly at the man for the rude interruption and says, "There are many terminals here, sir. Could you not possibly use another?"

"Look, huntress, I have business to conduct and a short amount of time to do it, and you, dear woman, are in the way."

Mathew begins to stand up to make his position against the obnoxious man, but Rosetta presses her hand against his chest with some amount of force, and since Mathew does not have much momentum, is forced to sit back down. "It's alright, Mathew; this man obviously cannot see past his own needs to the desires of others. If he wants this computer, he'll have it." She nods politely and smiles at the man, then moves out of the way behind Mathew's chair.

"It's about raring time," says the man, and sits down in the chair between Mathew and Korsaume. He turns the chair to face Mathew, then looks up at Rosetta, and says, "Do you mind, huntress. This man and I have some things to discuss…quietly."

"Oh, by all means," she shakes her head at the man giving him a condescending glare.

She stomps off toward the opposite side of Korsaume.

"Now," whispers the man, "I understand your name is Mathew Arnold, and you are the captain of the Vortex class Planetary Cruiser 'Vibrant.' Is this correct?"

Mathew looks at the man with no small amount of confusion and says, "Get to the point, please."

"I was told that if you arrived on this orbital base, I was to give you this message." The man hands Mathew a data storage card and softly says, "I'm to tell you that the password to get to the information on this disc is hidden behind your name plate on the door of your cabin. Do you understand what I just told you?"

"Of course… I'm a pilot, not an idiot."

"Hey, I'm just doing what the man told me to. Have a great day, Captain Mathew." The man smiles, stands up, looks back at Rosetta, and says, "I'm sorry for my rudeness. Please take this as small compensation for your putting up with me."

He hands her a small hand-held computer, pulls out a small machine from his coat pocket, and unfolds it. As he does so, Mathew, Korsaume, and Rosetta all watch him. The noise he makes unfolding the machine grabs the attention of the three on the other wall, as well as some other people in the room and a couple people walking by the room.

He presses a button on the long unfolded machine and in a flash, his body dissipates in an energy field of electrical golden-yellow static, and he is gone. The machine falls to the ground and immediately fries its internal wiring.

Rosetta grabs a metal-mesh glove out of a pocket and picks up the hot piece of smoking metal. "It's a one-person tesseract machine. He's anywhere between here and K'l-tarnos right now."

"Wow. I didn't know they made those kinds of tesseracting devices," says Korsaume.

"People do, but their illegal. The destination is nigh impossible to predict without a large computer, or exact knowledge of what's between the machine and the destination. He had to be an Agent."

"An Agent," replies Mathew, "Of what…?"

"An Agent of Nation; a group of people who do the Solar Union's dirty work… I don't like running into them. They're always mean, crude, and they like to feel up women like me." She turns to Mathew, "I've met one before today."

"How can I get one of those," asks Lacendu.

"You can't," is the reply from Rosetta, "they're illegal."

"Oh…yeah, you just said that…" Lacendu says quietly to herself.

"Back to work, folks," says Mathew, "We don't have much time."

While the crew turns back to the terminals, Rosetta looks at the hand-held computer the man gave her, and turns it on. On the monitor, she reads, "Strager Fortune was last seen on Onarus in the Poscertelle system, Quadrant 90778. His current photograph is enclosed. Latest sources tell us that Strager is looking for a woman named Sherise Felder, of which there is no current photograph. Sherise is believed to be a high-ranking official of the Solar Committee, but there is no evidence of this. All women with brown hair and brown eyes are asked to be cautious around this man. Please take a moment to familiarize your self with his photograph, and pay particular attention to his eyes, and the tattoo on his left pectoral. If you see him, please contact the local authorities immediately."

Rosetta turns off the hand-held computer and pulls two cards from it. One contains the data stored on the drive, and the other seems to be a funds card. She walks over to the wall and scans the card. Silently to herself, she reads, "Five thousand currency. No designated requirements. Use at discretion. What is this? No one goes around helping a bounty-hunter!"

She places the cards in her pocket, walks over to Mathew and says, "Pull up a note-screen."

Mathew looks up at her, looks back at the computer, pulls up a note-screen, and looks back up at her.

"My portal-address is 'bounty dot firemark dot seven nine one three one.' Feel free to call me any time. I have to run." She begins walking away.

Mathew finishes typing it in, and turns to her. "Rosetta…"

She turns back around, "Yes?"

"Thank you for your help today, as well as your company. I hope to see you again." He smiles at her.

She returns his smile and with brightened eyes she answers, "You will."

When Mathew turns to Korsaume, she looks over at him and smiles her usual guarded smirk. Turning back to her computer, she half-sings, "Mathew's got a girlfriend…"

"Shut up," he says looking back at the terminal and typing with a pleasant smile on his face. At this, Korsaume brightens up a bit and softly laughs to herself. The moment is short-lived and she puts on a straight face again.

*****

It is three hours later when all the crewmembers are away from the terminals, data storage cards in hand, and they are led back to their ship with the assurance that everything is in order.

The Corporal says while leading them back down the corridor to their ship, “Are you certain I cannot talk you into staying aboard our station to enjoy our humble hospitality?”

“Corporal, you have been extremely pleasant and helpful. We greatly appreciate all you and the crew of this fine station have done for us.” Mathew turns and heads into the ship.

“Corporal, your work here has been exemplary, as has the work of your crew. We will recommend your station for a star when we speak to our supervisors. I’m certain your station could stand another star after its title in the Solar Union’s data banks,” says Korsaume.

“Yes, ma’am,” smiles the Corporal.

“Great working with you, Sir,” says Agoparn to the woman, and holds out his hand. The Corporal takes it and they shake hands. Agoparn is the last to enter the ship.

Agoparn stands erect looking at the beautiful Corporal as he presses the button that closes the shell door. He gives her his nicest smile, and she waits for the door to completely shut before giving her own back.

When Agoparn enters the cockpit, the others are standing around Allen who is at the file storage system, starboard side behind the pilot’s chair. “You know, everyone,” Allen says, “It’s going to take some time to sort through what all of you found.”

No one moves. He adds, “A long time…”

Still no one moves.

“Alright… I just thought I’d warn you.”

Allen begins pulling up information and doing more direct searches for information. While he is working, Vaskette turns to Mathew, “A very cute young woman all dressed in red. Were you thinking of bringing her aboard…” she thinks for a second and adds, “Sir?” with a smile, a nod, and a wink.

The others turn their heads, except for Allen, who continues his work, but noticeably listens intently.

“She’s a bounty hunter…”

"…aaaaand…"

"…And she's cute."

"Very cute," interjects Korsaume.

"Yes, very cute… And she seems to like me. I won't say I don't feel the same."

The others are smiling and/or nodding their heads.

"She's a bounty hunter…"

Allen stops for a second to say, "You just told us that."

"Well, I said it with a purpose. She's got her own ship, and a big job. Some day she may be hunting for me. Or, she might have friends that are hunting for me right now. Heck, that guy that tesseracted out of the room may have been a bounty hunter."

"Doubtful," says Korsaume. "If he was, you'd either be dead or captured right now. Your girlfriend said he was an Agent of something called Nation."

"She's not…" he begins, and then decides to leave it alone, and smiles instead, thinking about the huntress.

"Hmmm…" says Allen.

"Hmmm, what," asks Lacendu sitting in the chair on his right, elbows resting on the counter in front of her, hands covering her face.

"Well, it seems I have three wanted ads with photographs. I'm pulling up the photos right now."

The first photograph is a picture of Lacendu, with her hair up. In the picture, her hair is red. She is wearing a dress with flowers. "Yeah, uh, Lacy, you might want to take a look at this."

Lacendu looks at the picture, and reads aloud, "Lacendu Ruric-Trester, went missing on March eighteenth, twenty-eight seventy-three; uh, how long ago was that?"

Mathew takes the queue, "About six months ago."

She continues, involved now, "Lacendu goes by the nickname 'Cendu' and has blonde hair, green eyes, and is twenty-three years of age. She is a teacher at Segnar's Physics and Calculus College. Her husband, a planetary dignitary, says she has bulimia, though she has never been tested."

Vaskette adds, "Well that explains a lot. At least now I know how to treat you."

Lacendu continues again, "Her husband, Kalchek also states she had never been off her home world, leading officials to believe she may still be on or near the moon Mercedes, or it's planet, Falgone. Kalchek Trester is offering a fifty-eight thousand currency reward for her living return. If you see this woman, please contact your local Solar Union office, or you can reach Kalchek directly at 'official dot trester dot zero zero zero eight one.' Great," she says looking at the others, hopeful, "how do I use the address to contact my husband?"

"Well," says Mathew, "you can use the communications channel as soon as we get in range of your planet. Korsaume can look up your planet in a few minutes on the charts," and this to Korsaume, "if she doesn't mind…"

Korsaume gives him a quick glance. "Uh, sure, Captain, I'd be glad to." She smiles at Lacendu.

Mathew adds, "If I'm correct, though, your home world is on the opposite side of the galaxy, and without a tesseract, it will take us a little over a year to reach communications range on this vessel."

Lacendu doesn't even act like she cares. She seems much happier now that she knows something about herself. She gets up from her chair and heads through the cockpit door toward the cabins.

During this, Allen has been working steadily to pull up additional info.

"Here we go, friends. The next one is…" he trails his voice off as if announcing something great and pauses when the picture comes up. "It's me!"

"Well…?" hangs Vaskette.

The picture shows Allen with blue eyes and black hair, combed straight back, and a military jacket on. He reads aloud, "Allen Pendergras; went missing on March eighteenth, twenty-eight seventy-three. His girlfriend, Laina Ursek began looking for him when she found out that he did not report to his class at the Solar Union Military Academy on Halgar Beta on the nineteenth of March."

"Didn't Lacy's info say she'd been missing since March eighteenth," asks Vaskette.

"Now that you mention it, I think you're right," says Mathew.

"I'm detecting a pattern," says Korsaume half-heartedly.

Allen persists, "Allen is an extremely talented strategist, and is top ranking in his class at the Academy. If you see this man, you are asked to contact blah, blah, blah, blah, blah, or you may contact Laina at 'graduate dot ursek dot three three two four six.' So, I'm a strategist … and let me guess; Halgar Beta is on the opposite side of the galaxy…"

"That's probably a valid guess, Allen," says Korsaume. "I would venture to say that all of us are from the opposite side of the galaxy."

"We'll look up all of that when we all have more info on ourselves. Keep looking, please, Strategist Allen." Mathew places his right hand on the back of Allen's chair and looks intently at the screen.

"Alright." Moments pass. Allen finds a promising file and opens it. It turns out to be nothing. "Well, that's everything on this disc." He pulls the disc out.

"Try this one," says Mathew handing him the one the man gave him.

Allen plugs it in. "It's password-protected."

"Oh, yeah," says Mathew, "wait just a moment, please."

He walks quickly out of the room, and a moment later comes back with his nameplate pulling a sheet of paper off the back of it. He looks all over the sheet, but sees nothing.

Korsaume holds out her hand, "Let me see it, Captain."

He hands it to her. She looks all over it again. "What prompted you to look at this?"

"The man told me it would be behind the nameplate…" Mathew's voice trails off as he turns the nameplate over. "Aha! There it is. Allen, the password is 'traitor.' That's an odd password." At this last part he looks at the others.

Allen types the password in quickly and the computer begins to hum. He looks at the disc, but before he does anything, the files open on their own and a voice file begins, "Hello, one and all. You must be wondering by now who you are and what your purpose is. That, I cannot give you... I am certain that the best purpose you could have right now is to find out more about yourselves. You will find a few of you listed on missing persons data bases the galaxy over. However, you will not find enough from these to remember anything. I am sorry, but the memory of you as a person has been completely erased from all data banks, as well as your minds. I am not the one responsible, but I know who is. It is best that you do not know for now. Traitors are so difficult to spot. You were placed aboard this ship as a means of escape from those who want to use your abilities for darker purposes … a war. You are on the opposite side of the galaxy from your captors to keep you from their reach. The less you know about them, the better off you are. One day, I will join all of you and we will find a way to stop your ex-captors from their evil plots, but you are best served right now by me staying where I am to do what I can to stop these people. I know a lot of this sounds cryptic, but I do not believe that I have much more to give you. Along with my voice on this card, you will also find three missing-persons ads. One is for Mathew, one for Allen, and one for Lacendu.

"I was the one who wrote your names on sheets of paper and placed them in your pockets. I was the one that got you away from your captors. I was the one who had your ship tesseracted across the galaxy. I do not expect you to be appreciative, nor do I expect a reward for keeping you out of harm's way. I do expect to see you again, though you will not know me. When the time is right, I will find you. Godspeed, friends… Your friend, Chrinsole."

"Can we play that file again," asks Mathew.

Allen looks through the folders, "I don't think so. It looks like it permanently erased itself. I don't know how. I didn't think files could permanently erase themselves from data discs, but this one seems to have. Whoever this Chrinsole is, he must be pretty powerful, or have access to some high-tech equipment."

"Great," Mathew says sarcastically. "How about that info on me…?"

"Pulling," states Allen.

It is not long before a picture of Mathew shows up on the screen: black hair, yellow-green eyes, and a pilot's jacket.

Mathew reads, "Mathew Arnold, twenty-eight years old, went missing on," and all of them quote the date, "March eighteenth, twenty-eight seventy-three," and then he continues, "Mathew graduated from piloting school four years ago. He had top honors, and is considered by most to be the best pilot in the known galaxy. He flew many maneuvers in the war two years ago, and was given the Hosker Medal of Honor in twenty-eight seventy-one for his heroism in flight against the enemy.

"His two sisters, Aiya and Zeger are looking for him, believing him to be alive. If you see this man, or have any knowledge of his whereabouts, please contact your local Solar Union authorities, contact Aiya directly at 'sedger dot arnold dot five one one one three,' or Zeger at 'sedger dot arnold dot five one zero eight three.'"

"Well, that seems to be good news for three of us, but what about the rest of us?" asks Korsaume.

"We have a mission, now, Lieutenant; in three parts… One, make our away to the opposite side of the galaxy… Two, find out about ourselves while we're heading back to our homes on the opposite side of the galaxy where everyone who knows and loves us lives… And third and final, live to see Chrinsole and help him stop the ones that tried to use us for some dark and evil plan. Does that sum up everything?" Allen asks.

"I think that's pretty much all of it," replies Vaskette.

"Except that Chrinsole told us not to go back," states Korsaume.

"Yeah, and if he were in our shoes…" Allen replies.

Agoparn walks over to stand behind the pilot's chair, and looks out at the planet.

Mathew joins him. "Are you alright, Parn?"

"Yes, sir… I'm just wondering if there's anyone out there looking for me."

"Chances are high, man. Think about those of us who know there is, though. We know about them looking for us, but we can't go to them. There's no telling when we'll be reunited with our friends, families, and lovers. The best thing we can do is find a way to get our memories back, if possible." Mathew puts his arm around the engineer.

"Good point," says Agoparn.

The other three join them.

Mathew pulls his arm off Agoparn, goes around and sits down in the pilot's chair. "Shall we see if we can hunt for some more clues to who we are?"

No one answers for a moment.

Finally, Korsaume speaks up, "At your leisure, Captain."

Mathew turns on the communications display. "This is Captain Mathew Arnold of the Vortex class Planetary Cruiser, designation 'Vibrant,' serial number 7 – 8 – 1 – 0 – A – 9 – 8 – 1 – 3 – X – 2 – 0 – 7 – 0 – 6; requesting permission to disembark."

Moments pass with no answer. "One moment, Captain," comes the reply. A couple of minutes pass before the next statement. "You are now clear to disembark. You have three minutes to clear the station's buoys."

"Understood. Captain Mathew, out."

The ship's docking shell closes, and the maneuvering thrusters engage. Slowly, the ship turns away and heads toward space, passes a beacon buoy, and forward-thrusters give a small burst pushing it further away from the station.

Soon, the ship is far enough away to push main thrusters, and the "Vibrant" is off.

Episode 2
Zephyr

OPENING:

"…Those things that bring us higher in our minds, and what makes us laugh, or love, we see as good. Is "good" then a placebo? Should we, therefore, rid ourselves of those horrible things that make us cry, or feel pain? If so, then we must take what we prescribe ourselves…"

The "Vibrant" floats through space. The lights are out, and a planet hangs on its right, suspended as if by some mystical force in the blackness.

The planet is mostly orange, with some vertical white and light red wisps.

Inside the ship, the passengers sleep soundly in their quarters, with the exception of one.

"I hate this! I hate this! I hate this! I've got to get off this ship!" Lacendu repeats this over and over to herself as if its harsh syllables will somehow make her wake from a dream.

She becomes disoriented and feels sick to her stomach once again. She leaps up from her bed, opens the door, and runs to the infirmary, barely making it to the sink. She does not hear the sounds coming from Vaskette's room.

Vaskette has heard her crew-mate's pain and pulls on a robe and ties it around her waist. Walking out of her room which opens into the infirmary, she sees Lacendu standing over the sink, wiping her mouth with a sterilized towel.

"It's getting worse, Lacy," she says coming up behind her and patting the young woman on the shoulder.

"Yeah…!" Lacendu breathes heavily as if she'd been running for hours. She places her hands against the sink counter, straightens her arms to hold her self up, and lifts her face up to breathe in deep, her eyes closed.

"One more dose of amabroprepsenol for tonight. Any more in the next twenty-four hours will cause your heart to dry out, and we can't have that."

"I understand."

The doctor walks over to the medical drawer and pulls a vial of the drug from a pile. Before she closes the drawer, her other hand grabs a syringe. Plugging the vial into the empty needle as she walks over to Lacendu, she prepares herself to inject the substance into her blood one more time.

The two walk together to Lacendu's room and Vaskette helps her onto the bed. Lacendu pulls the covers up just over her breast, leaving her arms exposed.

Vaskette injects the drug directly into her internal jugular.

The drug has near-immediate effects, softening Lacendu's heart causing it to beat slower, but more effectively, allowing the oxygen she breathes to flow fluidly through her arteries and veins. Her stomach calms, and within minutes, the sleep she has been mentally fighting off rapidly takes over.

Eye movement slows and her pulse wanes. Her chest stops heaving, and finally she's out.

Vaskette has sat on the edge of the younger woman's bed during all of this, softly stroking her medium-length blonde hair. Vaskette's mind goes back to the picture from the disc given them by the man, Chrinsole. At the time the picture was taken, longer than six months before, Lacendu had short blonde hair, cut in the "bureaucrat's wife" style of the times. Even then, her green eyes told on her. She was losing sleep then, and now the cycle was continuing. Lacendu could not remember who she was, though. She could not even remember her own name a week ago.

Now, on the opposite side of the galaxy, this young teacher had the same symptoms of bulimia as before her memory erasure. Added to the horrors of this mental illness, her unfortunate crew-mate was suffering space sickness as well. There was something else, here, though, and Vaskette believed she'd figured it out. It was there in those soft green eyes of hers.

*****

"Mathew, I'm concerned for Lacy."

"You woke me from a wonderful dream about sexy blonde women on a beach near sunset to tell me you're concerned for Lacy, and four hours early on top of that…"

"Shut up," and then she thinks about the statement and adds, "Sir."

"Come in." His arm stretches out behind him, his palm facing forward after turning on the light to his room.

"Thank you," says Vaskette, walking past her captain and seating herself on the chair near the desk.

"Now, what is it about Lacy that concerns you, Doctor? I mean," he pauses, gesturing as if he admits he has concerns of his own, "besides the fact that she's bulimic and throws up while we're all trying to eat…"

"What I mean, Sir, is I believe she was taking amabroprepsenol before she was kidnapped six months ago. The drug wears off too fast, and that kind of wearing-off doesn't happen over-night. It takes years."

"I don't suppose you're going to get to the point tonight while I still have time to sleep, and hopefully finish my dream. So she was taking amoeba-something-or-other… So what…?"

"Let me finish. It might take a moment." Vaskette breathes out annoyed with having to explain. "There are only two reasons anyone would take amabroprepsenol. One is space sickness. All the stuff does is settle the heart-rate causing the patient to feel more comfortable with his or her surroundings."

"I see. And this means what to our crew-member?" Mathew unfolds his arms that he folded somewhere in her speech and seats himself on the side of his bed.

"Well, let me give you the second reason; but first, the drug is given for space sickness, and only in extreme cases. Passenger vessels carry the stuff for one-time doses. This 'crack' is supposed to last for days. Use anywhere else is illegal."

"OK, so she's been in space a few hundred times."

"No-o-o-o… The message stated she'd never been off her home-planet of Segnar. I believe she's been taking this drug habitually."

"You just said it's illegal."

"That's right. I did."

"So how do you suppose she got her hands on the stuff?"

Vaskette ignores his question and continues, "Without being closer to her home planet, there's no way for me to get records on any of her standard teacher's medical check-up records. Unless someone specifically looks for this drug or does a precise analysis on her blood, they'd never detect it. The drug is often used by addicts for that very reason. People who have one dose often desire another, especially if they tend to feel anxious a lot."

"Is it possible she was having anxiety; stress from her job?"

"Or an over-bearing bureaucratic husband…? I would say that's a good possibility, but again, without more data from her home world, I can't say for certain…"

"Well, then, we've got our work cut out for us."

"Yes. I don't feel I should give her any more doses of that amoeba-stuff…" She smiles at him.

Mathew is too sleepy to notice her joke. "What do you suggest, doctor?"

"She needs help. I recommend a rehabilitation center."

Mathew rubs his eyes. "…And how long will this take…?" He yawns.

"It's not a quick-fix. Drug rehabilitation hasn't made any large strides for over four-hundred years…" Then to her self and rolling her eyes away from him, "…amazing how I can remember stuff like <u>that</u>…" She shakes her head.

"Well, I don't see any reason why we can't leave her at a center and continue our search for clues to who we are… Besides, a medical facility like that should be able to get records on her via tesseraction…"

"That's a good point."

"It's not like we're her best friends. I mean, we hardly know her, and medical staff members are trained to handle this kind of stuff, right?"

"Keep telling yourself things like that," she stands and smiles at him, "and you might start believing it… Captain…"

"I'm always justifying my decisions, aren't I…?" He lays his left hand on the side of his head, reaches his right arm backward and stretches.

"You could say that…"

"I wonder if I did this before I lost my memory…"

"I would say that's a good possibility…"

"Why are you constantly agreeing with me? Can I be wrong once?"

"Parn said if we voted a captain, we don't question his or her judgment. Besides, I'm a doctor, and doctors are trained to have a pleasant bed-side manner."

"Well, you're at my bedside…"

"You're pretty bright for someone so tired."

"It can't be helped. You've got me almost as concerned about Lacy as you are. I may never get back to sleep."

"I can give you something for that."

"That amoeba-stuff…?"

"Actually, I was thinking of something more like a kick to the head."

"If you think it'll work, doctor…"

"Good night, Captain." Vaskette smiles and turns to exit. "Light off?"

"Please."

Mathew lies back as she closes the door, and he sees nothing more for almost four hours.

*****

Agoparn sits at the computer station of the engine room looking over the displays. He is so enthralled in what he's doing that he does not notice Korsaume sneaking into the room.

Silently, her footsteps bring her within a couple feet behind Agoparn and she says, "What are you doing, Parn?"

He almost jumps out of his chair. He spins the chair around to look at her in the face. "I'm sorry, sir. I didn't hear you come in…" He pauses for a moment preparing to turn back around, then stops. "How long have you been standing there?"

"I think I asked you a question, first…"

"Yes sir… I'm going over the readouts to make sure everything is in order. We haven't been docked for over a week. The energy supply is running low."

"I was only standing here for a few seconds before I spoke. We missed you at breakfast this morning…"

"Oh, uh, yeah…too much to be done, not near enough time to do it… Food is a luxury I don't have time for."

"Well, engineer, if you don't eat, you can't keep your strength up," Korsaume says, leaning onto the control board with her arms and turning her face to look at him, "and if you don't keep your strength up, you get sick or die. If you get sick or die, I have to kill you, and then where would we be? This machine doesn't go anywhere without a pilot and an engineer. That's why both of your rooms are on the top floor of this crate. The rest of us are expendable. So, I suggest that you begin making time for food."

Agoparn looks at Korsaume for a moment in disbelief. "Sure. No problem, Lieutenant."

"Excellent. The captain says we're going to a planet not too far from here called Ablose. We believe there's a drug rehabilitation center there, and the doctor believes Lacendu has a drug addiction. We'll fuel up when we get there."

"Understood, sir…"

"I'm glad. I'll head back to the cockpit. Keep us afloat, Engineer." Her last sentence is almost sarcastic.

Agoparn watches the beautiful woman walk away from him.

She's only about five years younger than me, he thinks. Why do I feel like she's my elder?

When she is out of eyesight, he turns around and rereads the displays.

*****

"So, Captain," says Korsaume walking into the cockpit, "How long will it take us to get to Ablose?"

"According to your star chart readings, the fuel gauge, and distance, I'd say about a day at present speed. If our engineer is up to the task, we might be able to go a little faster; a minimum of nineteen hours."

"Let's just hope Lacendu holds out that long. The doctor is scared to give her another dose; afraid it might kill her."

"I know," he says breathing the words out as if he wished he would never say them again.

Korsaume walks up to the pilot's chair and leans in to him. "You seem sincerely concerned for her."

"She's going through many of the same things we are. She has no memory of who she is, what she's doing here, or why. She's suffering anxiety from knowing that somewhere across the expanse of the Milky Way her husband is looking for her right now. Add to that a medical condition and drug addiction and anyone in her shoes would be <u>begging</u> to get off this tin-can."

"I hadn't thought about that. I guess this is why we made you Captain." She pats him on the shoulder, messes up is uncombed hair, and walks away.

Mathew is silent for several moments. He soon hears footsteps behind him. He makes a jabbing assumption. "What is it, Korsaume?" Though he wants to be sarcastic, his voice comes off more lovelorn than anything else.

The voice behind him is not female, but the male voice tries desperately to sound like Korsaume, and fails miserably, "I'm just coming in to see you, dear."

"Sorry. She's been in and out of here so many times in the past two hours I was beginning to suspect there was no one else on the ship than her and myself."

"I thought you liked that bounty-huntress." The voice was Agoparn's.

"If you're thinking I'm starting to fall for the Lieutenant, you're WAY off base, engineer." Though the words sound stiff, Mathew's voice is endearing now. "What did you want, by the way…?"

Agoparn begins, "Is it my imagination, or does Korsaume sound bossy?"

"I think you're right. I think it's in her nature. What brought you to that conclusion, Parn?"

Agoparn's voice becomes a whisper. "The Lieutenant came into the engine room a little while ago and got onto me for not eating breakfast."

"Well, she's obviously concerned."

"I don't know about that, but I do believe she's throwing her weight around; what little she has…"

"Are you falling for her, Agoparn?"

"Hey, now… She's a pretty lady, and she's the closest to my age on this ship; but no. I'm not. I'm trying to tell you that if the Lieutenant becomes too consumed with her position, we should vote on a different Second-In-Command. Now, don't get me wrong. She's a likable woman and she is good at her job, but I'm pretty sure I speak for everyone when I say we don't want any of us to have too much control."

"I agree with you, Parn," Mathew turns his head to the Engineer to look him in his eyes. "Let me know if it happens again and I'll confront her about it. I do appreciate your concern, but I honestly believe it is part of her core personality; something that can't be taken away no matter how much memory they erase from us. She's just acting in the only way she knows how, and eventually she'll come to terms with her predicament and settle in to her place onboard the ship…"

Agoparn stands up. Aloud now, he says, "I'm sure you're right, Captain. I'll let you know if it happens again, sir."

"Thank you, Agoparn. By the way, I think we can get to Ablose in nineteen hours if we push the engines. I wanted to check with you to see if we could do that. Do we have the energy?"

"What's the alternative?"

"Twenty-four hours…"

"I'll see what I can do. You'll have a report on your engines display when I know for sure."

"Wonderful. I look forward to it."

Agoparn turns and walks out.

Mathew sits in the pilot's chair thinking about all the things he said to Agoparn.

He's right, Mathew thinks. There's something going on with Korsaume. I'm betting it's a power-struggle. Maybe I should have voted her for Captain. Maybe that's what she expected me to do when she said she was going to vote me to be Captain. I hope this isn't a power-struggle. I seem to think I dislike those…

He smiles in spite of himself about the same moment a read-out comes up on his engines display.

"Good ol' Parn," he says to himself. "Ablose, here we come…"

*****

A knocking brings Lacendu out of her deep sleep. In her drugged and drowsy, heavy-eyed state she moves, and in her mind she opens her eyes and sees the door opening. It's a man. More than that, it's her husband, Kalcheck Trester; and though she can't remember what he looks like, she imagines him tall with a medium-growth beard, hair a deep dark red like that of a hard fire, and bright, happy mage-blue eyes. A tuxedo ensemble finishes out her vision of her husband, black with a white under-shirt, and a suite tie with 45° angled, sharply multi-colored lines.

He looks down at her in her bed, smiles his gentle smile and seats himself beside her. "I have been looking for you, my love. Now that I have finally found you, we will never be parted again. I am taking you home."

To Lacendu, an eternity drifts by as she stares into his loving eyes.

In reality, another knock at the door brings Lacendu to. Her eyes shoot open, and as they do she regrets it. Her eyes burn from being opened and the orbicularis oculi muscles over her eye sockets punish her by forcing her eyes shut once again. Knowing she cannot open her eyes enough to get to the door, she just says in a voice she feels is more than loud enough to be heard through it, "Come in."

She hears her own voice and knows that the person standing outside the door could not have possibly heard it. "Come in," she says again, a little louder.

The door opens, but Lacendu dares not look up. Her eyes hurt too much.

It's Vaskette's voice. "How's my gorgeous patient, this afternoon?"

Groggily, Lacendu speaks up, "I'm suffering, but I don't feel sick to my stomach right now."

"Well that's a good sign. The drugs are holding up this time. It's probably because I gave you more than the recommended dose."

"How soon is it going to be before I can have another dose?"

"Well, I'd say a couple of days. I've given you so much of that stuff in the past three days that you should probably be dead right now."

"I'm dead anyway."

"Don't say that!"

"No, I mean I'm dead to everyone I ever loved. People I can't even remember. And more specifically, I'm dead tired…" Her voice trails off.

Vaskette laughs gently. "Well, as long as those are the <u>only</u> two 'deads' you are for the next few decades, I'll be alright."

Lacendu just smiles', barely opening her eyes to see Vaskette's warm smile over her, and closes them as fast as she can. "So, what now, Doctor?"

"Well, we're headed to a nice, happy planet called Ablose, where I can help you recover from the bulimia and, if all goes well, I'll help you get over this horrid space sickness as well."

"Is there really such a thing as space sickness?"

"Well, officially it's motion sickness, but there is the added problem of being in an environment with fake gravity. Planetary gravity has its up side."

"I do believe, Doctor, that you're trying to be funny."

"Hey, I am funny," says Vaskette pointing a finger at herself and smiling at her own joke.

"Alright, Doctor. So, what's on Ablose for me?"

"Medical facilities of all kinds…"

"Oh, good… That's all I need. Another infirmary with a million doses of cures for all that ails me…"

"Hey, it'll be good for you, Lacy."

"Yeah, I guess so. I'll look forward to it." Lacendu readies her mind for sleep again, and then realizes she has another question. "About how long will it be until we get there?"

"About fifteen hours. Parn's pushing the engines pretty hard; probably harder than he should. Mathew's piloting us past an asteroid belt between here and the planet. We're hoping to be there before you have another bout."

"You mean, before I throw up again…"

"You're a bright woman, Lacendu Ruric-Trester."

"Yeah, I'm real bright."

"Hey, we're all of us learning about ourselves once again." Vaskette stands at the door looking at the blonde-headed woman lying in the bed. Lacendu makes a move that tells her she's really tired and wants some sleep. The doctor says no more, turns the light off, closes the door and leaves.

Walking down the small hall past the showers, she moves along up the stairs toward the mess hall.

Arriving, she finds Mathew, Korsaume, Agoparn, and Allen seated around the table having lunch.

"How's our 'Sleeping Beauty,' Doctor," asks Allen raising a cup of water at Vaskette.

"Well, she'll be alright for a little while longer," Vaskette begins making a move to sit down at the table, "but I am going to have to say that if we don't get there pretty quick, she's going to go through her usual formula. She's in a bad way, gang." She seats herself beside Allen.

Mathew looks over at Vaskette. "You know I don't think I like your tone, my friend. I'm thinking we should have it out right here, right now."

"What do you suggest, Captain; a food fight?"

"Nah. I was thinking something a little hotter, like poker…"

Vaskette looks over at the captain. "I thought you were piloting us through an asteroid belt…"

"I was, but the belt was fairly small at the point where we crossed through. We were out of it surprisingly fast, and I was hungry."

"…and bored, it seems…" says Korsaume, raising her eyebrows and smiling.

Everyone smiles.

"Fine, sir… Poker it is." Vaskette pulls a box of cards from behind a small storage compartment on her left, opens it and pulls out the deck. As she begins to pass cards out to everyone, she says, "Standard five-card-stud; three's are wild. I'm only doing this because food fights are messy. If there were a better game," at this she looks at everyone's face, "we'd be playing it." She smiles.

"Wow," Mathew looks around at them, "the doctor's really opening up…"

"I originally thought I was an old stick-in-the-mud."

"You were," says Allen.

"ENOUGH!" she says triumphantly as she finishes handing out cards. "Let's play!"

*****

Lacendu lies in her bed sound asleep, dreaming of being back on the station orbiting Straite-mogue, where the crew of the "Vibrant" had been stopped only a week prior. She was seated at the same terminal she had been at when they were there. She continually tried to type words into the computer, but the screen remained blank. Behind her, she heard voices, and when she turned around, there was Mathew, Korsaume, the blonde-haired huntress Rosetta, and the man that had come to visit Mathew. The man held the machine that she remembered tesseracted him away. He looked at her hungrily. "You are Lacendu Ruric-Trester. I know you. I know what you want. You want to be a mathematician for the Solar Union, doing the calculations necessary for building faster ships, stronger weapons, and determining future advances based on the history of humankind. You know much, Lacendu, but there is one thing you don't know. That one thing is what you are searching for. If you can find it, you will be one step ahead." By now, his hands and arms are animated and he seems to be pleading with her, his eyes wide and anxious.

"What if I can't find it? What do I do then?" She is upset by his pleading, and finds herself feeling insecure.

"Then you are doomed, of course." He waves her off, saying it as if it should be obvious to her.

Lacendu looks at the man, shocked at his words.

"What did you expect, Lacendu? Did you expect you could fight what you know to be true? You're missing something; a very important piece to the puzzle. Not your past. Not who you are. Not what you had known. Those things are irrelevant now. You can't fight what you know to be true. You know…"

"Know what…?"

It is too late. The man does not bother to answer her. Instead, he pushes the button on the machine once more, and his body dissipates into nothingness.

She remembers little of this as her eyes open suddenly, her stomach wrenches and she rolls over on her left side and throws blood up all over the floor. Tears well up in her eyes and she cries loud and hard, heaving over and over. When she is finally through, she beats her stomach a few times with her right fist. Then she rolls back onto her back feeling the tears stream down the sides of her face, her pharynx burning from the acid. She swallows twice, but the taste does not go away. She pushes herself up onto her elbows and grabs the cup of water in the wall on her right. She gulps down the entire cup, places it back into the dispenser, and when it is filled up again she swallows the whole of the liquid in a matter of seconds.

She sets the cup back, drops down onto the bed, throws both arms to her side and breathes a heavy sigh of relief. Now her eyes won't shut. She stares at the ceiling breathing hard; that taste still in her mouth.

She thinks about the blood on the floor beside her and desperately dreads looking at it to clean it up. She sets herself for it, gets out of bed and wets a towel; leans down to the floor to get a glimpse of where she needs to clean, looks away quickly, and begins scrubbing the warm metal floor.

*****

"This is Captain Mathew of the Vortex class Planetary Cruiser, designation 'Vibrant,' serial number 7 – 8 – 1 – 0 – A – 9 – 8 – 1 – 3 – X – 2 – 0 – 7 – 0 – 6; six people aboard; all systems functional; requesting permission to dock on planet for fuel, repairs, and medical care. Please respond."

Moments go by, and a response is forthcoming. "Planetary Cruiser 'Vibrant,' you are clear for landing. Longitude 78°, Latitude 43°, more info when you get closer… Ablose Space Flight Council Center, out."

Mathew reads the information provided on his display via satellite from the Council and mentally plans the ship's descent to the coordinates given. The ship continues its slowing movement to the planet's surface.

It is a matter of just over an hour before the "Vibrant" settles against a docking station several hundred meters over the planet's surface.

Vaskette comes onto the cockpit with a smile in her voice. "Captain, I've done some research by way of the onboard data retrieval system. Ablose has two Rehabilitation Centers, and one comes highly recommended by the Council of Solar System Affairs. It's been rated as a nine-star Center, the highest rating for a Rehab within five-hundred light-years."

"I'm going to assume by the happiness in your tone that this is a really good thing…"

"That it is, Captain."

"Excellent."

"I would also like to request that the rest of us take this opportunity to rest and relax on the planet's surface. There are many places for us all to go; get away from the stuffiness of this small craft."

"Agreed, Doctor… Everyone gets off this thing within the hour. Have Korsaume set up the payment for staying docked for three days."

"Understood, Captain… I'll let the Lieutenant know."

"Thank you, Doctor," Mathew says. He presses the intercom button to the engine room. "Agoparn, shut down the engines. We're going to be stopped here for a few days."

"Yes, Captain…" comes the reply.

Korsaume enters moments later. "Captain, I need to speak with you."

Mathew turns his head to Allen who is seated behind him on his left.

"Allen, please leave us for a few minutes."

"Yes sir, Captain," Allen rises from his chair, walks past Korsaume and exits the cockpit.

Korsaume walks haughtily up to the pilot's chair and leans down to speak into his ear. Even though she speaks in a whisper, her words are harsh. "What do you mean 'we're staying on this fragged planet for a few days'? We've got places to go! We need more information!"

"You missed the most important part: we've got a crew-mate that needs our help!" Mathew rises from his chair and turns to face his Lieutenant. "Last I heard I was the Captain of this vessel. If you want to question me, you may do so. You know I don't have a problem with that…so, question away…"

She looks more than a little surprised by the Captain's sudden change in demeanor. She swallows noticeably, and then breathes out. "My apologies, Captain. I guess losing my memory is causing me to lose my mind as well."

"No problem, Lieutenant. We're all feeling the effects of what's been done to us, and being cooped up in a small ship doesn't help matters. While we're here, we will find as much information as we can. There's no telling what we might have at our disposal on a planet where medical technology is everywhere. There might be medical records on each and every one of us and if there is, I want that information."

She thinks a moment. "I couldn't agree with you more, Captain."

"Anything else, Lieutenant…?"

"No sir."

Mathew breathes a breath of relief. He frowns at her. He can feel his hands shaking a little, so he puts his hands behind him and folds his fingers together.

He looks at her eyes and she does not seem to notice. She looks past him at the planet that will be their home for the next few days, opens her mouth and cocks her head. Smiling at the Captain nervously, she says, "It looks like a nice planet. I suppose there are some fun things to do here…?"

"The doctor says there are many things for us to do while we wait to hear what can be done for Lacy."

"Great. I look forward to some time away from this crowded ship."

"Get out there and have some fun. Relax. That's an order, Lieutenant."

"Yes sir." She smiles nicely, as nicely as possible after being put in her place. Turning, she walks away from him, shaking her hips in a sexy way, hoping he'll notice. She does not turn around.

He doesn't notice. He grabs the disc with the address Rosetta gave him while they were on the station, turns toward the inside of the cockpit, and stops for a moment. He breathes in the stale air of a ship that needs a new oxygen tank.

I won't miss this thing for the next few days, he thinks.

It's not long before the ship is empty, and Mathew and Agoparn stand near the closed shell of the ship speaking with the man who will be responsible for replacing parts and cleaning the vessel.

"Also," Mathew adds, "if the oxygen tank needs replaced, please see to it."

"Will do, Captain," says the young man.

Mathew and Agoparn walk away.

Agoparn smiles, "That guy couldn't have been more than nineteen. Why do you suppose he was put in charge of our vessel?"

"He's a likeable enough fellow, sharp and bright. I'll bet he was just the man for the job."

"I guess you're right. I just assumed that they would send someone older, wiser, and more knowledgeable."

"You mean someone like you…?"

"Well, you know…" Agoparn doesn't know what else to say.

The two walk down the corridors and through the checkpoints, down elevators and escalators to the large open commons area. Hundreds of people walk back and forth, some to their ships, and others away from theirs. No shops are to be seen here other than some eateries, and the room is so much larger than the station at Straite-mogue they visited not long ago.

The ceiling is glass, and the sun shines down into the room making the people look like orange humans.

"Quite a nice planet… I'll bet there are thousands of beautiful women looking for a man like me."

"Agoparn…you're a nut."

"Hey, you got yourself a woman. I don't see why I can't."

"She's not mine. At least not yet... And I didn't say you couldn't have a woman."

The two laugh as they join the throng.

*****

The medical vessel carries three crew-members, and two passengers. The passengers are Vaskette and Lacendu.

Lacendu is out right now, lying on a medical bed, being prepared by two of the crew for tests. Vaskette is overseeing the preparations, and handing out the equipment the two nurses need for their job.

"How far away is this facility," she asks arbitrarily.

"Not far," says the female nurse. "We'll be there shortly."

"Oh, good... I'm really excited about being in a hospital," Vaskette smiles. "It's been a while since I've had a chance to see the latest health technologies."

"How long have you been in space," the male nurse asks as he writes something on a chart in his hand.

"Oh goodness; a very long time; at least six months... Perhaps more..."

"That's a long time to be away from civilization. You may need some personal therapy. It's not recommended for doctors to be out of the loop for such a long time. Their skills digress." He says this as he reaches up his right arm; pen in hand; to punch a few buttons on the wall.

"I'll take you up on that offer. I need all the help I can get..."

The two nurses continue their work while the doctor walks over to the bed. She strokes Lacendu's hair.

The female nurse is standing over Lacendu's left arm, poking a needle into her. "You care a great deal for your friend."

"Of course... She's the only patient I've had for a while."

The two nurses continue their work around the doctor.

It is not long before the ship moves downward to the Rehabilitation Center.

*****

"We have a possibly bulimic patient suffering heavily from motion sickness from being onboard a space-faring vessel." The team of medical doctors walks swiftly alongside the rolling bed. One of them is Vaskette who has been verified as a trained physician. The person pushing the bed is the young female nurse from the ship. The one speaking is another doctor walking behind them reading from a chart.

Lacendu Ruric-Trester is rolled into a room and the doctors begin their tests, using information they glean from Vaskette as they go.

Hours pass and Vaskette walks out of the room folding her arms and breathing a silent sigh of relief.

Another doctor whom she has come to know over the course of the tests walks out and pulls his protective mask off. "It's worse than you thought?"

"It is."

"She has bulimia, and a drug addiction that has been going on since she was a little girl."

"Who could have done this to her?"

"Hm. I wish I could answer that. Getting information here from a planet on the opposite side of the galaxy could take months. We don't have data-tesseraction capabilities anywhere within a thousand light-years of here."

"She's addicted to corbyuposterine. That stuff doesn't just kill. It mangles everything inside the body over the course of time. Little girls can't get this stuff."

"I would say her parents or legal guardians gave it to her. They were probably addicted, as well, and in a weak moment in their lives decided to give some to her."

"That drug is one of the most addictive anti-stimulants known and next-to-impossible to get a hold of…"

"We have a supply of it in cold-storage."

"Sure. What Rehabilitation Center doesn't? But I can't just take the stuff and give it to her. It would kill her. She's been without it for far too long, and giving her more of it after so long will kill her even faster. The crew can't afford to lose her."

"She's a vital member of your crew, then…"

"Well, she would be if she could ever wake from her bulimic, drug-induced state long enough to help…"

"What do you know of her?"

"Not much. We pulled some info from a news terminal on the station orbiting around Straite-mogue. It only told us she had a husband looking for her, and that she was a Mathematics teacher on the planet Segnar."

"Segnar," the man repeats and presses the backs of his fingers to his chin. "That's a fairly good distance away. It's the collegiate capital of the galaxy. You have to be pretty smart to get into the colleges there. You must have to be a super-genius to be a teacher!"

"She's got a good mind. I haven't seen her in action, yet, but I get the feeling if we ever do, we'll all be blown away."

"Well, I can't do much for her here. She needs rehabilitation treatment. Corbyoposterine is a tough drug to get free from."

"No kidding."

They look at each other for a moment, and then they turn to go back into the room.

Vaskette walks over to Lacendu who is barely awake and vaguely aware of her surroundings. "How are you holding up?"

Lacendu doesn't seem to notice her question. Her voice is hoarse, "What's the prospect, Doctor?"

Vaskette leans down close to Lacendu's face. "The tests are giving us a lot of detail. We'll be able to find a treatment for you soon. You just rest. You're planet-tethered. No more space travel for a while."

Lacendu smiles really big and grabs the woman-doctor's hand.

Vaskette smiles back. "You're going to be fine," she says, reassuring her friend.

The blonde suddenly seems incoherent and fades back off into sleep.

*****

Korsaume enters the Venotronic terminal and dials the number she remembers by heart. Her credentials got her in and even prioritized her call.

She waits for a moment for the terminal to get the request to the terminal on Baitronoc, a place she is most familiar with…

A Solar Union logo comes on the display, and then a 3-D image appears of the man she needed to speak to.

"Have you completed your mission, Sherise?"

"No sir. Things got a little complicated."

"I didn't pay you to have complications… I paid you to do a job, and I expect you to do it! There are five people that should be dead right now, and you're telling me they're still alive?"

"Yes sir. I believe you have a traitor on your end. He stopped my assassination. Now, he threatens to blow my cover. If Chrinsole has any reason to believe…"

"Did you say 'Chrinsole'?"

"Uhhh…yeah; do you know him?"

"Of course…! He's been a thorn in my side for far too long. Now that I know that he had his hands in this matter, I will dispose of him at once!"

"Be careful. He's a tricky devil. He stopped me, and I never even knew about it until a week later when I awoke on a planetary cruiser with the galaxy's finest in war."

"How much do they remember?"

"Not much, sir. The memory erasure was an evident success. The hardest part is playing along with them. I'm going to need their help to get back. Chrinsole's seen to that, and he's not making it easy for me."

"Look Sherise…"

"Please, call me Korsaume."

"Fine…! Look, Korsaume, the longer those five stay alive, the more danger you're in. If they even catch a hint of what you are up to, you won't make it back here in one piece; perhaps not ever. I've got a lot for you to do here. The galaxy's most proficient weapons expert is over a million light-years away from where she needs to be with few options of me reaching her when I need to. The sooner you dump their dead rotting carcasses and get back here, the better off all of us will be."

"I understand, sir. I will do my job, come hell or high water. You will hear from me in one month."

"Good. Don't be late!"

The image of the man moves as if to press a button on his screen, and the image soon disappears. The Solar Union logo comes back on, and then fades to nothing.

"Great!"

*****

Mathew stands in a waiting line. He sees Korsaume walking out of one of the Venotronic terminals and she seems more than a little upset. He finds himself wondering if she has found someone she likes. She does not notice him but instead walks off almost in a stomping rage. It is evident by the way she carries herself that her call was not a good one.

Only three other people are in front of him, and he waits patiently. Another walks out, and two of the people ahead of him walk into the two empty terminals. The person in front of him, a woman who looks like she has business to attend, glances at her watch several times. She seems nervous. He over-hears her say, "I don't have time for this. I'll miss my flight!"

She walks away, and he is next in line.

A third person leaves one of the Venotronic terminals and he is offered the spot. He smiles and looks down at the disc in his hand. He plugs the disc in and pulls up the note-screen. There, encoded on the disc is the beautiful wavy-blonde haired bounty-huntress' address. He punches it into the computer and moments later, a call is sent through. It takes some time before anything happens. He waits patiently, but nervously.

Finally, after an eternity, he hears the voice he remembers. "Hey there, Mathew," her tone is pleased. "What's going on?"

"I just thought I'd call you. I just arrived on a planet called Ablose."

"I'm familiar with it. What took you there?"

"One of our crew members was sick. She needed medical attention."

"That's the place to get it. You don't have a doctor on board?"

"Actually we do, but she doesn't have the means to determine the correct procedures for cure."

"Ah! I see. Well, it's good to hear from you. I'm currently on my way to a planet called Steg. Have you heard of it?" She can tell by his face he has not. "You haven't been in this sector for very long, have you?"

"I can't hide much from you."

"Where are you and your crew from?"

"You might not believe me."

"Try me." Her voice becomes insistent.

"Well, we're from the other side of the galaxy."

"Really… That makes sense. What did you do? Tesseract?"

"Actually, yes…"

"Well, I'd love very much to talk some more, but I'm hot on the trail of my prey. Next planet you get to, give me a call. I should be able to talk longer then."

"I'll do just that. It was nice to hear your voice again."

"Same. I hate to waste your money on such a short call. I'll make up for it sometime. Say, a dinner at a fine restaurant on a small, out-of-the-way planet where the sunset is the deepest purple and two moons shine brightly…?"

"I take it you have a specific place in mind…"

"Yeah; it's called Farrend, and it has a fantastic steak-eatery."

"I can't wait."

"Neither I. Have fun on Ablose. Take care; and say 'hello' to your crew."

"I'll do that, Rosetta."

"Please! So formal. Call me Seta."

"Alright, Seta. I'll see you soon."

"Wonderful." A smile in her voice concludes the conversation, "Bye…"

The communication ends, and the terminal kicks out his disc. He takes it in his hand and holds it tight against his chest. "Bye."

He steps out from the Venotronic terminal and looks at the long line of people waiting patiently, and impatiently, for their chance. The woman in charge points him away from the terminal and he nods at her walking away.

He walks for a while, knowing where he's going, but dreading going there. He wonders why he should feel that way, but he wants so much to call the beautiful woman again and speak with her for days on end. Someday, he thinks.

Soon, sooner than he preferred, he walks up to the table that contains some of his crew; Korsaume, Allen, and Agoparn.

"…Any word on the Mathematician?"

Allen answers. "…None yet, Captain. Agoparn was just over at the terminal trying to contact the Rehab Center."

"The nurse on the other end said Lacy was still in testing, and Vaskette was heading the work," Agoparn adds.

Mathew looks over at Korsaume. "What about you, Lieutenant?"

"What?" She seems surprised, and looks up at him as if she didn't hear him.

"I saw you come out of the Venotronic terminal. You looked a little angry. Is everything alright?"

"Oh, I was contacting a man about a possible source of data on myself, but it was a dead-end."

"Oh. I'm sorry to hear that," says Allen.

The four of them sit in quiet for a moment.

"Well," starts Mathew, "I guess we could order some food. I want some real sustenance while we've got the opportunity."

"Good idea, Captain," says Korsaume. "I'm starving, and lunch couldn't come quick enough."

*****

Vaskette is asleep, her head on her folded arms which sit on a table. Her body is contorted in a seat like a cock-eyed "S." The last of the other doctors walks out of the testing room and places her hand firmly on Vaskette's tense shoulder.

Vaskette wakes and looks up with half-open eyes at the woman.

"She's fine for now, Doctor."

"Oh, good… I guess I fell asleep." She moves to straighten herself and pull her shirt down around her waist.

"Yes. The other two left about an hour ago." The woman seats herself on Vaskette's left.

"How long have I been like this?"

"About four hours. You've been awake with the patient for quite some time, so we decided to let you get some rest. We were all rested before the two of you came in."

"…very nice of all of you. I needed the nap." Vaskette yawns, placing her right hand over her mouth.

"Don't get up. Lacy needs to be left alone in the dark for some pure sleep. She's been under test-lights all day. We've been poking and prodding for nine hours taking every test we can take. There's not much we can do for her. She needs to want to get better, and she'll have to go through the ritual of rehabilitation just like everyone else in her condition. The first step is getting her to admit she needs help. From there, she'll practically cure herself of the addiction."

"What about the bulimia?"

"We figured out what's causing that…"

"Really? What is it?"

"She's pregnant…" the doctor replies.

"You've got to be kidding! I never even thought to test for that… Did the baby suffer any damage from the stuff I gave Lacy?"

"Thankfully, nothing we can't repair. We are working on a treatment that should help with the healing process for both her and the baby."

"Doesn't sebolaratine keep medications from hurting unborn babies, or shutting down the immunity system?"

"Sometimes, but we were about to try a dose of it on her about an hour ago and realized the condition she's in wouldn't tolerate it."

"Yippee…" Vaskette says sarcastically.

"We also tried some newer, hard-core solutions like ventro-gel and pergifarimine, but neither of those tests was successful. You've got a rare case in this woman." The woman smiles at Vaskette. "Well, it's time for me to get out of here. I don't envy your position. You can't just clock out at the end of your shift. If she still needs your help while on the ship, you're the only one who can help her. You don't have the luxury of stepping out for a breath of fresh air and a hot cup of java."

"Alright; thanks so much for the reminder, Doc."

"I'm just trying to tell you that I empathize with what you're going through. None of the others, or I, would care to be in your situation. If there's anything else we can do, please let us know. We're going to do everything we can for Lacendu, and that's my promise to you; doctor to doctor."

"Your offer, as well as your assistance, is appreciated. I imagine she and I will still be here in the morning. Will I see you then?"

"Absolutely, Doctor Smith."

The two smile at each other, Vaskette just slightly out-of-it.

The other woman doctor walks away, not looking back.

Vaskette rises from the table and walks back into the room where her crew-mate lies breathing easy for the first time in over a week. She steps back out and walks over to the terminal. She dials the station, and a voice on the other end asks, "Name of party…"

"Crew of the 'Vibrant,' please…"

"One moment…"

It takes much longer than a moment. At last, she sees the four other members of her party standing in front of her in the monitor.

"What's up, Doctor?"

"Hey, Captain; it's not necessarily good news. She'll recover, but it's going to take a while. Her system is rejecting just about everything we would normally use to cure her of the addiction. If she hadn't been on corbyuposterine, a highly-addictive anti-stimulant that stays in the system and resists infection-fighting cells, we would have a cure. Years of being on the drug has caused her body to be more sensitive to motion, thus the space sickness. The bulimia seems to be genetic, but we can't prove that until we can get some medical records from Segnar, and they're telling me that could take several months, perhaps a year, to go through the proper channels and to freight the data here."

"You look really tired, Doc," says Allen, smiling at her.

"I am. I just woke from a four-hour nap, but it wasn't near enough. I've been up so much with Lacy I'm not getting the rest I need to think clearly."

"What are you going to do about it, Doctor?" Korsaume gives her standard half-glare.

"Well, Lieutenant, she's out for the night. They've got a room just beyond where Lacy is staying, and they set it up with a cot for me. I'm going to fall asleep in there and they'll wake me in the morning when the doctors come in."

"You do know it's only seven-thirty night planet-time, right?"

"No, I didn't, but since they won't be in until about seven tomorrow morning, that gives me almost twelve hours of decent sleep."

"Well, Vaskette," says Mathew, "Take care of yourself and our resident Mathematician. Keep us updated."

"I'll do that, Captain. All of you have a good time planet-side. There's plenty to do. Don't hang around in a bunch, either." She motions with her hands. "Split up and go somewhere you want to be. Speaking of which, Captain, did you call your girlfriend?"

"I did. She was a little busy, hot on the trail of that Strager fellow."

"You notice he no longer denies that she's his girlfriend…" says Allen, nudging Mathew with his elbow, a crooked smile crossing his face.

Vaskette smiles, as do the others.

"Mathew begins, "I thought she meant a girl," he pauses for effect, "friend. I didn't…"

He's cut off by Vaskette, a wide smile on her face, saying, "There you go again, Captain, trying to justify yourself…"

He slaps his forehead with the open palm of his right hand. "I've got to quit that!"

Everyone laughs, and Korsaume shakes her head at him, looking up at the ceiling.

Vaskette speaks up, "I've got to get. I need my beauty sleep."

"We understand," says Mathew, recovering from the embarrassment. "Have a good night's sleep and make our crew-member better."

"I'm on it, Captain. No need to fear when I'm on duty."

"I know, Vaskette. You're the best physician in the galaxy, right?"

"So I'm hearing, Sir. Good night."

She punches the button that ends the transmission and immediately turns around not bothering to pay attention to the screen as it gives its standard Ablose

Planet Communications emblem and says, "Thank you for utilizing our network. We hope your call was pleasant and that you come to us again for all your communications needs."

The hallway lights are beginning to get to her. She enters the room once more and looks at her patient.

She speaks softly in Lacendu's direction, "Good night, Lacendu. Sweet dreams."

She walks through the dark room, missing everything she could knock over from so many hours of walking around in it. She walks into the small room in the back.

The room is cool, but it is a pleasant change from the heat of the hallway, and the cold of the testing room. She sits down on the cot, removes her shoes and lies back onto the thin mattress, pulling the covers up as she does. She reaches up to turn off the light, and as the darkness encompasses her, her mind stops running and sleep overtakes her.

*****

It is almost nine night planet-time when Korsaume walks into the shop. She is the shortest person in the room full of bounty-hunters, police officers, disreputables, and rough-and-tumbles; and she's the only female.

She pays no attention to them, focusing directly on the man behind the counter. "I need weapons."

He says, "I'm going to need to see some I.D." but he barely gets it out of his mouth before she flashes her badge at him. "You need say no more, miss. What can I get you?"

The others just turn and walk away from the counters. Some leave.

"I need some assassin's rifles. Give me the best ones you've got on the market. Nothing substandard because if they don't work, I use them all on you; every one of them!"

"Hey, you won't get substandard merchandise here. I sell only the best. You got a big job? A presidential candidate…? A political leader perhaps…?"

"I came to you because I heard you had top products. I was also told you don't ask questions. Did the man I heard that from lie to me?"

"Oh, no, miss. I was just trying to make conversation."

"I'm not here to converse. I came to buy weapons."

"Alright – alright – alright… I get the picture." The shop-keeper turns and walks to the back, returning moments later with two rifles.

"Carbon ultra-pitch super-HOP's; full sights, permanent markers, laser-guided techs; I take it you have some sulfide-mono-nitrate and trained bullets…"

"Uh, trained bullets are illegal."

"So I take it you have trained bullets for these things."

By now everyone is looking at the counter. "Hey," he says quietly, "I heard you the first time, but there are police in…"

She doesn't let him finish. She flashes her badge at the nearest officer. "OUT…! ALL OF YOU! NOW…!"

The police usher everyone out.

After they all leave, she continues, "You'll be closing early and remain closed for three days as you get rid of all evidence of my presence here. You wipe this place from top to bottom. I don't even want my smell to linger here. Now, GET ME SOME TRAINED BULLETS!!!"

Episode 3
Write On the Stars

OPENING:

"...Pertaining to those beings which we find attractive, we can only estimate what their lives are truly like. Sometimes, those who show signs of outward beauty show nothing on the inside but black, inky emptiness. Thus, we submit that if there is nothing inside beautiful people, ugly people have everything..."

The cold of the night sweeps over him. He knows better than to be out in this weather, but never the less he walks on carried only by the knowledge that he has a reason for doing this. His mind races as he wonders which way he had taken to get here. His eyes rage with pain for sleep and his body numbs from the wind. The darkened streets all seem the same.

Allen Pendergras was just going to enjoy an hour or two out on the town and then head back to the hotel. Somewhere between a little arcade near the outskirts of town and the station where the ship was parked, he got lost. What's worse, he thinks, is the fact that he is supposedly a strategist. "Some strategist," he mumbles aloud to himself.

The dark night sky shows no stars, and no moon. Of course, that doesn't mean there's no moon. He knows that the reflective circle of rock is probably just hiding behind one of these giant buildings. If only he could find it, he would know which direction to walk. He remembered looking up at it during the day from the floor of the large open room in the center of the station.

A hover-car flies up and stops by him, and he recognizes it as the same one that flew by a few blocks back. The window goes down and inside, a man with a police officer's hat asks him, "Do you need a lift?"

"You have NO idea how long I've been waiting to hear someone ask that."

"Get in."

Allen walks around to the other side of the craft, opens the door, and pulls himself inside.

"Where are you from," asks the police officer.

"Well, that's really hard to describe. My crew and I are visiting your fair planet."

"Ah, you need to get back to the station."

"Actually, we're staying in a hotel around here somewhere. It's just a block or so away from the station."

"Do you remember the name?"

Allen thinks for a moment. The heater blows hot air on his face forcing his eyes shut and he tries to stay awake and focus on the question.

"I believe it was the 'Anchor.'"

"What about the 'Port.'"

"Yeah, that was it."

"Good; I'll take you there, since there's no hotel called 'Anchor.'"

Allen smiles at his mistake and wonders just what his problem is. He knows he can remember things easier than this. Why then, is he having so much trouble?

Minutes pass, and the officer sees that Allen is fighting sleep, so he lets the man be. It isn't long before the hover-car pulls up to the front of the hotel.

"Your stop, Mister…" The officer taps Allen on the shoulder.

Allen awakes. "OH! My apologies, officer, and my appreciation… You're a God-send." He opens the door and begins to get out.

"I'm just glad I could lend a hand. Take care."

"You do the same, sir." Allen closes the door and watches the hover-car fly off down the street. Then, he turns around and walks into the hotel lobby, up the flight of stairs he had been up the same night before, and arrives at his room.

He uses his pass key to get in, closes the door behind him, and walks over to the bed. He can feel sleep rumbling inside him, trying to take over. He pulls off his coat, shirt, shoes, and socks, lies down on the warm bed, and when his head hits the pillow, he falls asleep.

*****

It's almost mid-day planet-time when Allen awakes and realizes his stomach needs food. He gets off the bed and walks over to the small refrigerator. He looks around for something he feels like eating, but nothing seems very good to him. He remembers the evening before, the cuisine the crew, minus Vaskette and Lacendu, ate at the fancy restaurant next door to their hotel.

His stomach growls at this and he knows what he must do. He pulls on some fresh clothes, washes his hands, combs his hair, and goes downstairs to the hotel lobby. The evening before when he was lost in the down-town area for almost an hour flashes across his mind, and he is almost embarrassed by the fact that he could not remember how to get back. Worse yet, he even now cannot remember where he got lost, much less the directions to the arcade.

"Something's wrong," he says to himself, and then looks around at the other people in the area. He walks past the lobby floor and through the enclosed walkway to the restaurant. Then, he thinks of something he feels he needs to do first.

He changes direction and takes a communications terminal that's empty. He dials the portal-address for the hospital where Vaskette and Lacendu are staying. It takes a minute or so to get through, and when the nurse on the other end picks up, he asks, "May I speak with Doctor Vaskette Smith, please?"

"Who may I ask is calling for her?"

"Tell her it's a member of the 'Vibrant' who needs assistance. She'll understand."

"One moment, please."

Soon, the screen changes from the nurse to an empty hallway, and he sees Vaskette exit a door and walk up to the terminal. "What can I do for you, Allen?"

"Hey, I guess I should ask first, how are things going with Lacy?"

"Well, at least you're polite. She's doing well right now, and seems to do just fine as long as she's all drugged up. The problems start when the drugs wear off. This is taking way longer than I was hoping."

"Any prospective treatments…?"

"We've got two promising ones that we found on a medical research site by a doctor who specializes in drug-rehabilitation treatments. He's had three patients with addictions to corbyuposterine, and two of them showed signs of recovery within a matter of weeks. The other one is still undergoing treatment, and he's looking for another source for the cure. He's interested in Lacy's case and wants to try a couple of his ideas on her."

"Wow. You've been busy."

"We have. Now, what is it that I can do for you?"

"Oh, well;" he pauses to think, "I had a problem last night. I am pretty good at figuring out directions and finding my way around places. I didn't have any problems in the crowded areas of either station. Somehow, though, I got lost on the streets downtown. I'm thinking there's something wrong because I thought I was following the route I took there precisely to get back."

"Hm. Why do <u>you</u> think it happened? Were you focused on something else?"

"Well, you see, that's just it. I was focused completely on the directions I had read to get to the arcade. Reversing it should not have been a problem. I'm a strategist. I should be able to understand directions."

"Strategists only need to have a good grasp on the directions of others, not on their own whereabouts. That's how strategists work. They pay more attention to what's around them at the time; not what used to be around them."

"Are you saying there's nothing wrong with me?"

"Not necessarily, but I could do a simple test to see if your short-term memory is malfunctioning. It's a pretty simple test, and I don't even have to be present to do it. I'll send the information to your room. Take it at your leisure and send it back to me. I'll take a look at it."

"Great. Thanks, Doctor."

"No problem. You're part of the crew; lucky you; and for the crew, physicianing is free." Vaskette smiles.

"I do believe you made up that word."

"Doctor's prerogative," she says with a grin. "Have a good time, and keep in touch."

"You've got it."

The screen goes blank and Allen exits the communication terminal. He looks to the right where the food is, and then to the left where the test is. The test can wait.

*****

Korsaume sits on a rock over-looking the city. She came here sometime two nights ago after buying two carbon ultra-pitch super-HOP rifles and a heavy 'second-skin.' She's been awake the entire time. Though the wind blew and the cold froze her face, she rarely noticed. Now, the sun shines down on her, and the 'second-skin' is warm, causing her to sweat. She still does not notice. Nor does she care.

One rifle sits behind her, lying down, barrel facing east. The box of trained bullets sits beside her on her left for easy access. The other one sits on her lap, barrel facing west. She knows this. It's an assassin's job to know what's around her.

The city; a very big city at that; say a metropolis of silver-toned titanium; shines brilliantly in the orange sun of Ablose; so much so that she must squint up her eyes to keep the glare from hurting her retinas.

Her mind has been blank for most of the time. Twice, she thought of falling asleep but decided against it. Now, her mind races as she thinks about her job; the one she was paid to do.

She has no love for Chrinsole; the man who stopped her from killing the five people who are now her crewmates; the man who knocked her out and shoved her onto a small ship with those same people she was hired to kill; the man who sent that ship to the other side of the Milky Way, perhaps to teach her a lesson in love for one's fellow man. Now she knows it: she hates him. He ruined her life. It will take her years to get back to where she belongs if she stays with this crew and doesn't finish her job. It will take only a month or two if she kills them now and heads back to her home via some other means.

An assassin is not supposed to feel empathy for those she's paid to kill. An assassin is trained to kill. Nothing else…

So is it possible, she thinks, that there are circumstances when an assassin cannot do what she was paid to do? If so, is this situation one of those circumstances? She does not have an answer. Everything inside of her screams to help these people. Her head tells her to do what she was paid to do, get it over with, and get over it.

She is so scared that when the bullet goes through their soft skin, their warm purple blood, and their internal organs or that pliable white and grey matter, that she will look down at their bodies and wonder if there wasn't some other way for things to be. If only things were different. Say, if she had not been paid to kill them… Perhaps if they had erased her memory as well, then she could be one of them body, soul, and spirit, and none of this would be happening to her.

She hates to admit it, but she likes them. Mentally, her mind fights the thought. Her heart embraces it. Out of all of them, she is the only one who can remember her life beyond two weeks ago, and she knows that she has not had a moment where her heart told her what to do since she was eighteen. Since she became a weapon's expert for the Solar Union's subdivision, CHE, she has been trained to let her superiors, or money, tell her what to do. As far as she knew, her heart stopped beating when she was nineteen. Now, she feels it beating stronger than ever in her breast.

Blood beats strongly through her veins and for the first time since she can remember she is actually scared to kill someone.

She knows nothing else to do but sit there until she figures this out, regardless of how long it takes.

*****

Vaskette takes another vial of another substance, (perhaps substance five million; she can't remember now), and places it in the hypodermic needle. She pushes the back of the syringe until drops of the substance spill onto Lacendu's blood sample.

She takes the sample with the drops of substance and places them under the intra-violet electro-microscope and pushes a button on the side. She watches as the substance slowly melds with the blood sample. She zooms in on a particular section centering a random section where the green substance meets the red blood cells, white blood cells, and plasma. She blinks her eyes a couple of times, tired of looking through the glass of this machine.

Suddenly, something catches her eye almost out of sight near the bottom of the scope. She moves the scope down to see it just in time. The substance joins with the red blood cells. She watches carefully to see if the white cells attack it. She's seen this before, but she figures she should watch to make sure. One of them took almost two minutes to react.

She waits, motioning for someone to join her. It takes a moment, but two of the doctors come over, and she watches the clock on the black around the vision of the scope. She is thankful that pushing the timer button on the microscope is so automatic.

She waits patiently. The seconds tick by too slowly, but they begin to add up. Four minutes pass. Five… Six… Soon, it has been almost ten minutes, and the white cells have not even touched it. She knows what the red cells should look like, so she begins checking the others where the green substance meets up with the cells. Sure enough, the red blood cells are absorbing the green substance. The white cells don't move. The red cells fill up with the substance, and then move away to allow empty red cells to come to the front.

Twelve minutes pass when Vaskette decides to get up and away from it. She stands up, but the stress from the past two and a half days is just too much. She drops to her knees, and her arms fling out in front of her to keep her from falling on her face. "It's working." She breathes a heavy sigh, closes her eyes, and tears come. She cannot stop them, nor does she desire to. "I have a treatment for my friend…"

As the words come out of her mouth, two of the doctors who have worked so hard with her for so long pull her up from the cold metal floor and help her to her cot in the room just beyond the one they've been working in.

"Easy does it, Doctor," says one of them to her as the two lay her down.

"I can't believe it. Don't tell me I'm dreaming. I don't think I could handle it…"

The two smile at each other. The other one says, "It's not a dream. However, I suggest you get some rest and dream about something nice for a change."

"Sure. No problem."

The two doctors exit the room and one turns off the light as she leaves.

As they leave, another is administering a dose of the green substance into Lacendu's internal jugular, and Lacy doesn't flinch. She's been through so many of them, she hardly notices. She is awake, though, and she opens her eyes. "What's going on? Where's Vaskette?"

"The doctor is asleep in her temporary room. You need to rest as well. We believe we've found something that will help you to overcome your addiction. It's going to take some will-power on your end as well, but the best thing you can do right now is sleep."

"I've done so much of that already. I feel so useless."

"Don't worry about it, Lacendu. You're going to be fine, now."

Lacy rolls her eyes into her eyelids and looks at the half-lit darkness where sleep has found her for so many days, and this time is no exception. She is overtaken in a matter of moments, but before she fades out, she looks at the three doctors still in the room with her. They are watching her reaction, and she desires to give them a nice show, but her body does not respond. The dance number instead plays in her head, and she imagines being a little girl on a stage in front of her parents and family. She does not wonder if her family is her real one. The only important thing is that she performs her best for them. She dances her heart out, and when all is through, she receives no ovation. She gets nothing from her family. Their smiles disappear along with their features and they become faceless. Fear is evoked, and she feels her heart racing. She stares at the chairs full of people without eyes, noses, mouths or ears, and she cries out. Then, nothingness…

*****

Mathew walks through the garden palace, a spectacular mansion where the king and queen used to live, back when there was a king and queen. Ablose' final king was a stalwart man with brazen eyes, a short finely trimmed beard, and a trusting smile; or at least that's the way he's portrayed in the crystalline image of him on the front lawn. His wife was an elegant woman with short fluffy hair and soft penetrating eyes. They stand monumental with one arm each around the other and their other hands out as if welcoming cherished friends. This is the image of Ablose: a welcoming, warm, friendly environment. There is much to be seen here, and surprisingly it's not boring him.

Mathew finds himself wondering if he has ever been on a planet such as this back before his memory was erased. He wonders if there were other beautiful homes such as the one he is now walking through anywhere within a thousand light-years of his home-world.

His mind races as he begins to wonder about the war that had raged on the opposite side of the galaxy; a war he was supposed to have been a part of, decorated for his acts of patriotism aboard some kind of fighter; a war that even now he does not remember…

He realizes he has missed almost half of his walk-through due to this line of thinking and decides to give it a rest until he's back aboard his vessel. For now, he still has almost an entire day to do as he pleases.

Next, he finds himself thinking about Lacendu and Vaskette, the latter working on some kind of addiction cure for the former. How he wishes they could just not have to worry about any of it so they could enjoy their visit in this wonderful world.

Instead, the two of them are stranded in a medical rehabilitation center under fluorescent lights working with tubes of drugs and vials of blood on cold hard floors in sterile sheets, clothes, needles, and any number of other things.

He looks up again and realizes he just missed the other half of his walk.

"Well, this was useless, now, wasn't it…?" A couple nearby overhear him.

"What's useless, sir," asks the man.

"Oh, I didn't recognize that I said that out loud. My apologies…"

"No need to apologize," says the woman. "Do you truly feel this place is useless?"

"No, Madame. I do not. I was thinking how wasted our trip to this planet will be for two of my crew. They sit in a Rehabilitation Center kilometers from here, and I doubt that either of them have left the confines of the facility. I wish they would have time to see this…"

"What's wrong with them," the woman asks.

"Well, there's only something wrong with one of them. The other's a doctor. The doctor needed access to some better medical facilities than we have aboard the Planetary Cruiser."

"Ah, a Planetary Cruiser..." says the man, "I've been on one of those before."

"It's a 'Vortex' class ship. I suppose it's no older than five years."

"Do you transport people?"

"Well, for now that's what we're doing, considering that everyone aboard are my crew and my crew take up all the crew quarters."

"Six people, I take it..."

"Yes sir."

"Well," says the man, "Where are you headed?" The woman smiles at Mathew.

Mathew thinks that something is up, but he is scared to say anything about it. Instead he answers, "We're headed to the opposite side of the galaxy..."

Both stop and look at each other. The man says, "That's a year away on a Planetary Cruiser. I don't suppose you'd be willing to make a stop with a couple passengers, would you?"

Mathew looks a little confused.

The woman adds, "We'd be willing to pay you. We have plenty of funds."

"Oh, it has nothing to do with payment, although I'm sure we would accept it. I guess I just never thought about taking on passengers."

"Well," says the man walking up to Mathew and handing him a card. "Here is a funds card with fifteen-thousand currency. I'll give you the access code to it if you and your fine crew will take us as far as Pikornauc'for."

"I guess I'm not familiar with where that's at, but I absolutely must speak with my crew before I take you on."

"I completely understand. You just hold on to that card and this," the man gives Mathew a sheet of paper with something scribbled in bad handwriting on the in of the folded side. “That’s our temporary portal-address. Contact us when you decide to take us.”

Mathew is surprised at their audacity, but doesn’t show it. “I’ll let you know as soon as I can.”

“Great,” says the woman. “It would mean a great deal to my husband and me.”

Mathew smiles at the two of them and thinks, Great; one more group of people to worry about.

*****

Agoparn stands in a small elevator with a beautiful woman who has agreed to show him around her ship. The woman’s name is Ardelle and she looks thirty, though she’s probably closer to forty, he guesses.

The elevator takes its time, a blessing he feels he does not deserve as he stands against the wall looking at her amazing frame. It is evident that she is aware of his probing eyes, but she seems comfortable with it as she watches the elevator numbers go up the numeric scale, a grin from ear to ear. In this case, however, those numbers are not floors, but meters above the ground.

The elevator finally stops, and Parn doesn’t notice, nor would he have ever if she had not moved toward the door. “Are you going to stand there?”

“No, Ardelle. I was just thinking…”

“About what,” she asks innocently as if she doesn’t know.

His face turns a light red from embarrassment, but she helps him save face by pulling him by his arm into the junction coliseum where her ship is docked.

“Amazing,” is the only thing he can think of to say. He ponders for a moment and adds, “Your ship must be at least seven times the size of our Planetary Cruiser.”

“It’s closer to nine if you’re flying on a ‘Vortex’ class, which you said you’re on.”

"Yeah," he says looking over the edge of the railing at the lower side of the ship.

"It's a tenth generation Star Axis, call letters 'C-72.' She's one of the finest there is."

"I don't doubt that one bit," Parn smiles at her. "How many crew members you got on board?"

"About sixty-three… It'll hold eighty, but we also tend to use the empty space for cargo-runs and food. I think I could empty out a room if you wanted one…" She smiles big at him and winks.

"That's sweet of you, Ardelle. I don't think my crew would get where we're headed if I took you up on the offer, though."

"Speaking of which…"

"Please, don't ask. I don't know if I could explain it even if I completely understood myself."

"Well, I didn't become captain of a vessel like this by not asking questions and my ship is staying docked for at least a week. So, where are you headed?"

"My best guess, I think we're heading home."

She is silent for a moment, but only until she realizes he is not going to say more without some additional probing. "Home is…" she says leading him.

"Somewhere on the other side of the galaxy…"

She seems stunned for a while, and then says, "Then what brought you and your crew here?"

"That's exactly what we're trying to figure out. We believe, based on some info sent us by some guy we've never met, that we saw something or found out something we shouldn't have, so we were to be killed. Someone found out about us and saved us from the people who were going to kill us, but we still don't know much more than that."

"Interesting… So, you're all victims of happenstance. I don't suppose you remember what it was you saw that someone didn't want you to see…?"

"None of us have figured that one out, yet."

"It sounds really complicated, and I must admit, a little difficult to believe. The good thing is that I like you because you seem trustworthy. Anyone who can seem trustworthy to an old space-faring woman like my self must be a pretty good chap. So, since I have no reason to doubt you, I believe you…"

"That's comforting to know, Ardelle."

She takes him by the arm and the two head into the ship. "Oh, come now, we're beyond that, Parn. Call me 'darling.'"

*****

Allen sits at the table in his room, bored with the test, but he continues anyhow feeling he must know more about himself. He has spent the last two hours working on it and as he concludes the questionnaire, he wonders what Vaskette will say.

He walks over to the communications terminal and sets the electronic notepad in the slot. Information is automatically sent back to the Rehabilitation Center. He sits back on the bed and waits.

It's only a matter of minutes before Vaskette answers the call.

"Hey, Allen..." Her face appears on the screen, and she is looking down at the data.

"How does it look, Doctor?"

"Just a moment…" She leaves the screen and he watches as she enters through a door on the right. He looks at the small hallway with fluorescent lights and white walls with red trim.

It is about a minute later when she walks out.

"Good news, Doctor…" he asks.

She doesn't answer him. Instead, she brings her right hand up to her face placing four fingernails between her teeth and holding the tablet in her left.

"You're not giving me much hope here, Vaskette…"

"I'm sorry, Allen. I'm fairly confident noone's ever seen results like this before. I went and asked some of the other doctors for assistance. None of them have ever seen results like this, either."

"That's scary…"

"Not really. I'm wondering if the rest of our crew would have the same or similar results." She looks up at him and removes her hand from her face. She takes a deep breath. "I'm going to have all of us take one of these. If these results are what I think they are, I believe the memory erasure may have affected our short-term memory. I'll need to run a few tests on myself first. I'll get back with you. Thank you, Allen."

She turns off the monitor, and Allen lies back down.

"Wonderful! I hope I didn't start something…"

*****

Korsaume sets off from her spot with a new outlook. She has both rifles in her arms and the box of bullets attached to her ammunitions belt.

She walks down the hill that she had been flown up by a hover-car. She is practiced at this kind of thing. She's been in situations where she had to climb down the face of a steep cliff after being awake for nearly fifty hours and no food. Yes, she was younger. Yes, she was in better shape. She doesn't care. She has a mission now, and she needs to complete it quickly before she changes her mind.

She arrives at the bottom of the hill in minutes and begins her walk back to the city. It's slow going at first, but the high-rises of titanium silver gleaming orange in the light filtering through the feathered clouds brings a beauty unique to this planet, and she enjoys every step as much as anyone can who has decided that five people must die.

*****

Lacendu awakens in a motorized chair in a hallway. She has no idea if she's anywhere near her room, but things are constantly changing around her and she soon realizes someone is behind her pushing the chair. Her body is too weak for her to turn her head to see who, and her throat is so dry she dares not speak.

Instead she watches as the tiles on the floor pass her by too fast for her to determine the multi-colored dot patterns on them, but in the back of her mind her subconscious has already determined the pattern in its succinct multifaceted design, though it does not bother to share the complicated data with her consciousness.

She feels half asleep, but her eyes seem held open by some invisible force, and she is certain it is all due to the fact that she has had nothing but sleep and intravenous sustenance for far too many days.

Her mind wanders off to the ship, and she suddenly finds herself believing that the past two weeks have all been a dream. She has been here for months, now and she realizes that nothing is truly what it seems. Now, it all makes since to her. She fumbles for more information like what brought her here, and why. No answers arrive, and she becomes aware of the fact that the ship, the crew, the memory-loss, the arrival on this planet for treatment is all real. She is addicted to some drug she can't remember, and she is on the opposite side of the galaxy; or at least, that's what she's being told…

"Are you awake, Lacendu?" The voice is Vaskette's, and it speaks so gently that Lacy first believes she made it up herself. The tiles on the floor tell her differently.

"My throat," she manages.

Vaskette hands a bottle of cold water to her. Amazingly, her left arm reaches over to her right side and grasps the bottle with little effort. She sips the water and feels its icy tastelessness stop on her dry, spongy tongue. She takes more and as the liquid fills her mouth refreshing her cheeks and freezing her teeth she swallows. The damp fluid travels down her esophagus shooting an indeterminate chill through her body, and she craves more. After two solid weeks of nothing but water on board the ship, she honestly believed two hydrogen atoms combined with one oxygen atom could ever taste so wonderful.

"How do you feel," asks Vaskette.

She does not answer right away. She takes a few more gulps of the liquid and smiles to herself. "Much better…"

"I'm glad. We worked really hard on you."

"How long have we been on this planet?"

"About three days."

Lacy starts. "I thought we were supposed to leave on the third day…"

"We were, but your health is more important to my self and the crew to just leave without finding a cure."

"I take it you did…?"

"We found something that will help. Much of it's going to depend on you…"

"Well, with friends like the five of you, I don't think that will be too much of a problem." Lacy smiles again as the two pass around a corner. Lacy looks down the long corridor with its bright fluorescent lights and lavender walls and says, "So, when can we leave?"

"As soon as possible… Mathew wants to get to our new destination by the end of next week."

"So you've spoken with him…"

"Yes. Just this morning before the other doctors and my self picked you up out of your bed and sat you in this thing. By the way, I thought I'd let you know … you're pregnant."

"I'm what…?" She tries to look around at Vaskette, but her body is too sore. "How long?"

"About a month and a half. There's a slim chance I can pinpoint the date, or give you any idea whose it is until we get closer to home, but it's definite."

They're both silent for a minute. The hallways are quiet and the rooms are empty.

Lacendu thinks for a moment and finally says, “Let’s not tell the others just yet, alright?”

Vaskette pauses and asks, “Are you sure?”

“Yeah. The others have enough going on without having to protect me at every turn because of this…”

While she speaks, a figure steps out in front of them at the end of the hall and points a gun at them. The figure has black clothes and a dark hood on, making it impossible for the two to figure out who it is, but both quickly realize they need to move.

Vaskette pushes the wheel chair with Lacendu in it through one of the open doors and dives into another room. Both women slam the large metal doors shut. A bullet hits Vaskette’s door and penetrates it skimming her left arm as she pushes the lock. The force of the bullet passing spins her around and pushes her to the ground.

How in the world did that bullet hit me? she thinks to herself. The weapon wasn’t angled this direction…!

She clinches her teeth at the pain.

Vaskette lifts herself up with her other arm and peaks through the hole in the metal door made by the projectile and looks at the other door where she pushed her patient through. No holes.

The figure in the hallway moves in-between Vaskette’s view and the other door. Vaskette peers upward and sees the gun aimed once again at her.

She leaps away from the door and lands hard on the cold floor, as the back of her head hits a metal pole of the first bed. She feels herself close to unconsciousness from the pain, but she struggles to keep herself awake. She pulls herself to her feet via the bed and prepares to lunge at the intruder.

Her head pounds from the adrenaline rush as well as from hitting the pole. The figure tries the door, but it’s locked. A moment goes by, and then the sound of another trigger being pulled, and metal exploding as a bullet penetrates the door handle. The wall near the door handle shatters and the metal of the door within twelve inches disintegrates.

The figure kicks the door open keeping the gun in front of it. Vaskette leaps at the gun to push it away but the figure seems to be able to see her coming and pulls the gun downward which causes Vaskette to trip and fall against the remains of the metal door. As she passes, Vaskette sees the figure has a set of goggles on, and she assumes it is probably allowing the figure to see in the dark.

Her injured arm hits the metal door hard and the blood already spilling from the open wound splatters on the door leaving a trail as she falls hard down on the cold floor. Her nose hits the ground about the same time as her knees. Her nose goes numb and she realizes it's now broken. Her neck jerks around involuntarily away from the pain as the rest of her body hits the ground with a thud. She knows she's too injured to get away, but her survival instinct kicks in and she thrusts her right arm out grabbing the figure's right leg and pushing with all her might.

Thankfully, it is enough. The figure falls hard to the floor just as the gun's trigger is pulled again, and the bullet hits the back of Vaskette's left thigh.

She feels herself being pulled away by her left arm. Vaskette winces at the pain, but allows the movement as she realizes the person pulling her is Lacendu.

Vaskette pulls herself along with her right arm and feels her head touch plastic. Putting all the pieces together in her mind, she pulls herself up and lobs herself into the wheelchair. As she rises, she is assured by Lacendu's help and the woman pushes the wheelchair as quickly as possible down the hall as another bullet is fired from the figure's gun. More bullets are fired, and this time Vaskette knows it is not from the gun of the figure. The police have arrived.

The two women no longer care. They race down the corridors at Lacendu's top speed. More weapons are discharged and they hear someone running toward them. They do not turn to find out who it is, but Vaskette is sure that anyone with trained bullets won't be easily stopped by the police.

"Why would anyone want to kill you, Vaskette?"

"No questions just now," the doctor manages, "just get us someplace safe..."

"Where would you suppose I roll you to, dear Doctor," asks Lacendu, panting.

They soon reach the front lobby where several other doctors and staff members stand around chatting. Two of them are doctors Vaskette has been working with.

"Well, now," says one, "this is a switch."

The other notices Vaskette's injuries. "What happened to you, Doctor?" she asks with much concern.

"No time to chat right now. We're being hunted down. Someone got in here and tried to kill me."

"This way," says the first. He leads them around a corner and into a back room.

As he locks the door, the three of them hear bullets being fired, and people in the lobby screaming.

"That does not sound good…" Lacendu says, almost inaudibly.

The man doctor adds, "No, ma'am, it does not…"

"The killer is using trained bullets. If he has our body signatures, those bullets will go through any material to get to us. We've got to get out of here."

"Easier said than done, Doctor Smith," says the man.

"Look, Doctor Fields, we don't have time to argue about whether getting out of here is easy or not. It's got to be done, and it must be done now!"

"I find myself agreeing with Vaskette," Lacendu puts in nodding at the man.

"Fine, then, let's move." He walks to the end of the room and begins mixing some chemicals.

"What are you doing," asks Lacendu.

"I'm making a compound that will explode these walls outward. We'll need to run once the wall is down…"

"I've got an additional idea," says Vaskette. "He seems to be after me. If I can add some of my own body chemistry to some of these compounds, perhaps I can fool the trained bullets…"

"Smart," says Doctor Fields.

Lacendu comes over to Vaskette, "Let me do the mixing. You just tell me what needs to be done…"

"Fine…! I hope you can handle some blood right now, because you're going to have to carve some of my skin and blood off. I suggest…"

"Seriously…?" Lacendu gives Vaskette a fowl look of disgust.

"I suggest you take it from my left arm where one of the bullets skimmed me," Vaskette continues.

"That's gross." Lacendu convulses and takes a hard breath.

"We don't have time for this convo… Give me a knife and I'll do it myself."

"No. I'll get it. You start pulling the chemicals you need. Just tell me how much to cut."

Vaskette begins pulling vials and glass bottles around on a table with her right arm. Lacendu pulls a scalpel and sets it against Vaskette's injury. She winces at the sight of the blood. "How much do I need to slice off…?" Again she convulses, almost throwing up.

Vaskette turns her head down at the scalpel. "Just start slicing… I'll tell you when to stop."

Lacendu begins dragging the surgical knife downward from the bullet wound. The skin slices easily with blood pouring through the lesion. She turns her head for just a moment to swallow, takes a deep breath as she feels the knife continuing its journey downward into her friend's arm, and then looks back.

"That should be enough," says Vaskette gritting her teeth and breathing a little hard herself. "Pull outward so it will come away, and then slice the other side at the same depth."

Lacendu obeys, against her will. She finally finishes, and as Vaskette grabs the piece of skin covered in her own blood, Lacendu drops the knife and forces her self back against the wall, hands pressed hard against it and tilting her head upward to keep from vomiting.

"Come on, Lacy. I really need you to be strong for me right now. I need your assistance."

"No problem," says Lacendu. She pushes her body away from the wall and goes around the other side. "What can I do to help?"

Vaskette points to some vials. "Pour both of those into this bottle," she says setting a half-full glass container of clear-blue liquid. Lacendu follows the instructions as Vaskette drops her skin sample into the same container. Both of them watch as the skin sample begins to dissolve.

"I hope you're both almost done," says Doctor Fields, "because I am done."

"Great," says Vaskette. "I think we're ready. Can you pour this all over the floor near the door, Lacy? Save some of it, though. We might need it, later."

Lacy begins decanting the liquid near the door as Doctor Fields turns a table over and pulls it away from the outside wall. Vials and containers fall to the floor, some shattering. Chemicals begin flooding together in strange mixtures, and in some spots the combined chemicals start melting the floor, or start small fires.

"You sure made enough noise, Doctor," says Vaskette. "The last thing we need is that killer to hear us."

"Actually, that was precisely the plan," he says.

"Lacendu, come here," Vaskette says as she wheels the chair around behind the table.

Lacendu stops and ducks behind the table. Doctor Fields throws one of the vials of his concoctions at the wall and it shatters leaving a large spray of liquid on the wall. Then he throws the other and as this glass shatters and the liquids mix together, explosions begin to erupt all over the wall tearing through to the outside. Light pours into the room.

The male doctor picks the table up and runs at the wall. As it hits, the remnants of the wall break apart and he falls forward onto the grass. Vaskette and Lacendu follow behind him, Lacendu pushing her doctor in the wheelchair.

Vaskette stops a moment to dispense some of her body chemical onto the edges of the wall, and then the two of them follow along behind Doctor Fields.

A bullet punches through the door just as Vaskette turns around, but it is tricked by the chemical and explodes on the floor, effectively leaving a gaping hole in the door and the floor. The figure kicks the door down and walks just inside. It sees Vaskette and pulls its gun up to fire again. The trigger is pulled and the bullet turns right and detonates on the wall, collapsing the room's infrastructure. The right side of the ceiling falls. The figure jumps away to the left and lands hard on the ground. As it lands, the figure pulls her mask away and furrows her brows in the direction of the three running away.

"I thought this would be easier," Korsaume says.

*****

The three of them arrive at a station not far from the Rehabilitation Center they just left. Lacendu is pushing her doctor's wheelchair and they all try to look inconspicuous as they walk toward the restrooms.

Vaskette has already passed out, and Doctor Fields hands Lacendu his funds card and tells her to go get three tickets while he works on Vaskette's injuries.

Lacendu walks up to the counter and stands in line for several minutes, and finally gets to the front of the line.

"Three tickets to the station," she says.

The man looks at her for a split second, looks back down at the controls in front of him. "Three?" he asks, repeating to make sure he heard her right.

"Correct."

"That will be six hundred currency," he says.

Lacendu hands the man the funds card, the man runs the card through, and then takes three tickets from the machine in front of him and hands them to her with the card.

Lacendu takes them and walks over to stand outside the room she saw the doctor wheel Vaskette into and waits.

A short while later the man pushes her friend out, still in the wheelchair. She still looks pretty bad, but at least her wounds are bandaged and cleaned.

The three of them go to the tram, turn in their passes, and seat themselves on the first car.

Lacendu looks out the window and sees Korsaume walking in carrying a large duffle bag and a gun-case. Korsaume buys a ticket and walks onto the tram finding a seat near the three.

"Hi, Korsaume," says Lacendu, smiling really big. "You won't believe the day we've had."

"Really," says Korsaume giving Lacy a half-smile. "I don't think you'd believe mine, either, Lacendu."

"Vaskette got shot at twice by some jerk in a dark suit."

"Yes," adds Doctor Fields, "the jerk was using trained bullets."

"No kidding," says Korsaume. "Aren't those illegal?"

"I believe you're right, Korsaume." Doctor Fields says.

"I'm trying to figure out who would want to kill us," Lacendu remarks.

"Well, aren't the police involved?"

"They probably are by now, I'm sure." The male doctor rips some of Vaskette's shirt away and presses it against the long cut on her left arm, bleeding from under the temporary bandage. "We thought we should just get away while we had the opportunity. I'm certain the police will figure out who's involved and why…"

"I'm sure they'll catch him," says Korsaume. "I've heard nothing but good about the local law-enforcement on this planet."

"A weapon's expert should know," says Lacendu. "I was kind of curious what kind of weapon you have there in that case…"

"Oh, this…" Korsaume laughs thumbing at the case, "It's a carbon ultra-pitch super-HOP. I found it fairly cheap at a weapon's shop and just <u>had</u> to have it."

"You speak of it like I would a new dress," Lacendu smiles at her.

"Well, would you expect anything less from someone who can't remember what kind of weapons she owned prior to some massive memory loss? This is a very rare and powerful weapon…"

"No doubt..." The male doctor frowns at the woman and leans his head back only moments before the tram begins moving.

*****

"Agoparn," says Mathew watching the man and a beautiful, middle-aged woman on his arm walking toward him. "Who is the marvelous beauty at your side?"

"Captain Mathew, this is Captain Ardelle of the 10-Gen Star Axis C-72," the older man says by way of introduction.

Mathew holds out his hand. "Captain…" he says with a nod and a smile.

"Captain," she nods back taking his hand giving him a smile that becomes her.

"I'm expecting Allen here, soon," Mathew says. "I've been trying to raise Vaskette, Lacendu, and Korsaume for hours, but I've heard nothing from them. I just got word that all three of them are on a tram back here and should arrive any minute."

"Did you hear about the incident at the Rehab Center," asks Allen walking up.

The three turn toward him. "No," say Mathew and Ardelle simultaneously with a look of concern.

"Well," he begins as he stops only feet from them, "evidently the center was visited by an assassin that tried to kill Doctor Vaskette. In the process, the killer murdered seven other people. Trained bullets were in use."

"Oh, my," says Ardelle.

"What are trained bullets," asks Agoparn. Mathew adds an inquisitive look to the man's question.

"I was wondering that, myself," says Allen. "The broadcast says they're explosive projectiles that track body chemistry. Evidently, they can maneuver around and through other objects, choosing not to explode until they reach their target, or have gone a certain distance."

"They can also be programmed to explode in proximity," Ardelle includes with a look of concern. She looks back at Agoparn.

Agoparn looks back at her, then at Mathew. "I hope they're all alright."

"I do, too," Mathew says. "I can't have my crew dying on me when there's so much to be done… Shall we head for the tram station to greet them?"

"Let's," says Agoparn.

The four of them head off toward the tram station.

*****

Korsaume gets up as the tram pulls to a stop. Lacendu gets behind Vaskette's wheelchair and pushes her out into the aisle. Doctor Fields stands up behind them, and the four get off together.

As they pass through the gates of the station, they are greeted by Mathew, Agoparn, a woman, and Allen.

"Captain," says Lacendu, "I'm so glad to see all of you again…"

"Yes, sir," says Korsaume. "…And who is Parn's friend?"

"I am Captain Ardelle," says the woman.

"Welcome to our own personal Hades," says Korsaume.

"Korsaume," says Lacendu with a tilt in her head and a stunned look on her face.

Mathew kneels down before Vaskette as Doctor Fields walks around to her right side.

Doctor Fields speaks, "The good doctor's blood has dried by now. Unfortunately, I believe it has done so around and through her bandages."

"…And just who are you," asks Mathew looking up at the man.

"I am Doctor Thaddeus Fields. I've been working with your doctor here since she arrived at the Rehabilitation Center. I must admit I'm more accustomed to seeing Lacy lying on a bed under a surgical light; not standing up with a smile on her face."

"I feel much better now than I did a week ago," says Lacendu.

"Are any of you the least bit concerned for the doctor," asks Mathew with a matter-of-fact tone.

"Sure," says Doctor Fields, "but she'll be fine. All she has is a bullet hole in her left leg, and a large knife incision and skim on her left arm, and a broken nose. I can have her fixed up in no time. Injuries, I can treat. It's those blasted psych problems that're so blasted difficult…"

"Question, Doctor Fields," says Lacendu, "those bullets exploded when they hit the doors and disintegrated a rather large area when they passed through. Why didn't the one that went through her left leg do the same…" and then, after thinking about it, she adds, "…though I am glad it didn't…?"

"Hm." Doctor Fields thinks for a moment.

"Maybe I have an answer," says Korsaume. "I mean, I am a weapon's expert."

"Right, Lieutenant," says Mathew, a little perturbed, "now how about that answer…"

"Well, at such a close range, the bullet probably went several feet into the ground before it exploded. Normally the bullets explode on impact. If she were less than one or two feet from the weapon's barrel, and if it was a trained bullet, or a hyper-gleam stream bullet, it would have passed through her and then tried to turn around and come back before it exploded."

"That makes sense," says Mathew. "Now, what about that medical attention, Doctor Fields…? My crew member is passed out in a wheelchair with bullet wounds…"

"Let's get her to one of the medical rooms here in the station. I'll get her fixed up real quick."

*****

A few hours pass with the other six at a table when Doctors Fields and Smith walk up. Vaskette has bandages around her left arm and leg, and her face looks flush.

"Are you alright," asks Lacendu smiling at Vaskette.

"I'll be fine, thanks to the nice doctor."

"We're very glad," says Korsaume, giving a half-hearted grin. "We weren't entirely sure you were going to make it."

Lacendu elbows Korsaume. "The Lieutenant speaks for herself. I, for one, was certain you'd be fine. You're the finest doctor on any planet, and you were at the hands of the second finest doctor on any planet. Between the two of you, I bet you could reanimate dead people…"

"Very funny," says Vaskette smiling lightly at the patient she's had for the past week and three days.

"Well," says Mathew, "if the two of you will have a seat, I have a proposition for my crew…"

"Oh, really, Captain," says Allen with a smile, leaning back in his chair.

As the two doctors seat themselves at the table, Mathew continues. "I was approached by a nice couple who want to be taken on board for passage to another planet. I believe they called it Pikornauc'for."

"I'm familiar with it," says Ardelle. "It's a planet about eleven light-years from here. In your vessel, and at maximum speed, it should take about six weeks."

"Is it in the direction of the opposite side of the galaxy," asks Agoparn.

"Well, it's closer to the core of the Milky Way. That particular area isn't exactly fun, though. There are pirates, thieves, Raiders, little or no law, and most currency is not accepted. You should probably take some tradables with you for good measure."

"Which way are you headed?" asks Mathew.

She smiles at him, "Unfortunately, I'm heading in the opposite direction for a week or two. Of course, that's after our ship is restocked, which won't be complete for another day or so..."

"That won't do," says Mathew. "We need to head out pretty soon. Today or tomorrow would be best."

"Especially if I've got an assassin after me..." says Vaskette.

"Good point," says Mathew, "Also, we will be an additional fifteen thousand currency to the good for it. We can pick up some tradables, as Captain Ardelle suggested, before we leave and perhaps on the way." He looks around at the group, spending most of his gazes on his crew. "Do you all want to think about it first, or do we want to put it to a vote immediately...?"

"You're the captain," says Allen, "or do I need to keep reminding you of this...?"

"You're right, Allen," Mathew smirks, more at himself, as he points a finger at the man across from him for a moment. "We'll take a vote right now. All in favor raise your right hand."

Vaskette, Lacendu, Agoparn, Ardelle, and Allen all raise their hands.

"All opposed..."

Korsaume raises her hand.

"Your reason, Lieutenant..."

"I don't see that it matters... I am out-voted..."

"Your opinion as second-in-command does matter to me, Korsaume."

She pauses for a moment to think. "Where will we put them? All the crew quarters are taken up by the crew..."

"Well, we do have an observatory that we can put shades up so that folks on the outside can't look in; and it does have a door on it..." says Agoparn.

"What do you think, Lieutenant," Mathew asks after looking at the man.

"I hadn't thought about that. I suppose since we have a place for them, we'll need to get a bed for them to sleep on, and some additional supplies, so I don't see any problem with it; and you did say we'd get an additional fifteen thousand currency for the job."

"Wow, Lieutenant," Lacendu smiles, "you make it sound like a horrible necessity."

"You know, Lacy, I've noticed you seem to be completely surprised at just about everything I do. I'm still learning, too."

"Oh, yeah," Lacendu concedes. "I guess I should learn to be less surprised. I feel so much better since this morning. The adrenaline rush of running from that horrible person trying to kill my doctor seems to have helped quite a bit, too."

"Then it's agreed. We'll take on the couple and get away from Vaskette's would-be killer. We leave before sundown." Mathew arises from the table. "I'll call the couple to let them know the good news. The rest of you have your duties. Let's get this done."

"Yes, sir," say Allen, Lacendu, and Vaskette randomly.

All of them get up and walk in their various directions to prepare, with the exception of Korsaume.

After everyone's out of earshot she folds her arms and mutters to herself, "Wonderful. I'm never going to get my job done. My attempt at Vaskette was an atrocious failure; and I wasn't entirely sure I wanted to kill her in the first place. I guess I'll have to work on that, sometime…"

*****

Mathew stands at the threshold of the docking shell just inside the ship awaiting his crew. The couple has already come aboard, and he watches as Korsaume walks up carrying three duffle bags and two gun cases on her shoulders.

"Hello, Lieutenant."

"Hello, Captain." She stops in front of him. "Do we have tradables on board?"

"Yes. Each of our quarters has been stocked with them for our own purchases, and we have stashes in the infirmary and the engine room for ship and medical necessities. I also took the liberty of separating out the remaining balance of our mutual card into individual currency cards for each member of the crew. Those are in the crew quarters as well."

"Good thinking, Captain. Everyone will appreciate that…"

"Now, about those guns…"

"Yes, sir; what about them…?" She eyes him with doubt and a frown.

Mathew pulls her aside into the infirmary. "I saw on the report that the weapon used to kill those seven people in the Rehabilitation Center, and almost killed Vaskette, was a carbon ultra-pitch super-HOP, which just happens to be the same type of gun you are carrying in your two gun cases…"

"What are you saying, Captain; that I would kill our only on-board doctor?"

"Of course not, Lieutenant…but an expert like you might have some insight into the type of person that would… Lacendu did tell me you got them cheaply, and that you came onto the tram just after the incident at the Center. Did you, perchance, purchase them from someone before entering the station?"

"No sir. I bought them three nights ago at a weapon's shop."

"I see – and if you think of anything that might help the authorities on this planet capture the assassin, I hope you'll give them a call immediately…"

"Absolutely, Captain…! I don't like the idea of a murderer running around looking for our Doctor any more than you do. If I can do anything to assist with this horrible person's capture, you may be one hundred percent assured that I will!"

Episode 4
Red Horizon

OPENING:

"...As in most cases that are beyond our control, we often feel like we must do something to affect a better outcome. However, this is a myth as much as it is to think that we are the ones who caused the trouble in the first place. If we are to ever recover from this madness, it is we who must stop to think that if it is beyond our control, that we should then let the tide carry us to shore; however far away that might be..."

Every light in the ship is on. The thrusters fire at maximum levels propelling the vessel forward at a high velocity. A star above it to the left, yet still several million kilometers before it, glimmers off of the hulking metal creature.

Inside is mostly silence, with the exception of computers working, gears grinding mildly in the background, and the voice of Doctor Vaskette Smith.

"First things first," she says. "I thought you all might like to know, Lacendu," at this she gestures as the woman, "is pregnant."

Congratulatory remarks are made by everyone, with a word or two of thanks from the receiving party. She smiles in spite of herself; a grin that stretches her face out in joy.

Vaskette commands attention once more, though. “As for he test results, they are positive. Our short-term memory has been affected. Whether that’s the result of the memory erasure, or if we all had some trouble before the supposed incident is anyone’s guess at present. I’ll need to run some in-depth studies on our physiology before I can make a pure determination.”

“Can it be treated, Doctor,” asks Mathew.

“I have some temporary cures. All the stuff does is help the brain pathways stay opened up for long periods of time.”

“Side-effects…” Korsaume asks with a touch of sarcasm.

“Minor, but not without their problems… You’ll remember pretty much everything for days on end from the time you awaken to the time you go to sleep.”

“Like what, exactly?”

“Exactly…? Everything; like using the restroom and how long it took; every step you take up and down the halls. Minutes will seem like days, or longer…”

“It’s worth it to me,” says Allen. “Can I have one right away?”

Vaskette smiles, “You most certainly may.” Then turning to the rest, “Feel free, all of you, to make your way to the infirmary at your leisure and I’ll give you your shot.”

“More shots…” says Lacendu quietly exasperated, rolling her eyes.

The crew gets up and moves into their normal positions.

Captain Mathew Arnold sits down at the pilot’s chair in front of the ship’s main controls. Lieutenant Korsaume sits behind her captain on his right two chairs back at the weapons and tactical display. Allen, who normally sits immediately behind the captain’s chair on Mathew’s left at the external/internal sensors, heads downstairs with Doctor Vaskette and Lacendu Ruric-Trester. Agoparn heads to the engine room.

*****

About an hour later, Captain Mathew heads down to get his shot. As he walks down the stairs to the lower level, the couple the crew took on only a week ago approaches him.

"Captain…" says the man loudly as if to get his attention.

"I was quite aware of you, Mr. Folzandine; you and your lovely wife. There is no need to yell." Mathew smiles at them. "Is everything alright?"

"Oh, yes," answers the woman.

"The room, meals, hospitality of my crew…?"

"Of course," smiles the man with some amount of impatience. "It's the orbital ribbon station your engineer said we would be reaching at the end of the week…"

"Steg… What about it…?"

"We certainly cannot be seen there…"

"You're not 'wanted,' or anything, are you?"

The man and woman stand silent for a moment. "Well, we're not criminals, no…" says the man.

"...But you <u>are</u> wanted…"

The woman looks at the Captain with fear, "We were caught in the middle of an incident where it was believed by the local authorities that we were the cause of someone's death. The law enforcement in this sector is looking for us."

"I thought Ablose was in this sector…"

The couple move out of the way as Mathew finishes down the flight of stairs and walks around the corner, stops and turns to look at them.

"Do you have different identities to keep from being noticed on other planets?"

The man looks at the captain with a saddened face. "You have uncovered our secret, it seems."

"I assure you both, it wasn't hard. Both of you return to your cabin and I will be there when I've received my shot from the doctor."

"Yes, Captain," says the woman, and the two walk away back up the hallway.

Mathew watches after them, then turns around to see Vaskette positioned leaning against the wall with her arms folded.

"You overheard, I take it," Mathew says to her softly.

"I did. I was cleaning up behind the wall over here before I heard them stop you at the stairs."

"…And you used your doctor's prerogative to eavesdrop…?" He smiles at her.

"I don't like this; carrying around fugitives from the law…"

"Are we?"

"I don't know; but I do see your point: hypocrites we are to point fingers?"

"It is valid…"

"Yes, it is, Captain. So," she says standing upright away from the wall, "shall I drug you now?"

"Does it hurt?"

"Only as much as any other needle entering your skin at the base of your neck and injecting fluids directly into your bloodstream."

"You make it sound like I'm just going to die," Mathew says as Vaskette turns and walks to the counter to put on gloves. Mathew nods at Lacendu who sits in a chair nearby.

Lacendu stands and walks over to Mathew. "Have a seat, right up here, Captain." She pats her hand on the small surgical bed.

As the captain sits down, Lacendu pulls Mathew's shirt collar downward as Vaskette comes toward him with a vial and needle, and pulls on the plug of the needle to fill it.

"You're scaring me, you two…" he laughs.

"You have every reason to be scared," says Vaskette. "I'm going to stick a long, thick needle into your neck. It will only hurt for a moment, so be still."

Mathew closes his mouth tight and leans his head upward and to the right away from Lacendu's hands. He feels a sharp pain in his neck as the needle enters the jugular vein. It goes away, but the feeling of metal separating skin stays, and he has a slight light-headedness that he can only suppose is the drug flowing into his brain and causing an almost-instantaneous effect.

"You should feel a tingling in your brain for a few minutes," says the Doctor. "It will wear off and your memory will be affected within the hour. You'll begin remembering things like the exact moment you awoke this morning, every moment of getting dressed, all steps you've taken today, and every move you've made at the pilot's chair."

"Oh good... I was just trying to remember something I thought of to make my job easier about the same time I woke up this morning. Perhaps it will come back to me."

"It will, dear Captain, with a myriad of other things you might just as soon forget..." says Lacendu, sounding as if she speaks from experience.

*****

Mathew walks into what would normally be the observatory with thoughts driving rampantly through his brain.

"The door was open, so I made my entrance without knocking. I hope neither of you mind."

"Of course not, Captain. This is your ship." The man rises from the side of the couple's bed. The woman lies stretched out on the other side and pulls her arm up under her head sensually.

"Now, about our earlier discussion: did you get the currency from the," he pauses for effect, "incident..."

"The, uh, incident we speak of was," the man begins.

His wife finishes, "rather complicated. We were entirely victims of circumstance."

"Since I don't know of what trouble you might be in, much less do I have access to newscasts about things on Steg at this time I can only take your word for it… As for my crew and me, we, too, are victims of chance. We're not sure exactly how we got to this side of the galaxy. We might also be fugitives from the law, but none of us are certain of that, yet. We're heading back to find out, come-what-may. I suggest the two of you allow for yourselves to stay on board while we restock on the orbital ribbon station at Steg. We will not mention we have guests on board. You can have my word on that…"

"Captain, we are greatly appreciative of you and your crew's hospitality, as well as your silence. We will definitely take you up on your offer to stay hidden aboard your vessel," says the woman. The man turns to face her as she speaks.

"My wife is right. You will gain much more than the measly currency we gave you for this deed."

"Whether we gain anything by this or not, our sole interest is in getting back to our homes. Carrying you on a leg of the journey is just an act of kindness we can perform on our way. The two of you take it easy and stay out of my crew's way. We'll be there in about three days at our current speed."

"We understand," the woman interjects. "All pleasantries aside, which seems to have made up this entire conversation, we will do as we are told, regardless."

Mathew nods at her. "Thank you. Have a good rest." He turns away and heads back down the corridor, up the stairs and back into the cockpit.

"That shot took an awful long time to get, Captain," says Korsaume not even turning to look at him. "What did Vaskette do to you; put you into cold storage for a few minutes?"

"Actually, I was greeted by our passengers on the way to the infirmary."

"Captain," says Allen turning to face Mathew as he sits down in the pilot's chair, "I don't know much about them, but I think there's something going on with them that they're not telling us…"

"I agree with you, Strategist – especially since they simply told me so during our conversation." Mathew turns the chair around to look back at Allen. "They fear going to Steg."

"We're only stopping at Steg so you can see your girlfriend, Captain; no offense. We don't absolutely have to stop there, you know. I'd hate to be caught with fugitives on board."

"As long as none of us says anything, I see no reason we should fear stopping at the station. They said they will stay hidden. I think we'll only allow three of the crew off at a time so the others can keep an eye on the ship. We may be toting them around for a few weeks, but that doesn't mean I trust them."

"Very wise, Captain," Korsaume says. "You're getting better at this…"

"Thank you for the vote of confidence, Lieutenant."

*****

"Orbital Ribbon Station Z – R – Z – 1 – 9 – 5 – 7 around Steg, this is Captain Mathew Arnold of the Vortex class Planetary Cruiser, designation 'Vibrant,' serial number 7 – 8 – 1 – 0 – A – 9 – 8 – 1 – 3 – X – 2 – 0 – 7 – 0 – 6; six crew members aboard; all systems functional; requesting permission to dock on station for fuel, food, and a little relaxation. Please respond."

"Vortex class Planetary Cruiser 'Vibrant,' you have been identified and your request approved. Please cease ship propulsion and we will have your ship towed to the docking station. Prepare your docking shell for connection and allow our systems to take over. Respond."

"All requests clearly heard and understood. Instructions have been followed. We await tow."

"Lieutenant, please take over ship controls and have Lacendu and Agoparn join me at the docking shell."

"Will do, Captain," says Korsaume standing up while pressing two buttons, and holding down a third, "Agoparn and Lacendu, please report to the docking shell immediately to rendezvous with the Captain."

Mathew walks through the door of the cockpit and into the mess, grabs a few small items, and then walks down the stairs where Agoparn and Lacendu are already waiting.

"Hey, Captain," says Lacendu.

"Lacy, you seem to be a lot better. I trust those drugs the doctor has been giving you have been working well for you…?"

"Yes, sir," she replies. "I haven't thrown up once from motion. However, I still have trouble holding down all of my food. About one in four meals comes right back up…"

"That was more than I needed to know, Lacy," says Agoparn with a frown.

"It's OK," Mathew speaks, "I'm glad you're feeling better. Now, the two of you are the first ones I want off this ship. You will stay off for five hours, and then return. Agoparn, you will replace Allen, Lacendu will replace Vaskette, and I Korsaume. The two of you will relax on board the station and enjoy yourselves. That is an order."

"I'm so proud of you, Captain. You're getting much better at commanding your crew," Agoparn smiles.

Lacendu adds her own smile to Agoparn's and Mathew smiles back at them.

"Parn, have you had your shot?"

"Yes, Captain; four days ago…"

"The doctor said we should have one every few days. Go get another. How about you, Lacy," he turns to the young woman.

"Just yesterday…"

"Excellent. I should probably get mine again before we leave the station. Would you do me a favor and remind me?"

"Certainly," she says smiling, placing her hands behind her, grasping her fingers, and moving in a quarter-circle from the thighs up.

Mathew glances at her with a smile belying his happiness at her recovery from the sickly woman he knew only a week and a half ago.

*****

Only about ten minutes pass when the ship is docked and Mathew and Agoparn are going over the necessities of refueling, stocking, and paying for it, while Lacendu walks off happy and smiling on her way to the promenade.

"Fill up the fuel cells. We'll need food supplies; feel free to make the choices…"

"With the exception of those soup rations," adds Mathew. "I don't think any one of us liked that stuff…"

The man behind the counter looks up at this. "Those are my personal favorites."

"Well, then," says Mathew, "keep those for yourself, and give us the rest."

"Are you buying?"

"Yes."

"By all means, sir…"

"Also," says Agoparn looking once at his captain, and then back at the man, "the observatory is off limits. We have some valuables in there that we want to keep safe."

"Understood, Sir; the notation has been made. Anything else sirs…?"

"I believe that will be all."

"It will be ready for you within two hours."

"That's fine. We'll be here for about eleven hours, so just leave the ship and we'll find you when we return."

The man nods as the two leave and head in the same direction as Lacendu.

"On your way to see your girl, hey, Captain…?"

"The bounty-huntress, yes," Mathew responds.

"You really don't like us calling her your girlfriend, do you…?"

"Not exactly, since I really don't know what awaits me when we return to where we belong. Who knows, I might have a girlfriend, or a wife, and maybe even a child or two. I don't know if I'm the type, but I'm certain I like this girl. I find myself hoping that I don't have anyone waiting for me at home. I'm just not sure I want to take the chance."

"Chance is what led you to this side of the galaxy. Chance is what got you involved with the woman you now enjoy thinking about. Chance is now all you've got to hold you together until we get back home and find out what we can do to help that man end whatever caused our exile."

"You have a point, my friend. Perhaps you also have a wife or girlfriend back home. I think in your shoes, I'd find Captain Ardelle a comfort and a nice aversion from the road ahead."

Agoparn smiles, "I think you and I are both in the same boat, woman-wise. I'll make a deal with you: I won't tell your 'wife' if you won't tell mine…"

Mathew smiles back at Agoparn. "Deal…"

*****

"Well, it's about raring time!"

"It's good to see you, too, Seta." Mathew looks deep into the eyes that he has not seen face-to-face in two and a half weeks.

Rosetta Firemark stands before him with her arms outstretched, her tiny frame looking like a lamp with arms and a head. She is clad in a violet dress very similar to the hard red leather dress Mathew saw her in when they met. The color of the dress draws her purple eyes out into brilliance under her wavy blonde hair.

"You look beautiful, Seta," he says opening his own arms and engulfing her with them.

The two embrace for several minutes, the right side of her head pressed to his neck, and her hands clasped around his chest.

"I was wondering if you'd make it before I left…" says Rosetta.

"I had no way of knowing for certain you'd still be here when I arrived. Did you get your man?"

"Actually," she says pulling away a foot or so from him, hands still on his sides, "that's the only reason I was still here. I did capture him and turned him over to the Solar Union authorities. They made me wait here until they arrived, which took nine days. You just missed them, as a matter-of-fact…"

"I hate to say it, but I'm glad I did…"

The two of them smile at each other, and Rosetta wraps her right arm around him releasing her left arm, and the two begin walking down the promenade together.

*****

Lacendu walks merrily along looking at shops. She feels wonderful, knowing now that she is on her way to recovery, and that the space travel has been so easy for her the past few days, as opposed to her first week on board the "Vibrant."

Her mind meanders through the past few days, spent in the infirmary not because she must, but because she has made a dear friend in the doctor, Vaskette Smith. She thinks, too, about her husband, a man whose face she cannot remember, his love she cannot feel, and his presence she cannot hold. She wonders if she loved him, or if she married him for money, or even out of necessity. She speculates on whether or not she had children, or had even discussed the possibility with Mr. Trester, who even now searches everywhere for her.

In short, she is oblivious to the man following her; and though she sees him once in a while as she turns around looking at all the different things to buy; dresses, trinkets, equipment, computers, etc.; she does not recognize the fact that he is everywhere she is.

It is almost an hour before he makes his move, and as she seats herself at a small table in an open restaurant after ordering a local delicacy, he sits down across from her.

"Excuse me, miss," he starts, "I believe I know you."

She ignores him, but smiles with friendly lips as if he were some long-lost boyfriend she still likes. Her hand moves to cut the meat, and tender as it is, easily slices through, forks the meat and lifts it to her mouth.

"You are Cendu Ruric, from Segnar Physics and Calculus. You were my teacher about two years ago…"

She pauses with the meat pressed against her teeth, preparing to chew. She pulls the meat away, thinks better of herself, and stuffs the bite into her mouth.

"Don't you remember me…?" he asks.

Through a mouth full of food, her face goes straight and she mumbles, "Of course. You were my star pupil."

"Actually, I was your worst student."

"Oh."

"…But I got a great job out here doing mathematical equations for the building of stations on the planets in this sector."

"Look, um…"

"Ersisk Feinjurburg."

"Ersisk," she continues after swallowing the chewed meat, "I honestly don't remember you. I try not to remember teaching on Segnar, and I dread the idea of that time being brought back to me. If you want to say more, please leave Segnar and all it stands for out of the convo."

"Bad time there, hm?"

"What did I just tell you, Ersisk? Either leave Segnar out, or leave; preferably both."

The young man seems exasperated and places his hands on the table before him. "Miss Ruric; I don't know what has happened to you. You used to be a very nice lady, and my absolute favorite teacher. To be honest, I even had a crush on you for a while after I broke up with my last girlfriend. The thing is that, seeing you here, well it brings back memories for me. Pleasant ones that I want to remember."

"Ersisk, you are a sweet young man; of that I have no doubt." At this point, she places her right hand on top of one of his, keeping her fork in her left. She gives him the sternest look she has. "I am on a mission of the utmost importance. This is the first chance I have had to relax and get away from the ship by myself without being sick or hurried. I have four glorious hours left to myself and I desire to utilize every one of them by myself." She raises her eyebrows. "That means without ex-students, or passé memories of things I no longer wish to reflect on."

"I comprehend. Please accept my apologies for making your day so horrible."

"I accept your apology. I didn't mean anything bad by it. I was just really looking forward to being alone. Your presence brings up things I am trying to forget."

"Oh." The man turns around to walk away.

As his back turns to her, she realizes she may have missed a golden opportunity and her eyes widen as the full appraisal of the situation hits her. She decides to try anyway.

"WAIT!" She almost shouts it.

The man is more shocked at her loud voice than anything. He turns to face her, staying standing. "Yes, Ma'am…?"

She thinks for a moment. "Perhaps your presence would be accepted on one count." She does not continue, but instead brings her palm up to her chin and closes her fingers around her cheek.

"What might that be, Miss Ruric," the man asks slowly, as if her condition might not be acceptable.

"Do you have any old news data from Segnar and the surrounding sectors?"

The man thinks for a moment. "I do have my old books still, and I believe I kept a couple of papers on the plights of that area from my 'Current Events' classes. Some of those papers might have footnotes on what you're looking for…"

"How much do you want for them?"

He pauses, and then asks questioningly, "I thought you said you wanted to forget…"

She smiles, "I lied…"

He thinks a little longer. "All of them?" He raises his eyebrows pondering.

She does not bother to answer; she only nods.

"I never thought about it. I guess a couple hundred currency would be nice."

"Would you accept one thousand even? I'll forward the funds to whichever account you desire immediately." She looks up at him and smiles.

"Wouldn't you like to have the merchandise in your hands first?"

"Certainly… Go get them. The sooner you bring them to me, the faster you'll get paid."

The man looks almost excited and practically runs away from the restaurant area. Two enforcers step forward to slow him down, have a few words with him, and then release him.

Lacendu is practically ecstatic at the prospect of gleaning even more information for herself and her crew. She eats rather quickly now with anticipation.

*****

Agoparn stands at the large picture window at one of the lower levels. The window has a direct view of the planet Steg. His legs are apart, and his arms are behind his back with hands clasped. There is a smile on his face.

He watches as the planet below spins slowly from his vantage point; the swirling colors of white, blue, and orange, with some touches of violet and red. Though other people walk past him both behind and in front, he hardly notices them. His mind is absolutely transfixed on the globe below him. So much so, in fact, that he does not notice the young girl running along in front of her mother; nor does she notice him.

"Observe, Adrent," her mother calls just a little softer than a yell.

The child has turned her head up from the floor at her mothers call and the right side of her head hits squarely on Agoparn's right leg. The rest of her body follows and the impact against his fairly muscular thigh and shin is enough to just stop her in her tracks. She hits the floor, buttocks first, pushing her hands back to keep herself from falling any further away. She shakes her head and looks up at the man. "I am regretful, Sir."

"That's perfectly alright," says Agoparn bending down with his left arm outstretched to her to help her stand up. "And you need not call me 'sir.' My name is Agoparn."

The mother finally reaches them with a man at her side that Agoparn assumes is the father. "I am very regretful, Mr. Agoparn, that my daughter was not providing attention to where she was tracking."

"Your daughter tracks," he asks, almost to himself.

"Oh, I am regretful again; my dialect is dissimilar. 'Going' is the term I believe you would employ."

"Where are you from," Agoparn asks to the three as a group.

"We're from Passelket," answers the man, "on the internal disk of the second limb of the Milky Way."

"Interesting… How far away is that?"

"Of seven sectors…maybe fifty weeks of passage," replies the woman, "on a zero seven Celestial class Star Expeditioner passenger vessel."

"May I suppose that you know the travel time for a Vortex class Planetary Cruiser?"

"I've never heard of that type," says the man with a thumb on his chin, the other arm folding its hand into the elbow of the other.

The woman adds, "Nor include I…"

"I stake I could construct the numbers," says the girl matter-of-factly and looking up at Agoparn.

"Adrent, don't be inane." The mother places her hand on the top of the girl's head and looks down at her daughter as Adrent looks up.

"Except, Maternal, I consider I can. We did erudite diverse star crafts in university."

Agoparn is surprised at the young girl's vocabulary. "Adrent, you are quite schooled in your use of language, and I am willing to wager you very well could configure time and distance based on differentials of vessel types."

"Might I, Maternal?" Adrent pulls a small, flat, circular object from a pocket in her shirt.

"Certainly you may, dearest one," says the matriarch.

The girl opens the flat object and sets it in front of her. The object floats in mid-air and comes alive with lights as it begins projecting a keyboard, monitor, and several other images that seem to be peripherals.

"Agoparn," she speaks, "you stated it was a Vortex class Planetary Cruiser?"

"I did," Agoparn affirms.

She types for a few minutes, re-quoting the other man's information about the distance and time. "Considering the velocity and dimensional differentials in the two space faring vessels, the estimated distance from here to Passelket, the lone other object I need to identify is your vessel's traveler tally…"

"You mean how many people we have on board…"

"Yes, Agoparn…"

"We have six crew members, and two passengers. The two passengers get off on a planet called Pikornauc'for, and we'll be heading the rest of the way to the inner Milky Way."

"Superior… We discontinued provisionally at Pikornac'for on our way here. It is about nine light years to Pikornac'for from this point, and you'll doubtless replenish there, even however you won't require to." She continues to type in her calculations. "It will take your vessel approximately two hundred forty days, together with replenishment of supplies and fuel to attain Passelket."

"Oh, yea," he says half-heartedly. "That's nearly eight months of travel time…"

"Yes sir," replies Adrent folding her disc after turning off the imagery. She places the disc back into her shirt pocket on the right side of her abdomen and hands Agoparn a small disc no larger than a shirt button. "Here are my calculations. You may receive this to computate your trajectory and speed when you arrive to your ship."

Agoparn looks at the mother first who nods her approval, and then accepts with his left hand the very small disc from the girl. "I am much obliged to you all for your assistance in this matter."

"It is the slightest we can achieve for my descendant bashing into you as she did…"

Agoparn smiles; "I assure you that that was more a pleasure than impedance, Miss." He looks down at Adrent, bends to one knee, and holds his right hand out. She takes it. "A pleasure allowing you to bump into me that way, Adrent..."

"The pleasure is mine, Agoparn." The girl's entire face seems to smile.

"Near now, Adrent; we must exit. We have much distance to traverse at present." The mother pats her daughter on the back and the three of them walk off.

Agoparn looks down at the small disc, then back to the picture window. He smiles again, turns his body back around to face the planet, and proceeds to watch the planet change before his very eyes.

*****

Korsaume and Allen work in the cockpit at their assigned stations taking inventory, configuring flight plans and preparing the "Vibrant" for departure in just under seven hours.

"I hope the Captain was able to meet with Rosetta," says Allen cheerily to himself.

Korsaume unassumingly adds, "I do, too, Allen."

"You know, Lieutenant, I think I know why you're always so down…"

She is at first upset with him, but remembers quickly that he does not know she still has her life's memories. She turns around in her chair, "You think I need a man in my life…?"

"It couldn't hurt…"

"And just who do you suggest I take as my partner? You…?"

Allen's face turns beet-red. "I hadn't thought about that…" he mumbles quietly to himself. More loudly, "Actually, I was thinking that when you go out this time, see if you can meet a few guys, talk to them…and don't be so stand-offish."

As she turns her chair back around to press more buttons and finish her work, "So you think I'm stand-offish…"

"Let's just say you act standoffish," he says pushing the word 'act' hard. He gets up and walks over to Korsaume.

She knows where he is standing and half-looks at him in a couple of glances between watching her fingers pressing buttons on her terminal. "Acting is doing, Allen. If I act standoffish, I am standoffish. Did you ever think there might be more to it?"

"Like what?"

"Like, maybe I don't WANT a man in my life right now…?" She stands up and walks off to the back, and stops at the hallway entry. "Don't bring it up again, STRATEGIST!" The word 'strategist' comes out very sarcastically.

He stares after her as she walks down the hallway. Even though he can no longer see her and she is out of earshot, he says, "I was only trying to help."

*****

It takes about forty-five minutes for Ersisk to show back up, but when he does, Lacendu knows she has hit pay dirt. The young man has a duffle bag with him, and he literally lugs it from his shoulder and down to the table in front of her.

She has been finished with her meal for most of his absence, and she readily welcomes the large bag full of books.

"I found more than I thought I had," he says unzipping the container.

"I would have guessed," she says smiling as the two of them stand in front of the bag and pull books, discs, and papers from it. "You must have kept everything!"

"Actually, I just stuffed all my used books in here when I left Segnar. I was going to sell them at the college bookstore, but I never got around to it…"

"I suppose you were also going to sell your papers to those students who had the money…"

He looks a little shocked at her. Ersisk then places his right hand on her left hand and says, "You know, I don't have to sell these to you."

"I was just kidding," she says smiling very big and laughing, "I did the same thing in college. I kind of figured everyone did."

"I most certainly never did…"

"My apologies; I can see I have upset you. I assure you it was unintentional."

He stands there for a moment glaring at her. "You really did sell your college papers to other students?"

"Yeah… It was half of my college tuition…" She laughs again.

Ersisk laughs with her for a moment. "A thousand currency, huh…?

"Would you like that liquidated, on a funds card, or in an account…?"

Ersisk hands her a funds card. "If you could just transfer it to this card, I will be on my way."

"Uhuh," she says shaking her head. "For a thousand currency, I expect you to tote this bag back to my ship…"

He thinks for a moment. "Fine…a thousand credits for a bunch of books, papers, and discs delivered to your ship. Just give me directions."

"I'll do better than that – I'll take you there."

Ersisk smiles at her and the two begin piling the books back into the bag, he zips the bag up, and the two walk back to the "Vibrant" with the bag in tow.

*****

Korsaume stands at the door to the docking shell with her arms folded. The door is open and the ship's hallway as well as the station's hallway is empty. She contemplates taking her gun out and shooting Allen at his terminal. "No. That would leave a big bloody mess all over the cockpit, and I'd never get out of here. Besides, the Captain would never forgive me for messing up his workspace."

"Is that so," says a voice from above her.

Her first instinct is to pull her seven-eighty from her jacket pocket and point it upwards. Whomever the voice belongs to is now looking down the barrel of a gun designed to blow holes through twenty feet of solid metal from point blank, or up to three hundred yards.

"It's so." She looks up at a hole in the station's shell dock.

"You're Sherise 'Korsaume' Felder, right?"

"What if I'm not?"

"Then I've got the wrong person. I have a message for her."

"Not here, you don't..." She shakes her head as she says it.

"Then where…?"

Korsaume looks down the hallway, then back into the ship listening for anyone coming. Once she's satisfied, she looks back up. "What are you in?"

"A single-pass port-flyer…"

"You weren't planning on living much longer, were you…"

"I do what I'm told, lady; just like you!"

"Move…"

"What…?" he begins to ask. She raises her arms up, grips the metal around the hole and pulls herself up into the craft. "There's not room in here for two."

"There is, it will just be a little cramped, that's all…"

In moments, Korsaume is inside the small craft with the man, face to face.

"I'm Sherise. You will call me Korsaume. Now, what can I do for you?"

"I was sent by your boss to find out where you stand on finishing your job. He heard about the incident on Ablose."

"What about that Chrinsole fellow?"

"I don't know a Chrinsole."

"I told him I would finish my job and I have every intention of doing so. It just may take a little longer than I at first hoped."

"That's not in the bargain. If you're going to kill them at all, you get rid of them today, or I will get rid of you."

"There's only one of you, and two of me…"

"Excuse me…?" he says with a dour face.

She presses the seven-eighty to his chest.

"Actually, there are more of me," the man says, "I'm not the only one on this ribbon station that knows what you're supposed to be doing… If you don't finish the job, they'll finish for you, and you'll be included in the finishing…"

Korsaume places her gun back into her jacket pocket.

"Now what, Sher – Korsaume," he asks.

"It looks like I have no other choice. I do have one question." She does not await a confirmation. "How do I get back home when my job is complete?"

"We have personal tesseraction devices available with us. We will give you one when you have killed the other five."

Korsaume thinks. "Very well, lackey. But I want my personal tesseract device now."

"If you don't do your job, there will be no opening to the end-point of the device."

"Is that a no?" she asks.

"Yeah. That's a no…"

"Then I take my leave," she says.

The man is silent as Korsaume drops to the floor below, and he closes up the hole he made with a steam welder. Within moments, it is as if there had never been a hole there at all.

"Wonderful," she says just after the welding is complete. "What do I do now?"

*****

Mathew and Rosetta sit at a booth not far from her ship; a Star Field class Stellar Cruiser. The booth has no table; just red plush seats set into the wall. The booth sits at the corner of one of a seemingly infinite amount of junctions.

The two are laughing, possibly at a joke, or something else they mutually find humorous.

"Oh, to be with you, Mathew…" she says grabbing his left arm in her hands and pressing her right cheek to his shoulder, a beautiful smile on her face.

"You could be with me."

"And how do you suggest I do this?"

"Well, you could follow my crew and myself to Pikornauc'for and travel with us from there."

She looks at him and takes a moment to think.

"You could do some bounty-hunting at the inner-galactic planets."

"Hm," she sighs, "I think I could handle that."

"So, you will?"

"I don't need to think about it. I would come aboard now if you all had room for me."

"Believe me, I wish we did. I would pull you aboard immediately." He pulls his left arm free of her grasp and places it over her head and around her back, his left hand on her left shoulder.

The two of them sit comfortably for several minutes, silent, her head on his upper chest, and her left hand over his heart. She feels the rhythm beating inside him and her stomach settles as the beat soothes her mind, his warmth heating her own heart.

They are rather suddenly interrupted by gunfire.

Both look up in time to see Korsaume running through the hallway directly for them, her head turning occasionally, a gun in her right hand as she pulls the trigger several times at a man running after her.

"Korsaume," yells Mathew, but his word is cut short as Rosetta pushes him to the ground as a ray from the chasing person hits the wall behind where they sat. Mathew and Rosetta are both on the floor about seven feet from the booth. Korsaume runs up to them and helps Mathew pull his girlfriend behind the wall.

Another shot from the man skims the wall and slices a hole right through it hitting Korsaume's right hand. She drops her seven-eighty.

"We've got a problem, Captain."

"I would never have guessed if you hadn't said something," he says picking up the gun while Korsaume nurses her hand.

The two switch places. Mathew and the man chasing his Lieutenant trade a couple shots, both missing each other even when the rays burn holes through the walls.

"This looks like quite a dilemma you've got yourself into, Korsaume," says Rosetta dusting herself off after arising from the floor. She takes a hard breath. "What did you do, cheat at a game of cards with a gang of hustlers?"

"Actually, it's much worse than that." She squeezes the wound hard and blood drips from between her fingers to the floor.

"Perhaps we can talk about it after we come away from this alive," says Mathew, almost as a question. He turns the corner once more and fires just as the other man does the same. The other man does not get a shot off as the ray from the seven-eighty hits the man squarely in his upper right chest. "I got him. Shall we go?"

The three of them run down the corridor to where the man lays with a hole through his shoulder. He winces in pain, looks up at the trio, and glares at Korsaume. "Don't forget, Sherise," he smiles at her, "you're going to die, now. You cannot turn the tide. You and your friends will not live to see tomorrow."

The man takes a small box from his jacket pocket and presses a small button. Right before their eyes, his body disintegrates.

"Another tesseract," says Mathew. "Where do we get some of these?"

"Actually, Mathew," says Rosetta, "that was a suicide box. He's dead, with no evidence he was ever here."

Korsaume looks at Rosetta, then at Mathew. "We have much to discuss, Captain," she says as seriously as possible.

*****

Agoparn comes through the doorway of the "Vibrant's" docking shell and up the stairs immediately to his right. As he reaches the top of the stairs, Lacendu greets him.

"Hey, Parn; we're all having a meeting in the mess. You're invited."

"Great," Agoparn cheerfully says.

He walks with her into the mess where Mathew, Rosetta, Allen, and Vaskette sit at the table. Korsaume sits on the counter on the left where the sink sits.

"Have a seat, Engineer," says Mathew candidly. "Korsaume just had an epiphany."

"If you didn't sound so terse and grave, I would think you were kidding."

"He's not," says Korsaume. "Please." She gestures to the booth.

Lacendu sits down after Agoparn touches her left side in a signal to sit in the only empty spot in the booth. He stands next to her.

"I am not Korsaume," she begins. "My real name is Sherise Felder."

"That explains that," says Rosetta with a harsh look, referring to the man who killed himself calling her by her first name only a half-hour earlier.

Sherise looks at the bounty-huntress for a moment, but forgoes any rebuttals. Instead, she continues, "I am indeed a weapons' expert and tactician. There's one big difference between the five of you, and myself." She pauses for a moment making certain she wants to divulge this information. "They did not take my memories."

The other five seem very surprised, and Rosetta gives her a severe look.

"Then," starts Lacendu, "you know what happened to us…" She almost smiles.

"No. Unfortunately that is not so. I arrived after your memory loss. How they did it, I don't know. My sole purpose was to dispose of you."

All of them look alarmed. Mathew says, "So you were the one that tried to kill Vaskette on Ablose."

Vaskette looks up with widened eyes and a deep breath. "YOU…?"

"Wait," says Korsaume, "before you pass judgment, I must tell you that that was the biggest mistake I've ever made in my entire life."

"Not quite," says Lacendu, "your biggest mistake was not telling us all of this when we first woke up!"

Mathew looks over at them calmly. "Hold off just a moment, Ladies. Korsaume is being honest with us now. That counts for something."

"Not much," says Lacendu folding her arms and turning her head away from the Lieutenant.

"Thank you, Captain," she says and proceeds, "The reason I have been so upset is because when I awoke I didn't receive just my name on a sheet of paper, but a note from Chrinsole stating that I would not be able to make it back home without the five of you. I knew it was so because I have no experience flying star vessels. I saw no reason to kill any of you until the opportunity was right. As the past three weeks have unraveled, I've grown accustomed to all of you and, unfortunately for someone in my line of business, quite attached."

"And what is your line of business, Sherise," asks Vaskette rudely.

"I do the Solar Union's dirty work; or at least I used to. I worked for a group called the Caste of Hierarchical Electorates. I've killed many people as a job; many of them very similar to you. I never had the opportunity to get acquainted with any one of them, like I have you."

"Very convenient, since you're now being hunted down," adds Rosetta. "What happened? You didn't get your job done and now someone else is here to finish it…?"

"Both of those statements are correct. When I failed, practically on purpose, to kill Vaskette, my boss found out and sent some people like me to do what had to be done."

"Practically on purpose," Vaskette says sarcastically.

"I will repeat, good Doctor, that after getting to know all of you, I had no true desire to get rid of you. I was very upset with myself for harming you at all."

"What do we do, now," asks Allen giving her a scowl. "Now we're caught in a battle for our lives."

"You've been in a battle for your lives for months," says Korsaume, "only now, I'm included in the battle."

"So you want us to protect you," asks Mathew.

"Not even close," she starts, pushing her hands against the sink counter. "I suggest we all find a way to get rid of those men and women now doing what I used to do. My boss, ex-boss now, will send more and more after us until he gets what he wants."

"And can you tell us about ourselves?" Lacendu smiles suddenly, showing teeth.

"I don't know any more about you than you do. Like I said, your memory was erased after I was paid, but before I was sent to kill you. The only information I had was what you looked like, with approximate vicinity where all of you might be…"

"Were we together at the time?"

"I believe so. I arrived on the moon of Mercedes, where you were all supposed to be in stasis pods. It was dark out, and I used my normal equipment to hunt for your shuttle. When I came upon your shuttle, I prepared my weapon to kill all of you one at a time."

"You make this sound so easy," says Vaskette.

"It was easy; at the time. That **is** what I did for a living. I was recruited by the CHE when I was fresh out of the academy, at the ripe age of eighteen. I went through years of rigorous training and study to become a heartless, cold-blooded killer. I was threatened with my life to keep my institution in the organization's rites, and in the end I did so with enjoyment.

"Back to my story: I got ready to fire upon one of you; I think it was Agoparn; when someone came up behind me. I did not get the opportunity to see who it was before I was dropped to the ground unconscious and the next thing I knew I was laying on my back on a star chart table."

Nobody says anything for a moment.

Allen speaks next, "So, if some of those people on the station are out to kill all of us, and they're all weapon's experts and tacticians just like you, what chance do we stand of escaping here with our lives. Might it be you just feel guilty and are prepared to do us all in…?"

Chaos ensues. Vaskette, Lacendu, and Agoparn all agree with Allen's rationale of the situation and proclaim so loudly. Rosetta calls for them to hear Sherise out while Sherise tries to speak.

Mathew finally stands up and talks over all of them. "ENOUGH!!!" The room settles down. "We've only known each other for a few short weeks, but we've been in these cramped quarters for most of it. If we all admit facts to ourselves, it is very possible that any one of us could be keeping secrets from the others. We hardly know each other."

"How can you stand up for her, Captain," says Vaskette harshly. "If she's been lying to any one of us in this room it's to you!"

"Agreed, Captain," Agoparn admits.

"Unless you're keeping a secret from us as well…" says Lacendu.

"That's paranoia," Sherise shakes her head.

"I think Lacy has every right to be paranoid now," says Mathew looking at her. "…as do we all. Vaskette is right. You have kept many secrets from us. I am standing up for your rights, which I probably shouldn't be doing right now; so I suggest you come out with what you, as the resident weapons' expert and tactician in our group, think we should do."

Korsaume takes her eyes away from Mathew's and points them down at the floor, glancing a few times up at everyone and back to the floor. She heaves a sigh breathes out loudly. "I don't have any suggestions for us as far as staying here. I personally believe we should leave immediately, while we're all still alive. Chances are they'll begin chasing us, and the Solar Union will make us all wanted criminals. That means we won't be able to go to Pikornauc'for. The first chance we'll get to land anywhere is at the inner-galactic territories."

All of them sit to think for a minute.

"I say we leave Sherise here and get away while we're all still in one piece," Allen states, almost as if he says this only because he must.

"All in favor," asks Mathew.

As all of them raise their hands, Sherise looks at her captain with shock. "Are you serious?"

"You're votes are tallied, and Sherise Felder stays on the ribbon station. All those in favor of keeping Korsaume on board with us, raise your hands," he says.

All but Rosetta look at him with some confusion.

The bounty-huntress speaks; "Very clever, Mathew." Then to the crew, "Korsaume is a nice woman and a strong spirit for a tactical officer, as well as a weapon's expert. I would venture to say that you all need her as much as she needs you."

"Who are you to speak," asks Sherise. "You're not part of the crew."

"On the contrary," Mathew says, "she's with me, Tactician. All in favor of allowing Korsaume on board as our tactician and weapon's expert…" Mathew's hand goes into the air.

Rosetta raises her hand, followed by Agoparn, then Allen and Lacendu.

Vaskette folds her hands together and looks at her limbs stretched out before her. "Does this mean you're not going to try to kill us, now?"

Sherise sighs tiredly. "Vaskette, when I said, 'that was the biggest mistake of my life,' I meant it. I wanted to follow through with my job, as I had been trained to do, but my experience with you here kept me from trying as hard as I would normally have. I am grateful that you survived, and regret my mistake. I would love to be able to make it up to you, but I have no idea what would ever possibly do…"

By now, the others have put their hands down.

Vaskette continues to stare at her arms in front of her on the table. "You could start by apologizing."

"Doctor Vaskette Smith," Sherise begins without hesitation, "I am deeply sorry for my actions. Will you forgive me?"

The Doctor sits for a moment longer. "All those in favor of Korsaume joining our crew," she asks in her Captain's place.

All but Sherise raise their hands simultaneously.

"Then it's settled." Mathew turns to Sherise with an outstretched left hand. "Welcome aboard the 'Vibrant,' Korsaume. Will you take your place as tactician and weapon's expert among my fabulous crew?"

Sherise looks at Mathew with tears in her eyes; then to the others. She swallows hard as the trickles of salty water make their solemn way down her face passing her nose, then her lips, and finally hanging delicately from her chin. She takes his hand firmly and shakes it, smiling at him. Her eyes flood up and she pulls her hand gently from his grasp, grabs a towel from behind her and tries to dry her eyes. She sniffles a bit as she dabs her face of the water. "I will, Captain."

The door to the mess opens up slightly, and Mr. Folzandine peaks his head in. "Did I hear correctly that we won't be stopping at Pikornauc'for?"

"Excuse me, Sir," says the captain rather loudly, "this is a private matter, and I told you hours ago to stay in the observatory!"

"Oh, I did not mean anything by it, Captain," he says. "I just could not help overhearing about your disheartening predicament, and I thought maybe I could help in some way."

"How do you think you could help us," asks Allen.

"Oh, we'll think of a way," comes a woman's voice from behind the man at the door.

There is a sound of the cocking of a rifle, and Sherise instantly knows what it is. "That's my super-HOP!"

"Correct," says the man. "I believe we shall receive a plenteous prize for your capture. We have already informed the station that criminals are aboard, and they are on their way even now." He smiles to himself.

"I thought you were criminals," says Mathew plainly.

"That's what you get for thinking, my dear Captain," the man says dryly. "I said there was an incident. I did not say what kind. A man paid us to go to Ablose where you were and to try to get aboard and make certain you came to Pikornauc'for. However, since you won't be going there, I figured our deal was off. So I made another one. I really hope you don't mind, but I suppose it is irrelevant whether you mind or don't mind, just as long as we get paid, and arrive at Pikornauc'for."

"I, for one, could care less whether we're aboard your charming little vessel when we get there, or on a passenger or carrier vessel," says the woman.

"I couldn't agree more, My Love."

Episode 5
Singularity

OPENING:

"...Still the ever-beast, the wilde Cornusis runs rampant and unhampered through the wilderness of Pikornauc'for, its streamlined body moving like a freight-carrier on its way to the station. Its form is that of wonder, and its eyes blaze with the essence of the darkness where it makes its home..."

Mathew awakens suddenly from a bad dream. It is unfortunate for him that the bad dream seems better than the reality he wakes up to. The holding-cell is rather small and cramped, and the pillow below his head sits on the cold, hard floor where the rest of his body lays in a state of near-frozenness. He looks over to his left where the form of his girlfriend, Rosetta, is stretched out on the small bed made for one. She gave him the pillow the evening before and her head rests on her jacket, which she folded underneath her. One of the jacket's arms hangs off the head of the bed.

The lights are out in the cells, but just outside the bars are the fluorescent lights of the Enforcer's office shining into the cell, and keeping him from staying asleep for more than an hour or two at a time.

He hears some snoring coming from the right side of the cell, and knowing who's in it, he believes it to be Agoparn's, but it could be Lacendu's; he's not entirely sure.

He lays back again to rest, but the lights and the cold floor keep his eyes from remaining closed long enough to fall back to sleep.

"It's been a long night," he mutters to himself quietly.

"Are you awake, Love," asks Rosetta.

"How could I be asleep?"

She rolls onto her right side and looks down to the floor where his head rests solemnly on the pillow. "Would you like to join me?"

"That bed is only built for one, Seta."

"I'm sure we can manage. I hate to think you're cold down there when I'm all warm and comfortable up here. Come on…"

Mathew gets up gladly while Rosetta pushes herself as far against the wall as possible. Mathew lies down next to her on the remaining two feet of the bed and wraps his left arm under her head. She rests her head on his shoulder and places her left hand on his gently rising chest. Both of them fall asleep rather quickly, and Mathew manages to spend the rest of the night asleep.

*****

"Time to get up," a voice spoken plainly echoes through the metal walls of the cell chambers, and lastly through their ears.

"Just one more day, officer," says Rosetta groggily.

"Come on, dear," says Mathew raising her up with his arm. "It's probably important."

"You're tripping exact, Captain Mathew Arnold," the officer states. "It's very important. It seems you're all wanted by the Solar Union. Everyone, that is, with the exception of the bounty-huntress, which just makes her guilty by association."

The crew is being roused by the conversation and wiping their eyes.

"So how much are we worth to the 'Es-Yu,' Enforcer," Allen facetiously asks.

"I said you were wanted…I said nothing about you being valuable."

"Are you saying we're worthless," asks Vaskette. Not looking up she sits on the edge of the bed, which Allen was kind enough to let her use through the night.

"Now, now," he says, "I didn't say that, either. According to the records, you're wanted dead. It specifies 'dead.'"

"That figures," says Korsaume. "I suppose now you're going to stick us in sealed body bags, alive of course, and let us suffocate while you send us back to Tcheckine via a CHE-provided tesseractor."

"Actually, I'm just going to turn you over to the Solar Union Representatives that happen to be on the station at this moment." The man sits down at his desk as a group of seven men and four women, complete with large guns at their sides and dark-green leather suits on, walks in. He begins to sign the hand-held giving the eleven of them permission to take the crew away.

"Hello, again, Preston," says Korsaume sitting back onto the bed and folding her wrists over each other. She gives the man a pleasant smile.

"Hello to you again, Sherise. It's strange to have you on that side of the hunt…"

"It is a little different."

"That's what you get for not finishing what you started. I thought you knew better," says one of the women. "To think I used to look up to you…"

"Now you admit it, Ostra," Korsaume blandly states.

"Enough with the pleasantries," says Preston Wiggins. "Retrieval squad, get into place. Prepare to take the crew of the 'Vibrant' into custody." He turns his attention to the people behind the cell bars and speaks, "Luckily for the six of you, we respect the station's rules and regulations. We have to wait until we get you all on board our ship before we can kill you."

Mathew stands forward near the bars. "You said 'six.' Does this mean that Rosetta is free to leave?"

"Certainly… We have no specific orders on what to do with the friends of our prey. I think she'll be tortured enough knowing she couldn't help her friends and lover."

Rosetta, right arm around Mathew, turns to face him directly, sliding her other arm around his chest, a furrow in her brow and a tear on her cheek; though her face angles down to his chest, her deep purple eyes look up into his. "Don't be too sure about that…" she says loudly enough to be heard by the eleven Solar Union officials. Then to Mathew, "I love you. With all my abilities, I will find a way to be with you again."

"I believe you." Mathew smiles at her, leans into her face, and they kiss for a long moment. For the two of them it's not nearly long enough.

Mathew's arm is grabbed moments later and his body is pulled away from hers, and the two suddenly feel everything in slow motion. Though time seems to be going slower, the unhurried movie they both watch from their different angles does not last long enough to keep.

"This has got to be a testament to our abilities," says Korsaume as the crew is ushered out the door of the Enforcer's office. "It took eleven of you to get six of us… What does that say about our abilities? We <u>are</u> the best in our fields…"

"You <u>were</u> the best in your fields," Preston corrects her. "Once you're dead, the food chain moves up."

"…And I suppose the Solar Union will grab them and do with the new group what they did with these five in the hopes that the newbie's will follow the CHE's grand design and do as their told?"

"Since I don't know what the Solar Union wanted with the finest in war, I really couldn't tell you, but I am going to assume that those other six have been chosen, sent to do what they were asked, and completed the mission; whatever that mission was."

"Can't you see you're being used?" She knows it's a futile attempt, but she tries anyway.

"Oh, yeah; we've all been being used since we were born. You think the Solar Union Committee doesn't know who will be chosen to join them in their lofty positions once they're grown up? Or how about you, when you were a child…do you think they had not already prepared to invite you into the CHE?"

"Wow. When you put it that way, Preston, we're all doomed," Korsaume says with as much sarcasm as she can muster.

"No, you're doomed. Only those who do what they're told live," he says with a smirk.

This conversation occurs as the six crewmembers are marched down a long corridor toward the CHE team's ship.

Korsaume looks around at the eleven looking for an opportunity to escape. She knows Preston is watching her for just such a move and when she feels his weapon tapping her on her left side, she knows what it means: head forward.

*****

Rosetta walks past the guards and out of the Enforcer's office several minutes after her boyfriend and new crewmates left. The Chief Enforcer held her for several minutes to keep her from 'interfering with Solar Union activities,' as he called it.

She stops just out of sight of the guards and looks down a random corridor. It is only seconds before a blonde haired man in a dark green uniform approaches her. He has a mono-pulsating sonic open-circuit pistol at his right side.

"I've seen one of those pistols before," she says to the man as he stops in front of her. "It is Solar Union protocol for committee members…"

The man shushes her and smiles. "You are Rosetta Firemark…" He says it more like a question than a statement.

"I am…"

"You know who Mathew Arnold is, correct?"

"Um, yes. You're too late, though. Your CHE friends, whatever the CHE is, took them away about five minutes ago."

"Trant," he exclaims grabbing a small communications devise from a pocket. He speaks into it, "They've already been taken into custody by the CHE. Move to intercept at the Star Journey immediately." He then turns to Rosetta, "Follow me, Huntress…"

"You mean you're not with the CHE?"

"Not anymore," replies the man and adds, "Speak less…run faster."

The two dart through one of the corridors and as their feet hit the metal floor, the sounds echo through the hallways, matching the rhythm of her heart.

He continues with a steady voice though he is running hard, "The man who kept your new crewmates alive has cut all ties with the CHE and has begun his own work outside the Solar Union's watchful eyes. He took the opportunity before he left the CHE to talk several people still loyal to the populace of the galaxy into joining him. That's all I can discuss with you at present, but I assure you that I'm on your side."

It is only a matter of moments before they turn a corner and see the seventeen people they're looking for with four others Rosetta did not expect.

"My friends made it here before us…" he comments to her as the two get to within ten meters from the large group in the middle of the corridor.

"Preston Wiggins, by authority of the Solar Union I demand that you release those six people immediately!" The man commands authority with his voice, and Rosetta is suddenly very glad she met him.

Preston turns to face his adversary. "That's a very humorous comment you make, Drekker, since you and your crew of dissidents are no longer part of the Solar Union."

"We're more a part of the Es Yu than you or the CHE will ever be. We're still loyal to the people."

"Like the CHE is not," yells one of the ladies pointing her gun at Drekker preparing to fire.

Preston places his left hand on the woman's weapon to lower it. "We obviously have different views, Drekker, but I assure you that there is a mutually beneficial term we can reach with each other. For instance, we can take these six back to Tcheckine, you may return with us in your own vehicle, and we will be more than happy to turn these rebels over to you at that time…"

"You really have a lot of gall," says Rosetta to Preston.

"Actually, it's a good idea," says Korsaume. "Maybe you should take him up on it."

"Whose side are you on," asks Mathew in surprise, "or was I wrong in thinking you'd changed your evil ways, Sherise?" He says her real name with obvious distaste.

Rosetta is a little shocked at their sudden outbursts. "Mathew, sweetheart, this is not the time," she says to her boyfriend.

"SHUT UP," he yells back at her. "Korsaume, you are the lowest life-form of low life forms. You should be dragged to a science lab and studied under a microscope. I think they might actually find a heart in there; along with your uni-celled brain!"

Korsaume slaps him. "Look here, you overgrown embryo," she says walking up very close to her captain, their eyes locking, "Your crew would follow you to the pit of hell, and it seems that's exactly where we're all about to go. You got us into this mess, and I really don't see your immense genius getting us out of it, so why don't you take your stupid crew and get on the floor and let them kick you a few times!"

"I think I will," he yells at her. "Crew…drop!"

Suddenly, the six of them fall quickly to the floor, as does Rosetta, as the five people in green open a cross-fire at the unprepared eleven CHE people. One of them realizes what was going on rather rapidly and drops to her knees about the same moment the weapons begin discharging. She points her gun at Vaskette before any of them have the instinct to stop her, and the discharge hits the Doctor in her back. Her face already to the wall, she hits it as she falls forward.

Eight of the CHE members are felled before they have an opportunity to get their weapons pointed. The other three duck down behind their fallen comrades and try to quell the firefight. The woman who shot Vaskette is neutralized within seconds, and the other two soon realize they are outnumbered. Preston is one, and the other is Ostra.

Preston stands up pulling with him Lacendu as a hostage. Ostra takes her queue from her leader and grabs the injured Vaskette, who is in severe shock, and pulls her helplessly to her feet. Both are facing away from each other and they use it to their advantage.

Preston begins, "This fight is over, children. We will take these two to our ship and be on our way. The other four will die soon enough; it just may take a little longer; that's all."

"Out of the way," says Ostra forcefully to the four between them and their ship. "Move it or the good lady gets it."

"She's already got it," says one of the men moving to the side to allow them to pass. "She may already be dead."

Drekker moves closer to the people lying on the ground followed closely by Rosetta who more ducks down to walk giving her head clearance from gun-fire. She sees the eight CHE members lying on the ground with wounds that don't look like they'll heal any time soon, and notices that three of them aren't breathing.

Rosetta tries, "You can't get away from here, Preston. You won't be cleared for departure. I've already called ahead before we got here not to allow your ship to depart."

"Whatever," he smiles at her. "Solar Union gets top priority!"

"Not when there might be a bomb on board meant for your annihilation. I would hate to think that someone was trying to kill employees of the Solar Union…" She smiles giving him her poker face.

At first, Preston is disinclined to believe her, but as he looks at her his mind begins to falter.

"Go ahead, mister know-it-all. Get in your ship and see how far you get. The bomb-squad is already on its way down here to give your good vessel the thrice-over to safe-guard your flight from here." She pauses a moment for affect. "Like I said, you can't get away from here. At least, not with your dignity intact…" she laughs.

Ostra pulls her hostage around to face the same direction as her leader. "What do we do now," she almost whispers it. "If we can't leave quickly, they'll have the upper-hand…"

Preston looks regretfully at her. "They already have the upper-hand. I think she's bluffing, but I can't read minds…"

Mathew rises from the cold metal floor, his arms feeling the rush of cool air from the vents above his head. The air makes his arms feel even colder, but he manages to keep a steady chin in the midst of his discomfort.

"It's a simple equation, Preston," he says with a look that says he knows something, "you drop the two girls and I give you my word I won't let anyone here fire upon you. You might, I repeat 'might,' get away from here with some dignity."

"Well you certainly don't expect me to trust you, do you," asks Preston. "Besides, I've still got a job to carry out…"

At this, Korsaume rolls over on her back and sits up. "Preston," she says, and then adds, "Dear Preston… Don't you think that I would have had a very compelling reason to keep these five alive? They have something more than value as dead prey to you."

"Like what," asks Preston.

She didn't think he'd fall for it, but she thinks quickly, "I've had almost three weeks to kill them; nine if you include the time before my assassination was stopped and I awoke on the 'Vibrant.' I didn't do it because I found out the real cause of why their memory was erased…"

"Why is that," comes from Preston while Mathew simultaneously looks over at her and asks softly with one raised eyebrow, "You did?"

Now she really reaches into the back of her mind putting some of the pieces of the puzzle together, even if they don't fit. She makes it up as she goes, "I found out that these five people were to start a war. Their very presence, mixed with their lack of knowledge about who they used to be and their expertise in piloting, strategy, healing and medicine, mathematics, and engineering could be combined as a dangerous catalyst to assist the Solar Union in taking over all the remaining parts of the galaxy that refuse to accept the Committee's leadership. I quickly realized this, and since my presence with them was unforeseen, I figured I could help my CHE leaders fulfill that goal. Your being here has ruined everything, you dolt!"

"Why should I believe you?"

"Like I said before, I've been traveling with them for almost three weeks. I know them much better than you do. Even the reports don't do their genius justice. I believe that when their memories were erased, they were programmed. Some combination of words will cause them to switch into that mode and I believe that that combination is on the 'Vibrant.' I've been searching its database since I figured out what was going on, and I haven't found the word-combination yet..."

"Then why did our leaders send the twelve of us to kill all of you?"

"Have you heard of a man named 'Chrinsole'?"

"Yes. He left the CHE leader's circle a couple of weeks ago. I hear he did so under duress..."

"Chrinsole was responsible for stopping my assassination of these people. The CHE might think he de-programmed these five. I don't blame the CHE for wanting to start from scratch. Think about it, though, Preston; if I can get the ball rolling again, the Solar Union Committee can take over this side of the galaxy at the same time as the other side with the new six-member crew there that we haven't been hired to kill."

As Korsaume completes her last sentence two enforcers walk up followed by the Chief Enforcer.

"I'm not certain, yet, what to think of this situation," begins the Chief Enforcer, "I know I just released six of you to the nine on the floor and the two holding hostages, and the huntress I released without incident. What I can't figure out is why Solar Union officials are lying beaten on the floor and four additional folks in green outfits stand holding guns at their sides. I admit that it's possible I missed something, but I assure all of you that I have overheard everything, and have the entire occurrence on video. There's just one more thing I need to know…" He steps between his two men and out in front of them to stand very near Rosetta. "Why should I let ANY of you leave this station now?"

Everyone is silent for a long moment.

"Come, now. One of you must have an answer. Four men in dark green outfits open fire on Solar Union Officials escorting six wanted fugitives. Three of the Solar Union officials seem dead to me," turning to one of his men, then the other, "do they to you, gentlemen…?"

The two men nod.

"Now, two of the officials are using their captured prey as hostages and having a philosophical debate with two of the six they were sent to capture about the underlying reasons for the Solar Union's decisions about six people none of them even seem to know. So, what do all of you suggest I do? Let all of you go and pretend this incident never occurred? By the way, Preston, there was no phone call about a bomb on board your ship, so be assured for now that none of my Enforcers will be searching your ship. You can rest easy, now, as I escort everyone to holding cells until someone comes to straighten things out…"

"Just out of curiosity, sir," says Allen standing up, "who will be coming to 'straighten things out.'"

"I don't expect you'll need an answer to that," says Preston. He looks at Ostra and the two of them back slowly toward their ship.

Mathew's eyes widen and he looks back and forth from the Solar Union people pulling two of his crew away, and the Chief Enforcer. "You can't let them do this!"

"Actually," the Chief Enforcer replies, "I don't have much of a choice. They're Solar Union Officials. Legally, I can do nothing...and they're holding hostages which I have no desire to put in danger."

They allow the two officials to get to their ship with Vaskette and Lacendu.

Mathew balls up his hands into fists and stares down the Chief Enforcer. He pounds the wall beside him as hard as he can with the left one, injuring his hand and sending an echo through the hallways. Through clenched teeth, he says, "You may not be able to do anything about this, but we can!"

"I can't allow you to leave..."

Mathew's eyebrows furrow hard, he breathes heavily, clinches his teeth tightly, and looks like he might literally explode.

"Are you really going to stop us, Chief Enforcer," asks Korsaume.

"I don't see any other options." His eyes narrow to slits, daring her.

"We could tell our leaders we were caught off guard..." says one of the other enforcers. The other one agrees, "I think we could do that..."

The Chief Enforcer turns to them. "You two are in league with these folks, or something?"

"No sir," says the second, "but those officials are toting hostages..."

The Chief Enforcer seems a little upset, but turns to them. "I, of course, cannot allow everyone of you to leave. I must keep some people here to give you a reason to come back."

Rosetta steps forward. "I'll stay. Mathew would have a reason to return for me."

"Me, too," Allen adds. "I'm not absolutely vital on the ship, but..."

Mathew cuts off Allen. "Allen, I disagree with you. I will need you to help us figure out how to get Vaskette and Lacendu back."

"I'll stay, Captain," says Korsaume. You do NOT need me. You men are quite capable of using weapons when you need to. I also have full faith in your abilities..."

"Thank you, Lieutenant Tactician. We appreciate your faith in us," says Mathew.

"Wow, I've been promoted?"

"Oh, well; perhaps it was a slip of the tongue…" Mathew smiles at her through his still-clinched teeth.

Korsaume smiles at Mathew. "Bring our doctor and mathematician back to us, Captain…"

"I'm all over it," and then to the Chief Enforcer, "with your permission, Chief Enforcer…"

The Chief Enforcer pauses for a moment. "Go! We'll discuss the terms of your punishment when you return…"

"With your permission," says Drekker, "I request the honor of joining you. You may need me if they reach the secret tesseracter…"

"Very well, sir," Mathew says, "you may join us on the 'Vibrant.' I expect no less than complete loyalty from you."

"Believe me, Captain, you'll get nothing less than you expect."

The four men walk down the corridor to the 'Vibrant' while the Chief Enforcer makes preparations for them to depart immediately.

*****

"Do we have their flight path from Steg, yet, Drekker?" Mathew sits uncomfortably in the pilot's chair working the controls as the ship flies further and further from the orbital ribbon station.

Drekker looks over the controls and glances at Agoparn who sits in his chair, looking like he's still in pain from hitting the floor so hard. Drekker looks back at the screen. "I'm receiving the information right now, Captain. It looks like they're heading toward Quadrant 91281, Latitude 438, Longitude 19, 164-square thruster burst."

"Matching directions is the easy part, but we don't have that high of a thruster burst," says Mathew.

"It's OK," says Drekker. "We can compensate for that by switching to a repulse engagement using Steg's planetary gravity."

"We can utilize that this far out," asks Mathew.

"Captain," begins Drekker, "I am certain that if you still had your full memory, you would have thought of it. You started utilizing the procedure in your war days, and believe me, I have studied the war and your name comes up a lot in the archives…"

"Great," says Mathew smiling, "I'm a war hero and I don't have a single thing to remind me of my seemingly great exploits."

"You have me, Captain," says Drekker.

"Now there's a comforting thought," says Allen continuing to punch buttons.

"…Anything I need to do, Captain," asks Agoparn with some gruffness in his voice.

"Yes, Parn," says Mathew. "Turn off all engines and reverse the ship; head for Steg in exactly 180 degrees of our destination."

Agoparn looks at the back of Mathew's head with a strange look, but does what he's told. "Heading is now 180 degrees of our destination, Captain," Agoparn says with a dour note.

"Now, Parn, restart thrusters…"

Agoparn sighs, but punches some buttons anyway. "Reverse thrusters in effect, Captain. I'm waiting for the part where I say, 'WOW, Captain, that's a really neat trick.'"

"We're getting there, Engineer. Maximum thrusters…"

"Maximum thrusters, Captain."

"Counter-charge the hull."

"Counter-charging the hull, Captain…since it only affects the nose of the ship I think I see where this is going…"

"Speed, Allen."

"One hundred six percent of maximum speed and rising, Captain," Allen says.

"When it reaches one hundred sixty-three percent, flip the ship around, Engineer," says Mathew.

"Wow," says Agoparn, "this is turning out to be a neat trick…"

"One hundred thirty percent, one hundred forty five percent, one hundred sixty percent…" Allen gives the count.

"NOW!" yells Mathew.

The pressure inside the ship is tremendous, but tolerable for all of them as their seating belts are stressed as well as their bodies. The ship turns back around.

"Speed continuing to rise, Captain," continues Allen. "One hundred eighty percent and rising slower now; one hundred ninety percent, one hundred ninety six percent, two hundred percent, two hundred three percent…"

"Hull straining under pressure, Captain," says Agoparn, "this ship was not built for these speeds."

"…And our crewmates aren't worth the chance, Engineer?"

"Now, now, good Captain, I didn't say that. I just wanted to warn you for future adventures…"

"Thank you for your input, Parn," says Mathew.

*****

Ostra sits at the controls guiding the Triumph class Stellar Cruiser to the secret tesseracter. To Preston, "Our bosses won't be happy with us, Sir."

"I think that, under the circumstances, we were fortunate to get what we got. I imagine that our next mission will be to kill this Chrinsole fellow and all who claim to follow him. He's a nuisance, and so are his men…"

"I agree, Sir. Where are our prisoners?"

"After the injection you gave them, they're in Amitora's cabin sleeping soundly. I want to deliver them alive now and kill them in front of Skien myself."

"Great idea, Sir. There's nothing better than showing your boss how you disposed of the traitors than right in front of him…"

"I hope you're not being sanctimonious, Ostra."

"No sir. We lost some good friends, today."

"Agreed."

"What do we tell Skien about the others?"

"We'll tell him exactly what happened. Chrinsole is still involved and the entire CHE will want him cremated and his ashes placed in an ancient urn after this incident."

"I know I wouldn't mind seeing him rot on a lonely planet with no tolerable atmosphere…slowly…" She pauses and looks at her charts and read-outs. "We'll be coming up on the tesseracter in a few minutes."

"Great. I'll enter my pass-code in about two minutes. I don't want to alert anyone else to our presence until it's too late for them to do anything about it."

*****

"Kinetic force still has us going at about one hundred seventy percent of maximum, Captain."

"Good, Parn. We should be coming up on their ship any moment now…"

"Aren't they going to spot us, Captain?" Allen glances at Mathew as the Captain turns around to look at his tactician.

"Only if they've got their sensors running… I don't believe they know we are chasing them."

"Captain, they're trained in the same school as my men and I. They're running sensors, and unless you have another trick up your sleeve; one that I haven't read about; we will be spotted," remarks Drekker.

"Question, Allen," says Mathew, "how soon will we be up on their ship?"

"Another three minutes, Captain," Allen replies.

Two and a half minutes pass in silence. Mathew stares straight ahead as the thruster-fire of the Triumph class Stellar Cruiser comes into view.

*****

"Preston, Sir, we're being followed," says Ostra. "They'll be up on us in a matter of seconds."

"We'll be entering the tesseracter in a matter of seconds."

"Should I burn the remaining fuel to get us there faster, Sir?"

"We'll be out of fuel when we reach the other side of the tesseract."

"There will be a ship waiting for us there, though…"

Preston pauses a moment; "Do it!"

*****

"Captain, they just started going faster…" Allen blurts out.

"I didn't think that was possible," Drekker says angrily pounding his fists on the terminal in front of him. He looks down at the counter ambiguously, then out the front window.

"How long until we reach them now, Allen," Mathew asks.

"They're going about the same speed we are…almost. We should overtake them in another twenty seconds…"

"What is that?" Mathew stares in surprise.

Allen and Agoparn both look out the window at the large circular object as light and electricity begins forking from one side to the other. Without slowing down, both ships come upon the object within a second or so of each other as the light and electricity conglomerate into a bright orange field. Suddenly, everything goes black.

*****

Locked in a large room, the people who remained after the shoot-out in the hallway sit quietly awaiting word on the two ships.

Naturally and without thought, they all have reformed their cliques, with the Solar Union persons who were not severely injured at a table on the left, the "Vibrant's" very own Korsaume sitting with Mathew's girlfriend, Rosetta, on the opposite side of the room, and the four remaining members of Chrinsole's group standing in between.

The two ladies don't sit quietly.

"So, what do you think Mathew will do to those 'agrauves' when he catches them," asks Rosetta.

"Knowing the Captain, he'll give them two options and then apologize for having only two. Then he'll ask their forgiveness for bothering them with the options and beat the life out of both of them…" She can't keep a straight face and her smile increases as she says this, until she finishes with a giggle.

Rosetta laughs. "You know him pretty well."

"It's something you get used to while on the ship for days at a time with the man. I won't say he doesn't exude authority when he's not making excuses for every little thing, but he seems more than a little insecure."

"And what about you, Korsaume…? What would you say is your weakness?"

Korsaume thinks for a moment. She knows what the woman's point is. She knows that Rosetta Firemark is using the opportunity to find out just how serious she is about changing her ways. "I'd say it's not being able to follow orders…" She smiles, looking down at her hands on the table.

"That can be good, sometimes, you know…" Rosetta places her right hand on the woman's left hand and clasps it.

"I know." It is almost a hoarse whisper.

The two sit in silence for a moment. Rosetta gently removes her hand and places it back with her other.

"Do you have any weaknesses, Seta?"

Rosetta takes a long pause before answering, "Yeah."

Korsaume gives her new friend a cock-eyed look and smiles as if expecting a better answer.

"Yeah, I have a weakness. It's for cute guys who seem unsure of themselves."

"Mathew radiates that, for certain."

"Yes, he does." She furrows her brows at Korsaume and adds, "I wonder how he switches into his authoritative mode."

Korsaume opens her mouth to speak making a sharp but quiet smacking sound in the process, "I've noticed he does that well when he realizes people might think less of him."

Rosetta gives a half-smirk and says, "…Perhaps it has something to do with his previous life; a life he can't remember."

"I wouldn't know. I never do background work on my targets. It helps to do that kind of job when you don't know anything about them."

"Is that what stopped you this time…you got to know them?"

"Most definitely…" Korsaume nods her head.

*****

"WHAT JUST HAPPENED!!!"

Preston sits down at the controls near Ostra and begins pressing buttons.

"Sorry, sir," says Ostra. "The tesseracter did not complete."

"WHY NOT…?!"

His continuous shouting angers her. "…BECAUSE THERE'S ANOTHER SHIP RIGHT NEXT TO US, SIR!" Then a little less brutal, but still with force, "The machine only had enough energy to tesseract one ship, not two. When it read the other ship, it shut down automatically."

Realizing he needs to calm down, Preston asks, "Does it have enough energy to try again?"

"No sir. We're stuck here until we can get some more Photonia."

*****

"Where are we," asks Mathew. "Did the gateway work?"

"No, sir," says Drekker, "It shut down when it noticed two different ships approaching."

"It may just be me, but I'm having mixed feelings about that…" says Allen. "Returning home would be a nice thing."

"Let's focus," says Mathew. "We've got shipmates to rescue."

A flashing light indicates a message being received, and Drekker alerts Mathew. "Captain, I believe Preston is trying to contact us."

"Put them through," Mathew says.

The next voice the four hear is Ostra's. "This is a truce message," she comments. "We request a temporary respite. We will return your crew members to you at the ribbon base around Steg."

"We have a condition," says Mathew.

"We are not in the mood to negotiate, Captain," they hear Preston's voice.

"This is not a negotiation," Mathew retorts, "It's a requirement. There's no 'take it or leave it.'"

A long pause.

"We're listening."

Mathew waits a moment giving them time to think and then continues. "You and your men will retract the bounty on our heads; all six of us; allowing us to leave the orbital ribbon station and continue on in peace."

"One moment, Captain," says Ostra.

The four sit in silence for several minutes.

"What do you think they're talking about?" Agoparn sits comfortably in his chair, arms crossed around his pudgy belly, a large smile on his face.

Drekker answers, "I'm betting the two of them are having a nice argument about what the difference is between a negotiation and a requirement."

Preston comes back on about the same moment Drekker finishes his sentence.

"I don't see that we have a choice, considering you've got us at a disadvantage…"

"I don't see any disadvantages," says Mathew. "I see a couple of tweaks who have no way to get back home holding my crew. You have plenty of choices here, but only one will keep you and yours safe from me!"

Allen looks at Agoparn who looks back with eyebrows raised. They smile at each other. Allen whispers, "That's one clever way to get out of being ambiguous…"

Preston continues over them, "Follow us back to the ribbon station. We will detract the bounty on your head and let your crew go. Don't think for a second that once all of this is cleared up that I won't chase you down, though."

Mathew admits, "I had no such thought. You are free to do so, but the next time you take us, you will take all of us, or I will make certain you don't live beyond the day…"

It is evident that Preston tries to reply, but Mathew hits the communication button shutting him off. "Agoparn, set a course to follow exactly the path their ship takes back to the Steg Ribbon Station. If they try anything, use a secondary offensive maneuver on their clock…"

Mathew gets up from his chair.

"Sir," Drekker begins to ask where he's going.

"You have your orders. I'll be back in a few minutes."

Mathew walks through the hallway to his cabin. Entering, he closes the door behind him and lies down on his bed to think. His left forearm is draped across his chest as it heaves with every breath, and his right forearm lies harshly on his forehead, the back of the hand resting gently on his left temple.

What is going on? This whole succession of events, I am CERTAIN, is not what we signed up for. Why are we in this mess? What are we supposed to do? We're no closer to finding the answers Chrinsole told us to seek. Here I am having serious doubts about leading all these people back to our home-worlds just because I'm not confident in my self, instead of being concerned for their safety once we get there…

*****

It is twenty minutes before the two ships are safely connected to the ribbon station once more and the crews, (one with their captives), are being escorted back to the room where their friends and co-workers sit waiting.

While Preston and Ostra join their group, and Drekker stands among his friends, Mathew, Allen, and Agoparn seat themselves with Rosetta and Korsaume.

"Did anything exciting happen while we were away?" Allen smiles at all of them.

"No, Allen," says Korsaume, "although it's unfortunate. I would have loved to sink my teeth into those people I used to work with…"

"Very vampire-like of you, Lieutenant," says Agoparn half-heartedly.

"They didn't mistreat you, did they, Korsaume?" Mathew disconcertedly asks.

"Only verbally," she says, hesitates, and then adds, "…and maybe a little with their eyes…"

"Well," Mathew says, "we'll have to deal with them a lot more on our way back home…"

"Why do you say that," asks Rosetta gripping Mathew's right hand in her left and giving him a concerned look of her own.

"You're not taking us with them through a tesseract, are you," asks Korsaume in surprise.

"Not quite," Mathew says holding his left hand up as a sign to keep her from getting worked up. "We pretty much, by accident, stopped them from getting back home. They need more photonia to get their tesseract up and running again."

Rosetta smiles, "Excellent. Considering that no one around here is producing photonia, they won't be getting back home before you do…"

"That's where the problem comes in. It's now a chase. We're going to try to elude them, and they'll be hunting for us. Since Vaskette and Lacy will be out of their sleep before the others, we'll have a slight head-start."

"I think you might be missing something, Captain," says Korsaume. "We're also under arrest…"

"No problem with that, either," says Agoparn. "They're going to cancel the warrant here so we can be on our way."

"That would make sense," she remarks. "Preston loves a good hunt…"

"Now we need to decide what we're going to do with two ships," says Rosetta.

*****

During the four hours that pass while the crew of the 'Vibrant' awaits the awakening of Vaskette and Lacendu, the others head to the ship traders. Rosetta and Korsaume discuss on their way down what the crew's needs are with Mathew, Agoparn, and Allen.

As the five come up to the front desk, Korsaume begins the negotiations with the man behind it. "We need a ship, and we're willing to trade two for one."

"What do you have, dear lady," asks the old-ish man with white hair and a hard face.

"We have a Star Field class Stellar Cruiser about nineteen years old, and a Vortex class Planetary Cruiser about five or six years old."

"…And what are you looking for, Miss?" The man smiles at her. "Those two types of ships are worth a lot to me in the tight market for ships in this area at the moment, especially in trade…"

"A Celestial class Star Expeditioner would be good. I saw one on my way in," answers Rosetta.

"Yes, Ma'am," says the man, "I have a zero-seven for sale. I would need additional funds for the trade, though."

"How much," Mathew asks in a commanding voice.

"About sixty-thousand currency…"

Mathew looks annoyed. "I'll give you fifty-thousand, and the two ships as mentioned. Take it or leave it."

The man looks appalled, but looks at the five and says, "Deal."

Mathew and Rosetta turn in their identity cards for their respective ships, and the man hands them the one for the zero-seven. Then the man escorts the five to their new ship to take a look around.

Agoparn immediately starts checking the engines and verifying its condition.

The ship is much larger than their previous vessels combined, with capacity for over a hundred passengers. Though it is not as fast as either of their prior vessels, it is still one of the fastest vessels available, and they all agree that they can use it to trade later when they find the vessel they really want.

*****

Hours pass as the five prepare the zero-seven for departure, and Vaskette and Lacendu finally arrive pushing a large hover-cart with the group's belongings from the 'Vibrant.'

The seven meet in the mess to discuss what to do next.

"I don't think there's any question about the direction we're heading," says Mathew, who is interrupted by Allen.

"To the inward planets…"

"Yes," Mathew says, "so if any of you have any suggestions, now is the time for them. Rosetta has a pretty good grasp on this side of the galaxy, so I'm placing her in charge of secondary command decisions."

"Agreed," says Korsaume.

"…And Korsaume is my Lieutenant, taking the place of Sherise, who we kicked off the team…" He smiles at her, and she smiles back.

"Thank you, Captain. I am honored to fill that position."

Mathew continues, "The rest of you will keep your regular duties based on your expertise."

"I might have something for us," says Agoparn.

The entire crew looks over questioningly at the man who sits with his arms folded.

"I met a young girl named Adrent while on my little getaway here on Steg. Her and her mother are from the inward planets, specifically Passelket, on the internal disk of the second limb of the Milky Way; about seven sectors away."

Allen interjects, "That's nearly a year away on this thing…"

Agoparn continues, "Yes. They said they were riding a 07 Celestial Class Star Expeditioner, too. So this may be the very vessel they traveled on…"

Mathew looks up at his girlfriend who stands not far from him. "Unless our second-in-command has a better idea, we'll head toward Passelket."

"None, Captain," says Rosetta. "I'm not familiar with that planet. It's probably on the first or fourth quarter of the disk."

"What does that mean," asks Vaskette. Everyone glances at her, and she responds, "Sorry. I'm not knowledgeable about the inward part of the galaxy…"

Rosetta explains, "The galaxy was split into four sections, kind of like a pie. The first quarter contains Earth. The second is left of the Earth facing the disk in the center of our galaxy. The fourth is where you are now, and the third is to our left facing the disk from this side."

Korsaume adds, "The first quarter contains the only Dyson-sphere known to exist, and that is where the leaders of the Solar Union do their decision-making. The further away from the first quarter you get, the harder it is for the Solar Union to keep tabs on everyone, so they have several satellite groups in the other three quarters, and each of them have their own ideas about how everything should work."

“That answers my questions,” says Vaskette, palms up in front of her as if giving in.

Lacendu looks as if she wants to say something and Mathew points at her and nods his head for her to say it. She glances at him, then down, and says, “Nothing.”

“You sure, Lacy…?” Mathew looks at her inquisitively.

“Yeah…”

“Anyone else…?”

There is silence for a while, and Mathew continues. “Did anyone find anything out about any of us while here?”

“I didn’t,” says Agoparn. “I was a little busy.”

“I think we all were,” says Vaskette. “I’ve spent entirely too much time on this station and wish to depart quickly and quietly.”

“Agreed,” says Rosetta and Korsaume together. They look at each other and smile.

“Supplies,” asks Mathew toward Agoparn.

“The team sent to do that should be done by now. I can go check.”

“Fine; you do that. The rest of you get to your stations and prepare for undocking within the hour.” Mathew arises and heads toward the door.

“I’m impressed,” says Korsaume quietly to Rosetta as the entire group starts conversations and heading out the door of the mess. “Mathew has grown quite commanding since you joined our team.” She smiles.

“I seem to have that effect on him,” Rosetta laughs gently.

The two walk off behind the others, followed finally by Allen who stops to listen to everyone’s conversation at the same moment. He takes it all in and gathers everything they say to each other.

“At last,” he smiles to himself. “I’m starting to be able to do what that medication Vaskette is giving us is supposed to do. I feel like I can think clearly.” He scratches his forehead for a moment, closes the mess door, and follows behind them at a distance, turning right to head up to command.

*****

Lacendu sits in her room with the door locked. Knowing she cannot do much until they need a math problem solved, she sighs to herself and picks up the first of the books the young man gave her two days ago and opens it up. She realizes she did not even read the cover, so she closes it on her thumb to read it: "Serious Calculus Calculations for the Mathematics Expert." It is more of a workbook in which the student can type notes in and answer questions. The young man obviously did not do well in the class, but he did not fail. On the cover is a red "sixty-two" in her handwriting.

She plugs in the keyboard to the notebook and an electron-impulse screen rises from the book. She opens a file of a recording of her voice.

"Good afternoon, Class," her voice begins, "My name is Cendu Trester. You will call me 'Professor' as long as you are in my class. Once you leave my class, you can call me whatever you desire." Laughter ensues, much of which belongs to the young man since he was closest to the audio-input device of this book.

"I will not put up with abuse of my material, and if you try to sell notes, voice-recordings, or outlines to other students past, present, or future, you <u>will</u> flunk my class. You have been warned.

"Open your books to the first page." Pages turn, and typing sounds echo through the microphone. Moments pass. "I am not much on semantics, so I like to get right into the class and get it all out of the way. The sooner you learn what I'm teaching, the sooner you can get out of here and do what you want with your life.

"Now, on page one, write your name." A long pause with sounds of writing, typing, and throats clearing… "Good. Let's move on to page sixteen. Chapter one; knowing your subject matter… Please read down these two pages and answer the questions."

Another long pause occurs, and she starts typing the answers to the questions figuring most of the calculations in her head within seconds. A few she uses the pad to make the calculations. The book's internal computer already knows the correct answers and checks hers against what it knows, grading her immediately after every answer.

She gets every answer correct.

Her voice continues. "For those that got less than fifty percent on this test, you're in the wrong class." She hears herself go on to dismiss three students. Their names do not seem even remotely familiar, but she does not expect them to.

"Some of you have been studying ahead. For those that do, you will pass this class, even if you don't do well… Anyone who follows along as we go won't necessarily be so lucky. I am being up front with you, so I expect all of you to be up front with me. If you are not prepared for class every day, you will be dismissed. If you are dismissed three times, you are out of my class. If you fail more than two sub-tests, you will be dismissed from my class. If you try, you stand a chance of passing my class.

"For the rest of you, let's begin. Chapter two; something new…" The subject matter seems entirely too familiar with her, but the events occurring in the audio recording of the classroom is not. She listens intently to try to find out more about herself. Sometimes she skips forward, or reviews a particular part she hears of herself that doesn't seem like her.

She finds out that she did have a sense of humor, and that her stuffiness was solely for the class. She is jovial with many of the students by the third class recording, and the students are calling her "Misses Calculator" by the fourth.

She smiles from time to time as she listens to herself go on for about forty minutes in each class experience. She gives them very little time to catch a break, so typing continues almost incessantly during the entire class.

Just before the end of the fourth class audio recording, there is a knock on the door, and she recognizes it as Vaskette's. She jumps to her feet from the chair and hides the book and equipment, stands up, presses the front of her blouse with both hands, and calmly walks to the door and opens it, preparing a smile for her friend.

The door opens quietly and there before her is her doctor. "Hi," she says with wide happy eyes.

"Hey, sweetie… Is everything alright?"

"Yeah…! What's going on?"

"Nothing… I just wanted to stop by and see how you're doing. It sounded like you were talking to yourself."

"Oh, I was just reading aloud to myself. I bought a book. I find reading it out loud helps me to focus on it."

Vaskette cocks her head a bit and smiles. "Well, if you'll come with me, I have another treatment for you ready, and you're past your time to get a shot…"

"Oh, yeah… I forgot all about that stuff. I've been feeling a lot better lately," she begins, closing the door behind her and walking alongside her friend. "This ship is so big," says Lacendu after they've been walking for a bit.

"Yes," Vaskette replies almost haphazardly.

A long pause, and then Lacendu continues, "I could so easily get lost here."

"Yes," says Vaskette, again sounding distant.

Lacendu looks over at her friend. "Are you ok?"

"Yes."

"You're speaking in one-liners. I think you're lying."

Vaskette hears the word "lying" and wakes from her daze. "Oh, Lacy, I'm sorry. I've got other things on my mind."

"You haven't told me what happened on your little get-away from the ship the other day…"

"Yeah, not much happened. I ate dinner, found a shop and looked around. I was going to buy something, but I decided against it."

"Why didn't you? You could be happy now…"

"Yeah, I guess. I just figured there was no one to show it off to… It was a real pretty outfit, but it just didn't seem like I'd have any place to use it."

The two walk silently for a minute. A sound behind them stops them dead in their tracks.

"Um, are any of us in their rooms right now?" Lacendu does not look at Vaskette.

"Not that I'm aware of…"

The two turn and walk to where they think they heard the noise. A small room where some supplies were placed, the door closed, is where they end up, and Vaskette opens the door.

The lights are off, so she turns it on.

The supplies are stacked to the ceiling; food, drink packages, and toiletries. On the floor is a can of food from one stack. The two look at each other and smile.

"Well, if that's all it is, we've got nothing to worry about," says Vaskette. "We must be moving…"

*****

Captain Mathew sits in the pilot's chair. His crewmembers, Agoparn, Korsaume, and Allen sit in their assigned chairs, and Rosetta sits not far from him.

"Captain Mathew Arnold, your ship is cleared for departure. Safe journey..."

"Thank you, Steg Control."

Mathew runs his hands over the controls as if he'd been doing it for years. He thinks very little about it, other than the fact that he is amazed that he can so easily fly the vessel, even though he remembers nothing about ever having done so. The controls are completely different from those of the Vortex class Planetary Cruiser, and though this one is a bit slower, he is sure it will provide them with safe passage for a while until they can find a faster one.

The large vessel pulls away from the Orbital Ribbon Station around Steg, clears the buoys, and speeds up to its maximum speed within a matter of minutes. As it does so, Mathew finds himself thinking about the events of the past few days, and what will happen now that their enemies know they are alive and well, and on their way back to stop whatever the Solar Union officials are planning. Whatever it is, and whoever is the cause, Mathew is certain that the people he works with now are more than capable of stopping them. His uncertainty is the group of people now on their trail… A group that his Lieutenant knows enough about to be concerned; and this concerns him, as well.

Episode 6
Stellar Remorse

OPENING:

"Sometimes the thing or things we fear the most are derived from the inevitable feeling of isolation, with an undercurrent of uncertainty. The fact that we as a people are now searching the unending cosmos for a sign that it is not all for naught only proves that we have not overcome fear in and of itself, but rather isolated our uncertainty..."

The zero-seven Celestial class Star Expeditioner, now the home to six people that don't belong to this side of the galaxy, and a seventh that does, races at its optimum pace toward the center of the Milky Way Galaxy.

Though it is traveling at a high rate of speed, it seems the ship makes no headway to its destination.

Aboard the vessel, Rosetta sits alone in her room looking through information she found via her bounty-hunting contacts. The information is on her boyfriend, Mathew Arnold. She found additional information on the others, but does not concern herself with that right now. She wants to know more about the man she almost instantaneously fell in love with.

After reading for several minutes, she crinkles up her face involuntarily at the thought of presenting the data to him. It seems he was a barely likeable person before, having an overbearing attitude, along with an ego about being the number one pilot known in the galaxy. He had several girlfriends, but none lasted longer than a few months.

His sisters, Aiya and Zeger, are very sweet ladies; or so the data reads; and they have a reward up for his safe return home.

Rosetta had contacted Zeger just prior to Mathew's arrival on the Orbital Ribbon Station around Steg to let her know that she had found Mathew, and they were on their way back, but the communication was one way, and there was no way for the info to get to Zeger faster than about two weeks, which meant Rosetta would not be able to hear back from her.

She pulls the disc out of the mini-computer she was given by the man at Straite-Mogue and plugs in the disc full of data on Vaskette.

Vaskette was a member of the Doctors for a Better Life, Superior Physicians Organization, and several other high-profile leagues for extremely talented doctors and physicians. She was very humble, and hated being a doctor, but was so talented at it that she was consistently the top-rated physician in every league.

She had a boyfriend, but no record of him after her disappearance was on any file she was able to obtain.

He obviously didn't care much for her, Rosetta thinks to herself.

The information she obtained seems endless and mostly useless, but she knows that the people she now travels with would love to have any piece of their life, no matter how boring or unsavory. People can always change…

She makes the decision to stop reading the data and give them each their own discs, but she knows they will be angry with her for not giving it all to them sooner, so she sits comfortably into a large chair near her bed to think over how best to present the discs to them.

*****

"Where's Rosetta," asks Korsaume walking into the mess where Mathew sits alone.

"In her room, I suppose," he replies.

The two are quiet after this as Korsaume goes to the food-producer and punches in the items she wants to eat. The food items are dispensed onto a plate inside the machine to maintain sterilization, and the plate is ejected onto a small table extending away from the machine, and right in front her.

She picks up the plate and seats herself across from her Captain. She picks up a fork and takes a bite of the meat she chose, and as she begins chewing, she looks at Mathew with inquisitive eyes.

She finishes the bite and asks, "So, how does it feel to fly a bigger ship?"

He sits with his elbows on the table, finishes chewing his food and swallowing, then looks up at her with eyes a little wider than usual. She can see the entire area of the irises, and the white around them. He seems bored to her.

"It's different. I must admit that it is a bit less claustrophobic than the planetary cruisers."

He does not look like he is going to continue, so she presses him for conversation. "…And how do you like having your girlfriend aboard with us?"

He smiles. While she thinks he just enjoys the idea, he is smiling knowing she wants him to open up to her.

"You know, Lieutenant, I was enjoying sitting in here alone and in peace. If you wanted a full-fledged conversation, all you had to do was ask…" He laughs at her and shakes his head gently.

She is a bit surprised at the fact he did not just go ahead and answer her question, but she's learned to take this kind of thing in stride, so she asks, "Captain, would you converse with me about random thoughts concerning our lives since Steg?"

They both laugh lightly at this, and Mathew seems almost uncomfortable at the way the question was staged.

"It is nice to have Seta on board. She is a wonderful woman, and quite irresistible, not to mention more beautiful than the morning sunrise on Ablose."

"That's saying a lot, Captain. I saw the Ablose sunrise twice, and both were unique and incredible."

"Do you mind if I ask you about Sherise?"

It is rather sudden, and Korsaume is entirely taken aback. Her stomach clenches for a moment, and she swallows hard. Next, she finds herself breathing heavily. She did not expect to be caught off guard like this, and she is not accustomed to it.

She looks down, around, and finally back to Mathew. "What…do you want to know, Captain?"

"No, not as your Captain…as your friend…" He leans back a little and places his left hand on the left side of his face, thumb just under his ear, the next two fingers pressed to his temple, and the last two curled against his cheek.

"Oh. Alright…" Still, she cannot believe he made her feel this way.

"On Ablose, what were you…" He stops, knowing this will not get a good response. He tries again. "…What was Sherise going through … thinking … when she was there debating what to do about her orders?"

She takes a deep breath and prepares herself for the answer she hoped never to remember again. "Well, Mathew, I was thinking about getting back to my old life, doing what I thought I was supposed to do. I sat on a hill for two days looking at the city and debating with myself about why I was doing what I was ordered to do." She pauses to think. "I had never been around a group of people like you, and I suppose that's what the people who gave me orders wanted to ensure. If they can get a person to look solely at himself or herself and never have acquaintances or friends of any kind they won't think twice when they are ordered to kill someone."

"So, then, it must have been a hard decision for her to make when she decided to go ahead and try to kill Vaskette…"

Tears well up in her eyes; "Mathew, you have no idea how horrible I feel about that…" She blinks hard over and over to keep the tears from falling.

Mathew sees the tears as they gather at the base of her eyes and begin to stream down her face slowly. He arises from his seat and walks around the table to her, seats himself by her, and places an arm around her shoulders. She does not move her arms or her body. Her hands try to wipe the tears away, but every tear they clear, two more stream down to take their place.

She tries to continue, "Even while I was running through the hospital firing that weapon, I caught myself several times intentionally misaiming. If I could have, I would, but those bullets are set to seek and destroy. I didn't know…"

Mathew hands her a small napkin and she uses it to wipe her face, sniffling as she tries to blink away the remaining tears.

"I didn't know how I truly felt about all of you until I tried to kill Vaskette. Being so close to all of you," she pauses again, grabbing another napkin, and trying to correct her high-pitched crying voice, "Being so close to all of you was something I wasn't expecting. I'm so glad I didn't kill Vaskette. I would hate myself right now."

"You probably would never have told us you were the one if you'd actually finished her off, would you…" Mathew seems vaguely despondent trying to sound sympathetic.

She looks at him harshly, "you didn't have to put it like that…'finish her off…'"

"Sorry. Bad word choice…"

"…And, no, I would not have told you if I'd actually killed her. None of you would ever have forgiven me if I had…"

"No, we would not have…" He removes his arm from around her and gets up to sit back in his place.

She folds her arms and feels a sudden realization come over her. "You knew, didn't you…?"

Mathew stops. "What makes you think that?"

She separates her arms and places them on the table in front of her on either side of the plate and leans forward. "When you asked me about the gun…and when I came on board while we were preparing to leave Ablose…you had a look in your eyes. I saw it, but I thought I was pretty good at covering myself. I was too proud to see it, but I see it now. I see you look at me, and I know you knew."

Mathew does not turn around, and does not sit down. "I had my suspicions," he says looking down at the table, and placing his right hand on it as if to steady his body. "There was no way to know for sure without doing a full scale investigation, but I didn't know you still had your memories, so I was thinking maybe it had to do with the brain-washing. I was scared that it might happen to all of us…that all of us might snap and try to do the same thing to each other…a safety measure I figured they could program into us if they could do such a good job of erasing everything in our brains except what we needed to know."

"There's something I didn't tell you, or anyone for that matter…"

"There was a sixth person…?"

Her eyes widen in surprise. "How did you guess?"

"Don't know. I'm good at these guessing games…give me another one…" Mathew turns around, seats himself, and looks across the table into her dreading eyes.

She smiles very quickly, laughing, and then sobers up immediately. She speaks slowly and deliberately. "The sixth person was a lot like me. I knew him. He was the best weapons expert known in the galaxy. I hated him for being chosen above me, so I raised my weapon and killed him first. The rest of you were just business, if you don't mind my saying so."

"Of course not…" he says, and then almost to himself, "Why should I?"

"I don't mean it that way…"

"I know, Korsaume. That doesn't stop me from being upset, only keeps me from ridding our ship of the possibility of betrayal."

"So everything you said was false. You don't trust me."

"It has little to do with trust of you, and more of the chance of mistrust by the others of everyone else. For all any of us know, each of us is the only one without memory."

"I understand what you're saying," she says. "And I understand why... My main question is, do you trust me, and do you trust everyone else?"

"Honestly," he says questioning and pauses, "I do; but I fear that if the others have too much time to think about it, they may begin to question each other's loyalties."

She places a fist on the table and looks down at it. "I'm sorry, Captain; I haven't had the training for this kind of situation."

"Oh, and if I have, could I possibly remember it...?"

Korsaume breathes out heavily, and her mouth opens slightly in the middle, making her look a little pout-y. "I'm sorry, Mathew. I'm sorry for everything. I'm sorry for lying to you, all of you, for those three weeks. I'm sorry for the pain and trouble I caused you in the first place. If I could take it all back, I would. You have to believe that if you believe nothing else."

"Korsaume, I'm not here to pass blame or beat a dead horse. I'm concerned for your welfare from the others on board."

"I can take care of myself, Captain. I'm a weapons expert."

"Do I leave it at that, Lieutenant?"

"Please do, sir. Although I'll appreciate any future sticking-up-for-me you're willing to do."

The two sit in silence after this for quite a while until Mathew gets up from his seat and leaves the room quietly.

Korsaume sits alone now. She allows her body to relax and press into the seat. "I guess I managed to do what I've done all my life; lose the only friends I have..." She pushes her food tray away and folds her arms, closes her eyes and sits in silence.

*****

Allen sits with his back to Agoparn reading control panel readouts of shipping lines in the vicinity. Agoparn sits across the command deck from him at the ship's engine controls, which face forward.

Though the two have rarely spoken to each other, today seems different, for they are both in the mood to talk.

Allen starts, "So, Parn, tell me about your time on the ribbon station…"

Agoparn sits back in his chair, reaches up his arms behind his head and relaxes; a custom he seems to do almost without even thinking about it. He smiles and simply says, "I spent most of my time staring out one of the big picture windows at the planet below."

A moment passes before Allen turns his chair to face the engineer and says, "I was kind of interested in how you got the information about Pikornauc'for…"

"Oh," Agoparn raises his head in acknowledgement and then returns it into position, "A little girl named Adrent ran into me while I was looking at the planet."

"She ran into you," Allen emphasizes "she" and "you."

"Quite literally… She wasn't paying attention to where she was going and ran right into my right leg. She was a cutie, and very kind. Her parents were right behind her and we all got to talk a bit. The family is from Passelket, near the center of the Milky Way; a fifty-week trip from Steg on this vessel. The girl was quite educated in her use of the English language, even if it was a completely upper-class dialect."

"I've never heard an upper-class dialect of the English language," Allen starts, and then looks over at Agoparn, "at least not in the last four weeks." Then he smiles.

Agoparn smiles back. "What about you, Allen…? What did you do on Steg?"

"Oh, not much," he begins. "I went to an armament supply store for a bit, but couldn't remember the names of the weapons and other items, so I left there, grabbed a couple books to read and went back to the ship and read. Thanks to the injections the good Doctor has been giving us, I was able to read and retain the stories, and evidently I'm a speed-reader…"

"You don't say…"

"About fourteen hundred words a minute, one hundred percent comprehension…"

"Intriguing," is Agoparn's reply. As he says this, he unfolds his arms and places them back down in front of him, turning the chair to look directly at Allen. "'Question while we're sitting here alone…"

"What?" Allen says this half-heartedly as he continues to read displays.

"What do you think about Korsaume, truly?"

Allen suddenly stops what he is doing and looks down at the floor as if he were thinking of an answer. Then he turns his head toward the door to the bridge, and when he is satisfied that no one is present but the two of them, he looks Agoparn in the eye. "I'm just not sure."

"Neither am I," says Agoparn. "She was treating us all really rough, and now she's a little school girl with charm and charisma. I would love to say she's changed, but how can all of us be certain without reading her mind? I want so badly to trust her, but I admit to being a bit of a skeptic."

"As much as I hate to admit it, Parn, I have to agree with you…"

The two of them are interrupted as they hear footsteps enter, belonging to their Captain. "…Hate to admit agreeing with Parn about what, Allen," he asks walking past the two of them and seating himself in the Captain's chair. He turns it to face them, folds his hands in front of him and places his elbows on the arm-rests. He does not smile or frown. He is completely straight-faced.

The two straightened up the instant they heard his voice, and now both of them look awkwardly at Mathew.

"Well, Captain," Agoparn begins, "I am a bit skeptical about the change in Korsaume. I'm certain most of us on board feel this way, Sir…"

"I don't deny it myself," says Mathew. "I, too, have had my doubts this week. I am sorry you both seem to feel this way, and since I don't know what else to tell either of you, I'm just going to have to let it go at that. If you don't trust her, you don't trust her."

The two men do not actually look at each other now, but they both look off toward the direction of the other as if they could see the other through the side of their heads.

Allen seems a bit uncomfortable, but soon recovers. "Captain, I don't mean to sound like I don't trust her. Some part of me does not, and I can say that with confidence, but everything in me screams to go ahead and do so. Does that make any sense whatsoever?"

"It does," says Mathew. "It's called 'human nature.' We all have a natural desire to trust everyone, but after we're disappointed the first time, we always have a twinge of mistrust in others thereafter. For instance, how do I know the two of you aren't faking your memory loss as well…?"

Both men suddenly look shocked, their eyes widening at Mathew, an awed expression on their mouths.

"How could you even think such a thing," says one, and the other says simultaneously, "I never thought of that."

"We just have to trust each other anyway. While you're admitting mistrust for the one person who has seemingly let you down, also admit that without all of us working together, we're not going to live much longer. We've got trained killers on our tails. We don't have time to consider anything else. If we don't trust each other, who can we trust?"

Allen and Agoparn both settle down realizing their Captain is correct, and they both go back to what they were doing before.

*****

Lacendu sits at the desk in her cabin reading material of hers she picked up from an ex-student on Steg. She has come to know herself fairly well through these books, and the math quizzes and calculus problems contained in them keep her brain occupied.

She is looking over her fifth book for the day when she hears a noise outside. Then she hears footsteps, and another door closing. She does not think much of it, but then decides it is probably Vaskette and decides she wants to tell her about the books.

She quickly gets up, opens the door to her cabin, walks down the corridor and knocks on Vaskette's door.

There is no immediate reply, so she knocks again.

Soon, she hears someone stirring inside and the door opening. Vaskette stands before her in a long evening gown, and the light off in her cabin. She yawns, opens her eyes a little but quickly shuts them because of the light from the corridor. "Is everything alright, Lacy," she asks.

"Oh, I didn't mean to wake you. I heard footsteps in the corridor, and a door closing, so I assumed it was you."

"Footsteps and a door in this corridor…? We're the only two in this corridor; or even in this wing for that matter…"

"I know. It was suddenly obvious to me that it wasn't you when you came to the door. Now I'm scared…"

"Scared…? What is there to be scared of, Lacy? You know everyone on board. If someone's sneaking around, then you should go upstairs and find out who's missing, or if anyone came down here…"

"Good idea," says Lacendu and she quickly scurries away up the stairs.

Vaskette closes the door and starts back toward her bed. In her sleepiness, she feels a sudden pang of doubt in herself and goes back to the door to lock it. Then she turns back to her bed and quickly drifts to sleep.

Lacendu knocks on Rosetta's door. "Seta… Seta… You in there…?"

Rosetta comes to the door and smiles when she sees Lacendu. "Hey, girl; what's going on…?"

"Nothing … just checking to see if you've been down to Vaskette's and my corridor in the past few minutes to get some supplies."

Rosetta looks at the woman hesitantly, and replies, "No…" She shakes her head as the word comes through her mouth.

"Oh. OK. Thank you." Lacendu smiles, then turns and goes toward the mess.

She enters the small dining area, and there on her immediate right is Korsaume.

"Oh, hey, Korsaume," she says.

"Hi, Lacy," Korsaume replies. Her face is lit with a smile, but her voice sounds indifferent.

"Um, did you go to Vaskette's and my corridor for some supplies in the last five minutes…?"

"Lacy, I can honestly say I have not been to your wing at all. I'm sorry, but it wasn't me. Maybe one of the boys did. Have you asked them?"

"Not yet. I'm going to them next. Thanks." Lacendu hurriedly exits the room.

She arrives in the cockpit next. There sit all three of the males in their respective chairs.

"Captain," she says loudly. "Uh, all of you guys…"

All three of them turn around.

"Have any of you been to the port side living quarters in the past five minutes?"

"I haven't been down there all day," says Mathew.

"I've never been over there," says Agoparn.

Allen replies, "I was there early this morning for a couple items, but I haven't been back since."

"I can vouch for him," says Agoparn. "He's been up here with me for the past three hours or so…"

"Then, Captain, I'm afraid we have an unwelcome guest onboard," Lacendu says matter-of-factly and then moves to the side away from the door and backs up against the far wall on the starboard side.

*****

Mathew leads his crew, minus Vaskette, to the Port side lowest-level living quarters. Rosetta stands beside him on his right, Korsaume on his left, both with guns in hand.

Mathew knocks hard on Vaskette's door. "Doctor, please come out for a moment."

There is complete silence from within. He waits a bit and knocks again. "Doctor, this is your Captain. I need for you to come out, please."

More silence. He tries the door handle.

"Let me at it," says Korsaume.

Everyone steps back a ways. Korsaume levels her weapon at the door handle and raises her voice quite loudly. "Doctor, if you're inside, you should step away from the door immediately. I do not want to hurt you. I am going to burn the door handle off. Step back away from the door immediately."

"I don't think she's in there," says Lacendu.

"Better safe than sorry," says Korsaume as she fires the laser-gun at the door. It works like a torch, only faster. Within a matter of seconds, the handle melts right off the door, and Korsaume kicks the door in. She is prepared to say the word "doctor" as she moves down close to the ground giving Rosetta a place to cover over her head, but they are both speechless at what they see.

"Welcome," says the man inside. "Your good Doctor couldn't talk at the moment. You see, I told her not to say anything to you. If you want her to live, you'll all do exactly as I say. Do I make myself clear?"

He moves Vaskette toward the door, a weapon aimed at her head. "Just start moving along this corridor toward the front of the ship. There's a storage room there. I just want all of you to be comfortable and safe in that room..." He smiles at them.

"Nice to see you again, Marcus," says Korsaume placing her gun on the floor while Rosetta does the same behind her.

"Don't hurt her," says Rosetta needlessly, frowning at the man.

"Like I said, as long as all of you cooperate, this will be quick and painless for all of us. Well, I take that back; it will be quick, but the lack of pain will only be temporary."

The group moves toward the front storage room quietly.

Korsaume speaks to her crew. "Gang, this is Marcus. Marcus, these are my friends. I'm sure you know who they are…"

"Of course I do. I did my homework."

"Of course," parrots Korsaume. "Gang, Marcus is another one of the group we met on Steg. He is what we refer to as 'clean-up.' Anytime a member or members do not fulfill their role, he goes in and does it for them. He 'cleans up' after them. It's a specialized position that I used to be a part of…"

"…And you did it well, Sherise. That is, until you decided to side with the enemy…" His harsh words are meant to make her upset. She knows it.

"Oh, I guess they didn't tell you…my name isn't Sherise anymore. It's Korsaume, and I'd greatly appreciate it if you would call me by it."

"I'll call you whatever I want to… For now, I'll just call you dead meat. Oddly, though, I'm not going to shoot you myself. I'm landing this craft at the nearest habitable planet and letting someone else take over for me. It's the clean-up crew I'm with. They're newbies and they need a good lesson."

He makes certain that everyone is in the room and closes the door. On the outside, he uses a laser-gun to meld the door shut against its frame, then goes up stairs to the cockpit and flies the craft.

"Now what," asks Lacendu?

"Well, first of all, Lacy, I'm sorry I didn't listen to you earlier," says Vaskette.

"There's no time for regret," says Korsaume. "Is there a way out of here?"

"Not until we land," answers Mathew. "These panels come off pretty easily… We can use one of the light fixtures to work the first one off and work our way through the three layers and kick out the last panel…"

"How will we know when we land," asks Allen. "These things are made to be inertia-proof, at least as far as what we feel goes…"

"We'll just have to wing it," says Rosetta.

"When I last looked at the planetary sensors," says Agoparn, "we were in a category four star system, and there were two habitable planets; one a class 1, the other a class 2. With any luck, we'll land on the class 1 planet. Escape should be easy."

*****

It is over four hours later when they hear footsteps coming down the corridor. Allen is still stationed with his head at the top of the ceiling, ear against a small duct for heating and air ventilation to listen to the engines. They already have the wall panel off.

"I think it already powered down," he says. "I heard the thrusters kick off, but I can't tell if we've landed."

"Let me try," says Rosetta. "Hurry…"

The two switch places. Rosetta listens intently. "I don't hear gyros," she says.

"Gyros keep artificial gravity onboard the ship. That means they aren't needed. We must have landed," says Korsaume.

"How can we be sure we didn't land on one of the 'other' planets," asks Lacendu.

Mathew turns to her and says simply, "Do we give them what they want, or do we try to bust out of here and hope for the best?"

"I'm with you, whatever you decide, Captain," says Agoparn.

"I as well," says Rosetta, "but I assume that was expected."

"All of us are with you, Mathew," says Vaskette. "Say the word and we'll rip a giant gap in that wall, come-what-may."

"The word is given," Mathew says.

They pull out the layers between them and the outer hull, and then all of them immediately start kicking hard against the thin metal sheet on the outside wall of the ship. Lacendu and Vaskette are not accustomed to this and quickly give up nursing their feet, legs, and hips. But it is not long before the wall begins to give way and the metal is torn apart away from its surrounding segments.

At the first break in the metal, Mathew peers out through the crack. "I see sunlight. We could just be close to a star, but we'd all be being sucked through this little gap, too. I'm going to assume we've landed on a hospitable planet. Shall we continue?"

"I hear you in there," says Marcus from outside. "You making all that clamor isn't going to get you out of this. I'm not frightened by your outburst."

"Oh, no," says Vaskette loudly and slowly, drenched with sarcasm, "He's on to us, everyone. We should quit trying to scare him. He's so big and tough. We'll never make it out of here alive!"

Lacendu stands next to her doctor friend, her right hand covering her mouth as she tries hard to keep the laughter contained.

"Don't play his tricks," whispers Korsaume to the two whole-heartedly. "Let him be. He won't know what hit him when he comes through that door."

By now, the others are done kicking, and they are looking down at the ground only eleven feet below them.

"We've landed," says Marcus. "My friends are not far from here. As soon as I get word they're parking nearby, I'll be opening that door. Don't try anything stupid."

"We wouldn't dream of it, Sir," says Mathew as he helps Agoparn jump through the hole to the ground below. Agoparn is followed by Allen, and then Korsaume, Vaskette, Lacendu, and Rosetta.

"That ended all too well, Captain Mathew. What's going on in there?"

"We were just taking our frustrations out. We're a bit wiped out, now, though. Sorry for the noise level. We'll keep it down now."

"That's so nice of you," says Marcus.

Mathew jumps out.

The seven of them begin looking around. What they see is worse than they expected, though not too terribly awful. The ship is parked at the edge of a desert near a forest-like area. The "forest" is more of an over-grown flower-garden with plants as tall as trees, and blossoms the size of elephants. They are within three hundred yards of it, so they all start running that direction to get out of the heat of the day.

It is several minutes before all of them get into the forest, three of them completely out of breath, all of them drenched in sweat.

"I didn't realize how out of shape I am," says Agoparn panting.

"Thankfully," says Korsaume turning her head toward them, "this planet is human-friendly with oxygen and lots of plants. You should have no problem catching your breath."

"We're not far enough away from that ship for my taste," says Mathew. "Let's move out. We'll walk from here; keep to the plants and out of direct view from above if he decides to use the ship to hunt for us."

The seven people begin walking through the thick foliage.

The flora is wild and multi-faceted with beauty and color. The group travels for well over an hour before they come upon a giant plant with a base as big around as a house, and evidently it is being used as one.

All of them walk up to what they assume is the door, and Mathew knocks.

It takes some time, but finally, someone comes to the door. It is an older man who is well dressed in buffed dress shoes, black slacks, a button-up shirt that is tucked in, and a bow tie.

"How may I assist you," he asks in a rough but friendly voice.

"My name is Mathew Arnold. I am the Captain of a space ship. We just landed here for repairs and supplies, and we were hoping you could point us in the right direction."

"I will allow my masters to do that. Please enter…" The old man moves with the door and puts his arm out as if to welcome them.

They enter and are seated on a comfortable plant-like sofa in what they assume to be the living room.

"I will inform my masters of your presence," he tells them and walks up a flight of stairs on the far side of the room.

The place looks like the inside of a plant, mostly green with long lines up and down the wall in random patterns, as if the plant had been carved out. Much of the furniture also looks like plants imbedded in the plant structure. There are also metal and wood items, but most of these are very small.

It is only a few minutes before a young man comes down the flight of stairs with the older man behind him.

"I am not accustomed to having visitors," says the young man without even looking at them. "I suppose I should count my blessings this day." Finally, he reaches the bottom of the stairs, turns to face them, smiles and says, "To what do I owe the honor of a visitation from strangers?"

The rest of the group looks at Mathew. Mathew smiles and says, "I apologize that we are not from your world, so I do not know your customs. If there is some sort of custom for my speaking, please make me aware of it…"

Rosetta whispers over to him, "Quit apologizing and answer the nice man." Then she looks up and smiles really big at their host, her eyes mostly closed as if nothing is wrong.

Mathew continues, "We were on our way to Pikornauc'for, and we had some trouble on board our vessel. We stopped here for repairs and supplies. We were hoping you knew of some way to assist us."

"I am sorry," says the man. "We do not have space-fairing vessels on our planet." At this he walks over to stand in front of them, talking as he moves. "This is a planet that is mostly plants. Our entire inventory of metals is imported. We have learned to cope with this by taking techno-organic science to its extreme. Plants do everything for us including travel, living, water and food preparation, and numerous other things we are constantly discovering uses for this fine flora."

"Amazing," adds Korsaume. "An entire planet built around organic technology. I didn't think it was possible."

The man looks somewhat condescendingly to the woman, then at Mathew. "Does she hold some kind of position over you that you would allow her to speak?"

Korsaume sits with wide eyes and immediately looks down.

"I apologize for my Lieutenant's vocalization. She often makes comments such as this. She is more informed of such matters, so I allow her to tell me things I do not know. For instance, I did not know organic technology existed. Evidently, she did not, either."

The man looks at Korsaume again, then back to Mathew. "If that is your custom from another world…I can accept that. Here, we do not allow subordinates to speak unless directly spoken to."

"I should introduce you to my crew right quick. Perhaps that will help clear any misconceptions you might have of us. This woman to my right is my girlfriend, Rosetta. Next is my Lieutenant and second-in-command, Korsaume. Then Allen, Doctor Vaskette, Mathematist Lacendu, and our ship's engineer, Agoparn… I hold the position of Captain because I can fly the ship, but none of us are over the other."

"I see," says the man. "I was not aware of such possibilities. However, you should know that in traveling in a group such as yours here, you should have one leader, and that leader should make all conversation. If you wish to get assistance from others, they will not be as forgiving as I. I live here with my wife and servant, and thus I have come to accept things out-of-the-ordinary. My nearest neighbors are over forty kilometers away."

At this, most of the crew is noticeably disheartened.

Agoparn stands up and walks over to Mathew to whisper in his ear.

"Ah, good idea, Parn." Then to the man, "You mentioned you utilize plants for travel. Perhaps we could get a ride to the nearest city…"

"That is a possibility," says the man. "I will arrange transport for you and yours. I will welcome you to stay the night in my home. I have plenty of room for all of you."

Mathew looks at his crew, and everyone seems agreeable to this arrangement. "We would be honored to accept your hospitality."

The man seems quite excited about this and turns to his servant. "We shall have company tonight, Boston. Please prepare seven rooms for our guests."

The old man bows and walks back up the stairs.

"My wife is preparing food. We do not have meats on our planet, but we have many substitutes for it which taste most similarly to it. I hope all of you like vegetables and fruits."

*****

"WHAT DO YOU MEAN THEY ESCAPED?!!!" Preston and his crew have landed in their spaceship just behind Marcus' clean-up crew, and the eighteen of them stand outside the zero-seven Celestial class Star Expeditioner, the other ships lined up beside it.

Marcus points to the hole only five feet over their heads. "They escaped by kicking a hole in the ship's outer-hull."

"HOW COULD YOU LET THEM GET AWAY?!!! YOU'RE A CLEAN-UP ARTIST!!!"

Marcus yells back at Preston, "YOU SAID NOT TO KILL THEM! THAT'S ALL I KNOW HOW TO DO IS KILL! THESE PEOPLE ARE JUST AS GOOD AS WE ARE, AND WITH THEIR DIFFERENT TECHNICAL ABILITIES WORKING TOGETHER, THEY HAVE A BIG ADVENTAGE OVER US! YOU WANT ME TO DO MY JOB THEN LET ME!!!"

"Fine," says Preston angrily at Marcus. He turns to his men. "You have new orders. If you cannot find a safe and quick way to capture our prey, they are to be shot on sight. No questions asked. That goes for Sherise Felder as well. The traitor gets no special treatment. She is not to be taken alive! Understood?"

The men give their agreements to the command. "Marcus, you and your men take the North side. My group and I will take the South side. Spread out in open-pan pattern."

"Now we're talking," says Marcus.

The two men wave their crews forward, and they spread out, guns in hand to look for the crew of the Celestial Class Star Expeditioner.

*****

The crew is sitting around the heating plant as the cold of the night comes in through the open windows. They have been talking for a while, joking and laughing and having a general good time. Things finally settle down and they are talking about preparing for sleep.

Rosetta waits for a bit and when silence continues, she speaks, "I hope you're not all going to be mad at me…"

"Why would we be mad at you," asks Korsaume. "You're our best friend."

"Well, you're not going to be happy, that's for sure…" Her mouth curves down on the left side as she says this.

Mathew grabs her right hand. "I'm sure whatever it is you think we're going to be mad at you about isn't that big of a deal. Go ahead and tell us…"

"Alright, here goes," she begins. "I have information on each of you that I got through my bounty-huntress contacts. It's not a lot, but it's enough. I was skeptical about bringing some of it to your attentions because some of you were not that, um…"

"You're saying we weren't always nice people," asks Agoparn.

"Something like that," she agrees and continues, "I was seriously considering hiding some of the information from some of you, but then I realized that wouldn't be a good idea because if you ever found out you'd all hate me. I was going to confront all of you with it at dinner in the mess, but as you probably noticed, things changed…"

"So you've already read much of it," says Lacendu.

"Yeah…"

"Well, that's alright, Seta," Lacendu replies, "I've got a bit of a secret myself."

Everyone looks at her expectantly.

She goes on, "On Steg during my time away from the ship, I met an ex-student of mine. He had a bunch of his old textbooks from my classes and I traded him some currency for them. I've been studying them in my room."

Mathew looks at Korsaume, and she gives him an understanding nod about their conversation in the mess earlier in the day.

Mathew says somewhat comfortably, "I figured things like this would happen. We're all individuals. We all have things we don't want the others to know, and not all of us know everything about ourselves, though we're discovering it day by day. Rosetta knows our predicament, so I don't blame her for not telling us immediately."

"This is an awkward position for all of us," admits Vaskette. "Without memories, we're all re-learning not just about ourselves, but about how to work with other people. It can get difficult, I'm certain. I'm sure there are a few facts in my head about surveys on things similar to this…"

"Assuming, of course," adds Korsaume, "that anything like this has ever happened before."

"Two words for you, Lieutenant," says Vaskette, "Controlled expirements…"

Korsaume acquiesces.

"Admittedly, we are all just going to have to change this behavior of not letting the others in on our secrets. Sure, there are some secrets the rest of us don't need to know, but a triumph for one of us is a triumph for all. We should keep that in mind when, for instance Lacendu finds information about herself. We could all have rejoiced at this if she had just come directly to us and told us. We could all have learned about her together. Or Sherise being up front about the fact she still had her memories. Thankfully, we've left Sherise behind and traded her for someone far better. Korsaume has proven herself time and time again. Rosetta could have been up front with us about the information she got from her contacts. But let's not cry over the past. From now on, if you're all in agreement, we tell each other informative secrets we discover about ourselves. Is everyone in agreement?"

"I'm there," says Lacendu smiling.

"Me, too," adds Korsaume.

"Me, three," Allen states…

Agoparn and Vaskette nod their heads in accordance.

"Great," says Rosetta. "Perhaps you'll all allow me to tell you what I discovered. I promise I won't give any pertinent details to the group, but I'll be glad to tell those things in privacy later."

"Awesome," says Allen. "Any info on me…?"

"That was a little selfish of you," says Lacendu.

"No, no, Lacy; it's quite alright. He who speaks first learns first," Rosetta says. "Allen, your parents died almost four years ago in a freak accident in a space vessel. Your girlfriend, Laina Ursek, started a campaign for you when you disappeared. She really cares about you. I sent out several one-way messages to people all of you knew, and one was to Laina letting her know you're alright and that you're heading back as fast as you can.

"You have a teacher in the Ingrametin Defense Academy who really liked you and wants to see you finish the class.

"You were not much of a Solar Union supporter, and according to notes from one of your teachers, you felt the Solar Union was headed for disaster, and would not last in its current state."

Allen does not look directly at her during her speech, but instead looks at the table in front of him. When she finishes, all he can say is, "Oh…"

"Lacendu," Rosetta turns to the blonde-haired woman, "I don't know what information you gleaned from the books, but I'll give you what little I know…

"You were a book-worm and despised computers. You had never left your home planet of Segnar where you became the top Professor of Calculus in the galaxy at the top school in the galaxy which also sits on Segnar.

"You had a nice home with your husband; a Mr. Trester; and you were both planning on having children soon."

Lacendu makes a glance at Vaskette to keep quiet as Rosetta continues, "Your husband is a head member of the Solar Union Committee."

"The same Solar Union Committee that gathered us and then tried to have us all killed," asks Allen.

"I can't say for sure," Rosetta answers. "However, knowing what little I do about the Solar Union and its inner workings, I'd have to say that's a good possibility."

Lacendu sits uncomfortably, and then stands up. "I'm going to go to bed."

Vaskette excuses herself as well and follows her friend up the stairs.

Rosetta forces her upper teeth to catch her lower lip and wrinkles her face. "That didn't turn out as well as I'd hoped…"

"It's OK," Mathew says. "You don't know what little we do know about our previous lives. Perhaps we should call it a night and try again tomorrow."

"I agree," says Agoparn. "I'm sleepy and ready for a good night's rest."

"Off we go, then," says Korsaume, and everyone but Rosetta and Mathew leave the table and go up the stairs.

"Things are getting a little touchy with your group, Babe," she says to him and lays her head on his shoulder.

Mathew raises his right hand and places it on the left side of her head lovingly as his left arm moves down around her waste. "Yes. I'm a little scared for all of us. There're just no books on what to do in this situation; um, that I'm aware of…"

The two smile at the same time, and then they go upstairs for sleep.

*****

Marcus' men surround the plant-like home. Marcus and his second-in-command stand in front of the door waiting for someone to answer their knock.

It takes quite a bit of time, but finally an old man comes to the door in a pair of pajamas. He says drearily, "How may I assist you…"

"We're looking for seven people; three men and four women. Have you seen them," asks Marcus.

"Yes, they arrived here earlier today asking for directions…"

"Did you give them directions?"

"My master did, I believe. He has arranged for their transport to the city tomorrow…"

"So they are present now," Marcus asks excitedly.

"That is correct…"

Marcus keeps cutting the old man off excitedly, "They are escaped convicts from the planet Steg. Whatever they told you, it is most likely lies. We are to take them immediately for transport back to Steg to stand trial."

The old man looks upset. "Sir, the planet of Steg has no jurisdiction or power over this planet. If you wish to take them for trial, you must wait until they leave this house. My Master will be most upset at you for interrupting his sleep."

"Oh, we do not intend to interrupt your Master's sleep. If you will simply allow me and my men to enter, we will take them without commotion."

"My apologies, sir, but you do not understand the customs of our world. If you desire to do anything more, you will have to do it in the morning. I will not allow you entrance into my Master's house at this late hour."

"I tried," says Marcus to the old man. He turns to his second-in-command, "Didn't I try?"

"Yes, Sir," the commander agrees.

Marcus turns his gun on the old man and fires.

The man yells as loud as he can as his body falls limp to the floor. Surprisingly, his scream is much louder than his quiet speaking voice would have let on. Many of the crew is awakened. They are quick to get out of bed and run into the hallway.

"What's going on," asks Agoparn quietly.

Mathew motions everyone toward the Master's bedroom. The Master of the house and his wife are also awake. "What has happened," he asks, while his wife runs down the stairs.

"I'm not sure, Sir, but I believe someone has entered your home…" Rosetta answers.

Mathew asks, "Do you have any weapons?"

"No, I'm afraid I do not," he says.

At this moment, they hear a scream come from down stairs, and the Master's wife screams Boston's name.

"Is there another way out of here," Korsaume asks, looking at the Master with intent.

"Only down the stairs and out the front door," he says.

"Are there more levels to this home of yours," asks Allen.

"NO!" He says it quietly, but seems frustrated by the questions.

"Then we're going to have to get creative," Mathew says quietly. "Everyone, let's go into the Master's bathroom."

The eight of them step silently and enter the bathroom.

"What's in here," asks Korsaume of Mathew.

It is not Mathew, but Allen that answers. "This is a plant, Captain. There are many options right now. Where do you want me to begin?"

"We're probably going to have to make a few cuts in your home," says Mathew.

"That is inappropriate behavior toward our flora," says the Master.

"Unfortunately, we don't have much of a choice at the moment. They won't let you stand in their way, either, sir. They'll kill you as quickly if you try," Vaskette says.

Allen looks back at everyone. "Have we reached an agreement? I need to get to work…"

"Do it," says the Master.

"What do we do," asks Mathew.

"Just let me do my work," is all Allen says as he tears through the outside wall of the plant. "Korsaume, Rosetta, push on the side of the wall on either side at the top. We need to peel it downward."

Allen looks out of the hole he has made for men on the ground and sees no one.

"I'm going to go down first and distract them. Don't worry about me. Find the transportational plant and get as far away from here as possible. Whatever you do, though, don't go back to the ship. They'll expect that."

"We can't work without our chief Strategist," says Mathew.

"You won't need me for a while. You will, however, need the Master, Mathew, and Korsaume to continue. Protect Lacendu, Vaskette, and Agoparn. You'll need them on board the ship. As for me, if you don't see me again, just know that I did this for all of you…"

Allen begins climbing down the outside wall. Mathew looks over the edge at him. "Return safely to us, Allen Pendergras. Don't do anything overly stupid…I mean other than this…" Mathew smiles at him.

"Enough, Captain. Come down after me and go east." Allen continues down and reaches the ground in a matter of seconds. He then runs off around the house to the west.

Korsaume and Rosetta help Vaskette and Lacendu to use the peeling of the plant's outer skin to slowly drop them to the ground. Then the two use the second layer for the same purpose, followed closely by Agoparn and the Master. Mathew climbs down the same way Allen did, and the seven of them run off to the east.

While running, Mathew turns to the Master. "Where is the plant transport?"

"Just up ahead about forty meters."

"How do we use it," asks Korsaume.

"It's fairly simple. One or two of you stand on the budded pod for a few seconds and it transports you through its internal underground stems to its other bud…"

"Interesting," says Mathew. "Let's do it."

"A word of warning," says the Master. "There are three possible outcomes on this plant. When you stand on the bud, you must face the direction you want to go; southeast, east, or north. Somehow, the plant knows which way you're facing and does what it needs to do to get you to the right bud."

"We understand," Agoparn says.

They arrive shortly and Vaskette and Lacendu are first. They face directly east toward the city, and the plant's bud closes around them. When it opens again, they are gone. Korsaume and Rosetta are next, doing the same thing. Then the Master goes alone.

"You ready, Parn," asks Mathew turning to the Engineer.

"Yes, sir," Agoparn replies.

They stand on the bud, and just as they are facing themselves and standing still, they hear voices behind them.

"There they are," shouts one.

"Get them!"

At this, Agoparn turns around and Mathew turns to his friend, "NO! DON'T!!!"

"Ah, frag," is the last thing Agoparn says, scrunching up his face at his error before the buds fly up around them and they are pushed through the stem of the plant.

*****

Allen lies face down quietly in the underbrush of the forest about three hundred yards from the plant house. His left arm was hit by gun fire, and now he is being hunted.

He is grateful he grabbed his black cloak before leaving his room, and now he uses its full length to cover himself entirely under the black night sky. The moon shines up beyond the mountain to the north, and he is a good sixty meters from where the moonshine hits the ground over it.

He stays there waiting for his enemies to leave. They hunt through the floral forest with their infrared gun sites for the young man. They have been looking for about thirty minutes, and they don't seem to be giving up.

He smiles at this and thinks to himself, I sure did give them a run for their money. I hope everyone else made it away all right.

*****

The Master arrives on the bud at the center of the city. Waiting for him is Vaskette, Lacendu, Rosetta, and Korsaume. The Master steps off the bud and turns to await the remaining two.

They stand there for several minutes…nothing.

"They were right behind me," says the Master. "I hope those attackers of my home did not catch up to them."

"Me, too," says Korsaume.

"Is there a place here we can stay where no one will know we're here," asks Rosetta.

"Yes, I know of a place."

"Good," says Korsaume. "The rest of you go with him. Rosetta, return for me when you get there. I'll wait here for them. There's still a chance they just got on a little later, even if they were attacked."

"Yes, Lieutenant," Rosetta says smiling at her.

The four of them leave, and Korsaume runs to a small place where she won't be seen on the city street and hides, awaiting the arrival of her Captain and Engineer.

*****

"I am SO sorry, Captain. I didn't realize what I was doing until it was too late," Agoparn says sadly.

"It's alright, Parn. At least we made it out alright."

"You should have continued to face east, Captain. We would have arrived in the city."

"I just didn't know what would happen to you. Maybe only one of the two people must be facing the correct direction."

"I wonder what would have happened if we were both facing in a direction of different buds."

Mathew smiles and laughs at the thought. "Well, we don't have time to debate it. Let's get moving. I don't know which way to face from here, so we'll just have to find someone around here that does…"

*****

Korsaume is hiding behind an item she assumes to be a garbage bin when the plant bud closes up and opens again. "Finally," she says to herself.

Just then, two armed men from Marcus' group are standing on the bud as it opens, and she quickly ducks back down behind the bin. The two men step off, and the plant closes up again moments later. Two more…

This continues until there are eight men, including Marcus, standing near the plant bud.

Marcus turns to his men, "Spread out and find them. Shoot to kill. No mistakes; do you understand me…?"

"Yes, Sir," the men reply quietly but military-like.

Korsaume sits back against the back of the garbage bin and faces the plant wall of what she believes to be an office building.

Oh, great, she thinks. Rosetta will be back shortly, and I have nothing to protect her with…

She sits there quietly, her heart racing, listening to their footsteps as they fan out through the city streets…

Episode 7
Universal Life

OPENING:

"Garenoljola's plant life is subservient to its human population, but only due to the work of a man who was willing to believe that bio-organic technology could be achieved through a true relationship between human and flora. Garen Rhinistadt was just that man and his work was left on his planet when he died. Most did not believe that this technology could ever exist, and those same naysayers, if they were still alive, would be eating their words right now..."

Agoparn and Mathew run through the open field of flora. Though the flowers are beautiful, the two men are trying desperately to get through the field to the water about a kilometer away. Both of them have been without water for two days, and have tried several things to get some of the refreshing liquid, like breaking into plants and drinking what little they could get from the stems, and similar attempts.

Now, they are approximately a half a kilometer from the water-front, and a large chasm stands between them. Though this seems odd, there is a small bridge across to a large plant-like structure on an island in the center of the chasm. They cannot see around the plant structure, but they assume there is another bridge on the opposite side, so they cross the first bridge and enter the plant.

Inside, they move up the walkway passing stores, and people buying and selling on either side. The ceiling of the "hallway" inside is extremely high, perhaps twenty meters. The place looks more like a cavern small in width. It is mostly dark inside except for the lights from the shops, and a few lights sitting alongside the walkway.

The floor is completely uneven making their walk a little complicated, and occasionally one of them steps into a small hole in the floor and almost falls over, partly from the onset of dehydration. They shake from their need for water, but both force themselves to move onward.

Soon, they come to the top of the floor and they see the remainder of their trek through the plant heading downward.

It is at this point that they are greeted by a woman who introduces herself as:

"Metta Codiance. Welcome to Bydiovo Alurcit. Can I help you gentlemen…?"

Mathew looks disgustedly at her and with a dry, raspy throat says, "Water…"

"Right this way," she says flirting with her eyes.

She brings them to two barstools at her shop, goes around the counter and pours some water into two large cups. "On the house," she says setting the mugs in front of them.

The two take their respective refreshments and guzzle them in one gulp.

"Wow, you two really are thirsty," she smiles, stressing the word "are." "Perhaps you'd care for more?"

Both nod an affirmative, and they are treated to a second helping.

Agoparn recovers first and says, "We apologize…we have nothing in the way of payment for you."

"Oh," she says dissatisfied. Her big smile becomes somewhat less of its former glory, but she still seems friendly. "Where are you two from?"

"That's a good question," Mathew says. "We're not from this planet…"

"Ah, you're traders…?"

"Not quite," says Mathew, "though if we could get our ship here, we could trade you some items for your generosity."

"I'm sorry, fella's; payment first, generosity second. No disrespect to your line of business, but since I don't know for sure that you speak the truth…well, let's just say it's bad for business."

"We understand, Metta," Mathew says swallowing hard as he finishes the second cup. "No hard feelings for the woman who single-handedly saved our lives from dehydration…"

"We were going to go down to the ocean…" Agoparn begins.

"Oh, you don't want to drink the water around her, gentleman. It's un-filtered…" She seems quite believable as she says this. "You guys really aren't from this planet, or you'd know that the ocean water is completely undrinkable…"

"Why is that?" Mathew asks.

"Well, legend has it that the man who brought bio-organic technology to this planet, Garen Rhinistadt, used up a lot of the planet's natural resources to accomplish his work to make this planet completely supported by plants. The waste and by-products left behind by the amount of energy and resources he used to bond plants with human-nature was all dumped into the ocean, forever polluting it. Only the Sahragett and Jylicupid plants can strain the pollutants from the ocean water. Otherwise, you need to find a lake or mountain stream."

By this time, the two men have recovered enough to go on.

"I suppose it's a good thing you stopped us, then," says Mathew. "We are in your debt…"

At this prospect, she regains the smile she had when they first met. "I like the sound of that," she says joyously.

Agoparn looks at his Captain and says quietly, "Um, that was probably the wrong thing to say, Sir."

The woman is turned around, and the two decide this is the perfect time to make their escape, so they rise from the stools and walk back the way they came in. However, it is not long before the woman notices and shouts for someone to get them for payment.

*****

Rosetta had been heading back to the transport flower-bud in the darkness of the night when she saw them; two men with guns, and dressed in Solar Union military outfits. She hid quickly and allowed them to pass her. She immediately realized the men had followed her and the four others through the transport bud. Chances were that Korsaume had been caught and killed, but Korsaume had hidden and the four crewmembers, along with the man of a house far from here, managed to find each other.

That was two days ago, and the five of them are now hiding in the top floor of an office "plant." Actually, there was no floor above the one below them until the group of five carved it out for themselves and dumped the substance they removed into a garbage bin downstairs during the second night.

The men had searched their building from top to bottom and had not found them.

They watched just five minutes ago as the eight men Korsaume saw come through the bud transport went back through it.

Finally, they were free…at least temporarily.

They wait for night-fall once more and exit the building through the front door being careful not to alarm any person sleeping on the living quarter's level.

They exit the city westward and stop for the night in the forest on that side of the city.

"I like this planet," says Rosetta. "No bugs…" She smiles at this thought.

"I take it you've been on a planet with bugs," asks Vaskette.

"Yes. I was on a planet called Fergose not long ago hunting for a woman who was trying to take her two little girls away from their dad. She hid in a forest-like area kind of like this one, except with trees. I had to have help on that run and of course had to split the money with him, but the reward money was enough to make out like a bandit, if you'll excuse the comparison."

"...And what of the bugs..." asks Lacendu.

"Oh, uh, yeah, they were monstrous...enormous. I'd say they were the size of a child's fist. I had to have a pint of blood put back into me afterward."

Everyone laughs at the idea.

She looks up at them without a smile. "I wasn't joking."

"Oh," most of them say at the same time.

"Did it hurt when they poked into you," asks Lacendu.

"You have no idea," Rosetta answers pontifically shaking her head. "I'm not saying they were big, but they carried off one of the girls..."

"Now you're joking, right," asks Vaskette.

"This time, yes... But the bugs were huge and vampiric. The two girls were suffering as well. You'd think the mother could have picked a better place to hide. They were all hospitalized for two weeks, and the mother was sent to a camp-prison on Vegauris Theta." She thinks for a moment. "I guess giving you the name of the planet was useless."

Vaskette looks up at Rosetta, the moon shining delicately off her eyes. "I'm so glad we all got this opportunity to get to know you, Seta. I can see what the Captain likes in you, even if it's not my style."

"You're saying you don't like me," asks Rosetta.

"Not quite. I like you as a person, it's just that I'm sitting here thinking if I had to spend a lot of time with you, our personalities would clash."

Lacendu is surprised at her friend's straight-forwardness. "Vaskette, that was irrevocably impolite."

"Now, now, Lacy, the Captain just finished giving us a spiel about being open and up front with everyone about any secret concerning ourselves. I just don't want a bunch of contention later on when we're all back on a ship heading home..."

Rosetta smiles at the two of them. "I do apologize. I guess I get a little contemplative when I talk about my previous hunts. It's a curse to be sure, but I will try to refrain from over-communication when I'm around you, Vaskette. Thank you for being honest with me."

"No problem, Seta," she says, and lies down on the soft blue-green grass. "Good night."

Lacendu follows suit, followed closely by the Master. Korsaume is already asleep.

Rosetta looks down at them. "I guess I get first watch for the night," she says, almost questioningly.

"If you don't mind," says the Master. "I don't think I could keep my eyes open another second."

Rosetta stands up and walks away from them a few yards and sighs heavily. She closes her own eyes for a moment, and there she stands under the beautiful, large moon wondering where her boyfriend, Mathew, is; wondering if he, too, is standing somewhere not far from here with his eyes closed thinking about her.

Silently to her self, she says, "Mathew, I miss you."

*****

Allen runs through the brush and foliage toward the desert where their ship parked. He knows there should be a couple of others there as well, and it does not take him long to get there. The man-hunt for him lasted two whole days, and finally they all went to the Master's house to rest. He was glad to have this opportunity to escape. They certainly seemed serious about catching him.

Several times they had almost caught him, and if it had not been for his great skill as a strategist, he would probably be dead right now. The injections the Doctor has been giving him for two weeks are really working well, and he feels like he can retain memory better. However, the last dose is beginning to wear off, and even though he does not need as much to keep his mind fresh, he knows he is going to need another dose if he is going to save his friends.

He starts thinking about trying to fly one of the ships but quickly throws that option out as he realizes he has absolutely no skill at flying spacecraft. He will have to stick with what he knows best, and that means he will have to beat the men that are after him at their own game.

He knows he is nearing the desert's edge, and sure enough he arrives in moments after thinking about it. There, only a few hundred meters away are the four ships. The one on the left side is a smaller craft; perhaps one of the ones used for getting under sensors of other ships. The next one is the zero-seven Celestial Class Star Expeditioner which belongs to him and his crew. The other two he does not recognize, but they are big, ugly, and have tons of weaponry; obviously meant for extreme combat situations.

He looks around and tries to figure out if there is a way he will be able to tell if others are watching for just such a move from him. He has no idea how many of them there are. He has only counted the ten looking for him.

He decides to chance it. Preparing to run as fast as he can, he counts down from ten. On zero, he makes a break for it. He feels his feet hit the hardened dust, keeping time with the rhythm of his heart. He imagines his body being riddled with holes by the enemy as he reaches the ship, his body falling to the ground, and his last thoughts being of Korsaume. It is at this moment he realizes he likes her. He decides to brush that aside until this ordeal is over…both thoughts…

He arrives at the ships unharmed and stops to look back. Nothing.

He goes to the back of the ship on the far right and starts working to open it. It takes some time, but he manages to trick the sensors into agreeing to open the door by telling it that it needs to decompress while in a planetary atmosphere. It is an old trick, and he is not even sure how he remembers it, but he does, and the stairs slowly descend from the base allowing him entrance.

He climbs on board and rapidly begins pulling weapons and force-shields from the stock-pile in the armament room. Then, he goes to the cockpit and sets the systems for complete overhauls, which he knows will cause the computer system to reboot, and could buy them all about a week.

He piles the weaponry and defense systems outside the ship in the sand using a large shovel-like item he finds in the clean-up compartment. He proceeds to do that with the other two ships which do not belong to him and his crew.

Lastly, he prepares the ship to the right of the Star Expeditioner to overload its system circuits so that no one will be able to get in from the outside. When the door closes, he uses one of the lasers to meld the door to the ship.

He proceeds to do the same thing to many of the moving parts on the outside of the vessel, and then does the same thing to the other two ships. Then he goes into the Star Expeditioner and repairs the hole in the front that the crew kicked through to get out.

His work is finished here. Now it is up to the rest of the crew to get back here so they can get off this planet…

*****

Mathew and Agoparn are seated in an upper tier of the plant-building. In front of them is a man who they assume is in charge of the security force in Bydiovo Alurcit.

The man is quick at getting to the point. “I understand you two came in and got something to drink form Metta’s shop, and then walked off without paying for it. She tells me you claim to be from another planet. Is this correct?”

Mathew realizes immediately it is a trap. If he answers the second question, which is what the man wants, then it will sound like they are admitting to the first as well.

“She offered the drinks to us ‘on the house.’ It was only water.”

“That does not answer my question. Did you, or did you not walk off without paying for your drinks?” The man asks this leaning into Mathew’s face.

“Exactly as you have worded the question, yes, we did not pay for the drinks.”

“…And you claim to be from another planet…?”

"No sir. We did not claim to be from another planet. I did, however, tell her we are not from this planet."

"So you claim ignorance of the law. Is that it?"

"Well, I would claim that, but there was no law that we could break when she offered us the water 'on the house.'" Mathew is frustrated, and he believes he now knows why there are not many visitors present in Bydiovo Alurcit.

"Yet the two of you walked away while her back was turned. Anyone would assume you were trying to escape."

Mathew hates lying, though he is not sure he did prior to the memory erasure. Now, he hopes he is doing the right thing, even if deep down inside he is not sure.

"We just needed water. She told us that the ocean water was not drinkable. I told her we were in her debt, and she acted like she was going to take us up on that. We did not want to spend any time in respective servitude at this moment as there are members of my crew elsewhere on this planet. We just want to find them and get the heck off this planet."

The man stands in silence for a time.

Finally, "So that's it. Do you think that based on that little speech that I should just let the two of you go without you paying for services rendered?"

"As much as we would both like that, sir, I have to say that I don't expect you to do that based on your statements prior to this moment."

The man nods his head. "You're right. I don't know what to do with you two now. I could put you in prison, but what chance would that do of correcting your attitudes. I could make you pay off your debt to Metta's shop by working, but there would always be the chance of escape. You leave me in a difficult predicament."

Mathew tries anyway, "We would be glad to leave you be. We did not want to land on this planet anyway. We were forced to land here. Then we; my crew and I; got split up and Agoparn and I just wanted directions to a city. We just don't know what the city's name is, or we'd ask you for it."

"I really don't care what you want, Mister. I want to know what I'm going to do about your complete disregard for our fair city's rules and regulations. I also don't care if Metta offered you two the planet… Water on our planet costs money, and there is no such thing as a free lunch. Don't tell me you've never heard that!"

Mathew bows his head in disgust. "I don't know what to tell you, sir. We did not want to be here, but we are. We did not want any trouble, yet here we are. We did not want to get captured, yet we were. We do not want to stay here another minute, but I'm guessing you have some kind of plan to the contrary, and we'll be here until you've determined we're no longer a threat to you and yours. Am I correct in that assumption?"

"That about sums it up, Mister," says the man.

The two are left in solitude. The room is small, and there is a small slit in the plant where light comes in. Otherwise, the room is completely unlit. They are seated against a non-linear wall, more like a cave. The only exit is through the small opening in the floor which is covered by a metal plate that can be lifted to allow passage up and down. There is a small desk against the outside wall, but it is not very-well put together. There are legs on the left side, but the right side is propped up on a portion of the plant that is not carved straight. On the wooden-board desk is a small cup with a pencil standing up out of it. There is also parchment paper with a regular rock on top to hold it down. The light filtering in from the small slit shines on the floor. The sun is shining bright above the plant and the clouds in the violet sky move across their field of vision through that slit.

"What now, Captain," Agoparn says, his head bowed, eyes open, staring at the floor.

"I'm not sure, Parn. Things have gotten a little out of hand…"

"I'm quite certain none of us signed up for this kind of stuff. What did we do to deserve all of this?"

"Good question, Parn. I'm not sure."

*****

It is finally morning, and Korsaume is the final watch. She waits for the other four to rouse themselves by picking some fruits from the plants in the immediate vicinity. She hands them to the Master so he can verify their edibility. He approves all of them and the five start eating.

The fruit is quite delicious, though Lacendu, a very picky eater, only likes two of the five different kinds.

They talk and laugh and discuss their adventure with Rosetta and the Master so far. Vaskette and Lacendu leave out the part where they were attacked by Sherise on purpose, and Korsaume is glad. The Master and Rosetta ask questions, and the three try hard to answer them as they go. The Master is quite surprised at what they have gone through and thrills to the idea that five people have no memories of their previous life beyond four weeks ago.

It is during the current set of events being told that Rosetta rises from her seat on the grass and walks a couple meters away. Lacendu gets up and follows her.

Lacendu comes up behind the woman and asks, "What's wrong, Seta?"

Rosetta looks north at the violet sky. "Where is he, Lacy?"

"The Captain is smart, and so are Agoparn and Allen. Heck, they're the best in their respective fields; better even then those eight men who came through the transport bud. Better than those guys who chased us around on Steg. You don't think he isn't looking for us right now, do you?"

"That doesn't mean I'm not worried about him," Rosetta says turning to her new friend. "I want so badly to go find him, but I'm scared that we'll go through a transport bud and get to the wrong place and we'll all miss each other. The only thing I can think of is to stay right here and hope he makes it…that all of them make it."

"Come on back and let's discuss our options. Who knows, maybe one of us has a bright idea…"

The two women return and Rosetta says to the others, "I want to go find him. Them…"

The others stand up.

Korsaume places her hands on her hips. "What kind of search pattern did you have in mind?"

"I'm not sure," Rosetta answers. "I'm not a coordinator. I was hoping one of you might have an answer."

"You are a huntress," says Vaskette. "That's what you are good at. If anyone can find and track Mathew and the others, it would be you. You're barking up the wrong tree if you think we're going to have answers for finding someone."

"Not true," says Rosetta. "We have a mathematician, a weapons specialist, and a man who knows the lay of the land."

Korsaume shakes her head once, her oily, uncombed hair falling down around her face. "Seta, you tell us what you want us to do, and we'll help. We are just as concerned about the boys as you are, and we want to get off this planet. Head up the search; take charge and I'll follow you."

"I will, too," says Lacendu.

"I've got no place else to go right now. Searching for lost crew members is about the best thing I could do right now," the Master states.

Vaskette nods her approval when Rosetta looks over at her.

"Fine… We should keep someone here at this bud in case one or more of them come here. We should also keep one person at our entry point, which I'll check first to see if he and Parn went back there…"

Korsaume interrupts her. "As much as I hate the idea, Seta, I just want you to realize that even though Mathew and Parn are the best in their respective fields, it's quite possible that if our enemies caught up with them there at the transport bud or elsewhere…" She does not finish.

Rosetta looks deadly at the weapons expert. "I don't want to think about that right now. Either way, though, I have to know."

"As do I," Vaskette points out.

"I suggest we leave Vaskette on this end. I'll need Korsaume, Lacy, and you," she points to the Master.

"Please, call me Staton," he says.

"Alright, we leave Lacy and Staton at our original entry point. Korsaume and I will search for Allen, and hopefully Mathew and Agoparn went back there and hid waiting for us. When Korsaume and I get back, Lacy and I will go north, and Korsaume and Staton will go south. I'll search for any possibility that Mathew and Parn went there, and depending on what I find, I'll come back for the rest of you and we'll all go hunting together."

"Good plan," says Korsaume. "Let's do it."

The five head back to the center of town. They get a few odd stares from the locals, but no one seems to feel this to be entirely out-of-the-ordinary. Vaskette hides between two plant buildings, and the four of them travel through the transport bud to their original departure. When Rosetta arrives with Korsaume she checks the ground.

"There are a lot of footprints here," she says without looking up. She continues searching for telltale signs. "Mathew and Agoparn did not come back this way. Allen hasn't been here either, that I can tell, but I'm not certain of that because a couple of those men are his approximate size and weight." She turns to the other two. "Hide here and wait for us. We won't be long, if we can help it."

Lacendu and Staton hide in the brush while Korsaume and Rosetta run off to the east, back toward Staton's home.

It does not take them long to arrive, and when they get there, they see two men standing guard outside the front door.

"Oh, great," says Korsaume. "Do you think they have Allen?"

"No," she says, "look at the ground outside. There are no signs of men carrying anyone in; no signs of struggle which I'm certain Allen would have put up. No blood on the ground. I'm not one hundred percent sure, but I don't see anything that would say otherwise. Let's go around and head back to the ships."

"Weapons," Korsaume asks…

"That's the general idea." Rosetta smiles at her.

The two head south around the back of the house staying out of ear-shot, and make their way back to the edge of the desert, checking for signs that others are nearby.

"I don't see anyone," says Korsaume. "Should we make a run for it?"

"I'm going to try. You should stay here."

"Not a chance," says Korsaume. "I might miss all the action."

"Fine; follow me." She turns to the woman smiling big, "…and try to keep up."

They start off running as hard as they can toward the ships. Korsaume sees it…the glint of metal that does not belong at the level it is, or where it is against the leg of the Star Expeditioner. She jumps at Rosetta forcing her to the ground. No shots ring out.

"What are you doing, Korsaume?!" Rosetta spits out a mouthful of dust and looks behind her at Korsaume who lies on top of her.

"There was a gun pointed at us…"

"Oh. Well, why didn't the person fire?"

"I'm not sure…"

They look up. There underneath the shadow of the Star Expeditioner stands a man with a long black coat on. He waves at them.

"It's Allen," Korsaume smiles, and then laughs. "He's alive!"

The two women stand up and run to the ship.

"I'm so glad to see you two," says Allen. "Is everyone else alright?"

"Everyone but Mathew and Agoparn were for certain fine when we left them. We're not sure where the Captain and our Engineer are at the moment, but we're going to find them. Care to tag along?"

"I'd love to," is his response.

"Got any more of those," asks Korsaume pointing at his gun.

Allen smiles big; "Do I have any more of these…" It is a statement, not a question, and he stresses the letter "I." He digs up a couple other guns and hands them to the two women. Korsaume grabs a couple other items from the hole and then allows Allen to cover it back up.

Rosetta uses a few tricks to cover up the fact that there have been holes dug in the vicinity, and then the three run back to the forest.

It is nearly two hours that Vaskette, Lacendu, and Staton have been left alone when the three arrive back at the original transport bud. Korsaume and Staton head south and stay there. Rosetta, Lacendu, and Allen go north.

Rosetta searches the ground again and finds evidence that the two men they are looking for have been here. She points off to the west. "They went that way. Let's go get the others and meet back here."

Rosetta goes to get Vaskette, and Lacendu goes to get Korsaume and Staton.

It is about thirty minutes before all six of them are present and accounted for.

Vaskette smiles at Rosetta and nods her affirmation. "Good job."

Lacendu hugs Allen. "We're all glad you're still alive," she says happily.

"Me, too," Allen says contorting his mouth in a half-smile that quickly becomes whole.

"As thankful as I am for Allen's safety, my current concern is the other two. Let's move out," says Rosetta.

The six of them follow her through the brush.

Korsaume looks back at Staton. "Why does one of the buds come here, sir?"

"Well, there's a city not far from here to the east. The nearest city to the west is close to the coast about twenty kilometers from here… It would take them a couple days to reach it if they went this way."

"They've been missing for a couple days," says Rosetta. "Are there any other bud transports this way?"

"Not that I am aware of," says the Master, "but I don't come this way. Bydiovo is a runner's port. I can't imagine anyone wanting to go there."

"Two men without weapons who don't know the territory and trying to escape from several men with weapons who want those two men dead…I'd say if

I were in they're shoes, I'd just pick a direction and go. I wouldn't care if there was a city nearby or not…" Vaskette says ruefully.

"Good point," Staton says, half to himself.

"We've got a long journey ahead of us, folks," says Korsaume thinking ahead. "Let's save our breath. We're going to need it. I highly recommend not speaking unless you have something vital to say."

Two clear their throats, and one sighs and rolls her eyes.

*****

It is the next morning when the head of security in Bydiovo Alurcit comes back up through the door and into the small room where Mathew and Agoparn sleep soundly, heads resting on the back of the plant wall.

"Good morning, gentlemen," the man says to them.

Mathew wakes from his slumber and yawns wide, blinking his eyes fast and hard to get rid of the water in them. He looks over at Agoparn and notices he's still asleep.

He proceeds to nudge his friend with his elbow, and moments later Agoparn wakes to pain in his lower back from sitting in the same position all night. He leans left to stretch the muscles in his back, then to his right. He would lean back as well, but the wall is in his way.

Then, the man in front of them has the nerve to say, "I hope you both slept comfortably…"

He pours the two men drinks of water and walks over to them. He holds up a glass to Mathew's lips.

"No thanks," says Mathew. "I don't have any money to pay for that."

"Ah, drink it," he says harshly. "You need it so badly…" The man lifts the glass and Mathew allows the water to fall into his mouth and his dry tongue absorbs it quickly as he swallows whatever goes down the back of his throat. It is quite refreshing.

The man does the same for Agoparn, who gladly accepts it.

When he is finished, he says, “I thought about your punishment last night and this morning, and I have finally decided what it shall be. You will serve in the mines below for five days. I think that is punishment enough.”

“Mines…? What do you mine,” asks Agoparn.

“We use certain plant roots as stimulants.”

“You get high off the inedible portion of plants,” Mathew asks.

“Well, when you put it like that, yes.”

“I don’t see any reason to help your people kill themselves,” says Agoparn. “I decline.”

“I do, too,” Mathew says.

“Actually, you don’t have a choice in the matter. You’ll both be taken by chains to the mine below the city through a secret gate. You’ll both work for five days. You’ll receive provisions for your work, minus two large glasses of water each on the first day. When your time is up, you’ll be taken to the entry point of the city where you entered, and you will leave…” Then he adds, “…and never return.”

The two men look at each other.

The man is true to his word. Five minutes pass, and six men arrive to chain them and drag them down to the mine.

As they enter, barely under their own power due to the weight of the chains, they take note that there are openings on either side of the large cavern, which fall directly into the chasm. There are not many workers, but what are there look worn and in need of a bath.

Mathew and Agoparn are separated and shown how to cultivate the plants, which thrive in the dark and damp atmosphere of the cavern. All around them is evidence of the plant above; roots that are as wide around as three hundred grown men.

The small plants have minute pockets of orange glowing matter inside their leaves. The blossoms are beautiful in shape, but it is difficult to make out their color in the darkness.

They are given several small tools to work with, and an entire row of plants to work on. Then, they are left alone to do their work. There is a supervisor for every three people, and Mathew and Agoparn are closely monitored.

The mine is more a dark green-house than a mine.

Mathew begins pulling some of the roots on the plants that have already grown to their full capacity. The portions of roots he cuts are then placed in a small bucket which hangs around his neck. When the bucket is full, the supervisor comes by, takes the basket and replaces it with an empty one.

At first, Mathew and Agoparn have trouble adjusting their eyes to the low light, but they soon become attuned to it and can work fairly quickly without too much complication.

If it were not for the fact that they work for their very life's essence, the two would not bother, but their senses gave up two days ago when they were almost to the point of dehydration. The little water they've had since then has not made up for that fact.

So, naturally, when the end of the working day comes and the two are led to separate cells and watch people in the cells near them receive water and bread, their tongues go numb with thirst.

Mathew soon passes out from necessity, but no one is there to notice, and he lies there on the hard ground until the next day.

*****

Rosetta checks the ground and looks ahead. There is an ocean vaguely in view in the early morning light. The water looks violet under the reddish sky. Mathew and Agoparn came this way. She is now certain of it.

The group of six exits the forest and enters a large field of wildflowers. They are tired and exhausted, but seeing the ocean and the tall plant-city ahead of them gives them renewed strength.

Until Staton informs them that the water is not drinkable, they are excited about reaching the shore. Afterward, they seem a little less so, but the thought of finding their lost friends keeps them going.

It is not long before they reach a chasm before the plant-city, and the moment Staton sees it, he realizes what city it is…

"Uh, we don't want to go in here," he says matter-of-factly.

He does not continue.

Finally, Lacendu pipes up and says, "…yes, you said it was a runner's port…"

"These people are insane. This is Bydiovo Alurcit; basically it's a town full of drugged-out people who will steal your money for any reason they can find; and the local authority helps them do it for a small fee. I've read several articles on this place, but anyone who's smart stays away from here…"

Korsaume, Rosetta, and Allen give him dirty looks.

He clears his throat and adds, "Or people not from this planet which come for visits and haven't read anything about it…" Then he smiles at them.

"Nice save," says Lacendu turning to him and giving him a half-smile.

"What do you think, Korsaume? Can we handle it," asks Rosetta.

"You're leading," she answers.

"Yes, and you're our beloved Captain's second-in-command. I want your opinion."

"Oh, why didn't you say so…? I say we go in there and tell them how it's going to be. If they try to fight us, we blow them all to kingdom-come!"

Everyone but the Master turns to look at her and gives her their most rough look.

Korsaume holds up both hands in a stopping fashion. "I was kidding about that last part…" Then she opens her eyes wide and raises her eyebrows nodding her head, "…honest."

Staton does not turn around. "Actually, that's probably the best idea." Then he turns his head to Rosetta. "I'm not kidding."

"You really feel that strongly about these people," Vaskette asks.

"I'm all for going in, guns-a-blazing," states Korsaume, "but I think we should start by finding out if they're even in there…"

"They went in, Korsaume," Rosetta says, "but they haven't come out this side. I'm not saying they haven't gotten away, they just didn't come back out here."

"Do you think they're prisoners," asks Allen.

Korsaume answers quickly, "Well, we've got an expert strategist. We should utilize him."

"I agree," says Allen. "Just let me go in, and all of you hang out here."

"Good idea," Rosetta says. "We'll hide out here."

"I should go with him," Staton declares. "I know this world. I might be able to get him out of trouble if things go wrong…"

Rosetta looks at Allen. "I think that's a fine arrangement. Get to it."

The remaining four head south to make a temporary place to stay and Staton follows Allen into the plant-city.

The two men walk into Bydiovo Alurcit together, Allen in front, guns in hands.

They are promptly met at the door by what both assume to be a guard. He is tall and muscular, and his irises and corneas are both deep red. "Excuse me, sir," says the man, "we do not allow weapons in here."

"I kind of figured you wouldn't," says Allen. "So I'll just stand here at the door. I need to find two men. One is a Captain Mathew Arnold, and the other is Agoparn Schroet."

"Yeah? What do they look like," is his gritty response.

"Well," Allen begins, "Mathew is in his late twenties, six-foot-four, yellow-green eyes, and black hair. Agoparn is in his early forties; five-foot-eleven, brown hair, brown eyes, and is slightly overweight. Have you seen them?"

The man thinks for a moment by placing his right hand under his left armpit, resting his left elbow on his right forearm, and wrapping his thumb and pointing finger around his strong, pronounced chin. His eyes look glazed over as he looks off to the southern sky. "Let me think…" A long pause, "I think we had a couple visitors that fit that description come through a couple days ago. I don't remember if they stayed or not, though. I haven't heard anything about them since then, so I assume that unless the second shift caught them doing something illegal, they'd be gone by now, or living in the apartments if they decided to stay."

Allen looks at Staton with a questioning glance. Staton takes the cue and asks, "I would like permission to go to the apartment manager and find out. Would you take me to them?"

"I'm sorry," says the man placing his arms at his side as much as possible. The bulging muscles make it difficult to accomplish realistically, but he tries. "I have to stand post until mid-day. You may go through, though. We do not restrict access to friendly people into our fair city."

Staton looks at Allen and nods his head. "I'll be back soon. If not, I recommend getting away from here and never returning."

Allen says, "You know we can't do that. They're our friends."

"Just like my wife and butler were mine when those men busted down the door to my home…?"

Allen realizes this man has done much for them despite his unpromising circumstances. "Point received, my friend." He nods his head at the Master and walks back to the wooden bridge to wait.

*****

Staton arrives at the door to the apartment manager's office and knocks loudly. It takes a few minutes before someone comes to the door, and he is quite certain the young girl in front of him is not a manager.

"Excuse me, miss, but I need to speak with the manager of the apartments."

The young girl gives him a "drop-dead" look and says, "Who are you?"

"I am a Parasentinel of the Garenoljola Council. My name is Staton Vauren. May I please speak with the manager?"

"I'm sorry, Staton, but Parasentinels do not knock. They enter at their whim. If you're really a Parasentinel, you'd know that…"

"Actually, Parasentinel's are required by law to knock first and ask to be invited in; they only enter at their whim if they are declined entry. So, are you going to invite me in, or not?"

"Not." She closes the door and locks it.

Staton pulls out a pass key and uses it to open the door. He closes the door behind him and follows the young girl to a small room in the back.

Without so much as blinking, the girl stops, looks at the three men seated around a table, and says, "Parasentinel Staton Vauren wants to speak with the apartment manager." She turns and walks out.

The man on the far side of the table stands up. He is short and balding, but the hair on the sides of his head is black with no signs of gray. His eyes are dark and receded into his head, brows covering them making his eyes almost black in the candlelight. He has bags under his eyes as if he has not slept in days. His stubby hands hold five round cards, the standard deck-type of the planet. He does not smile, or frown, but his jowls show as he says, "To what do we owe the pleasure of a Parasentinel in our humble city?"

The man on the left laughs and says, "Parasentinels do not visit our city. They're scared of us…"

"Most of my brethren in the Council are, yes. My presence here has to do with two men who came this way. Their names are Mathew and Agoparn. They are not from this planet, and the men are wanted by the Solar Union."

The man on the left stands, pounding his fist on the table as he does… "We do not pay homage to the Solar Union. Why would we care what they want…?!"

Through this, Staton keeps a calm voice. "You should not care what the Solar Union wants… However, you should care about the platoon of agents on this very planet looking for them. Word came to them that the two men might be here. They asked me to take them into custody. That is what I am here to do…"

"Well," says the man behind the desk as the one on the left sits down, "I am sorry to say that we do not know of these two men, nor do I have anyone in my apartments by those names."

"Then, perhaps you will take me to the head of security…" says Staton. "That is not a request."

The man behind the table still standing gives a loud huff and walks around. "You're cutting into my wins," he says glaring, then haughtily stomps off through the door and across the living room.

Staton follows him and the two men head down the tall ladder to the tunnel below. They walk along the narrow path with shops on either side receiving waves from practitioners and shop-keepers as they head west. It is only a matter of moments before the man turns left toward a dark alcove where a door sits back away from the walk-way. The man opens the door and enters a small room where another man sits behind a desk. "Here you are, Parasentinel."

The man behind the desk's eyes jump wide open and he stands holding out his hand. The other leaves the room. Staton walks over to the man holding out his hand, but does not extend his own.

"Parasentinel, Sir," he says putting his hand down. "I am the head of security here in Bydiovo Alurcit. How may I be of service?"

"Well," Staton starts, but before he can get another word out, the man interrupts him.

"Can I offer you a cup of cold water, sir?"

"No, thank you. I'm here for one purpose. I need to find two men, and I believe they came here."

"I see." The man is obviously troubled by this. "Do you have any information on them?"

Staton sits on the chair in front of the desk. "Yes. They go by the names Mathew and Agoparn…" He knows already he does not need to go on. "You know them…" It's a statement.

"Yes. We have them in custody." He shakes his head.

"What did they do?"

"They were caught trying to escape without paying for services rendered."

Staton shakes his head. "People these days... Well, they're in trouble with the Solar Union. I have a group outside the city waiting for them. You should release them to my custody. I will rid your city of these bandits."

"Nothing would please me more, sir. I'll grab the prisoners and have them taken outside under duress." The man exits through another door behind Staton.

Staton exits the main door and heads back toward the entrance where Allen still waits, guns in hand. The Master explains what the head of security told him, and the two men wait for their two friends.

Only a minute or so after Staton finishes giving Allen the information, Korsaume runs across the wooden bridge shouting at the two men. At first they cannot make out what she is saying, but they soon realize she is pointing behind her. The two men look up and see what she is pointing at...a group of men walking this direction, and they already know who it is...

"Ah, frag," says Allen. "I didn't think they would try to follow us."

Korsaume arrives just as the head of security comes back with Mathew and Agoparn who look tired and worn.

Staton turns to Mathew and Agoparn, "You're both under arrest for crimes against the Solar Union. If you have anything to say in your defense, it will be heard before a judicial structure in a planetary system of your own people."

Korsaume immediately realizes what is going on and plays along.

"Staton, Sir; the agents are on their way. We should take these two men out to them." Korsaume says this slightly nervously, but the head of security does not seem to notice, excited to be of service to such important people.

"Agreed," says Allen.

"On your way," says Staton standing aside for Mathew and Agoparn to walk past.

Allen takes his cue and holds his guns to the men's backs. "Move out."

The two do not argue or talk; they do not look like they could if they wanted.

All five begin to run across the bridge as quickly as possible.

"What now," asks Staton… "Your enemies are closing in, and chances are they can see us from there."

"What is south of here," asks Mathew.

"Well, there's another city approximately ten or twelve kilometers that direction."

"We couldn't possibly outrun those men, Captain," says Korsaume as the five of them reach the end of the bridge and turn right along the chasm.

"Who says we have to outrun them, Korsaume," asks Allen. "We've done a pretty good job of outsmarting them all this time…"

Korsaume does not give a retort, but she acts like she wants to.

The group of five meets up with the other three, but do not stop, so the three women begin trying to keep up.

"Where are we going," asks Lacendu.

"Less talking, more running," is the Captains reply.

The eight people run hard and fast. Only Korsaume turns once to see the men hunting for them gaining ground.

"Captain, we're not doing a great job here," she says.

"They've decided to forego capturing us and go straight to killing," says Allen.

Along the chasm, the group comes upon a set of ruins; obviously not of floral design. It seems to be made out of bricks and mortar.

"Where is this place," asks Mathew as the group gets inside a small clearing with a wall between them and their hunters.

Staton gathers his breath and responds, "I believe it to be the ruins of one of the original cities built in this region by the Lourdes of Arbitration. They were the ones who colonized this planet nearly five hundred years ago."

"Nice history lesson, Staton," says Korsaume, "but that's not helping. Where are we?" She emphasizes the word "where."

"On the map, about a kilometer south of Bydiovo, and approximately twenty kilometers west-northwest of my home…"

"Well, then," Mathew says with a rough smile. "We'll just have to make a stand here."

"What do you suggest, Captain," asks Rosetta.

"Well, we've got the top mathematics expert, strategist, and weapons expert in the galaxy at our disposal. You three have about one minute to come up with something." Mathew smiles at them. "The rest of us are going to go hide. Korsaume, take command…"

Korsaume rolls her eyes. "I hope this isn't a sign of things to come," she mutters to herself.

"Can you calculate odds," asks Allen looking directly at Lacendu.

"Uh…um…yes. I can…" she says nervously, her eyes not glued to any one thing or one person.

"Great," he replies. "What are the odds that the three weapons Korsaume and I have on us could take out those eight experts back there?"

Lacendu thinks hard for a moment. "Uh, about four to one, assuming you two can get more than two shots off per second, and…"

Korsaume cuts her off. "That will have to do. We can start by dispersing them into separate groups temporarily. That should increase the odds."

"Actually, no it won't," Lacendu says calculating. "You'll make yourselves more vulnerable. Keep them in a group and fire on the things around them. That should keep them confused."

"I like the way this girl thinks," Allen says. "Let's do this. Lacy, stay behind us; Korsaume, let's fire on the trees and walls as those men get to them. When they think they've got that figured out, we'll fire directly on them."

"Good thinking, Strategist," she says peaking her head out over a piece of wall. "…And good timing… They're here. Allen?"

The two come up with guns aimed over the wall in different directions and pull the triggers of their respective weapons.

Korsaume's hits a tree knocking it over. Allen's hits a small wall at its base causing the top to wobble and fall toward the men. Two of them are caught under the old heavy brick-like wall and the rest are hit hard by branches of the tree as it falls from about three feet from the ground. Three are hurt badly by the thick branches. Two just get scratches on their faces. The two men trapped under the wall are severely injured, and Marcus has his left foot caught under part of the wall.

Marcus pulls his foot out carefully by digging a hole in the dirt under his foot. It takes a few minutes, but afterwards, he stands up and brushes his jacket, shirt, and pants off.

"Nice job," he says loudly. "You caught us off guard and did what we didn't expect. Most of my men are injured."

"The odds are in our favor, now," Lacendu says back at him from behind the wall.

"Obviously," he says limping forward a couple steps.

Two of his men stand up behind him and start helping their friends. A third finally struggles to his feet, barely able to hold himself up under his own power.

"You should give up now," says Korsaume. "You're out-gunned, out-maneuvered, and out-classed. You don't stand a chance."

"I don't know about that," he says raising his gun at the wall.

Mathew sees it from his vantage point hidden in the brush and yells, "MOVE!!!"

The three behind the wall hear it just as the blast hits the bricks knocking it over. They make it out of the way, but just barely. Rocks and dust catch the backs of their legs as they get far enough away and turn to face him down.

"When I go down, I'm taking as many of you with me as I possibly can," he says smiling, gun still in hand, aiming straight at the three.

Without a voice, a rock comes hurtling over their heads and straight for Marcus. He sees it, but it is too late. As he tries to move out of the way, Korsaume and Allen take their shots with their sonic-wave weapons. Marcus is flung through the air at some of his men which were, until now, standing and helping their friends. His body hits them with such force that they are all knocked down into the tree limbs.

"Let's move out," Korsaume says turning around.

The five hiding get out of the underbrush and the eight of them head out as quickly as possible toward the south.

*****

It is a few hours later when they arrive at the city of Yianger Shide-oak. Staton makes the arrangements for what Lacendu keeps referring to as a "flying-plant ride," and the group is under-way about twenty-five minutes later.

"It's not a 'flying-plant ride,'" Staton explains. "It's a Sargostic Air-Weed. It flies on simple principles of air-lift and photosynthesis." He then spends the next thirty minutes explaining how it works, though only Agoparn and Rosetta seem to understand.

About an hour and a half goes by as the "pilot" lands the Sargostic Air-Weed near the ships in the desert. After everyone gets off the plant, it returns to the air with its leaves spread out far and glorious.

"Well," says Staton, "I don't know where my wife and butler are or what's become of them, but…"

Allen clears his throat. "I'm sorry to say that your butler is dead. Last I saw your wife she was tied up on the second floor next to the hole we made in your restroom."

Staton looks at Allen wide-eyed, mouth open.

Allen swallows hard. "Um, that probably wasn't the best way to handle that…"

Staton sighs. "If I've lost my wife, then I have no reason to go on, and if not, then I have no reason to go with you. I'll head back and tell those men chasing you what has happened. Hopefully, they'll have mercy on me and leave me alone."

"Would you like some help, Staton? You've helped us this far. We have no reason not to try to help you," Mathew states with sympathetic eyes.

"No. You folks have had it far harder than I. Those men may be chasing you all over the place, but I know one thing: there is no reason to harm any of you. I've seen you folks in action, and how you treat each other. Anyone with your care for each other has no reason to be hunted this way by the Solar Union."

Korsaume says, "Well, we don't have time to tell you the whole story, but if there's anything we can do for you before we leave, name it."

"Well, I could probably use a couple of those guns you have for protection…"

Korsaume and Allen each hand him a gun with a smile.

"Anything else," Mathew asks.

"That will do. Thank you all for your assistance; and these guns…" Staton tries to smile.

Allen holds out his hand to shake, "Actually, we owe you much more than two guns. You helped us get around in this strange land. We would never have made it if it hadn't been for you."

"I agree," Mathew says. "We wish you the best in your future. I hope your wife is safe and well."

Staton does not bother to continue, but turns around and walks away in the late evening sun as it starts going down behind the not-too-distant forest. His steps are slow and tired, but steady and deliberate.

The remaining seven watch him for a while and then turn to go into their ship.

Mathew pushes Korsaume a bit off to the right with his shoulder as they walk until they are far enough away for him to whisper to her without the others hearing.

"Honestly, Korsaume, is there even a slight chance that his wife is alive?"

"Honestly, Captain," she says with a tear in her eye.

She pauses for a while.

The door to the ship opens downward and the other five walk up.

"You coming, Captain," asks Agoparn stopping midway up the stairs.

"Yeah, just a moment…" Mathew replies.

Korsaume faces Mathew with her face tilted down, and her eyebrows furrowed. She swallows hard looking up at his face with her eyes only. She blinks a few times.

"No."

Episode 8
High Tide

OPENING:

"There is a saying among the traders and planetary money-mongers who scour their small portion of the galaxy for anything that will make them wealthy. The saying is only known to the traders and money-mongers, but those outsiders who have heard portions of it say it has the words 'horror' and 'death' in it. If it does, then it is possible that the saying is heard only by those who get in their way..."

The darkness of space envelopes the large white ship in its firm grasp. The zero-seven Celestial class Star Expeditioner is home to seven people who, at the moment, are fairly happy.

Five members of the crew have been given information about their lives prior to a complete loss of memory. They cannot remember beyond five and a half weeks ago, so the information presented to them now drives them all into excitement.

The five crew members; Mathew Arnold, Allen Pendergrass, Lacendu Ruric-Trester, Agoparn Schroet, and Vaskette Smith; read the info Mathew's girlfriend, Rosetta Firemark, had found and has now given to them.

Though she had been reluctant to give it to them immediately, their recent adventure has only proven to her that she cannot keep anything from her new friends.

A few of them are smiling the more they read but Mathew and Allen are both noticeably upset about the information they received.

Mathew reads a note from a report from his superior, Kelli Frembondac, a female officer of the fleet. It is a very simple note, and he reads it to himself. "...Commander Arnold may very well be a masterful pilot, but his overbearing attitude and his complete disregard for direct orders make him bad stock material. As well, he is a male chauvinist and has on numerous occasions made advances to his female commanding officers including this Captain. I cannot, in good conscience, recommend him for promotion, or for any other position but field duty. He is a hazard to his command. As such, I recommend that he continue his piloting in which he excels."

He had not read much prior to this, but having read this small note only a few minutes after receiving the data, he feels remorse for his attitude prior to an inexplicable memory loss; an attitude he cannot possibly remember.

His hands bring the small computer down to his lap, and he closes his eyes as his head bows. He does not know if he wants to read anymore, so he stands up and walks out of the mess toward his living quarters. Korsaume and Rosetta both look at each other and Rosetta makes a move to go after him.

"I've got this," Korsaume says holding the other woman's arm effectively halting her.

Korsaume leaves the room to follow Mathew.

*****

A knock on the door lets Mathew know he has company. He stands up from his bed having just sat down. He walks over to the door and opens it carefully. Korsaume stands before him with her neck compacted on its self and her head leaning slightly to the right, eyes wide in curiosity, and a semi-smile holding the center of his attention; attention he does not want to give at the moment.

"May I come in," she asks.

Very dishearteningly, he turns and walks to the bed leaving the door only a quarter of a meter open. "Sure. Why not…?" His voice is deep and saddened.

"What's wrong, Sir…?"

He does not answer right away, sitting down on the bed, placing his face in his hands, and leaning his elbows on his thighs. Moments pass as Korsaume pushes the door near to a close and walks over to sit down beside him.

She speaks. "I'm betting you read something on that report you didn't like… Is that accurate?"

He only moves his face away from his hands long enough to be sarcastic. "What was your second clue?" His face goes right back into his hands.

"Mathew, we're your friends. If there's something bothering you, you know you can talk to us." At this, she does not give him an opportunity to answer, but continues, "So, why don't you talk with me…?"

Mathew shakes his head in disgust and removes his hands from his face, opting now to place his forearms along his thighs and hanging the same hands off his knees. He sighs heavily one time, knowing she won't leave this alone.

"Evidently I was a real creep in my previous life," he admits. "I was, and I quote, 'a male chauvinist, bad stock material, and a hazard to my command.'"

"Well, I know someone very well who used to be awfully similar in that regard. You might even remember her. Her name was Sherise Felder…"

He does not answer her, so she goes on. "I'm betting, too, that that is not what you are upset about…"

Mathew looks up at the ceiling. "Rosetta has read all of this and knows…" He pauses. "She knows how I used to be."

"Hm." Korsaume smiles to herself looking away from him at some random spot on the floor. "It's about a girl…"

At that, he smiles slightly. "Isn't it always about a girl…?"

Both of them laugh.

Mathew pretends to clear his throat. "I just don't know what to do. I was hoping that I was a much better person in…" He is not sure how to finish the sentence.

She tries to finish it for him. "…in your previous life…?"

"In my old, dead-and-gone life…a life I can't even remember!"

"…A life that, if you could remember, would make you the same person now as you were then. You've had a truly rare opportunity that only four other people in the galaxy that I've ever heard about can share – an opportunity you also gave me only a week or so ago – the chance to start over."

Mathew glances at her, but quickly turns away. "You know, I guess it is kind of funny that we've all wanted information on who we are, including my self. Now that I have it, I wish I didn't…"

"Well, knowing who you were before can help you to keep from becoming the same thing now. Use the knowledge you now have to make yourself a better person."

"Good advice from my second-in-command," he says smiling at her.

"Captain, you are the most wonderful person I've ever had the privilege of serving under. Besides, I'll bet you'll find some better information in the data your girlfriend retrieved for you." She pats him on the back and rises from his side.

"Thank you for coming to talk to me, Korsaume. It really helped."

"Well, you would have done the same thing for me. In fact, I believe you have…twice." She smiles down at him. "I'm only repaying the kindness you have shown me."

"It does not go unnoticed," he says smiling back at her and standing.

He takes her in his arms and hugs her, which she returns gladly. After he releases her, she walks to the door.

Holding the handle in her right hand and standing half-in/half-out of the doorway, she leans against the door post and turns to face him, smile still intact.

"Keep reading, and if you need someone to talk to about anything else you find, don't hesitate to come to me."

He looks at her in the dim light of his room with the bright light from the hallway shining past her making her seem dark against it. He had never really paid much attention to her before, but here in this moment, he finds her beautiful and attractive. He bows his head a bit, fixing his eyes on her face. "Thank you." He blinks a few times.

She closes the door behind her, and Mathew is left alone with his thoughts.

*****

Rosetta is sitting at the table with a smile on her face when Korsaume re-enters. Rosetta stands up and walks over to the other.

"Is everything alright," she asks.

"Yeah. Mathew was upset by something he read…a note calling him a chauvinist and bad stock material…"

"Oh. Yes, I did read that," Rosetta answers with the left side of her mouth pulled back.

"That's exactly what he was scared of; that you had read it and would think less of him…"

"I would never think something like that. I guess I assumed he knew me better than that."

"He probably does; but would that stop you from feeling guilty if the roles were reversed…?"

Rosetta thinks for a moment with her chin squarely against the web between her thumb and forefinger and her left arm across her chest, left hand holding up her right elbow. "Well, probably not." …And this to Korsaume; "I should go talk with him."

Rosetta walks away as Korsaume sits down next to Vaskette.

Vaskette does not look directly at Korsaume, and as she continues to read she moves away from the Lieutenant putting space between them. Korsaume immediately picks up on this and moves right, closer to the edge of the cushioned bench, giving Vaskette room.

Korsaume decides the best way to get back on Vaskette's good side is to talk with her, so she tries. "So, Doctor, what have you learned about yourself so far?"

Though Vaskette still feels betrayed by the other, the thoughts going through her mind are simple; 'if we're both going to be on this ship together, I guess I'll have to talk with her…' "I was the best known doctor in the galaxy. I was top of every class, the leader in every physician's organization that exists in quarter one of the galaxy, and I had a boyfriend that evidently didn't even care about me. He's not even looking for me…"

Korsaume smiles, "It sounds to me like you were a little too busy for a relationship."

"Well, I must admit that it would be nice to have a man in my life. I'm all for being a great doctor, but even people like me need someone to complete their lives."

"Perhaps so," says Korsaume, "but just think; if you had had a boyfriend or husband, would you have been the best doctor in the galaxy?"

At this, Vaskette looks over at Korsaume with a dull look. She blinks a few times. "I hadn't thought about that, but it doesn't really matter, does it? If I hadn't been the best doctor in the galaxy, I wouldn't be here now…"

"…And if you hadn't been here now, someone else would have, and I can't think of a nicer, smarter, or more caring person than you that I'd rather have with us now."

Vaskette feels a small rush of relaxation, but keeps in mind who it is coming from. With her half-frown still intact she simply says, "Thank you."

"Hey, I really mean it."

"I have no doubt that you do," Vaskette replies turning back to the small hand-held computer and scrolling through to read more.

Allen had left the room at some time during the two women's discourse. Besides Vaskette and Korsaume, only Lacendu and Agoparn remain.

Korsaume looks around the room and decides to leave it all at that. She exits the mess and walks toward the control room.

Lacendu looks up at Vaskette after Korsaume is sufficiently far away. "Wow, Doctor; do you think you could have been any colder?"

"Leave it alone, Lacy," she replies softly.

"No, I think you should go apologize to her. You were really mean to her."

"That wasn't the point and you know it! Now, leave it alone!" At this Vaskette stands up and walks out of the mess.

Agoparn looks at Lacendu. She notices his look and glances back at him. "What," she asks.

"Nothing," he admits, and then turns back to his reading.

"You think I could have handled that differently?"

"I'm not saying anything. I won't get involved." He says this over his hand-held computer while pretending to continue reading.

She stares at him for a moment longer and then goes back to her reading.

*****

Korsaume arrives at the control room to find Allen sitting at his seat, right elbow on the control panel in no particular spot, and his right hand on his head. She does not bother to talk to him, but instead sits down at her control panel.

She's not sure what to do, so she plays with the controls doing things she knows won't make any difference to the ships destination or its performance. Allen seems oblivious to her for quite a while.

Finally, he opens his left eye to see her across the room punching buttons. "Is there a problem?"

"Yeah! This whole galaxy has gone completely mad and it's taking me with it," she says almost too loud for the subject of the statement. At the utter futility she feels at the moment, she exhales loudly and falls toward the control panel, her forehead hitting the top of the panel just a bit too hard. She is hurt by it, but she is too frustrated to care.

"Is it just my imagination, or is no one getting along today?" He removes his hand from his head and leans back in the comfortable chair.

"It's not your imagination," she mumbles, her face too close to the control panel. "I think we're all having a bad day."

He folds his arms and looks at the ceiling. "It all started when we got our hands on this information about ourselves."

Korsaume lifts her head up a bit from the control panel and looks at him. "So you think Seta was right about not giving that data to the five of you like she was originally not planning to do?"

"I don't know. If we had all known what we were going to get, we might not have wanted it, but since we didn't have any reason to believe the information would upset us, there was no way to make any other decision than the one we did."

Korsaume lays her head back where it was. "Thanks for being totally confusing, Allen."

Allen decides to change the subject. "Hey, 'you wanna' know what I found out about myself?"

"Sure. Why not…?" The words are slurred.

He suddenly realizes that what he was going to tell her about what he learned was not as great as the way he had asked the question. "Oh. Well, I guess I was quite the military mind in the academy. But I was also a jerk about it. I rubbed it in other's faces and made them feel; well, let's just say I was a bully."

"That doesn't sound like you," she says lifting her head again. Her eyes remain closed, but she does not seem to feel as bad anymore; almost as if what Allen is saying is helping.

"No, it doesn't. I guess I've changed."

"Oh, don't get me wrong," Korsaume says smirking. "You can still be pretty mean… You're always making jokes at our expense."

He looks at her a little surprised.

"It's OK," she says opening her eyes and looking over at him. "It's part of your charm."

"Thanks…I think…" He stops to think. "You really think I have charm?"

She stands up and walks half-way across the room, stops and looks at him. "Don't push your luck," she says smiling. She walks away through the door.

*****

"Vaskette…"

Vaskette stands in the infirmary near the sink. She just finished throwing up, and she is now wiping her mouth with a damp cloth. Her head is tilted upward, and her eyes are closed. The cloth hangs over her right hand, and her left hand is on the counter helping to hold her up.

"Vaskette, are you alright?" Lacendu enters the infirmary and waits at the door looking at her friend facing the same direction she is.

Vaskette does not speak. Instead, she lifts her left forearm and holds up her pointing finger in a "just one moment" gesture. Lacendu remains quiet and looks at the floor.

Vaskette rinses the cloth off under the cleansing liquid that comes from the faucet. It is evident that the doctor is trying to relax her body. She dry heaves once and lifts her head back up in its previous place, eyes closed. She breathes heavily and long.

She finally feels she has pulled herself together and washes the cloth once more. Then she throws the cloth into the cloth-cycle machine for further cleaning and looks up at Lacendu. "What can I do for you," she asks; her heart not in it.

Lacendu looks at her with a frown. "I just came to apologize."

"You have nothing to apologize for," Vaskette responds dismissively with a wave of her left hand and shaking her head as she walks toward the other side of the room.

"You're wrong. I should have kept my nose out of your business."

"Korsaume tried to kill me."

There is silence between the two of them. Both of them were together when that incident occurred only a couple short weeks ago. They know how each other reacted when the secret came out. Vaskette was in a lynching mood immediately afterward, but the rest of the crew was rather forgiving.

"Yes. She did."

"I thought you were going to say something like, 'No, it was Sherise that tried to kill you…'" Vaskette says this with a large amount of sarcasm and does not even look at her friend.

"How can I? They're one and the same person," is the response.

"Thank you! Thank you for agreeing with me!" The statement is said with a harsh edge.

"I don't blame them, Lacendu … do you?"

Lacendu tries to remember the last time Vaskette called her by her full first name. She feels hurt by the demand. She does not know what to say.

The two ladies just stand there in their spots, not turning away. Vaskette faces a wall with instruments of her trade hanging on it. Lacendu stands at the doorway, the door almost closed, facing the doctor.

Vaskette speaks up. "I was a very nice person before. I was very likeable; very liked; and well-behaved… I was a Christian; a believer in God; something that most of the Milky Way has completely forgotten about. Why is it, then, that I'm having such a hard time forgiving now…?"

Lacendu continues her silence, just listening.

"What happened to me, Lacy? What happened to the world I used to know? Was I happy? What was life like then?" As she talks, her eyes begin to tear up, and her voice becomes strained.

She continues despite this. "I don't remember anything! I don't remember who I was, or how I became who I was. I can't remember who was in my life. What's going to happen when I get back to my old life and I can't pick up where I left off?"

The pain in her voice is evident. Lacendu is having her own trouble, and she does not hear every word her friend says, but she tries to listen carefully and with some empathy. She continually thinks about all the things she has learned about herself, both from the books and essays given her by an ex-student, and the data given her from the Captain's girlfriend.

"Listen to me, being all selfish and stupid when there are others on this ship going through the same thing I am. I'm such an idiot!"

"Now that's going too far," says Lacendu. "You are most definitely entitled to some self-loathing, just like everyone else here. And just in case you didn't notice, most of us are in that state."

"Yeah, I noticed." The way Vaskette says it makes Lacendu feel there is more to it.

"You noticed how everyone is going through what you are right now…?"

Vaskette turns to her finally and looks her in the eyes. "And you've been going through it since Steg?"

Lacendu stands frozen for a moment. "I was hoping you wouldn't bring that up."

"We're friends, Lacendu. I've seen the way you've been acting since we left Steg. You've been acting just like I am now. I didn't know what to make of it at first, but during our conversation in the Master's home, it all became clear." Vaskette's voice is slightly raised and sounds somewhat distrusting.

During the small silence that ensues, Lacendu realizes she is breathing hard.

Lacendu calms herself.

Vaskette takes a few steps forward, but is still some distance from Lacendu. "Why didn't you want to tell us?"

"I," she begins, but fails to finish. She tries again. "I don't know why." She looks at the ground as if it will have understanding toward her.

Suddenly, Vaskette's voice is loud. "Oh, come on, Lacendu! There's bound to be some reason why you wouldn't tell the rest of us that you found information about who you were prior to our memory loss! Or did your memory even get erased?! Perhaps you've been faking it all this time; just like Korsaume…!"

Lacendu's eyes widen in fear and she backs up just enough that she unintentionally closes the door. The sound of it shutting startles her. "NO!" Her eyes fill with tears. "NO! Vaskette, it's not true! It's not!"

"Then why," Vaskette says, the pitch of her voice is raised now out of hurt. "Why did you wait so long to tell us?"

Lacendu wipes her eyes. "I was afraid, Vaskette. I was afraid of…of what someone might say."

"Or maybe what we would do," Vaskette responds with a mixture of hatred and sadness.

Lacendu's body crumples against the door and drops to the cold, hard, metallic floor. She weeps bitterly. Through the tears that stain her shirt and touch her tongue as they drip from the top of her lip, she says, "I don't know…" Her voice trails off.

Vaskette's own eyes, filled with tears, look at her friend on the floor. She leans on the chair in the middle of the room, hesitating. She waits for a moment, then another, and finally pushes her right foot forward. It is all the momentum she needs to get over to her friend and fall hard to the floor to hold Lacendu.

At first, Lacendu cringes at the feeling of the other putting her arms around her, but she soon realizes that the sound she is hearing in her right ear is that of Vaskette whispering, "I'm so sorry, Lacy," over and over again.

*****

"Hey," Mathew says looking up at Rosetta as she enters. He watches her as she walks over and sits down beside him.

"Hey, Hon," she replies. "Korsaume mentioned to me why you walked out."

"I figured as much."

"You know I don't hold that against you. You are the sweetest man I've ever met, and I've met a lot of men in my line of work." She reaches her left arm around his shoulders and squeezes her hand on his right arm effectively scrunching him between her left hand and her body. Then she puts the left side of her head on his right shoulder.

"How is everyone else taking all of this," he asks with concern in his voice.

"I'm not sure. I haven't seen many reactions to the data, just a lot of intent faces as they read."

"Then I guess I'm the only one…" he says this almost as a question. "You know, I wonder if it was such a great idea to get this info. I was better off not knowing all that stuff about myself."

"…And if I'd kept it all to myself, like I was seriously considering doing, you'd all be mad at me for that, too…" She smiles.

Mathew pauses. "Do you remember when we met?"

"Of course," she says grinning at him.

He does not look at her, though. "I told you that I had a memory response at the name of the computer store…"

She thinks hard. A pause, and then, "Yeah, I do remember something about that. It's a very vague recollection, but I think I do…"

"I worked at a Meager's store just after I got out of school; a year before I went into the military…"

"Hm…" she ponders his statement.

"That would mean…" he begins.

She finishes it for him, "that your memory wasn't completely erased."

"We should confront the others with this. Would you help me gather them in the cockpit?" He stands up.

"Sure."

*****

"I have reason to believe that our memory may not be completely gone," Mathew begins.

There is silence from the other five members of his crew. Rosetta sits comfortably beside her boyfriend with an expressionless face. The longer the silence lasts, the more uncomfortable she seems.

"…Aaaaa-nd," Korsaume replies.

"OK," Mathew says quickly with some amount of embarrassment, "When we were on the station after we first awoke from…whatever we were out from…I remembered something…"

"And you didn't think it would be really great to let us all know about it sooner…"

Mathew seems even more embarrassed, but he continues. "Well, I didn't know for sure at the time. I wasn't sure where or why I remembered it. It was a shop, and after reading the information Seta gave us, I found out I used to work at one of those stores before I went into the military."

"Uh, Captain," says Allen. "I hate to interrupt, but I'm reading some vessels just coming into sensor range. They're big."

"Can you get specific readings," asks Korsaume.

Allen begins a feed to Korsaume's console.

"It's not looking good, Captain," says Korsaume. "The information Allen is feeding me here is showing up as Raiders."

"Raiders are bad," Rosetta mumbles. Then more out loud to anyone who will listen, "Raiders are the aggressive traders. They tend to take what they want and leave smoking piles of rubble in their stead…"

"…Thus giving a bad name to the good traders, I suspect," Vaskette comments, feeling useless as she sits down near the back of the room to keep out of the way.

The rest of the crew goes into action. Korsaume begins punching buttons on her command console. Lacendu seats herself near the tactical control panel with Allen. Agoparn turns to the ship's output readings. Rosetta stands at Mathew's side as the Captain turns to face out the window.

Mathew turns to Rosetta and Korsaume. "Suggestions…?"

"Run like frightened little bunny-rabbits," Rosetta says.

"I'm tending toward agreement with your girlfriend, Captain, though I have a gut feeling their sensors probably detected us over twenty minutes ago and the only reason we can see them on ours is because they know there's no hope for us…" Korsaume says with some amount of disgust.

"We could try to look like a derelict," Allen comments.

"Not even an option," says Rosetta. "They have life-sensors as well. They know how many of us there are, and most likely are cross-referencing to any and all data they have on anyone in this sector."

"…Which means," says Lacendu, "that most likely they already know we're fugitives from the Solar Union."

"True, Lacy; so they won't think twice about blowing a hole through the command deck to rapture all our cargo."

"Maybe someone could throw in some good news, too," Mathew says turning back in time to catch a glimpse of the three ships as they come into view.

Everyone is silent.

"I was hoping you'd give it to me audibly," he adds.

"I have none," says Rosetta apologetically.

"Nor do I, Captain," Korsaume adds. She turns to Allen. "Allen, you're our strategist. Some strategy would be really great right now…"

"Believe me, Lieutenant; if I had a strategy against these guys more than six weeks ago, it's not coming to me now."

"Odds, Mathematician…?" Mathew asks.

"Our survival, Captain," asks Lacendu.

"Any odds you have for anything we have or could do would come in really handy."

"Nothing's coming to me, dear Captain. I don't have enough information on hand."

"Someone give me something. We're at their mercy currently with the information I've been given thus far." Mathew sits uncomfortably, his stomach in knots.

Rosetta speaks up. "It's a long shot, but you could send a coded message to the OI/ITSO."

"…And that stands for…" asks Vaskette.

"The Office of Inter/Intra-Planetary Trade and Sales Organization… They're not known for interfering with those under attack by Raiders. They usually get involved in the clean-up, though."

"What about allowing them to board us," asks Mathew. "Maybe if we cooperate, our lives will be spared."

"Unlikely, Captain," says Rosetta, "but it's the best chance we stand that I've heard so far."

Mathew continues, "If we go to where the cargo they'll most likely rapture is on our ship, we'll stand an even better chance of them letting us live until they get aboard, right?"

"Now why didn't I think of that," asks Allen.

"I have no idea, Allen, but right now, it doesn't matter. Rosetta; Korsaume; what is their most likely target cargo?"

"Tradable goods," Rosetta states.

"Anything worth something on the main markets: foods, valuables, et cetera," Korsaume answers.

"What's the most valuable cargo we're carrying," asks Allen.

"You mean besides our lives," Agoparn asks half-smiling, his arms folded.

Two people laugh lightly at this.

"I think I can see where you're going with this," Allen states. "If we can match their greed with something valuable to them, we can barter for our lives."

"Currency is the most valuable possession we have," Korsaume responds. "And we have quite a bit of it. We can't give it to them in our cards, but we can trade the promise of those funds as a deal on a nearby orbital station."

"Fizicarmoe is the nearest orbital station. It's a refueling station. It has very little traffic; and it is remote, and not exactly known for being under the watchful eye of the Solar Union," Rosetta concludes.

"That's a start," Mathew says. "Let's shut down the engines, prepare the docking clamps, and get into the most valuable section of the ship. I'm hoping looking like we're cooperating will improve our chances."

The group does as the Captain says and then proceeds to level four where the main food stuffs are stocked.

*****

It is over an hour later. All the main systems are shut down with the exception of artificial gravity, air-conditioning, and life support. The entire crew sits in a small room with food. No one is hungry. They are sitting uncomfortably when they feel a small nudge on the ship.

Agoparn picks up a small computer from the floor and hits a button that remotely connects itself to the ship's main systems.

"What's going on out there, Parn," asks Rosetta.

Agoparn moves some controls, gives the computer a few simple verbal commands, and says, "It looks like they're trying to take over main controls through a 'vuldact' connection."

"I didn't think this ship accepted 'vuldact,'" admits Rosetta. "I think it's too new."

"I'm inclined to agree with you, Miss," Agoparn says, not looking up.

"…Someone want to clue me in, here? What's a 'vuldact' connection," Lacendu asks.

"It's a very old type of ship-to-ship signal connection," Agoparn explains. "They used them during some older wars. They would use small remote-controlled flyers to get near big ships. These flyers would send out audio signals; which many old ships used to run on; and take over the main controls, change all passwords almost instantaneously, and shut down all systems, including life-support. The people inside suffocated within mere hours, and many battles were won that way."

"There is still a huge graveyard of derelicts a parsec or two from here of just such ships," Rosetta adds. "They've most likely been picked bone-dry by now by the kind of Raiders we've chanced upon. They take everything, integrate it all into their systems, keep the best, and trash the rest."

"Well, you two," Mathew says, "thanks for the history lesson, but what about those ships out there?"

Agoparn smiles at his captain and looks back down at the controls. "Well, sir, it looks like they've given up on that 'vuldact' thing and are preparing to hook directly to the shell."

"They're going to try to enter on foot," asks Vaskette smiling at Agoparn.

"It would seem that way," Allen answers.

"Can't we do something," Lacendu asks, stressing the word 'something.'

"Not without them knowing. They already know right where we are, how many, and…" begins Rosetta.

"Yeah, you said that before, I think…"

"Yes, I did, Lacy. I don't mean to repeat myself."

Lacendu waves her off almost uncaringly.

Mathew looks at everyone in turn. Only a few are looking up at him and meet his eyes as he crosses theirs. He sighs. "OK. I had one idea, but I'm out. Let's have options. I want every option, and I don't care how wild and crazy it sounds." He looks at the person seated on his immediate left. "Allen…?"

"Weapons in hand, take them by surprise; if that's possible. Blow them to bits as they enter the clam." Allen looks down at the floor as he says this.

Mathew looks at Vaskette next to him.

"Flood the entire ship with mezzacastraphine; put them all to sleep. I could give us all anti-agents that would wake us all up first. The problem is I don't think I have enough to fill the ship, and I don't know how many of 'them' there are…"

Mathew nods at her and then looks at Lacendu.

"I could sing to them…"

Everyone laughs nervously.

Agoparn.

"I'd love the opportunity to hack their ship, but I don't know what they're running. If they have some of the newer computers, I could get caught in a feedback loop and be left in a coma or dead. I don't want to chance it unless it's a last resort."

"I understand, Parn," Mathew replies.

He looks at Korsaume, next.

"I really like Allen's idea. You know how I love guns and blowing holes in things."

"…And people," Vaskette says. Her eyes widen quickly as she looks up at Korsaume. "Uh…"

Mathew eyes Vaskette, as does Allen and Rosetta. Korsaume gives a reluctant smile. "No problem, good Doctor." Her face goes flat again.

Rosetta.

"This is not my official idea, but I still think sending a coded message to the OI/ITSO would be wise. If we hold out long enough, it's possible they might show up."

Mathew puts his right hand to his face, left hand under his right elbow to hold the arm up, chin between his thumb and pointing finger. "How long do you think it would take them to get here?"

"Anywhere between a couple hours and a couple weeks…" She notices the looks she gets quickly and adds, "But a small chance is better than no chance whatsoever."

"It's a good place to start," says Mathew. Then to Agoparn, "How long would it take you to code a message with Rosetta's help?"

Agoparn looks like he's getting ready to speak, but Rosetta cuts in. "I can send it from my hand-held. I just didn't want to do it without your permission. It would take all of a minute or less."

"Do it. Did you have an idea, too?"

As she punches buttons on the small hand-held given her when she first met this crew, and without looking up, she says, "Yeah. We have a small escape ship in the upper dock. We could use it, launch it quietly and slowly, and get under their ship and hide."

"What about that whole 'they already know who we are, where we are, and how many of us there are' thing," Allen asks with a harsh sarcastic edge to his voice's tone.

She looks up from the small hand-held and gives her questioner a quirky smile. "The launcher has echo-suits."

Everyone looks at her blankly, with the exception of Korsaume who raises both eyebrows and gets a smile of her own.

Rosetta continues. "The outside husk of an echo-suit is designed to exude room-temperature. It can hide us after we get outside. We'll all be nice and cozy inside the suits, and they won't be able to detect us."

"How did you know we had those," asks Mathew. "I don't think any of us knew this ship had them…"

"They came from my ship. I and my assistants used them for all kinds of things. They're especially helpful in freezing temperatures. They won't freeze over, so you can still move. I've never done a space-walk myself, but I'm willing to give it a shot if a couple of you are. I only have three."

"We'll have to exit the pod before it gets too far away," says Korsaume. "The Raiders will blow it to kingdom-come as soon as it's away from the ship far enough not to do too much damage."

"Agreed. Who's coming with Korsaume and my self," asks Rosetta.

Mathew looks at her and states, "I'm going to stay on board. Agoparn and Lacendu are staying with me for certain. I'm going to need all the help I can get negotiating with the Raiders."

"I agree, Captain," says Korsaume.

"I'm sorry, but I don't," says Agoparn. "If you're planning on attaching us to one of the other ships, you're going to need my expertise."

Mathew looks at Allen. "Are you up for some non-lethal negotiating, Strategist?"

"I'm willing to give it a shot, Captain," is his reply.

"Then, we have a plan. Korsaume's in charge of the space mission. Agoparn takes over once you get on and/or in the ship. He knows his way around engines. Take the ships out, but leave me with as many people to negotiate with as you possibly can manage."

"Understood, Captain," says Rosetta.

"The rest of us will grab guns and ammunition and meet our guests at the shell to begin negotiations. We'll use sapphire shields for protection from gunfire for as long as they last."

Allen looks at Mathew gravely. "Um, that will use up my entire supply, Captain… I only bought three, and they don't take a lot of damage."

"If we play our cards right," Mathew says as Korsaume, Rosetta, and Agoparn head out the door, "we won't have to use them all. Plus, we'll get you some more when we get somewhere where that's possible."

"Very kind of you, Sir… Shall we move out?"

The four remaining crewmembers head toward the shell to pick up weapons and defenses along the way.

*****

"Put the suits on quickly and sit down." Rosetta almost already has her suit on as the other two are pulling the seals apart.

Rosetta sits at the controls. Agoparn, between sealing his suit, grabs his computer and enters the control to open the escape launch bay. The small ship starts as the bay doors begin to open exposing the launch bay to the vacuum of space and causing the small ship to be slowly pulled out.

Agoparn and Korsaume have their suits on shortly after, and the three of them enter the exit-lock seal. Decompression occurs only moments later, and the three of them are pulled out of the small room as the door opens to space. The three of them use the inertia to float toward the docked ship.

Almost a full minute passes, and a projectile is launched from the docked ship at the pod, which is destroyed upon impact.

"Well," remarks Korsaume to herself, "There went our only other means of escape…"

"It's alright, Korsaume," Rosetta answers. "We've got the best this galaxy has to offer in means of war on board the smaller ship. I don't think losing a small pod will pose a problem."

Agoparn smirks, "I don't mean to be a smart-alic, but let's focus on the job at hand, ladies."

As their bodies float freely toward the other ship, twisting and turning slowly in a jumble of acrobatic motions, the two women grin.

*****

"Captain," Lacendu says shyly as the four of them make their way to the weapons room, "I don't know how to tell you this other than to just say I don't think I've ever used a weapon before…"

"It's pretty simple," Allen says, "They're all point-and-click…"

"It's the pointing I'm having a hard time with," she says. "I can do trigonometric calculations in my head, but I don't think I could pull the trigger of a gun aimed at another human being…"

"Don't think of them as human beings," says Vaskette. "Think of them as bad little numbers that must be erased from the equation."

"Clever," Mathew says smiling.

"Oh, yeah, real helpful," Lacendu says giving a crooked look at the wall near her.

They soon arrive at the weapons room and Allen begins handing out guns, ammunition, and shields to the other three, and finally takes some for his self. "I hope you don't mind that I kept my favorites for me," he says holding up two very large guns. "Korsaume would be jealous if she knew I had a mini-super-HOP…"

"Great," Mathew says as if he did not even hear Allen. "Let's get this show on the road."

The four members walk toward the shell. It takes only a few minutes to get there, and by the time they do, Allen realizes their ship has already been invaded. He pushes all of them into a small room and quickly and quietly shuts the door.

The lights are off, and he does not bother to turn them on.

"What the heck's going on," asks Lacendu harshly, but in a whisper.

Allen shushes her and says softly, "They're already aboard. We've got to find out how many and where they are. I'm the one to do that. The rest of you stay here and if anyone enters this door, shoot to kill."

"What if you enter the door," asks Vaskette.

"Trust me, Doctor; I won't be coming back in this door, regardless of what happens. I don't want to be on that end of Lacendu's gun…" He says this with a smile in his voice, but the darkness makes it impossible for them to see each other.

"Good luck, Allen," says Mathew.

"Thank you, Captain. It seems I've been doing a lot of this recently, doesn't it…?"

"Yes it does, but don't think for a second that it goes unnoticed."

With that, Allen pulls the door slightly ajar, looks around, and then exits.

The others are left alone in the dark, unsure of what will happen next.

*****

Korsaume is first to hit the ship, and she does so rather harshly against her right shoulder. She winces at the pain.

"Are you alright," Agoparn asks. "I heard that through our communicators."

"I'll be fine," she responds through clinched teeth.

Agoparn hits next, followed closely by Rosetta. They each use whatever small crevices in the ship's hull they can find to clasp on to with their hands. Agoparn is surprised at how well he can feel through the skin of the echo-suit. Though he knows in his mind that the hull of the ship he is feeling is quite cold, the suit tells him it is body-temperature.

The three of them make their way to the engines, which Agoparn immediately begins to tear apart with their help. It takes only a few minutes, but the engines are effectively shut down.

Korsaume makes a change to her communication device to call the Captain. "Sir, we've shut down the Raiders' vessel. We're making our way to the connection. Slow going, right now, though…"

"Understood," Mathew's voice comes across very quietly, and in a whisper. "Allen is loose in the ship. Be careful."

"Very good, sir," she responds. Then to her group, "Sounds like the Captain is in hiding and letting our Strategist handle the miscellaneous riff-raff."

"I'll make sure to say a prayer for the riff-raff when this is all over," Agoparn says.

The three of them make their way around the ship to the connection between the two ships.

"What now," Rosetta asks.

Korsaume looks at Agoparn. "Can we do anything, Parn?"

Agoparn looks at Korsaume, then at Rosetta, then off into space and thinks. A moment passes and then, "I bet we could make those other two vessels play games."

"Play games?" Korsaume looks at him with a quirky smile.

Rosetta looks off toward one of the remaining two ships, then to the other. "What's your game plan, Engineer? We're a little far away, and I want to be inside our ship when we get the heck out of here."

"If I play this right, we won't need to leave in a rush," Agoparn says with a proud tone. "It's going to take all of us working together, though. Korsaume, do you know what those vuldact remotes look like?"

"Yes. I've used one or two; modified, of course."

"That's where I'm headed with this. I'm going to connect to one and make a few modifications. That will require one of us to get back into our own ship, though."

Rosetta smiles. "I think I see what you're going to do."

"So, how do we get back into our ship?"

Korsaume looks at the connection they are on. "Well, I'm accustomed to getting into ships through connection ports, but not without a piece of Strephecyne. Do you know where I can get some?"

"Strephecyne would come in handy, but the closest thing we've got to it is this suit. You use them to get in, though, and you're going to open the inside of the ship to space." Rosetta looks at Korsaume.

Korsaume looks back at Rosetta. "I just need someone to help me get into the airlock."

Rosetta looks appalled. "…And how do you propose to get in from out here?"

"Oh, don't worry. We have an amazing engineer at our disposal. If anyone can get me in there, it's him. Once I'm in, the two of you can do what you want to out here."

"I just hope Allen's taking care of things inside. If he hasn't yet rid us of the men already aboard our ship, I'm certain he's got a plan to and has already put it into action."

*****

Allen is standing with his back against a wall. He holds two guns, one in each hand. He knows that just around the corner there are eight raiders. He already has his plan in his mind: empty both weapons at the ketotronic panel behind them and on either side of them. That will draw their attention in multiple directions. Chances are high he will be shot at, and possibly injured in the process, thus forcing him to try to avoid being shot at…

What he has not figured out, yet, is how to round them up without more damage to their ship than is necessary. Five shots to the ketotronic panel will likely put a hole in the hull exposing them to space and he desperately wants to keep as many of them alive as possible, his self included.

He comes up with a better plan. There's a floor above them, and one below. If he throws one of his smaller guns in the middle of them, setting it to fire, he can shoot at it and make it explode, knocking them out cold as they fall to the floor below. One problem he does not like is that he will probably be knocked unconscious by the blast along with them, leaving him an easy target to any remaining Raiders.

His timing will have to be perfect with the two sapphire shields he has on him. Worst-case scenario, he will be badly injured, but still able to haunt any remaining Raiders on board.

He decides this is his best option. He quietly lays the large gun in his right hand on the ground, pulls the smaller gun from his jacket and flips the switch. The blue meter on the top begins glowing and rising up the viewer. At about a quarter up he tosses the gun into the middle of the group as he pulls the gun in his left hand and aims it. He pulls the trigger while the thrown gun is still in mid air while he takes the two sapphire shields in his right hand and clamps the buttons against each other turning them on and surrounding his self with a force field strong enough to hold off more blasts from his own weapons than any three ketotronic panels of this very ship could ever take.

The blast from his weapon hits the small gun in mid-air and an explosion goes off that thrusts the eight men against the ketotronic panels and knocking them unconscious, simultaneously punching holes in the floor and ceiling. Collateral damage is everywhere, and Allen is included as the sapphire shields shut down almost instantaneously as it takes the brunt of the blast. Allen is thrust against the wall behind him, leaving a large dent in it. He is out cold for only a few moments. When he comes to, he is lying on the cold metal floor on the lower story below the hole he created. The eight other men are lying nearby. They do not move.

As he rises from the ground, he quickly realizes his body is in sore shape. He is bent over, but on his feet nonetheless. The gun in his left hand is damaged beyond repair.

He casts it aside and goes to check for pulses on the injured Raiders. It seems all of them are dead, most likely having taken the full force of the explosion.

He limps off toward the room he pushed his crewmembers into.

*****

Agoparn pulls the locking mechanism off the outer panel near the connecting juncture and forces the airlock to open from the outside. Korsaume pulls herself into the airlock and helps close the door from the inside. She watches out the small window, waving goodbye at Agoparn and Rosetta, smiling at them as she does.

She turns her attention to the inner door. The locking mechanism is more complicated than Agoparn made it look, but she follows his instructions to the letter and soon has the door open.

Once inside, she turns her attention to the enemy ship.

*****

Rosetta and Agoparn, still on the outside, move away from the airlock. "How do you do all that stuff, Parn," she asks.

"I assume it took years of training, but for some reason I don't recall," he says. "It just comes to me..."

He looks at her with one side of his mouth pulled back.

The two of them crawl their way back to the top of the ship where the escape craft bay is still open to space. As they slowly make their way in that direction, they see the two other ships rising from below their ship.

Rosetta pushes a button to contact Korsaume. "Um, K..."

"Go ahead," they hear her voice in a quiet whisper.

Rosetta continues. "We might have a problem, babe. Those two other ships are getting into a sentry formation."

The hushed whisper of Korsaume comes through clearly. "Frag."

*****

Mathew, Lacendu, and Vaskette stand motionless and silent in the dark room. They've been there for about a half hour, their eyes slowly growing accustomed to the dim lights along the wall and the small lights of the keypad near the door.

Finally, there is a knock on the door. Lacendu aims the gun at the door, and Vaskette follows suit. Mathew walks to the door and presses a button on the small panel.

"Anyone inside," they hear from the receiver. "This is Allen. If you can hear me, I've taken care of eight of them, and I'm heading around. I suggest the three of you find a new room to hide in. I've found two of the leaders checking rooms. They've checked the bottom three floors and are headed this direction. I'd say you have three minutes before they get here."

They hear nothing more from him but steps as he walks off.

They wait two minutes and Mathew slowly opens the door, peeking out for others in the hallway. Soon the door is open all the way and the three of them exit the room making their way quietly through the hallway.

A noise behind them prompts them all to turn around. Mathew looks at Lacendu and whispers, "Face forward. Watch for a trap."

Lacendu turns back the way they were walking as Mathew and Vaskette slowly move the opposite direction. Mathew stops Vaskette after a few feet and continues forward without her. "Turn your vale shields on, ladies."

He takes two steps forward and stops when a figure jumps out from behind a wall, gun in hand, aimed at him. Mathew already has his gun aimed, and the figure seems to realize immediately that it is outnumbered. Mathew holds his hand up at Vaskette not to fire. She pulls her finger off the trigger.

The figure steps forward.

Mathew speaks first, "Stop. Tell us what you want."

The figure stops walking. "Coshma allit fo-erm'I hetsmant."

Mathew looks confused. "I don't understand."

It moves a hand up to its helmet and presses a button, then speaks again. The previous syllables can be heard quietly under the translation. "Immediately drop weapons yours."

Mathew realizes instantly that they are trapped. He yells quickly, "FIRE!"

Blasts go off from every gun in every hand present.

Lacendu is firing in the direction she is facing. She notices her shots are bouncing off some kind of field. "Captain," she shouts, "these guys are invincible!"

Mathew stops Vaskette with a gesture and yells for Lacendu to cease fire.

The figure in front of Mathew stops firing as well. Mathew knows their shields may not have enough power for more hits, and the figure has taken no damage whatsoever.

Vaskette faces her weapon at the ground and looks over at Mathew. "We're screwed, aren't we, dear Captain?"

Mathew looks back at her. "It looks that way, Doctor."

Episode 9
Stabilized

OPENING:

"...Something is amiss. I knew when I came aboard I would be able to leave my imprint. At least, I thought I would... Instead, my imprint has left me entirely, and no one is here to remember me. I am alone, and finally I realize things were better where I was." - The final words of Chandra Emors'e, a trader in the mid-2400's whose skeletal remains were found aboard a derelict shuttle she commandeered during her lifetime. The shuttle was found in 2802 in the Sendracates system on the third arm of the Milky Way, over four hundred fifty light years from where she was last seen.

The zero-seven Celestial class Star Expeditioner is stationary in space. Attached to one side is an unknown-class ship with an unknown designation. Crawling their way up toward the top of the Star Expeditioner are two humans in echo-suits.

Rosetta and Agoparn arrive in the launch bay. Its walls are devoid of instrument panels. A single strip-light runs horizontally along the center of the walls on all three sides, lighting the inside of the bay with minimal light. The two of them turn around to face outside the bay only to see two very large vessels that seem to be staring them down.

"What now, Lieutenant?" Agoparn asks standing erect against the wall.

"I have absolutely no idea, Engineer." She stands beside him shaking her head. "We need Allen."

Agoparn smirks. "I wonder how he's doing."

*****

All weapons are firing.

Allen Pendergras stands with his back to his Captain, Mathew Arnold. Along side the two men are Vaskette Smith and Lacendu Ruric-Trester, back-to-back, guns in hand.

"This isn't going as well as I'd hoped," Allen yells above the sounds of laser fire and shields being hit.

"I can think of better ways to spend our day," Mathew yells back over his shoulder.

"Less talk, more firing," Vaskette warns.

As the fire-fight continues mercilessly, the Raiders try to close in, but the weapons now in the hands of the four shipmates continually push the enemies back.

When Allen first arrived on the scene, he had dropped a small charge behind three Raiders and blasted it, the charge erupting in a plume of smoke and knocking two of the Raiders down and out.

He had not expected to see his three friends surrendering, and he definitely would not stand for it. Now, standing together, these four are alone, back to back for the first time ever, and fighting the worst enemy they have yet to come up against.

A call from Korsaume, Mathew's first Lieutenant and the ship's resident weapons expert, informed the group that the other two ships had become aware of the goings-on aboard the Celestial class Star Expeditioner and had moved into a "kill" formation. In other words, when the Raiders made it back to their ship, the Celestial class ship would be left and destroyed, along with anyone on board.

This meant that the crew of the Star Expeditioner had to be the ones aboard the Raider vessel.

Korsaume is currently seeing to that.

*****

She walks smoothly and silently through the corridors. She is trained at this type of maneuver, and having the opportunity once again to sneak about with weapons in hand is thrilling her mind.

Korsaume realizes she cannot give any Raiders the chance to communicate with any others, so if she finds a group she will have to take them all out at one time; something she is trying to work out in her mind even now, even though she has not come across a single Raider since she began her search aboard this large vessel.

She still feels pretty bad about leaving Rosetta and Agoparn outside in the darkness of space, and Rosetta's communicae concerning the other two Raider vessels moving into a sentry formation has been on her mind constantly. For the first time in as long as she can remember, she feels scared. Though her heart is beating a little faster than usual, it is still steady; something she is trained to work through.

She soon arrives at the command deck of the ship. It is silent, and one Raider is seated in the center chair. She glances around the room once more to make sure, and then quietly makes her way around the left side watching the person in the chair. She glances back at the door to make sure she has not been followed, but maintains her view of the chair.

With her back to the wall she raises the gun into firing position.

She pulls the trigger.

Nothing happens.

There is silence for a long moment. Finally, "Welcome to my vessel."

"Actually, it's mine, now," she retorts. "I'm commandeering it."

The figure, in full Raider gear complete with helmet, looks her direction. "I'd like to know how you think that."

She waits a moment to come up with a witty remark, but finds none. Instead, "Just because my gun quit working doesn't mean I don't have some tricks up my sleeve."

"Well, isn't that nice," the voice behind the mask states obtrusively.

Immediately, Korsaume realizes it is a female voice, masked by some kind of vocal-altering device. "So, what's your name, Miss?"

At this, the figure seems startled. The figure removes the helmet, and underneath is a young woman with somewhat long, stringy blonde hair. Her face is slender, if a little long, and her eyes are penetrating. She wears a smile, unusually long for a mouth, yet no smile wrinkles seem overtly present.

The woman tilts her head a little, pulling off more of a smirk now. "You are very bright for a normal human. Come closer."

"Who said I'm normal?" Korsaume asks facetiously taking a couple steps forward.

As she stands within about six feet of the female Raider, Korsaume realizes there are blue and red lines in her face. At first, she thinks they are veins and arteries, but she quickly realizes they are too straight for such attributes. She looks harder and becomes aware that there are additional colored lines including golden yellow, green, and silver. These other lines are almost hidden by the outright obviousness of the blue and red lines. The lines seem to be purposefully placed along her facial features, accentuating small curvatures in the woman's face.

The woman looks at Korsaume knowingly. "You see something … different about me."

"Yeah" is Korsaume's only response as she nods her head.

Korsaume did not think the woman's smile could become any longer or fuller, but it somehow does. The woman indulges in the attention she is receiving.

"My name is Shivranikka. You may call me Nikka for short. Your name is...?"

"Korsaume..."

"Welcome, Korsaume, to my humble command ship." At this, the woman stands up and walks in a semi-circular path a quarter way around Korsaume and stops, staring blankly at her guest, her hands behind her, smile intact. "What is it that you see, Korsaume?"

"If I was forced to hazard a guess, I'd say you've had a techno-fusion-engraft. That's only a guess, mind you..." Korsaume glances over her shoulder at the door and sees no one.

"Don't worry. There will be no other persons coming through that door. I'm quite capable of taking care of myself, as you most likely also guessed."

"I did, at that," Korsaume manages.

The woman faces to her left and walks across the command deck. The wide viewport is full of stars in various shapes and colors. At the far left of it, a sun can be seen gleaming off the edges of the viewport window. The light glints off of the red, gold, silver, and black surfaces of Nikka's suit.

"I was engrafted with a technology far advanced for its time." She is not even looking at Korsaume as she speaks; a sign of overt confidence, which Korsaume does not desire to test. "The man's name was Xychocappla. He was a genius with organic-technology."

"We just came from a planet of organic technology."

"Oh, really," Shivranikka asks turning to face Korsaume once again. "Tell me of it."

"Plants are used for transportation, housing, and electricity, as well as for food and liquid."

Shivranikka looks genuinely surprised. "Intriguing. I must check this planet out for myself. Otherwise, though, I suppose I should adjust my explanation. Xycho was a specialist in carbonic technology; specifically human-machine integration. His first few hundred attempts caused some..." she pauses, thinking of the best word to use, "disruptive resuls...

"People, animals, and plants eventually became something akin to robotic statues…worthless in the grand scheme. Eventually, he perfected his work. I am his end result."

Korsaume eyes the woman carefully. "You killed him."

She throws up her hands as if tossing handfuls of nothing above her head, her smile unbroken. "He was useless after he perfected his science." Her hands come down, loosely swaying at her sides. She sighs, shifting her body weight to her left side and blowing at a tuft of hair that falls down in front of her right eye. "He became distant… And God knows he certainly was afraid to let me have control."

"Shivranikka Napercolten, from the planet Mount Ligmon-Ardreptipol…?"

"You've heard of me…?"

Korsaume's eyes narrow to slits. "You were diagnosed with Siverchan's disease in 2443. You became a despot until the planet's leaders kicked you off your home world for trying to take over the government."

"Wow. You seem to know more about my history than even I."

"You and that techno-fusing geek were given a one-way ticket through a tesseract and told never to come back."

"Yes, well, believe me, honey," she says walking haughtily toward Korsaume, stops about three feet from her, bends at the waist and points at her, "I have no intention of ever returning to that side of the galaxy."

"So you'll just be satisfied with taking over this half, hm?"

Shivranikka waves her accuser off uncaringly, turning her back on Korsaume and walking back to stand in front of her chair. "Call it what you will. I've no desire to be a dictator. I just don't feel that people can make the right decisions without me…that's all."

"Well, you certainly have a flair for the dramatic, Nikka. The HX-discs don't do you justice by any stretch of the imagination." It is a ploy Korsaume doubts will work on a woman who is hardly trying to cling to what is left of her humanity.

"I still have my sanity, if that's what you're suggesting, Korsaume."

"Yes, though 'sanity' is so relative."

Shivranikka moves so fast Korsaume does not have a chance to blink. She finds herself being held up by her throat with the woman's left hand around it, not quite strangling her. She speaks rapidly as her voice turns harsh, yet maintaining her smile. "You would love to try and get me into some witty banter so you can come up with a plan to stop me. Believe me, many have tried, and all of them have failed. Don't think for a second you'll be doing anything more than providing me with cheap entertainment for the next few decades until I see fit to have you shoved out an airlock into the vacuum of space and laugh heartily at your demise as your lungs implode, your eyes pop out of their sockets, and finally you become emaciated as your blood boils and your head explodes. I've done it before and I'll do it again, dear one!"

Korsaume is dropped to stand once again on her own two feet, and just as quickly as she moved over, Shivranikka is back at her chair standing in front of it. Korsaume struggles for a moment to regain her breath, bent at the waist until she can stand.

"It's beautiful, isn't it?" Shivranikka's voice is again soft and fluent. "Space…? The stars…? The planets…? The 'Milky Way,' as it was once called? It's mine, now. I'm commandeering it; a phrase I believe you used once, recently."

Still trying to get a handle on things, Korsaume stands motionless, rubbing her throat where the mechanical hand held her for such a short amount of time.

"You move fast for someone who's over four hundred fifty years old," Korsaume comments reluctantly.

Shivranikka stares out the window. Looking aloof, she states dryly, "Thank you."

*****

"So, Engineer…any ideas, yet?"

"None are coming to me right away," Agoparn says contemplatively. "…You?"

Rosetta looks at the two ships with her new friend. "What about that 'hacking' thing you were talking about…?"

"Is that our last resort?"

"That's my guess at the moment, considering we haven't heard from Korsaume in over twenty minutes and can't get through to her…and the Captain and the rest of our crew are in a fire fight for the fate of our ship… Do the math."

"I need a couple things."

"Name them."

Agoparn looks around the empty hangar. "Well, for starters, I need a way to plug my brain into a computer."

"You can do that?" Rosetta looks genuinely surprised.

"Well, it's kind of complicated, but the ultimate answer is, 'yes.'"

"OK. How do we plug your brain into those ships?"

"We don't. I do. Let's go get that vuldact connector they tried to hack our ship with, and we'll go from there."

*****

"OK," Mathew says aloud. "I'm almost out of ammo and we're no closer to getting out of here than we were before."

"No worries," Allen replies. "They're almost out of ammo, too. We'll be doing some hand-to-hand soon."

Lacendu gets a half-frown on her face. "That's when we proceed directly to getting our butts kicked, right?"

"…Or evaporated into nothingness," Allen answers.

"Odds are against us, Captain," says Lacendu.

“My apologies if I don’t hug you for your statistics, Lacy,” Mathew says. “Ah, frag! I’m out of ammo,” he frowns as his gun dies abruptly. “I’m not sure how much longer this shield will hold out, either…”

Allen wraps his arm around Mathew’s neck. “Hold on, Captain,” he says. Allen turns his gun on the wall beside them blowing a hole through it. He pulls the Captain in with him. They are quickly followed by Vaskette and Lacendu.

“We’re losing the battle and the war,” says Lacendu once inside the room.

“Not just yet,” says Allen. “Remember what I am…”

He walks over to the wall and attaches the three unused vale shields still on him to the hole he made just as the Raiders get over to it and aim their laser rifles.

The shots echo off the shields.

“That won’t hold for long.” Allen grabs Vaskette’s gun and aims it at the floor, out of sight of the Raiders, setting the controls for a lower, less forceful blast. He pulls the trigger and cuts a hole in the floor. The metal flooring falls below. “Jump through,” he says to them.

Mathew is first, followed closely by Vaskette and Lacendu. Finally, Allen joins them.

“They’ll be following us soon. Let’s move.”

They exit the room and run down the hallway, while the Raiders shoot a whole through their floor.

“Where are we heading, Allen,” Mathew asks.

“I’m hoping those eight Raiders I took out earlier are still unconscious. We could use their shields.”

“Fantastic idea,” Mathew replies. “And if they’re not…?”

“Be thinking up a plan ‘B’ while we’re running,” Allen answers.

The four of them soon arrive at the gaping hole in the ceiling.

As they stop, Lacendu looks at it and then at Allen. “You did that?”

“It’s a little messy, isn’t it,” Allen smirks looking back at her.

There are six Raiders there. "It looks like two of them survived just fine," Vaskette remarks.

Allen looks around at the unconscious Raiders. "Well, if anyone's thought of a plan 'B,' I'm ready to hear it. The other two shot their wounded and took their guns and shields."

Lacendu exhales, pouting.

"Well, Captain," says Vaskette, "If we could get to the infirmary, I might be able to come up with some solutions."

Mathew looks at Allen inquisitively.

Allen looks at his Captain. "I'm confident enough that I can get us there in one piece," he states, "though I'm not so sure about staying there for very long."

Mathew looks at Vaskette. "Any needs along the way?"

Vaskette looks at Mathew, then at the bodies against the downward-pitched flooring of the level above. "One of those Raiders might do…"

Mathew and Allen each take an arm of one of the Raiders and pull it up and forward following Vaskette and Lacendu through the opposite corridors from which they came.

It does not take long for them to arrive at the infirmary, and the door is closed and locked.

"That won't hold them for long if they figure out where we're at," Allen states.

"That's OK," Vaskette says. "If I can figure out some things really fast here, we won't need to hold them off."

Vaskette removes the helmet and looks into the face of a young man.

She feels his face, and then gets a dour look on her own. "This man's been dead for quite a while," she states, confused.

"What do you mean," Mathew asks.

"His body is stiff. Dead…"

"Oooh," Lacendu frowns, grossed out. "We're fighting dead people?"

"That can't be right," Allen says.

"What are those markings on his face," Mathew says looking at the man in the suit.

Vaskette looks closer. "I can't be sure just yet…"

She grabs a surgical knife from a drawer and walks over to the man. Placing the sharp edge along the young man's face she digs it deep and pulls downward. A small amount of blood swells outward around the knife as she pulls down cutting something else along the way; a tougher spot here and there… She pulls gloves on and pushes the cut apart looking at the lines which seem to encompass his face.

"Those are wires," she states in surprise.

"What…what does that mean," Lacendu asks.

Vaskette looks at her friend. "They're cybernetic-enhanced humans…"

"What does that mean for us," Mathew asks.

"It means I can't stop them with simple gases and the like," she says. "However, I might be able to come up with a concoction that would melt away at them. The problem in that lies in the fact that I don't think I have the right chemical elements."

"…And just where do we need to go to get the stuff we need," Allen asks.

She looks at them all in turn, shaking her head. "We don't have any of it on board…"

*****

The vuldact connection device was difficult to remove from the side of the Raider vessel but only a few minutes were all they needed. Now, Rosetta and Agoparn pull themselves along slowly toward the bay of their own ship.

"Once we get this, what else do we need to do," asks Rosetta.

"I'll need some simple linking wires with step-connectors on either end. They're plenteous in the walls of our ship."

"That's so handy," she replies.

The two arrive in the bay once again and set the vuldact flyer on the floor. Then they turn their attention to the wall beside them and, between the two of them, pull a panel off the wall.

"That wire right there will do," he states, pointing to a thick green wire.

They pull two other panels loose around the hole of the other and find where the wire connects. They pull the links loose and Agoparn takes it to the vuldact device. Putting one end to the device he finds a connecting juncture and fits the link into it.

"Will that do," Rosetta asks.

"Just a moment…I'll find out." He takes the other end of the wire and places the link against the right side base of his neck. "I can feel an electrical current," he says, not looking up at her, "but I'm not sure I'll have enough to link up."

"Then we need a transformer," she says. She walks back to the wall and looks up and down inside. She finds what she is looking for and carefully removes the small box from the holding cell.

She turns and hands it to Agoparn. "Will this work?"

Agoparn takes it and places it against the suit on the right side of his neck. He pushes the link into one of the circuit stages and holds it in place with his right hand.

Concentrating, he focuses his attention on the electric current he feels through the suit. Pushing himself he is finally able to make contact with the device's electronic brain.

"Exactly what are you doing," Rosetta wonders aloud.

"It's pretty simple. Our brains function a lot like computers, with electrical impulses. If you have a stimulus implant like I do, then you can focus the center of your own sending electrical wave barrier through a link wire like these and force the computer to respond with certain types of calculations. Since a vuldact connector does a lot of thinking and electronic calculations on its own, all I have to do is give it simple mental and verbal commands and it will obey as far as it can."

"You're a genius, Engineer," she states smiling.

"Rosetta," comes the sound of Mathew's voice over their communicators.

"I'm here, Mathew," she replies. "What's up?"

"I got some bad news…"

"I don't want any bad news, Babe," she replies.

"No, but you'll need it. These Raiders have been combined with technology. They're living machines."

Agoparn's head droops as he lets out a disgusted sigh.

"Did you hear that, Dear," Rosetta asks.

"What…someone breathing out?"

"Yeah," she says. "That was the sound of your Engineer giving up."

There is silence on the other end for a moment.

"I'm sorry, Parn," Mathew says. "I felt you might need to know."

"No problem." Agoparn sounds sad.

"What were you two doing up there?" Mathew requests.

"I was getting ready to use a vuldact connector to hack one of their ships," is Agoparn's response.

"What will stop you," Mathew asks.

"If they're cyborgs, there's no way I can keep up with the calculations at the speed I would need to…"

Lacendu's voice comes over the communicators. "Parn, I can do complicated calculations in my head. Can you give them to me as you receive them?"

"Not fast enough verbally," he states.

Rosetta speaks up. "What about another connector to a computer readout device?"

"Good idea," says Agoparn. "If I can send the signals I receive to the communicator in my suit, and if you can connect one of your communicators to a readout display screen, I should be able to feed you everything I get so you can type me answers back."

Allen's voice comes over the communications channel. "We need to put Lacendu in a room by herself in as secret a place as we can find. The rest of us will need to stand guard and protect her at all costs."

"Agreed," Mathew's voice responds.

Vaskette's unhappy voice can barely be heard behind them. "Yay."

"Great," Agoparn says. "While you guys are hooking up, I'm going to fly this vuldact connector to one of the ships ahead of us."

"Sounds good," Mathew says. "We'll call you when we're set up."

"Understood," Rosetta replies.

Rosetta takes a magnetic strip from the same hole in the wall and places it around Agoparn's neck. It straps loosely together and the metal transformer box is pulled close. She places a couple strips of wire between the step link and the circuit stage to keep the wire in place.

"You should be good to go, Parn."

"Thank you," he replies, a little nervous.

She is on her knees beside him, her left hand on his back. "Are you going to be alright?"

He looks at her through the face shield. Smiling, he answers, "I'll be fine. I'm going to go over there, do my best, and if it's not good enough, it's not…"

She smiles back at him, pausing a moment for effect. Nodding her head, she states boldly, "It'll be good enough."

He turns his face to the task at hand, and gripping the sides of the vuldact body, he mentally commands it to move forward. At his request, the machine responds with immediate force and both he and the machine are flying slowly toward the ship on the left.

While he is in the space between the two ships, Mathew comes back over the communications channel. "We're ready in here, I think."

"Great," Agoparn says. "Let's test it. Lacy, I'm going to give you a simple command that will require you to type back to me as many different combinations as possible. Are you ready?"

"Do it," she replies.

His mind thinks of several different small equations and the information is sent to the communications device's relay circuits via a small electrical current. In under three seconds her response is received in his brain, perfectly calculated.

"Wow, Lacy, you are good..."

A smile in her voice is reassuring, "Yeah..."

Another minute brings him to the underside of his chosen ship. The vuldact maneuvers around for the bottom to connect to the metal hull of the vessel.

His commands are short and succinct, and the vuldact connector reacts with almost instant readiness.

He begins the careful procedures of hacking the ship's main brain.

"Just out of curiosity," Allen interjects in everyone's ear, "won't these kinds of people know what we're trying to do?"

"Probably," Agoparn says, "but considering they're using it on other vessels, there's a good possibility it doesn't work on their ships."

"So, how do you plan on doing it," Allen asks.

"Just wait and see," he says. "I need complete silence for a little bit."

*****

Korsaume sits down in one of the command deck chairs. "So, what now, Shivranikka?"

Shivranikka does not answer.

"Look," Korsaume says rolling her eyes, "if you don't want me here, I'm not going to stay."

"You can do whatever you want," is the curt reply.

Korsaume sighs. Giving the woman an unnoticed dirty look, she asks, "You're not very good at this bad guy thing, are you...?"

Shivranikka, still with her smile, turns her face toward Korsaume with a finger to her lips. "Shhhh... I'm watching your friend try to hack my other ship."

Korsaume's half-hearted leer becomes straight rather quickly, and her eyes open wide. "Oh, no…"

Shivranikka hears Korsaume's remark and her smile widens a bit, but goes right back in place.

"I can do whatever I want, huh?"

"Sure. There's no way you can harm me. I have complete control over this entire ship."

"Yeah. I figured that out a long time ago. You have control over your little minions, too, don't you?"

Again there is no response from Shivranikka.

Korsaume stands up and walks out of the command deck, down the hall, and stops at the junction to the engine room. Quietly to herself she looks to the right at the opening between this vessel and their own, then at the door to the engine room, and says softly to herself, "…Whatever I want, huh?"

She walks into the engine room and sets down her useless weapon. Standing before the large metal cylinder which houses the energy the vessel runs on, she looks around the room. There are few controls; a sure sign of newer technology than the one her and her crewmates presently command.

She breathes in a long breath and looks down at the base of the metal plate. Finally she pulls a panel loose and looks inside. She speaks out-loud knowing the smiling woman can hear her. "Don't mind me. I can't hurt you. I'm just curious."

Over the ship's intercommunication board comes Shivranikka's voice; "Seriously, Korsaume; I used to be human, too, you know… Curiosity kills."

"I have one, too. Power corrupts…absolute power corrupts absolutely." Korsaume smiles to herself as she pulls on a loose cable.

"Korsaume, if you weren't so demeaning, you'd be a lot less fun."

Korsaume looks up as if Shivranikka were standing next to her. "I'll take that as a compliment. It's not often I get honest opinions from fellow members of my gender." She turns her head back to the opened panel and begins to pull the wire out. It goes quite a ways back; something she had set her hopes for. The wire pulls to a stop, and she yanks hard. It does not budge.

She begins to remove the panels leading to the end of it. After pulling nine panels off she is able to reach back and pull the link out of the circuit stage.

"What would you need that for," Shivranikka asks.

"Replacement cables are always important."

"You're up to something," Shivranikka states. "I'm already working on some countermeasures."

"You do that. I'll be here when you figure it out." Korsaume smiles in spite of herself.

*****

"I'm in," Agoparn says for the others to hear, though Lacendu already knows.

Agoparn continues sending the information he receives into his mind from the vuldact connection through his communicator via the transformer, and Lacendu reads the calculations and finds answers for him to circumvent the system.

Lacendu stops. "Parn! Back up two."

"Why?" he asks.

"I recognize the codes."

"How could you possibly recognize the codes?" Mathew asks.

"How should I know, Captain?"

She types in another code and he responds to it immediately running backward through the system script.

"Lacy, these are cybernetic encodings…" Agoparn tells her.

"Neat," she happily responds. "Now let's finish these 'agrauves' off."

"You're speaking my language," Rosetta comments.

Agoparn and Lacendu continue their seamless operation of hacking the ship for several minutes in silence.

Finally, "Lacy, I think I've arrived at the main console."

"I'm sure of it," she calmly states. "Let's try a shadow shut-down."

"Good idea," he replies. "If all of them are cybernetic, we should have no problems from them after that."

The procedure is carried out.

*****

"Hm…"

"What," asks Korsaume?

"Your friends are quite resilient." Shivranikka's voice sounds a bit disturbed.

"Why do you say that?"

Shivranikka is silent for a long moment. "They shut down my other two ships."

Korsaume smiles at this. "Yes, my friends are very resourceful."

"You had no idea they could do it, did you…?"

"Well, I wasn't sure," Korsaume says blandly, "but I would never put it past them."

"Exactly who are you and your friends?"

"Well, like I said before, I'm Korsaume. What I didn't say before was that my real name is Sherise Felder. My companions are Mathew Arnold, Agoparn Schroet, Vaskette Smith, Lacendu Ruric-Trester, and Allen Pendergras. We also have a bounty huntress on board named Rosetta Firemark."

"I've never heard of you," Shivranikka laughs, then adds, "…any of you…"

"No big surprise there," Korsaume remarks. "We're not from this side of the galaxy."

"You're children," Shivranikka says. "Playful, rotten children… That's all you are; and I will see to it you're all punished severely for interrupting my…"

Korsaume stands up and harshly says, “Look here, **techno-witch**! **You’re** the one that came interrupting **our** lives. We were fine **without** you. We had **no** desire to interfere with you or yours. You entered **our** ship without request, barged in, and sent **your** men in to kill **us**. You tell me we’re the ones that are interrupting you?! Punishment goes to those who do wrong. You’re in **our** way, not **us** in **yours**!”

There is silence for a few more minutes as Korsaume grabs the copper wire and begins wrapping it around the metal cylinder of the engine.

“You know,” Shivranikka finally says, “there aren’t many people I respect. In fact, there are none. However…you…? You, I can respect. You will make an excellent commander in my army.”

“I have no intention of ever being anything in your army. Not even a chair.”

Though Korsaume cannot see Shivranikka on the command deck, she knows the wicked cybernetic woman is smiling once again. “Let me guess…you’re going to say, ‘You don’t have a choice.’ Is that it?”

“Actually,” and there is a smile in the despot’s voice, “I was going to say, ‘You will make for a fine enemy.’”

Korsaume is taken aback. She continues coiling the copper wire around. “You’re just full of surprises, Nikka.”

“Just wait till you get to know me,” comes the reply.

*****

“I’m just curious,” asks Allen, “how fast can computers do these same calculations you two were doing…?”

Lacendu answers, “About four seconds, on average.”

“…And how fast were you two doing them?”

“About one and a half seconds, on average,” Lacendu matter-of-factly responds.

Allen looks over at Mathew. "Those poor cyborgs never stood a chance."

Mathew grins. "Of course not…They're dealing with the finest this galaxy has to offer."

Suddenly, a crackled communication comes over everyone's receiver. "Crew of the zero-seven Celestial class Star Expeditioner; are you in need of assistance?" They can barely make out what is asked.

Mathew walks over to a wall and presses a few buttons. "Please repeat your message."

"With whom am I speaking," comes the voice?

"This is Captain Mathew Arnold of the zero-seven Celestial class Star Expeditioner Everhold. Please repeat your message."

"This is Captain Ardelle Xysteck of the 10th Generation Star Axis Cargo Carrier Varrie. Are you in need of assistance?"

Agoparn's voice comes over the communications, "Captain Ardelle; this is Agoparn Schroet."

"Parn," the woman's voice draws out the name as she responds with excitement. "It's so good to hear from you. I thought you folks were flying a cruiser."

"It's a long story," Mathew says, "which we'll be happy to tell you all about at a later time. At present, we could use any assistance we can get."

"Name it," she states.

Mathew speaks into the communicator, "Rosetta, can we get Parn away from those ships fast enough for them to come in guns ablaze?"

"Captain," she says, "I'm quickly learning not to put anything past any of you… What do you think Parn?"

Agoparn's voice is happy. "I'll head straight down. I can be far enough away in about three minutes, but these two ships exploding will probably propel this vuldact device at about three or four times its fastest speed."

"Actually," Lacendu states, "you're looking at a much faster outward thrust of around sixty to seventy times. Within four seconds of that kind of explosion, you're looking at traveling around eight hundred kilometers per hour."

"I can't withstand that, Captain."

"No," Lacendu says, "but if you travel toward the ship that's coming in, they can pick you up along your projected path as they're firing their main guns."

"Great idea, Lacy," Mathew says. "Captain Ardelle, did you hear all of that?"

"I sure did, Captain Mathew. Agoparn can aim his craft at latitude 97145, longitude 43577. He'll be safe with us."

"Understood…"

*****

"Your friends are tres resourceful," Shivranikka states with mild anger.

"My friends are the top experts in their fields of study, ranging from flying vessels, to fixing them, fixing people, mathematics, and strategy."

"…And what skills do <u>you</u> possess, my dear Korsaume?"

"I'm a weapons expert."

"Ah, you deal death."

"You could say that."

"That's good, because I just did."

At that moment, Shivranikka is standing at the door to the engine room. Korsaume looks over at her. "So, you think my friends are pretty clever…?"

"More clever than you… You can't even get your gun to work."

Korsaume eyes the woman as she picks up a small computer board. "I was thinking about that, too," she says. "I think I figured out why my gun didn't work."

Shivranikka begins walking toward Korsaume but does not look like she will actually come close enough to touch her. "Intriguing… Carry on." She stops, legs apart, and folds her arms.

"Well, you're running a class L engine. These engines," she gestures at the cylinder with the copper wire she pulled and soldered the ends to at the top and bottom, "are designed to pull energy from wherever they can. The energy output is confined to a certain type; dyprase photoneuric energy…something these types of engines do not absorb. That is the energy module used in Xycho's computer-organic hybrids, if I remember my studies."

Shivranikka looks a little nervous, still holding her smile intact, "Very good."

"If you run on Dyphoto energy, your metal body would be desensitized, thus making it vulnerable to magnetic destabilization." At this, Korsaume presses a button.

The energy in the iron-alloy cylinder spins at an accelerated rate and the whole thing becomes a giant electro-magnet. Shivranikka is pulled from her spot without a chance to move. She is pulled to the cylinder in a matter of a couple seconds, her back against it. Her smile remains with her.

Korsaume sits down on the console. "So, what do you think of our resourcefulness now?"

The woman's arms are pulled back around the cylinder. She does not breathe. "I think you have outwitted me."

"Oh, come on," Korsaume says. "I don't believe that for a second. You could easily have seen where I was going with all my talk…"

"Possibly true, my dear Korsaume," she says, "if it were not for the fact that I know nothing of physics…" Shivranikka laughs heartily as if she's won something over the other.

Korsaume shakes her head and sighs. "You really are mad, woman."

*****

The plan works almost perfectly…almost. Agoparn pulls the vuldact connection off and it flies awkwardly through empty space to the coordinates of the directions given, and as the Star Axis comes racing forward, its shuttle dock doors open, the vessel fires two full blasts at the two dead ships. They explode in under a second sending a shockwave that thrusts Agoparn and the vuldact device forward at an alarming rate and shakes the Star Axis wildly. The dock doors close as the shockwave pummels the ship, and Agoparn is knocked loose from the device and both hit the back wall with the impact of a jump from forty feet.

Agoparn is knocked unconscious, but the Captain of the ship is prepared and has some of her crew standing just inside the doors to enter the shuttle dock as soon as it decompresses.

Still reeling from the impact, and well-shaken, Captain Ardelle radios back to the crew of the zero-seven Celestial class Star Expeditioner. "We have your crew member. He is out. I don't think those two Raider vessels were supposed to explode like that…"

"I'm sure of it," Lacendu retorts. "They had some kind of explosive devise set up to keep others from rapturing their cargo…"

"We appreciate what you've done for us," Mathew says to the other Captain. "We'll take the remainder from here."

The communications channel to the Star Axis is disconnected and Mathew turns to his remaining crew. "Rosetta, meet us inside at juncture eight. We're going to see about the Raider vessel connected to us."

"Understood, Captain… On my way…"

It is several minutes when Rosetta shows up still in her space-walk outfit, the helmet removed.

Mathew eyes her, gives her the once-over, and smiles. "You look good in that."

She smiles at him. "I bet you do, too…"

"OK, lovebirds, let's get going while we've still got the chance," Vaskette says, shaking her head once quickly to fling her hair back.

As they move into the connection between the two ships, they see two Raiders lying on the floor.

"They look dead," Vaskette says, unemotionally.

Mathew and Allen both hold up their guns, aiming them at the two motionless figures. Mathew looks at the doctor. "Be a dear and go check for us, would you…?"

Vaskette eyes her Captain giving him a crooked look. "…But of course…"

She walks over hesitantly and pulls the helmets off, commenting under her breath, "I don't know how I'm supposed to know if they're dead…they're all robots…" She feels around for something to indicate they are no longer functioning. Tilting her head down to listen intently at their heads, she hears no mechanical noises coming from their brains. "I'm going to assume they are no longer in a functional mode, Captain."

Mathew looks at Allen. "Is that good enough for you?"

"It'll have to do, Captain," he grimly states.

"Let's move out, then," the Captain says turning his head forward and moving through the connection joint.

As the group makes their way into the dark walls of the Raider vessel's corridor, they hear something from directly in front of them…talking…

The talking is cut short and Korsaume comes into view in the room directly ahead. "Well, it's about stinkin' time you folks showed up. I got rid of our pest problem." She smiles at them, pointing into the room.

Vaskette and Lacendu look at each other inquisitively.

"I'm serious," Korsaume adds, "come in and lookie what I caught."

As the group makes their way through the door, they see a woman in a Raider suit wrapped halfway around a giant metal cylinder.

"Who's your new friend, Korsaume," Rosetta politely asks.

"Ladies…Gentlemen, I'd like for you to meet Shivrannika Napercolten, from the planet Mount Ligmon-Ardreptipol…our side of the galaxy…" Korsaume makes a grand gesture at the woman.

Rosetta speaks up. "If that's Ms. Napercolten, she should look a lot older…"

Korsaume looks questioningly at Shivranikka. Shivranikka shakes her head.

Korsaume looks at her crewmates with a look of sarcasm. "Pay her no mind when she talks. She's an evil despot, with delusions of grandeur."

"Is she dead, too," Vaskette asks, stressing "she."

Shivranikka suddenly has a look of extensive wisdom and greatness about her. For the first time since Korsaume met the woman, she actually looks serious.

The madwoman begins, "I am not dead. Not in the sense you will all be dead, soon. I was given a chance at immortality through the great works of Xychocappla. He is indeed a genius. His mathematical equations and chemical balances between man and machine were far advanced for anyone but myself to fully understand." Suddenly, she smiles again. "Because of his work, I can stand before you today, majestic in my glory as the dominator of the gathering of humanity in its simplicity and humility; mighty in my strengths as the galaxy's most precious possession; a lifetime of peace I bring to all under my tutelage; and with you…all of you…as my protégé's, we will follow my shining example, and light of eternal love and expansion of our greatness beyond the stars themselves as we embark upon the journey intended at our inception…" At no point does she ever look her audience in the eyes.

"Wow…she doesn't even breathe," Lacendu comments.

"She doesn't need to," Korsaume explains. "She is speaking from a soundboard created by the technological virus inside her. Her physical body is no longer functioning in full capacity. Her brain is kept alive by stimulants perpetuating through the wires and devices set up in her."

Vaskette looks at the floor. "I didn't know that was possible."

"Don't look depressed about it," Korsaume states. "It was only theoretical science when Xychocappla began his work on it nearly five hundred years ago. His studies were abandoned. He and this witch were sent through one of the first tesseract devices to this side of the universe."

Suddenly, Shivranikka is mad. Her voice erupts, and it is evident her humanity is not completely gone. Still not even glancing at her audience, she loudly proclaims, "Yes! They thought there was no hope for me! They said I would never be able to take over a planet. I stood my ground against them and still they could not see my simplistic desire for man and woman to live together in peace and harmony. No! Instead, they came up with a silly notion that I had some kind of disease, and that they needed to be rid of me as if I was the disease itself. They stuck me on that hunk of scrap metal with that blowhard Xycho at their first opportunity and sent me away without even so much as a 'by-your-leave.' I believe in the benefit of my design to enable all men and women alike to rise above the rank-and-file of their modern governmental laws, rules, and regulations…their moral and spiritual divisions and entrapments…yea, even their perverted science and disruptive wars and petty squabbles. I will conquer all, and when I have finally conquered all, I WILL…" *breath,* "…HAVE…" *breath,* "…PEACE!!!" The woman's smile is completely gone, and if her head were not being pulled against the giant engine/magnet, it would hang down, defeated.

"What disease did she have," Vaskette asks, looking at Korsaume.

"Siverchan's," Korsaume says, almost sadly.

Vaskette looks plaintively at the woman against the cylinder, and walks forward standing before someone she would love to have as her patient. "I'm so sorry, Shivranikka."

Vaskette walks out of the room.

Everyone is silent for a moment. Finally, Allen asks the question on everyone's mind… "What is Siverchan's disease?"

Korsaume looks at him. "It's a fully-enveloping mental desire to control everything, and everyone. It's said to be untreatable, though I don't doubt for a second that if Shivranikka was still human and alive, our good doctor could cook up a remedy."

At this, Shivranikka again starts in, this time on the basis for her disbelief of the disease she had been diagnosed with so many years ago.

Everyone quietly walks out of the room, and Agoparn, looking back sadly, closes the door behind him.

As they are headed for their own ship, the door between the two vessels shuts. Shivranikka's voice is heard throughout the ship. "You will not leave me here," she says. "Not alone…"

Korsaume looks up as if the woman was somewhere on the ceiling. "Shivranikka, we're not going to leave you here alone. We're going to destroy your vessel."

Everyone waits for a response from the woman, but there is none.

Korsaume tries again. "Do you hear me, Shivranikka?"

As if Korsaume had never spoken, Shivranikka says, "I have seen to it that you will never be able to leave this vessel."

"What's that supposed to mean," Allen asks.

Just then, they hear the sounds of the ship disconnecting from their own. The vacuum pressure between the lock is filled quickly making unmistakable sounds outside the door.

Suddenly and without warning, they are all thrust backward and fall against each other and the walls and door of the hallway. The ship seems to be moving, but not under its own power.

"What was that," Vaskette asks pushing herself off of Mathew.

A communication channel is opened into Rosetta's headset. "Is anyone alive in there…?"

"That doesn't sound promising," Mathew replies looking at his girlfriend.

"We're alright," Rosetta states, a little haggard.

"What happened? Is everyone there?"

Rosetta looks around at the group as they all are getting up to their feet. She proceeds to do the same. "What happened from your perspective?"

"The Star Expeditioner blew up. I thought you were all aboard it."

"No, we're all on the Raider ship," Rosetta says. "What could cause that kind of blast?"

"I'm guessing it was a feedback loop caused by multiple incinerator devices," Captain Ardelle states. "At least, that's what venotronics is telling me."

Allen and Korsaume both look at each other. "The Raiders' guns," they say together with some surprise.

"Guns did that?" Vaskette asks.

"An overload in the chamber, hooked to the power supply of the ship, would cause a feedback through any open channels and blow the ship from the inside out," Allen says.

Korsaume finishes. "...Which means those cybernetic bodies weren't dead, just temporarily inactive while Shivranikka was distracted."

Mathew looks at Korsaume. "If she still had control of those robot people, could she still be in control of this ship?"

Korsaume looks concerned. "I would say that it's perfectly feasible, Captain."

"Great," Lacendu says. "What now...? All our belongings are gone...destroyed. All the information we got from Rosetta...all the food and clothing, tradable goods...A mad woman has it out for us, as well as complete control of the ship we're on. Things aren't looking so great for us..." She promptly sits down on the floor in exasperation.

Everyone looks at Lacendu for a moment as she lets out a heavy sigh.

Rosetta speaks up. "That is rather defeatist of you, Lacy."

Shivrannika speaks again. "Defeat... You slew my companions Shallajohne and Forgiven. You destroyed their vessels. It is only right and fair that I do the same to all of you."

There is silence. The machines in the vessel can be heard above the quiet, turning and twisting...performing their functions.

Finally, "What do we do now," Vaskette asks?

Mathew gets a renewed look of vigor. Not looking at anyone in-particular, he says, "We find out just how much control Shivranikka exerts over this ship." He pushes past his companions, and walks down the corridor to the command deck. Allen, Korsaume, and Rosetta follow closely behind.

Vaskette sits Indian-style against the opposing wall, facing Lacendu. "Lacy…"

"I finally thought things were working out for us," she explains, seeming about to erupt in tears, but refraining. "I was finally really useful to everyone. I helped stop the bad people from destroying our ship and killing us, and now we lost everything." She looks up at her friend for anything comforting, letting out another sigh.

Vaskette sits with a mild look on her face; part concern, part sadness. "I know what you mean," she says. "When we were in the room and you were doing your thing, I felt so proud of my friend. I knew you must have been feeling on top of the world when you were typing answers to Agoparn faster than those machines could figure them. It was a high you didn't want to come down from, but with all the things that have happened in just five minutes, it's destroyed all our feelings of excitement. You're right to say we've lost every thing we had; but we have not lost each other."

Lacendu breaks down and cries. Vaskette puts her hands on the other's shoulders and they sit in a semi-silence as tears stream down their faces.

*****

Mathew sits down in the commander's chair and looks at the controls. "This stuff isn't even in my language, and I still know what to do," he says.

Korsaume looks at her Captain as she stands in the weapons center, computer consoles all around her. "I'm glad someone does. I'm clueless, here."

Allen stands in the tactics center looking around. "I have an idea how everything works, but I'm not sure it's correct."

"Only one way to find out," Mathew says. "Allen, put us up with the Star Axis."

Allen types in a few commands while looking down at them. Something clicks, but the ship doesn't move. He tries again, a few different commands; still nothing.

Mathew looks around at him with half a smile. "Allen…?"

Allen looks at Mathew, closes his eyes, and feels the control board. His mind races as he pushes a few buttons, pulls a lever on his right, and taps at a keyboard. When he opens his eyes, the ship still isn't turning.

"What's wrong, Mr. Pendergras," Mathew asks.

"I'm not sure, Sir."

"Actually, Captain," Rosetta says, "the reason we're not moving is because Korsaume, Parn, and I dismantled the engines." She turns to him and shrugs, "It seemed like a good idea at the time…"

Mathew speaks into the communications display on the left of his chair, "Captain Ardelle of the Star Axis; this is Captain Mathew Arnold of the Raider vessel Saiar Ria Contract." He reads the name in the language it is written in on the top side of the viewport. "Please respond."

"Captain Mathew Arnold, your communication is received. We are standing by with your Engineer. Please prepare your ship for docking procedures," Ardelle's commanding voice is heard throughout the ship.

Mathew looks over at Rosetta. "You heard the Captain," he says with a smile.

Rosetta looks down at the control board. "Um, Mathew…er, Captain, I don't know this language, either."

*****

An hour later, the vessels are joined and the two Captains meet face-to-face. Agoparn is standing by her side with a wide grin, happy to be near his female friend once again.

"You're serious about flying that thing onward," Captain Ardelle says, half-asking, half-stating…

"It's a big learning curve for some of my crew," he admits, "but I don't see we have too much of a choice at the moment."

"Well, you're all welcome to travel with us to Ascension City," she says. "With my vessel leading yours, I should be able to explain things to them when we arrive, allowing you to park that behemoth near ours. It will give you a little clout on the planet…as much as a freighter Captain's clout can give…" She smiles at him.

"We would be honored to have an escort," Mathew says with a smile of his own.

"What about that woman on your engine…?" she asks, having been on board for a few short minutes with Agoparn as he gave the engine room a once-over.

"Oh, she'll be quite helpful to us at some point, I'm certain," he states.

Episode 10
A Lit Path

OPENING:

"According to all known accounts of the Travesty of Light, a commentary on the building of the first 'Dyson-sphere' Baitronoc; which began in 2348 AD and was completed nearly two hundred forty years later; the builders; a group known as the 'agrauves;' were slave labor. This is to say the Solar Union, a fledgling organization at the time, kept track of around four hundred million slaves spread out over eight billion square kilometers... a falsehood to be sure. This implies that the 'agrauves' were never paid, causing a following uprising, which would have lasted a great many years. Thus the reason for the hatred of the 'agrauves' would be unfounded. Thus the 'agrauves' were nothing more than sadistic charlatans with a sense of purpose." -- A quote from Keeper Gadilon Shonger, 114th head of the Solar Union, and founder of the Lights for Humanity.

Korsaume walks through the corridor of the Saiar Ria Contract; an advanced vessel with technology ripped from any vessel the Raiders who previously owned this ship could get their hands on. She has in her hands the diary of a person who is dead … unofficially.

As she enters the engine room not looking up, she takes a seat next to Agoparn whose day has been entirely too long … not because he is having any trouble. In fact, far from it … mostly because the woman who is unofficially dead just will not shut up…

He wipes his eyes to try and stay awake despite the fact that he has only been awake for about seven hours.

"Do you think the Captain will let me take a break," he asks, not even glancing at Korsaume.

Without diverting her eyes from the large book, she comments, "A break…? What do you think this is … a job?"

"Jobs are supposed to be work. This is torture." He looks up at her.

"I don't think you're supposed to get a break from torture, either…" Korsaume looks in the general direction of the dead, evil despot, Shivranikka, strapped and magnetized to the engine core of the vessel. "Nikka, do you think you could take a nap or something?"

Shivranikka, not one to speak plainly, makes her speech, "My nemesis, Korsaume, you should know by now that I do not need sleep or rest. I am capable of going for years without so much as a bat of my eyelashes. Pouring rain, magnetic storms … not even the vacuum of space could put me out for a moment's time."

"Yeah, yeah…we've heard all of that. Could you knock yourself out for a few and give Agoparn a rest…?" Korsaume knows in the back of her mind that the woman is too far gone to care about such matters.

"Even if I did, you know that I could keep part of me conscious enough to know if one of you were trying to hurt me…"

"Nikka," Korsaume says standing up agitated and walking a little closer to the despot, "is there even a remote chance that you can answer simple 'yes' and 'no' questions with a simple 'yes' or 'no?'"

Shivranikka's incessantly happy smile beams at Korsaume, a steady laser-like focus that, if it were made of light, would punch a hole through the ship.

"Yes, it's possible. Yes, I could. Yes, I might. In backwards order of the questions asked me."

Korsaume takes a quick mental jaunt through her previous questions at the confusing way the techno-witch made her statement. She sighs. "Look, Nikka, we've been very nice to you. None of us have yelled at you, or talked bad about you behind your back. All I'm asking is that you not talk for a little while, so that you're not being disruptive to our Engineer's work."

Shivranikka pulls her smile back a little further. "My dear Korsaume, I thought you wanted me to be a better bad guy."

Korsaume rolls her eyes and turns to look at Agoparn, whose back is turned to her. "Parn, you have my permission to walk out of this room for an hour and relax somewhere. I'll inform the Captain, and take over your responsibilities for the allotted time if necessary."

Agoparn turns around to look at the Lieutenant. "You have no idea how wonderful an hour away from here would feel."

"Oh, I do have an idea," she replies with a half-smile, nodding her head.

Agoparn immediately stands up and exits the engine room, leaving his commanding officer alone with the despot.

Korsaume turns back around to face the blonde-haired beauty whose body consists mostly of metal, and whose brain and body are kept alive by wires, metal, minerals, and dyprase photoneuric energy, the latter of which is produced by the very cylinder the woman is held helpless against.

The Lieutenant sits down on the console, still holding the diary in her hands. "You've gone through a lot," she states.

Shivranikka gets a cold smile on her face and turns away from her enemy.

Korsaume continues. "Your journeys are that of great exploits on the level of some of the greatest pioneers of the last five hundred years."

"Well, as you stated, I am nearly four hundred fifty years old. That's plenty of time to do all the things I said I did." It is the first time Korsaume has ever heard Shivranikka answer so formally.

"The planet you dubbed yours…is there really a tesseract device nearby?"

Shivranikka glances back at her, then away again. "When I was last there … about sixty years ago … the device in question was still there floating near a forgotten system."

Korsaume lifts her left hand to her forehead and scratches her temple, then places the pointing finger along the edge of her face, folding her fingers inward and resting the middle and thumb tip on her cheek.

Shivranikka adds, "You will not take me to the other side of the galaxy. I shall not go back there!"

"Nikka, someone as powerful as you should have no fear of returning to her home."

Shivranikka acts like she does not hear Korsaume. The smile is gone, and in its place is the temperament of a child in the middle of a temper tantrum. "If you take me back there, you shall be even more my enemy. I shall see to it that you are torn limb from limb when I am freed to roam the galaxy and begin my quest again to control the planets of the third and fourth quarters of the galaxy. When I rule, all shall bow to me, and all shall…"

Korsaume is moving toward the door.

"…Where are you going?" Shivranikka demands, her smile returning.

"We talked about this already, Lady. If you're going to start in on your 'conquering the galaxy' trips, I'm not going to pay attention to you."

The despot makes a sound akin to a laugh, smiles wider, then reforms her regular daunting grin and says, "You really are a great enemy. I enjoy our moments together."

Korsaume shakes her head as she exits the engine room, closing the door behind her.

*****

"…And this symbol is the character 'aush' which, in its dialect, forms a compounded phrase…" Mathew says, standing next to Rosetta, his left arm around her shoulders.

"So, let me get this straight. With this set of symbols," and Rosetta pushes six buttons in succession, "I would be telling the ship to set up a perimeter shield on the forward hull." She looks at him for approval.

"No…you would have to hit this button, too," he remarks, reaching in front of her and lightly tapping an orange button with a different symbol.

"OK. I thought you said that one was the 'crea' symbol, which would put four running streams off each side of the shaft…" She points for effect.

"Yes. When used with the 'larr' symbol, here," and he taps another one, which she had pressed, "which puts a dyprase field from the loading lever across the bottom and top of the front of the ship."

She takes a few steps away toward the back of the deck. She closes her eyes and sighs, then opens them again at Korsaume's approach.

"Captain, I gave Agoparn an hour of reprieve from the engine trouble. Do you want me back there for now?" Korsaume stands about three feet away from Rosetta, but looks at her Captain instead.

"No, Lieutenant. That's fine. You both need a break, anyway," Mathew answers.

Korsaume takes a knowing look at Rosetta. "Not going very well, I take it?"

Rosetta simpers, "What was your second clue?"

"You shouldn't work her so hard," she tells Mathew, walking away. "I thought you were supposed to be nice to your girlfriend."

Mathew walks behind Rosetta to place his hand on her middle back. He looks at Korsaume who walks to the forward right console and takes a seat. "I'm trying to help."

"Yeah, well, I don't like other languages, Mathew. The one I speak is difficult enough," Rosetta states mildly, but upset.

"I'm sorry, Seta." He says it very gently.

"Don't take it so hard, Rose," Korsaume says. "He's really a nice guy, once you get to know him."

Rosetta looks over at Korsaume with a mean look. "Yes, he is. …And don't ever call me 'Rose' again!" She walks out of the command deck with a huff.

Mathew watches her leave, and then turns to his Lieutenant. She looks back at him with an inquisitive look.

"I didn't mean anything by it, Captain…"

He glares at her for a moment; then relaxes. "I know." As if giving in to all that has happened, he takes a seat in the commander's chair and asks, "What have you found out?"

"Well, since our captive likes to talk, I've found out how many ways she wants to take over the third and fourth quadrants of our galaxy; no two of which, by the way, are ever the same; that she both loves and hates Xychocappla for what he turned her into; she thinks I'm her great arch nemesis…"

"Anything of interest…?" he interrupts to ask.

"Oh, there was one thing," she says, standing up and handing him the diary. "You're going to love this one. She says that sixty years ago there was still a tesseract gate floating through the Groonacalta system. According to maps of that sector, which we so handily have aboard this vessel, it's only about three sectors away. Add to that the fact that there's a planet not far from there cartographers named 'Plenawald,' after Isaac Plenawald of Pripeter fame, which Nikka calls 'her planet;' more specifically, she calls it 'Mine.' I have reason to believe there is a nice big bucket of Photonia energy reserves still in a stasis chamber there which could power the tesseract device."

"Now that's the kind of information I was hoping to hear," he says, handing the diary back to her after glancing over the pages she had turned to.

Mathew looks out the viewport window with his right elbow on the armrest, his hand holding his head up. "After we get stocked and ready at Ascension City, we'll definitely want to check it out."

Korsaume gives Mathew a questionable look. “About how much longer will it take us to reach Ascension City?”

“Captain Ardelle said it would take about four weeks, total. Another three days should see us there…”

“Wonderful. I’ll go exploring some more of this ship. I’m sure there’re a few places I haven’t looked into, yet. There’s no telling what that old devil-woman is hiding here.”

Mathew puts himself upright in his chair. “Be careful, Lieutenant. That woman is dangerous. I don’t trust anything about her.”

She smiles at him, shaking her head as she says, “Neither I, Captain.”

*****

Lacendu sits in a chair in what has become her bedroom. It has no bed, though; only a chair, table, sixteen computer terminals, and a floor space that would put the command deck to shame. In the center of the room attached to both the floor and the ceiling are matching ‘bubbles,’ for lack of a better term. They are orange-red and glowing, surrounded on the rim with a metal container of some sort. The orange-red glow of the ‘bubbles’ push energy between them; and Lacendu has spent most of her time in this room, alone, trying to figure out just what its purpose is. She took it upon herself at the onset of their voyage on this ship to at least have this to do, so as not to be bored. She was fooling herself.

Typing away at the console, she reads the output on a screen with multiple geometrical shapes which she continuously manipulates with commands and programs in her attempt. Little by little she has worn away at the puzzle in the center of the room, but consistently she has been just on the edge of the discovery, forcing her to think outside the box, but also wearing away at her emotions to the point where, only fifteen minutes ago, she yelled at her best friend, Vaskette. Lacendu has had little sleep.

She is soon up again and walking across the floor space to another computer on the opposite side of the room from the only door in or out. As she sits down at the console, the door opens.

"Not now," she says aloud and annoyed. Her voice reverberates off the metal walls back to her.

The door closes, but she knows the person came in due to the sound of footsteps echoing in the room.

"What do you want," she asks, giving in.

"Lacy…"

It is Allen. She knows his voice, and she is not in the mood to be bothered by him. "I repeat my question…What do you want?"

"I just wanted to check on you to see if you're alright. Do you want something to eat or drink?"

"Vaskette sent you in here, didn't she?"

Allen's voice softens a bit. "Actually, no… I came in here of my own accord. However, she did mention you yelled at her."

"Figures…"

"You're having a rough time trying to figure this out, aren't you?"

"What would make you think that," she asks with a sarcastic smile, turning in her chair to rest her right arm over the back and look at her traveling companion.

"You know, it is often said by many that taking a break from your labor can bring the answer." Allen stands straight with his hands behind his back, and with an air of someone who should be trusted. It is his customary stance, and those on board have come to respect him because of it, if not directly acknowledging that his attitude is the main cause.

She lets out a long sigh, most likely of relief, and turns back around to face the console. "You guys have had things to do for nine or ten weeks…however long we've been together…and I've had nothing to do." She stresses the word 'nothing.' "Now, I've got something to do and all of you complain that I'm working too hard."

"That's because we haven't seen you in any part of this ship except this room since the day we got stuck on this ship. You have hardly eaten; only what Vaskette has brought you in her friendship to you. Perhaps it would be wise to take a small break and see the others. I know we'd all like to see you."

Lacendu does not respond with anything more than additional typing at the keyboard in front of her. A few moments pass, and just as Allen turns his head and looks to be doing the same with his body, she says, "You're a strategist. What do you think of this ship and that woman in the engine room?"

He looks uncertain at the woman's back, not sure why she threw in the "…You're a strategist…" part. "What do you mean?"

Lacendu stands up and walks over to the bubble in the center. Allen is standing just off to her left in the middle of the floor between the bubble and the wall. She looks down at the glowing light. "If Nikka is in control of this vessel, why are we able to do stuff with it?"

"Ah." He understands now. Her question was that of what Shivranikka's ultimate game is, if indeed she controls the vessel. "My first thought is that she is not completely in control of the ship. I think she was more in control of the Raiders who controlled the ship. That's just my main guess, though. Alternatively, if she is in control of the ship, she would be best suited to retaking the ship if we were not on board. To that end, it would be better for her if we get to where we're going so she can continue her journey."

There is silence between the two of them except for the hum of the two bubbles below and above. Lacendu's eyes are transfixed on the one at her feet in front of her. Finally, "She's extremely powerful. She got that way by means not even understood by us. If she is planning to take control of half the galaxy, what would she need to do it?"

"Well," he says, remembering what Korsaume has told them about the diary, "she would need what Xycho-what's-his-name used to transform her into what she is so she can do the same to others so she could control them."

"Right," Lacendu says, "which brings me to my point. I think I know what's in all those rooms we can't get into."

Allen eyes her carefully. “You mean…?”

She looks up at him. “I also think I know what this is.” She pauses a moment, then, “We need to have a meeting with everyone.”

*****

It is the first time in almost four weeks that the whole team has been together in one room. The room they transformed into a dining area, though little in the way of food exists aboard the ship, has become their temporary meeting room for the evening.

Rosetta and Mathew are the last to enter. Both look across the room at Lacendu with the same surprise as the others when they entered.

Rosetta smiles and says, “Lacendu… It’s so good to see you again.”

The two of them take a seat at the empty booth nearby.

“What’s going on,” Mathew inquires.

Allen looks at Lacendu, and then speaks first. “Lacy has some ideas she wants to share with us.”

Though the others make sounds or gestures for her to begin, she hardly notices, heading straight to the point. “If Shivranikka has plans to take over the galaxy, she would need some sort of way to control those around her. Since we know she can control machines after a manner, like she controlled the Raiders, we know that her plan must include making more like her. In order to make more like her, she would need the equipment necessary for doing this. Since she needs the equipment for this, she needs a big ship to carry all that stuff on. Since she needs a big ship, she has this. Since she has this ship, then my best clue is that she is either toting all the stuff she needs to make more like her on board, or she is using us to go back to the very place where that equipment is.”

Korsaume looks over at Mathew in shock. “Plenawald!”

Mathew looks up at her. “You could be right. But if she’s toting it on board already, we would be playing into her hands by taking this vessel to Ascension City. She could control the entire planet in no time at all…”

“What’s ‘Plenawald,’” Lacendu asks.

“It’s the planet where Shivranikka was transformed into her current state,” Korsaume answers.

Agoparn gets a dour look on his face, pulling his left hand up to rest his face in, and leaning his elbow on the table. “Wait. If she is planning on taking over people and converting them to cybernetic beings, why hasn’t she already done that with us…?”

Korsaume looks down at the floor. “Thankfully, that’s one mistake I’m very glad I made,” she replies. “She considers me her nemesis; and by extension the rest of you as well. She wouldn’t turn her enemies into beings like her. We could destroy her…or at the very least stop her. She needs people who she can manipulate, and she can’t do that with us.” She looks up and around the room at the crew.

Rosetta looks almost sad. “We played right into her hands, then…”

Korsaume looks at Mathew’s girlfriend. “Not quite… She had no idea who she was dealing with. I think she has just been playing along. Those who are very powerful don’t need to push their agenda. She will live an extremely long time, especially since it’s nigh impossible to kill her, so she has all the time in the galaxy to make small changes that will work to her advantage. She most likely only sees us as a means to an end.”

“She’s using us,” Lacendu states, cocking her head and looking across the room at her Captain.

Everyone sits in stunned silence for a long moment.

“One more question,” Rosetta says, “Can she hear us right now?”

“No,” Mathew says looking over at her. “I had Agoparn disconnect the audio sensors throughout the ship where he could.”

“…The first time I’ve ever been happy in four weeks that I couldn’t get into those rooms,” Agoparn states. “I don’t want to be a cyborg.”

Allen looks over at Lacendu. “Didn’t you say you know what that bubble in your room is for?” he asks.

Lacendu looks up at him. "Yes, I did." Then to the rest of the crew, "Let's take a field trip."

*****

"Wow," Rosetta exclaims, her voice echoing through the room. "I haven't been in here, yet." She walks over to the left and stands against the wall.

"It's rather majestic and large for a room of its kind," Allen concurs.

Lacendu is center of attention, though, as she says, "I've been trying to figure out what this thing does since we came on board. I was certain I almost had it figured out, but it wasn't until I began including the thoughts I gave you earlier about Shivranikka's possible ultimate ends I got in my head when Allen was in here a short while ago that I finally concluded the reason for this device. I think she has turned this whole ship into one big device to make people technologically-enhanced like her. They would simply be moved through the stages of development from one room to the other and come out of the ship with all the things that make her tick."

"If that's true," Korsaume states, "then it would explain why she doesn't know much else. She is so single-minded about this that she doesn't think about anything else."

"Is it possible, then," Rosetta asks thinking aloud, "that her mind really is dead, and the computers trying to hold her brain together are narrowly focused on the last remaining thoughts she had before her physical body died?"

"Not only possible," Vaskette says, "but completely likely. We could use that to our advantage."

"First, though, we need to find a way to sever her control of this ship. The longer we stay here on her terms, the less likely we'll be to win," Mathew says.

"Maybe a trap…?" Agoparn suggests. "How about a chance to download the rest of her mind into the ship…? We could make her believe that I was going to do it, like I sort'a did when I hacked the other ships, and just accidentally leave the download device near enough for her to do it."

"The drive we would use to do something like that would have to be completely self-contained, but look like it was part of the ship…" Lacendu adds.

"…But you're missing one thing," Korsaume points out, "her mind already is in a device; and one she's not completely ready to give up. No; we need a way to force her to abandon her body."

Vaskette looks around. "I could start cutting her up to study her. It might take a few days to keep the illusion that I'm really doing it for study purposes, though."

"That means we'd have to slow this ship down a bit, which means contacting the Star Axis without her knowledge," Mathew states.

"Don't you think she would notice if this ship slows down," Lacendu innocently asks.

Agoparn looks at her with a grin, "I can fix that, no problem. I can keep the energy usage constant with our present speed. All I need is a place to divert the extra energy."

Allen says, "The generators on the top of the ship… They're completely separate from the main ship, only hooking up for power reserves. Have Captain Ardelle pull one off, drain it, and put it back on, and then connect it to the main circuit boards on the running streams…"

Rosetta smiles in spite of herself. "This stupid ship is finally starting to make sense, now…"

*****

The crew; everyone except Lacendu; heads back toward the front of the ship. Mathew, Rosetta, and Allen go to the command deck. Vaskette walks with Agoparn and Korsaume to the engine room.

As Agoparn opens the door and steps inside he looks back at Korsaume with a half-grin. "Thank you for that nice break, Lieutenant."

"No problem, Engineer…" she says, looking at Agoparn, and then at the engine core. Her face goes blank and she stops mid-stride, staring at the large cylinder.

Agoparn notices the look and turns toward the cylinder as well. Vaskette bumps into Korsaume, unprepared for the abrupt halt.

"What's wr…" Vaskette begins, looking at the engine core with them. "Oh, dear... That could be a problem."

"Didn't we leave a mechanized woman helpless against that engine core," Korsaume asks.

Agoparn's head is facing between the cylinder and his superior, his eyes transfixed on the engine core. "There aren't two of these…that I'm aware of," he says.

Korsaume reaches toward the wall on her left and presses a button. A signal rings and she speaks toward it. "Captain … um … there's a slight problem with our plan, now…"

"What's wrong," Mathew asks through the system. "Don't tell me she's not there."

"Alright…I won't tell you."

"…Heading your direction," he responds, and the intercom system is shut off.

It is only a matter of seconds before Mathew, Rosetta and Allen arrive behind them.

"Where did she go," Mathew asks.

"That's a great question," Agoparn states, "and one I'm not particularly dying to know…"

Korsaume turns to look at Mathew, then at Rosetta. "…Lacendu's room?"

"Possible, but we just came from there. There aren't any access panels out of this room, so she would have had to go through the hallway," Agoparn answers.

Allen does not hesitate. “There are four levels to this ship. She must have gone down a tier, but where would a crazy cyber-witch go?”

“I don’t know much about crazy cyber-witches, but if she overheard our conversation, she would know what we have planned, but I don’t think she would have too much trouble countering anything we came up with if she already knew she could escape the engine core,” says Vaskette.

“…And that’s precisely what she’s aiming to do,” says Mathew. “She was putting up a front to find out what we would do, and is now taking countermeasures to ensure her own survival.”

“Then we’d best get started on a few of our own,” Allen states.

“Yes, but if she can hear us,” Rosetta says, “then there’s no use in making new plans.”

“Good point,” Agoparn agrees.

“Then what are we going to do,” Korsaume asks, looking directly into the eyes of her Captain.

“I suggest we stay together as a group,” he responds. “Let’s get back down to Lacendu.”

“That might not be as easy as you think,” says a feminine voice over the intercom system.

Korsaume takes a few steps forward. “What are you up to, Shivranikka,” she asks to the ceiling.

“Well, my great nemesis,” the voice says with glee, “if I told you that, this wouldn’t be anywhere near as much fun.”

“Trust me,” Korsaume responds, “this hasn’t been any fun at all since the whole thing started. If you have Lacendu, we need to know that she’s alright. I want to hear her voice, and I want assurance that she will remain that way until the end of this.”

“Oh, Arch Enemy of mine,” Shivranikka says in her usual cheerful sound, “I have not touched your friend, as of yet. She is quite safe, and not being turned into me, at the moment. However, it is a card I can play at any time. From here on out we play to the final finish… I have shut down most of the controls to the ship. Life support will remain on, though; I want you to at least try. As for propulsion, ship communications of any kind, and food or water, those are all gone. I thought about turning out the lights, but then I really want to see the looks on your faces."

"If all communications are off," Mathew asks, "then, how can you hear us?"

There is silence.

Korsaume turns to face the rest of her crew. "Now, the communications are turned off. She's going to try to pick us off one at a time, if her diary is any guide."

"True," Allen says. "Plans are going to be worthless from here on out. We're going to have to work together each step of the way."

"I agree," Korsaume says.

"Fine," Mathew states. "Korsaume is now in charge. The rest of us move with her."

Korsaume looks at Mathew, then at Allen. "Alright, Sir… With all due respect, Captain, I choose Allen for my Lieutenant."

"I can't think of a better person suited for the job," Mathew admits, smiling at Allen.

"Thank you, Captain," he says, looking at Mathew, then at Korsaume and, "er, Captain…"

"Weapons won't take her out," Korsaume says. "We're going to have to go for some different strategies, and that's where Vaskette comes in."

"Me," Vaskette gets a horrified look on her face. "What am I supposed to do?"

"You're the only one here with any clue as to any type of details on cybernetic humans." Korsaume says.

"Cybernetics at her level is still theoretical," the doctor states with a sincere face. "I don't have a clue how it could have been done four hundred years ago, much less how we could do it now."

"Nevertheless," Mathew says, "it's been done, and if anyone in here can figure out how to stop this mad-woman, it's going to be you."

"What do you need," Allen asks, smiling at her.

"Well, if I still had the data I ran on the guy in our other ship, I would have a start, but I'm not sure we're going to get a sample from Shivranikka," she replies.

"Wait," Agoparn says, "if Shivranikka is really planning what we thought she's been planning, then those rooms we haven't yet been in might hold the clues we need."

"Great idea," Korsaume says. "That's where we'll begin. Let's move out."

*****

Twenty minutes pass quickly as the crew, minus their mathematics expert, makes their way to the armory for weapons and shields, then to the first major room to which they have thus far been unsuccessful in opening.

"I didn't want to tear these doors off, but the predicament we're in calls for it," Allen says, shifting a large gun into his arms and setting the controls. "Laser torches work well, even if they are a little slow against this material."

He aims the gun at the edge of the door and fires a steady, low-level stream at the metal door. The beam slowly begins to eat away at the metal, and it is not long before there is a long rectangle carved out of it. Allen raises a leg and kicks at the door, but his foot bounces off of it and he jumps up and down on his other leg, holding the first.

"Ouch! That was stupid," he says, squinting up his face, his eyes closed.

"You carved right through it," Korsaume says, bending down to look at the door. I don't see anything holding it in place.

"You're right," he responds, finally letting his foot to the ground slowly. "Nothing is holding it in place, necessarily. It's a large, heavy, metal door, and it's around sixteen or so centimeters thick. It isn't going to budge just because I kick at it."

Korsaume stands up. "Oh. I hadn't thought about that, really," she says.

Mathew smiles and says, "Perhaps we should all just get together and push it in."

Four of them put their hands and shoulders against it, their feet hard against the ground for leverage, and push as hard as they can. It moves slowly, but it does move, and in a matter of moments it falls over with a loud crash, allowing them to get inside.

As they clamber in through the makeshift doorway, they are each in turn stunned at what they see. The room is about fifteen meters deep and approximately thirty meters wide. Each wall is lined with a row on the floor, and one against the ceiling, of pods with humans inside. Machines on the floors, ceilings, and walls are working on the humans in the pods. Parts from the next room back flow into the room along a conveyer, and the machines take the parts they need and hand them off in a dance recital of technology.

Vaskette gets a healthy smile on her face. "This would be a great start," she says.

"What are we looking at here, Agoparn?" Korsaume asks.

"I suppose you want details," he asks.

"That was the general theme," Korsaume replies, giving him an odd look.

He walks over to the machines, careful not to get in their way, and picks up a part from the conveyer belt. He gives it the once-over and looks up at her. "This one is shaped like an extractor unit used in the old naval battle ships. They're designed for simple transformations of one material into another. It looks like it's been outfitted with some things I'm not so sure about."

"Some kind of way to turn material into energy," Vaskette asks?

"That would be my guess," Agoparn replies.

"Yes, but what would it convert to energy," Korsaume requests. "They don't eat, they don't sleep… What could they possibly use for those things?"

Vaskette's eyes widen. "The human body is constantly absorbing minerals, vitamins, and other nutrients and transforming them to other materials. If one simple machine was added to keep those materials inside the body so that all waste was renewed, there would be no need for additional substance or excrement."

"Wow," Mathew says nodding his head, "that's…pretty gross…"

"It's all part of being human, Sir," the doctor responds.

Agoparn is looking around the room. "I don't think these guys are ready to be released just yet," he says. "We might be able to take one out of here for further study."

Vaskette walks up to one of the pods and peers inside, looking intently at the face. "Well, I can see they have some red, green, yellow, and gold lines running under their skin. They're at least far enough along that taking one out for study might produce the results we want." She looks over at Korsaume.

Korsaume looks at Agoparn. "Let's do it."

Agoparn and Allen walk over to the pod together as Vaskette moves out of the way. Agoparn looks over the pod carefully, searching for anything that will make the job easier.

He finds a small locking mechanism and pulls hard on it, but it does not budge.

"Do you think you can pull that little trick you did with the door here," Agoparn asks Allen.

Allen raises his gun once more, but before he can pull the trigger a mechanism from the ceiling rips the gun from his hands too fast for him to try and maintain it.

"Now, now," says Shivranikka's voice. "We can't have that, can we…?"

"I thought you said communications were shut down," Vaskette yells at the ceiling.

"That is correct, dear one, but that does not mean I cannot hear or see you, or talk to you… Isn't this fun?"

Allen looks at Korsaume. “She’s a child,” he states incongruously with his normal tone. “She’s toying with us.”

“…Common in Siverchan’s disease,” Vaskette replies… “They have impulsive desires to take anything they can get, and keep anything they take. You can only expect more of this from her.”

“So, she’s not going to make it easy for us,” Mathew states. “I say we make a new plan.”

“What did you have in mind, Captain,” Korsaume asks, turning to him.

Everyone else turns to face him.

“What?” Mathew looks a little stunned.

“Well,” Korsaume says, “you didn’t become our captain for no good reason. If you have a game plan, let’s hear it.”

“Oh.” He stops to think for a second. “Well, this ship has two portions. There’s a large section on the back of the ship which can be disconnected. Let’s go back there and get in it. We could jettison it away after we find Lacendu.”

“That would require us to find Lacendu,” Vaskette states the obvious.

“…And I bet you I know right where to find her.”

*****

A few minutes later, the crew members arrive at the room where Lacendu locked herself away.

“Why do you think she’s here,” Agoparn asks.

“Well,” Mathew replies, turning toward the Engineer, “we’ve determined that Shivranikka acts like a child. We’ve also determined that she’s at her best playing mind-tricks on us. It’s her natural response to those she perceives as her enemy. She’s been doing it to you and Korsaume since we came on board…all of us, actually.”

Mathew opens the door and the crew steps inside.

“Hey, guys,” Lacendu says, looking up from her work. “Did we save the day again?”

Everyone but Mathew seems a little embarrassed.

"What's wrong?" She gets a concerned look on her face.

"Nothing," Allen says, walking out of the room shaking his head.

The rest of the crew does the same, with the exception of Vaskette. "I'm going to stay in here for a bit," she tells them, closing the door as the last of them exit.

"Let me guess," Rosetta says once the five of them are in the hallway. "You think Shivranikka is in the engine room, still…"

"I do," Mathew says with a half-smile.

"You're enjoying this, aren't you, Captain," Korsaume asks, eyeing him with a smirk of her own.

"No…well, maybe a little." He shrugs. "Shall we…?" He gestures in the direction of the engine room.

They are there in only a matter of moments and enter together.

"Alright," Korsaume says with a give-in. "You've played your little game." She walks around the cylinder. "You can stop…" She stops suddenly. "Captain…"

"She's not there?" Mathew asks.

Korsaume looks over at him. "See for yourself."

The rest of them walk around the cylinder. Nothing but the copper wiring…

"Now what," Agoparn complains.

"If she overheard our discussion about jettisoning the other portion of the ship, she may have headed back there." Rosetta cocks her head a little at her companions.

"Good idea," Mathew says. "Let's go."

*****

Two minutes later the seven of them arrive at the door to the secondary escape shuttle; literally the entire last quarter of the ship, designed to carry everyone on the first three quarters away in case of an emergency.

Mathew stands at the door and presses a button that releases a cover to a control box on the right side of the door. The control panel is displayed in the language of the remainder of the ship, and is lit up in unusual patterns.

"Impressive," comes a voice through the speaker near the door. "How did you do that?"

"How did we do what, Shivranikka," Korsaume asks.

"How did you find me so quickly?"

Mathew looks back at Korsaume. "What is she thinking?"

"I'm thinking," Shivranikka says coldly, "that you can't stop me, now. I've taken the crew I needed, destroyed the rest, and shut down your entire ship. It's my ball, my bat, and we don't go home until I win…"

"Alright, then," Rosetta replies; "You've won. So, what do you do now?"

"We all go home," is her reply.

Suddenly, mechanisms pop all around them, and the noises of a ship pulling its self apart can be heard in front of them. Firing thrusters are heard and through the door's window they see the last fourth section of the ship rapidly moving away through space.

Through the window of the secondary door of the escape ship they see Shivranikka's face; the cold, calculating smile of someone who knows how to play games. Her voice is heard through the speaker again. "I enjoyed our little game. You tried so hard to outthink me that you didn't even notice the things that were happening right under your nose. You may be the finest in war, but you still have your weaknesses…" They see her face move away from the window, and her hand shows in it for just a brief moment…waving goodbye.

Almost every one of the crew sighs in unison. Some stare in surprised wonder.

“I can’t believe this,” Allen says leaning against the corridor wall, his head facing the ground. “She bested us.”

It is very silent for a long moment.

“I’m sorry, Captain,” Korsaume says. “I failed. We should have just left you in charge.”

“No. It was my decision to put you in charge. I didn’t figure it out until we talked about it in that mechanical room.” Mathew turns and leans against the door.

Agoparn speaks up, “We do need to go get this ship working again. There’s no telling what she did to it.”

“Chances are all she did was shut it off,” Korsaume says. “It would be consistent with everything else she’s done.”

“Aren’t we going to go after her,” Rosetta asks, giving a mean look at Mathew.

“No, Seta…we’re not,” is his reply. “We have something far more important to deal with, and it needs our attention.”

“What’s that?” Rosetta requests.

“There’s a war on the other side of the galaxy that still needs to be stopped,” he answers. “I say, we stick to our plan and not let something like this take over our priority list. So we got beat. We’re not down and out. There’s a galaxy that needs saving. It needs us. That’s what we’re going to do.” Mathew walks off down the corridor.

Rosetta waits until Mathew is out of earshot before smiling, looking at the others, and saying, “That’s my man.”

*****

Hours pass as the crew turns the power to the ship’s controls back on and restarts all the processes that had been going when they were en route.

Finally reviving ship-to-ship communications, Mathew makes a call to Captain Ardelle Xysteck of the 10th Generation Star Axis C-72 Cargo Carrier Varrie.

"Hello again, Captain Mathew," her voice says through the channel. "What happened over there?"

"Well, first, Captain Ardelle, what happened out there from your point of view?"

There is a brief moment before she answers. "Your ship suddenly shut down and was basically coasting. When it began to slow down, we were sure there was a problem. We've been maintaining course with you and trying repeatedly to hail you with no response. That began nearly an hour ago. What happened? Why did you jettison the escape section of your ship?"

"Well, do you remember that techno-witch we had on board?"

"How could I forget?"

"She escaped in it."

Captain Ardelle makes a sighing sound through the speaker and responds, "How in the galaxy did you folks manage to let her escape."

"It's a long story, Captain, but once we get propulsion back up and running and get back on track, I have a feeling it will be something we'll have time to cover. About how far are we from Ascension City, now?"

"...About a two days' journey, Captain."

"Perhaps you can tell me how far away we are from the Groonacalta system?"

Captain Ardelle's voice becomes grave. "You don't want to go there," she states. "They say it's full of all sorts of evil."

"Yes. My Lieutenant said there's a planet named Plenawald there."

"That's rumored to be the source of the evil," she says. "Don't get me wrong. Just because I'm a space-faring woman doesn't mean I believe all the rumors and legends, but it's best I pass them on to you for safety's sake, than to just pretend it doesn't exist. No rumors exist without some basic truths."

"That techno-witch we were carrying is from there."

"All the more reason, dear Captain, for you to stay away from there... Besides, Plenawald is a big planet. It requires a huge amount of energy to get off the ground."

Agoparn walks up behind Mathew and taps him on the shoulder. "Sir, the propulsion drive has been checked and rechecked. We're good to go, at your command."

"Perhaps you and I can discuss this further when we get to Ascension City," Mathew says to the woman. "My engineer says everything is in order."

"My crew is ready, Captain Mathew," she states.

"At your leisure, Captain Ardelle...Lead the way."

*****

"I still don't understand why we aren't going to try and stop Shivranikka," Lacendu says, sitting in her chair, tapping away at a computer.

The room she had sheltered herself in for the past couple weeks has become a bedroom of sorts. Vaskette and Rosetta helped her bring a cot and some necessities in and set them up. The door is open, and the two women are seated in chairs near Lacendu.

"Well, Lacy, it's going to take a long while before Shivranikka even gets somewhere where she can begin her domination plans again. She still has to recreate all the stuff she made on this ship, and find people willing to follow her. The odds aren't exactly in her favor..." Vaskette smiles and looks at her blonde-haired friend. "But, look who I'm telling that to, huh...?"

Lacendu looks up and over at the doctor. "I suppose you're right. I don't have enough data to calculate her odds, but I'd say if she did have the capability right now, the chances of us hearing the phrase 'Galactic Queen Shivranikka' a year from now wouldn't be too far a stretch for my imagination."

"A nightmare of a daydream, to be sure," Rosetta adds.

"Suffice it to say, Shivranikka took up way too much of our time as it is. We would have been far better off never having met her," Vaskette states, cricking her neck and looking up at the high ceiling with an uninterested look in her eyes.

"Actually," Rosetta says, "according to Korsaume, Shivranikka may just have been our ticket to reaching your homes sooner than we had planned."

"How's that," Lacendu asks, stopping what she's doing and turning her chair to face Rosetta full on.

"Korsaume found Shivranikka's personal diary and read through it. She found a passage where the old woman said something about a tesseract device near a planet she was on."

"That 'plena-what-ever' planet," Vaskette gives Rosetta an inquisitive gaze.

"Plenawald… It's where Shivranikka was turned into her current form."

"Yeah, we heard her say that in the dining room," Lacendu states, agreeing. "Do you think the Captain will want to go there?"

"I believe so," Rosetta responds. "There may be some photonia, there. That's the stuff they use in tesseract devices."

"What is photonia," Vaskette asks. "How do they make it?"

"It's not made, per se," answers Rosetta. "They find dying stars and suck the photons out of it. Then they mix it with a few things and use it to power up tesseract devices."

"Doesn't a tesseract need two devices on each end," asks Lacendu.

Rosetta nods. "Normally. The problem with only one is that you don't know exactly where you'll end up. Calculated jumps are risky without a receiving device. You could end up inside a star, a planet, or any number of inhospitable places no one would really want to be. Getting the right mix of photonia for the jump is also difficult, because it determines how far you travel. Either way, though, a tesseract will work with only one device. Folded space is folded space."

"I guess I don't understand the concept of folded space," Vaskette says.

Lacendu replies, "It's like a sheet of paper. You draw two dots on either side of the page; where you are, and where you want to be. Usually, the quickest route between two points is a straight line. Tesseracts forego the line. Crinkle up the sheet of paper in the middle and join the two dots together, then just walk across. That's basically what a tesseract is. It's nearly instantaneous. The problems with it lie in the fact that it takes up so much energy to perform, and that horrible little crinkle in space between the two spots. Eventually, it will probably mess up our poor galaxy, and we'll all have to go somewhere else."

"Many people believe that and refuse to live between access points, or travel through them," Rosetta states. "That answer coming from a mathematics expert would give me pause about going through another one."

The ladies continue their conversation for a long period, mostly about menial and trivial things before Rosetta bows out and heads back up to the command deck.

She arrives to find Mathew in the Captain's chair, Allen at his spot behind and to the right of Mathew, and Korsaume sitting at a console on the front right.

"How are things going up here," she asks, walking up beside the chair.

Mathew turns his head to look at her. He reaches his left hand out to her and she takes it in her right hand. She leans up against the chair and breathes deeply.

"Everything's moving along rather smoothly," he answers her. The two kiss and Mathew stands up. "Would you mind taking over for me for a few minutes?"

She gives him a confused face. "Sure. What's up?"

He smiles at her, a reassuring one; and then winks. "Korsaume, may I see you privately for a few minutes?"

"Sure, Captain," the Lieutenant says, not looking up. She punches a few buttons, pushes the chair back a bit, stands up, and walks around it toward him.

The two of them head just past Allen into the Captain's room, and Mathew closes the door behind them.

"Have a seat," he says, motioning with his right hand at a long, red chair akin to a sofa, connected to the wall on the right. He takes a chair in the center and sits across from her; a small, long table between them.

"What's wrong, Captain?"

He stares at the table as he speaks. "I want to know more about our side of the galaxy. I want to know what you know about the CHE's vendetta. Sherise is the person to give it to me." At this point he looks up into her face. "I hate bringing up that fact, but we are heading into more and more danger the closer we get to our homes, and I want to be prepared."

When she first sat down, she had moved into a somewhat comfortable position. At this, she sits up rigidly and formal.

"I'm just curious why you waited until now to ask me…Sir…"

He breathes in big, and lets it all out at once. Pulling his head straight up with more force than is necessary, he looks her square in the eyes. "Today proved to me something I still, unfortunately, wasn't entirely certain about…your loyalties."

She gives him a blank, appalled stare.

He holds up a finger in protest. "Don't get me wrong, Lieutenant. You've proven yourself over and over these past few weeks. I trust you. Now, I believe I know where your loyalties lie, and I am confident that I can believe what you have to say when I ask you about the CHE."

She sits back into the plush sofa, still seeming to maintain a formal air about her. She clasps her hands together between her knees. "Sir, the CHE is all I've ever known. There isn't much that I can say about my loyalty to them. They're still my comrades, regardless of our stances against each other. However, the knowledge we possess may very well find my comrades back on our side some time in the near future. I don't count them out completely.

"As for the information you are requesting, I hold nothing back other than the few things I've been sworn to secrecy on."

Mathew interrupts. "Tell me about the political climate where our homes are. I want to know what things have been stirring in the nest."

She sits forward again, and seems with her motions to be bracing herself. "Things aren't going well in the political system. Many believe that the Solar Union is heading for a downfall that will annihilate their way of life. They think 'the Committee has allowed too many stepping stones to be removed from the path to peace,' as one politician put it.

"Some fear the Committee puts too much trust in the 'brain,' a supercomputer invented a few hundred years ago which was set up with the 'knowledge of good and evil;' mankind's morality encoded. The people who believe this feel that the 'brain' may not be completely trustworthy, and that the steps it is leading our galaxy into is a path which will exacerbate, if not fully be the cause of, the downfall of our civilization.

"As to my personal feelings, I have been trained not to feel anything. I act upon decisions based on the training I have received. In the CHE, I wasn't allowed to have feelings. They were seen as a sign of weakness; as you could probably imagine, with someone in my line of work.

"I've assassinated presidents of planets, kings of nations, political heads, mistresses, and unfortunately, even little children who were innocent. I did my job. They told me where to go and what to do and I did it, with no emotions attached. Many people in the CHE are tied to the same account as my self. Our goal is to see the Solar Union succeed, even when we disagree with the Committee."

Mathew pulls his body forward, leaning over his knees. His elbows rest on his thighs, and he folds his fingers together, and finally lays his chin on those. "Is that something the 'brain' set up for the government?"

"From what I've been told, yes… According to accounts of the 'brain's' set-up in the late 2300's, early 2400's, it was the 'brain's' idea to create the Solar Union and set up a group of checks and balances; similar to that of the United States of America on Earth from 1800 through the twenty-second century.

"The CHE was created as the bodyguard of the Solar Union Committee, as well as its enforcing right arm. On the same token, the Solar Union was to be held accountable by the CHE, so that the CHE was as much the enforcer of the governances of the Solar Union as it was overseeing that they stuck to the ordinances laid out by the 'brain.'"

"Is it possible the 'brain' was just a big, sick joke," Mathew asks her.

"Sir," she asks, wide-eyed.

"I'm sorry," he responds quickly, leaning back into his chair once more. "I don't mean to sound sarcastic. It's definitely not you." He glances at the floor. "I just don't think that morality can be contained in a box…you know what I'm saying?"

"Yes, sir," she answers.

"If I've got my clues correct, I'm guessing the 'brain' told the Solar Union that a war was needed. We were gathered to participate in that war and help the Solar Union win, and we refused, based on our own moral standards."

"That would seem to be correct from the little information we have so far, Captain," she states.

"If we made a moral choice not to start a war, then my first question is simply, 'why did the 'brain' think we needed one?'"

She raises her eyebrows a brief moment in contemplation. "Interesting… Your second question."

"If the Solar Union wanted us to start a war, and the CHE is supposed to keep a check on the Solar Union, then wouldn't it be naturally right that if our moral choice was to not start a war, that the CHE would be correct in trying to stop us?"

Episode 11
Someday the Rain

OPENING:

A shining example of the works of man, Ascension City is the masterpiece, the penultimate of the cleverness and creativity of some of the finest minds in the galaxy. The planet itself is the masterpiece of a Mastermind, Whose abilities far exceed man's own.

Lacendu and Vaskette are the only two on the command deck when the large planet, Ascension City, comes into view. They are seated in front of the console which is usually utilized by Korsaume. At the moment, the remaining five members of the crew are asleep.

The planet is little more than the size of a person's fist from twenty feet away. It is a red globe that glimmers and glistens in the glow of the star on the near right; Ascension City's very own star, Allcauri IV.

The two ladies are huddled together with a blanket over them.

"I can't wait to be planet-tethered again," Lacendu says.

"How have you been holding up, Lacy," Vaskette asks. "You haven't had a dose of that cure I had for you in a number of weeks."

"I guess that's why I was so adamant about not leaving that room," Lacendu answers. "It helped get my mind off the fact we've been flying through space."

"What did you think of the last planet," asks her friend. "The plants; the cool breeze; the neat little flower-stem ride…?"

Lacendu smiles in remembrance. "The plant rides were fun. I wish we'd had more time to enjoy them instead of running for our lives."

"Well, let's hope we won't be running from anybody on this one," Vaskette adds.

They sit in quiet and solitude watching the planet growing closer and closer.

*****

There is a knock on Mathew's door. Mathew, sound asleep, rouses from his slumber groggy. His eyes open a little and then quickly close again. He flings the thin sheet off his body and pulls himself up and his feet and legs off the side.

Another knock on the door brings him breath enough to speak. "Who is it?"

"It's your girlfriend," he hears Rosetta's voice.

"Come on in," he manages.

The door opens and in walks the beautiful golden-haired bounty huntress in a pink slip. He can only see the outline of her hair and slip from the light in the hall. He closes his left eye to try and keep his right eye on her, but soon switches off, then blinks a few times.

"What's going on," he asks.

"I was just informed by our illustrious doctor that Ascension City is coming up directly in front of us," she answers sitting down in a chair next to the door.

The door closes and the two are left in the dark.

"Dim light," Mathew states, and the sensors in the room receive the command turning a dim light on around the middle strip on the wall, and one around the top edges of the ceiling. The light is a baby blue that sets off the room really well, but not their skin so much.

Mathew yawns wide.

Rosetta looks across the small room at her boyfriend in a pair of shorts and grins to herself. His hair is ruffled and misshapen. "Are you going to get up," she asks.

"Actually, I was seriously considering staying in bed and letting someone else handle the parking." He yawns again.

"Well, don't look at me," she replies. "I haven't learned enough to do parking for this black behemoth."

"First we have to get past the three checkpoints on the way into the territory. If they blow us to kingdom-come, parking won't be an issue."

"Oh," Rosetta exclaims, standing up and walking over to sit down beside him, "don't even talk like that. I have quite a bit of confidence in the Star Axis Captain. She'll get us through them with no problems."

"Captain Ardelle already told us they would probably board us. Three days wasn't near enough time to clean up the mess on board…"

"…For that matter, neither was four weeks," she responds with some sarcasm.

"Well, how were we supposed to know what all Shivranikka was toting on this thing?"

Rosetta lays her head on Mathew's shoulder. "I'm just saying…"

"I know…"

*****

Mathew and Rosetta arrive on the command deck fully dressed to see the planet of Ascension City about half the height of the viewport, and almost perfectly centered. Mathew sits in the Captain's chair, and Rosetta takes her place to the forward left of him at a set of control panels in a near-complete circle. She stands in the center of them.

"I hope I've got this stuff down," she says. "Captain Ardelle's instructions were explicit, but complicated."

Vaskette and Lacendu stand up between the tactician console and the veiwport window at Rosetta's statement.

"I'm sorry," Mathew says to them. "Did we bother the two of you?"

Lacendu pulls the left side of her mouth back. "Not really."

"You're both welcome to stay," he states.

The women turn to look at the planet.

Allen walks in at that moment and takes his place. "Are we ready to get this show under way, Captain," he asks.

"When Korsaume arrives and Agoparn says he's ready," replies Mathew.

Korsaume enters. "Did I hear my name?"

"No…" Allen looks at her. "We were talking about the other Korsaume on board…"

"Smart-alic," she says with a half-grin striding over to the tactical console where Vaskette and Lacendu still stand facing out the veiwport window.

"It's a beautiful planet," Vaskette says. "I can't wait to land."

"It will be a nice break from the past few weeks," Korsaume states.

"Who would have thought I'd want to have a mundane day," says Allen.

There is a moment of silence before Agoparn's voice comes over the communications channel. "Captain, everything is ready on my end. We should be coming up on checkpoint number one in about three minutes."

"Thank you, Engineer," Mathew replies. "Prepare for docking procedures at their behest."

Agoparn's voice is heard again. "Terminal compliance accepted, Captain. 'Awaiting outside source commands…"

At the same moment Agoparn's voice begins, a signal heralds a communication channel from the Star Axis.

"Captain Ardelle, this is Captain Mathew of the Saiar Ria Contract. What can we do for you?"

The Star Axis Captain's voice is heard clearly, "Captain Mathew, I just wanted to inform you that we have contacted the first checkpoint and explained the situation. I noticed your ship is prepared for docking. You're playing this well."

"We're all a little sleepy over here," Mathew says. "The clean-up hasn't gone as well as we'd hoped, but we're trying to stay on top of things."

"I understand, Captain. If there's anything we can do to assist, let me know. I'll be boarding with the Checkpoint Officials for reassurance."

"We'll be waiting, Captain Ardelle. Saiar Ria Contract out…" Mathew cuts the communications channel and turns to his crew. "Boarding should occur within thirty minutes. Stick to the instructions, answer all their questions, and we'll make it through this just fine." Mathew stands up. "Everyone is to meet at the docking shell in twenty minutes. No tardiness. We want to make a good impression."

"Yes, sir," most say in unison. Lacendu turns around and watches Mathew exit the command deck. Then she turns to Korsaume. "Is it just me, or is he finally becoming more…what's the word I'm looking for…?"

Allen, "Bold…?"

Rosetta, "Sexy…?"

Vaskette, "Commanding…?"

Korsaume, "Secure…?"

Allen, "Overbearing…?"

Korsaume, "Annoying…?"

"You guys are a lot of help," Lacendu finally stops them. "The word I was thinking of was 'confident…'"

The rest begin agreeing; "Yeah." "Mmhmm." "Oh, right." "You bet…" "Confident…makes perfect sense."

Lacendu rolls her eyes and shakes her head.

"Perhaps we should go get dressed," Vaskette says to her friend.

The two exit the room.

*****

The docking shell opens and the Checkpoint Officials with Captain Ardelle and one of her subordinates enter the Saiar Ria Contract. Standing in stripped-down Raider uniforms are the seven crewmembers.

Ardelle looks at Agoparn and winks, a smile on her face. He returns a smile and nod.

The head official speaks first, looking at a slim-sheet computer. "Captain Mathew Arnold, of the Saiar Ria Contract…"

Mathew answers, "That would be me, Madam."

She glances at him, looks him up and down with all the finesse of a club-hopper, and then says, "Of course… Introduce me to your crew, Captain." She holds the slim-sheet behind her back and stands with her legs slightly apart; a hopeful sign of commanding representation.

Mathew looks and points at each of his crew in turn, "Our Lieutenant and Tactician, Korsaume Felder; Mechanic and Engineer, Agoparn Schroet; Mathematics and Computer expert, Lacendu Ruric-Trester; Weapons and Strategist, Allen Pendergras; Shields and Analysis, Rosetta Firemark; Doctor, Vaskette Smith."

The official looks at Rosetta. "I understand that you were born here…is that correct, Bounty Huntress?"

"Yes, Madam," she replies.

"What brings you back home," the woman asks, not looking at her.

"I have offered to help this crew," Rosetta replies. "And there is a more personal matter…the Captain and I are in a relationship."

"Was this before, or after you joined the crew?"

"Our relationship began before I joined the…"

"Very good… Engineer," she cuts Rosetta off and turns to Agoparn, "What is the condition of this vessel?"

"Madam, the Saiar Ria Contract has been given a good thorough check three times in the past two days per regulations. The engines meet or exceed all expectations provided by your government." Agoparn hands her a small hand-held computer. "You'll see in all instances that the wiring, controls, regulators, energy outputs, and storage capacitors are all fairly new and in excellent working order."

The official looks through the streaming data and hands the small computer back to him. "Well done, Engineer." Finally, she looks directly at Lacendu, whose head has been facing down at the floor the entire time. "Look at me, Computer expert." Lacendu looks up, but averts her eyes. "Look at me, Computer expert," this time a little louder and more forceful; eliciting Lacendu's eyes directly into her own, "I want an account of the technology aboard this ship."

Lacendu reaches her hand behind her and pulls a hand-held similar to Agoparn's and hands it to the woman. She swallows hard.

"Can you speak, Computer expert," the official asks.

"Yes, Madam. The computers all work and do the stuff they need to, Madam," Lacendu stumbles through.

"They all work, and do the stuff they need to…"

"Yes, Madam."

The official looks through the device's streaming feed. "This is quite a list of computers. Where did you pick all these computers up at…?"

"They were on board when we got here, Madam."

The woman hands the device back to Lacendu. "Yes. I read in Captain Ardelle's report that you folks kicked the Raider's out on their heads, and that the Raiders destroyed your other vessel. What was it, again?"

Captain Mathew clears his throat. "It was a Star Expeditioner, Madam."

The woman turns to Mathew. "All your belongings were aboard, Captain."

"Yes, they were, Madam."

"Do you have a complete list of the items destroyed on your previous ship," she asks.

"We do, Madam." He reaches his hand out to Korsaume who hands him a slim-sheet, which he hands to the official.

She reads through it thoroughly. "You had quite a bit of cargo," she says. "Star Expeditioners carry people, Captain Mathew; not cargo." She looks up at Mathew, staring him down.

"Under normal circumstances, that would be correct," he states. "We are traveling to Quadrant One."

"Quadrant One," she replies, almost in a mocking tone, "What is in Quadrant One so important…?"

"Our homes, Madam," he bluntly states.

The official stares at him a moment with a blank look. "What brought you here?"

"The Solar Union, Madam. Lieutenant Korsaume is with the CHE."

"Is that so," she asks, her eyes a little wider. At this she turns to Korsaume. "Name, Rank, and Number, Lieutenant."

"Sherise Korsaume Felder, Rank One, number seven-seven-zero-nine-alpha-zeta, top-level…"

The official looks up the number on a wrist-computer on her left forearm, and then looks upset. "Rank One…"

"Yes, Madam."

The official swallows. "What is your business, Lieutenant?"

"To see these people safely back to their homes in Quadrant One, Madam."

The woman hands the slim-sheet back to Korsaume. She looks at her assistants. "Pass them on to Checkpoint Three for station-landing," she says, and this to Korsaume … "Do you require anything for your stay?"

"Nothing I can think of right off hand, Madame."

"Is there anything else we can do for you…?"

"That will be all, Madame," Korsaume says, nodding her head once at the woman. "You're dismissed."

The woman turns on her heels and walks out the door. Her entourage follows quickly.

As the door closes, Ardelle looks around at the crew. "That turned around rather rapidly for you…"

"Did you see the way she acted when she found out I was a CHE member?" Korsaume asks.

Lacendu nods. "That was a bit bizarre."

"Let's not dwell on it right now," Mathew says. "We still have a ways to go before we reach the planet. Let's get prepared; we've still got one stop to make before we dock with the orbital station."

Ardelle and her crewmate exit and head back to their ship as the crew of the Saiar Ria Contract walk back up to the command deck.

*****

It is a matter of hours, after both ships are searched thoroughly at checkpoint three, that they soon arrive at the orbital ribbon station around the planet, Ascension City.

A jaunt on an external railway to the only opening in the planet's crystalline shell around the atmosphere is short, and contains everyone from both ships, and a few others which just came in to dock about the same time.

Each person is then taken individually and "piped" down through an energy stream to the glass surface sixty kilometers above the uninhabitable surface of the planet.

The planet's body is made up of the heaviest elements known to man, including many radioactive ones, making life on the surface impossible. A glass-like substance was designed, and with the help of anti-gravity bots, was pieced together over the planet's surface to give the remaining one-hundred fifty kilometers of atmosphere to the people who live on it.

The crystalline structure around the planet is natural, and only one hole was punched in it to get all the things necessary through it. The orbital ribbon station allows for transport to, amid, and from the planet.

As for the governing body, they are not very interested in the affairs of the daily lives of the citizens, choosing instead to live their own lives. They are only called upon when decisions are needed, so the people who live and travel here are free to go about their business; as long as that business does not interfere with the rights and privileges of other people who also have their own business.

Imports are the most common. Not much is produced on the glass-like surface, except energy, which is one of only two exports. The energy comes from the stems and vials of the radioactivity of the actual planet's surface itself forced upward toward the glass-like surface, gathered, and converted to power trillions of homes, offices, resorts, and any number of other structures in place.

Basically, it is the center of commerce in the third quadrant of the galaxy.

Water is actually derived from the air around, as it is plenteous at the level the glass-like structure was built at. All used water is filtered, the harmful and non-essential elements harvested for other uses, and the purified water super-heated and released into the air for the water-derivation plants to reuse all over again.

As to consideration for the glass-like structure the humans live on, most people who visit are extremely unnerved to see sixty kilometers of open space between them and the ground. However, few, if any, people born on the planet have a phobia of heights. Rare cases have occurred where the structure collapsed in spots, and radiation was a threat, but procedures are in place to find and fix those problems before they occur. To be sure, the glass-like substance is more a "film" which is super-radiation-resistant, and the little radiation that does get through is quickly taken up by bots and utilized for energy.

Resorts are plentiful; mostly for the tourists who desire to see the amazing structures built on a see-through film sixty kilometers above a radioactive planet surface, and the odds and ends they can pick up from the other side of their home from here. Exotic, strange, and bewildering animals from surrounding planets are brought and caged for viewing, and uncommon elements such as platinum and gold are stored and shown; some of it even given away to visitors in minute amounts as an attraction for visitors so that more currency is spent on this one planet in one year than all the planets in the third quadrant in the same elapsed time.

All of this is information Rosetta and Ardelle give to the crew of the Saiar Ria Contract as they stand in line waiting to be pushed down through the energy stream to the glass surface.

"I just want all of you to know this is free time for us all," Mathew says to his crewmates. "I want all of you to take a breather. Relax, let your hair down, and do something for yourselves. We all need a break from each other, and from the monotonousness of the past few weeks."

"I'm looking forward to it, Captain," Lacendu says with a great big smile. "Except for the part of being able to see through the ground I'm walking on… That part won't be so great."

"It's alright as long as you don't look down," Rosetta says laughing.

"I don't suppose any of your bounty-hunter buddies are here," Vaskette says as a question to Rosetta.

"Oh, there's a few. It will be nice to see them again, for sure, but if you're thinking they might have a bounty out for us, I seriously doubt it. We'd have known about it by now."

"Well, that's a sigh of relief for me," Allen says. "I can't wait to get some rest."

As they continue to talk amongst themselves, the line gets smaller, and soon each of them are taking their turn on the trip down the energy stream through the planet's crystalline structure. The trip is astoundingly beautiful, if a bit unsettling as it takes about six minutes to reach the landing platform; a non-glass structure that looks more like a sea-side port with shops and restaurants.

The crew meets together at one of the restaurants at Captain Ardelle's request and they all enjoy a fabulous meal.

Afterwards, they are greeted by a man in a long silver gown who verifies their identities and hands them each pamphlets of information on things to do and places to visit on the planet.

Then, they all split up. Captain Ardelle takes Agoparn with her to travel to her favorite resort about half-way around the planet. Lacendu runs off by herself to look at shops. Vaskette heads for a hotel to get some sleep. Surprising everyone, Korsaume grabs Allen by the arm and the two walk out without saying a word to the rest.

Mathew and Rosetta are left alone in the lobby.

"Well, what do you want to do," Mathew asks, polite as can be.

"I don't know," she smiles delicately, "What do you want to do."

"Now, let's not start that," he says rolling his eyes.

She giggles at him. "Maybe we should find something we both enjoy and go do that."

"How about we go see where you were born and raised…?"

"Alright..."

The two of them head out into the open air and Mathew looks up at the immense light-reddish sky with clouds so high up they are barely visible. "One hundred fifty kilometers of atmosphere above us, huh…?"

"Yes…"

He looks down at the ground to see a dark red mass beneath his feet, swirling eddies of matter in black and dark blue; a long drop if there were nothing directly underneath him. "Sixty kilometers of emptiness below us…"

"That's about the size of it," she remarks, half hanging on his arm.

He looks straight ahead, shakes his head, and then looks at her. "So, how do we get there?"

She looks out on the expanse of the massive metropolis before them. "We look for the folks in the green jackets. They sell boarding passes to people to travel on the rails."

It takes them almost no time to find one, and soon they are boarding a long railcar to Dauverzleigh; Rosetta's birthplace.

"Are your parents here," he asks while the train is in motion.

"Yeah. They still live here. I try to come visit them once a year. I didn't make it last year…"

"What do they think of your work…?"

"They don't like it. They think I should find something else to do."

"You did…"

"I know. I want them to meet you and then I want to tell them I quit bounty-hunting… They'll absolutely fall apart." At this, she laughs.

"What…?"

"I was just thinking about how the last time I was here my mom said something like that… She said, 'If you ever find a nice young man to settle down with and quit bounty-hunting, I'll absolutely fall apart…"

"I'm not so sure I want to see your parents in little pieces on the ground… I might feel a bit awkward trying to introduce myself."

*****

Agoparn and Captain Ardelle arrive at the small station where the world-round rails pick up tourists and deliver them all over the globe. Agoparn has been consistently shocked and amazed at all the technological wonders of the planet thus far, and anticipates the rail ride with the enthusiasm of a child on his birthday.

It is not long before railcar number forty-eight six eighty-two is carrying them both far away from the metropolis and whisking them toward the northern resort more than fourteen thousand kilometers away. At a rate of three thousand kilometers an hour, the ride is not nearly as long as he would have hoped, as the two have an entire one meter by two meter room to relax in and talk. The talking is short-lived, however, and soon they become embroiled in each other's arms hugging and kissing.

The ride is over far too soon for either of them and they make their way out of the railcar and into an open stretch of gardens, glass ponds, and small buildings with people walking around in silver robes, or sitting out in long stretch chairs enjoying the afternoon sunshine from Allcauri IV.

"It's amazing," he says in awe.

"Yes. That's what you've said about everything else so far." She smiles at him.

"I meant every bit of it," he replies, almost in a stupor.

She pulls his arm forward. "Come on. Let's go get checked in."

They walk quietly and unhurriedly forward down the steps into the long stretch of the sunken grounds where the gardens are placed in nice rows and columns. Unique and wild plants surround them in potting pools which run about three meters wide and ten meters long. At each break, small topless gazebos with beautifully carved columns extend upward to about five meters high. They walk down the center toward the pool, and Ardelle talks him into wading through it on their way across the platforms. She assures him the walk to the lobby is plenty time-consuming and he will dry off long before they reach it.

*****

Lacendu looks through shops along the east side of the metropolis outside the main doors of the station, oblivious to the people around her. She is much more entertained by the trinkets, jewelry, and clothing of the area. Thus, she is completely caught off guard when an older woman, probably in her early seventies, confronts her.

"Hello, young lady," the woman says with a somewhat haphazard smile.

"Hi," Lacendu replies innocently almost without paying attention.

"You look like the picture of my granddaughter," the woman says looking squarely at her.

Lacendu is taken aback and decides to go with it. "Really…? Where does your daughter live?"

"Oh, last I heard she lived with her parents in Quadrant One."

"That's where I'm from," Lacendu says, thinking little of it.

"What brings you to Ascension City, dear one," the woman asks.

"Well, some traveling companions and I are heading back there. We had to take a journey to Quadrant Four a few months ago, and now we're on our way home."

"That's wonderful," she says. "Do you have a boyfriend, or anything?"

"I'm married."

"Oh."

"What is your son's name," Lacendu inquires.

"Actually, it's my daughter, and her name is Phaylene Armausta. She married a nice young man a couple decades ago. I don't remember his name."

"Have you met your granddaughter?"

"No, I haven't," the woman says with some sadness looking at the ground.

"How about I play your granddaughter for the day and you can show me around Ascension City…?"

"Oh, that would be wonderful," the woman responds with joy. "Perhaps later you can come over to my place for some food and drink and I can show you pictures of my granddaughter and her family."

"I would like that very much," Lacendu states with a grin. "Shall we?" She points her head in the general direction she had been going earlier and the two walk down the walkway looking at shops.

*****

Korsaume and Allen walk quietly, not saying much to each other. If at all, most often it is a remark to laud the builders of the metropolis. They don't even touch each other, and Allen has been keeping his questions about her actions to himself.

Finally, he decides to say something, but after having thought about it for nearly an hour, he is still unsure of what to say to her.

"So…"

"What…?"

"What made you decide to hang out with me?" He smiles at her, a bit sheepish.

She knows why he asks. She is not entirely certain of the reason herself. She notices her face is wrinkled a little as she looks back at him, but does not try to hide the questioning look, deciding instead to keep it in case she realizes something else later. "I suppose I needed someone to hang out with…someone to talk to."

"Everyone needs a friend, Korsaume."

"I know."

"You've acted like the most friendless person in the galaxy since…" He is not sure if this is coming out right. "Um…"

She stops suddenly, causing him to stop and take a few steps back to face her.

"I'm sorry. That didn't come out right."

"No." It's not in answer to his statement. "No…" She says again, pausing and shaking her head, thinking. She looks up at him and gives her peculiar half-smile. "You're right. I've acted like a real witch since we awoke on the 'Vibrant.'"

"You've really warmed up since I got the chance to know you; what with all we've been through in the past however many weeks it's been, now."

"Seven."

"Seven weeks, then… OK. We've been through a lot. You've remained something of a mystery. You never open up."

She smiles at him. "How surprised you'd be if you'd heard some of the conversations our Captain and I have had."

"No doubt," he retorts.

The two almost simultaneously begin walking again in their previous direction, hardly noticing the people that are going around them as they walk slowly.

"What would you like to know about me, Allen?"

"Well, for starters, tell me about your life."

"There's not a whole lot to tell, Allen. My parents were upper-Echelon leaders in the Sharcuran Knights. As far as I know, they still are."

"Both of them…?" he asks. She nods, and he continues. "What are the Sharcuran Knights?"

"Think the old Secret Service, or maybe the Knights of the Round Table; or even the Templar Knights. They fight all the secret battles for the Solar Union, apart from the Solar Union. They're their own entity, and their own law… After I was born, I was raised by them in a military fashion, and the Solar Union already had dibs on the rest of my life after I finished school. At the age of ten, I was taken against my will and forced to live under the CHE, and learn their rules; their language.

"I was trained in every fighting technique available and knowable. They taught me to kill. When I graduated from the CHE School of Procedural Tactics, I could take apart any mechanical weapon and put it back together in a matter of moments. I could fight with any weapon on me, and even devise ways to utilize anything in my surroundings as a weapon. Killing was all I could do, and when the CHE ordered me to kill, that's what I went and did. I did it until about ten weeks ago.

"I've assassinated presidents, world leaders, and high ranking members of underground and secret societies. I've killed 'Well-Knowns' and unknowns, debtors, laymen, and slaves. I've been party to mass murders. You name it; I've done it … if it involves the death of anyone who did anything against the CHE. It was my job, and it was all I knew."

Allen hides well that fact that he is a bit shaken at this information. "That's why you told us that you were not allowed to know your prey on a personal level; that you might not be willing to do your job…"

"Yes. We were given orders and were taught that any order given meant the surety that those in our sites were worthy of death, and that anyone protecting them was as worthy, or more so, for trying to stop us from doing our job."

"Then you got to know us…"

"Yeah." She nods her head and smiles at him with her face still mostly toward the ground. "I don't think five people without their memory could be knowingly responsible for something they did before they lost their memory. I don't know what all transpired before I came to do my job; but if all the stuff we've learned so far is any clue you five are the least worthy of death than anyone I've ever met."

"I'll..." He clears his throat. "...take that as a compliment."

"You should. I don't give out compliments for free, you know..."

"...You mean I have to pay for it?"

"No. I mean you've earned it."

*****

The entry to the city of Dauverzleigh is astoundingly beautiful and the designs of the buildings, mostly of textured, colored glass-like substances, are intricate and delicate; completely artificial and gratuitous, but simultaneously grandiose.

The streets are wide and full of walking people. The buildings' doors are held open and patrons walk in and out in endless streams like rushing rivers.

After the railcar stops at the station, Mathew and Rosetta step off amid the crowd of passengers, both boarding and debarking. Mathew particularly feels engulfed and insignificant.

She grabs his hand and pulls him behind her through the traffic and they somehow manage to make a quick path to the outskirts of the throng.

Against the cacophony of the people speaking over each other, Rosetta turns to him, her face close to his. "My parents live up there." She points to a rather tall building, a skyscraper over a hundred stories high. The lower portion is hidden by the other buildings surrounding them, each at least six stories, and many closer to twenty or more.

Mathew at first estimates the building to be a block or so away, but soon realizes as they come around a corner and see the length of the road ahead of them that it is nearly two kilometers distant.

Soon, the two are away from the masses enough to walk side-by-side and he puts his arm around her shoulders and she her left arm around his middle. They chat and laugh on their way, passing the time to the large skyscraper with each other, and hardly noticing the time it takes them to get to the main doors.

"Doors" is actually a limited word in this case, as the entryway is open to the outside, and the archway is nearly six meters wide and three high. The inside hall is well over three times that, and golden-hued architecture is layered, covering the structural beams and walls.

They walk up the majestic stairway and through the hall into the main room. As they stroll across the half-kilometer of floor space with royal red, gold, and silver interlaced carpet, they are occasionally met with looks, stares, and smiles by people Rosetta recognizes, but whose names she does not remember.

Moments later they are on an elevator to the eighty-third floor where her parents live in one of the many plush condominiums.

Nearly a half hour after exiting the train they arrive at the door of her parents' home and Rosetta rings the buzzer.

They wait a long while for someone to come to the door, and as it opens, a smile swells on Rosetta's lips showing teeth, and the face of her mother is quickly revealed behind the large metal door.

"Seta!" her mother almost shouts reaching her arms out and taking a couple steps forward. She is met by Rosetta's own arms and the two embrace. "Oh, my girl… My little girl came home once again." Their bodies separate, but their arms remain in a semblance of the hug as the mother looks Rosetta over. "You look none the worse for wear, dear."

"You're looking really good, too, Mum."

They release each other and the mother ushers them in. "So, who's this nice young gentleman you've brought with you? …and may I say it's about time."

"Mum, this is Captain Mathew Arnold of the starship Saiar Ria Contract."

Mathew holds out his hand.

"Oh, there'll be none of that in this house," the mother says. She grabs him in a hug and he follows suit.

As she releases him, she motions them through the somewhat large foyer into a sunken living room where two large, long, plush couches round the edges' circumferences sit with a low but wide table made of pure silvered glass. "Have a seat. There will be no formalities here. If you're hungry or thirsty, say so and the servant will be more than happy to oblige. I'll be right back with my husband."

Mathew looks over at her. "Servant…?"

"Oh. My apologies, Sweetie… They pay servants here very well. They're not slave labor, like the 'agrauves,' or anything."

"Good," he says. He leans back into the comfortable sofa and almost instantly feels the sofa filling up any empty space around his body. It's a bizarre feeling like lying down in putty, but he rapidly grows accustomed to the feeling and almost instantly finds himself drifting to sleep. He cannot help it, and within a moment he is out.

*****

It is near nightfall when Agoparn and Ardelle finish checking in. They are each assigned a small space for sleeping and changing clothes. They are also given thin silvery robes, bags with some personal hygiene items, and directly encouraged to spend the night under the stars.

Ardelle explains that at nightfall, all the lights which would illumine outside go out, and the stars are bright and romantic.

The two place the bags they were given in their six-by-ten "rooms" with a small, one-person bed in each, and a nightstand with a reading lamp, and enough room in the drawers for the items, and proceed to get into their robes. The "rooms" are very little that at all. They are pillared at the corners, and drapes which hang down to the ground provide the "walls." The drapes are thin, but cannot be seen through, though the sun- and starlight is reflected into the room through them, providing natural lighting. The starlight at night is dim and soothing; a light violet color which seems to hasten and enhance sleep.

They pull back the curtain between their rooms and open the back drapes to the reflective pool in all its pure, calm beauty. There are partitions between the individual rooms' backs with steps leading down to the edge of the pool, and the two of them sit down on the steps behind Ardelle's room, their arms around each other, and their heads leaning together in the gentle wind which sweeps across the water cooling them to a relaxing temperature.

"Mmmm," Ardelle groans. "Could it be any more perfect?"

"Perfect doesn't begin to describe it," Agoparn replies in his softest voice.

It is quiet with the exception of an occasional flying creature which seems to have found this place as wonderful a place to stay as the two of them. It flies across the open sky from one side of the pond toward the other distant side, and after a few minutes, returns again, seemingly looking for just the right place to land.

"What are you thinking," asks Agoparn.

She grins, though he cannot see it, and answers, "I was thinking this was the best idea I ever had."

"You've been here before..."

"Yes, but not with someone... At least not with anyone I cared about until now."

Agoparn's chest heaves lightly once in a laugh; not at her, but at her charm. "Well, I'm glad you care about me."

"Parn," she whispers, and then is silent for a few seconds. Her voice becomes a little louder, but not by much. "Parn, I want to go with you."

"You have no idea what we're up against."

She pulls her head away from him suddenly and looks at him, as he in turn looks at her. "What...? Are you in trouble with the Solar Union?"

"Something like that…"

"What did you do?" A dour look envelops her face…

"Well, first we wouldn't go along with their plans for us, and then we wouldn't lie down and die for them…"

She smirks. "Are you teasing me?"

He shakes his head and looks at her with an innocent grin. "No. We were asked to do something for them, and we agreed among each other that it wasn't the right thing, so they decided to get rid of us. After someone helped us escape to this side of the galaxy, the Solar Union sent the CHE after us to kill us, and we managed to escape them and strand them temporarily on a planet. I'm sure they're working hard to find us."

"What did they ask you all to do?" she asks.

"Well, we're all still fuzzy on the details, but basically they wanted us to be a part of a war, or start one, or something like that. All we really know is that it has to do with a war."

She looks even more confused. "What do you mean, 'you're fuzzy on the details?'"

"Um, well; our life's memories were erased. At least, everything that had to do with who we are and where we came from. The knowledge of our specialties remained intact. I don't claim to know how they did it, but, well…they did."

"So, you don't know anything about who you were?"

"Not before about six or seven weeks ago…"

She pulls her arms away from him and moves over a little, and then clears her throat. "So, you could be married."

He looks at her with some shock. "Oh, no, no…" he states. "Rosetta found some data on us and it turns out only one of us was married, and that was Lacendu. She was married to a fairly high-ranking Solar Union official."

"What about a girlfriend," she asks.

He takes a few glances down at the ground, and then back at her face which is turned away from him. "Well, I, uh… I had one, but evidently she didn't care much for me. Everyone else's friends and loved ones started campaigns to find them. My 'girlfriend' ran off and got married." He clasps his hands together in front of him and bows his head.

She sighs deep. "I'm sorry. I didn't mean to ruin the moment we had."

"No, that's OK. I started it."

"Yeah, but you meant it to be romantic, and I had to go and ask a bunch of questions…" She shakes her head in frustration.

"It's alright. You should know all of that if we're going to be involved with each other."

She sits quietly by herself; then places her left hand on his right shoulder. "Maybe we should get some rest. We can talk more in the morning. It's a wonderful night for sleep." She smiles, rolling her head down closer to her chest as if trying to look at his bowed face.

"Yes, I suppose it is." He lifts his head and looks up at the night sky. "It is definitely a beautiful night."

The stars shimmer and twinkle in a reddish glow evoking feelings of deep warmth within him, and although the moment with his girlfriend has passed; he hopes only temporarily; he stands up and reaches his hand down to her to help her to her feet. She accepts and stands up and the two lie down in their respective beds with the drape still open between them, and the backs still open for the gentle breeze to blow in, and they are both sound asleep in moments.

*****

Lacendu and the older woman whom she has come to know as Srulé arrive at the woman's home after a few pleasant hours of looking at shops. As the sun began to set, the two made their way to Srulé's home not far from the center of the metropolis.

The woman closes the door behind them and as she does so, the lights come on in the house. The main entry room, something equivalent to a living room, has a vaulted ceiling with curved walls. The archways to other rooms are high, wide, and rounded on the top. There is a huge sofa to the left of center, and directly in the center is a holographic projection screen for entertainment.

Hanging throughout the places she can see immediately are strands of some type of metal coil shavings which Srulé refers to as "hamunimungs." They glow in the dark with an aural effect between each other, and when the woman has the in-home computer turn the lights off for a moment, the auroras are so amazing that Lacendu can only stare in awe.

"How do they do that?" she wonders aloud to herself with a stunned hanging of her jaw.

"They're magnetic lightings which project toward each other. The fact that they're coiled makes the light between them give off an aurora effect."

Lacendu shakes her head in amazement as Srulé tells the computer to turn the lights back on. So, the young blonde relegates her mind back to the room.

"Here," the woman says walking toward a rounded dresser that fits snuggly up against the concave wall. On it are a small chest and a holographic picture album between two large golden candle-holders with large white candles in them. The woman lights the candles with a fire-stick and places it back in its holder.

Lacendu walks over to the dresser as the woman picks up the picture album. It begins cycling through the images it has stored, and there before them are pictures of a blonde-haired girl who could easily be Lacendu at an earlier age.

The woman smiles in reflective thought. "The last time my daughter and son-in-law sent me anything, they included a card with these images in it. That was only five short years ago. There's about fourteen years worth of images in this, and you can see my granddaughter grow up right before your eyes."

...And they do. The pictures show the young lady growing up, with people surrounding her like friends, family, and acquaintances.

About half-way through the show, the woman says, "I received a letter from them about a year ago stating that my granddaughter was a teacher of mathematics on some important planet, and that she was getting ready to get married to a nice young politician."

Lacendu instantly loses her breath and her eyes widen in shock. She looks at the revolving pictures in front of her, and a sight catches her eyes; that of the young blonde-haired girl on a stage receiving her diploma. The scene seems familiar to her; too much so; and Lacendu passes out on the floor.

*****

Allen and Korsaume walk through the hall of the hotel where the crew's sleeping quarters have been arranged by Ardelle. Korsaume knocks on the door to the women's room and Vaskette opens it moments later dressed in a blue silk robe. Her eyes are drooping and she blinks several times as she half-heartedly tells them to come in and turns away to lie down.

"Are you alright?" Korsaume asks of the doctor.

She breathes in loudly, but the noise is unintentional. "I'm so tired." Then she yawns. "What've you two been up to?"

"Just walking around the city," is Korsaume's polite but curt response.

Vaskette smiles in their general direction. "Sure." She slips into the bed and pulls the cover over her breast, holding it with her right hand over her heart, and props her head up on her left hand, the elbow of which is pressed into her pillow.

"Have you heard from Lacendu?" Korsaume inquires.

"Or anyone else, for that matter," Allen adds.

"Nope… I've been asleep since I got here. I don't know why I'm so tired."

"We've all been through a lot in the past several weeks," Allen states unnecessarily, "so this time to relax is what we all really needed, and we'll each take it in the manner that best suits us. For you, it's probably sleep."

Vaskette rolls her eyes and lays her head on the pillow facing up at the ceiling. Her eyes are soon shut and she drifts off to sleep.

Korsaume looks over at Allen and gestures for him to move with her to the room across from the beds. They both stand up and quietly remove into the other room and sit at the table next to the kitchenette. The light in the kitchenette is on, and the game/exercise area next to them is dark.

Allen sits back in the seat and places his hands on the table in front of him.

Korsaume leans forward onto the table and looks down at her hands, looking at his from the top of her vision, but without his noticing she hopes. "I enjoyed having a friend today, Allen."

"Korsaume," he responds, "it was great to have you as my friend today, too."

She looks up at him. "It doesn't have to end today, you know…"

"Oh…?" He nods his head in understanding. "Well, then, I hope we can be friends for a very long time."

She looks off to her right closing her eyes, uncertain of what to say next.

"What did you think about that monastery we toured…?"

Her eyes dart upward, but still in the same direction away from him and she breathes in contemplating. Finally, she looks directly at him and answers, "I thought it was unique and intriguing. I can't say I've ever liked monasteries or cathedrals much. They always made me feel uncomfortable. I guess it's because those kinds of places are known for repentance, and my job required too many sins to be committed."

His eyebrows raise and he cocks his head at her. "So, there is something you're scared of…"

"Look," she responds with a shake of her head and a short, silent laugh, "I admit that I don't like going into those places, but it's not because I'm afraid of them. I just feel uncomfortable; like I don't belong there. However, this one was different and I found the design thoroughly refreshing when compared to some of the other ones I've been in."

"I really liked the water fountain in the main sanctuary. It didn't look like the others I've seen."

"Remember, too, that it..." She stops and looks at him in suprise, and then away from him.

"What...?"

"You remembered something like that?" she asks looking him square in the eyes.

He pauses a second and thinks. "You mean fountains in the main sanctuary...? Is that unusual?"

"Yes."

He ponders that for a long moment. "You mean that I wouldn't remember something like that if my memory were completely erased...? Is that what you're saying...?"

"Well, I can't say for certain," she says, "but it would seem to me that if you could remember that many churches have water fountains; something that's not normally in a strategist's repertoire; it could be plausible that you actually are remembering something..."

He thinks about it. "Why wouldn't you think it wouldn't be in a strategist's repertoire...?"

"Well, think about it," she answers, thinking quickly, "when you first awoke on the 'Vibrant' you stated you remembered something about a game of chess. So, let me ask you something... What are the pieces on a chess board...?"

He looks away for a second, then back to her. "King, Queen, bishops, knights, rooks, and pawns..."

"What are the standard colors," she asks.

He doesn't give it a second thought. "Black and white..."

"How does each piece move...?"

"Well, the king can only move one space at a time; the queen any direction as far as she wants; the bishops diagonally as far as they want, the rooks forward and sideways as far as they want; knights forward or backward two steps and sideways one, or visa-versa; and the pawns can move only one space unidirectionally, except for their first turn, and only forward except when taking an enemy."

"Here's the kicker," Korsaume adds. "What is the most common element chess pieces are made out of…?"

"Well, they…" He stops short, looks at various spots on the table, opens his mouth to answer, and cannot. "I… I know I should know something like that…"

"What's the classic element used to make chess pieces," Korsaume asks. "That might be easier."

"I honestly can't think of it…" He looks at her. "I don't get it. Why can't I remember that…?"

"Your strategy skills do not necessitate the need to remember what everything's made out of," she answers.

"Yes, Vaskette and I had a similar discussion on Ablose."

"So, you see the possible importance of you remembering something like a water fountain in a sanctuary. Were you an avid church-goer?" Korsaume is almost excited, now.

"As far as I got through that information Rosetta obtained about us, I didn't see anything in there regarding it, but I can't exclude or negate the possibility…"

"Ultimately, it doesn't matter, anyway. Even if you were not, the fact that you could remember something like that might suggest your memories aren't completely erased."

"…Just like the Captain was saying a few weeks ago, right before we discovered those Raider vessels heading our direction…" He has a look of almost fond memory.

"Yes. I think there's more to what the Captain said than even he realizes. My guess is that the Solar Union, or whoever did this to all of you, did not erase your memories, but instead blocked the ones your abilities wouldn't need, so that you wouldn't have your life's history to draw from in making your decisions."

He looks up at her. "In other words, we would have followed blindly."

"Then, when you needed your memories restored they could give you an un-inhibitor of some kind to free your past memories for whatever purpose you or they might need them for…"

"If you're correct about this, then it's possible that all of us could be starting to get our memories back naturally," he says. "I wonder if Vaskette can obtain some information on this kind of stuff somehow."

"I'll speak with her about it first thing in the morning. Let's get some sleep."

"Good idea," he says standing up. "I'm pretty tired myself."

He walks out the main door into the hallway and goes to the men's quarters using his pass key to get in.

Korsaume exits the building and walks the streets of the metropolis once again. It is close to the midway point between dusk and dawn, and she is not even close to sleepy. Her mind is going non-stop as she makes her way to the Venotronic stations.

Arriving at the main office she walks through the doors, which are now shut, but not locked. A man stationed as guard holds up his hand. "Excuse me, miss. I need to see your pass card, please."

She holds up her right wrist for him to scan. After he scans it he immediately steps out of her way. "My apologies," he states with a simple bow and a gesture for her to continue.

She enters the Venotronic terminal and dials the number she remembers by heart. Her credentials got her in and even prioritized her call.

The call goes through to Baitronoc, the Solar Union symbol is displayed, and after a few minutes, the man she last saw about six weeks ago stands before her once again.

"Sherise," he states with a sour note in his voice, "or shall I call you Korsaume, again. Did you finally decide to do your job?"

"Well, sir," she begins, "actually I wanted to let you know that their memories seem to be returning."

"If those memories return, they'll…"

"I'm not worried about it. They already know I was going to kill them."

"Interesting… So you told them, did you?" At an affirmative answer from her, she continues, "…And what did they have to say about that…?"

"At first they were all upset at me. One still seems to hold a grudge, since I tried to kill her after our last discussion."

"So, if you haven't completed your mission, why are you calling me?"

She looks directly at his face. "Sir, first, you should know that they're headed back to Quadrant One, and they have some ideas on how to get there sooner than later."

"What else?"

"That they're allowing me to come with them."

"Your plan all along, wasn't it… To deliver them into my hands…?"

"Actually, Sir, there's a third thing I need to tell you."

"What's that…?"

She smiles at him. "I'm coming for you. As for the CHE…I quit."

Episode 12
Dreams and Shadows

OPENING:

"Somewhere between the center of the galaxy and the last star on the longest spiral arm; the farthest edge of the same; humans lost their humanity. We've fought so long and hard to keep ourselves upright that we no longer remember how to lie down. So instead, unrest rules us, and we find ourselves in the midst of unnatural hatred and fear. It's a common dilemma found in those who lose sleep at night; they become irritable and restless and only sleep can heal them. Will humanity ever realize this and put distance between their dreams, goals and visions, and the simplicity of life? I quote, 'Beware the inner darkness…'" – Li Monscane, Contemplation on the Crisis of Man, page 368, chapter 15

Doctor Vaskette Smith stands over her troubled friend. Two days ago Lacendu fell into unconsciousness at the home of a woman who, as it turns out, is her grandmother.

Korsaume and Allen had been near enough to be present when the nurses toted Lacendu into the hotel per Vaskette's instructions. Vaskette, being the patient's officially recognized doctor, had immediately taken charge of the entire procedure. Her first goal was to check on the baby, which it turns out is just fine, to her relief.

Mathew and Rosetta arrived only a few short minutes ago.

"Were you able to get in contact with Agoparn and Ardelle," Mathew asks as he enters the hotel room and notices the two are not present.

"We left a message with the office there," Allen answers, keeping his eyes on Lacendu, "but it's a vast complex. They said it could be a couple of days before they receive the message."

"There's something worse than all this, though," Korsaume states.

Everyone glances at her.

"We're going to have some visitors who want to retain us for pick-up by the CHE," she continues.

"You mean your friends made it here, too," Rosetta asks.

"Not quite," Korsaume says. "I called my old boss at the CHE and quit."

Mathew looks at her with a bit of discomfort. "You couldn't have waited until we were leaving the planet to do that…?"

"Well, at the time it seemed like a good idea," she replies, not hiding her disgust. "Besides, Captain, I didn't know that Lacendu was in a coma, either."

"Wait," Vaskette says, "Isn't your old boss on the other side of the Galaxy?" She doesn't wait for a response. "How could you contact him if he's way over there?"

Korsaume sighs. "Venotronic terminals have built-in light-drive coilers. They send data at thirty times light-speed. With certain types of access cards, those coilers are activated and the transfer rates move to light-speed-times-thirty making communications with the opposite side of the galaxy near-instantaneous."

"Why didn't you tell us this sooner?" asks Vaskette.

"It never came up…" is the response.

"As much as I hate to break your banter up, Captain and Lieutenant, how was your trip, Captain and Rosetta," Allen inquires.

"It was nice," Mathew says, smiling at his girlfriend.

"My parents are proud of me for hopping off the bounty-hunting game, and they absolutely adore Mathew." Rosetta smiles broadly and wraps her right arm around him, and he his left around her.

Allen gives them a fast squinty look that hints at a smile. "You can tell your parents they can't have him. We got dibs on him."

"I'll do that," Rosetta nods at him.

Korsaume folds her arms in a huff. "Am I the only one in this room concerned with the fact that we're all about to be under house arrest and jailed; maybe even killed?"

"I'm concerned," Vaskette says, leaning over her patient and placing her closed mouth on Lacendu's forehead. "That would make it exceedingly difficult to take care of my best friend."

The room goes silent.

Mathew finally speaks up. "Chances are good that they're not going to let us off this planet regardless. So, if anyone has options on getting back to our ship without causing chaos and killing, I'm in the market for them."

From the kitchenette and game room area an older woman enters the bed room. She walks carefully and shyly. "I might have a suggestion."

"Who are you," Mathew asks.

"I'm Srulé; Lacendu's grandmother."

"Oh," Mathew and Rosetta say in unison, staring in a bit of shock.

The woman continues. "As much as I'd like to keep my granddaughter here, the CHE isn't known for leaving their prey alive; and I can't let that happen to my granddaughter. Before I tell you how, though, I want to know why. Why is the CHE after her?"

Mathew clears his throat. "It turns out that we were to be part of a war the Solar Union was starting. They wanted us to do some things we didn't agree with and we refused. So they had our memories wiped with plans to start over with us. A CHE member was sent to kill us, and she was stopped by a man who sent us through a tesseract to Quadrant Four. We're on our way back to stop the people who did this to us."

Srulé looks at Mathew with some distrust. "Dear Sir; that sounds far-fetched."

"Trust me, Miss," he says, "It sounded far-fetched to us as well, but without our past memories, we have no reason not to believe."

"About that, Captain," Allen says tapping Korsaume's right arm with the back of his left hand.

"Oh, yes," Korsaume begins. "Do you remember when you were discussing with us about your memory at the name of the establishment on the orbital station around Straite-mogue?"

"You mean right before we began tracking the Raiders, which ended up being our current ship…?" Mathew pulls back the left side of his mouth in obvious contempt.

"That's the incident I was referring to, Sir. Anyway, I caught something Allen was saying a couple days ago about something he 'remembered.' It was something so simple, but piecing the clues together rather quickly I realized he hadn't been near a church establishment since I'd known him until the other day when he and I were walking around."

"What was it he 'remembered' about a church establishment?" asks Rosetta.

"…Fountains in the main sanctuary."

"I think that would fall under the header of 'common knowledge,' Korsaume," Vaskette says facetiously looking her way, but not at her.

"I don't think so, Doctor," Korsaume states. "Think about it. That might be a piece of information a priest would need, but I wonder if Mathew, Agoparn, or Lacendu remember something like that…?"

"To be honest," Mathew says, "I hadn't really thought about it, but now that you mentioned it, it seems like I knew it all along."

Vaskette shakes her head and sits down in the chair behind her to look at her friends. "What you're talking about is a concept called 'association.' It's common in people who develop amnesia, as well as those who intentionally subconsciously forget tragic events in their past. The pieces in the puzzle are there; it's just that the pieces are turned over. In order to rediscover that information, something has to cause them to turn that piece over, like a game of 'memory.'"

"So, what you're saying is this kind of thing is simply explained away," Korsaume asks with delicate force.

"Not exactly, Tactician. What I am saying is that we don't have amnesia or self-causative memory barriers, or anything like those. Chrinsole said our memories were erased. Anything we associated with our abilities as doctor, mathematician, pilot, strategist, or engineer, respectively, and no matter how simplistic they might seem to us, would still be in our memory; even if they are in obscurity. What you're describing would mean our memories were inhibited…not erased."

"Is that not possible…?" Korsaume asks.

"I'm not currently aware of any technology that could erase specific memories, nor inhibit them; but then I'm only a doctor, not a neurologist."

"Yet, here we all are," Allen says, opening his arms out as a gesture to everyone present. "Our memories **are** inhibited, or erased, or whatever… Obviously, your technical knowledge stops somewhere between doctor and neurologist. I'm not implying by that anything more than that you have your specialty, as we all do, and neurology isn't on any of our lists, either. So, if you could be wrong, then let's assume for the sake of argument that Korsaume is right and our memories are inhibited, as you suggested she was saying, and not erased. That would mean that either Chrinsole lied, or didn't know the facts."

Vaskette looks annoyed. "Yes," she sighs.

"Then, is there a way to search for inhibitors in our brains," Mathew asks.

"Inhibitors exist for every function of the human body in every place including the brain. The problem is I'd have to know what I was looking for because things that inhibit memories in our brains exist naturally. It's how we shut off memories in certain cases, or remember things from when we were children that we've long since forgotten. It comes back to that word I used earlier; '…association.' Since I'm not aware of how inhibitors would be placed in our brains in patterns that would cause us to forget our previous lives only, and not our knowledge, it could take years."

"Oh," Korsaume says looking sad.

Vaskette looks frustrated, and suddenly she throws the device she has in her hand down on the ground, stands up and walks out of the hotel room, slamming the door behind her.

Korsaume sighs. "I was just trying to help."

"It's not you, Lieutenant," Rosetta says in an attempt to help. "Her best friend is lying unconscious… We weren't exactly facilitating her work with our questions."

"Let her go for a few minutes. She'll be back," Mathew states. "As for that assistance;" and at this he turns to Srulé, "what can you do for us…?"

Mathew and Rosetta take chairs nearby.

Srulé sits on the bed next to her granddaughter. "Have you ever heard of a group called 'Nation'?"

Everyone looks at each other.

"I haven't heard that name since we first came to this side of the galaxy," Mathew says.

"Their headquarters are here…"

"How could you possibly know that," Rosetta asks. "They're the most secretive group in the third and fourth quadrant. I doubt very much that the Solar Union even has that kind of information on them."

Srulé smirks at Rosetta. "Dear one, I work for them."

Everyone's eyes widen with uncertainty.

"If you want to get out of this alive, you'll need to trust me…"

Rosetta glares at the woman. "Trust you…? You're a member of a secretive under-government for half the galaxy, doing what you will, going where you choose, and with no regard for the underpinnings of our society and you want us to put our faith in you…? You have a lot of gall, Lady."

"Well, Rosetta, you're actually the only one present who knows enough about our organization to make even those remarks; even if they are wrong. However, I assure you, I have my granddaughter's best interests at heart, regardless of what my leaders think."

"So, why did your man give me the information on Strager Fortune?"

Srulé smiles and nods at her questioner. "That's simple, deary. He was hunting for Sherise, and we weren't quite ready for her to end her journey with the crew. We figured if we could keep him from finding her, we would have a better chance of keeping the rest of them alive. All the more reason to make sure you found him first. When our man found out Mathew was kind of sweet on you, he took it upon himself to give you the information, and the money. Count it a bonus."

"So," Mathew says interruptively, "If you're really a member of this underground organization, how is it that you don't know who we are or what we're about?"

"Actually, I asked because I wanted to find out what you know. However, you should know that the longer we stay here, the higher the risk of the CHE discovering your whereabouts and we can't have that…" The woman pulls out a small metal object and presses a button.

Korsaume looks at it, and recognizes it immediately.

"Mathew," she says, "Didn't I see you with one of those in your hands when we first awoke on the 'Vibrant?'"

"Yes," Mathew states. "I had no idea what it was, but I've still got it. It's in my pocket." He pulls it out and looks at it.

"What is it," Allen asks.

Srulé laughs. "That one is probably the one Chrinsole gave you folks. He probably half-expected you to push the button. It's a tracking device … undetectable unless you have the exact signal output and are scanning for it."

"You know Chrinsole, as well…?" Korsaume asks upset.

"I know him very well. He is a great man," she replies. "You'll be interested to know, though, that he is the man responsible for creating 'Nation.'"

*****

Lacendu's mind has effectively shut itself down. Basic necessities like breathing and her heartbeat remain active, but for the most part she is completely unconscious. Oddly, though, thoughts are occurring. They are in the very back of her mind, and she is scared…actually, maybe more nervous.

Lacendu's eyes open, but close almost immediately. She is not sure what she saw, but it is dark above her and light below her. With her eyes closed, the light below her does not register against her eyelids.

She senses she is seated in a chair, and grips the sides under the seat, which is warm against her hands.

She feels nervous about opening her eyes, but she finally makes herself do it, and what she sees seems justifiable in her mind.

Above her is a vaulted rock ceiling as if she were in a cave. Her nervousness disappears as she looks at it, easily forty meters above her head.

She smiles at the calm effect the green-lit rocks over her has on her emotions.

Then she looks down…

The lights are coming from two chasms; one on both sides of her; and her chair is positioned on a long, half-meter rock ledge between the two chasms…or perhaps separating them.

Before her the rock ledge extends seemingly endlessly, and the chasm on the right exudes dark blue light while the one on her left gives off a brilliant golden-yellow, tinting the ceiling a light green.

She shutters briefly which causes the chair to fall off to the left. As she senses it, she rolls off the chair onto the rock ledge, stomach first, grasping the sides hard with both hands, as she turns her head to the golden-yellow chasm to see her chair fall out of sight and disappear into nothingness. Her heart pounds hard in her chest.

She looks up at the section of rock wall which had previously been behind her. About sixty meters away the rock ledge opens into a hall-like cave where she assumes whoever placed her here got her in through, and evidently left.

Her mind races to who would do this and where she is, but she can think of no answer.

She debates whether to make for the hall-like cave and decides it would be best. Without looking down she begins pulling herself along the ledge.

About halfway there, a man steps out of the hallway, a gun pointed at her. Behind him is Shivranikka.

"Shivranikka," Lacendu exclaims. "This is your doing…"

"Not quite, dear," the techno-witch states with her quirky smile. "You have this man to thank for your current choices."

She does not recognize the man, but she quickly realizes that it must be Chrinsole. Though she never saw the video file the others did, she knows it must be him.

"I can't let you exit, Lacendu Ruric-Trester," he says. "You have come from the blue chasm; not this hall. Will you choose to go back into the blue, or will you go into the yellow?"

She knows the answer, remembering the chair. She rolls off to her right.

*****

Mid-afternoon is stunning and beautiful for Agoparn and Ardelle who walk hand-in-hand in the general direction of west. The smell of large amounts of meat being cooked over a natural wood fire (part and parcel to their coming to this place) permeates the air around them, wafting into their nostrils; and though they just ate some of it, it still smells wonderful. Air filled with the remnants of a low-hanging cloud nicely offsets the sun shining so brilliantly overhead. The air is slightly cool as they walk away from the fire toward the trains.

They received the message concerning Lacendu about four hours ago, but were unable to make the train between then and now. They had to await the next one, which is scheduled to depart in about a half hour.

"What did the last report say about Lacendu," Ardelle finally asks.

"The note said she was still in a coma," Agoparn replies.

"Who sent it?"

"Vaskette... She says everyone else is at the hotel; including Lacy's grandmother."

Ardelle looks at him in surprise. "Grandmother...?"

"That's what Vaskette said, though I'm not sure how they know that for a fact without a DNA test of some kind, but who am I to say anything...?"

Ardelle laughs lightheartedly at him, thinking about all the things he has told her about his fellow crew and their plans here.

Their laughs quickly turn to blank stares as they watch three military hover-vehicles coming directly toward them about eight meters above the ground.

Ardelle stops Agoparn and steps in front of him with an upset look on her face.

The crafts hover around them, surrounding them in a matter of seconds.

A voice can be heard from the craft in front of them.

"Agoparn Schroet and Captain Ardelle Xysteck; lie down on the ground or we will be forced to use offensive methods."

"What do you want with us," Ardelle asks.

"You are wanted fugitives and you are under arrest."

Ardelle pulls out a device from a pack around her waist, turns to Agoparn and half-whispers, "Get ready to run."

She lifts the object over her head and turns her head back to face the main vessel.

"Bite me," she answers them, pressing the button.

An energy field erupts from the device, outward toward the hover-vehicles. Their systems fail immediately and they fall hard to the ground, shaking everything for kilometers around.

The glass-like surface seems to take some heavy damage, and Ardelle tugs on Agoparn's arm. It is all the motivation he needs as the two of them begin running hard and fast toward a small structure not far away.

When they arrive, Ardelle opens a door into the structure and turns to close it after he enters.

"We're going to have to do something I really didn't want to do, honey," she states.

"What is going on, Ardelle?" He stares at her in disbelief.

"When they were going over my ship before we docked at the orbital station, I was told you were a plausible threat to Galactic security. After spending three days alone with you, I've determined you're definitely not a threat…"

"So you've been spying on me all this time…?" Agoparn seems hurt and frustrated.

"Absolutely not," she replies in a harsh tone. "I was asked to watch you. I was going to do that anyway. Put this on."

As they were conversing, they were walking through the small structure. At a junction, she has pulled two suits off a rack and hands one to Agoparn.

He complies. "What are we doing, now…? Why are we running from the military?"

She laughs at him and answers, "That was no military unit, Agoparn…at least not one from this planet. Those guys were from a group called 'Nation.' I don't trust them as far as I can throw them."

"I've heard of them," he answers, "though, for the life of me I can't think of where…"

"Don't worry. We're going to take a very unsafe, but much faster way back to the hotel."

"…And you're telling me not to worry?"

They put helmets on and they are soon crawling through a duct, down a shaft, and to the underside of the glass about three meters, dangling off of a metal ladder.

"What now," he asks through the suit's two-way communications.

"These things are made to hover by use of the radiation emanating from the core of the planet. They're designed to withstand up to four hours of radiation before the human inside begins to cook. Don't fret, though. If you follow me, we'll be back at the hotel in about three hours and fifty-five minutes."

"I'm, oh, so assured, Ardelle," he says, sounding pathetic.

*****

Srulé sits uncomfortably at the stares from the people surrounding her.

Vaskette enters about that moment, turning the heads of everyone, to the relief of Lacendu's Grandmother.

"Hey, Doctor," Mathew gently says.

She shuts the door a little harder than necessary, probably unintentionally but completely unapologetically, and walks to Lacendu's bedside.

"...Anything exciting go on while I was gone," she asks, nonchalant-as-can-be.

"Not really," Allen remarks. "Are you alright?"

"Fine," she abruptly states.

"So," Korsaume continues, "Srulé, you said Chrinsole created Nation..."

Srulé shakes her head. "No, I said he was the man responsible for creating Nation. He oversaw the conceptual design, and how Nation would develop and work once it came into existence. He did it as a concept with no intention of ever actually creating it unless things went bad. His wife noticed things going bad and actually took his work on the concept and put it into motion here in Ascension City."

"Is Chrinsole still alive?" Korsaume asks.

"Mr. Chrinsole is. His wife died about six months ago."

Mathew looks at her with some concern. "Was that before, or after, he sent us here?"

"That would be before," she answers. "From what little I know, the 'six-people-starting-a-war' thing was part of a Solar Union experiment having to do with the 'brain.'"

"So, we were supposed to start the war..." Mathew places his head in his right hand, right elbow leaning on the arm of the chair, and looks off through the wall beyond the woman.

There is silence for a moment.

"What are you thinking, Captain...?" Korsaume asks.

"Well," he begins, "I'm thinking if we were supposed to start a war..."

"Is this about what you and I discussed last week in your office?"

"Yes." Mathew looks over at his Lieutenant.

"Are you going to clue us in, Captain," Allen asks, a bit perturbed.

Mathew looks at Allen. "I was originally thinking they wanted us to participate in the war and help them win. Now, we find out we were supposed to start it."

"That just makes what we have to do now even worse, then," Korsaume states.

"We," Vaskette asks. "You were not a part of the original six, Korsaume."

"No, but I am now, and don't think for a second you five are going in without me." Korsaume looks more than a little upset at Vaskette.e

"Don't count me out," Rosetta states. She points at Mathew, "I go everywhere he goes, even into the heart of battle..."

"Now, wait," Srulé exclaims, holding up a hand in a stopping gesture, "Who said any of you are going there. Our job is to keep you here."

"I don't think so," Mathew says. "We will not stand idly by while our government pulls off a war we didn't agree was necessary."

"Less necessary, more imminent," Srulé argues. "This was something that was going to happen with our without your help. The Solar Union just wanted to keep things from getting out of control. You six were to start it in a way that would keep the loss of life to a minimum."

"Who said there had to be any loss of life," Vaskette says. "Did the Solar Union ever think about that?"

"How should I know," Srulé asks. "You six were the ones doing this. I had nothing to do with any of it…"

"Then stay out of this," Allen says.

Srulé gives Allen a dirty look, but bows her head in submission.

"Well, regardless of what our plans are, we can't make them without all of us in agreement. That includes two people that aren't with us now…Agoparn and Lacendu." Mathew looks at them each in turn.

"I agree, Captain," Allen nods.

"What then," Srulé asks with little enthusiasm. "Do I take all of you to our headquarters, or do we all sit here and bum around until the CHE gets here?"

"If it weren't for the fact that we're in this mess, I'd say we should sit here and bum around, but our plans don't include 'Nation' if you're not going to back us…" Mathew states matter-of-fact.

"My granddaughter's life is at stake. If I have anything to say about it; and I assure you I do; I will not allow you to put her life in jeopardy!"

"With all due respect, Miss," Vaskette states, "We'll leave that up to the young lady, here."

"As long as she's in this coma, my wishes are to be obeyed. I am her guardian in this case."

"No arguments, Madam, but she won't stay in there for long," Korsaume states. "We've seen what Lacendu's mind is capable of, and if it's any indication she'll be out of it in no time at all."

*****

Agoparn is following closely behind Ardelle. Closely, by these standards, is about six hundred meters. The communications still work, but neither has said a word to the other since they began rocketing forward toward the main city, a distance of fourteen thousand kilometers away. Actually, that's if they were hovering on the surface of the glass. Since they are making a near-straight line, bringing them significantly close to the surface (about three kilometers away), they are really only about nine thousand kilometers away, and at a rate of twenty-four hundred kilometers an hour they are making good time.

Agoparn hears Ardelle in his headset. “Are you still with me, Dear?”

“Yeah…”

“I hope I haven’t hurt you,” she states. “I had no intention of spying for them. They asked me to, but I didn’t think they would come after us, either. I wasn’t spying at all. I really care about you.”

“I’m not concerned with that, Ardelle. I really don’t mind one way or the other, though I’m glad you’re telling me this. Even if you were spying on me, it would probably make our relationship a bit more interesting.”

Ardelle laughs.

“I’m sorry, Ardelle, but my mind is on my companions.”

“No problem, Parn,” she says in a comfortable voice. “We’ll be there shortly.”

*****

Lacendu has been falling through the golden-yellow chasm forever, it would seem. She is no longer frightened. She feels weightless and in a constant state of panic which she has pushed aside since she knows she has no control over ever stopping.

While her mind is certain this can’t be happening, her eyes tell a different story, and at this moment what she sees is real.

The golden-yellow light permeates every fiber of her being, warming her flesh, but chilling her heart. She knows that sooner or later she will land, and while she fears hitting the ground, the warmth comforts her in a way she cannot explain.

She can turn her head enough to see the wall of rock she rolled off of, but when she looks up she can't see the ceiling. She is too far away to see anything above her but golden-yellow, and far too high up to see a place to land.

As she is thinking these thoughts, she sees her chair coming up fairly fast. Not too fast, though, as if she were running toward it; maybe just jogging…

She soon reaches the chair and takes a hold of it, maneuvers into what she believes to be an upright position and tries to sit down in it. This takes a few moments, as the grasp on her chair keeps pulling off at odd moments, but finally she pulls the chair up to her buttocks and suddenly everything goes black. She is no longer in the golden-yellow, nor falling.

A sudden flash of light to the low left makes her realize she is in a room, but the light is all too brief. It flashes again, but this time it stays on.

It is the room she works in on the Saiar Ria Contract, and the flash comes from the floor in the center of the room: a bright blue bubble. Then the top bubble flashes on in a couple of short flickers. The energy stream between them comes to life, flowing rapidly and straight in the space.

She looks around the room and her eyes meet the open door just in time to see Shivranikka walk in with her customary smile. It is at this moment she realizes she is still clasping the bottom of the chair with both hands. She releases them from their grasp and places them in her lap as to try to show more firmness at Shivranikka, otherwise the woman might think her weak.

"So, Dear," Shivranikka begins, "Did you enjoy your fall?"

"I would have enjoyed it more if I could have known I would never see you again," is Lacendu's curt reply.

Shivranikka smirks. "You still don't know what this is, do you…?"

"Not really," Lacendu retorts. "I have a few ideas…"

"You do realize they're all wrong, don't you?"

"No. But since you just told me, I guess I have to come up with another answer."

"Oh, but you already have the answer, Lacy. Hasn't anyone told you, yet?"

"What…?"

"These bubbles were here in this room before I got this ship…"

Lacendu's eyes widen in disbelief. "You must be kidding… You had to have put these here. There's no way they could be that…!"

"Oh, they are, Dear One… They are…" Shivranikka laughs a long, wicked laugh, and then walks out of the room.

*****

Srulé exits the hotel room and walks down the stairs of the hotel having excused her self from the room for a breath of fresh air. When she exits the building she pulls from her dress jacket a small device which she sets over her head. As she does so she pushes a button on it and waits for the call to go through.

"Hello, Srulé," says the voice.

"Hi, Chrinsole. I have met with the majority of the group. Lacendu is in a coma and Agoparn is on his way."

"How is your granddaughter? Is she recovering?"

"She's got the best doctor in the galaxy working on her. I'm sure she'll be fine."

"I sent three enforcer vehicles after Agoparn and his lady friend but Captain Ardelle Xysteck used a 'feather' on them…"

"Where do people get those…?" Srulé half-asks this to her self.

"Irrelevant. When they're all together, I want to transport them to headquarters immediately. Stay with them and let me know when you're ready. I'll have my men take it from there."

"One other thing, Sir," she adds, "They're insistent on heading back to Quadrant One to stop the war…"

There is silence for a few moments.

His voice comes through softly. "This does not bode well…"

*****

"I don't like her," Korsaume states, and then adds, "I don't trust her."

"Do you think she's really Lacendu's grandmother?" Rosetta asks.

Korsaume does not answer, but gives Rosetta a look that says she doesn't know.

"I don't see that that's relevant," Mathew replies, "but I don't trust her, either. I think she's hiding something."

"I'm sure of it," Vaskette says standing up and turning to her patient. She feels Lacendu's forehead with the back of her hand. "I really wish she'd wake up so we could get out of here."

"If it weren't for Agoparn not being present, we'd be out of here with her over my shoulder," Allen says. "In fact, if she's not awake by the time Agoparn gets here, I'll do it anyway."

Vaskette looks at Allen. "I don't have the equipment to move her like that," she says making a face at him.

"She's just asleep," Allen says with naiveté.

"No," Vaskette says with annoyance, "She's in a coma. There's a huge difference. Her mind has shut down."

"Not according to that little device down there," he says. "That little brain thing has been going off the charts for hours…"

Vaskette gives him an odd look, and then looks down at the monitor on the floor. She gets down on the floor on all fours and begins punching buttons. "You're right. How long have you known about this?"

"Um, for hours, I suppose. About three, probably…" Allen looks at her with inquisitive eyes.

Vaskette turns around. "This isn't right. According to this she should be wide awake, or having a horrible nightmare."

Vaskette gets up on her feet and leans over Lacendu. She places a hand on the woman's stomach and pushes side to side for a moment. "Lacendu…"

She pauses a moment to give her friend an opportunity to reply, then she does it all again, repeating this about three or four times.

"I don't get it," Vaskette says sitting down on the edge of the bed.

"What does this mean," asks Korsaume?

"I don't know..." She lays her hands out with open palms and a shrug of her shoulders. "With brain patterns like that she shouldn't be in a coma."

"Then are you sure she's in a coma...?"

"She's not responding to verbal or physical stimuli. Until she does, I have to assume she's in a coma as the readout states, so we're not moving her." Vaskette takes another look at her friend and sighs.

*****

"I'm running out of energy," Agoparn says.

It has been nearly four hours and he has kept an eye on the readout on the side of his helmet off and on since they started off.

"I am, too," Ardelle admits. "Let's make our way up to one of the surface entrances. Slow down to eighty kilometers per minute on my mark..."

"Understood," he replies.

"Mark."

In seconds he can see her within forty meters of his position and he begins closing in on her and following her up to the surface.

He sees her arm pointing upward at a small spot and the two head for it. In minutes the two reach a hatch, just like the one they left from, and climb up the metal ladder.

Inside, the two of them take off the suits and exit through a door in what Ardelle believes to be the back of the building.

"That was different," Agoparn says reluctantly to his girlfriend.

She turns a smile to him, but turns back, grabs his left arm and pulls him along through a throng of people. "We need a ride back."

They hit the street amid thousands of people walking around and finally find what Ardelle is looking for…a taxi.

"Where can I take you two," the slightly-larger woman asks with a half-frown.

"City Main," Ardelle answers and hands the woman a card. "Fast…"

*****

Srulé gets to the hotel room and knocks. She is greeted by Rosetta who makes a grand gesture for the woman to enter. After she enters and Rosetta closes the door and goes to sit down, Srulé stands against a wall near Lacendu's bed listening to the continuing conversation.

Mathew, "…if it were up to me. But until we get there I don't think we should make any more sudden moves."

Korsaume looks at her Captain and replies. "I'm inclined to agree, Captain. There are several good things about our predicament. Only 'Nation' is concerned with us here…not the CHE. The CHE representatives who are trying to track us down don't know we have a new ship, and it's also likely they still don't know we're here, to our advantage… Lastly, we've got a high-class ship that won't make escaping here difficult once Agoparn rejoins us."

"That's assuming he rejoins us," Allen says with a grin. "The lady he's seeing, the Star Axis Captain…she's a looker…"

Everyone but Srulé smiles big…

"I'm confident he'll return to us," Korsaume says, almost as if trying to make herself believe it. "He's our engineer…"

"I'm not so sure," Mathew admits. "He may come back here, but I don't know if it will be to hop back on the Saiar Ria Contract; a ship he barely understands, and which even the rest of us somewhat fear."

"I just don't get the language thing," Rosetta says. "Where did it come from?"

Srulé speaks up. "You're flying the Saiar Ria Contract...Nation got the specs on it a month ago. It uses Morstone, and the language we read and speak today is a derivative of it. It's a mathematics language created nearly four hundred years ago.

"A group of mathematics experts took all the languages spoken by man and condensed all of them to mathematical equations. They found that if they included the emotion behind each individual word and added the emotions as equations, the words became more mathematically alike. So, all humans began learning and using Morstone until it became the commonly-used language we speak today."

"I think Morstone is a more complex language than what we read and speak," Rosetta states.

"You're right," Srulé replies. "That's why I said our spoken and written language is a derivative of it."

Vaskette eyes the older woman. "If it's a mathematical language, I bet Lacendu can use it..."

"The way you folks speak of her, I don't put anything past my granddaughter," Srulé replies.

*****

Now she is in a similar dream to that which she had many weeks ago. The vision of her as a child standing on a stage; there are people in the audience with no faces, except their smiles. They cheer for her as she dances. Her heart rate beats faster as she finishes her recital in triumphant glory. The audience stands and cheers, and as she smiles bright for her parents whom she stares at now, their smiles fade and their faces become completely blank. No eyes, nose, ears, or mouth are present on them, but the cheers continue from somewhere else.

As those cheers fade into nothingness, the whirring of computer terminals are heard. She turns fast to see Mathew, Korsaume, Rosetta, and that man from Straite-Mogue who tesseracted away. She is standing in the first day of their voyage from their awakening.

She now sees Korsaume's face; a hard, knowing face; and Lacendu realizes that Korsaume knew all along that she was the only one of them who still had her memory. Suddenly, Lacendu is frightened…intimidated by the would-be assassin.

The man, though… That man…

She could swear she knows him.

He holds that tesseract device in his hand, unfolded, his hand on the trigger.

His cold eyes look into hers with the depth-perception of the Reaper.

"Lacendu Ruric-Trester…do you remember me? I know you do. Have you remembered, yet? Have you remembered what you wanted to be? The brightest mathematician in the known galaxy working for the Solar Union, doing the calculations necessary for building faster ships, stronger weapons, and determining future advances based on the history of humankind… That's what you wanted to be. You know much, Lacendu, and there is something you must remember. You know what it is. That one thing you've been searching for … it's here."

He hands her the tesseract device and points to the trigger. She takes it in her hands.

"Push it," he says.

She shakes uncontrollably in fear. "I'm scared."

"Push it," he repeats.

"I'm scared of what I'll find." Her voice is shaking horribly.

"Push it," he says again.

"I don't want to," she says louder.

"Push it," he demands.

"I CAN'T!" she screams. "I CAN'T! I WON'T!"

"PUSH IT!!!" he yells at the top of his voice.

Without thinking, her hand is on the trigger squeezing it.

Everything goes blank.

Not black. Not white. Just blank…she cannot describe it even if she wants to.

There, amid the blankness, she is no longer terrified. She sees calculations written everywhere in mid-air. It looks like mid-air, anyway, but when she places her hands on one particular calculation, she is surprised to find there is a wall.

She looks at her feet and sees the floor, too, is blank…a glass-like substance. Beyond, far below, she sees the swirling of the planet's surface of Ascension City; the volcanic red, the misty dark blue, and the inky coal black.

A voice behind her whispers something, but Lacendu doesn't quite catch it; nor does she recognize the voice. She turns to find out who it is, but instead, she is suddenly on a planet. It is a beautiful planet, and in the dome of her college, she stands in line to receive her diploma.

"Lacendu Ruric," the man says. He turns to look at her, holding a small plaque.

The audience cheers. She looks out over them and sees her parents in their dress suits. Their faces are not smiling. Instead, they are stoic, as she always remembered them. Straight-faced and candid, Lacendu makes her way across the platform and shakes hands with the faculty until she gets to the man with her diploma. He hands her the plaque and she glances down to see her name etched in the titanium-alloy plaque with the school's name, "Segnar College of High Mathematics."

The voice behind her whispers again, and like before Lacendu cannot make it out.

"Who is it?"

The voice whispers again.

"What are you saying…?" Lacendu asks, almost pleading, and becoming more and more scared.

The voice whispers loudly. "Remember…"

*****

The taxi pulls into City Main about an hour later and the woman driver turns her head to them, both fast asleep. "Hey! You two! We're here."

They both rouse from their slumber, Agoparn with a twist of his head and a strong and winning attempt to open his eyes wide. Ardelle, her head on Agoparn's left shoulder, mouth open, keeps her eyes shut as she stretches her arms against her male companion and the side wall of the door.

They soon exit the vehicle, the woman hands the funds card back to Ardelle, and she is off.

"We should have asked her where 'here' is…" Agoparn suggests.

"Oh, don't worry. I know right where we are," she says.

They look around to see there is literally no one on the street.

"…And where would that be, Sweetheart?"

She looks around. "City Main…"

"I thought City Main was the main city…" Agoparn says to her.

"No. City Main is a place nearby the main city. The main city is called Troullerstead, though if you ask most of the people that live there they'll call it City Main. The people who live outside know that City Main is the nothing-metropolis next door. City Main was taken over by separatists, and is also, from my understanding, very likely the headquarters for 'Nation.'"

Agoparn looks inquisitively at her. "Didn't 'Nation' try to take us captive?"

"Yes."

"Then why would we want to show up on their doorstep…?" he asks with eyebrows raised and eyes wide.

She smiles at him. "I don't mind going to see 'Nation,' Honey. I just don't want to do it on their terms. Besides, it's what they would least expect, and the hotel your crew holed up in is only a few blocks away."

"What about the separatists? Are they dangerous?"

"Only if you look them in the eye…so…"

"Don't look them in the eye. Got it…" He rolls his eyes.

She smiles knowingly at him. "I understand your doubts, but trust me … I've been here before."

"It's not you I don't trust," he replies. "It's any group referred to as 'separatists.' It's those kinds of people I wish to avoid at all costs."

"Then let's get busy and avoid them. This way…" She heads off in the general direction ahead of them and between two buildings.

There are no signs for any building, and the architecture is brilliant, if bland. Few windows exist, and the ground; or the glass below their feet, rather; is practically clean enough to eat off of.

It is only a matter of blocks before they arrive at the back entrance of the hotel. Ardelle allows Agoparn to go in first. They stop by the reception computer to verify where their friends are staying, and then head up the stairs to the room.

A knock on the door brings a bustling inside, and then after it is evident that someone saw the monitor of just outside the door, the bustling becomes something more akin to excitement. The door opens and Mathew stands there with a smile.

"We thought you'd never get here," he states.

The two are welcomed in with relief, the door is shut, and both groups tell their account of the past several hours, to the dismay of Srulé.

Only a short while passes after the conversation settles down before there is one more knock on the door.

Everyone inside is silent as Mathew once again presses the monitor button to see who is outside. The crew and Srulé recognize him immediately. Mathew opens the door, and there before them is Chrinsole…the man who saved them from death.

He steps in, gives a knowing look at Korsaume, and then shuts the door behind him.

"Hello, friends," he says.

Srulé half-bows toward him and says with apprehension, "Senator."

Korsaume gives him a 'drop-dead' look, stands up, pulls a small weapon from her side pocket, and points it at him.

Everyone is silent.

"Hello, Sherise," he says with a grin.

"Just because these people have become my friends, and just because I cherish them, travel with them, and just finished quitting the CHE, doesn't mean I have any great love for you, Senator…"

Chrinsole releases his smile. "I didn't expect you would, Sherise."

"Her name is Korsaume," Mathew states.

Chrinsole looks at Mathew, then back at Korsaume. "Hm. So you took the name of your dead sister… I wondered how you'd get by here with your real name on databanks the galaxy over."

"Non-updated databanks," she says. "I've been a fugitive from the Solar Union for months. We step one foot in the vicinity of Ascension City and they treat me like a queen. My original rank and file number, something that would have been updated within two weeks at a planet like this, was on file, and they acted like I was God's gift to their fair planet. You're either playing a dangerous game for the fun of it, or you're a complete idiot…"

"Well, I'm not a complete idiot, so I guess that makes me the former, though I'd hate to admit to that, either…"

Allen stands up next to her. "As much as I like seeing guns pointed at people, perhaps we should let the man speak his peace," he states, looking over at Korsaume.

She looks back at him for a second, still keeping her eye on Chrinsole, and finally pulls her arm down. With a frown, she states, "Go ahead, Senator. Speak your peace."

"Well, I guess we need to start with answering the burning question: what really happened to all of you…?

"About eleven months ago I was approached by the Solar Union Committee. All ranking members of the Solar Union were asked to gather for a meeting at Baitronoc: the first Dyson-sphere in our Galaxy, and the only one in Quadrant One. It was a high honor for all of us.

"The meeting took place in the hallowed halls of the Solar Union's largest and most grand building. A simple question was posed... What will it take to keep the Galaxy on course? The general consensus of us all was to ask the 'brain.' This is a problematic issue, oddly enough, as only the Head Solar Union Keeper can pose a question to the 'brain.'

"It was evident through our studies, and many others, that the Galaxy was preparing to split into fractioned groups... This would mean changes in currency, ever-different laws from planet to planet, and many other hardships for the citizens of our Galaxy.

"To avoid that, a small committee of the Members determined that the Keeper should pose the question to the 'brain.' So he did. The answer the 'brain' gave was that a war was needed.

"Four months later, my wife found a vast study on the possibility of the 'brain' having been corrupted. The discrepancies in the 'brain's' answer over the last two hundred years were too innumerous to ignore. No, they hadn't caused any serious problems for the Committee, or the Galaxy that we could tell, but they were discrepancies nonetheless.

"One of the things suggested by the leaders to assist in this was that the six most gifted people in the Galaxy would be needed. Those six people would be responsible for determing how to keep the inevitable war from killing more than was absolutely necessary. As you're all most likely aware, wars are matchsticks for technological advance and productivity enhancement.

"The five of you present in this room and one additional man..."

At this he looks at Korsaume, who looks off to the ceiling and says, "Tyber Urching ..."

"...Tyber Urching ...were all asked to meet at Baitronoc, after which you were taken to an at-that-time-undisclosed location, which later I discovered to be the Solar Union secret base on Shimrabose around Antoinette.

"There, you were informed of your reason for being brought together. After countless hours of debate between yourselves and exasperating arguments with each other, you finally all concluded that a war was the last thing the Galaxy needed.

"Since the Solar Union was sure it was all of you who were wrong and not the 'brain,' they took you back to Baitronoc and had your past memories wiped. It took weeks of intense pressure on all of you, but the memories of who you were before that day were erased, and only your skills were left.

"You were then shuttled back to that same secret base where you were to begin your discussions anew. Waiting for you there was Sherise Felder, the number two weapons expert and tactician in the Galaxy. Since the Solar Union had taken the first from the CHE, the only other choice was her. She was to board your ship once it landed and kill all of you.

"I had been informed of this shortly before my wife died, hopped aboard the vessel as a diplomat, and stopped Korsaume from completing her mission. Then, I had members of my team fly the Vortex Class Planetary Cruiser 'Vibrant' to one of my more secretive establishments and paid to have all of you placed where you would awaken together at about the same time once the tesseract was complete."

Everyone sits in a stunned silence for quite a while.

Agoparn finally opens his mouth, and his voice is a little quiet. "How did you know Korsaume wouldn't have killed us all…?"

"I didn't," is his calm answer. "I had to make sure she didn't know how to fly a Planetary Cruiser. That part was easy. Making her believe you were all her best hope of survival was the difficult part, but putting a note in her pocket like the rest of you must have done the trick well enough, I suppose."

"What did that paper really say, Korsaume," Mathew asks, remembering the moment when they were walking down the hall together after first awakening.

Solemnly, she thinks for a moment. "Something about me needing all of you to get back home… That he would be there to stop me from ever completing my mission…"

"I do admit that I didn't expect all of you to be at Ascension City so soon, but I suppose it proves your worth to our Galaxy. That's one reason why I cannot allow you to continue your journey." Chrinsole smiles as if he's accomplished something.

"What makes you think we'd want to stay here?" Mathew asks.

"You can accomplish much more by becoming part of my organization and helping me coordinate the efforts of thousands of people who are doing what you're thinking about doing as a small group of six…" he answers.

They are all silent again for a short while, and Allen watches Mathew as the Captain sits with one arm on the chair staring straight out the window on the far side of the room.

"What are you thinking, Captain," Allen asks.

Mathew glances at Allen a moment, then back out the window with a soft grunt.

Vaskette takes a turn… "Captain…?"

Mathew shrugs a little, and then looks at the floor in the center between all of them. "I'm thinking that if you can't change the Solar Union with thousands of troops at your command and disposal, what makes you think we're going to be able to help you in even a remote way…?"

"Simple," Chrinsole replies, like it should be blindingly obvious to everyone. "You six have the know-how, the technical skills, and the integrity needed to put the Solar Union in its place. If you had thousands of people at your command…"

Mathew interrupts and continues, "We would turn into the Solar Union ourselves if we ever did solve the mess you claim exists."

"Captain," Korsaume says with frustration. "Any galaxy committee who takes six people from their homes, tries to coerce them into starting a war, wiping their minds clean when they refuse and trying it again is what I would call a mess…"

"I'm agreeing with Korsaume on this one," Vaskette states.

"…But you're all missing the one key factor in all of this," he says, standing up and walking around the edge of the room about ten steps. He stops, turns around and walks back, taking a knee to the floor next to his chair and looking at his left hand dangling off the arm. "The Solar Union didn't choose to do this of their own accord. They did it at the behest of a supercomputer…"

"The 'brain,'" Allen says, almost as a question.

"If we can find that stupid computer, we might be able to solve the problems from the inside out…"

"Hm…" Rosetta looks at the rest of the crew in turn with her brow furrowed. "He's got a point…"

"I know," Korsaume states reluctantly.

"He's right," Agoparn admits, looking at Ardelle.

Ardelle looks back at him and nods.

Vaskette stands up and turns to face Lacendu. Suddenly, Lacendu sits up in bed, her eyes wide. Vaskette jumps back in shock. For a moment, Lacendu just sits there, not breathing. Then, finally, she breathes in heavily once and starts gasping for air.

"Lacendu! Are you alright…?!" Vaskette is down beside her friend in a flash.

The young woman is panting, taking large quick breaths and letting them out too fast.

"Calm down, Lacy," Vaskette encourages. "Lacy, you're going to have to calm down or you'll hyperventilate."

Lacendu looks over at her friend as she feels her face go flush. Her mouth hangs open.

"Are you alright," Vaskette asks.

By now, all of her crewmates are gathered around her.

"Lacendu…?" Mathew has a sincere look of concern on his face.

"I remember…" she states suddenly.

"You remember…?" Vaskette asks. "Remember what, Lacy…?"

Lacendu looks around at all of them.

Her mouth closes once; she swallows, and then looks back down at the bed.

"Everything…"

Episode 13

Where the Stars are Broken and Crumbling

OPENING:

One of three things can happen when you start looking for your destiny. You'll give up and accept fate... You'll find your destiny... Or, you'll find someone else's destiny... Regardless, you always find something when you search. The ultimate question is, "What will you do when you find something...?"

Everyone sits in a stunned stupor. Some look at Lacendu, others at the floor or wall.

"Everything…?" Chrinsole almost looks worried, but nobody seems to care except Lacendu.

"Yes," she responds. Lacendu makes a move to get off the bed, so Vaskette, Allen, and Korsaume back away. She rises out of the bed while Vaskette pulls a needle from her arm and two cords off which were taped to her neck. "How long was I out…?"

"…Um, two days…" Vaskette answers.

Lacendu looks taken aback and stares at Vaskette. "Seriously…?"

"Yes."

Lacendu glances around. "Have you all been standing over me this whole time…?"

Some of them make a sound like giggling or laughing, but all feel relaxed suddenly. They move back to their places as Srulé begins, "Lacendu, I am your real grandmother."

Lacendu looks over at the woman. "I know. My parents showed me pictures of you a few years ago, and told me you lived on Ascension City… It's nice to finally meet you in person."

The two women hug, and then Lacendu sits down on the end of the bed looking at Mathew. "What do we do, now, Captain?"

"We've decided to go back to Quadrant One and find the 'brain,'" he answers.

"What do you plan on doing with it when you find it," she asks.

"I haven't got that far, yet."

Allen raises his hand. "I have a suggestion. Why don't we destroy it? It's caused enough trouble for one half of a millennium."

Lacendu turns her head to him and responds, "That wouldn't be good. The Galaxy is too reliant on it, not to mention the Solar Union. The Galaxy would fall into chaos if it was destroyed."

"Barring that, I don't have any suggestions," Allen says.

"Well, thank you for your input anyway," Mathew states. "Why don't we just go to Plenawald and use the tesseract device to head home. We'll use the few clues available to us to find the 'brain.' Does everyone agree…?"

His crew nods their approval; even Lacendu; and Rosetta and Ardelle state their approval.

"Are you coming with us," Korsaume asks of Ardelle.

"Well, I will need to speak with my crew, first. They are usually willing to follow me to the pits of hell, but this might be stretching things a little, and it is my ship," she replies with a smile.

Chrinsole speaks out, "I must state my disapproval one last time. This is suicide for all of you."

"Duly noted," Mathew says. "Does anyone wish to back out?"

No one responds.

"Very well," Chrinsole says. "I can't stop the finest crew this galaxy has to offer once they've set their mind to something. Shall we go, Srulé?"

Lacendu's grandmother turns to him. "Yes, sir…"

"Just like that," Lacendu asks. "You're just going to let us go?"

"Do I have a choice," Chrinsole asks. He looks at her knowingly, and she returns the same look.

"You did last time."

"Yes, and I made it, albeit wrong. I admit my mistakes. Will you?"

She drills an invisible hole through him with her eyes in the meanest face she can make, but digresses when he turns, opens the door, allows Srulé to exit first, and leaves without fanfare.

"That's that," Mathew says. "I want to get off this planet in three hours. Everyone is to meet at the orbital station-transport building in two."

He takes Rosetta's hand, she stands up, and the two of them exit the hotel room.

Korsaume looks over at Allen who looks back at her.

Korsaume says, to anyone in the room who will listen, "Is it my imagination or is all of this not turning out as planned."

"You're assuming there was a plan," Vaskette says with a smirk. "I don't mean that facetiously."

"Not taken that way, Doctor," Korsaume says standing up. "Well, we have less then two hours, so I suppose we should get ready to go."

Everyone sets about preparing their belongings and the few things they've bought on the planet for leaving.

*****

It is two hours later and the crew of the Saiar Ria Contract, including a newly-gained Captain Ardelle Xysteck and her crew of fifty-one (eighteen decided to go a different way), stand in line awaiting transport back up through the atmosphere to the orbital ribbon station around the planet.

The Saiar Ria Contract crew stands close together chatting about the planet and the things they enjoyed about it, and within twenty minutes they are at the front of the line and moving through the beam shaft upward.

The two crews make their way to their respective ships, and an hour and a half later the two ships are making their way outside the jurisdiction of Ascension City.

Mathew, Korsaume, Allen, Vaskette, Agoparn, Lacendu, and Rosetta stand around on the command deck of the Saiar Ria Contract.

"So, what's the plan, Captain," Rosetta asks. She is in long shorts, and her hands are on the back of her hips.

"I want us to hit Plenawald in the next two weeks. I think we can make it on this thing, and I believe the Star Axis will be able to keep up, or at the very least meet us there…"

"I believe so, Captain," Agoparn states after a look from his Captain gives inquiry.

"I have something I want to say," Lacendu says. Everyone looks her direction, a bit intimidating for the young woman. "Uh," she pauses to think about it, and then continues, "You should all know that I helped to create and design this ship…"

Everyone looks surprised.

"I designed it while I was in high school. It was purely experimental, but I submitted it to ship designs about five years ago, and I'm guessing they decided to design it and make it." She licks her lips, almost as a tick.

"You designed this…?" Allen asks.

"Well, I created the mathematics it uses…"

Korsaume looks around the room. "Well, that explains the use of the Morstone language being used all over it."

"Yes," Lacendu replies. "I learned Morstone and several other calculus languages in high school. That's why I'm a teacher."

"This is going to take some getting used to," Vaskette says, not looking at her friend.

"Well, when we get to Plenawald, I want to track down that Photonia. We need to find out if there's enough for both ships…" Mathew states.

"We won't need Photonia," Lacendu says. Everyone looks at her for more. "This thing can make it to Quadrant One in a matter of about twenty minutes."

"That's impossible," Korsaume says.

Agoparn stares at Lacendu. "I don't recall seeing a hyprogenerge drive on this thing," he states.

"It doesn't need it," she answers him directly; "It uses a streaming mega-mass drive."

"I've never heard of it," Agoparn says.

"Of course not," she tells them. "It's new technology."

"You invented this technology," Mathew asks.

"No, Sir. I designed the ship to use that technology. The drive was invented by a friend of mine from college. We worked on it with a few other folks and turned the plans over to the Solar Union. We never heard anything about it after that… That was five years ago…I believe I mentioned that already, though."

"Then we only need enough Photonia for the Star Axis…" Allen says with a smile.

"It would seem that way," retorts Vaskette.

*****

The days pass quickly and the two ships are orbiting around the planet Plenawald. After the two ships connect and some of the people from the Star Axis move onto the other leaving a skeleton crew on the first, the Saiar Ria Contract heads down to the surface of the planet.

*****

The crews exit the Saiar Ria Contract near an old village after three hours of searching the surface for the old derelict ships that brought the original settlers, as well as Xychocappla and Shivranikka.

"I feel sick," Lacendu complains to the rest of the Saiar Ria Contract crew.

"It's the heavy gravity," Vaskette explains. "You'll feel queasy and sick for a little while until you get used to it."

"This place is creepy," Rosetta says. "I've heard rumors about this place…legends. I thought they were just stories."

Everyone heads toward the small village. Most of the buildings are falling apart and coming down. There are people and animals all over the place, motionless, with computer lines running through their skin, and out.

"Very weird," Korsaume admits. "As much as I hate to admit weakness, I agree with Rosetta."

"Well, let's see if we can't spot that big bag of Photonia around here," Mathew states to the crews. "Spread out and search. I want at least five people together at all times. No one separates from your group."

The group splits up and begins searching the village, derelict parked nearby, and the woods around the two.

Mathew, Korsaume, Lacendu, Vaskette, Rosetta, and Allen all enter the derelict ship, taking note that most of the original equipment and the robots have been removed…no, torn from the ship.

Korsaume looks over a small console with much of the wires ripped out of the internal structure. "I'd love to know what really happened here…"

Allen walks down the corridor with the rest behind him and stops at the entrance to the command deck. "This is really old equipment. There's nothing here we could use…"

"Yeah," Lacendu remarks, "it's all five hundred-year-old technology. I doubt seriously that we could even melt it down and use it for something else."

The rest of the crew joins Allen and they begin going over the command deck thoroughly.

"Can you imagine ever living like this," Mathew asks. "I can't..."

Korsaume and Rosetta smile at him, and one gives him a nod.

"Exactly what are we looking for," Mathew asks.

"Photonia," is the answer from Rosetta. "It should be in a large bucket-shaped metal container with a large hole on the side, covered by a steptrycyne film patch."

Allen looks around at Rosetta. "Will it be any good if we do find it intact?"

"Photonia holds its charge forever, pretty much," she replies. "Remember, it's just a bunch of photon particles trapped in a container. They don't go anywhere unless there's an opening."

"That's assuming time hasn't done any damage to the container," Mathew states.

They are all a little surprised by numerous footsteps from the corridor.

"Captain Mathew!"

They all recognize it as Captain Ardelle's voice.

"Captain Mathew, are you in here?"

Mathew walks to the entrance of the command deck to find the woman with Agoparn and the men who followed her right behind her.

"What's wrong?"

"Look out that window," she states.

Everyone turns to look out the main windows. There, hitting the outside hull are small burning drops of some kind of liquid.

Lacendu gives an odd look at the window, then back at Ardelle. "What is that stuff?"

"Fire drops. They're prevalent on a planet called 'Phoenix Rain.' They can do a lot of damage," she answers them.

"Is this normal," Mathew asks.

"On 'Phoenix Rain,' people live underground. That stuff kills most forms of life. My guess is that either this is a rare occurrence, or the plants on this planet have adapted to it..."

"What do we do," Allen asks.

"We wait for it to stop," Ardelle states bluntly.

Allen glances again at Ardelle. "Where is 'Phoenix Rain...'?"

"It's on the edge of Quadrants One and Four. I went there when I first started on freighters. My dad was a freighter captain and did trips between the first and fourth Quadrants. When I joined his business I took over the four-to-three runs. He retired a few years ago..."

Most everyone looks back out the window for a few minutes to watch the fire drops come down in a storm of rain and then subside to a trickle.

Mathew turns to Ardelle. "Are your people alright? Were any of you injured?"

Ardelle turns to her crewmates. They hold up their arms and in the dim lights inside the others can see small marks on their skin and clothing.

Mathew raises his eyebrows a bit. "You guys need to get back to the Contract and get some medical attention...anyone not injured comes with us. We're going to see if we can find anything else as soon as this rain lets up..."

As if on queue, the rain subsides.

Ardelle looks over Mathew's shoulder and smiles. "Come on, Captain...say, 'We're going to make a billion currency as soon as we walk out of this ship...'"

A few laugh at this.

The two groups exit the derelict ship and the ones injured by the rain head for the Saiar Ria Contract for medical attention with Vaskette while the rest travel together to find the third group.

It does not take long. They come upon a small, sturdy building which has survived the fire drops just fine, and when the group emerges three of them are seriously injured from the rain and head back to the ship while the other two join the larger group and explain what they were doing prior to the start of the fire drops.

"It looks like someone made a marked path through the woods," one of them states. "We were going to follow it when the rain started."

Allen bends down to look at one of the marks; a piece of metal like a stake, with a red mark on the top. After going over it for a few moments, he stands up. "I really don't like this," he states with concern, "These are fairly new marks."

"What…" Lacendu asks, "You're saying that other people have been here recently…?"

"Yes, that's what I'm saying," Allen agrees.

"How new are they," Korsaume asks.

"My best guess, no more than a couple months…most likely just a few days…"

Mathew looks around at those with him. "We should get some weapons if we're going to follow these. Anyone who doesn't want to go along may stay at the Contract."

The group walks back to the Saiar Ria Contract and boards it to grab weapons and shields. They return to the marks within a half hour, minus four people, and begin finding the other marks following an odd path through a forested area that grows dimmer with the waning of the light which shines through the clouds which have since passed over head.

About twenty minutes brings them to a large hole in the ground with a small lake at the bottom. It is about four meters from the top to the water below.

Allen looks around at his crewmates. "The marks stop here."

"Why would they stop here…?" Mathew asks. "Unless someone specifically wants others to come here…"

"Or," Korsaume states, "If they intend to return here."

Lacendu squints her eyes down at the hole in the ground, balls up her fists and walks sideways a meter or so to the right.

"What is it, Lacy," Mathew asks, stopping everyone else and coercing them to look her direction, too.

She points down about halfway into the hole. "What do you all see there?"

Everyone surrounds her and tries to look for themselves. In the dimness of the planet, and the forest's darkness they see something metallic.

"It might be another mark…" Allen says.

"Could the marks continue on past this…?" Mathew asks.

"I highly doubt it," Korsaume says. "There doesn't seem to be any places in that direction that would hint at a path."

"Well," Mathew continues, "There must be a reason for that stake to be down there if that's what it is, so I say we investigate…"

"Agreed," Agoparn states, "I want to get to the bottom of this. No pun intended…"

A few give him a blank look as Mathew, Korsaume and Allen begin climbing down into the large hole.

It is a short while later when the rest are down at the water's edge staring at the stake and the small area near it where there seems to be a door.

"What is that?" Lacendu asks.

"Um, it might be a door, Lacy," Agoparn suggests. "Call it a hunch…"

Lacendu gives him a mean look. "I'm about to call you something, Mister Smarty-Pants."

Mathew begins, "Come on, guys. Korsaume and Allen are with me. The rest of you stay here and keep watch. If anything happens, I want to know immediately."

He wades into the water and swims to the other side, followed closely by the other two. Lacendu sits on the embankment of the water, and Agoparn sits beside her.

"Why do I always have to sit it out when the cool things go on," she asks.

Agoparn makes a small sound of a laugh. "Be glad they do leave you behind. If they get injured, you can help them and save the day. Not to mention the fact that you're always out of harm's way when anything does go wrong while they're in the thick of things wishing they were sitting here with you…"

Lacendu looks over at him with a look of gratitude, and the side of her mouth pulled back. "Well, when you put it like that, I wish they'd go into danger more often."

"Now, that's not what I meant," he says while lightly laughing.

Across the short lake, Mathew, Allen, and Korsaume climb out of the water only half a dozen meters away. The door is partly opened, and with a few strong pushes it opens enough for them to get in.

"We need a light," Mathew says.

Suddenly, random lights come on all over the room they're in. It is evident by the inconsistency that many of the lights have long since quit working.

"How convenient" Korsaume comments.

"What is this place," Allen asks.

"A better question would be, 'Why is this place at the end of those markers?'" Korsaume looks around the room and walks to one panel.

"Yes, that would be a better question…" Allen grins.

"It looks like it was meant for a launch pad," Mathew remarks walking forward to find broken glass on the floor and a door ripped off of its hinges.

The other two walk toward him and stand beside him, all of them looking inside a large cylinder room which stretches downward into darkness

"There used to be a craft in here," Korsaume states. "I wonder who used it."

"I'll give you two guesses, and the first one doesn't count," says Allen.

Korsaume gives him a mean-hearted grin. "You're suggesting that Shivranikka used the shuttle?"

"What would she need with a shuttle," asks Mathew.

"Think about it," Allen states as if it should be obvious. "This is a heavy-gravity planet. She would have needed help getting off of it."

Mathew continues, "So, do you think she built this place?"

Korsaume takes a short step just inside to peer upward. "Think about what we know of her, Captain. She's insanely powerful as a near-complete machine, but she's not particularly bright…"

"The worst kind of enemy," Allen says almost as a joke.

Korsaume practically ignores him. "I don't think she could have thought to build this place in a million years, much less in four hundred. No. Someone else built this place; she just used it."

There are footsteps coming from somewhere to their right, and the three of them quickly pull back and try to look into the shadows. On the wall about three meters in front of them is a glowing red box.

"A doorway…" Mathew states.

"Yeah, but to what…?" Allen asks.

More footsteps…

Mathew swallows hard, and both Korsaume and Allen hear it, but pay little attention as their own heart rates rise.

Mathew reluctantly walks quietly over to the glowing box and presses a bright red button. A door opens quickly and beyond the doorway is a hall. The three of them move slowly, weapons in hand pointing in front of them. The lights in the hallway all seem to work fine, and just a few decimeters beyond the door lie three decomposing skeletons in random positions.

They walk toward the footsteps slowly and with deliberation.

The footsteps stop beyond a door with an identical box nearby like the first. Mathew presses the red button, and this door opens revealing a vast room about sixty meters wide and two meters high.

In the middle is a chair, and almost everything else that looks like it was scattered throughout has been pushed to the edges of the room. There is a figure in dim lighting in the middle of the room.

The voice is female and easily recognizable.

"Welcome, friends. It sure took you long enough…"

They point their weapons down, more in exasperation, and partly out of futility.

Korsaume leans against the doorway breathing a sigh of relief. "Shivranikka, what do you want…?"

She stands up and in a heartbeat is within arm's reach of Mathew, but she is looking directly at Korsaume.

"Korsaume, my nemesis, the game isn't over until one of us has won…"

"There's nothing to win," Korsaume states. "We had no intention of meeting you. You attacked us. We just did what we could to keep ourselves alive."

Shivranikka shakes her head. "You really don't get it, do you…? This isn't about you or your friends. This is about me and my friends, and my goal. You stand between my goal and me."

"And what is your goal, Shivranikka," Mathew asks.

"Ah… The consummate negotiator…the Captain…always looking for a mutually inclusive answer to help everyone. Aren't you sweet…?" Shivranikka looks at Mathew with a sweet, innocent look like a young school girl flirting with an older male. Then she drops the look and straightens her arms slightly behind her leaning forward into his face. "Anything you could come up with would be mutually exclusive for us both," she states, maintaining her customary smile. "I can assure you of that. Your crew killed my best friends. You think I'm going to let it go at that?"

"So this is about revenge, Shivranikka," Allen asks. "If it hadn't been for you and your best friends we would have gladly passed on by."

"SHUT UP!" she yells at them. "It's not enough that you killed them, but you can't even take responsibility for what you've done!"

Mathew looks infuriated at her. His voice is strong as he speaks. "FINE…! You want us to admit to killing your friends…? Alright. I admit it. I admit that we were scared that you would kill us, so we took the opportunity to kill your friends first. We even had intent to destroy you and the Saiar Ria Contract. Are you happy?"

She pulls back a little with a satisfied smile. “Finally…the truth… It’s been so long since I’ve heard that from anyone…” Her smile practically beams, now. “As for me being happy, though, Dear Captain…?”

At this, she reaches out her hand around his throat so fast he has no opportunity to move, and without getting closer lifts him into the air by his neck, effectively choking him.

Mathew struggles for a moment with his hands around her arm, but finally just uses her arm to grip and hold himself in a position to where he won’t choke as badly.

“Put him down,” Korsaume states, giving her a death look. “I’m the one you want. Put him back on the floor.”

“No, no,” she says with her smile and a shake of her head. “You are the one I want, but taking you won’t satisfy me. I have to beat you…not kill you.”

“So, you want a test, then? …A game?”

“Isn’t it all a game, dearest enemy mine?”

“Put him down and let’s discuss the stakes,” Korsaume says with a give-in.

Shivranikka laughs hysterically putting Mathew back on the floor. He grabs his neck swallowing again and again while massaging the place her hands had been.

“The stakes… What’s at stake?” She turns her back to them and walks around in a small imaginary circle. “Alright…” She nods her head at Korsaume. “If I win, you must serve me willingly for the rest of your life.”

Korsaume looks at Mathew and Allen. Mathew looks back at her, but gives no indication as to his view.

Allen shakes his head ‘no’ at her. “You couldn’t possibly trust her,” he states. “I seriously doubt she would even play fair.”

Shivranikka looks genuinely upset. “DON’T TALK ABOUT ME LIKE I’M NOT HERE!” she screams directly at him. “If you don’t trust me, that’s fine, but you should know I trust you even less.”

He rolls his eyes at her, and then looks back at Korsaume. "It's entirely up to you, but I don't agree."

"I have to agree with Allen," Mathew states. "It is your choice, but I don't feel comfortable with this arrangement."

Korsaume looks at Shivranikka, and back to her crewmates. "What do I get if I win?" Korsaume asks.

"Then," she starts, thinking hard. "Then I will serve you willingly for the rest of your life."

"What's the game," Korsaume asks.

Shivranikka opens her mouth wide in a grin and giggles. "We're playing it…"

Without a hint, Shivranikka disappears off to their right so fast they barely notice the direction.

"I really don't like this," Korsaume states unnecessarily.

"Is this your first realization, or your second," Allen asks.

Korsaume hardly pays him attention. "What is she playing?"

Mathew looks at her; then at Allen. "What do you think the game is," he asks.

Allen thinks for a moment, picking a random spot on the floor to stare at for a few moments. Finally he looks up. "My best guess…? It's a toss-up between hide-and-go-seek and chess."

"Why chess," Mathew asks.

"Oh, no…" Korsaume's eyes widen into ovals. "Not chess…"

She turns and runs out the door followed closely by her companions. They are soon outside at the water's edge. Across the water where their crewmates and traveling friends were are the dirt and plants originally present. They look around the edges of the top of the hole they are in and see no one in the dimness. It is barely lit by a moon above and behind them showing down on the other side of the hole.

"I'm horrible at chess," Korsaume says, exasperated.

They climb out of the hole, walk around it and follow the metal markers back to the small village. Almost there, they see the Saiar Ria Contract still sitting in its place, and everything seems to be in order. The lights all over the ship are still on, lighting a very small area around it. It takes them about ten minutes to walk to it from the forest and they enter it preparing for anything…

"If this is chess, then she's already got most of our pieces," Mathew states with a sad look about him. "I'm ninety-nine percent sure our ship is empty."

"You're ninety-nine percent wrong," comes a voice over the speakers in the ship.

"She's going to finish the game where we left off," Allen states.

Korsaume smiles at them. "Then we have some knowledge about this that Shivranikka doesn't have… We took most of the stuff she had in it out and reconstructed much of the equipment."

"She's not going to make this a walk in the park, though, Lieutenant," Mathew comments.

"We should go to the infirmary first," Allen states. "That's where Vaskette and the injured would be if Shivranikka plays the way she did last time."

"Good idea. We stick together on this. I don't want any of us walking off away from the others," Mathew commands.

"I agree," Korsaume adds.

Allen looks at both of them. "Well, I guess even if I disagreed, both my commanding officers have given the same order so I don't have much of a choice."

They smile at him and the group of three head through the corridor, up two flights of stairs, and forward through the ship, soon arriving at the infirmary. The door is open and no one is inside, though it looks like people have been there recently.

They look around the room for clues, and then head for Lacendu's room, finding nothing there, either.

"Now, where," Allen asks. "Those are the first few things I can think of…"

"What about the room where the pods are," Korsaume asks.

"The door is still in need of repair, and that room still creeps me out, but it's the only other option I can think of," Mathew replies.

They head down to the pod room, which only takes a few minutes, and arrive a bit weary. They walk quietly into the room, taking slow deliberate steps.

There in the pods are the crewmembers of the Star Axis, including Captain Ardelle. However, Agoparn, Lacendu, Vaskette, and Rosetta are not in any of them.

Mathew looks upset. "She is not going to turn them into machines like herself!"

"Of course not," comes the reply from Shivranikka over the speakers. "I'm not completely insane."

"That's debatable," Korsaume replies.

Suddenly, from down the hall a shot fired hits the side of the doorway.

"What the…" Mathew begins just as a Raider comes through the door, weapon aimed. All three of them immediately hit their sapphire shields turning them on, but Allen is struck on the shoulder forcing him to turn around and fall to the ground, hitting a conveyer bar square on the chest.

"Frag! That hurts," he says, the clothing effectively fused with the skin around his shoulder. The wound is cauterized almost instantly, but the smell of burnt flesh is enough to make him sick to his stomach.

"Are you alright," Mathew asks of Allen above the sound of his weapon firing.

"I'll live," he replies standing up slowly in severe pain.

Korsaume gets a mad look on her face, pulls her super-HOP out of its holder and points it directly at the Raider, more coming to the door. She watches the readout on the back of the gun until it recognizes the identities of all the Raiders in its view.

"I really wanted to save these shots for you, Shivranikka," she yells to the air. "But for some reason I'm getting the feeling you're not about to let us last that long…"

She pulls the trigger and just holds it. Multiple missiles exit the shaft too fast to see, but they hit the first Raider and begin circling around the Raiders and through the walls and back blowing up all around their targets. The near-dead-humans are instantly damaged beyond repair falling to the ground in heaps and piles of human remains, suits, and damaged internal components.

The three crewmates stop firing.

Mathew looks at the dead Raiders. "Come on, Lieutenant. You couldn't have left something for us to use?"

"I could have," she suggests, "if they weren't so stinkin' powerful."

"It'll have to do," Allen states with a short smile. "I need a quick break. I'm hurting bad…"

Korsaume and Mathew gather to him and help him up to his feet. He sits on the conveyer machine behind him and looks at his shoulder.

Korsaume begins checking it over. "It looks pretty bad," she remarks.

"If it weren't for the fact that I want you to win against that witch, I'd sit this out and let myself get captured…"

Mathew smiles at Allen. "That's not a half-bad idea. Let's move out."

Korsaume and Allen both look at him with an inquisitive gaze. Korsaume pulls on Mathew's arm to tug him around a bit to get a better glimpse of Allen's shoulder. "Have you seen this, Captain?" she asks, pointing at his wound.

"Yeah. Now, both of you come on."

*****

The group of three arrives at the infirmary after dropping by the weapons room, which to their surprise is still fully stocked.

At the infirmary, Mathew and Korsaume use a few of the machines with the computer's help to treat Allen the best they can, and then leave him there and head for the back of the ship searching every room on their way there.

"Lieutenant, this isn't looking so good for us," Mathew says.

Korsaume shrugs. "What do you want from me…sympathy?"

Mathew turns around to face her, seeing something coming down the corridor they're in. "Well, there's another team heading this way. Are you ready?"

She turns around with her super-HOP aimed and checks the readout. "They're all enemy's," she states.

"Feel free to fire away at your leisure, Lieutenant."

She does, and the missiles take off exploding on impact of the seven beings in their Raider suits. This time, however, the explosions occur inside the Raiders' bodies and Mathew and Korsaume run over and begin picking up weapons and trying to salvage suits.

"That worked almost too well," Korsaume says.

Mathew glances at her. "Like you said, Shivranikka may be extremely powerful, but she's not too bright."

"…And I'm sure she heard you," Korsaume states under her breath.

They pull the suits off the near-dead-humans and begin using some tools they picked up from the weapons room to fix the suits. Then they suit up and pack the enemy weapons on the suits, grab their own weapons, and head for the back of the ship.

"Are you there, Shivranikka," Korsaume asks into the headset.

"Yes, dear; I'm here," they both hear in their earpiece. "You've done well for yourself."

"I'm about to do better," Korsaume replies. She looks over at Mathew who holds a small metal device with a single button. "Press it," she tells him.

He does, and a signal is marked with the device as it tells them which way the tracking device is, leading them through the corridors.

They soon arrive at the back of the ship to a small room they have never been in. Korsaume presses the release button on the box near the door to open it, and it does open.

Mathew and Korsaume walk in to see their crewmates and friends that were not in pods in the other room; and there in the center is Shivranikka, her smile intact.

Shivranikka stands up from the small chair she is seated in and with a shake of her head to toss her hair around says plainly, “Check.”

Korsaume looks over at Allen who is tied up and lying on the floor. She smiles back at Shivranikka and nods. “…Mate!” She presses a button on the device in her hand and a small box on Allen’s belt comes to life opening quickly and releasing a blue light.

Shivranikka suddenly doesn’t look so happy. “What is that,” she asks.

“Some call it a blue star…but you can call it a multi-energy hyper-surge.” As Korsaume talks, Shivranikka begins writhing and wiggling, trying to stand on her own two feet, but finally falling to the floor.

“What does it do,” Shivranikka asks with a question on her face.

“It causes devices which use dyprase photoneuric energy, among others, to surge. It’s great for stopping small pulsating energy guns and women named Shivranikka…” Korsaume now has a smile on her face, and Shivranikka lies on the floor unable to move.

Mathew stares at her. Without a smile, and more worried than anything, he says, “You enjoyed that.”

“Yes,” Korsaume admits. “A little bit too much, Captain.”

*****

It is a short while later and the crew of the Saiar Ria Contract stands around in the infirmary with Ardelle and two of her close friends from the Star Axis while Vaskette works on Allen’s shoulder. Shivranikka is also present, if unconscious.

"Do we have to take her with us," Lacendu asks. "I really don't like that thing."

Korsaume laughs. "It was her decision, Lacy. She said if I won that she would serve me willingly the rest of her life."

"Don't you think that was all a little too convenient, Lieutenant," Vaskette asks, leaning over Allen's body with one of her many medical devices. "The way you make it sound she left herself wide open for a loss... Quit moving, Allen."

Allen apologizes. "I don't like this skin-tissue regenerator," he remarks. "It hurts."

Vaskette bops him on the head. "The sooner you quit moving, the faster this thing can heal you and the sooner it will quit hurting."

"Alright," he states. "Anyway, I confess to having my own doubts, as well, but seeing what little I have of the way she thinks, I'd have to say that it really couldn't have been that difficult...no disrespect to your genius, Lieutenant..."

"Oh," Korsaume says, rolling her eyes, "Not at all, Strategist..." She sighs.

"All I'm saying is she's not too bright; for a machine, anyway."

Mathew glances around at his crew. "My real question is, 'Do we really want to take her with us?' What advantage will she give us when we get to where we're going?"

"You mean, besides annoying remarks about how she hates everyone and constant reminders of how she's the most powerful of all Xychocappla's creations...?" Lacendu folds her arms together and looks generally repulsed.

"That's an advantage?" Agoparn asks.

"Yes, besides that," Mathew retorts.

"Two words," Vaskette smiles, "'Canon fodder...'"

Everyone laughs.

"You all know I can hear you," comes Shivranikka's voice from her position a few feet away. She is lying on the table the crew placed her on over an hour ago.

"Well, little servant," Korsaume says folding her arms and walking over to her enemy. "You're finally awake."

"I don't sleep," Shivranikka states blandly, maintaining her annoying, incessant smile.

"Yeah, well, you're back, up and running," Korsaume replies.

Shivranikka sits up, moves her legs off the table, and stands boldly before Korsaume. "You play well…better than I expected."

Korsaume gives the woman an odd look with her head tilted. "You had expectations from me?"

"I expected if you did win that it would take significantly longer," the techno-witch states.

Korsaume gives her best 'drop-dead' look and says, "You give yourself way too much credit."

Shivranikka giggles at her new master. "I will keep my end of the bargain. What is my first duty?"

"We need to find that canister of Photonia. Where is it?"

Shivranikka looks around the room. "Where are my creations?"

Mathew steps around his crewmates to face the woman. "They're in the stasis pods in that one room…"

"I will have them get the Photonia container," she says. "It is far too heavy for one being to carry."

"Fine," Korsaume says. "I'm putting you in charge of that. Take a few of your 'creations,'" and she stresses the word 'creations' soaked with sarcasm, "and bring back the canister as it currently is with no additional incurred damage or change in its capacity of Photonia."

"You are very specific," Shivranikka says flipping her hair back. "Anything else…?"

"Not at present," Korsaume replies with candor. "Go."

Shivranikka walks out of the room and down the hall.

Korsaume waits until the woman is out of earshot and says to a flood of laughter from her crewmates, "I think I'm going to enjoy this."

*****

Two hours later Shivranikka and four of her minions arrive at the ground-loading bay on the left side of the ship, and they are carrying a huge dark grey container using only their arms and hands. Korsaume and Agoparn are there to greet them.

Shivranikka; "Where do you want this," she asks of Korsaume.

"Up the ramp, just inside against the back wall…" Agoparn replies.

Shivranikka and her minions stand there silently.

Korsaume sighs. "You heard him," she demands. "Carry that thing up the ramp and set it just inside against the back wall."

The five of them head up the ramp to do as they're told.

Agoparn looks at her. "This is going to get real annoying really quick."

Korsaume looks deep into his eyes when he faces her. "I'm willing to take what I can get on this issue," she states. "I don't like her, but we did make a deal, and she seems to be keeping her end of it. We'll just have to live with her inanities for now."

"For now," Agoparn agrees. "Hopefully, 'now' won't be too long…"

The two of them walk up the massive ramp and Agoparn hits the button to bring the ramp closed. It slowly begins to rise just as he and his commanding officer walk onto the floor of the storage compartment.

Korsaume glances to make sure the container is put down, stops in front of Shivranikka and asks, "How full is it?"

"Nearly complete," the woman replies. "You should have enough to go anywhere in the galaxy."

"Excellent."

"Where are you planning on going," the woman asks, getting an almost-dour look on her face, afraid of the answer.

"We're going to use it to get the Star Axis to Quadrant One," Korsaume replies.

Shivranikka seems relieved, maintaining her smile.

"…And then we're going to power up this ship's streaming mega-mass drive and meet them there."

Shivranikka looks devastated. "NO! NO! You can't make me go back there!"

"I can," she answers, "…and I will. We need your help."

"You don't need me that bad," Shivranikka states with a mix of fury and fear. "I was cast out by evil men who wanted nothing to do with me. They're not good enough for my presence." At this, she becomes animated standing closer to and face-to-face with Korsaume. "I am a god compared to them. They are mere gnats to be squashed beneath my feet. They will all bow to me one day, but they will do so on my terms and on the day of my choosing!"

"Shivranikka," Agoparn states, "the people that kicked you off that planet died years ago…"

She suddenly gets a strange look on her face, still staring at Korsaume. She glances down at the floor for a moment, then over at Agoparn for a solemn minute, then back to her master. "I had not thought of that."

"Then you don't mind going…" Korsaume says, half as a question.

"No, I still do not want to go," she replies. "I will not, unless you demand it of me."

"I do so demand…" Korsaume says matter-of-factly to the woman.

Shivranikka still looks quite upset, with furrowed brows, but regains her odd smile. "Very well!" She turns to her minions, gives them a nod, and the five of them all head back to the pod room.

"Good thinking, Engineer," Korsaume says with a smile.

"It just makes sense," he answers her. "I was about to laugh, but I didn't think it would help my relationship with her much."

The two of them walk back to the main portion of the ship to meet up with their crewmates.

*****

"…and according to Shivranikka, the other portion of our ship is orbiting the north hemisphere," Korsaume concludes, sitting in the Captain's office just behind the command deck with the rest of her crewmates.

"I want to attach to it before we head for the tesseract device," Mathew states. "Are there any issues with that?" He looks around the room at his crew.

No one makes a contrary motion, so he continues.

"Does anyone have anything else, before we get going?"

"I would like to say something," Lacendu says.

The crew looks at her, but not in the eyes.

"I'm not sure I want to go back…"

They are all surprised.

"What do you mean, Lacy," Vaskette asks.

Lacendu remarks, "I'm just not sure I want to do what we're getting ready to do. I don't know if we should be doing this… We could die, or worse cause the death of others."

They sit for a long silent moment, but Ardelle, who is sitting against the back wall stands up and steps forward. "Lacy, I see where you're coming from, but I can't help but think that if you didn't have your memories, you would not even be thinking that now."

"I know," she starts, but closes her mouth abruptly, then tries again. "I know, but I don't want my husband to die, and he's there waiting for me, wondering what's happening to me… I love him, and I don't want him to die."

"There are no guarantees in any of this," Mathew says, "but if we don't try, the Solar Union may get away with their ominous plans without anyone to stand in their way. Do you want them to keep doing things to others just like they did to us?"

"Of course not," she says. "It's just," she sighs, "I'm scared. I don't know what we should do."

"It doesn't help that we really don't have a plan," Korsaume states.

"Then we need to make one," Mathew agrees. "Lacendu and Korsaume, I'm putting the two of you in charge for getting a semblance of a plan together for when we find the 'brain.' I want a report on it in three hours. The rest of you hit the command deck and let's get this thing under way."

*****

"Captain Ardelle," Mathew says, calling to the woman who is now on the Star Axis with her crew. "We've set up the tesseract device with the Photonia. Commend your people for finding it so quickly while we were on Plenawald."

"I already have, Captain Mathew," she replies, "but I'll definitely let them know another commendation came from you and your crew."

"Lacendu," Mathew continues, "have you cracked the code to start the device?"

Lacendu's voice comes from the computer room she has made her own. "I believe so, sir, and I've also done a few calculations of my own…but without another device, my chance of being right about where they'll end up is fairly low."

"I understand, Lacy. I trust your abilities, the Star Axis crew has placed their lives on your calculations, and they understand the consequences of this decision."

"That's why I've tried to make sure there are no stars or planets in the line they'll be ending up…" she replies.

"Start it up," Mathew says to her.

"Done." She replies with a smile in her voice.

The Saiar Ria Contract floats comfortably within twenty kilometers of the large device, barely able to fit the Star Axis through the center of it, and completely unable to take the Saiar Ria Contract.

The device comes alive, crackling with yellow and blue light in the center of it. The center of the energy field suddenly begins to swirl around and soon envelopes the enter hole of the device.

The Star Axis, already in position, awaits Mathew's command.

"Captain Ardelle, we'll be with you in about a half hour to an hour. Is your beacon set up?"

"Yes, Captain," is the reply from the freighter captain.

"At your leisure, Captain Ardelle," Mathew says, and the crew in the command deck of the Saiar Ria Contract watches as the Star Axis moves toward the tesseract device and the energy slowly begins to envelope the ship. In moments the ship is fully beyond the entrance to the device and the energy field in the center flickers and dissipates.

"What's done is done," Allen says to himself, but just loud enough for everyone to hear him.

"Now it's our turn," Mathew states out loud. "Lacendu, have you and Korsaume finished that plan?"

Korsaume turns to him. Lacendu answers over the speaker. "Yes, Sir," she replies. "We both agreed that the 'brain' is most likely on Earth."

"Though we're uncertain where on Earth it might be…" Korsaume adds.

"How far away from Earth will we be when we exit the mass-line?" asks Rosetta.

"Several parsecs," Korsaume states turning back around and punching a couple of buttons.

"How long will it take us to get there," Mathew asks.

"About two days if we drag the Star Axis with us…" Lacendu puts in.

Mathew thinks for a moment. "We won't be taking them with us on that part. They didn't sign up for that and I'm not going to throw out the welcome mat for them on this one. When we get there, we need to have another assignment for them."

"I have a suggestion," Allen says with a smile.

"I thought you might," Mathew turns to the Strategist.

Allen glances at his Captain, and then faces the control board before him. While doing some calculations of his own, he says, "We should send them to Baitronoc to learn as much as they can about what's going on. If we go, we'll be caught for sure…but the Solar Union won't have them as enemies…"

"Good idea," Korsaume says facing him and smiling. She turns back around to look out the window.

"Are our own calculations and computers ready," Mathew asks.

"Yes, sir," Allen, Rosetta, and Korsaume say together.

"I'm ready down here," Lacendu adds right after them.

"Whenever you're ready, Lacy," he says.

"NO! I CHANGED MY MIND!" Shivranikka runs onto the command deck, eyes wide and staring out the window as the ship pushes forward and everyone on board feels the effect of a central mass. Suddenly, everything feels different and the main lights of the ship go out as energy crackles around the ship's hull.

Shivranikka's run slows to an abrupt halt and everyone is in their position, completely motionless as the massive ship begins to shrink to about one fourth its original size. The thrusters fire in two short bursts, pushing the increased mass forward about four thousand kilometers on the first, then twenty-six thousand kilometers on the second. Finally, the third thrust pushes them hundreds of thousands of kilometers per minute.

*****

"I wasn't able to stop them," Chrinsole says to his companions, "but I sure won't allow anything to happen to them."

The ex-CHE members of Chrinsole's group stand in a line in front of him.

"I can't go back there myself, but the four of you can. You know what's really going on there, and I want them protected at all costs. Those six people have no idea what they're getting in to.

"Are there any questions, gentlemen or ladies?"

The six people stand in their full body suits, weapons on their backs and at their sides, helmets in their hands. "No, Sir," each one says down the line to the last.

"Good. I want all of you on the ship ready to depart within the hour. Dismissed…" Chrinsole waves them off and they immediately head single file out the door of his office.

Two of his companions; Lacendu's grandmother, Srulé, and Dierdre Pachallo; sit in chairs on the opposite wall.

"You can't protect them forever," Srulé says with a rough face at him.

"I don't need to protect them forever," Chrinsole replies. "Only until this whole mess is over."

"It's evident they don't know what they're getting into," Dierdre says with her usual intense candor. "My question is, why didn't you tell them just what was really happening over there?"

"I figured it would be easier on them in the long run to find out for themselves."

"Based on their trajectory," Dierdre stands up at this with a slim-sheet computer in her hands and looking over at Chrinsole says, "They'll be exiting their jumps right in the middle of the biggest firefight our galaxy has ever seen."

"Well, I seriously doubt they would have cared even if we did tell them, sir," Srulé states. "They're overly determined to do this regardless of our knowledge."

Chrinsole folds his hands together behind his back, stands on the tip of his toes for a moment and then steps around behind his desk and sits down putting his arms on his desk. He breathes in and out hard once and looks at Dierdre holding out one hand. She walks to the desk and hands him the slim-sheet.

He takes a look through the information on the screen and hands it back to her.

Srulé stands up and walks to the desk standing next to Dierdre. "Have you informed Mr. Ruric-Trester of his wife's return to the area…?"

"I have not," he states. "Nor, do I have any intention of doing so. I don't expect them to find each other any time soon. He arrived on Phoenix Rain only a few weeks ago and has not made it back to Segnar, from last report."

"I feel sorry for him," Dierdre says with sincerity.

"I don't," Chrinsole blandly states. "He's part of this mess, and I doubt Lacendu knows just how much his involvement in the Solar Union has done to bring her and her friends to this point in their lives."

"So, what do we do, now," Dierdre asks.

"We do what we've been doing since 'Nation' started. We find a way to dissolve the Solar Union…"

Episode 14
The Whispering String

OPENING:

She spoke in a hushed whisper, possibly out of fear of being heard... "Sometimes...when I'm standing there, I realize there is more to me. More to who I am... The knowledge lingers like the smell of burnt toast. The brink is elusive...and though I search for that edge desperately, it doesn't take me long to realize I'm standing at it, my hands outstretched toward the fall...and I do it. I fall. I fall far below and wonder if I'll ever reach bottom..." Iakole Shihoun, after the Prelature of Hioma found her on a planet after four years alone.

"MOVE!" Ardelle shouts loud to her crew. She races to the front of her command deck just moments after a hit from laser fire knocks the ship for a loop and one of her crew falls over hitting his head on the floor. "I want all shields at max, take down all unimportant functions to use for power." She begins punching buttons on the console she stands at... "Readout, Lieutenant! What did we just get into...?"

Her first lieutenant looks over at his computer panel. "It looks like a war, Captain, but I don't need readouts to tell me that."

"Who are we between," she yells at him, half out of exasperation.

"The Solar Union's fleet and an armada of Agrauve vessels," he replies.

"What the heck did the Agrauve's do to tick the Solar Union off…?" She asks the question to herself.

"We need to get out of this firefight," someone says aloud behind her.

"No! You think…?" another yells.

"Down," the Captain yells above the noise.

The Star Axis C-72 takes another hit from fired shots, and then another.

"Our light shield is down by half," someone yells out.

"Keep the status calls to your self until we're out of this," the Captain shouts. "Focus on the job at hand!"

Additional shots are received on aft and starboard just as the ship exits the edge of the battle.

"Full thrusters," Captain Ardelle yells. "Get us as far away from this as possible and start the beacon for the Saiar Ria Contract."

"Captain," the Lietenant says, "that might draw unneeded attention from the two fleets."

"I don't care," she yells walking over to him and slamming her hands down on the console in front of him. "I don't want them to wind up in the same mess we were just in!"

The lieutenant looks at her in surprise first, and then in acknowledgment. "Understood, Captain…" He presses the button for the beacon to begin.

Captain Ardelle turns and sits partially on the edge of the console. "Someone get the doctor up here to help Jenley."

"Yes, Captain," someone says pressing another button on their console and calling for the doctor.

She walks off through the command deck. "Repair teams to the affected decks. I want this ship fully operational in two hours. Take what you have to from any downed ships in the area nearby. I'll be in my room."

Ardelle walks to the back into the Captain's room.

*****

The Saiar Ria Contract slows and begins to expand. The crackling of energy around the ship slowly begins to fade and Shivranikka falls flat on her face hitting her nose in the process. Her nose begins to bleed.

She pulls her self up from the floor looking at blood on the floor with complete confusion. She raises a hand to her face and wipes at her nose, and then pulls her hand from her face and stares at it agape with the other hand on the floor holding her body up.

"No way," she says. "How could this happen? I'm supposed to be invulnerable."

Vaskette turns to the techno-witch with realization. "The increase in mass and shrinking of your natural size must have separated your metallic structure somewhat when you returned to normal size. You should be alright shortly."

Shivranikka looks up at Vaskette. "I told you I didn't want to come here!"

"You were too late," Korsaume states blandly standing up in a huff and walking to the woman on the ground; "We were already under way when you came in…and don't try to get out of your verbal contract with me, now, Nikka." Korsaume bends down to look Shivranikka in the eyes. "You're mine." The Lieutenant stands up and walks toward the back of the command deck.

"Don't leave just yet, Lieutenant," Allen says quickly to stop her from leaving the room.

"What's wrong, Allen," Mathew asks turning to the man.

"We're coming up on a battle…and I mean fast…" he replies.

Everyone on the command deck looks out the front of the ship. In front of them are a large amount of ships and a bright spot between them, obvious to them as shots of lasers and weapons being fired off between two groups.

"They got it started anyway," Korsaume says walking back to the front of the command deck. "They didn't need our help after all…"

"What now, Captain," Rosetta asks turning to her boyfriend.

Mathew doesn't look back at her. "Track the signal of the Star Axis…" He turns to her now, "…and pray they're not in the middle of that…"

Rosetta looks back at her console and presses a few controls on the panel screens. "I'm picking up their signal about three thousand kilometers out to our immediate left. They look like they've been hit by something, Captain. Possibly laser fire, and maybe a projectile or two…"

"Let's go to meet them," Mathew says sitting down in his chair.

Allen presses controls and says, "Heading their way, Captain. We should rendezvous with them in about eight minutes."

Shivranikka wipes her nose again and sees more blood on her hand. "What about me…?" she asks. "Doesn't anyone care that I'm bleeding!?"

*****

Lacendu lies quietly on the floor of the large room near her chair and console. She has been unconscious for about ten minutes, just after the mega-mass device took effect. It happened slowly. She was turning just as the device began its process and it pulled her from her chair and caused her to fall asleep. She hit her head on the floor when she fell from the chair, and now she is rousing.

She begins breathing deep and opens her eyes to look around the room. It is completely dark.

"Captain," she says… She waits. "Captain…"

"What's going on, Lacendu," Mathew asks.

"The lights are all out down here. Is there power on the command deck?"

"We show there's power down there," Lacendu hears Vaskette's voice.

"Well, there may be power, but it's not in use," Lacendu responds. "Could you send someone down here to help me? I hit my head on the floor."

Vaskette replies. "I'll be right down."

Moments later Vaskette arrives and opens the door to the room to see Lacendu is still lying on the floor. "Lacy," the young woman hears and Vaskette is soon at her side.

"When did the power come back on in here," the doctor asks.

"You're kidding, right," Lacendu responds. "I can't see anything."

There is complete silence from Vaskette.

"What's wrong," Lacendu asks.

"Lacy, I think you have a concussion. You've probably lost your sight temporarily. I'll get you fixed up. Can you stand?"

"I think so," she says.

As she tries to stand Lacendu feels very dizzy and light-headed. As Vaskette tries to pull her up the young woman rolls out of her doctor friend's arm.

Vaskette says loud enough for the computer to hear her. "Allen, I need some help down here."

"I'll be right there," he replies, and only a few minutes later he arrives and helps Vaskette pick Lacendu up off the floor.

"Are you alright," Allen asks Lacendu.

"I feel dizzy…"

"I think she has a concussion," Vaskette tells him. "I want to run a couple of tests. Let's get her to the infirmary."

After the two help Lacendu to the infirmary, Allen leaves Vaskette to do her work.

Allen arrives on the command deck and Mathew immediately turns to him. "What's wrong with Lacendu," he asks with sincere concern.

"Lacy fell and hit her head and the doctor thinks she's temporarily blind from a concussion," Allen answers.

"Is anyone else feeling effects from that mega-mass thing," Mathew asks.

"I am," Shivranikka says, still kneeling on the floor with little joy of being there.

"…Besides the guest…?"

"I am," Korsaume and Rosetta say together, and Allen also gives an affirmative.

"Oh, good. I'm not the only one," the Captain says with a smile. "When we get to the Star Axis, we're all going to get ourselves checked out by the doctor."

"Yes, sir," Korsaume replies with relief.

"We're coming up on them in one minute," Rosetta says pressing some buttons. "It looks like they've already got some work on the damage underway."

As the Saiar Ria Contract comes within visible range of the Star Axis, the crew on the command deck can see the damage to the ship they sent ahead via a tesseract device.

"That doesn't look good," Korsaume states…

"Captain Ardelle," Mathew says, allowing the computer to carry his voice over the venotronic waves to the other ship. "Are you and your crew alright?"

"Captain Mathew," they hear Ardelle say, "you have no idea how good it is to hear your voice."

"What happened out there?" he asks.

"We exited the tesseract right in the middle of that firefight," she replies.

"Do you need any assistance," Mathew asks as his ship gets close enough to see the details of the other vessel.

"No, sir…I think we're going to hit the repair center nearby. There's a planet called 'Fenjac' about two light-years away, and we can be there in about two days. We have enough energy to get there without problems. Did you have anything else in mind," she asks.

"Not for your crew at this time. I would like to see you and your Lieutenant onboard for a short time. I have a proposition to make…" Mathew states with a smile.

There is a smile in Ardelle's voice, too. "I'm not entirely sure that sounds good," she responds.

"We'll connect to your vessel in just a few minutes and I'll lend Agoparn to your repair crew."

"That would be wonderful," Ardelle says.

"I'd like to help, too," Korsaume states…

"You heard my Lieutenant, Captain Ardelle…?"

"I did, Captain Mathew. We look forward to sharing your crew for our temporary repairs. I'll be aboard as soon as you're connected to us. Captain Ardelle, out…"

*****

"You want us to go where…?" Captain Ardelle laughs as if it's all a joke.

Her Lieutenant smiles, as well, with his eyebrows raised.

Mathew returns a smile but says, "I'm not kidding. I want you and your crew to go to Baitronoc."

Her chest still moving with some semblance of laughter, Ardelle says, "Captain, we have no right to go there, much less reason. Baitronoc is the center of the Solar Union. I seriously doubt we could even get on the Dyson-sphere, or even near it for that matter. They wouldn't even give us the time of day."

Mathew looks over at his weapons expert who steps up to the desk. Korsaume says, "They will if you have this…" She hands Captain Ardelle what looks to be a wristband.

Captain Ardelle goes straight-faced. "What is this…?"

"It's my saper-churrenii," Korsaume states. "It was embedded under my skin in my right wrist at my inception to the CHE. It contains secret information about my life that only the Solar Union and the CHE would have access to."

"That thing isn't metal, is it," asks Ardelle's Lieutenant.

"No. It's made of Strephecyne," Korsaume answers. "It has tripper pads in place of circuits, and cell-data generators. The CHE will want it, and you can trade it for access to the sphere.

"…And just as an FYI for you, the only way to get that thing is to kill me…"

"I'm not killing you, Korsaume," Ardelle says.

"What I mean is they'll see it that way. They'll assume you killed me and pulled that off of me," Korsaume looks at Ardelle as if she should have realized this.

"You think they'll believe I or someone from my crew killed the galaxy's most proficient weapons expert," Ardelle asks. "That's what I was trying to say…"

"Admittedly it's not the most likely thing in the universe," Mathew suggests, "but it is the only feasible way to get you and your crew onto Baitronoc without fanfare."

"Where are you all going," Ardelle's Lieutenant asks.

"We're headed to Earth," Mathew says.

"Permission to board the Star Axis to assist their crew, Captain…" Korsaume requests of Mathew.

"Dismissed, Lieutenant," Mathew says, looking up at her.

As Korsaume walks out of the Captain's room, Ardelle continues. "What's on Earth?"

"We believe we'll find the 'brain' there…" he states.

Ardelle and her Lieutenant look at each other for a brief moment.

"Captain Mathew, people have been looking for the 'brain' since it was created and set up. No one has ever found it. What makes you think you and your crew will, and what could possibly have made you think it would be there…?"

"Keep in mind, Captain Ardelle, that I have at my disposal the galaxy's best in weapons, strategy, and mathematics. Korsaume and Lacendu took the little information available on the subject which we had aboard this vessel, and with what little Shivranikka knew about the subject, since she is from that time, the three of them have about four different places they feel it could be. Earth was at the top of the list."

Ardelle and her Lieutenant stand motionless for a few moments.

Finally, Ardelle asks, “What do you want us to do on Baitronoc?”

“We want you to find out in as subtle a way as possible any additional information you can about my crew and me.” Mathew stands up and walks around the long desk to stand in front of Ardelle.

Ardelle sighs while glancing down at the floor, up at Mathew, down at the floor again, and finally settling on Mathew. “While I admit concern for your crew traveling to Earth; a near-desolate planet with a small population of highest society and little place in the way of landing; I seriously doubt I’ll talk any of you out of this.”

“Oh, now, I don’t know,” Mathew says with a smile. “I have a gut feeling you might be able to talk Agoparn and Shivranikka out of it…”

Ardelle and her Lieutenant chuckle at this.

Mathew adds, “Before you go, I’d like you to inform your doctor we need him to run some tests on us with regards to the mega-mass drive we just used.”

Ardelle’s eyes widen for a moment in a bit of surprise, but she holds her hand out to Mathew who takes it and shakes.

“I’ll do that, Captain.” the woman says to him.

The woman and her companion walk out of the room.

Rosetta looks up from her place on the sofa. Mathew sits down next to her and puts his arm around her shoulder.

“What do you think,” Mathew asks.

“I think we’re all crazy…” She stops for a moment. “I take that back…I know we’re all crazy. I think we’ll accomplish what we set out to do, regardless of what happens…” She turns her face to smile at him and meet his eyes.

He returns her smile and they kiss.

*****

Two hours allows time for the doctor to check out the crew of the Saiar Ria Contract and find they're alright, especially Lacendu's baby which doesn't seem to have suffered any permanent ill effects, but he highly recommends they not use the mega-mass drive a second time. It is also just enough for the crews to mingle and Agoparn to hang out with Ardelle before the two ships separate and head out to their destinations.

The Star Axis C-72 takes off, leaving the Saiar Ria Contract to its own devices.

The entire crew is in the infirmary once again.

"Can you see, yet," Korsaume asks Lacendu.

"A little," Lacendu says sitting up on the bed.

"It wasn't a concussion," Vaskette says to them. "Her proximity to the drive is what caused her blackout."

"What do you mean," Korsaume asks folding her arms against her chest.

"We used that drive without considering what it did or what effect it would have on us. I already tried to speak with Shivranikka about how she came upon this ship, but the only thing I could get out of her without a demand from Korsaume was that everyone on board was dead when she came aboard." Vaskette comes around the bed and sits down next to her friend.

"Could those original crewmembers be the ones she's using as her help?" Allen asks.

"Ew, gross," Rosetta says giving Allen a sour face.

"I'm just asking," he says.

"They could," Korsaume agrees. "It's her style."

"She has a style," asks Vaskette.

"Style, I'm not sure about," Mathew says, "but she is predictable."

"Predictable and annoying," Lacendu adds with her eyes closed.

"Well, we don't want to use the drive again unless it's absolutely necessary," Mathew says.

"Then you don't need me to get on our merry way," Lacendu says. "I'll go somewhere to get out of your way and wait until someone needs a mathematical calculation or an unnecessary statement..."

She stands up and opens her eyes to see where she's going.

"Out," Vaskette says in the nicest way. "I have a patient to see to and you all have a planet to get us to."

Mathew turns and allows the other crewmembers to exit first and follows them to the command deck. Shivranikka is long since gone, her blood staining the floor. They all step around it and fall into position.

"Point us in the right direction, Allen," Mathew says. "Whenever you're ready, get us going."

The vessel turns and in a matter of moments the ship moves forward and accelerates until it reaches its fastest thruster speed.

*****

Most of the lights are off throughout the Saiar Ria Contract and Rosetta walks silently through the hallways. She arrives on the command deck wearing her gown, bare feet, and her hair hangs loosely around her face, a little less curled than usual. The command deck is empty, barely lit, and a little cooler than she would prefer.

"Computer, raise the temperature of command about four degrees."

The computer follows the order almost instantaneously.

It takes just a few moments for the temperature to rise enough for her senses to accept it while she walks to the front of the ship to stand between the two front panels.

"It was quiet in here until you showed up..." It is Shivranikka's voice.

"Hi, Nikka," Rosetta says reluctantly.

Shivranikka steps from the shadows in the far corner and stands not far from her.

The two of them stare out the window at the multitudes of stars, and a golden sun shining gently on the right giving off a radiant glow into the left of the command deck. It is beautiful, and Rosetta just tries to take it all in.

"What do you see," Rosetta asks of the woman.

"Where," Shivranikka returns… "Out there…?"

"Yes. What do you see out the window before us…?"

"I see a place I hate. No, despise… I see a horrible little realm that will never accept me as their goddess."

Rosetta turns her head, but doesn't quite look at the other. "Do you want to know what I see, Nikka?"

"Not really, but I'm in the mood for something funny right now. Go ahead."

Rosetta feels a twinge of anger at the woman, but allows it to subside, reminded of whom she is speaking with… "I see an open place where men and women can live together in harmony."

"Harmony… That's such a funny word, don't you think, Seta…?" There is a sense of humor about her.

"There are funnier words in our language," Rosetta replies. "When I say 'harmony,' I don't mean music, or accordance. I mean that everyone can have a right to their own feelings, emotions, desires, and needs, without fearing that others will take it away.

"That's what law and order is based on. We humans need law and order because some of us tend to take advantage of our rights. Some believe that because we have rights that we have the right to take other's rights away. 'Law and Order' steps in when the rights of one interfere with the rights of another.

"We all have a right to live with each other, but sometimes we forget our other rights. If we don't like someone, it is not our right to kill them, or hurt them. However, we do have the right to never see them again if we choose."

Rosetta is silent for a long moment.

Shivranikka finally fills up the silence. "So you feel that if everyone realized this, we wouldn't need leaders and overseers."

"Oh, no, I don't say that. There's a place for everyone in a well-balanced society. Leaders are necessary, and in some sense I think overseers are, as well. The question I pose is this…What does the Solar Union think about our rights? Better yet, what about the rights of the six individuals who were sent to Quadrant Four away from their homes without their memories? Who gave the Solar Union the right to take their memories from them in order to force them to start a war…?"

Shivranikka gives Rosetta a crooked look. "That's three questions, dear."

Rosetta rolls her eyes and sighs, shaking her head.

"Besides that, who are the six individuals sent to Quadrant Four without their memories…?"

Rosetta turns to face the other woman. "You don't know…?"

Shivranikka shakes her head. "No."

Rosetta breaths in deep; "Actually, I guess there were only five. Korsaume still had her memories. Mathew, Allen, Lacendu, Agoparn, and Vaskette got their memories wiped clean. Lacendu only recently regained hers…"

Shivranikka's eyes widen in disbelief. "Really…?"

"Yeah…Really…" She nods her head.

Rosetta turns and begins to walk away folding her arms and using her hands to warm the sides of her upper arms.

"…And they were still able to rival me…?" asks Shivranikka.

Rosetta tilts her head up at the other, the left side of her mouth pulls back a bit, straightens back up, and she walks out of the room.

Shivranikka watches the huntress leave the room and then turns back to the front and walks to stand where Rosetta stood. She stares out the window for a long, silent hour watching the ship slowly pass the radiant golden glow of the star as it draws nearer and nearer and finally begins to fade behind leaving her in near darkness, with only the large cluster of stars in front of her to show light beyond those of the working consoles in the room.

*****

"We'll be coming up on Earth in about a half hour," Allen says to Mathew, who is seated in the Captain's chair. The entire crew is back in their places, with Shivranikka safely out of the way in the pod room.

"Have we been able to get information about Earth from trans-waves," asks Mathew.

"No, Sir," Rosetta replies. "I've been scanning the area for anything and all I get are trans-waves from two of Jupiter's moons, Mars, and a few stations circling the other planets…not to mention random waves from planets much farther away."

"Are there encircling stations around Earth," Korsaume asks.

"No, why," asks Allen.

"Just curious," she replies.

"I'm not showing any kind of protection around Earth from my sensors," he adds.

Mathew asks, "Does that sound like the kind of place the 'brain' would be…?"

Allen interjects, "If you want to hide something, you don't stick guards around it. That's the first sign something important is being hidden."

"Good point," Rosetta remarks.

Mathew stands up. "Korsaume, I want you and Shivranikka to meet me in the back shuttle in five minutes. I'll meet you there…"

"Where are you going," Korsaume asks turning her head from her terminal.

"You'll see," he replies.

*****

Ten minutes pass and Korsaume stands with Shivranikka just inside the door to the back shuttle.

Mathew arrives with a device in his hand.

Korsaume recognizes it immediately. "What do you want with that…?"

"I want the two of you to go down to the planet's surface, set it up perpendicular to the core, and start it up…" Mathew answers.

"What is it," Shivranikka requests.

"It's a pulsing D-1-9," Korsaume explains. "It's usually used to set up at blockades. It fires every second and does significant amounts of damage for long distances." She turns to her Captain. "Then what…?"

He opens his other hand. In it is another devise she recognizes.

"Where did you get a 'matter-seek?'" she asks with a smile, eyebrows furrowed.

"I've been increasingly surprised at the things in that weapons room we found," he states. "The people originally aboard this thing left it all behind."

"Speaking of that," Korsaume turns back to Shivranikka, "In what condition did you find this ship in…?"

Shivranikka doesn't look surprised at the question. "When I came on board, every person was dead. I was on the small shuttle Donnikynian and Forgiven built for their son and his fiancé. I was with Forgiven and Shallajohnne. We'd been traveling for well over seventy years avoiding planets and stars as much as possible.

"We came upon the Saiar Ria Contract about two years ago, and we'd been flying it for all that time when the six of you took over it…

"We attached the shuttle to the clam and began trying to figure out how to run the ship. The language is Morstone, which Xychocappla taught me while he was turning me into what I am now, so they and I were able to read much of the instructions and get it underway. We put the dead in the pods and set up the transfer into their current states. Most of them died on your ship. I had to rig all of them with a capacitor that could accept my mental commands; otherwise they'd just lie down limp on the floor and not do anything…"

"That explains why the ones we met were already dead," Korsaume responds.

"How many men were aboard this thing when you found it," Mathew asks.

"There were forty-six men…" she answers.

"How about women," Korsaume asks.

"There were fifty-nine women…"

"That's one hundred five," Mathew states. "Were they all Solar Union members?"

"They all had the Solar Union emblem on their uniforms," Shivranikka states.

"What did the Solar Union need with an experimental ship and one hundred five men and women…?" Korsaume furrows her brow at Mathew.

"They couldn't have been searching for us," he states. "Not two years ago… We were still home…" Mathew clears his face and smiles at the techno-witch. "Thank you, Shivranikka. If you don't mind, I'd like to finish our discussion when you return."

Shivranikka looks at him with curiosity. "Why do you thank me?"

"I appreciate your honest answers," he states.

She turns and walks off seemingly upset.

"I hope thanking her didn't offend her," Mathew says to Korsaume.

"Don't take it personal, Captain," she answers. "We'll get the job done and be back before you know it."

"Be careful, down there. I don't want anything to happen to either of you."

Korsaume smiles eloquently. "I'm so glad you care, Captain."

"No, I just don't want to have to go down there myself to finish the job…" Mathew replies.

Korsaume laughs, giving him a sour face. "Whatever…" She grabs the two items from Mathew's hand and turns to walk out.

Mathew exits and closes the door behind him. Then he watches as the shuttle detaches again to head to Earth's surface.

*****

Korsaume sits in the co-pilot's chair, allowing the machine-woman to control the main systems.

"What do you read, Korsaume," Shivranikka asks.

"I'm still not showing any defenses or ships coming to meet us. I'm also not showing much in the way of ground sites for earth-to-air def-off weaponry." Korsaume continues to check her readouts.

Shivranikka does not reply.

From their positions, they watch as the ground comes up quickly at them and within moments they are tilting the ship upward in preparation for landing.

"We have visitors," Korsaume states. "Hover vehicles are heading this way, less than a kilometer behind us."

"They're probably thinking they have visitors," Shivranikka says looking over at Korsaume. "I dare say we're invading their territory."

"With all due respect, Shivranikka, Earth is every human's home. No one should be able to claim a certain right to any piece of it. It is our origin."

"But of course, dear master," Shivranikka responds.

The vessel lands a minute later and the two women exit from the side clam, down the steps watching the hover vehicles come up to them rather fast. The two vehicles stop within meters of the women and seven females and one male step out, weapons at their sides.

"Welcome," says one of the women, most likely the leader.

"I am Korsaume," the Lieutenant says. "This is my assistant, Nikka." She looks over at Shivranikka, whose face is lit by the sun more brightly than Korsaume has ever seen it. The lines in her face are painfully obvious, and Korsaume hopes they won't notice and ask questions.

"Where have we landed," Shivranikka asks.

"You have landed on the property of the Lesser Corsythe Felluge College Campus…" responds the leader.

"We're not too familiar with Earth," Korsaume states. "Is that bad…?"

"It can be," the woman states, "…if you don't have the proper permits."

"What type of permits," Shivranikka asks.

"The kinds that allow you to stay here. All we need to do is see your permits, and you may land where you choose." The woman's voice is adamant.

"I can supply you my data. They're inside my ship. However, my servant has none." Korsaume looks a bit harried.

"Bring us your papers, and we will allow you safe passage," the woman states.

"Shivranikka, stay out here; keep them company. I'll be right back." Korsaume walks back into the ship. She returns moments later with a hand-held computer and walks toward the lead woman.

"Stop," the woman says. "Place the computer on the ground and step back."

Korsaume does as she is told and the woman steps forward to retrieve the hand-held. She reads over it and looks back up at Korsaume. "You are a member of the CHE…?"

"That is correct," Korsaume replies.

"We do not recognize the CHE's authority, Madame," the woman states. "You will need to leave."

"I can't leave right away," Korsaume tells her. "I have work I was ordered to complete, and I must carry out that order."

"I'm sorry, Madame…you will need to board your ship and leave," the woman reiterates.

Korsaume turns to Shivranikka. "We really need to stay here."

Shivranikka looks back at her master. "I understand."

In seconds, Shivranikka moves past all of the eight individuals relieving them of their weapons and breaking them into small pieces.

They all look at her in fear.

"What is she," the leader asks, pointing at the techno-witch.

Korsaume glances at Shivranikka and smiles, "Would you like to explain it to them."

"I am a hybrid machine-human. I am the culmination of the life's work of Xychocappla, a man far advanced for his time. He created a hybrid of technology and human physiology and made me the ultimate of all his creations. I run on the most advanced energy known to man…dyprase photoneuric energy…

"You cannot harm me. No matter what you do to me, I will never die. I am the penultimate human-organic technology hybrid. One day, you will all bow to me and call me your leader…your master. I will lead this galaxy to peace and prosperity, where all humans; men, women, and children; can live without fear."

The eight people look at each other during Shivranikka's speech while Korsaume sets up the gun on the ground.

When the speech is over, Korsaume starts the gun. It begins pulsing, punching a hole into the ground.

One of the other women from the group looks at Shivranikka, then at Korsaume. "Is she always like that?"

Korsaume nods and laughs. "Pretty much…"

The gun continues for several minutes and they all stand in silence.

"What are you doing," the leader finally asks somewhere in that time.

"I'm doing what I was sent here to do," Korsaume replies. "I have a job to do and I'm going to do it, with our without your consent."

"I repeat the question…What are you doing," the leader asks again.

"I'm drilling a hole about nine kilometers deep," Korsaume answers with her head cocked. "What's it to you…?"

"You are destroying the Earth," the woman states.

"No, just drilling a hole. People do it on all kinds of planets."

"What's done to Mother Earth hurts her," the woman remarks.

"Well, then, Mother Earth is getting an injection," Korsaume replies. "One which will save the lives of trillions of humans the galaxy over… You're a part of that, you know."

"I am not a part of this," the woman shakes her head.

Shivranikka looks up into the sky. "Korsaume, dear," she says.

"What do you want, now, Nikka…?" Korsaume looks at her servant annoyed.

"We have company."

"What kind…?"

"The kind that doesn't want us here," the techno-witch prates.

"I assume you're not referring to the ones in front of us," Korsaume says following Shivranikka's gaze into the sky. "What is that…?"

"I'm not certain," the other states, "but they have weapons powered and are preparing to fire."

"Can you do anything to stop them," Korsaume asks.

"Not without some help," she says.

"What do you need?"

Shivranikka looks at Korsaume. "You might want to close your eyes and not look forward…"

"Is this going to be a desecration," Korsaume asks.

"I'm not sure what that means," replies Shivranikka, "but based on the way you used it in the question, I will say 'yes.'"

Korsaume turns away as Shivranikka runs at the eight people knocking them over into a pile on the ground. She picks up one of the hover vehicles and hurls it at the coming vessel overhead. The vessel fires off a weapon which hits the hover vehicle causing it to explode only meters from the vehicle, knocking both out of the sky. The flying vessel and the remnants of the hover vehicle fall straight down from the sky on top of the other vehicle crushing it.

Materials from the crash fly at Korsaume's back, but Shivranikka is already there catching them in mid-air and throwing them to the ground.

"Will there be anything else, Korsaume," Shivranikka asks.

Korsaume turns to look at the destruction. "I guess the hole in the ground is deep enough now to throw in the 'matter-seek.'"

"I believe so," Shivranikka remarks.

Korsaume bends down and stops the gun, pulls the 'matter-seek' from a pocket on her jacket, presses the button to start it up, and drops it into the hole. "Let's get out of here while we're still in one piece. Check our shuttle for damage…"

Shivranikka does as she's told and finds three spots where shrapnel has damaged the hull. Korsaume walks over to join her, pulling from another jacket pocket a communications device. She stands near Shivranikka as the woman shows her the damaged places.

"Go ahead," they hear from the device.

"Captain, you should be able to begin the 'matter-seek' now…" Korsaume answers into the device. "Also, we have hull damage on the shuttle. We'll need for you to meet us in the upper atmosphere…"

"We understand," responds Mathew with much concern. "Is everything alright, down there?"

"Not exactly, Captain. We had a run-in with some folks, and they asked me for my permits. I showed them the CHE report, but they said CHE members didn't have access. Another vehicle came and was preparing to fire on us, but Shivranikka took care of that…" Korsaume smiles at the other woman.

They hear laughter on the other end. "Thus, the damage to the shuttle's hull," he asks.

"Hey," Shivranikka looks almost upset, "I was protecting my master to the best of my abilities. She gave me permission."

"He's not mad at you, Nikka," Korsaume shakes her head. "That's why he's laughing."

Shivranikka looks hurt, anyway.

"Don't worry about it. We'll meet you halfway and attach in the atmosphere about twelve kilometers up. Rendezvous in five minutes," Mathew says.

"Understood," replies Korsaume. She turns the device off, and then this to her servant, "Let's go."

*****

It is actually less than five minutes before the shuttle attaches to the back of the Saiar Ria Contract and they hover through the atmosphere above the hole Korsaume made on the ground.

Korsaume arrives on the command deck after asking Shivranikka to patch the holes in the shuttle. "Am I missing anything," she asks.

"Not yet," Rosetta replies. "We found sixteen various buildings, a buried city we believe to be the remains of a place called Dallas, and some old coins."

"Coins," Korsaume turns her head to ask. "Those haven't been used in generations…"

"I'm just curious," Allen adds, "how will we know if we do find it."

"I assume it will look like a computer," Korsaume states.

"What kind," Allen asks. "How big is it? Where will it be? It'll take over three hours for that 'matter-seek' to search the planet. What leads will we follow up on?"

Mathew turns toward Allen. "I see your point," he remarks. "While that thing is doing its job, we should check out Jupiter."

"I'm not so sure," Rosetta says watching her readout of the information being sent from the 'matter-seek.' "I think I've got something rather promising…"

"What," Mathew asks as he stands up and walks over to his girlfriend.

"Eleven hundred kilometers that direction," she points downward. "I think it's under the place where Japan used to be."

"Didn't it sink under the ocean about four hundred years ago," Korsaume asks.

At that moment, Shivranikka walks in. "Four hundred forty-one years ago," she states with blandness in her voice, as if everyone should have known it. "It was called Roalkudore by that time, and it was the hub of electronic computers at the height of Earth's electronic computer development until China created the technology we currently still use in our modern computers."

"We appreciate the history lesson, Nikka," Mathew says. "Have a seat. Allen, take us there."

The ship begins moving and is soon up to maximum planet-speed.

"How do we plan on getting down there," Allen asks. "If it's under water, that's not exactly going to make it easy for us…"

"We'll have to do some of our best work to get into it," Korsaume states. "The people involved in keeping the 'brain's' location secret I'm sure made it extremely difficult to get into it."

"We've got company," Rosetta says, rather loudly.

"What's going on," Mathew asks.

"I'm reading a large group of large ships." She turns to her boyfriend with eyes wide. "They're the Earth Sharcuran Knights force…"

"My parents," Korsaume says, looking behind her at her crewmates with deep concern.

"Who are the Sharcuran Knights, and what do they have to do with your parents," Rosetta asks.

"We don't have time for that. Vaskette, I need you and Lacendu up here now!" Mathew sits back down.

"I think we do need to know," Rosetta says harshly to Mathew.

"Seta, if it's enough to concern my lieutenant to the point of worry, I'm thinking we're not going to stand a huge chance here. The faster we resolve this, the better off we'll all be," he answers.

Allen interrupts. "They're preparing to fire a Shiva-response weapon," he yells.

"Evade," Mathew shouts.

As the ship moves sideways to the left, they see passing them a large energy rod crackling with yellow, gold, and blue.

Lacendu and Vaskette arrive on the command deck.

"What can we do for you, Captain," Vaskette asks.

"I really need you, Lacy," Mathew turns and points for Vaskette to sit down. "I need to know what this ship is capable of..."

"This ship...?" she begins. "It's capable of almost anything you want it to do."

"Like what," Mathew asks taking the young blonde to the desk near Korsaume and helping her sit down.

"Well, this thing is basically a computer program. It's built by computer programming for computer programming. It's based on a computer programming language. Tell it what you want it to do and it will do everything in its power to accomplish the task," Lacendu states.

"I don't feel comfortable with that," Mathew says as they are hit by a shot from one of the ships. "I want you to program it. You're better at that kind of stuff."

"Yes, Sir," she says pulling the chair up to the desk, locking it in place, and locking the belt around her to keep her in it. She begins punching buttons on the screen. "What are we dealing with...?"

"The Sharcuran Knights," Korsaume answers turning her head to the blonde.

"Dear God...What did we do to tick them off...?" Lacendu asks breathing hard.

Allen says loudly again, "They're preparing to hit us with that Shiva-response again..."

Lacendu punches several buttons. "It's a good thing I know what a Shiva-response is..."

"You can program against it," Allen asks.

Lacendu glances over and up at him. "I can program against a single blast. Maybe a double and triple blast... The more they shoot at us at one time, the less chance we'll have at evading it."

"Just like any weaponry," Korsaume says a little louder than she intended.

"That was the point," Lacendu replies, more than a little upset.

"Alright, people," Mathew says in a calmer voice, but still with a sense of urgency, "let's not be fighting with each other…Let's focus on the task at hand. I want options."

"Stand and fight," Allen states.

Korsaume is next. "I agree with Allen.

"We can take them," Lacendu says.

"Dive into the ocean," Rosetta says.

"Don't look at me," Vaskette says. "I don't have any suggestions. You all just do what you think is best."

Mathew turns to Shivranikka. "Your thoughts…"

"Who… Me…?" Shivranikka points to herself.

"Um, yeah," Mathew says. "I want your thoughts."

"Oh. Um… Stand and fight…like the others stated…" She looks a little embarrassed.

"I'm in agreement with the consensus," Mathew says. "Turn this thing around and face them. Prepare to fire all weapons when I say…"

"Weapons' ready," Korsaume says.

The ship turns quickly and they are soon facing a fleet of about sixteen massive ships hovering in the air.

"They've stood down from their weapons," Allen states, calm now.

"They are requesting communications," Rosetta says.

Mathew walks over to her. "Answer their request."

Rosetta pushes a button on her console. "Open."

"This is Captain Mathew Arnold of the Saiar Ria Contract. What do you want?"

"My name is Varnelle Choreegue, Admiral of the Sharcuran Knights, requesting you stand down from your weapons as we have done…" The voice seems a bit distant.

"I would like to fulfill your request," Mathew replies, "but I need some assurance…"

"You, Captain Mathew Arnold, are trespassing on our property. If anyone has the need for assurances, it would be us…"

"I wasn't aware that Earth was owned by any one individual group," Mathew states. "Last I heard Earth was owned by all humans equally, and if we chose to set down that was our right."

"In theory, that sounds well and good, Captain Mathew, but in practice, things are not so easy. We would like for your ship to settle down on the next planetary mass. We will escort you and then we would very much like to meet you and your fine crew in person."

Mathew gives the signal for Rosetta to turn off the signal, and after she does he turns to his crew. "What do all of you think…?"

"It's a painfully obvious trap," Korsaume replies.

"Agreed," Lacendu says.

"We've walked away from worse, Captain," Allen answers.

"Are you serious…?" Lacendu asks with sarcasm.

"I wouldn't worry about them," Shivranikka says. "I can handle anything they dish out…"

"With that, open the channel back up," Mathew says. After Rosetta has done so, he says in a more formal tone, "We will accompany you as you have requested. Allen, Korsaume; stand down from weapons."

The ship goes to normal mode and within moments the sixteen vessels are surrounding the Saiar Ria Contract and they are heading toward the land mass where China had once been.

It doesn't take long for them to reach the destination and they are soon landing on the ground and exiting the ship as a group.

Before them is a man in a black full body suit, and numerous other people, all of them with their chests jutted and their hands behind their backs. The man in front seems to be the leader, and Mathew immediately takes him to be the Admiral he spoke with…

"Admiral," Mathew says hoping.

"Captain Mathew Arnold of the Saiar Ria Contract," the man half-asks.

"I am," Mathew replies.

"You have a fine crew," the man states.

"Look, I didn't come here for pleasantries. No disrespect, Admiral, but we are on a mission of the utmost importance..."

"I admire that," the Admiral says with a smile. "You may call me Varnelle."

"What did I just finish saying about pleasantries, Admiral...?" Mathew looks at the other with annoyance.

"I know why your crew are here," Varnelle states.

"Oh, you do, do you...?"

"I can think of only a very few reasons anyone would have come to Earth... You are looking for the 'brain.'"

"Out of curiosity, what were the other reasons you could think of...?"

"Korsaume's parents, for one... The other is perhaps your need to get away from everything. The 'matter-seek' really gave it away."

"Are my parents here," asks Korsaume.

The Admiral all but ignores the question. "What do you want with the 'brain'?"

"I want to ask it a few questions," Mathew responds. "It was the cause of my crew and I being sent to the other side of the galaxy without our memories, and I want to know why."

"We all really want to know why..." Allen states, knowing he, too, will be ignored.

"Not really," the Admiral states. "You don't need to seek the 'brain' to understand the reason for your memory erasure... Nor do you need the 'brain' to give you the answers to any other question you seek. I have the answers to any question you might ask."

Mathew turns to Korsaume who in turn looks at Shivranikka. "Would you mind helping us out," Korsaume asks.

Shivranikka looks like she is about to do something, but suddenly falls flat on the ground. Korsaume rushes to her side, looks up at the Admiral with an inquisitive face and asks, "What just happened to her…?"

"She runs on dyprase photoneuric energy. We've shut her down to keep her from doing anything you might regret…"

"We might regret," Korsaume stands up in anger, stressing the word "we." "You have a lot of nerve…"

"We're the Sharcuran Knights, Korsaume… We are required to have a lot of nerve."

Mathew sighs, showing an intense amount of exasperation. Through clenched teeth he says, "Enough! What is the answer, if you're so smart…?"

"The answer to the reason six of you wound up on the opposite side of the galaxy is because of the question asked of the 'brain' by the Head Keeper of the Solar Union…the only man allowed to make any conversation with the 'brain.'

"The question was simple. It goes like this… 'What does the Solar Union need to do in order to protect its future?'"

"What was the answer," Lacendu asks after a long pause of silence from everyone.

The Admiral shrugs. "The answer was just as simple. It was this: 'The Solar Union must destroy the Agrauves.'"

There is another long silence.

"That's all?" Mathew asks.

The Admiral nods his head. "That's all."

Mathew is furious. "That is what started this whole stupid thing?!" It is almost a yell.

"Yes…" The Admiral's eyes widen, but not out of fear of Mathew, but more out of trying to persuade him he is telling the truth.

"You know," Agoparn says, speaking for the first time through all of this, "I'd hate to think we wasted a trip to Earth to see the 'brain' and didn't get to see it just because someone answered our questions before we got there." He pauses for effect looking down at the ground; then back up at the Admiral. "Is the 'brain' on Earth…?"

The Admiral smiles delicately, with diplomacy. "If I told you that, what would keep any of you from telling others unless I could assure you were incapable of ever doing that…?"

"Do you even know," asks Lacendu.

At this, the Admiral laughs a full, hardy laugh. "I'm the Admiral of the Sharcuran Knights. My sole goal in life is to protect the 'brain' at all costs. Half the galaxy understands that. If I were to make the Knights' home base on Earth, don't you think everyone would realize that and come to search for it…?"

Lacendu looks embarrassed. "That fact was kind of what led me to believe it would be here."

"So, what was it that the 'matter-seek' picked up," Vaskette asks.

"Oh, that… It's a giant computer created about six hundred years ago by the Japanese. They invented a super-computer to hold a massive multi-player video game. The goal was that any country which wanted to go to war with another could do so with said country via a computer game. They could fight any way they wanted in a virtual world, and the winner would win in real life without the physical loss of a single man or woman. Quite ingenious for its time, but as you can imagine it never quite made the cut…"

"Yes," Mathew states seemingly a bit upset, still, "People do have a tendency to want to take life and destroy rather than keep life and restore…"

The Admiral smiles at the Captain. "A true quote from a valid author," he states. "I didn't know you were familiar with the works of Sandrue Loure."

The Captain looks at the ground with his brows furrowed.

"What now, then," Mathew asks. "You just let us go?"

"Of course… Despite the fact that twenty-three of our operatives are dead, you, yourselves, have not done any real harm, though I dare say if we'd let Shivranikka run amok on Earth as seemed to be her wont, what would there be left for future generations. It is true that you can come and go on Earth as you please. All humans have a right to their place of origin, but there is still a need to preserve it."

"So that's it..." Mathew says. "We can get back on board and fly away."

"I would highly encourage it," the Admiral states, "though I have a feeling that Korsaume will want to stay for a little while."

Korsaume looks up at him with an inquisitive face. "Why me...?"

"You're parents would like to see you."

Her eyes widen. "Where are they?"

A man and woman step from the crowd of Knights near the Admiral. They stand side to side, their shoulders back, and a dour look on their faces.

"Dad..." She looks hard at them. "Mom..."

"Hello, Sherise," the father says, maintaining his straight face. "It's been a long time."

Episode 15
Shattered Illusion

OPENING:

He is my catalyst. If I am without him, I am harmless ... entropyc ... lethargic ... plain. When I am with him, I become something more. I become the missile. I become the thing others fear the most. I become death itself. If he can't stop me, no one ever will.

Gronsa Rudee, mental patient in discussions of his friend, Plecarr Norm, the two of whom were captured and imprisoned after destroying the mining camps on Jupiter's moon, Titan, in 2381

"We are disappointed in you, Sherise," Korsaume's mother says. "You gave up a firm career in the CHE to help five fugitives. That is not the Sherise I raised."

"No, mother, I'm not the Sherise you raised. Being out there in space with those five people made me something better than what you tried to make me into…"

Korsaume; her father, Clyburn Felder; and her mother, Ambeedra Felder; stand at the edge of the Asian continent overlooking the ocean. It is overcast and rainy. Occasionally they feel raindrops, but they don't seem to care.

"What made you decide to utilize your sister's name as your own," asks Clyburn.

"I needed something quick, and I knew the crew wouldn't be able to track it. Korsaume's death was so shrouded in mystery that I doubt even you two know what happened to her." She doesn't bother to look at them.

They do not answer her.

"OH, COME ON!" she yells at them, making a swooshing motion with her left arm, a maddened expression on her face. "Are you two so stubborn you can't even talk about her…?!"

"You were both so young," says Ambeedra. "It was an unexpected death. The fact that you still remember her; or even bring her up; shows just how young and inexperienced you still are…"

"If you had fulfilled your duties like a good little girl, you could have one day been a member of the Sharcuran Knights," her father says.

"Look… I'm already proud to not be a member of the CHE anymore. Don't make me glad I'll never be a member of the Sharcuran Knights, too. I'm a part of something much bigger…" she says. Her eyes fill with tears, though she tries to hold them back.

"YOU ARE NOTHING!" he replies facing her with an indignant face. "You were always second best. Your sister would have become something. You…?! You'll never be anything. You'll never go anywhere."

"WHY?" she yells back… "Because I'm not ever going to be you…? Is that the measure of all success…? Are you the gauge by which all true greatness is assessed…?"

He turns and walks away.

Korsaume's mother faces her. "You are nothing, dear, because you have nothing. You have no rank, no singular identity, and no work."

"I am something because I have great friends," Korsaume states through teary eyes. "I am something because I will help them succeed where you and dad always failed."

"Have it your way," Ambeedra remarks.

She, too, walks away following her husband.

When they are out of earshot, Korsaume drops to her knees weeping and banging her fists on the ground as hard as she can. Then she collapses on the rain-soaked ground, mud all over her face as she cries.

*****

Shivranikka's internal systems come to life again. She is unsure what happened, so she lies on the ground listening. The ground is cold, but she does not feel it, her sensory perception long having been taken over by the computers, organic wires, and venotronics inside her.

She can hear everything, and sift through it as separate and distinct. Afraid that whoever shut her down could do it again, she lies on the ground with no movement. She just listens.

*****

Korsaume arrives back at the door to the Saiar Ria Contract. The front of her body is muddy and wet. Her face is smeared with mud, evidence she has spent some time trying to wipe it all off. Her crewmates stand around waiting.

Fifteen of the sixteen ships have already left. The large open field not far from the ocean has dimples where the feet of the vessels held them up. It is midday where they are, and they have been on the ground for just over three hours.

Mathew intercepts Korsaume as she is heading up the ramp. Quietly he says to her, "You've been crying…"

"I'm fine."

"You're covered in mud…" he says.

"I'm fine," she says again, a little more harshly than she intended. "I'll be inside getting cleaned up."

Mathew walks over to the group of Sharcuran Knights huddled together discussing some subject he can't hear. He makes his way past them to the Admiral who coerced the Saiar Ria Contract's crew to land and discuss what they were doing on Earth.

"Excuse me, Admiral…"

"Yes, Captain Mathew?" the Admiral asks.

"I believe we are prepared to leave Earth. I would greatly appreciate it if you could turn our traveling companion, Shivranikka, back on…"

"That won't be an issue. She should be coming back on any moment. We shut her down only temporarily," he responds.

"Then we are free to leave," Mathew says more as a statement, though it is intended as a question.

"At your leisure, Captain," the other states; "For the record, though, I don't recommend a return trip to this planet unless it is as a visitor with harmless intentions."

"Believe me," Mathew responds, "I have no intention of ever returning to this planet for any reason…"

Mathew turns around and begins walking away.

"Captain," comes the Admiral's voice behind him.

Mathew stops and turns his body a quarter the way around. "Admiral…?"

"You might want to be gentle with your Lieutenant, Korsaume. She's not in the best of moods at the moment."

"I noticed. What did her parents do to her…?" Mathew looks upset.

"Let's just say that her parents aren't exactly proud of her…"

"Let's just say that, Sir."

Mathew walks away.

*****

The Saiar Ria Contract is well on its way through the Earth's Solar System when Korsaume arrives on the command deck. She walks up to the Captain's chair and whispers in his ear. He nods his head, and Korsaume walks over to Allen, places her left hand on his left forearm, and the two walk out of the command deck into the hallway and back into a random room near the middle of the ship.

"What's wrong," he asks.

She looks like she will cry any moment. Her lips tremble, she stops to focus herself, and then she speaks. "I just need someone to talk to…"

*****

Inside the ship, Mathew pulls Shivranikka aside.

Shivranikka's body slinks into a symblance of a standing position, and her head turns to the right slightly with her eyes aimed at his, her smile rapidly enveloping her face. "Yes, Captain?"

"About that subject we were discussing before you went with Korsaume…"

"I remember," she remarks.

He nods to her. "I'm sure you do. As for the Saiar Ria Contract, there were a hundred five people aboard … men and women. Any children?"

"No."

"How did you take control of the ship?"

"They allowed Shallajohne, Forgiven, and me to board after we connected our Raider vessel to the ship, and then we cut off the oxygen supply to the entire ship and allowed them to suffocate to death."

"…And then what?"

"Well, I needed more like myself, so I used the technology already on board to recreate the same technology Xychocappla used on me to turn them into my…"

As she is saying this last part, Mathew interrupts her, "Don't you dare say 'minions.'"

Her grin widens and she shakes her head affectionately and says, "You know me so well…"

"More than I was willing to admit," Mathew smiles back at her. "Seriously, though, how long have you been flying that thing around?"

"About two months."

"What about the Raider vessels?"

"We'd been using two of them for almost a hundred seventy years. Where do you think the Raiders come from?"

"You made them?"

"I invented them. I captured two trader vessels. The title came with the job…"

Mathew thinks about it for a moment. "I may have to sit down with you sometime and hear the whole story."

"It's in my journal," she says. "Korsaume had it, last I knew…"

Mathew smiles. "Yeah. I just don't feel comfortable going through a woman's journal…"

Shivranikka shrugs. "Well, aren't you the polite little gentleman."

*****

"Hey, Vaskette," Lacendu says, walking into the infirmary.

Vaskette is turned in her chair away from the door. She is seated in front of a computer, reading files.

"How are you?" asks Lacendu.

Vaskette mumbles something not quite audible to Lacendu, and Lacy walks up behind her, and then sits down in the chair on the left next to her friend.

"What are you doing…?"

Vaskette looks over at her and blinks a couple times, her eyes red. She breathes in with some additional realization, swallows, and looks at Lacendu like she hasn't had sleep in several days. "I'm just … looking through some … information, Lacy," she replies, speaking slowly, breathing in between her words.

Lacendu smiles at her friend. "What kind…?"

"Oh, just some medical data I downloaded while we were parked on Earth…" she says, turning back to the screen.

Lacendu's eyes widen a little. "Neat. I didn't know you'd had time for that…"

"I did it while we were circling the planet, and worked on it after we landed a little, too." Vaskette puts her head in her left hand, still typing things onto the keypad with her right hand.

"Anything interesting in there," Lacendu questions…

"There's some new info I missed out on while we were gone. It's nice to finally be able to catch up on the latest technical items." She speaks half out of lack of sleep, half out of feeling a little annoyed.

"I'm bothering you, aren't I," asks Lacendu.

Vaskette's voice is less occupied now, "No, of course not… You never bother me, Lacy."

"It's just…" She pauses, waiting to think of a delicate way to put it. "…we haven't spoken much since I got my memories back…"

"We've been pretty busy, Lacy," is the response. "Things happen. You have more work to do now with the ship."

"…But that doesn't mean we have to lose our friendship."

"Look, Lacy," Vaskette says, turning her entire body in the chair to face Lacendu, and spreading her hands out in an almost-welcoming gesture, "we're still friends. That won't ever change. We're on a top priority mission right now, and we have to focus on that right now. Our friendship is still there, but if we want to make things right in our universe, our specialties will be needed more and more from now on, so I don't want you to give it a second thought. When we win the day, we'll have all the time in the world."

There is a small tear at the bottom of Lacendu's left eye, but Vaskette doesn't even notice. Instead, she turns back to her computer.

Lacendu stands up and walks slowly and meticulously out of the infirmary. She goes into her room down the hall, lies down on the small bed in the corner, commands the lights off, and cries herself to sleep.

*****

"Captain, I'm getting a message from Baitronoc," Rosetta states.

"Play it," Mathew responds.

The message from Captain Ardelle of the Star Axis C-72 comes over the command deck speakers.

"Captain Mathew Arnold of the Saiar Ria Contract, you should know right now that we have landed on Baitronoc. This message is being sent with a non-standard encryption, so no one else should be able to crack it.

"They did accept Korsaume as dead and have allowed my crew to land and look around. We have found little in the way of information on your crew, and nothing on Korsaume whatsoever.

"It's looking like we might not get much of anything. One of my crew has already been approached by a Solar Union official of some kind asking why she was looking for information on you and Lacendu.

"Because of this, we have determined that this may not be the best place to get information... However, they are not allowing us to leave, so we believe there may be some problem.

"I can make no guarantees that we will be able to exit Baitronoc, nor can I guarantee that we'll be here when you get here. That is, of course, if you're coming here at all. My highest recommendation...? Don't...

Captain Ardelle Xysteck of the Star Axis C-72, signing off."

"What now," Rosetta asks with raised eyebrows when Mathew looks over at him.

"I want to know more about that war…" Mathew states.

"Where should we begin," asks Shivranikka.

"How about the Agrauves homeworld…?" Rosetta asks with a half-smile.

"That's as good a place as any. …And let's see if we can't go around that little war between it and us…" Mathew answers.

"It will be a three day trip, Captain, but the coordinates are inputted, and we're on our way," Rosetta replies.

*****

Korsaume has just finished explaining what happened between her and her parents to her new friend, Allen. She is crying again, and standing in his arms.

His arms are tight around her, her head on his left shoulder and her face against his neck.

Allen breathes slowly and quietly rubbing her back.

She pulls back from him a little ways and wipes her eyes. "I've never cried this much in my entire life."

"When was the last time you cried," he asks her.

She thinks for a moment, still wiping her eyes. "I was fourteen," she replies.

"Well, then, I think you were about due for a good cry," he says smiling at her.

She laughs lightly, but she can't seem to hold it. She sniffles before she says, "I know that what they said isn't true, but hearing it from them made things difficult."

"Well, just think… If you'd done things the way they wanted, you wouldn't be where you are, now." Allen leans his face down to the right a little catching her eyes.

She looks at him and smiles delicately. "You're right," she says. "I wouldn't have all of you as my friends, and I'd probably be stuck on the

'Vibrant,' unable to get it to go anywhere if I'd followed through with my original orders."

Allen straightens his shoulders. "I'm very glad you didn't."

She moves a little closer to him, wraps her arms around his middle and leans up to his face. "You've been my strongest proponent. I appreciate your friendship."

She leans toward his face, he to hers, and they kiss.

*****

"Lacendu..."

It is the Captain's voice, and she opens her eyes a little bit, stares at the blue glow between the bubble on the floor and the other on the ceiling. The sound of the energy is soothing, and she almost forgets her Captain just called her name.

"Lacendu," he says again.

"Yes, Captain...?"

"I would like to have your assistance on the command deck, if you would..."

"I would be happy to help," she replies sitting up and pulling her legs off the bed. "I'll be there shortly."

She stands up, watches the blue light for a little while longer, breathing deeply, and finally begins walking. She opens the door, exits allowing it to close on its own, and walks slowly and deliberately toward the command deck.

A few minutes later she arrives and walks up to the Captain's chair. She didn't realize it until now, but she had been walking so loosely that her feet were almost stomping on the floor. Everyone in the room is looking at her.

"Is there something wrong, Lacy," Mathew asks.

"I was just asleep," she responds, a bit despondent. "I didn't mean to stomp. I'm not upset, or anything...just sleepy."

"I understand," he says with a quick smile.

"May I speak with you, Captain…alone…?" she asks.

"Sure. Let's go in here." The two walk into the Captain's room behind Allen, and the door closes.

"What's up, Lacy," asks Mathew.

"I'm worried about Vaskette…" she replies. "She and I have been friends for a long time…well, you know what I mean." He nods his head as she continues. "Anyway, I think she hates me, now."

He looks at her awkwardly. "Why would you think she hates you, Lacy…?"

She pauses, looking down. "I think she hates me because I have my memories back."

Mathew chuckles silently, stops and looks at her keeping the smile and then chuckles a little more. He shakes his head just as she looks up at him with a crushed look on her face. She looks almost at the point of tears. "Lacy, she doesn't hate you. We've all made friends with each other on this ship. We're all in awkward situations, and I think even if she does have a problem it's probably more with her than you. I bet, if anything, she feels like you aren't going to want to hang out with her anymore. She probably feels like you're going to go back to the way things were before your memory loss and then she won't be able to spend time with you anymore."

"I never thought of it that way," she says with an understanding gaze off to the side. "I guess if I keep not talking to her as much as I used to that she'll feel like that even more."

"You've got it," he replies.

"Well, I guess I need to work on that." She smiles at him. "What did you need from me, Captain?"

"I need for you to do some programming of this ship. I have some ideas in mind, and you're the only one on board that knows what this thing is capable of… We're heading into the Agrauve territory, and I feel things are going to change quickly when we get there. You're the one we need."

Lacendu smiles at him, "Thank you, Captain, for trying to placate, but I don't really need it. I just need something to do, and so I will be more than happy to program the vessel I helped design… Where do you want me to begin?"

*****

Hours have passed, and most everyone is asleep…most everyone with the exception of Vaskette and Shivranikka.

Vaskette is alone in the infirmary continuing to read material she downloaded while the ship was around Earth. Shivranikka walks in, but the doctor doesn't notice.

The newest member of the crew walks quietly up behind the doctor and reads over her shoulder. "What are you reading, dear Doctor?"

"Hey, Shivranikka… I'm reading something about a new medical procedure. It's quite fascinating."

Shivranikka pulls the chair on the right back a bit and sits down next to the other. "What kind of procedure…?"

"It's one they use to repair internal organs after serious injury. Mostly this has to do with the heart and lungs, but there's a little about the liver and pancreas as well. There's a device someone made that does repair at the cellular level." Vaskette glances at Shivranikka to see if she understood what she was talking about, but can't read anything on the other's face, so she goes back to her reading.

Shivranikka waits a long moment before saying anything else. "Why would you want to repair someone who's been damaged that badly…?"

Vaskette gets a look of confusion on her face, but finally turns to her and replies, "I'm a doctor. I dedicate my life to helping people who are injured or ill. When someone comes into the infirmary with serious physical problems, I fix them."

"Could you fix me…?" Shivranikka asks.

Vaskette gives the other a crooked look. "Are you serious…?"

"I'm just wondering. I don't want you to fix me; I just want to know if you can..."

Vaskette looks down at the floor, and then back up. "I suppose I'm capable of ripping out the organic technology from you and repairing you, but I don't have the equipment or machines necessary to do that... Why would you even ask?"

Shivranikka looks at the doctor with a face that is almost angry. "I was hoping that maybe some day, I could die..."

"Couldn't you destroy yourself," Vaskette asks.

"I won't commit suicide," the techno-witch states quite loudly, sounding upset.

Vaskette hangs her head. "Sorry. I hadn't really thought about it that way...but I guess it would be suicide... It wasn't my intent to offend you."

"Not taken that way," she responds, regaining her smile.

"So, I thought you didn't want to die...that you wanted to take over the galaxy..." the doctor states.

Shivranikka looks off above her to the right and stares at the wall. "I thought I did," she says. "I've realized that if Korsaume can beat me, anyone could. If I can be beat, then I am not fit to be the leader of the galaxy."

Vaskette suddenly finds herself feeling sorry for the other. "That's silly," Vaskette replies. "The first step to anything is realization that you can't do it alone. People are made; designed; to work together. If you ever thought you could do anything without the help of others, you, too, would be remiss. Even if you became the leader of the galaxy, you'd need help. You can't be everywhere at once, no matter how fast you are...and from what I've seen, you're quite fast." She smiles at Shivranikka.

"I suppose you're right, Doctor." This time, Shivranikka uses the honorary title with reverence, and Vaskette feels like the woman might now respect her.

"Of course, I am," Vaskette says. "I only know it, though, because I've learned it myself... Excuse me. I need to go speak with someone."

Vaskette stands up as she turns the computer off, and then walks out the door.

Shivranikka watches the other woman walk out and then sits alone in the room with her thoughts.

*****

"Wake up," Vaskette says shaking Lacendu a little at the shoulder.

Lacendu rolls over and opens her eyes to slits to see who's trying to wake her. "What's wrong, Doctor," she asks.

"Hey, I just wanted to talk with you for a minute…" Vaskette replies.

"It couldn't have waited 'til morning," Lacendu asks wrapping the covers around her body and sitting up with her legs off the side of the bed. Her eyes are closed and she yawns.

"It couldn't have," Vaskette answers. "I had to apologize. I've been treating you like I'm upset with you… I am very sorry."

"That's OK," states Lacendu, her voice pitched a bit higher.

"No, it's not," Vaskette says adamant. "Really, I was sad for myself. I didn't know how you'd treat me, now that you have your memories and I don't."

"Oh," Lacendu exclaims, pulling her arms out of the covers and hugging her friend. "I will treat you like I always did," she states. "My memories won't affect our friendship. Besides, I bet you'll get your memories back, soon, too."

Vaskette smiles, her head on Lacendu's right shoulder. She faces the wall and stares at it with tears in her eyes. "Friends…?"

"Always and forever," Lacendu responds.

*****

"Captain, we'll be within visual range of the Agrauve planet in twenty minutes," Allen says.

Everyone is awake, and the entire crew is on the command deck in their positions.

"How are you coming on those programs," Mathew asks of Lacendu.

"Even after three days I'm still having some issues with a couple, but I think I've just about got them figured out, Captain," answers Lacendu.

"You have about twenty minutes to finish them," Mathew says with a smile.

"They'll be done, Captain," she says.

"What are we doing here," Korsaume asks.

"We're going to stop this war…" he states.

"Did you want to clue us in on just how you intend to do that," asks Rosetta.

"I'd love to," Mathew answers, "but I have my reasons why I'm not going to right away…"

"We haven't stopped trusting you," Allen says, "but we do want to be in the know on this if at all possible."

Mathew turns to Allen; then to the rest of the crew in turn who are all looking at him, now. "Alright… I intend to go to the headquarters and take the leader of the Agrauves hostage."

"Captain," Rosetta asks slowly.

"I didn't want you all to know in case we get captured…"

"I don't think that's going to happen," Lacendu states. "I'm done with the programs you requested, and I'm prepared to set them into motion at your command."

"He told you?" Allen asks.

"No, but I figured it out just now…" she says.

"Exactly how do you intend to do this, dear Captain," Shivranikka asks, entering the command deck. "The Agrauves are a warring people."

Mathew turns to her. "Would you like to help us out," he asks.

"Sure," she answers. "You know how I love to get my hands dirty…"

Mathew turns back to the viewport with a smile on his face, shaking his head.

The fifteen remaining minutes pass relatively quickly and the ship does not slow down, bringing the planet up rather quickly.

Defenses around the globe are started, and Rosetta begins receiving constant messages from defense command-posts. “Captain, we’ve got a request asking if we’re preparing to crash…”

“Ignore the request,” he states.

“Additional requests for our identification codes…” she adds.

“Continue ignoring requests,” he says.

“Yes, sir,” she says, punching a few buttons.

“Lacendu,” Mathew says looking over at the Mathematician, “set code four in the system.”

“Done, sir,” she replies after hitting a few spots on the console in front of her.

The atmosphere burns hard around the ship. Adding to these problems is the laser fire from the surrounding defense systems, and soon surface-to-air projectiles begin flying upward.

The ship begins maneuvering in patterns which escape the projectiles completely, and the ship’s hull turns the light from the lasers being fired into fuel.

“Are the light collectors keeping up with the laser fire,” Mathew asks.

Lacendu checks a read-out. “They’re having no problems at this point,” she states. “Another hundred or so and the buffer will have to be reset.”

“We won’t have to wait that long,” he says.

Mathew turns to Allen. “Sweep the citadel and land inside the cathedral…”

Allen begins checking the ground data for what Mathew is telling him, finds the information he needs, and programs the ship to get extremely close to the citadel.

"Shivranikka," he says a little loud, turning to her. "Go to the weapons room, if you will, and prepare weapons for us and your group. We're going ground fighting…"

"Korsaume," she asks, facing her master.

"Do as he says," she commands.

Shivranikka turns and runs from the room.

The Saiar Ria Contract sweeps right next to the citadel, rattling both the ship and the building. The vessel fires two shots at the cathedral blasting a huge hole in the top. The vessel pulls up right above the hole, slows to a hover and drops vertically to land in the middle of the massive building.

"Lacy, put program eight in and stay here with Vaskette. Agoparn, stay in the engine room and prepare for lift-off. The rest of us are going hunting…" Mathew says.

The remaining unmentioned crewmembers stand up and they head for the weapons room. A few minutes pass and they arrive at the ground exit, weapons in hand.

Mathew turns to Korsaume. "Let's leave about six of Nikka's men here to guard the ship. Everyone else with us…"

Korsaume looks at Shivranikka. "Please," she asks.

Shivranikka sighs and nods her head. "You could speak to me like I'm here, Captain."

"Well, you won't obey anyone else but Korsaume," he says, shrugging his shoulders.

"I'm giving up that notion as of now," she says. "You're her captain. If I obey her, I have to obey you…"

Korsaume smiles at her Captain. "That works for me…"

Mathew reaches a hand over to Shivranikka and places it on her left shoulder. "I appreciate any assistance you and your group are willing to give us."

Shivranikka rolls her eyes. "Yeah, yeah… Let's just do whatever it is we're here to do…"

"Drop the door," Mathew says. "Shields up… Prepare for enemy fire."

The door opens as Allen presses the release button. As soon as the fighters outside can see into the ship, shots are fired.

The crew of the Saiar Ria Contract begins firing back at the shields around the men and women Agrauves with their weapons aimed. Mathew and Rosetta cover the left side, Korsaume and Allen the right, and Shivranikka and her men walk right out into the middle and begin fighting by hand, taking full blasts and shaking them off like minor nuisances. They make quick work of the Agrauve soldiers, leaving them on the floor unconscious but alive. They remove the shields and guns from the bodies and follow Mathew, Allen, Korsaume, and Rosetta.

They make their way out of the building slowly along the half-kilometer walkway almost forty meters over the rock surface of the mountain. In the distance before them they can see the citadel where the leader of the Agrauves lives. It stands above all buildings on the rocky mountain. The sun shines down from above and behind the cathedral where they parked their ship, and as they step out into the light it becomes very hard on their eyes as it glints off everything in sight.

"Captain," Shivranikka says a little loud, "We have flying visitors…"

The group turns to the right where there are hundreds of Agrauves with guns, shields, and rocket packs, and all of them are aiming at the walkway.

"Protect the bridge," Mathew yells.

Shivranikka and her crew are quick as they stamp the shields on the sides of the bridge and turn them on along a lengthy stretch of it, and the crew begins walking more quickly while firing their weapons.

Meanwhile, the flying Agrauves are firing their weapons at the shields trying to break them. They quickly realize it is useless and they move ahead of the crew and begin destroying the bridge sections there.

"Now what, Captain," Korsaume asks above the noise.

"We need some of those rocket packs," he yells back.

Korsaume looks at Shivranikka.

"I heard," Shivranikka says with a smile.

She looks at one of her men. The man steps forward, lifts his left leg up onto her hand, puts his left hand on her right shoulder, and Shivranikka throws him into the air at a section of the crowd of Agrauves which is particularly dense.

He catches one, then another, and in mid-air and with fluid motion detaches the rocket packs and watches the men fall to their deaths.

"That's not quite what I had in mind," Mathew says…

Shivranikka turns her head to him and smiles. "Then, next time, be more specific…"

Soon, her man returns with nine packs and hands them to the crew, one to Shivranikka, and the remaining are split up between Shivranikka's men.

They put the packs on over their shoulders, strap them to their bodies, and Korsaume gives everyone a quick lesson on their usage, after which they are flying across the damaged section of the bridge with few problems.

By the time they land near the entrance to the citadel their shields are mostly gone. They make their way through one of the main entryways around the side of the citadel. It opens into a massive hall, and there is no one inside.

"What's this…?" Korsaume asks.

"This doesn't feel right," states Allen.

Mathew walks out ahead of everyone. "Get new shields out and start them. Let's move out." He says this as he tosses his used shield to his left and pulls a new one from his belt with his right hand, snapping it on the vest where the last one had been and turning it on.

The group follows his order and they begin walking through the massive hallway. At the end of the hallway, and up about six meters is a beautiful stained-glass window with the figure of a red quarter-moon near the upper center.

Mathew turns to Korsaume. "You're the one who's been here before. Lead the way, Lieutenant."

Korsaume nods and takes the foreground leading the group up a long flight of stairs which curve off behind the left side of the hallway and up over the top of it.

In a matter of minutes the entire group walks through another hallway to the end where wide arching doors are closed.

"This is the place," Korsaume says, nodding her head and raising her gun.

"Open it up," Mathew says to Shivranikka.

"Gladly," she replies walking right up to it and pushing the doors wide open. She keeps walking in with her smile intact looking around the room. She stops and turns to the crew.

The rest walk in to see seven people sitting around in chairs. In the middle between a man and woman is an older gentleman who seems to them to be an Agrauve.

"Anything else," Shivranikka asks.

"That will be all," says Korsaume.

She walks to the side and sits down in a large, high-back chair, resting her arms on the arms of the chair and getting comfortable. She looks around with a smile. "I could enjoy this…"

"Who are you," Mathew asks, pointing his weapon at the three on the sofa in the middle.

"We're the ones who did the job you and your crew couldn't," the woman replies.

"That's the leader of the Agrauves, isn't it," asks Korsaume.

The woman stands up and walks onto a large rug in the center of the room. "I'm you, Captain Mathew Arnold…or at least, what you should have been."

Allen points his gun down at the floor. "How could you do it," he asks, shaking his head. "How could you approve of a war…?"

"It was pretty simple," she remarks. "They told us you wouldn't…then they explained that the same thing that happened to all of you would happen to us if we didn't approve."

"So they forced you to agree to a war," says Rosetta.

A man stands up from the right side of the room and walks up to the woman's left. "It was never your place to approve or disapprove of the war," he explains. "Your job was to start it and figure out how it would work. We did our job..."

"It's over," the woman says. "Your crew has failed. The war has begun, and the Agrauves will die. Their people will fall, and the work of the Solar Union will go on like it's supposed to..."

Mathew steps forward. "You don't get it, do you...? Did they even tell you what their question was to the 'brain...?' Did they tell you what the Keeper posed? Did they even bother to tell you what the answer was...?"

"It doesn't matter," another of the six says, staying seated. "We did what we were told, and now we've got a new job."

"...And we'll fulfill it, where the CHE members sent to follow you in Quadrant Four failed..." the woman leader says.

"You forget," Mathew says. "They chose us first. We're the best there is."

The woman smiles at him and then laughs, "There's a difference between your crew and mine... We still have our memories."

"So you do," Mathew agrees, nodding his head. "...We're still better than you... We proved that by not going ahead with the war, and we're about to prove it again, right now..." He looks at his communicator, and speaks into it. "Now would be fine, Lacendu."

The top of the room they're standing in is ripped off, and there above them with light from the nearby star radiating into the huge room from both the surrounding sky and bouncing off the hull is the Saiar Ria Contract.

"We'll be taking the leader of the Agrauves with us," Mathew says. "Anything but total agreement from the six of you is unacceptable."

Korsaume, Rosetta, and Allen all raise their weapons as Shivranikka's four men walk right between the group and help the Agrauve's leader to his feet.

"What do you want with me," he asks in his rough textured voice.

"Just your cooperation," Mathew replies, "we're not here to harm you."

"You have it," he responds.

The ship maneuvers into position next to the room and the ramp is lowered into the room, the base landing directly on the floor on their left.

"Move it," Mathew says. "The six of you, feel free to stay here and enjoy yourselves as long as you like. We've got work to do."

"Just remember," the woman says after him while Shivranikka picks up the chair she was seated in and carries it aboard with her, "We'll be playing clean-up after your crew is dead and gone, so don't leave too much of a mess. I'd hate to think we'd have to spend the rest of our lives sifting through your remains."

"You're way too generous," Korsaume calls out as she reaches the top of the ramp.

"Anything else," Mathew asks.

"Yeah," she says, "Any fight you can walk away from…isn't finished…"

"Words to live by," Allen says with a smile as he presses the button for the ramp to move up.

The six of them stand up and watch the ship fly up into the sky.

The woman looks down at the underside of her wrist where a small display of a wrap-around computer is attached. "Did you get all of that," she asks.

"Yes, Maneesha," says the man on the screen. "You folks did your job well, and you will be rewarded accordingly."

As the display goes blank, the woman turns to her crewmates. "Let's get out of here…"

The six members walk through the large open doors and into another room where a small craft is stored. They enter it, the roof of the room opens, and the craft takes off in a similar direction of the Saiar Ria Contract.

*****

"They were waiting for us," Mathew says, slamming his fist on the panel nearby.

"They're us," Korsaume states with blandness. "They think like we do. I recognized the leader woman…Maneesha Huchan is her name. We worked together in the CHE off and on. I never really got to know her…we did our jobs, and occasionally those jobs brought us within speaking distance."

"How did they know where we were headed," Allen asks. "…'Them' thinking like we do couldn't possibly prelude them thinking Mathew would decide to take the Agrauve's leader hostage…"

"…Unless you're all being controlled," adds Rosetta.

"That's circular reasoning," Mathew says. "If they don't want us doing anything, they'd stop us by controlling us…"

"True," she admits.

"I have something to add," Shivranikka states with her usual smirk.

"What?" Korsaume asks in a frustrated huff.

"While we were on Earth, and I was out on the ground, I came to. When I did, I overheard one of the leaders talking. He said that he figured you all would try one of two things and that a group should follow you to see which one you would most likely do…"

"That would explain things," Allen says. "If we're being followed, they would know where we would strike and what our plans would most likely be when we got there…"

"Why didn't you tell us this sooner," asks Korsaume, a little rough.

"Well, it hardly seemed important at the time," she responds nonchalant.

Korsaume furrows her brows at the woman and clears her throat. "You and I need to sit down some time and have a long chat about the meaning of the word 'important.'"

"Well, if we're being followed, then we're going to have to try some creative approaches…" Mathew turns around to face his crew in the weapons room.

"What do you have in mind, Captain," Korsaume asks.

"Well, we've got the leader of the Agrauves. Let's start with ending the war..." he replies.

"...And just how do you intend to do that," the Agrauve leader asks.

Everyone turns to face him as he speaks, and then looks at Mathew.

Mathew says, "We walk right into the big middle of that war out there and let your people know we are holding you hostage unless they stop fighting and go home."

The Agrauve leader just laughs loud and boisterous. "You think my people will stop fighting because you have me...?" He stops laughing. "Listen here, you idiot. My people have wanted a fight with the Solar Union for four centuries. Ever since they used us to build their stupid Dyson-sphere and left our fathers unpaid for their two centuries of work, we've been gathering everything we can and preparing to fight. The Solar Union just started it a little sooner than we wanted them to, but we're definitely not going to back down."

"So the stories are true," Korsaume says. "I was always told that was a fable."

"Then you've been lied to," the man says.

"...And this war is useless," Mathew says. "The Keeper asked the 'brain' what was needed to keep things going, and the computer must have determined that since the Agrauves were never paid for their work that they would be upset and planning a war. The 'brain' would have been correct in the recommendation for the Solar Union to start one."

Allen looks at the ground. "If we had only known we would probably have made the decision to go ahead with it..."

"So, what, then," Rosetta asks, "Do we back down and go run and hide? Just because a war was going to start with or without you, does that mean it <u>should</u> be happening?"

"How do we stop a war that's been brewing for four centuries and was started by the Galaxy's second finest in war...?" Allen walks out of the room.

Mathew looks around at the remaining crewmates and traveling companions. "Let's get to the command deck."

"Where next, Captain," Allen asks walking up to his post as Mathew and the rest walk onto the command deck.

Mathew sits down before saying, "We're headed for the war."

"Isn't that the last place we want to be, Captain?" asks Lacendu.

"It's the last place I want to be," Vaskette mutters to herself sitting down at her station.

"It is," Mathew agrees, "but it's where we need to be if we're going to stop this stupid war…"

"Where do we begin," Korsaume asks sitting down and punching a few buttons on the console in front of her. "Do we attack them? If so, whom do we attack: the Solar Union or the Agrauves?"

"We can't attack the Solar Union and expect to do any good," Rosetta says. "They're too many compared to our little ship."

Mathew turns to Lacendu. "Can the mega-mass drive be dumped out of the ship," he asks.

"In theory," she admits. "I think Agoparn would be the person to ask…"

"I heard," Agoparn's voice comes over the speakers from the engine room. "The drive can be dropped. Do you want me to do that?"

"No," Mathew says. "If you can see where I'm headed, though, we may need to."

"I won't be a part of that," Vaskette says out loud standing up. "That's mass murder."

Mathew turns to her with force. "This whole war is mass murder," he angrily replies. "It was started with little thought, and based solely on a computer's idea whose abilities are in doubt…"

She looks upset, but she sits down. "Point taken, Sir," she replies.

"I'm sorry," Lacendu says, "but I have to agree with Vaskette. Dropping something like that will do more damage than it's worth…"

"Other options," Mathew says with a give-in.

Everyone on deck stops what they're doing, tensing up. Even Shivranikka who is standing against the back wall drops her head in thought.

The leader of the Agrauves, standing next to the techno-witch, smiles to his self. "You know…I tried to tell you all it was useless. The amount of damage you will need to do will have to destroy the Agrauves before they'll quit. We will fight to our dying breath."

"Why," Vaskette asks standing up and walking over to him. "Why do your people want to die so badly…?"

"Oh, it's not like that, Madame," he replies. "You've got it all wrong. We don't want to die… We're willing to die. That's the difference. We've known defeat. We have nothing left to fight for…"

"The Solar Union gave you an entire solar system to yourselves with the promise to leave you alone…" Lacendu says.

She is interrupted by the furious voice of the Agrauve. "…And they didn't leave us alone, did they…!? They couldn't even keep **that** promise. NO! Instead, they send you six to create a war between us, and when you all fail they throw you away and start again with a different group!" His voice quiets a bit, but not much. "No, they never had any intention of leaving us alone. They've known for years that we were preparing to destroy them, and they decided to get a jumpstart on it before we took their entire empire and their house of cards down in one fell swoop."

"So your people didn't feel that an entire solar system was payment enough for two centuries of work…?" Mathew says, facing forward.

The man laughs. "The Solar Union was a fledgling organization at that time. It was created by the whims of a super-computer designed for nothing more than to decide right from wrong…like that was so hard to do that they needed a computer to help them figure it out… The organization promised to pay our fathers for their work. An empty planet doesn't quite cut it, you know…? We had to build everything: our homes, offices, families, and had to bring almost every plant and animal that wasn't indigenous to it. You tell me if it was worth all the work we did to create that massive chunk of metal…"

"Well, when you put it like that," Vaskette says, "I think we should dump the mega-mass drive right in the middle of the Solar Union."

"I'm inclined to agree, anyway," Mathew says, "but not for the same reason."

"Isn't it a moot point?" asks Shivranikka.

"Why," the Agrauve asks to her.

She smiles, "With what I saw of the armada of Agrauve ships and the limited, but larger ships of the Solar Union, the ol' Es-Yu doesn't really stand a chance…"

Lacendu frowns, turning to Mathew who looks at her. "Shivranikka's right, Captain… The Solar Union doesn't stand a chance against that kind of fire power mathematically."

"I think we should turn our attention forward," Korsaume says. "We're coming up on the massacre right now…"

Everyone turns around to face out the window. What they see is indeed a massacre. The Solar Union fleet is slim; about three hundred massive ships still stand out of the thousands they saw when they first arrived.

The Agrauve fleet is decimated.

The Agrauve leader steps forward in awe, watching as the Saiar Ria Contract moves slowly through the mass grave yard. His jaw drops open and he leans forward falling onto his knees. "No," his voice almost silent; "…No…"

Mathew swallows hard. "What is this…?"

"It's a war-zone, Captain," Rosetta replies without thought.

"That's not right," the Agrauve shakes his head at the devastation. "We were supposed to win…"

"What destroyed those ships," Mathew asks walking over to Allen but keeping his eyes on the screen in the front of the room.

Allen is looking up until his Captain asks, and then he looks down and presses some buttons. "It looks like someone had our idea before we did…" he answers. "Those ships were destroyed by mass-implosion."

"Where did they get one of those drives…?"

"I'm reading an explosion about three thousand kilometers off the port side…" Allen states.

"Show it to me on the insert screen," Mathew says.

A small image appears on the top left side of the viewport window. There is a small burning light and a ship not far from it.

"I'm picking up traces of communications echoing off the remains of the ships," says Rosetta.

"Can you piece it together," asks Mathew.

"I'm not that good at this stuff," she comments.

"Lacendu," Mathew asks.

She sighs. "I'm working on it, now." She says it with a kind of contempt as she begins to punch buttons. She works for several minutes. "I'm patching what I put together to Rosetta's terminal."

"I see what she's doing," Rosetta remarks. "Give me a moment. It's going to be a patchwork, and it might stutter. I'm playing it…now…" She hits a button.

There are occasional hiccups and some static in the middle of words, but it does play.

"Vessel with weapons at the ready; STAND DOWN! I repeat, stand down!"

"Hello, Maneesha… It's so good to hear from you again…"

"You're going to give away our position…"

"Yeah, well, that's what we're here for, isn't it…?"

"You idiot… Stand down, now! I will fire on you…"

"…And risk giving away your position…? I don't think so…"

"Fire…"

"That's all of it, Captain," Rosetta says with her head bowed, and glancing at her boyfriend.

"Should we investigate," Allen asks.

"No." Mathew replies. "We've got other issues right now."

"Like where the sister of this ship is," Korsaume says a little louder than intended.

"We don't have to look far," Allen says. "Take a look."

The image on the top left of the viewport screen moves to the starboard side of the ship.

"There it is," Mathew says.

"Don't look now, Captain, but I just picked up another one near it," Korsaume states.

"Uh, Captain," Allen says, "permission to move the ship their direction…?"

"Given," Mathew replies.

The vessel moves into position to see the two other vessels like the Saiar Ria Contract. What the crew sees is far worse.

Mathew stares in wide-eyed wonder, almost shock. He takes a step backward and collapses into the chair behind him.

"It's a whole fleet of Saiar Ria Contracts…" Lacendu says in awe. She stands up and walks up behind Korsaume.

Korsaume shakes her head. "That's not right…"

"Sir," Allen says, "The first one we spotted is missing its mega-mass drive."

"What do we do, now…?" Vaskette asks.

"You die," says the Agrauve leader.

"If we die, you die with us…" Mathew says.

"Isn't that the point? They're trying to kill off the Agrauves. They know I'm on board. They'll destroy this ship if it means killing me…" he replies.

Mathew breathes out hard.

Amid the silence that ensues, there is a beeping on Rosetta's terminal. She looks down at the button flashing red. "Sir, we have an incoming call from one of the other ships like ours."

"Go ahead," Mathew says quietly.

She presses the flashing red button and it turns to green.

"Hello, Captain Mathew Arnold of the Saiar Ria Contract." The voice over the speaker is unfamiliar to all but Korsaume.

Korsaume stands up. Mostly to herself, but loud enough for everyone to hear, she says, “General Engall Fremthar…”

“Hello, Korsaume,” he replies. “I’m so sad to hear your voice.”

“Not as sad as you’re going to be…” she replies with an open amount of anger.

“Who is this man,” Mathew asks.

“As you obviously heard, Captain Mathew, my name is Engall Fremthar…but you can call me General Fremthar,” the voice responds.

“What do you want,” Mathew says in a calm voice.

“What do I want…? Now that’s a turn of events, isn’t it…? Six months ago you were ready to fight me to the death…”

“I don’t remember that,” Mathew replies. “I think you know that.”

“Oh, yeah, yeah, yeah…” he states with some humor in his voice. “You lost your memory… Amnesia, or something, I heard…”

Mathew stands up throwing his hands down to his side with fury. “I’m not asking again, General. Either tell us what you want or leave us the frag alone!”

He laughs. “Alright…alright…I’ll tell you; but first, I need for you to hear me out. You will stand down from any defense or offense your ship and crew are on. You will prep the Saiar Ria Contract for connection by my ship. You will all come aboard quietly, peacefully, and without any weapons or shields. Do I make myself clear…?”

The voice waits for a long moment, and no one on the command deck responds or says anything.

“I repeat…Do I make myself clear…?”

Mathew sits back down with a face clearly enraged. Through a long, loud breath out, and clenched teeth, he says, “Shut it off.”

Rosetta does as she’s told, but slowly, looking at the button as if it might hurt her if she presses it.

Everyone on the command deck except Shivranikka and the Agrauve leader are bewildered.

Allen speaks in a relaxed and worried tone, "What did we do in our early lives to deserve this…?"

Lacendu, still standing behind Korsaume's chair, looks over at Mathew. "Was one of those programs you had me write to the ship preparing us for this…?" she asks with a bit of fear.

"The lead ship is preparing to fire," Allen says.

"They're calling us again," Rosetta says with her hands at her side, her face staring at the button.

Shivranikka walks up beside Mathew. Her smile still intact, she says, "Let me talk to him."

Mathew looks over at the woman. "What do you think you can say to him that will change anything?"

She pulls the right side of her already-wide mouth back with an almost flirtatious look on her face. "There's nothing I can say that will change anything," she replies.

Mathew's eyes are on her with a thread of contempt. He turns to look at Rosetta. "Let them through."

"Captain Mathew Arnold, I asked you a question. When I ask questions, I expect answers," the voice of the General seems upset.

"Hello, General Fremthar. My name is Shivranikka Napercolten. You might have heard of me in your more recent reports."

"Yes," he replies. "I've heard of you. What do you want…?"

At this, they can hear quiet discussions going on in the background through the speakers.

"Now that's a new twist," she says. "You're asking what I want…" She laughs. "What I want…all I've ever wanted…was to be queen of the Galaxy. I guarantee you, Sir, that if you dock with this ship, you will give me the means to that end."

They hear his voice come through clearly. "Shivranikka Napercolten has been dead for years," he replies, as if reading from a script. "She was sent through a one-way tesseract with Xychocappla, both of whom were expelled from the planet Mount Ligmon-Ardreptipol over four hundred years ago.

"It's an interesting ploy, and one I'm not entirely certain how you came across or came up with, Captain Mathew, but I assure you it won't work. Now, back to what I want…"

"You already told us what you want," Korsaume says.

"Not exactly," he replies. "Those three things were just for starters. I want your cooperation so I can get what I wanted from the beginning. I want you all dead."

Episode 16
Juxtaposition

OPENING:

If you were ever looking for the way to the fountain of youth, you were going in the wrong direction. Everyone feels they need to go forward to find it. Unfortunately, going forward will only lead you away from it. The fountain of youth is in your past, and to find it, you must turn around. The problem with turning around is that you'll never get where you're going.

Her name is Sherise Felder.

Sixteen years ago, she was recruited into the Caste of Hierarchical Electorates. It was slow-going at first. She did rise through the ranks quickly, compared to most of her comrades, but in her mind, she was never the best.

Her insistence on constantly increasing her talents and abilities led to reading more and more material, practicing with larger and more dangerous weapons, and ultimately becoming a leading expert in everything that could do damage to anything.

With her extensive knowledge, and after seven years of solid training and following orders, she began getting her own assignments from a man named General Engall Fremthar.

He was a nice enough man with a solid background and extensive working knowledge of the Caste. He wasn't a General when Sherise began getting to know him, but when he became the highest ranking officer of the CHE, he personally requested she be under him. She was only one of five under the General, but even there she was always second best to the brown-skinned man she had come to know as "Urchin." His real name was Tyber Urching. He was good…and in Sherise's opinion, too good.

No matter what assignment she was given, his were always better. Of course, "better" in her opinion meant the same thing as "more exciting," "more dangerous" and "much more difficult."

Certainly and without a doubt the assignments given her were not without a great amount of risk.

At one point, she was given the job of assassinating a man who intended to take over a large corporation. As that event was unfolding, however, "Urchin" had been given the job of prying the lid off of an assassination plot against the Head Keeper of the Solar Union.

She remembers sitting in an assigned hotel room on the Agrauve home world after being ordered to find a band of crooks. If they did not come quietly, she was to kill all of them. With the help of an acquaintance, she tracked them all down near the hotel, offered each of them the choice, and when they did not accept her terms, she shot them each in the head…point blank. She felt no remorse. She had done her job.

There in the hotel room, on the sofa, relaxed and reading a slim-sheet computer with new weapon design manuals, a package arrived at her door. It was a small package with a simple note inside.

It read, "In the absence of a friend, you might find yourself wishing for one. If you know where to find one, however, you should look there. Falgone would be a good place to start…specifically, the moon Mercedes. If you remember me, I'll see you there. Have a safe trip."

It was her next order, and it came directly from the General.

In a matter of hours she had booked a transport to Darkcry, a planet two light years from Falgone. From there, she hitched a ride on a prison ship heading for Mercedes, where the Solar Union has a penitentiary and two offices.

She did her homework on the way there. At Darkcry, she picked up another package which contained information on her prey.

Mathew Arnold was from Shalokeer Raimoore III. Fresh from schooling at the age of sixteen, he got a job at a computer sales store. His accentuated knack for chauvinism got him fired fairly quickly, so in order to prove to his friends and family that he could do something right, he joined the military. It was there that he excelled, especially at flying ships. He learned every ship he could, and by the time he was twenty-four, he was the top pilot in the military. This only boosted his ego, but his leaders saw his potential and continually allowed him to head up flight missions. His ability to work with others, despite his chauvinism on the ground, made him the top choice for head pilot of the top squadron when a war occurred two years later. He was honored afterward for his bravery in combat, and use of his piloting skills.

She did her studies on the others as well, and when she saw the name Tyber Urching, her eyes squinted up and a smile swept her face. Whatever "Urchin" had done to deserve being on the other end of her super-HOP, she was more than happy.

She remembers it clearly…the emotions she felt at the sight of his name on her hit-list. His name immediately made its way to the top of that list in her mind.

After landing on the moon, she put on a space-suit and stepped out onto the uninhabitable landscape, following the coordinates given her by one of the upper managers. It wasn't long before she arrived at the place where the Vortex Class planetary cruiser was to set down.

She waited over two hours for that vessel to arrive, and when it did she didn't waste any time getting aboard. It was strangely silent, but she didn't care. Her top priority was to get rid of the six people lying in stasis pods in the observatory. She made her way there quickly, and once she saw "Urchin" in his pod, frozen with his eyes closed, the smile caressed her face. She leveled her favorite weapon at the stasis pod, and not wasting another second pulled the trigger. The missile hit the pod, exploding on impact and forcing it open, damaging the man inside permanently. He came out of stasis rather quickly and with eyes wide open, unable to breath, he watched as the woman he had come to know fired a second shot.

His body was incinerated right there. She didn't mind the gore. She had done this so many times before. She wasn't smiling at the grossness of his body being destroyed; she was smiling because before today she was second best. Finally, here in this moment, she was the top…the best. The General would be giving her the best jobs.

…And then everything went silent. She found out later that Chrinsole hit her on the back of the head, knocking her unconscious, and sending the Vortex Class planetary cruiser, designated "Vibrant," on a one-way trip through a tesseract. Destiny, she has now decided, is cruel…

*****

"They're connecting to the ship, Captain," Agoparn says.

The crew, with Shivranikka and the leader of the Agrauves, sit in the weapons room.

"What now?" Lacendu's face is worried.

"I hate to keep using Shivranikka's talents like we have been," Mathew says with a half-grin.

Shivranikka is turned away from the crew, facing the wall. "You should utilize me while you have me, Captain."

"Were you thinking of leaving," Korsaume asks.

Shivranikka turns to Vaskette with a simulated death-look, but her smile remains. She hopes the doctor won't say anything about their conversation two evenings ago. "Not at all, good Sir, but you never know what might happen…"

Now she directs her attention directly at Mathew, "It would be best if you utilized every advantage you have while you have it… That's what I do."

"…And you do it very well," Vaskette agrees with a nod of her head, being appeasing.

Korsaume gives an awkward look to both of them, but ignores it for now. "Would you be willing to do a few odds and ends jobs for us while we're docked," she asks of Shivranikka.

Shivranikka's smile only widens. "Of course, my dear Master, Korsaume… What would you and your hansom Captain have me do?"

Mathew gives Shivranikka a questionable look, but then more of an unsure one, and continues. "Do you know how to turn off one of these ships?"

"Naturally…"

"I would appreciate it if you and your men went aboard, rounded up all of the weapons and shields before their men can do anything about it, and I want you to shut it down."

"What do you folks intend to do, if you don't mind my asking," the Agrauve leader asks.

Mathew smiles at him, "It seems we're going to be doing a lot of this in the future, but…"

Rosetta finishes for him, "…we're going to take the General hostage…"

Vaskette makes a noise of exasperation while rolling her eyes. "Look, as much fun as that is…as much fun as the last time we did that was…I'm really getting tired of that kind of stuff. It seems the more we try to do good, the more illegal things we end up doing. Do you honestly think we'll get away with all of this in the end, Captain?"

Everyone is silent for a moment.

Mathew looks at the floor, and then back up at Vaskette. "Thank you for being the voice of reason, Doctor. You're right. Let's skip taking hostages and find another way."

"Do you still want me to gather all the weapons and shields, Captain," asks Shivranikka.

"Yes. Gather them and put them someplace where the crew on that ship can't get to them. We're going to have a chat with the General. I want your men to hold the crew in rooms until we're done speaking with the General."

"Well, nothing like morals to ruin my good fun," Shivranikka says with a shake of her head.

Mathew stands up. "Let's just get to work and worry about who's right and wrong when we get out of this mess."

Everyone stands up and follows Mathew out of the room. Meeting them there are Shivranikka's men, already informed of their job through the link she created in them. Around the corner is the clam-shell. The light on the side is blinking letting them know it is safe and awaiting someone to press the button opening the hatch.

Shivranikka and her men stand side by side and Allen punches the button to release the mechanism allowing the door to open, and it does so rather fast. As the door comes down, Shivranikka and her men are off past the General, taking his men with them.

The General looks around with a strange face, and then up at the people before him. "Who was that…?"

"That was Shivranikka…" Mathew replies with a straight face. "You'd be surprised what one can find on the other side of the galaxy."

The General suddenly seems very uncomfortable.

Korsaume walks up beside him, looks over at him with a rude glance, and then walks past him. "Let's go to the command deck, General."

The man looks around at the crew before him, turns on his heels in military fashion and follows Korsaume.

The rest of them walk behind him and follow them to the command deck.

"Have a seat, General," Korsaume says walking up to the Captain's chair and patting it once, and then walking over to the console where on their ship she normally sits.

The crew surrounds the captain's chair where the General sits down trying to look calm, but failing. "What's this about…?"

"Well, naturally, General, you don't think we would just let you walk right onto our ship and kill us all, do you?" Lacendu asks with her head tilted onto her right shoulder. Her blonde hair hangs off center, and strands from the left side dangle into her face.

The General pears up at the ceiling, "I see your point, obviously. So, what makes you think I'll leave all of you alone once you're gone?"

"I think there's been a miscommunication between us," Mathew says walking right up in front of the chair in the center of the room. "You have it in your mind that we deserve to die. I just want to know why…"

The General sighs. Breathing in loudly he responds, "I would think it would be obvious. My job is to keep wars from happening, or if nothing else to stop wars. I am responsible for the safety of the people of our galaxy. Sometimes that means killing a person, or a handful of persons, to keep civilization from harm."

"So you think we are going to start a war…" Mathew asks.

"Not anymore," the General answers. "I stopped the one your successors started, and I'm most certainly not going to allow you to start another…"

"Well, that's good of you, General," Mathew says turning with his hands clasped behind his back and walking toward the center front of the ship. He turns back around to face the man in the chair. "We have no intention of starting a war. We never did. We declined the offer the Solar Union gave us before they sent us off without our memories to try again."

The General's eyes narrow at the Captain of the Saiar Ria Contract. "What do you mean, 'without your memories'?"

"I mean, we can't remember anything before three months ago when we awoke on board a planetary cruiser in Quadrant Four," Mathew replies.

"…But you have the Saiar Ria Contract," the General says. "You're back here for some reason."

"The crewmembers of that ship were dead when Shivranikka Napercolten came across it. Whatever caused their death, it most likely has something to do with that mega-mass drive…" Korsaume says.

"Yes," he replies. "We realized its danger after our first use of it. That ship disappeared two years ago and we never heard from it again until now. To be sure, we were surprised that it was found at all. We've since then modified the way the drive works, and it doesn't cause the damage to human cellular tissue that it did in the beginning. You folks weren't foolish enough to use it, were you?"

"Unimportant, at the moment," states Vaskette walking around so he can see her. "We are trying to stop the people that caused our memory loss; the ones who tried to force us to start a war with the Agrauves."

The General gives a loud harrumph. "Your successors are still out there somewhere," he responds. "Do your plans include stopping them?"

"We only recently found out about them, so we haven't started any plans for them," Mathew says.

The General looks around at the crew of the Saiar Ria Contract, his eyes resting on the leader of the Agrauves. "What are your plans for him?"

"Originally, we wanted to stop the war without killing a bunch of Agrauves, so we took him hostage to see if we could stop it that way. Obviously we were too late," Korsaume says.

The General's left hand comes up to his face and he strokes his beard while his elbow rests on the arm of the chair. "I'll take the Agrauve leader back to his home world. If you folks really think you can get to the people you're talking about, I would encourage it. Naturally, I still have a stake in how this whole thing turns out, and I don't expect I'll be seeing you folks again for a long while. So, I want to send someone with you; someone who works for me."

Korsaume laughs. "I used to work for you. I quit because you wanted me to kill my friends."

"I was obviously wrong in that respect. You're back on my payroll."

Korsaume steps forward to stand beside Mathew. "You still owe me for my last job…"

"You didn't kill them," answers the General.

"I'm not talking about that. I'm talking about the job before that..." Korsaume steps up to the man and holds out her hand as if expecting something. "So, how about it...?"

The General stands up. "How about I don't kill you...? You folks stay out of my path, and I'll stay out of yours. How's that for payment?"

Mathew steps forward and with his left hand lowers Korsaume's right. "I think we've found some common ground, General."

"We'll be taking our leave now, if you don't mind," says Rosetta.

Mathew holds out his hand for the General to shake.

"You're in my path," the General simply states.

Mathew puts his arm down and walks away. His crew follows.

*****

The Saiar Ria Contract disconnects from the sister ship with the crew, and Shivranikka and men aboard. Shivranikka's men go to their stasis pods, nearly deplete of energy, and Shivranikka sits at the back of the command deck to rest.

"Where do we go from here," Allen asks politely, if somewhat nervous.

Lacendu looks at her control panel. "The war is already over. That's one battle we already don't have to fight..."

"No," Korsaume replies, "but the battle we do have to fight is much more deadly."

"...And the ground we have to fight it on is the most dangerous of all," Mathew says with contempt.

"Where...?" asks Vaskette.

He turns to her. "Baitronoc..."

"Oh, no..." Korsaume says, "We can't go there. That's the worst idea I've heard, yet."

"I didn't say it would be easy," says Mathew.

"Nor did you say it would be impossible, but it will be," his Lieutenant replies.

Allen is smiling, though no one is turned to look at him. "Impossible is our middle name," he says. "We've done the impossible several times if my memory serves me right."

Mathew turns his face to the strategist. "Do you have something in mind?"

"I have a few ideas, Captain…" Allen turns to Lacendu. "I believe with Lacy's help that we can trace the echo of that scrambled message we got and find out who those two ships belong to and where. If one of them is the one that's following us, we can grab their ship and use it…"

"Hm… Good point, Allen. If it's our successors, their ship would most likely get access to Baitronoc. We could use that to get there…" Mathew grins at the idea. "The two of you get together and work on that. How long do you think it would take?"

Lacendu turns in her chair. "If we get everything right, we could be looking at ten minutes max…"

"Go ahead. Rosetta, move this ship into the wreckage and shut down all non-essentials. I don't want that other ship to get a ping off of us for any reason," Mathew says.

Vaskette stands up and walks out. Shivranikka notices and follows quietly.

*****

Vaskette sits down at the computer console, but leaves it off. Instead, she drops her head onto her hands which are folded on the table. She doesn't care if it hurts right now.

Shivranikka is soon sitting next to her. "Hey, Doctor," she says in a hushed tone. She waits for a response, but gets none. She tries a little louder, "What's wrong, Dear?"

"What do you care, Nikka," Vaskette asks through a voice that sounds sad and annoyed.

"I have my reasons…none of which aren't personal and selfish, I admit, but that doesn't mean I don't care…" the long blonde-haired woman responds, her smile lessened, but still present.

Vaskette lifts her head up and tosses her hair aside. "I'm just sick of all of this. We're finally near our homes, but instead of going home and leaving well enough alone, we're going to go charging into the heart of darkness to save a day that doesn't really need saving…"

"Somehow I don't think you felt that way two and three months ago," Shivranikka says.

Vaskette shakes her head. "I didn't know what to think then," she answers, "and I still don't. I'm a doctor. Not some kind of warrior. I just want to go home. I want to get my life back, and it seems like everything is taken care of. Why can't we just…?" She doesn't finish.

Shivranikka maneuvers a bit to settle in her seat. "You know, Doctor, back when I was about twenty years old, there was a war. It started out for the right reasons, and everyone was happy with the reasons. Then, after a while, when it seemed like things weren't going the way everyone wanted, and things that started the war didn't seem to be relevant, there were many who decided the war should never have started.

"People get bored with war very quickly. Heck, people get bored with everything quick. Most often they just end up determining that if they can't have it their own way, or on their terms, then it shouldn't be…"

Vaskette's eyes widen slightly and she passes them from in front of her to the woman sitting next to her. "You're talking about Recongiere's Syndrome…"

"Whose syndrome…?"

"Recongiere…" She pronounces it 're-con-zhe-ay.' "He was a philosophical scientist near the turn of the millennium. He determined that people tend to reason until they run out of options. Then, they give in…"

Suddenly Shivranikka looks very happy. “So, then you see what I’m saying…”

“Yeah,” Vaskette says with a smile she doesn’t feel. “I just haven’t got there, yet.”

“…But you’re heading that direction, Vaskette. Eventually, you’ll get over your emotions here and move on to the point where you accept your position. I guess your best friend getting her memory back hasn’t helped, has it…?” Shivranikka knew before it came out of her mouth she shouldn’t say it.

Vaskette bangs her fists on the table and walks through a door at the back which leads to her room and shuts it behind her.

Shivranikka blows up at a tuft of her hair effectively blowing into her face. “Hm. I guess I went a little too far…”

*****

“We’ve tracked it down,” Lacendu says.

Allen continues. “I’m reading a movement track from two types of ships. One of them leads to a dead ship which has been shot at from the outside… There are no life-readings aboard.”

Mathew waits for him to tell about the other, and when Allen doesn’t, “…And the other track?”

“It moves into the debris field, Captain.”

“Shouldn’t that make it easier to track?” asks Mathew.

“In theory, Captain…” Allen quips.

Mathew doesn’t seem to take notice.

“I’ve got something alive in there,” Rosetta says. “It looks like a ship of some sort. Hm, make that: two ships…”

Mathew steps forward to the space between the consoles in the front. “View…”

The ship turns toward the area they are discussing and soon, with help of filters on the viewport they can see two small vessels hiding in the wreckage.

"How do we capture them without them trying to make a run for it…?" he asks.

"If they don't already know we see them, Captain," Allen says, "I'm not really sure."

"Prepare to fire at the material behind them. I want to force them in one direction…"

"I see where you're going with this, Captain, and I'm already on it…" Allen prepares to fire.

"Give them a 'red-rover,' Allen," Mathew says.

The shots are fired and material and debris hit the two ships coercing them to maneuver toward the Saiar Ria Contract.

"Transmit their direction," Mathew says.

Rosetta punches a few buttons and says, "You're on, Matt…"

"This is Captain Mathew Arnold of the Saiar Ria Contract. Respond, please…"

Allen speaks quickly. "They're preparing to move away…"

"Fire second shots," Mathew says.

More shots are fired at debris around the two ships and they are kept from moving away being buffeted closer to each other.

"I'm getting a transmission from one ship. The other remains silent," says Rosetta.

Mathew steps back to his seat and turns to look out the window. "I want both of them to respond. Fire third round shots, Allen."

The shots are fired around the two ships once more.

Mathew speaks to the open circuits. "This is Captain Mathew Arnold of the Saiar Ria Contract. Respond, please." This time he is much more forceful.

"Both are transmitting, Sir," says Rosetta.

"Can we get visual readouts from them," Mathew asks.

"We're transmitting visuals, Captain," says a voice from one of the ships.

"Left and right inserts," Mathew says to Korsaume.

Two images appear, one on the top left and one on the top right of the viewport window. On the left is a man with a helmet on. On the right is the woman leader of the six the crew met on the Agrauve home world.

"Well, it's good to see you again, Maneesha," Mathew says with his face scrunched up.

"Somehow I doubt that, Captain Arnold," she replies. "Now, what do you want?"

"It's pretty simple," he remarks. "I want your ships."

"I'm sorry," Maneesha says, "you can't have ours…" "C'mon, Captain, you've got one of the top ships in the fleet…" says the man in the other ship simultaneously.

"Well, I'm going to get one of them either way, so you can either give it up or we'll take it," Mathew says.

"You've got to be kidding," Maneesha says. "You don't even need our ship."

"Actually, we do," Mathew says. "We're willing to make a trade, of course…"

Maneesha leans back in her seat. As she does, two other crewmembers on board her ship can be seen on either side of her. The man on the other ship leans into the screen. "What's your plan, Captain?"

"Well, if I told you that I wouldn't need your ships…"

"You need both of them, Captain," the man asks.

"Look, the more you talk, the more I'm going to ask for. We're trying to make the decision easy for both of you…" says Mathew.

Maneesha looks at the rest of the crew around Mathew. "Is he serious…?"

Korsaume stands up to face the screen. "That would be a 'yes,' Maneesha. If you have to ask…"

"I don't see that you have us at a disadvantage…" Maneesha says. "I don't see why we would want to give up our ship."

"Well, naturally, you get this ship in return…" Allen says. "Can you think of anything better?"

"What do we need to do," Maneesha asks?

Mathew laughs at a thought he has. "I would have you two fight it out between you, but instead, I'm just going to trade this for both your ships…"

Maneesha looks upset and sighs. "I don't like you, Captain…"

Mathew smiles at her. "I don't really care, Maneesha. Dock with our ship and we won't hunt you down."

"You only have one clam," the man from the other ship says.

"You're right," Korsaume replies. "However, there is a huge cargo section which will hold the smallest ship. The other ship can dock to the clam. You'll both be on either side of the ship, so once we're gone the group with the best skills will get control of the Saiar Ria Contract."

Mathew walks to Rosetta saying, "You both have five minutes. I'll expect both ships to be docked in that time. We'll see you soon."

At Mathew's sign Rosetta cuts off the communications.

Lacendu starts laughing. "This is the most awesome thing we've ever done…"

*****

"WHAT!?" Vaskette half-yells, opening the door…

"We're packing and getting out of here," Lacendu says. "Are you alright?"

"I'm fine. I'm sorry, Lacy. I thought you were Shivranikka…"

"Has she been troubling you?" her friend asks.

"Oh," Vaskette says shaking her head, "It's not that as much as it is she keeps saying things that upset me. I still don't like her…" Vaskette picks up a couple things from the floor in her room. "…Or trust her…"

Lacendu watches her doctor friend with a face which is just on the edge of smiling.

Vaskette turns to Lacendu. "If you're going to be in here, you might as well help me out..."

"Sure," Lacendu replies walking to the other side of the room and picking up a few items.

There isn't much and they soon have everything on Vaskette's bed. Vaskette pulls a physician's bag from a compartment in a wall in the room and begins putting everything into it a little rough.

"What's really wrong, Vaskette," Lacendu asks walking around to her friend and placing an arm on the woman's shoulder.

Vaskette maneuvers aside away from the arm, and then reluctantly looks at her friend. "I'm sorry, Lacy. It's not you. I don't know what's wrong..." She sighs.

"Well," Lacendu says looking injured, "It's alright, Doctor. We're about to get into a couple of other ships. They're a lot smaller and we'll probably be able to spend more time together. We'll figure out what's wrong together...alright?"

Vaskette tries to smile while nodding her head. "Alright."

*****

Shivranikka and her men meet the group from the ship that docks in the storage bay. The men and women have Nation emblems on their shoulders, and when they exit the ship, they are obviously prepared for danger, weapons and shields on.

"You won't need those," Shivranikka says, smiling.

"That's alright," the pilot says. "We'll keep them anyway."

"Actually, no, you won't," Shivranikka replies, her smile widening. She points at the group and her men quickly remove the weapons and shields from them. "Now," she says, "If you'll all follow me, this will be really easy."

The group's faces are surprised and scared. They follow her and are surrounded by Shivranikka's men. They are taken to a room in the back of the ship and locked in. One of Shivranikka's men stands guard to make sure they don't try to get out ahead of schedule.

Meanwhile, Mathew and his crew stand at the clam shell when it opens and their weapons are already pointed at the other group.

"Wow," one of Maneesha's crew says, "What a welcome..."

"It's just for our protection," Allen says. "Let's move."

As the group is being walked to the back of the lowest floor of the Saiar Ria Contract they are met by Shivranikka and seven of her eight men. That group is placed in the room on the opposite side of the ship from the other group.

"What do you expect us to do in here," Maneesha asks.

Mathew walks off followed by most of his crew, except Korsaume who stands with Shivranikka and her men. "When we're ready for you to, we'll let you know that you can begin trying to get out of this room. The first group to the command deck gets control of the ship..."

Maneesha smiles at Korsaume. "You and I both know who will win that..."

Korsaume shrugs. "You're right, Maneesha. However, I assure you none of us are worried. To add to the fun, the ship will be shut down leaving about six hours of air inside. The other group is hearing the same thing you are right now through the communication systems, so both groups will be in the know.

"Just so you're all aware, there are weapons in the weapons room. It might be a great idea to go there first. All your weapons will be in there...both groups'. We're taking all of ours with us. Have fun..."

The door is closed and one of Shivranikka's men is left at the room.

Shivranikka and her men meet at the clam shell dock.

Korsaume meets her crewmates in the bay and they take the other ship out.

The Saiar Ria Contract is turned off by remote, and the two small ships are on their way toward Baitronoc.

*****

"Here we go," Rosetta says. "I found the logs of visual and audio transmissions out. I'm patching them through to you, Lacy."

"I'm getting them. I've got over three hours worth of video and audio on Maneesha to form some good visuals of our own. Most synchronic visuals are within tolerable limits…audio data and frequency compensable to create live-automatic strings." Lacendu is rummaging through the files quickly and with expert speed and efficiency.

Mathew sits in the front command control seat of the considerably small command deck piloting the vessel. It is about a third as large as their original ship, the 'Vibrant.' It's small enough that the rooms have bunks.

"You've got about one hour to prep it," Mathew says. "We'll be within audio/visual range in forty-five minutes."

"That's alright, Captain," Lacendu states, a smirk on her face, "I'll have a mock-up for you to test in about five…"

"Captain, you asked for updates on the status of Shivranikka's ship," says Allen.

"Go ahead," Mathew replies.

"They're keeping up with a literal one hundred percent accuracy."

Mathew turns to his strategist. "That sounds just like our Shivranikka."

Korsaume enters the pilot room with something less of a strut than normal. She sits down beside Allen and takes his left hand in her right.

Lacendu glances over and sees their hands together and smiles big to her self. She clears her throat in jest, and Mathew turns to her. Lacendu's eyes avert to Allen and Korsaume, but Mathew doesn't buy into it.

Instead, he says, "…And Lacy, how are you coming on that live audio/visual stream?"

"It's going pretty quick, now, Captain. I'll have something in a moment…"

Mathew presses a button and speaks to Rosetta. "Seta, update Shivranikka and her crew on our plans…"

"Yes, Sir, Captain," Seta replies.

"Captain," Allen begins…

After waiting a moment Mathew turns to him. Allen's hands are on the console in front of him. "What, Strategist?"

"Lacy's test is going to have to go live right away, sir. We've got company. Full Solar Union Battalion…"

Rosetta's voice comes over the communications channel; "Captain, we're being traced and called… They're calling for Maneesha."

"Lacy…"

"I've almost got it, Captain. You can't rush perfection…" She says it as if he's pushing her too hard, but she holds back making her voice sound more sarcastic.

"I'm not looking for perfection, Lacy," he remarks.

Lacendu looks at him. "That's good because I just patched it all to Rosetta's console…"

Rosetta's voice comes over the speakers. "Captain, you're on…"

"On view," he says.

On the view in front of Mathew is a screen with an image of a large woman commander. "Hello, Maneesha…"

"Hey," Mathew begins, hoping the job Lacendu just finished is working. "What do you want…?" He leans back in his chair trying to act like the woman he remembers.

The woman stares at the image before her, blinks a few times and says, "I just want to know why you decided to come home. Your mission isn't over, is it?"

"Over…? No, Sir. It's just…my crew and I have some information and we need to set down for a bit." He pauses, watching her face. Suddenly and without warning he leans up close to the monitor. "Come on… We've been out here forever. You can't expect us to stay out here. We've got human functions that can't be done while on your stupid old cramped ship quarters. This thing's giving me hives!"

The woman's eyes furrow, and when they do the overhang of her brows makes her eyes seem dark, almost black. "Did you meet with the crew of the Saiar Ria Contract…?"

"Of course…On the Agrauve home world, just like we were told… We were ready for them. They managed to make off with the leader anyway, but it was all in good fun. The CHE already took care of the Agrauve fleet."

"Yes, I heard. Did you inspect the wreckage?" The woman is intent, now.

"Naturally," Mathew says.

"What did you find…?"

Mathew suddenly feels a pang of doubt. Was the other crew ordered to find something? Did they find it? "A bunch of heaping rubble, piles of debris floating in empty space. What else do you expect anyone to find in a battlefield?"

"Did you find any trace of the weapon the Girancholle Shiaduce used to stop the war…?" The woman sounds upset at Mathew's playing around the fringes.

"If you're wondering if anyone will be able to tell what killed all those Agrauves, you needn't worry. Mega-mass worked like a charm…" Mathew smiles in spite of himself, and suddenly finds his thoughts on hoping it doesn't give him away. He looks down. "…And about that matter we discussed, Sir…" He knows he's taking a huge risk at this.

"It's taken care of, Maneesha. You and that other ship are now cleared to pass to Baitronoc. Feel free to check in with the Manager at the hangar bay. He'll let you know about that…" she pauses for effect; "…matter…"

"Yeah, yeah…" Mathew waves her off. "Whatever. I'll expect I won't be seeing you too soon…"

"Any time is too soon," the woman quips, and then signals to her communications specialist to cut transmission.

"We're out," Rosetta's voice comes over the speaker. "Great job, Captain…"

Mathew breathes in heavily and then sighs big putting his left hand to his forehead. "Never again…"

Korsaume obviously overhears him through the communications because she says, "Actually, Captain, once more…"

"Where," he asks.

"Considering you don't remember Solar Union-owned planetary and military installations, I'll forgive you for not knowing this, but they require direct voice-print and sequence numbers for landing privileges…" Korsaume responds.

Mathew rolls his eyes. "Great…" He looks at Lacendu. "Can you find a previous performance of that on those audio/visual records?"

"I'm already working on it, Captain," and she is, head over her console going over early data.

Mathew puts the ship on auto-pilot. "I'll be back in a few minutes. Inform me the moment anything comes up…"

"Yes, Sir," Allen replies with a nod.

Mathew steps around Korsaume in the small space of the piloting room and walks through the back door.

When he is safely out of earshot Lacendu turns her head, but doesn't quite look directly at the two behind her. Instead, she returns her gaze to the computer screen before her. "So… When did you two hook up?"

"Ascension City," Korsaume says with a smile in her voice. "Why do you ask, Mathematician?" She says Lacendu's honorary in a polite tone.

Lacendu whirs around in her chair rather fast. Her own face is grinning. "Just curious…" She leans her head toward the two. In a hushed whisper she says, "I think it's great… Why didn't you tell us?"

"If you didn't notice, Lacy," says Allen, "we've all been a bit busy. There just hasn't been time to discuss it."

Lacendu giggles at them. "Oh, there've been plenty of chances." Her eyes are a little squinted and she nods her head up and down sounding sarcastic.

Korsaume smiles back. "Alright, Lacy… Your point is proven. We just want to take our time."

"Oh, take your time…by all means, take all the time you need," she responds, her head going back and forth until she turns back to her console.

*****

Mathew arrives in the communications room. It is easily the largest room in the ship as it contains the small infirmary on the starboard side. It is simply a large room with many computers and the latest technology.

"Hey, Captain," Vaskette says. Her face is drained of energy, but there is a gentle warm smile on her face.

"Hi, Doctor. How are we holding up down here?"

"Fine," Rosetta responds.

Mathew looks at Vaskette directly with his eyebrows raised, awaiting a response from her.

Vaskette feels it and looks up at him from her seated position in a chair on the starboard wall. "I'm just waiting for someone to get injured so I can be of use."

Mathew feels uncomfortable suddenly, knowing that she feels worthless. He is unsure what to say to her. Instead, he walks over to Rosetta and stands next to her. "That was a little unfair, wasn't it…?"

She doesn't even look up. "Oh, you know I was just teasing you. I didn't mean anything by it."

"No…I know you didn't. I just figured I'd come down here and give you a hard time about it, anyway."

"You didn't have to do that," she says eyeing him. "I could have just as easily come up there to you…"

"I would have been all for that, but Korsaume went up there to be with Allen…"

"You're kidding." A broad smile creeps up on Rosetta's face. "How grand…"

"You're almost giddy about it," Mathew says with a straight face.

"Positively," she answers him. "I thought Korsaume was a stick-in-the-mud."

"Oh, she's still a stick-in-the-mud. Now, though, she's a stick-in-the-mud with a boyfriend." He smiles again.

They both laugh at this comment. They smile at each other afterwards, kiss, and Mathew walks back up to the pilot room.

"Did you hear," Rosetta asks of Vaskette.

"Yeah. I heard."

Rosetta turns to the doctor and leans back on the console she's been standing at. "You know, you've been absolutely boring for the past few weeks. What is wrong with you?"

Vaskette stands up mad. She throws her arms down to her side. "There's nothing wrong with me." She looks Rosetta up and down once. "What's wrong with you?"

"Hey, I'm just trying to help," Rosetta answers retaining her composure, though sounding a little rude.

"Well, help someone else. I don't need it."

At this, Vaskette stomps off out of the room, up the stairs, and to her bunk where she lies down, closes the bunk door, and covers up crying.

*****

"There it is," Mathew says. He pushes a button which allows the others where they sit to pull up the image he sees as Baitronoc's dark edges and large metal structure comes into view.

"Wow," Lacendu says in awe, shaking her head.

The massive construct encircles a star about five hundred million kilometers from Earth and took over two hundred years to build, and more than seven quintillion hands.

Much of the original structure has been dismantled, melted down on a planet in the same solar system, and brought back to replace old sections which have broken from stress.

It is more of a band around a sun. It circles at an estimated fourty-one million kilometers from the star, and because of the star's small size it is easy to maintain. The band is only seven hundred kilometers at its width and is made of metal from eighty-two planets within forty light years of the system.

The band-like "Dyson-sphere" contains over twenty-one billion humans and their plants and animals, their lives, their homes, and their jobs. It has come to be known as the hub of the galaxy for all laws and regulations, even if most of the planets closer to the center of the Milky Way disregard those laws and regulations.

The film cover over the inside of the ring is only three meters thick and see-through, but air-tight, and invulnerable to most structural breakage. Multiple monitoring stations around the ring scan the film for any sign of a breach, and when something even remotely resembling one is ascertained, the segment is covered, removed, and replaced. There is an entire economy dedicated to this one portion of the life on this monstrous metallic structure.

The place is not for the weak in heart.

Amid this, the structure is home to the highest-ranking officials of the Solar Union. More specifically, it is home to the Solar Union Committee: a five-thousand member group whose job it is to determine the best course of action for well over three hundred eighteen quadrillion people throughout the galaxy.

The question being asked of those five thousand people today is: are five thousand people enough?

"I don't like telling you this, Captain," Rosetta calls up to the pilot room, "but, you're about to be on again in about twenty seconds."

"Lacy," Mathew says in hope.

"I've done all I can to make it better, Captain. Good luck…" She presses a button which puts a list of stringed words, phrases and numbers in a sequence for him to read from. He scans ahead as he reads aloud, the computer filtering his voice automatically on the front end before the message is sent out through the ship's terminal communications display.

He reads, "This is Maneesha Huchan of the Simpra Core Regent vessel, designation 'R – S – F – 0 – 0 – 9 – 4 – 8' requesting permission to dock at main hanger."

"This is docking bay quartermaster Brian Shems to the Simpra Core Regent vessel… Your designation number is in process. One moment, please."

They wait patiently.

The quartermaster comes on again, "Your vessel is cleared for docking procedures. Vessel Skeer Morgan, please give us your designation code."

They hear a man's voice, "This is Stetler Viroa of the Skeer Morgan, designation 'T – L – 1 – 4 – 6 – 9 – 0 – 9 – 2' requesting permission to dock." His voice is mechanical and monotone, but it seems fairly normal.

"Skeer Morgan, your vessel is cleared for docking. Simpra Core Regent, hanger 8 – 9 – 2 – 1; Skeer Morgan, hanger 7 – 9 – 1 – 9."

"Understood," Mathew and Shivranikka say simultaneously.

The communications are turned off and Mathew gets out of his chair and walks to the back. "Let's go downstairs and meet," he says to the three others with him in the pilot room.

Korsaume, Lacendu, and Allen follow him downstairs. Agoparn meets them there moments later.

"Where's Vaskette," Lacendu asks looking around.

Rosetta presses a button for ship communications and says, "Vaskette, please report to the infirmary."

They all take seats and within three minutes Vaskette walks down the stairs, her hair mussed and unkempt. Her eyes are red, and the makeup on her face is running and blotchy. She sits down in a chair near Lacendu and breathes heavily.

"Are you alright," Lacendu asks quietly to her friend.

Vaskette yawns, "I was asleep."

Mathew looks at each member of his crew in turn. "This is it. This is where our quest ends. I want to know what we're going to do. What is our plan?"

"You're the Captain, Captain," Allen replies. "You're the one who's supposed to be making the decisions."

"It's more than that," Mathew states, "it's not about me, or any one person in this room. This event affects all of us equally. This is where it started, and it's where we're going to end it. I want to know what your thoughts are, and what we should do."

Vaskette raises her hand mid-way into the air; then sets it down in her lap when Mathew nods to her. "Why would we want to end this at all? I'm just curious." At the odd looks she gets from everyone, she continues, "I'm just saying that we're here. We're already to Quadrant One. We made a trip that should have taken over a year in less than three months. We've been through a lot of stuff to get here. Why don't we all just go home…?"

Her crewmates fall deathly silent, contemplating this.

Allen begins, "I think, at least for me, that the whole reason we should wrap this up is **because** we've been through so much. I don't know if I could go back to my home with the thought that what got me here is still out there, determined to fight what I know to be true."

"It's not about what we want, anymore," Korsaume says with thoughtfulness. "I just got my employment back, but if that's all I'd wanted, I would have gone with my boss and left the rest of you to your own devices. The reason I came along is because I want to see this thing through to the end. I'm not going to give up."

"There're still a lot of things that we haven't answered," Agoparn adds. "I don't think I could face my family; people I still don't remember; knowing that what caused me to lose my memory is still out there waiting for another opportunity."

Mathew says, “The ‘brain’ didn’t cause what we went through. I’m confident of that, now. I know what was asked, and what the answer was. What I don’t know is why the Solar Union chose us to start the war. I still don’t know why we decided not to go through with it.” He eyes Lacendu, who frowns, knowing the answer.

She begins; “When we were first brought together, we were told that a war was needed, and that it had to be between the Solar Union and the Agrauves. We were informed of intelligence which concluded that the Agrauves were already preparing for war. The Solar Union Committee wanted us to plan the war in a way which would cause the Solar Union to win.

“Even though we put our heads together and came up with several viable options, we determined that the Agrauves were way too well prepared, and that it would require direct intervention with mass murder which would ultimately amount to genocide…specifically, destroying the Agrauve home world; something that not even Mathew or that dark-skinned guy were willing to go along with.”

“That dark-skinned guy…?” Rosetta asks.

Korsaume smiles and says, “His name was Tyber Urching.”

“Oh, yeah,” Lacendu replies with a smile and nod. “Anyway, Mathew and Tyber were for the war, all the way; both of them being warrior-like and all…but when faced with the possibility of genocide, they were both against it immediately, so we didn’t give that as an option. In fact, Vaskette specifically discouraged it saying it would lead to even worse things.

“Since the group in charge of our study felt like we were holding something back from them they sent us to a big chamber where they systematically erased our memories of specific life events and our family and friends. They pretty much told us as much while we were all strapped to large chairs while they were preparing to do their thing on us. Then they drugged us, and I don’t remember anything after that until we woke up on the ‘Vibrant.’”

“Evidently, our memories weren’t erased,” Vaskette says, “…at least, yours weren’t, Lacy.”

Lacendu smiles at her friend, "Yeah."

"Well, then, it sounds like our plan would be to find out who's responsible for our memory erasure…" Allen says.

"I think it needs to go deeper than that," says Mathew.

Korsaume looks at the Captain. "What did you have in mind?"

"I think we should take it all the way to the top."

Lacendu looks surprised. "You mean, the Head Keeper."

"That's the idea," Mathew replies.

Agoparn shakes his head. "I seriously doubt they're even going to allow us to run around on Baitronoc, much less get in to see the Head Keeper. I'm pretty confident he's incessantly too busy to see us…"

Mathew smiles at them, "Then we need to make our way in to see him."

Korsaume shakes her head. "I don't see how. The building he practically lives in is the most secure place in the whole galaxy. We're not getting in there without an invite."

"Do you have that much doubt in our abilities, Lieutenant," Lacendu asks.

Korsaume shakes her head. "No, I just have that much faith in their security. I've been to that building multiple times. Every check is random…every camera is controlled and constantly watched…every guard is specially trained to keep people like us out. I just don't see how we could do it."

Mathew lightly kicks Korsaume's left leg with his right foot; not hard enough to hurt her. "What would it take to shut the place down?" He has a smile on his face.

Korsaume looks at her leg, then his foot, then into his face, and finally answers, "An act of God."

Mathew shakes his head. "Does Shivranikka qualify?"

Korsaume laughs at him. "She's just an act. No 'God' involved."

"Let's land first, get off our ships, and we'll get together and figure out something from there…" Mathew states.

Vaskette adds, "Assuming they don't shove us all in jail first and throw away the key."

"Always the optimist, Doctor," Allen says with his face down and his eyes peeking up at her, a smirk on his face to let her know he's kidding.

She practically ignores him, stands up and walks up the stairs and back to her bunk.

Mathew sighs, but not noticeably to everyone. "Dismissed…"

At this, everyone is standing and heading back to their duties…everyone but Lacendu who pulls Mathew to the back of the room.

"Is this about Vaskette?" he requests.

She nods, "I'm really concerned for her, Captain. She's becoming more and more despondent. I think she's going through depression."

Mathew breathes out, the sound audible to Lacendu. "I believe you might be right. What do you think she's depressed about?"

"I'm not sure, but it started happening before we got to Ascension City. Since then it's only gotten worse."

"So, you don't think this is just a phase she's going through, or that maybe she's jealous that you got your memories back and she didn't?" Mathew asks with obvious implications.

"She confided in me after we got that material on our pasts. She said a lot of things; but I think there was something in that material that she didn't tell me…something that is driving her to the brink…" Lacendu confesses.

"What do you think we should do, Lacy," Mathew asks, directing her attention to helping her friend.

"I'm not sure, Captain," she replies with a simple shake of her head, "but whatever we're going to do for her it needs to be fast. I've seen this before."

"Depression…?"

Her face becomes deadly serious. "She's contemplating suicide."

Episode 17
A Heartbeat

OPENING:

Forget what you know...what you remember. It has now become necessary to stampede the allurement of hope in humanity by building a failsafe. ...Or so they're calling it. The 'brain,' as most uneducated people tend to refer to it as, burdens the men and women who have to build it and it only weighs us down. Thus, I have built a back door, as all programmers do. It will serve someone well down the road if they can find it. All they need to find is Main Street.

Baitronoc is a beautiful place for those who enjoy the metal jungle. The people who choose to live here thrive on the confined, cramped quarters. More or less, those who live here love their claustrophobia.

The main city is Egra. The city is more like a large building, infrastructure housed in a single structure inside a large ring that encircles a star; a system within a system within a system.

The Simpra Core Regent lands in the hangar bay 8 – 9 – 2 – 1. It is a large hangar, big enough to hold the Saiar Ria Contract, and ships even larger, most likely. Thus, in comparison, the Simpra Core Regent is a mosquito in this large jar.

Vaskette pulls herself out of the top bunk over Rosetta's. Her clothing is wrinkled, her hair is horribly disheveled, and the areas around her eyes are black from makeup that should have been taken off a day ago.

Her legs are wobbly as she walks into the sanitary room for her daily bodily functions and a hot shower. She takes a long shower pushing her body to relax.

When she exits the shower room she puts on fresh clothing, fixes her hair in her customary fashion, and puts on fresh makeup. She looks into the mirror, breathes deeply, and presses her clothing with her hands.

Her eyes are cold, against her will. She doesn't notice, nor does she care. To be perfectly honest, she doesn't even pay attention to how she looks. She's just doing what she's always done for as long as she can remember which isn't very long…maybe, four months or so. It's just a routine, and routine is all she has left.

She exits the sanitary room to the greeting of Allen, who is the last to get into the room. He smiles at her, pats her on the shoulder as she passes him with her head down, and enters the room.

Lacendu is the next person to see Vaskette. "Hey, beauty queen…" Lacendu's smile is pulled further back on the right side of her mouth, as if fighting laughter.

Vaskette either ignores her blonde haired friend, or doesn't hear her. Instead, she walks around the woman with a fluid movement that tells Lacendu she's only in the way.

Lacendu turns to watch her friend walk through the hallway and down to the infirmary.

Vaskette sits down on the chair that she would normally have one of her patients in, but today she is her own patient. She picks up a sterile needle and a bottle of some substance which she injects directly into a large vein in her left arm.

No one is there to watch her, and she falls unconscious.

*****

"Are we about ready?" asks Mathew.

Rosetta walks up to him and stands beside him with Allen and Korsaume in the room directly behind the pilot room. Agoparn joins the four of them moments later, and within a few minutes Allen follows.

"Where's Lacy and Vaskette?" Korsaume asks.

"Lacy's in the sanitation room throwing up…she was waiting by the door when I came out, so she should be along any time, now."

"I thought she was over that, now," Agoparn says.

Korsaume shakes her head, "No, she's been doing that on occasion for the past few weeks. She still gets that motion sickness on these types of vessels, but she's getting used to it."

"…Or so she says," Allen remarks.

"Let's get downstairs and prepare for the great welcome we're going to get from all the thronging crowds," Mathew says with a step forward.

Everyone laughs at the joke.

They all know what they're about to face, and it won't be pretty. When the people in charge of the hangar bay see the seven of them exiting the Simpra Core Regent, they will know instantly that they're not the six people they sent away on the same ship, and will most likely send a full regiment of armed guards to escort them to prison.

The group is counting on the technological advances of the crew of the Skeer Morgan to help them through this endangerment.

Korsaume is the first to see Vaskette in the chair unconscious. She runs over to the doctor. "Dear, God, Vaskette…what did you do?" She pushes her friend's shoulders, shakes her, and puts her right hand up to the woman's face to move her head a bit. "Wake up."

By now, everyone but Lacendu is in the infirmary/communications room.

"Does she have a pulse," asks Allen.

Korsaume checks, and feels it fine. “She’s got a strong heartbeat.” She leans in close to the woman with her ear to her face. “She’s breathing well.”

Mathew picks up the needle and bottle. “It’s ‘caracubine;’ the stuff she was injecting us with every few days to help our short-term memory.”

“I don’t remember it ever putting me out like that,” Agoparn states; “How much did she inject?”

Mathew looks at the empty bottle. “Impossible to tell… I admit I never paid attention to how much she gave me.”

It is at that moment that Lacendu comes down looking as if she feels a little queasy. “What’s going on?”

Rosetta turns to the woman stepping off the stairs. “Vaskette injected herself with ‘caracubine;” and possibly quite a bit of it.”

Lacendu’s head tilts to the left and her eyes widen a bit as her mouth hangs loosely open only half an inch. “Mathew…” she begins.

“I didn’t forget, Lacy. I just didn’t figure it would look like this,” he says looking back at her. “Is there an anti-agent?”

Lacendu shakes her head. “I don’t know. What do I look like; a doctor?” She thinks better of herself and says, “I’m sorry, Captain.”

Mathew puts the bottle and needle into the sink. “No problem, Mathematician.”

Lacendu comes over between the other members of the crew and gets down on her knees in front of the dark-red-haired woman in the chair. Mathew looks at his crew and catches their attention to pull them away toward the door.

Lacendu begins trying to wake Vaskette. It is several minutes before Vaskette rouses from sleep. She looks groggily at Lacendu and smiles. “Hey, Lacy…”

“What are you doing? We’ve got to go, and you’re shooting yourself up…” Lacendu says, sounding quite upset.

Vaskette’s body moves slowly and she places a hand on Lacendu’s shoulder. “It’s alright. It’s just ‘caracubine.’ I know what I’m doing, too; remember…I’m a doctor…”

"Yes, I know you're a doctor, and you're a human, too," Lacendu says, "How much of that stuff did you plug in?"

"The usual dose," Vaskette replies. "I never use too much of this stuff."

"Well, we had a time waking you, Vaskette," Lacendu adds standing up and bending over her to help her up.

"I'm alright, Lacy…really," says Vaskette. "I'm just sleepy…"

"Yeah, you're acting just fine. What else did you take?"

Vaskette eyes her friend, "What are you implying, Lacy? That I drugged myself on purpose?"

"You're too happy," Lacendu says. "You took something to make you happy."

"No, I took something to make me rest. I'm tired."

"You just slept for four hours, and before that you slept nine hours with only a five hour waking period. You're in depression, and you need help," Lacendu says.

Vaskette, having just stood up and practically hanging on Lacendu, turns and slaps the blonde. She says quietly, "You shut up. I am not depressed. I'm a doctor; I know all the signs of depression."

Lacendu leans into her friend's face, her cheek throbbing from the slap. She whispers loudly, "I've had a friend before in your condition. She was suicidal, even if she didn't show all the signs of depression."

By this point, everyone near the door is looking to the front of the room where the two women are arguing.

Vaskette turns to Lacendu, balls up her fist and swings at Lacendu, connecting on her friend's jaw. Lacendu is knocked away, and because she was the only thing keeping Vaskette on her feet, the doctor falls over toward the chair where she catches herself with her right arm, her left hand pounding from hitting bone.

The others run toward the fight.

Lacendu is furious as she stands up and jumps on Vaskette with a blow to her back. Vaskette pulls herself up and turns with her right elbow to Lacendu's upper head. Lacendu; now on the floor in severe pain; sweeps at Vaskette's legs, knocking Vaskette forward onto the cold hard floor.

The rest of the crew is now nearby. Allen, Korsaume, and Rosetta pull Vaskette to her feet, the red-head trying to use the momentum to push her body forward to tackle Lacendu, since she's having too much trouble standing on her own.

Mathew and Agoparn are holding Lacendu to the floor, the blonde woman fighting them with her arms pinned.

Korsaume screams at her, "THAT WILL BE QUITE ENOUGH!"

"Yeah," Agoparn says with his eyes narrowed back and forth at the two women, "That's not what we're here for."

Vaskette, her arms being held, hangs her head and her legs give out. They allow her to fall to the floor, but hold on to her.

Mathew begins, "Vaskette, you need help. We're going to sit right here in this room until you tell us what's wrong."

Vaskette pulls her head up; tears are streaming down her face, with her red hair hanging over the sides of her face. "Ask Lacy. She knows so much about me, you know."

Lacendu tries to pull forward, her face red in anger, "I was just trying to help!"

Mathew and Agoparn rein her back. "That's enough, Lacy. I don't want to hear you right now. I want to hear Vaskette." He turns to the doctor. "Now, Doctor, what's really wrong."

Vaskette just breaks down. She weeps, and her body falls limp. She falls over to the left, her legs and arms pulling up into the fetal position.

Lacendu calms very suddenly and moves forward to be with her friend. Her own tears are showing now. "I'm so sorry… I'm so sorry." Her voice softens, but she continues to repeat it as if chanting it to her will heal her friend's heart.

Mathew and Agoparn release her to let her move next to Vaskette. Mathew sits back against the nearby wall, his stomach relaxing as he realizes he was on an adrenaline rush and his entire body was tightened. He breathes a sigh of relief. Agoparn looks his Captain's direction, but sits with his legs out beside him, and his right arm holding him up.

Korsaume strokes Vaskette's right arm. Vaskette's body is pulled up, and her head is resting on Korsaume's thigh. Korsaume is looking down and finds her heart breaking at the sight of the woman on the floor.

Vaskette soon realizes she's uncomfortable and slows her crying. After a few moments of sounds that seem more like whimpers, she tries to get up to her knees.

She breathes loudly for a few minutes before she opens her eyes. "I'm sorry, Lacy. It's not you."

Lacendu tilts her head down to try and look into Vaskette's face. "It's alright. I know you didn't mean it. I didn't mean to fight back…"

"You had every right," Vaskette replies. A long moment passes, and finally Vaskette begins; "You wanted to know what's really going on, Captain, so I'll tell you. I got the information from Rosetta. It was all really nice. I was the top doctor; of course. I was in every major doctor club, and had high honors when I graduated. I performed experimental surgeries with perfection.

"There's one thing I discovered I didn't have…"

Everyone is silent, awaiting the answer.

"I don't have love… I don't have a boyfriend, husband, or anyone in my life. I don't even have friends here. There's no one looking for me. My mom doesn't care where I am, as long as I'm making money and being a physician. She said so in an interview Rosetta retrieved.

"Do you all know what it's like to not have anyone wanting you to come home? I have nothing to return to. What's the use in coming back home if no one cares? The only thing the clubs would care about is who the next big thing is, and I doubt I could hold that title very long. No one ever does."

Korsaume swallows hard. "Yeah, Vaskette; I know just how you feel."

Vaskette, her hair still hanging around the edges of her tear-stained face, looks up into Korsaume's eyes. "You do?"

"Yes." She nods her head at the Doctor. "My boss doesn't care about me. No one was looking for me. They would have assumed that if I didn't come back that I was either dead or a traitor. If I'd ever been found as a traitor, I'd have been shot on sight. My parents don't even care."

Vaskette's eyes narrow at the Lieutenant. "I'm such an idiot…" She shakes her head in disgust. "I had no idea. I assumed that when you saw them that everything was fine…"

Korsaume silently laughs, a smile crossing her face. "…Not hardly… In fact, they pretty much told me I'm not their daughter anymore."

Vaskette rolls her eyes, "Oh! I'm sorry. I had no idea…"

Korsaume smiles at the other. "It's alright. I'll live. I found out I've got friends right here. It helps knowing that all of you care about me, even if I did try to kill you…"

Vaskette sighs, her face slowly becoming controlled. "Oh, Korsaume," she says lunging forward and hugging the Lieutenant. "Thank you."

As they pull away from each other, Vaskette begins brushing her eyes with her hands. "I don't know what I was thinking…"

Korsaume's head hangs down, noticing Mathew's look.

"I knew something was wrong," he says.

"Yes, Captain," she states, "That was what was wrong when I came back covered in mud. You were right."

"You know," Agoparn says, "Just because we're all about to go into that office and end this whole thing doesn't mean we can't all remain friends. I consider everyone here my friend and I'm glad I've had this opportunity to get to know all of you."

"I agree, Agoparn," Mathew adds, "I say we go in there, finish this thing, and find our ways home. I think it would be worth it to all of us to keep our friendship."

"You're all my best friends," Lacendu says.

There is silence for a short moment.

Finally, Vaskette looks around at everyone. "I'm very embarrassed."

"There's nothing to be embarrassed about," Korsaume remarks. "Instead of dealing with my problem I tried to hide it from everyone. I've learned to deal with deception and the like. You still don't even have your memories."

Vaskette looks down in surprise. "Actually…" She tries to stand up, but falls right back down. "I'm going to need some help getting up," she says.

Everyone begins getting on their feet and Korsaume and Lacendu help Vaskette stand up.

Vaskette continues, "I believe I do have my memories…" She looks around at everyone. "I do…" she says in surprise. "I have my memories… Help me get over to the console," she says to the two holding her up.

They help her walk over to the console and hold her up while she types some things into her computer.

"I just figured out how to get all of our memories back," she says.

"What do you mean," asks Agoparn.

"Well, I just figured out what they did to us…"

They wait for her to continue, and finally Agoparn says, "Go ahead, Doctor. What did they do to us?"

She smiles, but does not turn her head. "It's called 'magnified partitioning.' All humans have the capability of partitioning off memories and thoughts; things they don't like or don't want to remember. Evidently they made me forget about it, too.

"It's actually very simple. They drug us to no end with drugs that help us partition off information, and then tell us what information to forget. Extremely tragic events or intense emotions trigger the brain into de-partitioning. It's common in accident victims, or people who have been assaulted, raped, or otherwise treated poorly by loved ones or strangers."

Korsaume adds, "It's also part and parcel to my training as an assassin. We see so much every time we do a job…people we kill in ways I won't repeat. We're trained to not remember what we've done to them."

Vaskette turns her head with an almost fearful look on her face … more of someone appalled at what they are hearing.

Korsaume gives a quick, silent, breathed laugh, and then says, "Sorry…"

Vaskette nods. "You've got the general idea, Lieutenant. Anyway, back to what I was saying. The reason the guys haven't got their memories back is because men tend to have different types of triggers than women. For us, it's usually some kind of evoked emotion." She turns with her hands on the console to hold her body up. "For you guys, it's going to be a lot more difficult."

Mathew looks at Allen and Agoparn in turn. "I don't know about the rest of you, but I'm not overly concerned with getting my memory back."

Allen shakes his head. "Not really."

Agoparn looks back at the other two. "I'm not worried about it at the moment; though I wouldn't mind it if we get the chance."

Mathew walks to the other end of the group, closest to the door.

"Well, there's only one way to begin. We've got to go into that building and meet the man who started the whole problem." At this, Mathew turns to Rosetta. "Give Shivranikka her queue."

Rosetta pulls the small box from her waist and presses the button on it.

Vaskette turns to them. "You guys go on ahead. I'll stay here and do what I can to find an answer for you."

Mathew shakes his head. "No. Not with the condition you're in. Either someone else stays here with you, or we carry you along. You're not staying here alone."

Vaskette sighs. "I'm fine, Captain. I wasn't trying to commit suicide, and I'm not going to…"

"It doesn't matter," Korsaume says. "The Captain's right. When we walk out that door, they're going to know exactly who all is aboard this ship, and they're not going to confuse Rosetta for you. They'll know if someone's aboard, and they'll figure out that it's you and take you captive. We can't have that."

Agoparn walks to the back of the room and grabs a full body suit like the ones the rest of them are wearing, and walks it back to Vaskette. "Put this on, good Doctor."

Korsaume and Lacendu help her get into the body suit. It takes several minutes, but finally she is in it.

Mathew glances at Agoparn and Lacendu. "Help her. We're going out."

Agoparn and Lacendu take Vaskette under her arms and walk her to the door.

Korsaume turns around with her super-HOP in her hands, loaded, ready, and smiling. "Let's do this…"

The door opens, the ramp goes down to the floor of the hangar, and the seven of them walk down. As they head for the main exit, the doors to the bay open and guards in full body suits appear with weapons aimed.

Lastly, a man in a Solar Union Officer uniform walks in, hands clasped behind his back, his chin held high. "You are not the six member of the Simpra Core Regent. Who are you?"

"I'm Mathew Arnold, and this is my crew."

"Lying to the Baitronoc command is an offense. You are all under arrest for that offense. Come quietly, or we will be required to use force in your capture and detainment."

Mathew turns to his crew. Then, he turns back to face the guards. "Unacceptable terms, Sir," he says. "I guess you'll have to use force; if you can."

The guards march forward in quick succession to surround the seven of them, and the Officer walks directly up to Mathew. "I take it you're the group leader."

"I'm the Captain over this crew," Mathew nods.

"Then it will be many times worse for you." This to the guards, "Take them, by force if necessary."

The seven crewmembers of the Simpra Core Regent stand in place.

Very suddenly, wind is whipped around all of them and the guns in the hands of the guards are gone. Finally, Shivranikka stands in the center of the crew with all the weapons of the guards in her hands.

Mathew, without turning around to her, asks, "What took you so long?"

Shivranikka has a laugh in her voice. “It took a few extra minutes to get through all the security, Captain. I’m here, now, though, and my men will shortly arrive.”

“Always a pleasure, Nikka,” Mathew says.

The Officer, as are all the Guards, is stunned. “What just happened,” he asks.

“Officer, where is the nearest cell block,” Korsaume asks.

The Officer points to his right.

“Off you go,” she replies, nodding her head in the general direction. “Guards, follow your commanding officer.”

They all do as they’re told.

As they are all walking across the massive hangar bay, the doors open again and Shivranikka’s men step in.

“My men apologize for being late,” says Shivranikka.

“We’ll let it slide this time,” Mathew says.

It is a matter of a few minutes as their prisoners are detained in cell blocks and the sixteen-member group head through the halls to the surface of the ‘Dyson-sphere.’

Through one hallway, then another, they are constantly met by guards and officer who are pushed aside and their weapons removed by Shivranikka’s men.

“Where to, first, Lieutenant,” asks Mathew.

Her voice is strong, “We need to shut down the energy source to the main offices. It’s in a building nearby, and particularly difficult to get into.”

Allen laughs, “I don’t see we’ll be having any trouble with that…”

Lacendu remarks, “Unless they shut down Shivranikka like the Knights did on Earth…”

Shivranikka, her shoulders back and her head high, says, “That won’t be a problem. The organic technology inside me learns from past failures. If they shut me down, it won’t be for very long, as unlikely it might be that they can pull it off again at all…” Then, this to her self, “I love being a goddess…”

Korsaume rolls her eyes.

They arrive on the surface of the city. Above them they can see the star, always shining in through the thick clear film around the ring. In front of them is the large city of Egra; a massive complex of dark metal gleaming in the light standing at least two kilometers over their heads like a giant castle. On their right is another large structure which Korsaume refers to as Egra's energy source.

All around them, standing in their way, is an army of Guards and Officers of the Solar Union.

"STAND DOWN," says a man whose suit decorations show him to be a general.

"Hold up, Shivranikka," Mathew commands, seeing that she and her men are preparing to fight. Then he walks out in front of the group to face the general. "We're standing down."

The man walks forward to stand within a few feet of Mathew. "I ought to have my men kill you."

"Why? We didn't kill anyone on our way here. That should be evidence that our intent is not to kill. Those who live by the sword…" Mathew smiles at him.

"…They die by it… I'm aware of the saying, Sir." The general looks over at some of his men and nods; then he looks back at the group in front of him. "You're all under arrest."

"For what," Mathew asks. "What did we do?"

"You've proven yourselves a threat. Threats are dealt with." He says this leaning into Mathew's face.

"We're no threat. However, we knew that getting in to see the Head Keeper wasn't going to happen since our reputation already precedes us." Korsaume walks up to stand beside Mathew, her super-HOP pointed at the ground.

"You will never see the Head Keeper," the general says. "You'll be tried, convicted, and sentenced to death. That's already been concluded."

"Then you know who we are," Mathew says.

The man smirks, "Of course; everyone here knows who you are… The question is, 'what do they know about you…'"

Mathew glares at him.

"Oh…and about that group you sent ahead of you…the group from the Star Axis…?"

"Yes," Agoparn says, half out of fear.

"They're already in custody and they'll be tried and convicted along with you."

Mathew turns to Shivranikka. "I guess we're going to go to jail. You and your team have your instructions."

She smiles at Mathew, bows her head, raises her arms out to her side and her body begins to glow. The light even radiates through her clothes. Her legs lengthen making her taller. Her arms also lengthen, and soon, she is too bright to look directly at…

Mathew and his crew are already turned away.

Suddenly, Shivranikka's men are levitating off the ground, and then her own body as well.

"What is going on," the general asks.

Mathew grins, and then goes straight-faced. "She's drawing all the power nearby into her self. Her men are helping. Feel free to stop her." He turns to his crew, and as hovering vehicles begin falling out of the air, guns and weapons lose their power, and lights all over the place go out, the seven crewmembers walk toward the entrance to Egra.

The general walks with them. "I can't let you do this," he says.

"You don't have choice," responds Mathew to the demand.

The general takes a chance and tries to punch Mathew. He dodges it easily, realizing rather quickly what the man was preparing to do, but does not take a shot back.

Mathew shakes his head. "Don't try. We've got a lot to do, and little time to do it."

The man shakes his head. "I'm coming with you. It is my duty to protect the Head Keeper."

"Fine," Mathew shrugs. "Let's go."

They walk toward Egra's entrance. It takes several minutes; a long walk. When they arrive, the doors are closed and locked.

"They're in lock-down," Korsaume says. "It's automatic when the power goes out."

Allen makes his way through the group to stand in front of it. Pulling a small device from his belt he pulls a seal off one side and sticks it to the metal door. "Turn your heads," he says to the group.

They all turn as the device begins rapidly heating up. They feel the heat, and move back a few feet. The light from the heated object burns all around them, and the brilliance enters their eyes, even though they are turned away from it.

When the light finally goes out, they turn to find the door completely melted.

"Great," Vaskette says, "how do we get across the melted door…?"

Allen throws a small pellet onto the melted metal and it freezes over within a matter of moments. "Does that answer your question?"

"Where do they make all this stuff," she asks.

Allen glances at her. "Do you really want to know?"

"Not really," she responds, and Lacendu and Agoparn help her walk behind the group.

As they enter the large vaulted room, Guards and Officers are everywhere, guns and weapons aimed.

Allen pulls out another device and looks down at it. "Um, Captain, their guns are working…"

Mathew stops in his tracks and turns. "What do you mean, they're working?"

"Just like I said, Captain…their guns are working. They don't run on any of the variable energies Shivranikka's absorbing."

"What does this mean?" Agoparn asks.

"It means, we surrender," Mathew says, turning back to look at the guards.

*****

Each of them is placed into separate cells. The cells are cool and very dark. There are small blue lights recessed in the ceiling, but it only adds to the feeling of gloom.

A woman knocks on Mathew's cell door. "Mathew Arnold?"

"I'm in here," he says.

The door opens and she walks in. Instantly, lights are on all over the room, and the dark metal of the walls and floor are illumined. The door is closed behind her.

She holds her hand out. He thinks he'd rather not take it, but he shakes her hand anyway.

She smiles as she sits down in a chair against the wall. "Hello. I'm Radia Ihone. I'll be your group's counsel."

"I'm sure none of us care," he responds. "We've already been informed that we're to be tried, convicted, and killed."

She laughs. "You were informed incorrectly. That's a common tactic in the military here. They rarely kill anyone."

"Radia, I'm pretty confident you don't know enough about the situation we're in to fully grasp what they're willing to do."

She looks away for a moment, gathering her thoughts and continues. "I know plenty, actually. I know that your team was sent to the other side of the galaxy to gather information, and that you determined there was an internal problem here and wanted to get to the bad guys before they got away."

His head is resting in his left hand, the elbow of which is positioned on the arm of his chair, "Is that what they told you?"

"It comes from the highest official documents of the Solar Committee."

He laughs at her this time. “You really don’t know anything, then. If we were sent to the other side of the galaxy on a data-gathering quest, we weren’t informed of it, nor, did we determine there was some internal problem. We didn’t come here to stop bad guys before they got away, and even if we had, they’d have gotten away by now.”

She nods in understanding. “Well, obviously you don’t know enough, Mr. Arnold. Your team is being heralded as heroes. The information you provided the Solar Union led to the arrest of some deep-cover operatives of the Agrauves who infiltrated the highest echelon of the Solar Committee. Your names and faces are plastered all over the galaxy.”

He looks at her doubtfully, “Then why are we under arrest?”

“Obviously, it’s because the Committee feels you don’t know that the issue has been resolved. They sent me in to settle this whole thing peacefully and give all of you a place to spend the rest of your lives. I have been authorized to send you and your crewmates to ‘Apollo-Glenn In Freehurst.’”

“I can’t say I’ve ever heard of it.”

“Oh, I’ve been there. You’d all love it. It’s a beautiful planet. I highly recommend it.” She smiles big at him.

He leans back in his chair. “Maybe you can tell me all about it when we’ve completed our mission. We’ve got to talk with the Head Keeper.”

“I don’t think that will be a problem for galactic heroes,” she says. “I might be able to get you in a group session with the Solar Committee. They would all like to thank you for your bravery on a more personal level.”

Mathew leans his head back against the wall, shakes his head, rolls his eyes, and sighs.

“You seem frustrated, Mr. Arnold.”

In his mind, his only recourse is sarcasm. “No…really?”

“Am I correct to assume that you feel I am misunderstanding what your intentions here were?”

He knows she's leading him. "You are correct in our intentions. We came to stop bad people. The problem is, the bad people we were coming to stop are most likely still where they always were…in the Solar Union Committee."

"Whom are you accusing?" she asks, her eyebrows, raised.

Mathew leans in to her. "Who else…? The Head Keeper…"

She looks completely shocked. "You're accusing the Head Keeper of subversion?"

"That's the reason we want to see him…personally…and alone…"

Her face is red, bent slightly downward, and she looks at him through squinted eyes. "Just remember I was here to try to help all of you. You'll be lucky to get a jail cell in the deepest, darkest corner of the dreariest planet on the outer fringes of our galaxy back in Quadrant Four."

"Then, you'll forward my message," Mathew says with a nod.

She frowns, turns on her heels, and opens the door, exiting without fanfare.

"I'll take that as a 'yes.'"

*****

They have no communication with each other until the next day when the entire group is brought into a meeting room in chains and forced into chairs where they are shackled.

Allen says, "So, is everyone enjoying the wonderful room and board here?"

Vaskette seems to be the least interested of all of them. Though she feels she has dealt with the pain in her heart, she still does not feel certain she wants to continue. Due to her emotions at the moment, and even having heard the remark, she doesn't feel like answering.

Finally, Rosetta speaks up. She says looking at Mathew, "I missed being with you…"

He looks across the table at her and smiles.

Without warning, the door to the meeting room opens and the woman Mathew spoke with the day before enters. “Hello, everyone… My name is Radia Ihone. I’m your counsel for the trial.”

Mathew yawns. “So, there’s going to be a trial, anyway, huh?”

“I told you there would be, and there will be, Mr. Arnold.” She walks to an empty seat on the right side of the table and sits down. “The general counsel will be here momentarily…we’ll sit and wait.”

They are all silent until the door opens again and a man walks in. He is barrel-chested, balding, and dressed in a full suit. When he speaks, his voice is scholarly and highbrow. He turns after he enters and pushes the door closed, and then turns around to sit at the head of the table. “Hello. My name is Yckrenelle H’eurecc.” He folds his hands on the table before him. “I am the general counsel for the Solar Committee. I am here today with all of you to discuss the terms of your indictment of the Head Keeper.”

The crew turns to each other, and finally their eyes settle on Mathew.

“Captain,” Korsaume says as a question.

He lets out the breath he suddenly realizes he was holding in and bends his head down to the right. “I’m sorry, everyone. I had to give away my plan to get through to our counsel.”

Lacendu turns to Agoparn. “We had a plan?”

Korsaume is upset. “We did until our good Captain told them.”

Agoparn asks, “What happened to Shivranikka and her men?”

The man completely ignores the question. “I am to understand that you believe the Head Keeper has done something wrong…?”

“In that, you speak correctly,” Mathew says.

“Mr. Arnold,” the man begins, “the Head Keeper is above that sort of thing.”

“No one is above the law,” Lacendu remarks.

“I did not say he is above the law, Lacendu Ruric-Trester. I said he is above doing wrong…”

"That's a lie," she retorts. "Anyone can make a mistake; even the Head Keeper of the Solar Union. Admittedly I always believed him to be a great man, and very intelligent. However, I do know that he is capable of making mistakes."

The man stands up. He is angry, but it comes across more as acting. "The Head Keeper **is** the law! What he says is the rule!"

Mathew snickers at the thought. "Then we have nothing more to discuss. You've already got it in your head that we're wrong. This will be the most one-sided trial in history."

The man is furious now, but still it comes off as palliative. "You can bet your life it will..." He picks his briefcase up and walks out the door.

"That went well," Allen says with a grin.

"Their counselor is upset now, too," says Radia. "I brought him in here to try to work this out. You folks just blew your only chance."

"He had no intention of working anything out," Korsaume says. "You don't want my opinion, but I'm going to give it to you anyway: this whole thing is out of control."

Mathew moves forward, picking up the chair he is chained to, and moves closer to the Counselor. She looks at him nervously.

"Get us out of these," he says to her.

"I can't do that..."

"Then we'll get ourselves out," he responds.

He sweeps the legs of his chair out from under him to fall the other direction. Using the momentum he knocks her chair over, too.

As she is picking herself up off the floor, Allen is already around the table with his chair and lands on her back, knocking her head on the ground.

"Now, Radia; how about that release...?" Mathew asks.

The breath was knocked out of her, but she laughs anyway. "You people are crazy," she says through gritted teeth; obviously in pain. "I'm not giving you anything, now. I won't even be your counselor."

Allen removes a key from the woman's jacket pocket and rolls off of the woman over her head to lie against the door.

Korsaume retorts, "I don't recall ever asking you for counsel."

Allen moves his chair around and gets the legs under the conference table. When Korsaume realizes what he's doing, she joins him and the two use the chairs' leverage to lift the table up on its side longwise. It comes down on its side with a loud crash and the others nearby join them in pushing it against the door after Vaskette moves out of the way.

"I was the only one offering to help you," Radia says. "At least you had that on your side. You could be well on your way to 'Apollo-Glenn In Freehurst.'"

Lacendu's and Vaskette's eyes pop wide open. Lacendu says, "That's the most beautiful and exclusive planet in the galaxy."

Korsaume speaks next. "There's a reason it's so exclusive. It's the place they send people who are too smart for their own good, and who are a danger to anyone else. No one gets there without special appointment from a Solar Union Committee member. Most Committee members take their vacations there."

"Have you been there?" asks Radia.

"Yes, I have," Korsaume answers, "Twice. It's **the** place to be…"

Radia continues, "Then you know that it's a great place for people like yourselves… You'd all fit in perfectly, there."

"It's sweeping the dirt under the rug, though, Mrs. Ihone," Korsaume shoots back. "Instead of dealing with the problems at hand, the Solar Union has voted instead to stick their heads in the sand and ignore what we're trying to accomplish."

At this, Radia stands up, though in pain. "That's just it," she says, "you came in here guns a-blazing and you think that will help you get in to see the Head Keeper. That's the first sign of danger for the Solar Union… You seven are the first group to ever do that in Baitronoc's history. You should be proud of that and the fact that the Committee has chosen to give you a home where you can't be touched instead of pressing charges and having all of you lined up in front of a firing squad."

Moments pass, and everyone is quiet, looking around at each other. Radia's face is dour. Suddenly, the lights in the room go out, and there is a knock on the door.

"Korsaume…" comes a voice from outside.

"Shivranikka," Korsaume calls out. "Sorry…there's a large desk in front of the door. Give us a moment."

"No, no, Dear. Just stand back from it." The door is ripped from its place and the table is pushed down onto all fours. "I've been looking for all of you for several hours."

"Did they shut you down," Korsaume asks.

"They did, and worse, I'm afraid. They destroyed my men."

Mathew says, "That was to be expected, Nikka. By the way…Nikka, Radia; Radia, Nikka."

Radia is in shock and just stares at the blonde-haired woman with the wide smile. "How'd you do that…?"

Shivranikka laughs, but doesn't answer. "So, Master, what can I do for you?"

"You can start by getting all of us out of these stupid chains…" Korsaume replies.

Shivranikka wastes no time obeying the command and helps everyone to their feet as she does. "I hate to tell you this, Captain, but I killed numerous people on my way here."

Mathew looks annoyed. "Thanks for the warning. Now we've got that to deal with beside the fact of escaping custody."

"Maybe we can crawl through air ducts, or something," Lacendu says; "Avoid the hallways and such…"

"Not quite, Lacy," Korsaume replies. "This place was built with those kinds of things in mind. We'll have to go out the front door…"

"…And how do you expect us to do that," Vaskette asks, being the last person to have her chains removed.

Korsaume gives Vaskette a simple look. "I didn't say it would be easy, Doctor."

"Since when have we dealt with anything easy," asks Allen. "We've been doing things the hard way since day one, but that always seems to be the way we have to do them. I say, we just walk right out of here and straight up to the Head Keeper's office."

Shivranikka interjects, "I don't think I can stop all of the guns and the like on my own. I'm going to need some help, and I don't have the equipment to create new minions."

"Couldn't you use a different word," Lacendu remarks under her breath.

Shivranikka hears it, but ignores it as well. "Let's take Radia."

Radia is still in shock on her knees on the floor. "Take me where...?"

The techno-witch grabs the woman by the shoulders and pulls her to her feet. "You're my new minion. We need your help getting to the Head Keeper. You're going to help us, aren't you?"

Radia just stares.

"I'll take that as a 'yes.'" She turns to the crewmates. "Off we go, Dear Ones."

They all walk out of the room and up the hall. As they walk, Shivranikka is pulling energy from the surroundings, replenishing her reserves. Thus, every step brings lights to nothing and venotronic boards off-line. After she passes, the lights go back on and the boards come back to life.

"They're going to know something's amiss with all the power going down everywhere we go," remarks Vaskette.

"I agree, Shivranikka. Can you keep from doing that?" Korsaume asks.

"I can, Master, but then my energy would go bye-bye very quick. I might be the most powerful being to ever walk, but I need energy, just like everything and everyone else."

"Quite an ego you got going there," Radia says. "It's no wonder all of you are doomed. Pride comes before destruction..."

"Where is the Head Keeper's office in that structure," Mathew asks as they step out of the building they've been in for the past day and a half.

Radia's voice is whiny, "Like I'm telling you…"

Korsaume answers instead. "It's at the top, naturally. Shivranikka, we need a way up there…"

Shivranikka looks off to the right to see a hover-vehicle. "How about one of those?"

They all get on one of the vehicles and Shivranikka puts her hand on the dashboard. Wires come out of her hand and enter the venotronic terminals through the gaps on the board. The vehicle starts up and she coerces the vehicle to do something it wasn't made to do. It begins to fly up into the air over the city, straight for the top of the city of Egra.

"I didn't know you could do that," Radia says.

"You would be the person who would know what I can do," Shivranikka remarks with sarcasm.

The hover-vehicle lands on the top of the city. There are numerous windows covered in the same type of film they walked on at Ascension City.

Shivranikka walks up to one rather large window and places her left hand on it. Then, she pulls her right hand back and thrusts it forward like a punch, hitting her cupped hand. The pressure is too much for the window and it cracks under her hand. Next, the blonde woman pushes her right hand against the crack until it gives way and she can get both hands just inside. Lastly, she pulls on it, ripping the film window from its holding place and throws it over the side of the massive structure.

"Hm," she says with her usual grin, "I hope there was no one down there…"

They drop down through the window and begin walking through the halls. As they walk, men and women come out of their rooms to watch the group make their way to the Head Keeper's office.

"Which way," Mathew asks of Radia when they get to a crossway.

She points to the right.

Mathew pulls her to the left. "Like I'm going to believe anything you say…"

Korsaume stops at one particular door and says to the rest, "You all go on. I've got someone I need to talk to right now…"

Mathew turns to her with his eyebrows raised.

"It's alright, Captain. I'm not going to do anything stupid."

"Please don't," he responds.

The rest of the group walks on toward their destination while Korsaume tries the door. It is unlocked. The name on the door reads 'Raylo Bristane.' Korsaume recognizes it as Chrinsole Forgenbaugh's wife.

She enters to find the desk of the late wife of her enemy empty. The shelves, which were most likely once filled from floor to ceiling with slim-sheet computer books and reference material, are cleaned out. The chair behind the desk is neatly placed, and the lights are dimmed to the right degree. The light from the star shines in through the small windows around the top of the room giving the room a warm yellow, inviting feel.

She walks around the room looking at all the walls. Against the far wall she finds a small crevice. It is unnoticeable to the untrained eye, but hers are attuned to just this sort of thing. She pushes at it, claws at it, and finally pulls a small empty file folder from a drawer and rips off the top of it down to the paper-thin middle which she slides delicately into the crevice. Using this as leverage, she bends the paper around and lightly tugs at it.

With the patience of a master thief, she soon finds the small door in the wall coming open. When she gets it open about a quarter inch, she pulls the folder out and uses her fingernails to pry it open.

Inside is a small case made for a gun.

She picks up the case and opens it. Inside the case is a standard-issue weapon given to all Solar Union Committee members for their personal protection. It's designed to kill, no matter what part of the body it hits, and it's fully loaded…

*****

The group arrives at the door of the massive office of the Head Keeper. Shivranikka walks right up, tries the door, and when it doesn't open she rips it right of its hinges. Holding it in her hands, she walks in followed closely by the rest of the crew.

The office is at least six meters wide and five meters deep, and the ceiling is high. Near the back of the office near a long wall-window is a huge desk. There is a high-backed chair behind the desk, turned, facing out of the window.

A man's voice is heard from the chair. "Welcome."

Mathew steps forward. "Are you the Head Keeper?"

The chair is turned and there is a man in the chair. "Yes, I am, Mathew Arnold."

There are sounds behind them and they all turn to the door. Men and women guards in full body suits are aiming weapons at them.

The Head Keeper stands up. "It's alright," he says to the people outside the door. "I'm not in any danger."

"Sir, we've been ordered to come here and protect you," says one of the women.

"…And I'm ordering you to leave," he responds.

"Yes, Sir," she says, and turns around to walk away, followed closely by the other guards under her command.

The group turns back to the Head Keeper.

Mathew is obviously upset. "What is going on?"

"What do you mean, Sir?" the Head Keeper asks.

"There were no guards while we were in the conference room. There were no guards on our way out. There were no guards when we got out of the prison. There were no guards on our way here, and not a single person on our way through the halls tried to stop us. Now, I want to know what you're really up to," Mathew says.

The Head Keeper laughs. "If I thought you were here to kill me, believe me, I would have had guards posted at all those places."

"We were told by the Admiral of the Sharcuran Knights of the question you asked the 'brain,'" Mathew says.

The Head Keeper looks surprised. "Really…? I'm glad he informed you. I take it the answer wasn't satisfactory."

"You're right. I think there's something more," Mathew adds.

"Well, hear it for yourself, Mr. Arnold." He turns to the computer on the wall to his left. "Computer, play the entire sequence of my last discussion with the 'brain.'"

There is a clicking sound of the computer working on the file, and then it beeps twice and a three-dimensional image appears on the floor near it. The audio and video is crisp and clear.

It is a meeting room; extremely large, and containing what seems to be the whole of the Solar Union Committee seated in chairs around an empty floor. It is quiet for a few moments except for a few people clearing their throats, shuffling papers, and moving in their seats.

Finally, a soft voice, indistinguishable as male or female, begins…

"Hello, Head Keeper Phillip Dae'Lurgen. I am the 'brain.' You have requested a hearing with me, and I have connected to a venotronic computer near you to hear your question."

The Head Keeper's voice is heard next, and they can make the man out on the floor in the center of one side.

"Good Evening, 'Brain,'" he says. "I have a question. The question is as follows: The Solar Union is under threat. What do we need to do in order to protect the Solar Union and continue our existence?"

The 'brain' is silent for a long moment.

"The answer is simple," it responds, "the threat comes from the group of people known as the 'Agrauves.' You must destroy them before they destroy you. This is the way for the Solar Union to survive. Will there be anything else?"

"No…Thank you, 'Brain,'" the image of the Head Keeper says.

"Thank you, Head Keeper Phillip Dae'Lurgen."

After another moment or so, the image goes out.

"That's what happened," the Head Keeper says. "Any other questions…?"

Mathew says, perhaps a little louder than he intends, "You asked the wrong question! You asked how to keep the Solar Union going…"

"I don't get your meaning," the Head Keeper says. "The 'brain' was the one that started the Solar Union…determined how it would work, and how the system would work. Why would it think any differently now than before…?"

"The same reason people do," Vaskette says taking one step forward, her fists balled up, arms down at her sides. "There's an old saying that goes, 'You can't keep doing what worked one time.' Everything changes. Did you ever think about asking the 'brain' if the Solar Union should even still be in existence?"

The Head Keeper's eyes narrow and he contemplates this question.

Just then, Korsaume walks into the room, out in front of the group, and points the gun in her hand at the Head Keeper.

"I've heard most of your conversation," she says. "I want to know one more thing… Who all was involved in the discussions of the question asked?"

The Head Keeper looks more than a little afraid now, but says, "Well, me, of course…Keeper Filge Trimpston, Scientist Lori Precaudi, Senator Raylo Bristane, and Senator Chrinsole Forgenbaugh… Why?"

Korsaume turns to Mathew. "I think I just figured this whole thing out, Captain," she says as her arm goes down. "The Head Keeper isn't the problem, sir."

"What do you mean," Mathew asks.

"Chrinsole… He's the one…"

The Head Keeper's attention is raised and he looks at them in surprise. "He quit the Solar Union Committee four months ago," he says.

"Yes," Vaskette says, "He's now in Quadrant Three heading up 'Nation.'"

"I started 'Nation,'" he says. "'Nation' is a project I worked out with Raylo and Chrinsole... We designed it to help make things better in Quadrants Three and Four where we have little or no jurisdiction, especially toward the center of the Milky Way..."

"That's got to be it, Captain," Lacendu remarks. "Chrinsole, after his wife died, must have taken over the project and is probably trying to use it to destroy the Solar Union. How many things did he say to make us think the Solar Union was the problem...?"

"I don't remember exactly, but I see your point," Mathew responds. "It looks like we're fighting the wrong battle."

The Head Keeper looks relieved. "If you are all in agreement, then I would like to give all of you amnesty if you can stop the people of 'Nation' who are trying to bring down the Solar Union..."

"There's only one problem," Mathew says, "There's a group just like us out there in the Saiar Ria Contract that will definitely be standing in our way. We need you to inform them of our intents."

The Head Keeper looks worried. "I would, but I can't," he says. "Those people were hired by Chrinsole; they're following his orders..."

Episode 18
The Shadow in the Mirror of Lights

OPENING:

"...Like cattle we are lead from our floating homes in space. The building of the ring is done, and they have no more need of our skilled services. What now, I wonder? Will I find a new career on the planet-home the union has given us? Building the ring is all I've ever known. My dad, his dad, and his dad before him, all worked on this project. Why do I have to be the last?" The words of Shive'r Threnagen, the last Agrauve to be settled on the Agrauve home world after the building of Baitronoc

"Ardelle," Agoparn yells running across the large open metal floor between the city of Egra and the launching bays.

Captain Ardelle Zysteck stands with her crew, which have all been in custody for nearly two weeks on Baitronoc.

After securing amnesty with the Head Keeper of the Solar Union Committee if they can stop Chrinsole Forgenbaugh; the now leader of a band of enemy agents called 'Nation,' out to destroy what so many have fought so long for; Mathew, Korsaume, Allen, Vaskette, Lacendu, Agoparn, Rosetta, and Shivranikka got a release for Captain Ardelle and her crew.

While she and her crew got the Star Axis C-72 back with a few repairs, upgrades and modifications, Mathew and his group requested a new ship…one which the crew they placed on the Saiar Ria Contract won't recognize, as they would the Simpra Core Regent: the very small ship the group took from their counterparts.

Now, these two groups leaving Baitronoc have two missions: first; stop the counterparts, and two; stop 'Nation.'

The Head Keeper and the Officer of the Guards walk with them to the hangar bays, with Agoparn out ahead greeting his girlfriend who is walking behind her crew to the Star Axis C-72.

"You folks have quite a story," the Head Keeper states, "Perhaps when this is all over you can tell it to the rest of the Galaxy…"

"Do you think that would be wise," Lacendu asks of him. "Perhaps that might shed a less-than-positive light on the Solar Union and its inner workings. You don't want the average person thinking you're all weak…"

The Head Keeper smiles in spite of himself. "You're right… Let's all keep this whole thing to ourselves."

"Out of curiosity," Mathew adds, "are we really heroes with our faces plastered all over the news around the galaxy?"

"No," the Head Keeper admits, "That was something we use as a 'ploy.'"

"So she lied," Mathew continues.

"Not as far as she knows," the Head Keeper says. "She was told exactly what we wanted her to say to you, so she knew nothing else."

"Then you lied," Vaskette remarks.

The Head Keeper laughs. "I guess we did…"

"That seems to be going around a lot," Lacendu adds. "Chrinsole lied to us, Sherise lied to us, and the Solar Union lied to us. I wonder if anyone else is interested in joining in on the lies."

The Head Keeper stops, and as the group realizes it they stop, also.

He says, "I guess I should apologize on behalf of everyone involved in all this mess. …And you were right, Mr. Arnold … I asked the wrong question. The 'brain' shouldn't be asked how to continue doing what it's been doing. That's only in the best interest of the Solar Union. I will have a team look into determining the right question which would be to the benefit of the people of the galaxy. That's what's most important here, anyway, isn't it?"

"I believe you're on the right track," Mathew concludes before he turns around, and with the rest of his crew heads for the launch bays.

*****

Ardelle turns to see her boyfriend running toward her. They hug tightly, and then kiss. "I missed you, Parn," she comments.

"…And I, you," he responds with a sweet smile.

"So, what's on the agenda, now?" she asks.

"We're heading out to stop 'Nation…'" he answers.

"Hm. We're going to need more of those 'feathers,' then, aren't we, hon?"

"What are 'feathers,'" he asks.

She gently laughs at him, "Do you remember that energy-disruption device I used on the 'Nation' vehicles on Ascension City?"

"Oh, yeah… We probably will need more of those," he remarks, not really thinking about it. "Hey, I just wanted to let you know that when this whole thing is over, I want to marry you…"

She smiles at him. "I might like that… Ask me when it's all over and I'll let you know what I want."

Agoparn laughs at this, "Maybe I could have worded that better."

"Don't worry about it. I know you pretty well, now, so I didn't exactly expect you to get down on a knee with a ring in your hand…"

They hug, kiss, and he turns and walks into the entrance to the bays with his crewmates. They walk down the stairs and make their way to the launch bay where their new ship awaits.

As they enter the bay, they look at the ship; a fairly large vessel promising a fast and easy ride.

"They said it's a new type; a Nebulae Class Galactic Runner… It's called the 'Beyond.'" Allen smiles at the thought. "They said it's the fastest ship ever…"

"Hopefully it doesn't have one of those drives we used on the way here…" Vaskette says. "I don't think our bodies could make it through another jump from one of those…"

"Well, crew, I want to be in space in thirty minutes. Let's get on board and learn what we need to before we leave." Mathew walks forward.

"Wow," Lacendu responds facetiously, "A ship Mathew actually doesn't already know how to fly…?"

Mathew laughs. Rosetta catches up to him and grabs his hand and they walk together toward the ship, followed closely by Korsaume and Allen, Agoparn, Lacendu, Vaskette, and Shivranikka.

"This should be fun," Allen says.

*****

"What do you think," Allen asks Korsaume.

She returns a gaze and asks, "What do you mean?"

"What are we going to do when this whole thing is over?"

Korsaume laughs out loud. "You're assuming we'll survive…"

"I have no reason to doubt our survival," he says.

"No, but you do have reason to doubt we'll accomplish what we're setting out to do. Even with Shivranikka, it's still a matter of finding the people responsible and stopping them. Finding them is half the problem. That alone could take years…"

"Somehow, I doubt it," Allen responds. "I have a lot of faith in our abilities."

Korsaume moves closer to him and wraps her arms around his waist, and then lays her head on his left shoulder. "Your faith in the rest of us is what I like most about you. You've always been the one to stand up for all of us."

He returns her hug and strokes her hair. "I love you."

She giggles.

He backs up with a half-smile on his face and an appalled look. "I tell you 'I love you' and you laugh…?"

She is laughing now and moving toward him. "I've just never heard anyone tell me that. It's the first time I've ever had someone who cared about me…"

"So you laugh at me…?" He is laughing, now, too.

She grabs him as fast as she can and holds him tight, bringing her face right up to his. "You need to know something, Allen … I love you, too. I've never felt that way about anyone in my life."

He smiles at her. "I don't know whether to be happy or feel sorry for you…"

She pulls her arms away and fake-slaps his shoulder, taking a step back. "Well, I don't want you feeling sorry for me," she says in a matter-of-fact tone.

He laughs again for a moment. "Then I won't feel sorry for you. I'll just be happy."

She grabs him once more and holds him close, kissing his neck. "You do that."

Allen pushes the door to his room almost closed as the two begin kissing.

*****

Lacendu sits down at the controls of a Venotronic computer on board the ship in the communications room. She puts in the portal address she remembers now by heart and waits.

"Communications line open. Kalchek Trester will accept your call." The computer's voice is male, and sounds soothing.

The screen brightens and her husband is there on the other side.

"Hi," she says.

He smiles big at her. "I am so glad to see you, finally."

"I hear you've been looking for me."

He has a look of relief on his face as he says, "I have… I've been looking for you since we lost contact with each other. I received a message from a Rosetta Firemark about a week ago saying you were alive and well."

"Where are you, now?" she asks him.

"I'm on the slowest possible ship ever made, I had to rent it with the promise of return payment, from a guy on a planet called 'Phoenix Rain,'" he says. "I was there for two months; trapped there by a man named Chrinsole…"

Her eyes widen fast. "Chrinsole…?!"

"Yes. Do you know him?" he asks.

Her shoulders droop. "Yeah, we know him…We…"

He interrupts her. "We…? Who else is there? Where are you?"

"The group I'm with is the group I was with several months ago when I was ordered to go to Baitronoc…"

"What was that about…?"

"I'm not at liberty to discuss it, right now," she answers, "but I can tell you I'm glad to be back on this side of the galaxy. Maybe I can talk the Captain into meeting up with you and bringing you aboard…"

"I suppose it depends on where you're heading," he says.

"If I told you, you wouldn't let me go," she says with a reluctant grin.

"Why…" he asks, a little out of fear of what he'll hear.

"We're going to hunt down Chrinsole," she states.

"Oh, then, by all means, go hunt him down," he says with some excitement.

"I'm pregnant…" she adds.

His eyes widen. "You're… You're pregnant?"

"I have been for almost four months, when you made that excursion to Baitronoc for the council session. I'm not showing, yet, but Vaskette says I will be soon." She smiles broadly at him.

He smiles and nods. "Who's Vaskette?"

"Vaskette Smith, the doctor onboard the ship," she answers.

"Oh, yeah… I read about her; the galaxy's number one doctor…"

"That's the one."

"You're pregnant…?"

"Yes," she answers again.

He smiles. "Oh, Honey, I'm so happy. I'm going to be a dad."

"You are," she says, "and Vaskette has affirmed it is yours, since you're the only one…"

His face goes straight. "You know, I found out while you were gone that the guy I was told you were having sex with was lying. He was just trying to get attention."

She breathes out a quick, unnoticed, sigh of relief.

"I'm sorry I was so willing to believe him when he told me that. I should have known better. I married you for the very reason that you have always been an honest and modest woman."

She smiles to herself. "Well, I can't say much for that; or at least, I won't. I appreciate you letting me know."

His grin is still noticeable, but he looks at her delicately. "I readily wait to see you again in person."

She feels warm inside, and tilts her head to the left a little. "I can't wait to see you, again, either…"

He shakes his head, "You're pregnant…"

Her heart pounds in her chest, and she feels it, kicking at her like the child inside will be doing soon. She is excited, but scared. She can't help but wonder if she'll make it back at all.

*****

Agoparn Schroet walks around in the engine room learning as quickly as possible what he needs to know about the readouts and controls. He is familiar with almost everything in the room…the problem he has is the layout. While it is said to be easier to use, he's not so sure.

Mathew enters with Rosetta on his arm. "How are we doing, Engineer?"

He doesn't bother to look up from his slim sheet computer as he reads, glances at a console, presses some buttons, and looks back at the computer. "I'm getting there, Captain. I can't say I'll be ready right when you wanted to leave, but I'm trying as hard and fast as I can."

"I'm not overly concerned about the exactness of getting out of here in thirty minutes, but I do want to leave as soon as physically possible," Mathew says to his friend.

"You know, Captain," Agoparn says, turning to the Captain, "When we were on Ablose, we made a vow to each other… Do you remember it?"

Mathew thinks hard. "Not really…" he replies, shaking his head.

"I told you I wouldn't tell your wife if you wouldn't tell mine." He smirks at the thought.

"Oh, yeah…I do remember that… It turned out that neither of us was married…"

At this, Rosetta bumps Mathew and gives him an inquisitive look.

Agoparn turns to his Captain and puts the slim-sheet to his side, holding one hand on the back of a chair. "I used to be married…a long while back. She divorced me about seven years ago."

"You won't have to worry," Mathew says. "I won't tell her about you and Ardelle."

"Oh, I have no reason to doubt that…nor am I overly concerned. The thing is, Captain; I can't remember her. There's only a record of her existence in my life. To be perfectly honest, I'm not so sure I want my old life back." Agoparn looks contemplative.

Mathew remarks, "I know what you mean, Parn. After what I did read of my old life, I'm pretty sure I don't want to be the way I was…proud and arrogant, chauvinistic, and untrustworthy outside of combat. I hope Vaskette won't take offense if we ask her not to work on our memories."

"I wasn't thinking of asking, Sir," Agoparn states with something less than enthusiasm.

"Neither I, Parn," Mathew says. "Will there be anything else before I head to the pilot room?"

"Not at present, Captain. I do have one request, though…"

Mathew, having prepared to turn around, turns back completely to face the engineer. "Name it."

"No one in our crew deserves death. I don't want to be a hero, but if death is adamant about us, let's go out in a blaze of glory…"

Mathew and Rosetta both give Agoparn a blank stare. Shortly, though, Mathew's face contorts with the right side of his mouth in a smile and he silently laughs, his chest heaving as he does. "You might want to get the rest of the crew's reaction, Engineer. I intend to live as long as possible."

Agoparn returns his own smirk and shakes his head at the man he has come to trust implicitly; something that took a long time, but Agoparn feels is well deserved.

Mathew and Rosetta turn together and exit the engine room.

*****

Vaskette now has a place to be alone once more. She sits in the quiet and even requests of the computer not to let anyone interrupt her for the next ten minutes.

The door is closed, the room is silent, and dimmed red lights surround her as they shine from the center of every wall in big round globes which barely bubble out of the walls.

She buries her face in her hands and feels it…the feeling of crying again. She refuses to let it last, but the refusal is limited to her thoughts and her body rejects the decision almost instantaneously as tears well up in her eyes and become too heavy to stay there. Instead, two trickle down her face; one from each eye; around the edges of her nose, and stop at her lips where they hang delicately like two fragile flowers wilting.

She opens her mouth to speak, but nothing is emitted. She tries again.

"Dear, God…" There is a long pause as she swallows hard and tries to figure out what to say next. "I remember my Christianity. I wasn't the best, by any stretch. I've been so wicked for the past few months, doing things I didn't feel right about inside.

"I have my memories back, and to be honest, I don't even want them. They only serve to hurt me worse than not having them. The only respite I had was in my belief of You.

"So, I come here to this quiet place without the hassle of all the things going on in my life … the things we're about to do for what we believe to be for the betterment of humans the galaxy over…and ask You to help me. I don't know what to do next, or how I can make it through this, knowing there is no one waiting for me.

"I beg of You; give me something to pull me through this. I can't bare the thought of coming back home, having saved the galaxy, to my old empty life…"

By this time, the tears are flowing freely and pooling in her cupped hands and dripping down her arms into the folds of her elbows.

She stands up and wipes at her eyes, forcing herself to stop crying. She wipes her arms and breathes in.

The room seems a little brighter to her now, and she says, “Computer, dim lights further…”

It does.

Her breath is shallow and hot.

There is a knock on her door.

“Who is it,” Vaskette asks.

“It’s me,” Shivranikka’s voice comes over the speaker.

“Computer; lights,” she says just loud enough for the computer to hear, and then louder for the door signal, “Come on in.”

The door opens and Shivranikka, with her hands clasped behind her back and that old, familiar smile on her face as always, walks nonchalant into the room. “What were you praying for…?”

“You could hear me praying and you have to ask what I was praying for…?”

Shivranikka thinks, “Maybe I worded that wrong. Why were you praying…? Do you believe there’s really a God?”

“Don’t you?”

“I was never sure,” Shivranikka remarks, “My parents had always told me that ‘God’ was an old myth, like the Iliad.”

Vaskette sits down again on the chair and relaxes. “I’ve been a doctor for eight years. I’ve seen patients with belief in God recover more quickly than those who believed in medicine. Even a young woman I worked on a couple years ago who had full faith in me, I couldn’t save her, but a man who believed in God who I worked on at the same time and I gave three days to live made a full recovery and last time I talked with him he was still alive and he had no recurrence of the disease. You tell me if there’s a God.”

Shivranikka grins and says, “You’re the one who’s seen all that stuff. I haven’t, so I couldn’t possibly believe based on what you’ve seen. I believe each person must make the determination of the existence of God on his or her own. I've been around for a long time; four hundred plus years; and I've seen so many things that I could only attribute to a mastermind Creator, but to be sure, there was never anything I couldn't explain. I guess when the time comes, I'll know for sure."

"I've already made that decision," Vaskette says, "but I've been told everyone who has faith reaches a crisis point where they must either renew that belief, or refuse it and follow another path. I've chosen to renew my faith."

"You're a better person that I," Shivranikka says. "Would you like to be left alone?"

"No… That's alright. I'm done, now, so I guess I'd better go check out the infirmary facilities."

"If you don't mind a friend, I'll accompany you," the other says.

Vaskette stands up. "Let's go, then."

*****

"Agoparn…status on the engines," Mathew says.

He is seated in the pilot's chair with Rosetta at her communications post behind him not far away.

The command deck isn't quite as big as the one on the Saiar Ria Contract, but it is significantly larger than both the Simpra Core Regent's and the 'Vibrant's.'

Agoparn answers, "I've already primed the engines. This thing has never flown under its own power, Captain. It was recommended we allow the priming to last about two hours…"

"I'm guessing you know my answer to that, Parn," Mathew replies.

"Of course, Sir…"

Mathew turns his head to Rosetta just as Lacendu walks in and takes her seat across from the other woman. "Inform the Star Axis and the Launch Bay that we'll be leaving immediately and the doors need to be opened."

"Right away, Captain…" Rosetta replies. She begins talking into the headset she places on her head.

"Lacendu, can this thing be programmed, as well," Mathew asks.

Lacendu nods her head, but soon realizes the Captain won't hear that. "Yes, sir; but not to the extent the Contract could…"

"I want you to begin checking on programming this thing to outmaneuver the Contract's commands you made for it. Let me know if you need assistance with the movements…" Mathew says to her.

"I'm on it, Captain," Lacendu responds.

"Rosetta," Mathew says with a question in his voice.

"I just finished, Captain. The launch bay doors will be opening soon."

"…And the Star Axis…?" he asks.

"They're waiting for us on the outside, Captain," she answers.

Mathew maneuvers the ship in a full one-eighty degree turn to face the vessel at the launch bay doors and is in time to see them begin opening. It takes some time, but once they're open, the 'Beyond' moves forward and out of the hangar.

Mathew says out loud, but to no one in particular, "This is it…"

*****

The crew of the 'Beyond' is once again having a group meeting.

Mathew opens it up, "I don't think this is going to be easy. Most of you were there when we met the other crew like us. I've asked Rosetta to give us information on them."

He turns his head to her as she turns a slim-sheet computer on and begins reading from it.

"Maneesha Huchan, ex-CHE pilot. She was considered to be the best until Mathew took her place about four years ago. She is well-trained in ship maneuvers, and even studied under Craider Maans, a professor of flight theory on Segnar.

"Garmy Fingsbeau, two-time winner of the Ranston Doctor's Board Award, and followed Vaskette's career closely, making several lists, but never top place which Vaskette continually received.

"Flynn Porman, a heady strategist; he's an older gentleman and is considered to be the top hunter in existence, but his strategy techniques are a little wanting…thinks out of the box, with little ability to stay focused, making him more perceived than actually dangerous.

"Tex Dimbor is the weapons expert of the team. He's actually a bounty hunter for the Solar Union, having been on the top of that list for more than ten years consistent. His past was deleted from all major systems, so the little information I was able to get on him says almost nothing about who he actually is…

"Shayley Zimmancee is the mathematics expert, and she is most likely at least as capable as Lacendu. Shayley turned down a full ride to Segnar's Physics and Calculus College, which Lacy taught at, so she could do mathematics for a leading physics design company, and helped put their financials over the top.

"Finally, Reed Nemhollan is their engineer, and he's served on over one hundred vessels. He's in his sixties, but he's the highest paid engineer in existence. His work rivals Agoparn's, but Parn has had more experience working directly with the various engine types and his work is more focused on problem solving than Reed's is…

"…And that's the scoop on who we'll be hunting down, first."

Rosetta smiles, places her right leg over her left and relaxes with a glance to Mathew to let him know she's done.

"Just out of curiosity," Allen says with a quick raise of his hand, "what is our goal in this? Are we supposed to take them into custody, kill them, or what…?"

Mathew looks at Vaskette (who sits with her arms folded and is not looking at anyone) before answering, "I'm thinking we should avoid death at all costs…only if it's you or them."

Shivranikka makes the comment, "I could convert them to minions. I ran out of my last set for some reason…"

"We heard," Agoparn remarks, "and I'm very sorry to hear they were killed by the Guards."

"Aren't you sweet," Shivranikka says with an even bigger grin than normal. "I'm not worried about it. They were already dead…"

Lacendu rolls her eyes.

Korsaume pipes up. "We've got a strategist. Let's utilize him. Allen, why don't you come up with some plans and we'll discuss them in a few hours."

Mathew says, "Excellent idea, Lieutenant; Korsaume and I will go over it with you when you've completed it. Lacendu, how are you coming on the programming?"

Lacendu replies, "I've had the opportunity to start a number of them, Captain, but the programming for this ship is a little more complicated. It doesn't use the Morstone programming language; it's got the same cybernetic encodings we came up against a month ago when we were still on the Star Expeditioner and I hacked Shivranikka's other two ships with Agoparn. Hacking the ship is easy. It's the programming of new procedures not already in place that make it so difficult."

"It's alright, Lacy," Mathew says, "I'm not sure if we'll get the opportunity to use them, but if you can get at least some of them, I'd like to know as you do so I know which ones we have at our disposal."

"Yes, Sir," she responds with a quick smile.

"Is there anything else," Mathew asks.

Nobody answers, so he adjourns the meeting and everyone heads to their places.

As they walk away, Shivranikka grabs Vaskette and pulls her aside. After everyone is out of earshot she says to the doctor, "You're no good to me all depressed."

Vaskette looks appalled. "What are you talking about?"

"It's time," the other answers with a modest look on her face, her eyes wide and seeming suddenly innocent.

"Time for what…?" the doctor asks, confused.

"I want you to try to perform that surgery we talked about before…"

Vaskette looks upset, but nods. "Alright…follow me."

Shivranikka does, and they walk right into the infirmary, and Vaskette locks the door.

*****

Seven hours pass.

"Captain, I just received a response to my request on the last known coordinates of the Saiar Ria Contract. She was followed for a short time by a cargo carrier, but the carrier lost track of it as it needed to finish its run…" Rosetta is reading from a message on her screen.

"Thank you, Seta," Mathew replies.

He has been sitting quietly for about six and a half hours, flying the ship, and as the coordinates come across his screen, he makes a course correction and checks to see if the Star Axis following behind makes the same correction…it does.

He is oblivious to his physical surroundings until he feels something on the back of his chair and the warmth of his girlfriend's face against the right side of his head.

Rosetta places her hands on his shoulders and massages them.

At this, he realizes he has been very tense and breathes in deep, allowing his body to relax in her hands.

She says in his ear, "You're taking this harder than you should. You've been stressing out for a couple of days."

"I'm concerned," he says to her just loud enough for her to hear. "I think we're all stressed. I'm not sure any of the crew is relaxed. We need a break."

"Captain," the two hear behind them. It is Allen's voice.

"What's up, Allen," Rosetta asks turning to him.

"Well, I just figured you might want to know what I thought of..." He pauses, and then continues, "If the people who won are who we think they are, they're going to figure out we're looking for them and either hide, or attack..."

"How did you figure that out, Allen," Mathew asks.

Korsaume walks in behind him. "Are you ready to tell us your conclusions so soon...?"

"I thought you should know..."

"Know what," Mathew asks standing up and turning around.

"A message from our ship was intercepted by the Saiar Ria Contract about three minutes ago..." Allen replies. "...the last one we sent to the Star Axis..."

"That would mean they..." Korsaume begins, but she is cut off as the vessel is rattled, being hit from outside.

Rosetta moves to her station and sits down just as another jolt hits the ship. She catches herself on the console and straps herself in while Mathew sits down and does the same.

"Lacendu," Mathew half-yells out to the young blonde-haired woman.

"I'm sorry, Captain; I haven't finished any, yet..." she replies, knowing his question.

"Then, we'll just have to wing it," Mathew says to himself.

He presses a button on his console and a three-dimensional image appears over the console. He says loudly to Allen as another shot is felt throughout the ship, "Get to your post, Strategist. I need your help."

"He won't be able to," Korsaume's voice says behind them. "He's been knocked unconscious."

Rosetta turns to see Allen's head on the floor, blood under it.

"Get him to the infirmary and get up here to help me out," Mathew says, almost mad.

"Yes, Sir," Korsaume replies with understanding.

As another shot hits the ship sending it off track, and Korsaume drags Allen out of the pilot room, a message blinking on Mathew's console comes to life with Vaskette's voice. "A warning might have been nice, Captain."

"Sorry, Doctor…I don't have time to talk. We're under attack."

"Well, just for your information, I've got a patient in my room, and I need less rattling and shaking to perform the procedure…" Vaskette says.

"You're about to have another patient," Mathew replies. "Korsaume's dragging Allen your way with a knock on the head… It looked pretty serious."

"Alright, Captain," she replies, and closes the connection.

Mathew turns his head quickly to Rosetta, "Who else could she be working on, down there?"

"Agoparn or Shivranikka," Rosetta replies. "They're the only two left unaccounted for…"

Another shot pummels the 'Beyond,' and Mathew devotes his entire attention to using the three-dimensional image to try and determine the source of the shots.

"I've got it," Lacendu remarks. "I'm feeding you the info on where the Contract is firing from…"

"You're sure it's the Contract," Mathew says.

"Ninety-nine point nine percent, Captain. The maneuvering shots are consistent with the Contract's capabilities," Lacendu replies.

"Then why can't I find it," he asks.

"I have no idea, Sir." She says it harshly, but it doesn't seem intended that way.

Rosetta speaks up, "Captain, the Star Axis is calling us."

"Ignore their calls," Mathew says. "I don't want them involved in this until we can get into a better position."

"Understood, Captain…"

"Too late," Lacendu adds, "The Star Axis just got hit twice on their port side. The spots are damaged pretty badly, and they've lost power to their main engines."

"Fairly systematic, don't you think," Mathew says.

*****

Korsaume knocks on the infirmary door when it doesn't open at her approach. Vaskette opens it and assists the other woman in getting Allen strapped to a bed.

Korsaume looks over at Shivranikka on another table, and then gives Vaskette an inquisitive look.

"Don't look at me," Vaskette replies. "She asked me to do this."

"What are you doing?"

"I can't answer that," says Vaskette, "…Doctor/Patient confidential…"

Korsaume gives the red-head a questionable look and says, "Just make sure Allen gets fixed up. The Captain needs him ASAP." She turns on her heals and walks out fast.

*****

Korsaume returns to the pilot room and sits down in Allen's place, straps herself in, and says amid continued volleys from the enemy ship, "I'm back,

Captain. Vaskette's got something going with Shivranikka in the infirmary. I'm not sure what's going on, but she's got Allen down there and I told her you needed him."

"Thank you, Korsaume. We don't have the time to worry about Vaskette right now. Let's do our job," Mathew states with bland abruptness.

"I understand, Captain," Korsaume responds.

"The Star Axis is out of commission," Lacendu says out loud, mostly to Korsaume as an update.

Mathew turns his head slightly to the left so that Korsaume will hear him better, "What are your thoughts, acting-Strategist?"

"I'm still reading the info on the screen, but based on the last few remarks, it would seem our best bet would be to get behind the ship…"

"Bad idea," Lacendu says, "remember I helped build the thing. All they'd have to do is turn on the main shaft-thrusters and we'd be toast…"

"This ship is small enough that we could get next to the connection of the extra thrusters on the side and top…"

"Great idea," Lacendu says, "There's little protection on the steel rods holding them down. If we can hit one of the bars, we might be able to destabilize or even erupt the thruster containers and slow down the ship…"

"Korsaume, you're in charge of weapons as well. If I get you a straight line, can you hit it?" Mathew is maneuvering the ship in the direction of the Saiar Ria Contract.

His Lieutenant smiles and says, "Just remember who you're talking to, Captain."

"On my mark, then," Mathew says.

A short moment passes and Mathew shouts, "NOW!"

Korsaume presses the button on a console with a screen giving her a heat image of the area. A shot is fired and out the front of the window against the black of space they see the blaze from the projectile hit something in the distance and an explosion follows.

"Direct hit," Korsaume says with excitement.

Mathew is quick to respond, "Don't get ahead of yourself, Lieutenant. They have just as many tricks up their sleeves as we do…"

Korsaume feels annoyed at this but doesn't say anything, the left side of her mouth pulled back in response. "Sure, Captain…"

Vaskette is on the communications line directly to Mathew again, and her voice comes through clearly amid the next shot fired at their ship. "Captain, Allen is headed your way. I don't recommend he try any extended exercises right away, but he should be able to help you out up there."

"Great, Doctor… We look forward to him being up here with us," Mathew says to her.

More shots are exchanged before Allen arrives and takes his place allowing Korsaume to go to the other side of the room in front of Rosetta to operate the main weapons system.

"Good to have you back, Allen" Korsaume says as she sits down.

"Are you alright," Mathew asks.

"I'll be fine…just a little woozy, Captain," he replies.

Lacendu says in a tone louder than normal for her, "I'm sending all of you additional information on our latest situation. Allen might be able to use it."

Allen looks at his console as he straps himself to the chair. "I'm reading it now… It looks like you folks did a fine job without me."

"Not as good as we'd like, Strategist," Mathew answers. "Your expertise would be appreciated."

Another shot against their starboard side knocks everyone in the room around a bit. "We've got to stop getting kicked around or I'm gon'na puke," Lacendu says.

*****

"How do you feel, Nikka," Vaskette asks.

"Are you done already?"

"Not hardly," the doctor replies. "I've got a little ways to go; it's a lot more complicated than I figured, and I counted on it being extremely complicated even for me…"

Shivranikka's smile doesn't fade. "I have full confidence in your capabilities, Doctor. If anyone can make me human again, it will be you."

"That's the problem," Vaskette says, "It's going to take years for you to become human, again, but growing cells to replace the organic mechanics in your body won't take very long at all with the equipment I have on board. Humanity is a state of being, not a state of body."

The blonde-haired woman laughs. "That's why I like you, Vaskette. You have your wits about you and you're honest. I don't think I could ever be like you."

"You don't need to be like me," is the response, "you just need to be yourself."

"I've never followed advice from a physician," Shivranikka says, "but then, no physician has ever given me sound advice…until now."

"There's a first time for everything," Vaskette responds. "I need you to shut yourself down, now…completely…so I can finish my work. If you're still running, I can't remove all the implants and rebuild your internal genetic structure. You have to do it willingly."

Shivranikka looks nervous for once. "Very well," she says, and she does.

*****

"Can we take out the running streams," asks Rosetta.

"With the right hit," Korsaume answers. "It's going to take some maneuvering on Mathew's part, though. The angle we have to shoot into is along the top of the ship, which would require us making a strafe run past their most guarded area."

The 'Beyond' is struck again on the bottom of the ship as it is making a roll to the right and is knocked off course.

"We're not going to make any strafing runs if we can't get over that stupid ship," Korsaume says with too much force.

"Relax," Allen states, "I've got an idea."

"Out with it," Korsaume says. She seems upset with him, now.

"I said, relax... Captain, make a circle near the last shots fired..."

"Heading there, now, Allen," Mathew says pulling the ship around and moving into position in a circular pattern.

"Stay here for a while completing circles..." Allen says.

"I'm not sure what you're up to, Strategist, but I really hope I'm going to like this," Mathew says.

"They're preparing to fire again," Lacendu remarks out of desperation.

"Of course," Allen declares. "That's the idea. Captain, reverse the thrusters, NOW!"

Mathew does so, and the ship slows in the frictionless space and begins moving backward.

The shots move right across the bow of the ship, but don't hit it.

"Captain, use your three-D image to move backward over the top of the Contract," Allen shouts.

"Done," says Mathew.

The 'Beyond' maneuvers right to the top of the Saiar Ria Contract and Korsaume uses the opportunity to blast away at the running streams around the front shaft of the vessel, leaving it virtually defenseless.

"Nice work," Lacendu says. "I think I just got some new ideas for programming..."

"Captain," Rosetta says, "The Saiar Ria Contract is trying to contact us."

"Now, they want to talk," says Allen.

Rosetta continues, "The Star Axis is also trying to contact us, Captain."

"Put them both on," Mathew commands.

Rosetta presses the controls on her board to put both crews on their communications line.

Mathew pushes a couple buttons on his console to show the visual images of both command decks as three-dimensional images before him.

"Captain Arnold," Maneesha says, "that was a very impressive move…"

"I can't take all the credit," Mathew replies. "I've got some good help."

"Naturally, I'm calling to discuss our predicaments."

"Just for the record," Captain Ardelle says, "You're the only one in a predicament, lady. We may not be able to move, but we've got more than enough fire power to take you out."

"I'm aware of the Star Axis' capabilities," Maneesha abruptly says.

"It's alright, Captain Ardelle," Mathew says in a calming voice. "Now, Maneesha, we want to make a proposition."

"You want the Saiar Ria Contract back…I'm alright with that," Maneesha remarks. "We don't much care for it ourselves."

"No, that's fine," Mathew says, "we don't want it, either. However, we do want to come aboard."

Maneesha gets a smirk on her face. "Of course, Captain Arnold; we'd be more than honored to have your crew's presence on board this ship. We'll open up the clam shell for you; dock at your leisure."

The three-D visual screen for the Saiar Ria Contract shuts off, and Rosetta says, "The Contract just cut communications."

"I don't like that," Ardelle says. "You can't possibly trust her."

"I don't trust her," Mathew admits, "but we've got a job to do. I want to get it done."

"You're going to need help, Mathew. I don't recommend your crew going in there alone. Have us help you. My crew is anxious to kick some butt on that stupid ship…" Ardelle seems happy about this as she says it.

"You're more than welcome to join us," Mathew says. "We'd welcome your assistance."

"It's going to take some time for us to get our engine back up and running, Captain Arnold. We'll dock with the 'Beyond' once we get moving again."

"We'll see you folks shortly," Mathew replies.

Rosetta informs them the Star Axis has also cut communications, and Mathew presses a button to speak with Agoparn in the engine room. "Parn, prepare the docking clam for attachment to the Contract," he says.

"Right away, Captain," they hear over the forward speaker.

Mathew turns his chair to the crew in the pilot room. "I want us all to meet up in five minutes. Prepare yourselves with weapons, shields, and anything else you feel might help us against those six. I have a feeling they're going to put up a fight."

"Never in doubt," says Korsaume with a quirky smile.

Allen, Korsaume, and Lacendu all stand up randomly and walk out of the room.

Rosetta is up from her chair moments after and walks up to him, kneeling down next to his chair and putting her arms on the arm of the pilot chair, and her chin on her arms. "What are you thinking, Sweetheart?"

"I'm thinking this has 'long day' written all over it," he replies.

"Officially, it's close to night, and we're all getting pretty tired," she says. "I could tell everyone in the room was a little tense, even for a battle."

"You're right," Mathew says, "but what do you want me to do about it? If we sleep, the crew on that ship will definitely be blowing away at us, or leave. We've got to take the opportunity while we've got it."

"I agree. I'm just saying maybe we need to go by the infirmary and talk with Vaskette about some kind of shot to help us through what we're about to face."

"That's an excellent idea. I'm sure she has something that can help us. I just hope she's not doing something stupid with Shivranikka on the table," he says with some amount of fear.

Rosetta stands up and reaches her head over to kiss him on the cheek. "You're sweet, but you worry too much." She stands up and walks out the pilot room door.

Mathew sighs, shakes his head, and turns the chair back around to fly the ship directly to the Saiar Ria Contract.

*****

Korsaume knocks on the infirmary door.

Through the intercom she hears Vaskette's voice. "Is this an emergency?"

"We're all getting ready to board the Saiar Ria Contract," Korsaume states.

"I don't consider that an emergency," comes the reply.

Korsaume responds, "The Captain asked all of us to go to the infirmary for a shot."

"I know. The Captain just informed me of his request. There are needles filled with the injection he requested for each of you in a canister to your right. I hope none of you are squeamish about giving yourselves injections…"

Korsaume looks to the right and sees a small alcove with five needles filled with a reddish fluid.

"Come on, Doctor…there's got to be a better way to discuss this…"

"I'm not coming out until I'm done, Lieutenant. I am in surgery," Vaskette rejoins.

Korsaume gets upset at this and practically stomps off in the direction of the bridge. After only a dozen steps she sees Mathew and Rosetta rounding the corner heading her direction.

"Captain, you've got to speak with our insane doctor! She won't open up the door. She says she's in surgery..." Korsaume says, flustered.

"On Shivranikka," Mathew questions... "What does Nikka need surgery for...?"

"I have no idea, but whatever it is, I'm most definitely not liking it," the Lieutenant replies in a huff.

The three of them soon arrive at the door to the infirmary.

"Vaskette," Mathew begins through the intercom, "Please open the door. We just want to talk."

Vaskette's curt reply is, "Please don't make that an order, Captain. I'd hate to have to disobey a direct order..."

Mathew feels perturbed, but he doesn't let it get to him. "Vaskette, you and I both remember how this whole thing started with us on the 'Vibrant.' There is no hierarchy on this ship. I'm only 'captain' because I can fly the ships.

"If you'll also remember, though, we each agreed that if any of us was out of line we'd let that person know. Korsaume and I are both in agreement on this. You're out of line. I think..." He rethinks his statement. "...I believe you understand what I'm saying."

It is evident that Vaskette is turned away from the closest microphone to her position because the sound is slightly muffled. "Of course, I understand, Captain. I wouldn't be much of a doctor if I didn't... However, I'm right in the middle of a very complicated surgery and I don't have time for your incessant pedantry. I'll be done in a little while."

Rosetta asks the obvious question, "What did Shivranikka need surgery on."

Korsaume adds, "I was under the impression Nikka didn't need any help..."

"For the record," Vaskette says in a concluding voice, "I'm trying to save the last vestige of humanity left in Shivranikka."

Korsaume suddenly realizes the truth and collapses against the door, banging on it. "LET ME IN!" she shouts. "LET ME IN RIGHT NOW! YOU ARE NOT GOING TO TAKE HER ABILITIES AWAY FROM HER WHEN WE ARE THIS CLOSE TO THE END!"

Vaskette ignores the outrage while Rosetta and Mathew both pull her away from the door and shut off the intercom.

"YOU CAN'T LET HER DO THIS!" Korsaume yells at Mathew.

"There's no need to scream," Mathew says with some stress in his voice, turning away at the decibel level. "I can hear you just fine right here…and yes, I can let her do this. She's already said she's almost done…"

"Captain, she's taking away my…" Korsaume starts.

"You're what…? Slave…?" Rosetta asks. "She was never 'yours' to begin with. She's a human being, even if we don't like her style or attitude."

Korsaume's chest finally stops heaving, though she continues to breathe a little hard. She composes herself quickly, presses her hands to the jacket against her chest, and apologizes. "Sorry for that little outburst, Captain. I don't know what came over me. …And you're right, Seta. Shivranikka is not '**mine**…'"

She doesn't look at either of them, but instead walks off toward the clam shell door, her chest heaving in rapid breaths.

Mathew looks at Rosetta, who shrugs slightly and makes a questioning face.

"This is getting out of hand," Mathew says.

"You're telling me," Rosetta responds.

Mathew walks up to the door, grabs the small plate with needles, and hands it to Rosetta taking a needle for himself as he does. He places the needle's tip to his left arm where a vein extrudes and pushes it in pressing the button on the end down to inject the substance into his body.

As he pulls it out, he shortly realizes just how tired he was as his whole body seems to "wake up." He feels refreshed and energized, but he knows in his mind that it is a trick of the drug to help him feel like he just had several hours of sleep and rest.

Rosetta grabs a needle as he does this and hands the tray back to him.

After she injects herself, they take the tray down the stairs to the deck where the others stand.

"Where's Shivranikka," Allen asks. "We're going to need her assistance."

"We're not going to be getting that kind of help this time," Mathew remarks. He glances at Korsaume who, though she looks quite normal, is pouting.

Korsaume speaks up, "Well, let's get this trip underway... Are we attached to the Saiar Ria Contract?"

Agoparn turns away from the console he's been working at and says, "We just attached to it. I'm trying to open both doors at the same time."

"Shouldn't we be standing ready to fight," Lacendu asks.

"Good point," Mathew says. "Everyone get ready to fire once the doors begin opening."

The remaining crew members all stand at the ready, weapons in hand and aimed at the door.

Agoparn turns back to the controls and continues to try to open the doors.

"Is there a problem, Engineer?" asks Korsaume.

"Yes, Lieutenant...I can't get the doors open." He says this as if it should be obvious to her.

"Why not," Allen asks with simplicity.

Agoparn now tries very hard not to sound annoyed, but he says through gritted teeth, "I don't know..."

"This is going to be a short trip if they..." Mathew begins, but is quickly interrupted by Allen.

"Oh, frag... They're not going to do what I think they're going to do...are they?"

"What do you think they're going to do, Allen," Korsaume asks.

Suddenly, everyone of them are thrown to the ground.

"What was that?" Lacendu asks.

"They're moving the Saiar Ria Contract with us attached," Allen says loudly moving toward a wall to pull his body off the floor. "It's a classic trick. The crew allows their enemies to attach to the larger ship to surrender, and then as they try to open the clam shell doors, they move the ship. It can rip our ship apart..."

"Nice trick," Mathew says. "I'm heading to the pilot room."

"No, wait," Agoparn says. "They have their tricks, and I have mine."

"They're probably expecting that," Korsaume says. "You're getting ready to pipe the clam shell remote cell controls through the Contract's Venotronic filter and force it to open to space."

"How did you know," he asks.

"I've done that more than once, myself, but when you meet up with people like these, you can't do that. They'll be expecting it if the people Rosetta told us about are as smart as they sound."

"Then what **do** we do," Rosetta asks as Mathew helps her to her feet.

Korsaume points her super-HOP at the door. "Agoparn, are we still connected to the Contract?"

Agoparn steps away from the door. "Yes, ma'am," he replies.

Korsaume pulls the trigger on the super-HOP and a projectile explodes on the door blowing a hole through it leaving a five-foot circle where weapons begin firing through.

Allen screams as he is struck on the left forearm while everyone in the room is moving out of the way as the gunfire from the other side infiltrates the 'Beyond.'

The doors now try to open, but the holes produced in them keep them from opening all the way. Then they stop, and the smoke from the explosion continues to fill both sides.

Maneesha and her crew enter through the hole and stand over the crew with weapons in hand.

Mathew looks up at them from his place on the floor on the far left side. He coughs once and says, "Welcome to the 'Beyond.' Please drop your weapons and surrender."

Flynn Porman steps forward to stand next to Maneesha and laughs. "Aren't you the jokester?"

Maneesha turns to her strategist. "Don't give him what he wants, Flynn. He wanted you to laugh. It's a start on their mind games. Prepare to kill them all. Aim weapons…"

Episode 19
The Last Starlit Room

OPENING:

"If you're always going to feel like you're the one at fault, then you're always going to coerce yourself into believing that you're the center of the universe. No human can survive at the center of the universe..."

"How do you feel, Shivranikka," Vaskette asks, looking down into the eyes of her patient on the surgery table.

Shivranikka's face is flush and she looks different. The extensive smile is gone though it was there through most of the surgery despite the fact she had practically shut her internal organic systems down and Vaskette had her under intense anesthesia. She opens her eyes and looks up at her surgeon.

"I feel really weird."

"You will for quite a while," Vaskette says. "I had to rebuild most of your organs, especially your brain, and then restart all your bodily functions and download your memory from your techno-brain cells to your real brain. It's taken me several hours, and I'm surprised it was this quick. I expected it to take significantly longer. You're going to want to rest."

"We can't do that, Doctor," she says. "Our friends downstairs are in trouble."

"What do you mean," Vaskette asks.

Shivranikka says innocently, "They're getting ready to be killed."

"How do you know that?"

"I could hear everything going on during the surgery. Agoparn's trying to open the doors…" Shivranikka smiles at her, "You're going to want to hang on to something right now, Dear One…"

Vaskette grabs the stationary surgery bed as the ship jolts awkwardly toward the back. She barely manages to stay standing.

"We need to get downstairs with some weapons and help them…" Shivranikka says.

"What just happened," the doctor asks.

Shivranikka smiles at her friend. "Get me out of this stupid bed and help me up. We need to help them." As Vaskette un-straps the woman on the bed, Shivranikka continues, "By the way, you talk too much. It's no wonder you aren't getting along with your friends."

"What's that supposed to mean?"

"Exactly as it sounds… You didn't have friends before, either, did you?" Shivranikka doesn't care that she's making Vaskette feel worse.

"You weren't very good at diplomacy before Xychocappla, were you," Vaskette retorts, pulling the straps off the woman roughly, effectively hurting the blonde-haired woman on the surgery bed.

"Touché. Let's move."

Vaskette helps Shivranikka walk toward the door and opens it.

"We need weapons," Shivranikka says.

"From what you've said, we don't have time. Let's just go down there and make a grand entrance…"

"No doing," Shivranikka remarks. "Get a bottle of something that will explode on impact. Let's take that down there."

Vaskette runs off and grabs two bottles of substances while Shivranikka leans against the door, barely on her own strength. Vaskette runs back and helps the other down the stairs. They move as quietly as they can manage as an explosion occurs and they hear weapons fire.

"That doesn't sound good," Shivranikka remarks under her breath.

"You stay here," Vaskette says pushing the other against the wall and holding her up long enough for the blonde-haired woman to stand up straight under her own power.

Vaskette walks down and peaks around the corner as the other crew from the Saiar Ria Contract comes through a gaping hole in the clam shell door. She hears Mathew say, "Welcome to the 'Beyond.' Please drop your weapons and surrender."

She ducks back behind the corner and pauses, thinking to herself about how she's going to make sure the two substances land together and not harm her friends on the floor.

"Aren't you the jokester," she hears one of the men of the other group laugh.

"Don't give him what he wants, Flynn. He wanted you to laugh. It's a start on their mind games. Prepare to kill them all. Aim weapons…" She recognizes it as the voice of Maneesha Huchan, the leader of the other group.

She acts quickly and without thinking takes a glove from her pocket, pushes the two vials inside and turns around the corner tossing the glove into the middle behind the other group.

"What…?" one of the women asks as they look up and see Vaskette, and then notice a glove in the air as it lands behind them.

"Welcome to our world," Vaskette yells as the vials break on the floor near the clam shell doors and explode with a furious impact knocking those standing with their weapons in hand forward onto the floor.

A few of the weapons discharge, hitting the floor and walls, and an uncertain number of objects.

Vaskette runs into the middle of the room and helps Korsaume and Allen to their feet. "Sorry I'm late," she says.

"No, no; that's quite alright, Doctor," Korsaume says.

There is still a cloud of smoke in the air and they glance up toward the stairs as they hear the unmistakable sound of someone falling down them.

Vaskette leaps over Mathew and runs to help the woman to her feet. "Are you alright," she asks.

"I'll be fine, good Doctor," the other replies. "Great job, by the way…"

"Yeah…thank you for your help."

Meanwhile, Korsaume helps Mathew and Rosetta up while Allen grabs Lacendu's and Agoparn's hands separately to pull them to their feet with his right hand, still feeling the wound in his left forearm.

Lacendu's hands, which held a gun a few moments earlier, are empty as she presses her shirt to her chest. She seems disoriented. "That was fun. We'll have to do it again some time…"

Mathew looks at Allen's arm and says, "Go get fixed up, Allen. We'll deal with these folks."

Allen walks toward the stairs and Vaskette looks over his injury.

"Be glad we're not going to treat you the same way you were us," Korsaume says.

The group on the floor looks up at their new captors.

"I hate to tell you this," Maneesha says, "but you left one thing out in all of this."

"What would that be?" asks Mathew.

"You remember that other group you locked up?" She doesn't wait for an answer; she knows they do. "They work for us…"

Agoparn turns around to see the four people of 'Nation' coming through the hole in the door, bigger guns in hand pointing them at the crew of the 'Beyond.'

"Hello, Captain Mathew Arnold," says one. "You probably recognize me from the Steg Orbital Station. We helped you, but now we're taking you into custody. You're under arrest for interfering in the affairs of 'Nation' and its subsidiaries."

"I don't think we recognize your authority," Lacendu says. "In fact, I know we don't."

"It doesn't matter," he says. "Drop your weapons and you'll be given a cell instead of being taken to Chrinsole in body bags…"

Mathew glances around at his crew with him and nods. Everyone puts their guns on the floor.

Meanwhile, Vaskette, meanwhile, has already moved Allen and Shivranikka up the stairs to the infirmary, leading Flynn to ask, "What happened to the three over there?"

Mathew answers them.

The man nods to Garmy and Tex who move up the stairs quickly and quietly while Maneesha and her other crewmates get to their feet.

Maneesha practically yells at the man, "Breeshawn, I want them dead!"

"Chrinsole doesn't and his commands get obeyed before yours…" he answers.

"So…" Mathew says, "Breeshawn…that's your name. What was that other guys name…?"

"You're referring to Drekker," Breeshawn says. "He wasn't able to come."

"He was a nice guy," Mathew says.

The man harrumphs. "He certainly **was**…"

Maneesha and her friends prod the crew of the 'Beyond' through the hole in the clam shell door and walk them to the back of the ship, locking them in the same room as the crew had locked them in only a few days before.

*****

"Now, what," Allen asks. "I'm sure they'll be here any second." I'm sure you heard Maneesha's remark to the Captain while we were walking up the stairs…"

"Shut up and let me fix your arm," Vaskette says with annoyance. "…And yes, I heard her. That's why I locked the door when we came in. We'll be fine for a few minutes.

"Hey, I'm just thinking of our well-being…"

"…And I'm thinking of yours, Strategist; now hush…"

Shivranikka remarks, "You're both right. That doesn't make anything either of you are saying less important. Let's concentrate … what can I do to help?"

Vaskette finishes with the small device designed to assist in healing projectile wounds. "You're lucky," she says, "Usually those things go through people's bones. This one just skimmed the bone and cut through mostly meat."

"Maybe we can cook steaks when you're done," he says as a joke.

She doesn't seem to care.

"The door is locked, but it won't stay that way for long. Shivranikka, how do you suppose we get onto the Saiar Ria Contract without going through that hole in the clam shell door?"

Allen answers, "They can't disconnect this ship from theirs right now without opening both ships to space, so they'll have to cut off something. Since they're certainly going to try to get us on there and put us with the rest of our crewmates, we're going to have to take them out, first…and no, I'm not Shivranikka. Sorry."

"That's quite alright," Shivranikka says. "I wouldn't have even gotten that far."

Vaskette glances up at Shivranikka, then back down at what she's doing.

There is a knock at the door.

"Open up, or we will blast this door down."

"Maybe we should do what they say," Allen declares. He looks across the room at one of the medical machines. "Is that a rhinocrono-stimulator," he asks.

She glances over where he is staring and replies, "Yes."

Allen looks up at her and smiles.

"That would be very painful for them," Vaskette replies.

"It would, but the good thing is it won't kill them. We can take them out pretty quick after that and put them someplace safe, tied up of course, and go save our friends."

Vaskette looks a little upset, but says, "I think you're onto something. Let's do it."

She places the device she's been using to fix his arm on the surgical table and pulls the gloves off her hands and throws them away. "Don't put too much pressure on that arm," she says to him. "Give it some time to heal."

"I'll work on that," he replies. "You coming," he glances at Shivranikka.

"You two go ahead. I'm not able to stand on my own, yet…"

Allen and Vaskette move the device over to the door and Allen stands behind it as Vaskette stands against the wall and presses the button that opens the door.

"Come on in," Allen says as he presses the button to turn on the rhinocrono-stimulator.

As the door opens, the men are exposed to the energy beam from the machine and their skin is burned, mostly their faces. There are two of them, and they are injured severely, screaming and dropping their weapons falling backward against the wall on the other side of the hallway with their hands to their faces.

Allen turns it off and grabs the weapons while Vaskette helps Shivranikka to her feet and walks her to the door. "What now," Vaskette asks.

"We do what we've been doing since day one: we figure out what's going on and stop the bad guys," Allen replies.

Shivranikka remarks, "You might want to keep in mind that they believe us to be the bad guys. Should we stop ourselves?"

"If that's what it takes," Allen admits, knowing any other answer will open a conversation with the woman, which he is not prepared for at the moment. "Let's get out of here."

As they exit the infirmary, Vaskette presses the button to close the door and lock it, making sure it will only open for her and her captain.

They make their way to the back of the ship on the same level, Allen half-dragging the two men on the floor behind them.

"The exit is downstairs," Vaskette whispers.

"I know. That's why we're going this way. We're going to get a few suits on and see if we can find another opening," Allen answers.

"Is there another way into the Saiar Ria Contract," asks Vaskette.

"Of course, Dear One," Shivranikka replies. "It's at the back end of the ship on the underside of the escape vessel I used."

"Do you have a way into it," Allen asks.

"If you have suits for us, I can get us in without any problems. The escape section is a self-contained programming function, and it's actually used as an exit. I'll need an Ocmar device to crack it from outside, though…" she answers.

"We don't have those on board," Allen states, "but I think we can fake one with a couple different devices. If nothing else, we can blow the door open."

"Unlikely, Sir," Shivranikka says, "but I'd love to watch you try…"

"Have you ever done a space-walk?" Allen asks of both of them.

Vaskette replies negatively as Shivranikka says, "I love space-walks…"

Vaskette and Allen help the blonde into a space suit and Allen pulls the doctor aside.

"What did you do to her," he asks.

"She requested I pull the organic technology out of her," Vaskette replies.

"…Despite the fact that it was the biggest help we had…?"

"I'm not a strategist, Allen…. I don't think the way you do. When she offered me the opportunity to put my skills to the test, how could I have in a million years passed it up?"

"I see your point, Doctor. Is she up for this?"

"My expert opinion…? No. It's up to her, though. If she chooses to do it, I can't stop her, and she stands even less of a chance of survival sitting on this ship alone." Vaskette looks across the small room at the other woman.

Allen says, "Good point. We all go…"

*****

"What goes around comes around," Korsaume says. "Isn't it always true?"

"When did you become a philosopher?" asks Lacendu.

"I'm just saying, we did this to them, and they're doing it to us…"

Mathew walks through the center of the room. "Whatever they did to get out of here, they didn't leave us the same options. All the walls have been reinforced, the door is double-locked, and there's no material in here."

"…Not to mention the fact they removed all our weapons, including the ones I was hiding in my pants," Korsaume remarks.

"That's more than we needed to know," says Rosetta.

"Don't you have experience in this kind of stuff," asks Mathew of Rosetta.

"What…being locked in rooms with nothing but the clothes on my back…? No, I sure don't," his girlfriend replies. "I'm open to suggestions."

"Help me up," Lacendu says to Korsaume.

The Lieutenant picks the other up at the legs and holds her up toward the ceiling for Lacendu to pull the light filter out of its place. She drops the filter to the floor and reaches up inside.

As she does this, she says, "When I was fourteen, my cousin locked himself in his room. I didn't have authority to override the computer lock and I was the only other person in the house. I pulled the strephecyne sheet from a light fixture in the wall, purged the rotation lock on the light switch and took a magnetic pin from the lock mechanism to unlock the door. This is the same kind of door."

"Interesting idea," Mathew says. "How do you plan on getting past the guard just outside the door?"

"Hey, I do my part," Lacendu says, "and you guys do yours…"

She removes a strephecyne sheet and uses it to rotate the light switch just at the top of the indentation where the light connects. There is a sound of air filling the container and the light flickers a little, but stays on until Lacendu reaches her other hand up and pulls a magnetic pin out. The light goes out leaving the room slightly dimmer with the other blue lights around the top edges of the room.

As Korsaume lets Lacendu down to the floor, the mathematics expert holds up the magnetic strip. She says with a big grin, "Do you have a plan formulated, yet? I can get us out of this room any second."

Mathew looks over at Agoparn who is standing in the corner at the front of the room. "…Got any ideas roaming in your head, Parn?"

Agoparn smiles and shakes his head.

"Is there a problem?" asks Rosetta.

"Yes, there is," he replies. "I knew one of the people from 'Nation.' I can't quite place her, but I know I recognize her."

"From recently, or from before," Lacendu asks.

He knows what she means, "I think it was from before…"

"You mean, from before your memory loss," Mathew says with implication.

"Yeah, I sure do…" He considers the thought and continues. "If I can place her, I might be able to use that to our advantage."

"…As long as it was a good relationship," Lacendu remarks.

"Oh, I'm quite certain Parn can use it even if it was a bad relationship," Mathew says with a laugh.

"Has anyone forgotten that we want to get out of here?" asks Korsaume.

Mathew walks up to the door. "Lacendu, do your thing…"

She walks up next to him and drops to her knees holding the magnetic pin up to the middle of the door where the lock is on the inside. She inserts the pin into a small slit behind the bar on the side and maneuvers it a few different ways, then puts her left ear up to the door and holds up her left hand to everyone else to stay quiet. Then, she puts her left hand back on the door to hold herself up as she moves the pin into a few different places until she hears a click.

She holds up her right hand to Mathew with a thumb up to indicate it's unlocked.

Mathew pushes the door open quickly and Korsaume, Agoparn, and Rosetta follow him out, prepared to put up a fight.

"What is this," Rosetta asks.

There's no one outside the door.

"I don't like this," Agoparn states. "We would have had someone standing outside the door."

"I wouldn't," says Korsaume. "I would have set up some kind of perimeter at the four major points on the ship: the Bridge, the Engine Room, the Weapons Room, and the Infirmary."

"Then let's go to the cargo bay," says Mathew. "Would they expect that?"

"I would have expected it, but I wouldn't care. What are you going to do from there," Korsaume asks.

Mathew shrugs. "I haven't thought that far ahead," he says. "We should leave someone at the entrance to the escape section."

"Agreed," Korsaume says. "I might even suggest **two** people."

"Fine," Mathew says. "Lacendu and Agoparn, you two go to one of the rooms next to the escape shuttle entrance. The rest of us are going to the cargo bay."

"Yes, Captain," Lacendu and Agoparn say together and walk off.

Mathew looks at Korsaume and says, "Lead the way."

*****

"What are we going to do with these other two," Shivranikka asks.

"We're taking them with us…naturally," Allen says.

"How do you expect to do that," Vaskette retorts.

"We suit them up and drag them behind us…" says Allen with a bit of humor in his voice.

"Where do we get out of here," Vaskette adds.

"There's an upper level space walk exit in the top of the ship. Remember, Vaskette; I'm a strategist. I believe it was you who told me the things the Strategist looks at are only what are around him at the time. I took the opportunity when we came on board to look over the specs of the ship…"

Vaskette smirks and nods. "I did say that…"

They suit up the two men, and then themselves, and hold the men's guns to their backs while Allen helps Shivranikka along and they make their way up to the next level and enter the air lock where the air is removed and the outer door opens to allow them access to space.

Vaskette stands still and allows her body to slowly be lifted by the vacuum. She says nervously, "I'm having second thoughts…"

"You said you've never done this before," Allen comments.

"No. Doctor's aren't required to do this kind of stuff. I do know what space can do to people, though."

"Good," Shivranikka says. "Maybe you'll move, then, since the longer you stand still, the less likely you'll be to get hold of something."

Vaskette makes a slow move toward the wall and follows the two men who are still injured, and Allen who continues to hold a gun to their backs.

"How are you two men doing," Allen asks them.

One of them says, "My face burns. What was that thing?"

The other male answers his friend.

"You must be the doctor," Vaskette remarks to the second; "Garmy, I think they said your name is…"

"That's right; Garmy Fingsbeau" the man replies.

"Who's the other one," Shivranikka asks.

"Tex Dimbor," says the other.

Allen smiles at them, though they can't see it. "You two might want to hug, right now," he says.

The two men turn around to look at their captors.

"I wasn't kidding," Allen adds. "Hold each other."

The gun in his hand shows he means business and they grab each other slowly; slowly because of the vacuum of space, and partly because they really don't want to.

Allen places a magnetic strip around near their hands on either side and straps their legs together. "There," he says, "that should hold the two of you in a way which will make it easy for us for now."

He grabs one of their arms and pulls as he maneuvers around to fire the gun in small bursts to move them forward. Shivranikka holds on to Vaskette who uses her weapon in the same manner, and they slowly make their way to the underside of the Saiar Ria Contract.

As they get to the underside of the ship, Shivranikka immediately begins looking for the right section, and finds it rather quickly with the assistance of a light on the arm of her suit.

"Right there," she says, shining the light directly on a small crevice in the ship.

They reach it shortly and Allen makes an attempt to open it by hand.

"I already told you that won't work," Shivranikka says. "Aren't you ever going to listen to me?"

"Hey…Sorry. I had to try," he replies.

"Let me at it," she says moving closer to the ship with the items in her right arm. She let's them float around her and picks them up one at a time, setting them up until they're in the right place. She connects two pieces together and plugs a keypad into the top portion. Pressing the devices to the hatch and swinging around to rest against the ship she begins typing on the keypad.

After a few minutes, Allen asks, "Have you got something, yet?"

"Not yet. I'm working as hard as I can, but I'm not familiar enough with hacking computers to do this quickly," Shivranikka replies.

"…Implying you've hacked a few computers in your time…" Vaskette says with dismay.

Shivranikka holds up a finger to the plate of her helmet to shush them. For the first time since Vaskette performed the surgery, she realizes the blonde-haired beauty, despite her great age, seems so young.

Finally, Shivranikka remarks, "There… Got it; open it up, Strategist."

Allen moves to the hull door and turns the large metal handle in the indentation. It clicks and opens.

"Pressurization will set off the alarms in the main ship," Shivranikka adds. "We're going to want to go in with no additional air."

"That's fine," Allen states, "we won't need a whole lot."

"What about the depressurization as we open it," asks Vaskette?

"Oh, I shut that off," says Shivranikka, "at least, I think I did…"

They move and work together to pull the two men and themselves into the small enclosure and Allen pulls the door shut. Once inside, they allow a few minutes to pass before they open the hatch into the lower floor of the escape vessel, after which they pull themselves out of the enclosure and shut that hatch as well. The ship's sensors immediately kick in additional air from the compressors.

Once the ship's computer stabilizes the condition of the air in their section, they remove their helmets and breathe the stale air.

The lights are off, and as Allen turns them on, they begin to look around the lower floor room where lay ten men and women, dead and decomposing.

"Oh…I forgot about them," Shivranikka says.

They all plug their noses as the realization hits them that these men and women have been dead for months.

"You didn't bother to convert them?" asks Vaskette.

Shivranikka strains to breathe and replies, "They were on my list. I'm sure I would have remembered if I had my old brain…"

"Let's get out of here," Allen says, and they all move through the room to the main door and exit. They make their way up two flights of stairs to the main entrance to the ship.

*****

They move silently through the corridors of the lower level of the Saiar Ria Contract. Korsaume takes the lead, followed closely by Rosetta. Mathew brings up the rear.

They arrive at the door to the cargo bay, but before Korsaume pushes the button to open it, Rosetta stops her.

"What are you doing," Korsaume quietly asks.

Rosetta replies with a little force, "…You open that door and they're going to know right where we are…"

"How will they know that," asks Mathew in a hushed whisper.

"The same way I knew when any of the important doors were opened. The control panel I worked on up there had lights that flickered any time the infirmary, the cargo bay, and about seventeen other rooms were opened, including the clam shell door. We open it, and they're going to know…" Rosetta says this with curt enthusiasm.

"I get your point," says Korsaume. "What do we do? Are we going in there, or not?"

Suddenly, they feel a strong tug through the corridors.

"What is that?" Rosetta asks.

Mathew pushes the button to the cargo bay. "They just disconnected our ship from theirs, and that leaves a hole to space! Get in there, now!"

He practically pushes them into the cargo bay and slams his fist down on the button to close it. The force gets stronger as the large door closes.

Korsaume looks at the other two with surprise. "The others... Agoparn, Lacendu, Vaskette, and Allen..."

"Don't forget Shivranikka," Rosetta states.

"Shivranikka's not the one I'm worried about. She can withstand being in space. She's said as much..." is Korsaume's answer.

"Not anymore, Lieutenant," Mathew says. "With what the doctor has done to her..."

"Yeah," Korsaume replies, "don't remind me... I should kill her..."

"Let's not go too far," says Mathew. "We still need Vaskette, even if you don't agree with what she did to Shivranikka.

"I have a feeling Vaskette couldn't do anything to Shivranikka she didn't want the doctor to do... Shivranikka chose to have the procedure performed," says Rosetta.

"I was talking about killing Shivranikka," Korsaume concludes. She looks up at the bounty huntress. "When we all first came aboard the Contract, I explained to her about the disease Shivranikka had been diagnosed with: Siverchan's disease. Vaskette told us she would have loved to try to fix her."

"I remember something about that," Mathew says. "Do you think she tried to cure Shivranikka of that?"

"Doubtful," Rosetta says, "Shivranikka is mentally ill, and mentally ill people don't know they're mentally ill...especially not that techno-witch. Most likely, Vaskette only tried to take out the organic technology."

"That little…" Korsaume begins, pounding her fist against the door hard, hurting her hand. "She lost against me, and to keep me from being able to use her abilities, she has Vaskette take out the stuff that made her invulnerable."

"Now, wait," Mathew adds, "don't get mad at her. She has her rights, too…"

"Um, Captain, I hate to change the subject, but," Rosetta says, "If they know we're in here, as Rosetta implied, wouldn't they be just as capable of floating us right out the cargo bay door?"

"I wouldn't worry about that," Korsaume says. "They weren't trying to get rid of us. They just didn't want us roaming the halls. You heard what Breeshawn said…that Chrinsole wants us all alive."

"The Star Axis is still out of commission. Do you think they'll leave this area," asks Rosetta.

"…Especially if they leave the Star Axis crew behind…?" Mathew asks, "You can bet they will."

*****

"The door's locked," Vaskette says, trying the door to the main portion of the ship.

"What do we do now," Allen asks turning to Shivranikka.

The woman stares back at him, points at her self, and says, "What are you looking at me for…?"

Allen smiles and then laughs noiselessly at his mistake. "Old habits die hard," he replies.

Shivranikka smirks at him half-heartedly. "Kill those habits quickly and bury them." Immediately her face goes straight and she nods her head. "I don't know **what** we should do."

"I'm guessing we should wait," Vaskette says. "I think this ship is moving."

"I do believe you're right," Tex says. "They're taking all of you to Chrinsole."

"All of us, you mean," Vaskette retorts. "They're taking the whole ship."

"Where, is the question," Shivranikka points out.

"The place where 'Nation' is headquartered," Garmy answers.

Allen glances the speaker's way and asks with anxiety, "Ascension City?"

Tex and Garmy laugh. "Sure," Garmy says.

"I take it that's only a rumor," states Vaskette.

"Where are they taking us," Allen stomps the floor toward them with a harsh face.

The two men smile, and Tex answers, "Praimarre…"

Shivranikka gives a weird and inquisitive look at Vaskette and Allen. "Have you heard of the place?"

The look on their faces says they do…

*****

"Why do I get the feeling we're not going to like what happens, next," Korsaume asks to no one in particular.

"What do you mean," Mathew questions, turning to her.

"Do you remember what it was like the only time we used that stupid mega-mass drive," she asks.

"Unfortunately, yes…" Mathew says.

Rosetta looks at both of them in turn and frowns… "Not again."

…And it happens…

*****

…Their proximity to the drive drops them to the floor. Agoparn and Lacendu are both prostrate on the floor, dizzy and unable to function properly. Their eyesight is dimmed as they lie on the floor.

"Frag," Lacendu says, picking her self up off the floor. "I feel miserable."

Agoparn helps her to her feet. "I think we just mega-massed across part of the galaxy," he says to her.

"No…you think," she almost yells at him.

"Sorry. I forgot that you were in the main room when it happened," he responds. "I can't imagine how our friends are feeling, now, too…"

Lacendu pushes herself up against a wall and says, "Vaskette told me what that thing can do to our insides… It isn't pretty."

"I take it third time is not a charm," Agoparn remarks.

"You have no idea," she says. "Vaskette told me that the second time could cook us."

"That sounds about right," he says. "I feel well-done…"

"We're all going to need some serious medical treatment," she states.

*****

Mathew, Rosetta, Korsaume, Allen, Vaskette, Agoparn, Lacendu, and Shivranikka are brought to the command deck after being treated in the infirmary by Garmy.

Maneesha smiles as they are all lined up on the floor on their knees, hands tied behind their backs.

Lacendu is the only one to speak; "I don't feel so good." At this, she throws up on the floor, but without balance now she collapses on the ground in front of her and goes unconscious.

"Garmy…Tex… Take the teacher back to the infirmary and fix her up. One of you, clean up the mess she made…" Maneesha is practically giddy with excitement over the capture of this crew.

While Garmy and Tex pick Lacendu up and carry her out of the command deck, Flynn says, "Feel free to familiarize yourselves once more with the command deck of the Saiar Ria Contract. It's the last time you'll get to see it."

"Actually," Maneesha says, "I wanted you all to see this." She moves out of the way in a grand gesture to allow them to see out the front viewport. Maneesha adds, "Shayley, enhance their view…"

In the dimness of space, it is hard to make out the intricacies of everything. As Maneesha moves from their view and the image is enhanced digitally, the dim outlines become bright and clear. There is a station in front of the ship, prominent and beautiful; the gold hues of the nearby star glancing here and there on the edges of the layout make the view intriguing…a massive station of metal and other forms of material in the most complex design ever invented by man. "Welcome," Maneesha says triumphantly, "to Praimarre…your final resting place."

"I thought this place was a piece of fiction," Vaskette says. "It would have taken the entire 'Agrauve' population twice as long as it took them to create Baitronoc."

"You'd be surprised what people can do when they set their minds to it," Reed says, walking in from behind with a slim sheet in his hand. He walks up to Maneesha and hands it to her.

She looks it over, smiles, and hands it back to her engineer. Then, she walks to the center chair and takes a seat. "Sharrock, we've been cleared for connection at port seven. Prepare to set down."

"Yes, Captain," the woman of 'Nation' says from her spot where Allen once stood.

The Saiar Ria Contract rapidly moves closer to the massive construct of Praimarre, and soon they can see from the enhanced view of the city built high around a planet the size of Earth's sun the docking bay where the Contract will be setting down. Within minutes, they are inside and the ship settles down on the metal flooring.

"Shut down all unimportant systems and prepare to leave the ship. We return home victorious," Maneesha says.

Mathew and his crewmates, minus Lacendu, are forced to their feet and walked out through the cargo bay dock walking down into the massive structure of a bay designed to house a ship at least ten times larger than the Saiar Ria Contract.

Walking out to meet them is the man they recognize as Chrinsole. He approaches them with a somber face. When he speaks, his voice seems somewhat quiet in the massive structure of the bay.

"Welcome," he says. "I've been waiting for all of you to return to me. What say we go discuss this whole thing like grownups…?"

"What say you go shove yourself out an airlock door into the vacuum of space while we all watch," says Shivranikka.

Everyone within earshot stares at her, but it is the rest of her crew who give her dirty looks. She shrugs at them and says, "What…? I thought you all didn't like him…"

Some of them roll their eyes away from her, and they all face Chrinsole again.

Chrinsole seems genuinely crushed by the statement. "I didn't know you all felt that way about me… After all I did for you, you all hate me…?"

"Ignore the witch," Mathew says. "She doesn't speak for us as a group."

At a gesture from Chrinsole, they are all taken across the massive hangar bay and through a door in one wall and through several corridors as Chrinsole speaks.

He waits until they are in the corridors before he begins…he knows he won't be heard by all of them otherwise. "Perhaps I didn't make myself completely understand last time we were together. The Solar Union is doomed. I fought for years to try to help the Solar Union achieve balance, but no matter what we did as a group, it was always evident we would eventually lose and a galaxy of people would dissent and begin setting up their own governments with no one to look over them…"

Vaskette interrupts, "They've already begun. What makes you think that that would be wrong, anyway…?"

"You don't get it, Doctor," he continues, "That's not the point. People need some semblance of leadership, if nothing else to look up to as an example, even if that leadership doesn't have any real authority. The difference between the Solar Union and 'Nation' is that we actually have authority."

"You're a police state," Allen says. "No one will tolerate that…"

Chrinsole, arriving at a door and opening it for them, says, "Oh, they will, Allen. You can bet your life on it. In fact, you just did."

Mathew and his crew are forced into stationery chairs and chained.

"I'm having Baitronoc flashbacks," says Korsaume.

"We heard about that," one man says, "so we made sure these wouldn't budge."

Mathew laughs. "News travels fast…"

"So, this is what you do to people who are just trying to do what's right," Vaskette says.

"That's just it, isn't it," Chrinsole says with a smile, "you have no idea what's right and wrong…"

"I know that whatever it is you have planned for our galaxy, I'm sure your way isn't right…" Korsaume says with a dour face. "Your willingness to put people's lives in danger, erase people's memories, and deviously undermine the way our civilization works by intentionally asking questions in a way that gets you what you want proves you're ability to lead should be put under serious scrutiny. You were the one that fed the information to the 'brain' to ensure a war between the Solar Union and the 'Agrauves,' despite the fact that the Solar Union never kept their promise to them."

Chrinsole looks down at the floor, and then glances up at the people before him in chairs and smiles. At that moment, Lacendu is walked through the door in chains and seated among her friends.

"How are you feeling, Lacy," Vaskette asks.

"Better," she says. "I won't be able to ride on the Saiar Ria Contract again without dying…"

"I figured as much," her doctor replies.

"Back to our conversation," Chrinsole continues, "You're right, Korsaume. I did almost all of that. I did **not**, however, have your memory erased. That was someone else's idea entirely, and I told them I didn't want that done."

"You'd rather have killed us," Mathew adds.

"NO!" Chrinsole yells. He calms down immediately, "I was adamant that you not be killed. I was certain that if you could be made to see what I see you would all join me."

Dierdre walks in and takes a seat. In her hands is a slim-sheet computer which she is reading from.

Chrinsole says, "You're here to listen to what I have to say. If you still feel the same way you do now after all of this information is provided to you, you will, of course, be offered a place to live where you will be out of the way, but I will assure all of you your lives. I don't believe a group with the talents you have should be killed…far from it… You should be allowed to live out your lives in peace and quiet in a place where you can do no harm to others."

"We could say the same for you," Mathew says haphazardly.

Chrinsole laughs, but it is evident he is a bit nervous.

With a glance from Chrinsole, Dierdre begins… "The Solar Union was the idea of the 'brain' more than five hundred years ago. The 'brain;' its official name is the 'Paralaxian Modus Assurity Collective Response Divinerate;' was designed with the sole purpose of determining the direction the galaxy needed to go as a collective whole of individuals based on the complete integration of information obtained by all levels of official investigation. It was begun by people under the preeminence of a vast emergence of the highest rated psychologists of the time, and designed by the highest rated programmers of the time."

Chrinsole stops her with a gentle hand on her hand on the slim-sheet as he says, "This should help all of you to understand that this machine is capable of making mistakes. Any machine invented by humans, is capable of being like humans in the sense that we make mistakes. We all make mistakes. If we err in the design of a machine of this magnitude, do you honestly think that it could make problem-free decisions…?"

"That's why your wife had me do a linear shift matrix on that data," Lacendu says.

Chrinsole looks shocked. "That was you…?"

Lacendu harrumphs. "You weren't much on keeping up with what your wife was doing, were you…?"

"Lacendu, that information you compiled for her helped us design the concept for 'Nation.' My wife began with your information and took it a step further by designing a back-up failsafe against the fall of the Solar Union. Because of the data you sifted through, we figured out that the Solar Union would fall on its own in a matter of years."

"Then you misread the conclusions I made," Lacendu remarks; "That data was not intended to determine the end of the Solar Union; it was to determine what needed to be done to correct the problems before they got out of hand… Did you mention to anyone the other data I compiled?"

Chrinsole acts like he didn't hear a word she said. "The Solar Union will fall one way or another," he says. "Either they will fall on their own, or they'll fall with our help. The Solar Union will pay for their crimes."

"That's what this is about, isn't it," Mathew concludes. "You're getting back at them for something they did to you…"

"Yes, Captain Mathew. They ruined my life. They had my wife killed and took everything from my people and left us with nothing…" Chrinsole is obviously shaken.

Suddenly, almost everyone in Mathew's crew is struck by the same realization. "You're an 'Agrauve,'" Korsaume says what is obvious to them.

Chrinsole nods. "I am a descendant of the original 'Agrauves,'" he tells them. "My ancestor's were the ones with the last name, 'Agrauve.' They were the best builders of their time. The patriarch of the family was a mechanical engineering genius hundreds of years ahead of his time. He came up with an official design for a real Dyson-sphere, and created the machines that could help people make a real one. The newly-formed Solar Union heard about it and hired his family to go ahead with the building of it. He was put in charge of hiring additional workers until they could actually begin forming the structure, and then the Es-Yu gave them vessels and homes in space to do their work.

"Over the years, the Es-Yu forgot their promises of payment and considered what they had already done for the people on the payroll as payment in full. Though my people fought for many years over this, the Es-Yu continued to decline their full and final payment. Instead, they gave us a planet and said that was more than enough. Anyone can start a home on another planet. What we wanted was our rightful due…"

"It all comes together, now, doesn't it," says Vaskette with little or no emotion. "The 'Agrauves' raised you and sent you into the heart of the Solar Union to corrupt it from the inside."

"You are finally catching on, Doctor…" Chrinsole replies.

"Well, it doesn't take a rocket scientist to figure out what you're really after, then, does it?" Vaskette asks.

"…And all of this would explain why we were thrown to the other side of the galaxy…" Lacendu adds.

Mathew, Agoparn, and Korsaume all look over at Lacendu, and Agoparn asks, "How's that?"

Lacendu smiles in spite of her self. "It's actually pretty simple, Parn," she says, "after our memories were erased…or, actually, blocked…and our abilities were still intact, he felt they could be put to better use, but he had to get us out of the way until his other plans came to fruition. We very well couldn't be starting the war for the Solar Union. He had to let that one play out on its own."

"It didn't go the way you wanted it to, did it, Chrinsole," Mathew says. "The war, I mean…"

Lacendu continues, not allowing Chrinsole the opportunity to answer. "He was hoping that when we did return we would want to help him end things in favor of the 'Agrauves' to help ensure the downfall of the Solar Union."

Vaskette looks contemplative. "Thus, the reason he met us on Ascension City…"

"…And with Lacy's Grandmother already on his side, he had the means to help coerce us in his favor; but instead, Lacy got her memories back and it only put us on the offensive," says Rosetta.

Mathew smirks at his thoughts. "The group you sent to follow us already knew where we were headed and followed us to this side of the Galaxy to keep tabs on us. They used every maneuver at their disposal with our counterparts to capture us and bring us here."

Chrinsole smiles at the people before him. "You never suspected a thing, then, I take it…?"

The crew is silent.

Shivranikka speaks out, "So…let me get this straight. Your real goal, all this time, is to put the 'Agrauves' in charge of the Galaxy under 'Nation?'"

Chrinsole's neck straightens as he stares down the blonde-haired woman. "You're much smarter than I gave you credit for…"

She laughs hysterically, until she can hardly breathe. After a few moments and some odd looks from the other people in the room she finally calms down, but her smile remains intact. "Whoa…head rush. I forgot what it was like to laugh that hard as a regular human," to her self, and then to the others in the room; "…Alright, Chrinsole… allow me to tell you a story."

Suddenly, Shivranikka's voice switches into high gear, like when Mathew and the crew originally met her. "Before humanity shot itself into space as a commonplace occurrence in the lives of people who lived on Earth, there was a nation called 'America.' You might have heard of it… It was the 'center of Democracy,' they called it. Slowly, and not quite deliberately; though some would argue; that Democracy fell apart because the government tried to control everyone and everything just because a handful of individuals got too out of line. The government began spying on their own people, demanding that everyone get implants in their bodies so 'satellites,' which orbited Earth, could track everyone's movement.

"There was a massive uprising of people who didn't want to be controlled to that extent, and eventually the 'Americans' rose up and overthrew their government. Are you even slightly curious how they did it, Dear Sir?"

"Not really," Chrinsole replies.

Shivranikka looks upset for a split second, but says, "Humor me…"

Chrinsole stares hard at the woman. "Alright…" Then, facetiously, "Sure…"

"'Democracy,'" she replies. "The people voted the idiots who wanted to control their lives out of their offices and replaced them with people who would fight to keep the people's independence from jerks who wanted to have control of everything."

There is a long pause before Chrinsole asks, "What does that have to do with this?"

Shivranikka smiles at him and replies, "The only way you're going to be able to do what you're talking about is to create a policed Galaxy. You'll have too many supervisors, and not enough workers. Eventually, your police will fail with the uprising of the people the Galaxy over, and 'Nation' will fall; just like 'America' fell, and eventually the Solar Union, as well. Everything fails eventually. It's the nature of anything created by humans. As you mentioned yourself, even the 'brain' will fail some day. When it does, the way to be prepared is not to get control. The answer is to find what works for the present time."

"What is your suggestion," Chrinsole asks facetiously, humoring the woman at the other end of the table.

She giggles silently with her mouth pulled back almost to its old length. "Why…set me up as goddess of the Galaxy, of course…"

It is almost a complete let-down for those in the room other than Mathew and his crew, so accustomed to such insanity from the woman who they brought aboard against their better judgment. The crewmembers just shake their heads.

"I think he was hoping for something more realistic," Korsaume says.

Shivranikka gets a somber face and says sarcastically, "I am **being** realistic…"

Chrinsole laughs at her, "What you're really saying is that the Solar Union is failing, and 'Nation' can take over only a short period of time before something else will come along and take over 'Nation.'"

"That sounds right," the woman replies.

"Naturally, you would be correct. However, understand that I won't even be alive when 'Nation' falls, and thus it doesn't really matter at all." Chrinsole turns his head to two armed guards in the corner. "Escort our prisoners to their cells."

The guards follow their orders as Chrinsole, Dierdre, and the 'Nation' men and women present during the entire discussion all exit the room.

The crew is unchained from their chairs and forced at gunpoint back out into the white hallways of the extraordinary station.

As they are moved along rather slowly, Shivranikka begins chatting, half to her self, but she doesn't seem to mind if anyone hears her. In fact, she says it precisely because they will.

"I knew this was a bad idea. I told them I didn't want to come to this side of the Galaxy, but did they listen to me? Of course not… Instead, they dragged my fantastic, god-like body to Quadrant One, insistent that I would be alright…but look where we are, now. …Oh, and do they have any hope of getting out of the mess they got themselves into? Absolutely not! The enemy is shoving our lousy butts into cells with no intention of ever letting us leave. I gave up being the goddess of Quadrant Four for this…?"

Korsaume smirks and glances behind at the woman who agreed to be her slave for life. "Just in case you didn't know, we can all hear you…"

Shivrannikka replies, "I figured I was being ignored. People have been ignoring me my entire life."

"That's a considerably long time to be ignored…" says Korsaume. "Maybe you should look into a new career as a show-woman. …You ever thought about playing the part of a madwoman in theatre?"

"I wouldn't be ignored, then, would I," Shivranikka asks.

Korsaume grins. "That's about the size of it. What do you think, Captain?"

Mathew looks around at his crewmates. "I think she should stay out of show-business."

It is his final word on the subject, letting them know not to try anything; that he feels they should wait for a more opportune time to try to escape.

Moments later, they arrive at the detention area and each one is placed in a separate cell with a comfortable bed, and small table with prepared food on it, and a small hand-held computer for their amusement. When the doors are shut, they cannot speak with each other by any means, and they are left alone.

*****

"What do you suggest we do with them," Dierdre asks as she takes a seat on a sofa in Chrinsole's massive office alongside Srulé. Also in the room are Maneesha, Garmy, Flynn, Tex, Shayley, Reed, Breeshawn, Stetler, Foly, and Sharrock.

Breeshawn's answer is snappy and simple. "Kill them. They're a nuisance and they know too much. I'll never understand your desire to have them on your side."

Chrinsole seems upset by this. He stares Breeshawn down as he speaks. "I realize that you don't understand, and that's why you're on that side of the desk instead of mine."

Shayley is next to speak. "The planet Praimarre encircles is fully habitable, if a bit on the warm side. Throw them down there and see what happens."

"They're a bit too resilient, Shayley," Foly states; "they'd be off it in no time."

"I have a hard time believing that we'll keep them in those cells. With what we've heard of their capabilities, I wouldn't be the least bit surprised if every one of them escapes their cells in a matter of hours." It is Flynn who says this with a furrow in his brow.

"They're exploits have been exaggerated somewhat," Chrinsole says sitting down, his back to the multi-paneled window that overlooks much of the orbital station complex, where the planet's star shines in from the right making the room spectacular, but which no one inside seems to care about at the moment.

He folds his hands together to rest his head on them with the elbows pressed to his desk. "Their reputation is being blown out of proportion by the very fact that they have continually beaten some of the most well-trained trackers the CHE has to offer. Word just came in from one of our operatives inside the CHE that Preston and his crew just arrived from Garenoljola where Mathew and his crew stranded them over two months ago. That's saying something."

Everyone looks at each other, realizing the implications.

Flynn says, "Preston is the leading CHE Surge-Agent they have to offer. He is allowed to choose his crew and if the crew he picks can't get the job done, what hope do we have?"

Chrinsole releases his left hand and holds up a finger at Flynn for only a split second, a half-grin on his face as his hand then slowly falls to the desk and he picks up a slim-sheet computer to wave it gently at them. "I have this... It's the names and addresses of their families and friends. Use your imagination, folks."

Episode 20
Un Escalier de Soleil vers Sol

OPENING:

"They've done it. They've finally done it. We're all doomed, now. It's true because I saw it in my dream. All the manmade inventions that shoot us to the stars above are leading straight for destruction. The dream: Un escalier de soliel vers sol... a staircase from the earth to the sun. Watch us walk right up it and jump off the end, burning... burning forever..." Reviving My Dying Dream, *page 718, paragraph 3, written by Larson Oldran.*

Shivranikka sits in her cell room. If one knew her very well, he would say she's taking this quite well; being stuck in a cell all alone with no one to talk to; but none do. At least, no one still alive…

That's the problem. She seems to think that no matter where she goes the people around her; those closest to her; never seem to live long. Xychocappla, Shallajohnne, and Forgiven are only a few examples.

So, needless-to-say, she is taking this very well, all things considered.

"LET ME OUT OF HERE!!!"

Her fists pound on the door until they bleed. She bangs her head on the heavy metal door only once, and after receiving a throbbing headache and having to rest on the bed where the blood on her hands dries on the sheets, she is back up doing it again.

She doesn't care about the pain to her hands, and if the pain in her head hadn't about dropped her to the floor, she wouldn't have cared about that, either.

After three or four hours of fists banging on the door and screaming at the top of her lungs and her eyes tearing up from fear, her voice gives out and she falls back onto the bed once more to rest.

She can't control it, now. She cries her self to sleep, but she doesn't stay that way for very long. The anxiety is overwhelming. She hasn't felt this way in about four hundred years: the insatiable desire to be in control and have everyone around her look up to her; admire her…no, worship her. She had forgotten what it felt like, and now that she has it again, she cannot let it go. The fact that she has not slept a moment since the surgery over eleven hours ago is irrelevant, and she is here now with her thoughts, and that madness-inducing mental disorder, driving her to be in complete control of everything.

Not being in control; being in a room alone and in control of no one and no thing; is eating her alive from inside.

The fifteen minutes of sleep isn't nearly enough, but it gives her the strength to stand up at the door and begin again.

"LET ME OUT OF HERE, NOW!!!"

Pound, pound, pound, on the door…screaming at the top of her lungs again and again, the wounds on her hands opening once more and dripping blood; a perpetual cycle she cannot control. She cries incessantly, and now she finds inside her the strong desire to panic.

*****

Chrinsole sits at his desk in the massive office that is his. He is the head of a group of people now called 'Nation;' a group he did not bring together, but a group that now is his charge. His wife started the group only nine months ago, and after her death he took over.

The individuals who make up 'Nation' include some amazing inventors, strong and knowledgeable experts in over two hundred fields of endeavor, and an array of ex-CHE members, highly trained bounty hunters, and people who just want to see an end to what they believe to be the 'evil overlords,' also known as the Solar Union Committee.

His wife was a firm believer in the Solar Union. She felt strongly that 'Nation' would only be the new CHE, and she fought hard to bring that about. The CHE was corrupt from the inside; a caste of members more in the nature of a secret society equivalent only to the Sharcuran Knights of Earth: protectors of the "Paralaxian Modus Assurity Collective Response Divinerate," otherwise called the 'brain.'

Now, he and his team of experts and the like are the new protectors. They protect the people from the dark doings of the Solar Union, whose goals started out righteous and pure, but had, over time, become the judge, jury, and executioner of the people of the Galaxy.

Too much corruption everywhere in the hierarchy of the Society had now brought about a necessary change, and 'Nation' was it.

This is what Chrinsole believes. He knows deep down inside his heart that it is true. His teachers had trained him as a young boy on the 'Agrauve' home world, and he has learned his lessons well; seen the corruption first hand, and has even taken part in the simplest task of all: helping tear it down with the help of the very people who were trying to keep it from falling…the Solar Union Committee itself.

By being the one in charge of feeding the data to the 'brain' and allowing only that data which supported his needs, and by helping the Head Keeper determine the question to be asked of it in order to cause the Solar Union's downfall, he has almost single-handedly helped his people win the war they had been waging for years.

In other words, he has killed two birds with one stone. Now he is in charge, and he likes being in charge.

There is only one problem right now. He has to figure out how to get six people on his side. Specifically, the six people whose lives he had saved in the hopes that they would one day return and help him finish what he has started.

The slim-sheet computer before him containing data on the family of each member, and their friends, former colleagues, and past lovers, is sure to be the answer to his dilemma. It is a threat, and he hates that, but he doesn't see any other choice.

*****

Mathew sits in his room at the small white table with the small slim-sheet computer in his hands. He is reading through some news broadcasts when she comes to the door and opens it.

"Hello, Captain Mathew Arnold," she says.

It is Sharrock Vicksmith, one of the 'Nation' members aboard the Saiar Ria Contract on their way here. He doesn't remember her saying two words on the ship, but now she is here and asking him to stand up.

"Follow me," she says pointing a gun at him; a type he doesn't recognize.

He makes a motion with the slim-sheet in his right hand and she nods, approving him to take it with him, so he does.

The phrase, 'follow me,' isn't really very literal. She pushes him in front of her and gives him directions as they walk through the white corridors of the immense station 'Praimarre.'

They end up in a large room with two guards on either side of the door outside, and when the large doors open, there are two more guards inside. The room is fairly large and the walls seem even whiter than the corridors.

He is asked politely to take a seat in the middle of the room. He takes the chair and relaxes, looking from person to person; there are only three; and gets nothing from any of them, so he looks back to the small slim-sheet and keeps typing.

Several minutes pass with Sharrock staring at him before a man enters dressed in high-level 'Nation' uniform. "What are you reading," the man asks. With a gesture he dismisses Sharrock.

"It's some news from the area where I used to live. It was very nice of you folks to give us access to the latest info from around the galaxy." Mathew doesn't stop reading to speak, but the attention he pays the man requires him to reread a few words here and there unconsciously.

"May I have your attention, please," the man asks.

"Sure," Mathew replies with a shake of his head as he hits the stop button on the computer and lays it on a small desktop on his right. "What do you want?"

The man smiles inconspicuously and says, "You don't even want to know my name?"

Mathew thinks for a second noticeably, and then says, "No. Not really. I've met more people in the last few months than I probably met in my entire life before... I'm a little tired of meeting new people and trying to remember their name, rank, and everything about them. I'm tired and I want to go home. You are just keeping me from it."

"Oh, I don't think that's what you really want," the man says. "If you had really wanted to go home you wouldn't have gone looking for trouble with the Saiar Ria Contract."

Mathew laughs quietly and retorts, "There's no way to go home quietly and relax with people out to kill us. You and I both know the real purpose of Maneesha and her crew."

"Do I?" the man asks, just on the edge of sarcasm.

"So, Mister Whatever-your-name-is, go ahead and get what you have to say out of the way and take me back to my cell." Mathew now seems completely aloof.

The man sighs. "My name is Erick Remnath. I'm here to talk with you about your and your crew's real purpose for being here."

"We were brought here by the Saiar Ria Contract…"

Erick interrupts him by clearing his throat. "I know… I was briefed on everything that has happened since you were all requested to make an appearance on Baitronoc about nine months ago. My reason for asking will become evident as we go through this. Now, let's try again. Why are you and your crew really here on 'Praimarre?'"

Mathew sees no reason to lie to the man. "We're here to stop 'Nation' from their plots against the Solar Union."

Erick smiles and says, "Now we're getting somewhere. I've heard about your crew's abilities, and the situations you've all been through in the last few months only prove to me that if you've set your mind to it, you'll accomplish it."

"That's reassuring," Mathew says, almost happy.

"I didn't say it to reassure you. I said it because we don't want that. You're here to discuss terms with me to find a peaceful way for us to end this without destroying 'Nation,' and/or 'Praimarre.'"

Mathew laughs at the man and then says, "So, what you're saying is, you're scared we're going to do what we came here to do and you won't be able to stop us. The reason I laugh is because you actually believe there's a way to resolve this peacefully. At what point in your study of my crew could you have possibly had reason to believe anything we do has a peaceful ending?"

As Mathew laughs at this thought, Erick joins him. The two men laugh, but both seem uncomfortable.

"You are right about that," Erick says with no small amount of unease. "If you could, though, how would you resolve this peacefully?"

Mathew thinks for a moment. It doesn't take him long to come up with the answer. "'Nation;' every man, woman, and child; packs their belongings and goes home and tries to find a way to help the Solar Union find a mutually inclusive answer to our Galaxy's dilemma of total failure of its government… At that point, I'll be willing to take my crew and all go home." Almost as an afterthought, he includes, "Oh, and cancel the death threat on us by Maneesha and her crew."

The man puts his hands in his pockets and says, "Barring all of that, knowing that none of that will happen; except perhaps the part about taking the bounty off your heads; is there any other way?"

Mathew glances at different spots in his field of vision from the chair and then finally settles on looking at Erick, about a meter in front of him and replies, "Not that I can think of…"

Erick sighs and shakes his head. "What if I made a few suggestions? Would you be willing to hear my ideas on how to settle this peacefully? …And if so, would you be willing to consider my options…?"

Mathew thinks for a moment before replying affirmatively.

Erick begins by pulling his hands from his pockets and turning away from Mathew to walk around in front of him to make his statements seem well thought-out, and occasionally looking directly at Mathew when it seems natural to do so. "I … first of al l… I feel like maybe your crew doesn't have all the facts. Now, mind you, that's only my opinion, but in an attempt to be fair, I can see how you and your crewmates might get the feeling that 'Nation' isn't abiding by the law."

"Oh, they're abiding by the law," Mathew says, "It's just their own law…"

"Well, now, you might be right, Captain, but realize, too, that what their goal is requires that some laws already in place by the Solar Union may not make sense if they keep 'Nation' from its set goal…"

"…And what is that goal," asks Mathew.

"Well, I believe Chrinsole already went over that with you earlier, but for the sake of argument, I'll reiterate that here. 'Nation's' goal is to stop the Solar Union. We have no intention of destroying Baitronoc, or taking over it, or killing anyone, though any one of those things may be ultimately necessary if it comes to that. The goal is that because the Solar Union is no longer valid and has not increased in its ability to provide for its original laws and guidelines for the people it governs, change is necessary."

"I can see that," Mathew replies, "but I think you're going about it all wrong."

"In what way," asks Erick.

"In the way 'Nation' saw fit to rush my crew and me headlong into the great unknown, far away from our family and friends; our homes. Maneesha and her crew were given the same challenge we were given, but because we chose not to go to war with the 'Agrauves,' it meant that Chrinsole needed some reserves; people who would agree to whatever he had in mind. He made certain they were on his side while we were busy determining that what the 'brain' had chosen to do based on limited information was wrong, and then had them step in to do what we wouldn't. Just so you know: war is never the answer…"

Erick replies, "Some might say that war is necessary…"

"War is only necessary when people refuse to agree to disagree. Like you and me for instance; I could walk out of this room with a pleasant smile and feel good about myself right now, knowing I made the right choice because I chose not to kill you where you stand. Can you walk out of here at the end of this conversation knowing that I won't change my mind about the evil 'Nation' has planned for the Solar Union…if you get the opportunity to walk out at all?"

Erick seems very uncomfortable now, as do the two guards who stand behind him.

Erick turns to the two guards and asks them to wait outside. They are quick to obey. After the doors close, he turns to Mathew who is now standing up. The man jerks back a step instinctively. "Look, I'm not your enemy," he says in rapid response to a perceived threat.

Mathew tilts his head a bit and says, "I see my reputation precedes me more than even I was willing to admit. If you're not my enemy, then you're my ally, but you have said the exact opposite since you entered this room, trying to get me and my crew to go along with whatever 'Nation' intends for the Solar Union. I'm here to tell you, it isn't going to happen, Erick."

A voice over a speaker system in the room comes on, “That’s where you’re wrong.” It is Chrinsole’s. “You’ll stay right where you are, Captain. Don’t move an inch toward him or your life is forfeit. You have been warned.”

“You know,” Mathew says, “the great thing about handhelds that can receive information…they can also send information.” He reaches to his right and presses a small spot on the screen of the slim-sheet computer he came in with…

Suddenly, the power in the room goes out, including the lights.

Mathew’s voice is heard echoing in the room. “Erick, command the emergency lights on.”

Erick is quick to oblige. “Computer, emergency lights in this room…”

It is an acceptable command and the emergency flood lights come on.

Erick looks in front of him to find Mathew staring him down. “Whose side are you on, Erick?”

The man is startled, but says, “I’m on my own side. I take orders from Chrinsole…”

“What if I made a few suggestions? Would you be willing to hear my ideas on how to settle this peacefully? …And if so, would you be willing to consider my options…?” Mathew repeats verbatim what the man asked of him only a few minutes earlier.

Erick is a wreck of nerves. “Sure…”

Mathew smiles at the man and nods once as he says, “Good!”

*****

Shivranikka has given up her banging on the door, yelling and screaming. She is practically unconscious now, her knees on the floor, the front of her body pushed hard against the door with the right side of her face pressed. She would probably feel uncomfortable if she hadn’t injured herself so badly. This is almost a soft bed for her now.

She lost feeling in her knees and below because of the way she is positioned on them, but she doesn't notice. She is sound asleep when there is a ding from the computer informing anyone inside listening that someone is at the door, wishing to come in.

She doesn't hear it.

The door opens and she collapses backward, her head barely missing the leg of the chair. It is at this point she wakes up, realizing she is in severe pain.

She cannot open her eyes, she feels exhausted, and she cannot move her legs.

"Pick her up and take her to the infirmary," she hears a voice she doesn't recognize.

"It took her long enough to work herself down this far," says another.

Shivranikka feels hands caressing her body and lifting her, but she cannot move, and she is placed on a rolling bed, strapped down and taken somewhere and patched up, cleaned up, and returned to her room, laid on the bed, and it is not until her head hits the pillow that she returns to sleep…sweet, blissful sleep.

*****

"You can't really expect to drop all four of the guards outside this door," Erick says with serious concern.

"I can, if you'll help me," Mathew replies. "I'm going to do this with or without your assistance. Feel free to help, or not help; it's your choice."

"What are you going to do if I don't help," he asks.

Mathew turns to him with a hard look. "What **have** you read about me?" It is not necessarily intended as a question…more a way to get the man to think about it.

Mathew walks back to the chair, picks up the slim-sheet and places it in his jacket pocket. Then, he picks up the small table and takes it apart in a matter of moments, keeping the legs and table top in separate groups.

"Why did they pick you, Erick?" Mathew asks.

Erick glances at his inquisitor. "What do you mean?"

"You're scared of me…of us. You have little or no training. Why did they pick you to come in here and talk with me? It makes zero sense. If they know my capabilities, why would they stick a man in here who doesn't know what he's doing?" He doesn't wait for the man to answer. "When you entered the room, you were pretty straight-forward with me, telling me how it was going to be. Did they tell you to talk a big talk, or do you really think I'm that naïve?"

Erick looks confused. Mathew turns around to face the man and hands him one of the legs of the table. The man looks down at it in his hand, and then looks back up at Mathew.

Mathew uses the tabletop to pummel the man upside the head once. Erick drops to the floor on his hands and knees in severe pain. "Toss the table leg away from you."

Erick obeys, flinging it to the other side of the room. "What are you doing?"

"I'm not taking any chances," Mathew says. "If you really read up on us, you'd know we don't particularly have good luck with people who agree to assist us. Fool me once, shame on you. Fool me twice, shame on me."

It is the last thing Erick hears from Mathew as the Captain knocks the man in the head twice more, and the man's head hits the floor as he falls unconscious.

Mathew hangs a table-leg connector off his belt, takes one table leg in each hand and walks over to the door. Using the one in his right hand he smashes the control panel and the door unlocks and opens. As it does, he walks through the light smoke erupting from the door panel watching either side of his view. The two guards who were standing outside before are still there, and Mathew thinks how great it is that they aren't wearing helmets.

Using the table legs, he swings them at the men's heads, rapidly knocking them to the floor. He then steals their guns and hangs them from his belt, keeping the table legs in his hands. He knocks both of them in the head once more each for good measure, and walks back down the hall the way he came, keeping watch for the other two guards Erick sent out of the room.

He knows he's being watched by cameras throughout the corridors he walks through, but he doesn't really care. He has no recourse at the moment. Besides, he also knows that whoever is watching him through those screens already knows where he's headed. He can't very well go this alone. He needs all his crewmates to win this fight.

*****

"What now," Tex asks, a bit subdued; his customary choice in attitude.

Chrinsole doesn't even answer.

Shayley stands with her arms folded, and before she turns and walks to a chair she says, "You know what."

Maneesha and Flynn both seem extremely upset, but it is Maneesha who is always the one to speak, and loudly, her mind… She looks at Chrinsole with harsh eyes, her hair hanging down in her face. "You knew this would happen. You sent that idiot down there to 'negotiate…'" she says 'negotiate' with added stress, and continues, "…knowing full well that he would turn at the slightest pressure by that Captain Arnold."

"Of course I did," Chrinsole replies. "It has to end one way or another and the only way to end it is to have the twelve of you fight it out amongst yourselves. Meanwhile, I'm getting the 'Nation' army prepared for the fight we've been waiting for; so while you folks are in the hallways running amok, I'm going to be ending the Solar Union once and for all."

Reed, never one to speak unnecessarily, says, "So, what did you have in mind, Chrinsole? Did you plan your little suicide run from the beginning, or is it something you're doing on a whim?"

Chrinsole looks mad. "What's that supposed to mean?!"

Reed doesn't answer. He stands up and walks to the door.

The rest of the crew follows him.

Maneesha turns her head as her crewmates walk out the door. "If you need us, we'll be out in the halls…running amok." She walks out the door and doesn't look back. She slams the door behind her on the way out.

"How long did you have this planned," Dierdre asks.

"Not very long…but somehow I always knew it would come to this." Chrinsole walks around his desk and stands about two meters from his secretary who is seated on the opposite side of the middle of the room in one of the plush sofas. "I'm doing what's right for the people. You know that…"

Dierdre gives her boss a half-hearted glance and smile, but looks back down to her handheld computer. "You know those six people who just left your office aren't going to stay on your side, now."

"Well, they're certainly not going to help their counterparts. After it's all over, they'll know I was right and come back to work for me. I've seen to that." Chrinsole smiles at a thought. "Besides, I seriously doubt those fine folks who just left my office will return anyway."

"You believe the other group will win…" Dierdre responds, half as a question.

"Of course… They're the Galaxy's best…and when they're done, I've still got my ace in the hole with their families…" Chrinsole's smile fades.

Dierdre seems displeased. "I hope you're right…for all our sakes."

*****

Mathew arrives at the cell block where he was taken from and begins jamming the locks to try and get the doors open. The first one he actually gets to open contains Vaskette, and she assists him in opening other cells. Several are empty, but as they go, their other crewmates assist in finding the rest. Shivranikka's cell is one of them, and they find her sound asleep.

"Are you alright," Vaskette asks bending down to the bed next to the blonde-haired woman.

Shivranikka is groggy and says, "They helped me." There is a smile on her face. "They're not all bad… They patched me up."

"What are you talking about," Vaskette asks.

Shivranikka holds up her hands where patches are on the outsides of each hand. "They bandaged me up…"

Vaskette looks concerned. "What happened to you?"

"I went mad in here and couldn't control myself. I hurt myself really bad banging on the door. I don't know why… I feel something I haven't felt in a few hundred years…"

Realization hits Vaskette hard as she realizes Shivranikka is still suffering from her mental disorder. "I didn't even think about the Siverchan's disease… I'm sorry. I guess my surgery isn't complete, is it…?"

Shivranikka is looking up at the doorway, and Vaskette soon realizes someone is behind her. She turns to see Lacendu, with Agoparn right behind her looking over her shoulder. "Is everything alright," Agoparn asks.

"Yeah," Vaskette replies. "Help me get Shivranikka up and out of here. I'm guessing she might also be a bit claustrophobic…"

Shivranikka smiles at everyone, more out of habit than because she's happy, which she is not… "I don't remember being claustrophobic… Maybe I can get a second opinion."

"As soon as we're out of here, I'll give as many opinions as you want. Work with me."

Lacendu is beside them helping Shivranikka up.

Shivranikka pulls her right arm away from Lacendu quickly and says, "No disrespect, Teacher, but I can stand on my own. Same for you, Doctor…"

They allow her to stand up, and as she does she presses her pants legs down the back, and then her shirt. "I'm ready when you are…"

They exit the room together to find Mathew, Rosetta, Korsaume, and Allen standing to one side waiting. "Is everyone ready to get this show over with…?"

"I am," Vaskette says. "The sooner we do, the sooner we can go home."

"Agreed," adds Lacendu.

"I have a problem with all of this," Mathew says. "Just know that I think we're being set up. The guy they had interrogating me was a wimp and scared stiff of us. He was too easy to get rid of, and there were only two guards outside the door. Getting here, there were no guards on my way, so I think there's something up…"

"That would be my guess," Allen says. "It doesn't make sense any other way. Can Korsaume and I have those two guns…?" He smiles at this thought.

Mathew smiles back. "Of course…" He removes the two guns from his belt and hands one each to Korsaume and Allen. "Let's move out…and be on the watch for anything strange."

Lacendu says loud enough to be heard, but obviously to her self, "Define strange…" There is no answer from her crewmates.

They walk silently through the halls, making their way back the way they were brought in when they were incarcerated. They soon arrive at a large window which is on the left as they round a corner. Mathew is the first to glance through it, and what he and most of the crew see is almost unbelievable. The room is about a kilometer wide and just as long, about twenty meters high, and the ships are lined up almost perfectly in a square pattern with hundreds of men and women walking around, some working on engines and systems, others bringing equipment and parceling them out.

"No, way!" Lacendu remarks almost loud enough to be normal tone…

Agoparn nods his head toward the window at a glance back from Vaskette and she walks over to it, places her hands on the film and stares. "Unreal," she says. "What do you suppose they need all those ships for?"

"War, maybe?" Allen half-asks, eyeing the doctor.

She looks back at him and says in a matter-of-fact tone, "Oh… Yeah…"

"What do we do, now?" Korsaume asks, turning to their captain.

Mathew glances at the vast space, the floor about twelve meters below them, and says out loud, "There's got to be ten-thousand ships in that room…"

"You suppose," Korsaume asks. She says forcefully, "What do we do about it?"

Mathew shakes his head. "We need to find schematics for this station." He turns to Allen. "Where do you all think we could do that from?"

Allen looks at Lacendu with a small gesture of his hand.

Lacendu glances back at him, her face crinkles up like she tastes something terrible, and shakes her head. "Don't look at me. I'm not a computer expert…"

"Can you hack one of the computers," Mathew asks.

"Theoretically. It depends entirely on what programming language it uses. On top of that, I'd have to know what I was looking for… Schematics can be done in numerous ways…" she responds.

"I'd be glad to help, if I can," Shivranikka says.

"You may have that opportunity," Mathew says. "Allen, let's go find a computer for these nice ladies to hack."

*****

"What do you think we should do," Reed asks, looking directly at Maneesha.

Maneesha seems flustered and upset, but turns to him and says, "Let's just kill them. I want to kill every last one of them. I'm so sick of Chrinsole's constantly making them out to be better than everyone. I want to kill Mathew. The rest of you can kill your counterparts. I'll tell you right now, though…if you won't, I will."

Garmy shakes his head in frustration. "How do you suppose we do that?"

"Let's go to the weapons room," she says. "We have access to some of the most powerful weapons in the galaxy. Let's use them."

"I really don't like the idea of killing them," says Flynn. "They're good people. They don't deserve…"

Maneesha interrupts him. “Alright, you lead! What do YOU want to do? Beat them at a game of poker?”

“That might not be a bad idea,” Tex says. “We might actually stand a chance against them…”

Some of them laugh.

“Enough,” Maneesha says giving them all a dirty look. “Flynn, where do you think they’ll go first?”

He answers, “Best guess…? They’ll try to make their way off the station. They know a war is brewing, and they won’t want to be aboard when the war breaks out. They stand a better chance of survival if they get off this station.”

“Admittedly,” Maneesha says, “but you’re assuming they care about their own survival. The data we have on them suggests they’re more than willing to do what it takes to win, even if it means they might have to give up their own lives to do it.”

“I didn’t get that from the info we read,” Shayley states. “They’re just really good.”

“FRAG!” Maneesha half-yells it. “What’s the deal?! Is everyone in the galaxy goo-goo over those trippers…?!”

Shayley looks a little concerned. “I was just saying…”

“I know what you were saying,” Maneesha says with force, leaning into the words toward Shayley. “Now, let’s get this done. Weapons…now! Kill them…now!”

*****

“None of these doors open,” Allen says. “I’ve tried several of them. Even removing the box and disconnecting the power won’t let me in.”

Korsaume is standing next to Allen when he says this and looks up at him with a smile. Mathew sees it and shakes his head. “No…no, Korsaume. We don’t need you blowing holes in everything…”

“But, Captain,” she says nicely, “I like blowing holes in everything…”

"Just one," Mathew says with a sigh, giving in. "Only one door, though. Pick a door, and if it doesn't have a computer in it we'll try something different."

"Alright," she acquiesces.

She brings up the gun at her side, levels it at a random door nearby, and as the rest of the crew steps out of the way she pulls the trigger.

The door comes off its hinges and falls a few feet away, the top of the door landing on a desk. Smoke rises from the hole in the door.

The crew enters together and in the wall on the left is a computer screen.

"Good job," Allen says, nudging Korsaume with his right arm.

Lacendu and Shivranikka walk up to the computer screen and proceed to try to turn it on.

"It's not working," Lacendu says after a few minutes. "I can't find a power switch…"

Korsaume walks behind the desk, pulls a drawer open and feels underneath. First try a bust, she begins opening other drawers, and finally finds a small remote control box in one drawer. She pulls it out, points it at the computer screen and presses the power button. "How's that," she asks.

As the screen comes alive, Lacendu looks back at her and smiles. "It'll do."

While Lacendu and Shivranikka begin searching the computer for schematics for the layout of the station, Mathew walks up behind Allen, Korsaume nearby.

"Allen, take Korsaume with you," he says quietly, "and keep a watch out the door. I don't want any surprise visits."

"Agreed," Allen replies taking a few steps back, grabbing Korsaume by her left arm and pulling her to the door…

Lacendu pulls out her handheld and tries to link it to the computer. Within moments, she has the link and is controlling the screen through the hand-held using voice commands to activate different folders and programs. Minutes later, she has the schematics up and begins downloading them to the hand-held.

"Captain, you'll be happy to know we've done it…" Shivranikka says, turning to Mathew.

He replies, "Excellent. Once they're downloaded, let's get out of here and see what we can do to stop 'Nation.'"

"Captain," Korsaume says, running over to him, gun in both hands, "we've got company…"

"Maneesha," he asks her.

"Yes, sir. They all have weapons, and they also seem to have intent."

"They knew where we were already. That means they have access to a lot of information about this station," Allen says. "That might work to our advantage."

Agoparn has a bit of a surprised look on his face as he says directly at Allen, "I fail to see how…"

"Don't worry," Allen replies. "You'll see later."

Mathew and Korsaume are back at the door where Allen still stands, peaking out behind the wall occasionally to check on the progress of their counterparts.

Allen peaks around once more, and turns to Mathew. "I've got an idea," he says.

"Let's hear it."

"I could blow a hole in the window across the way as they pass. It would give Korsaume and myself the opportunity to get the rest of you out of this room. We don't stand a chance backed against a wall."

"You're the strategist," Mathew replies. "I trust your opinion." At this he turns to Lacendu and Shivranikka. "You ladies done?"

"Yes, sir," Lacendu says. "We were just checking for any other data we might need."

Everyone gathers around Allen and Korsaume who keep peaking out to find where the other group is. They wait patiently, and finally Korsaume looks up at Allen. "You ready for this?"

"They have sapphire shields on," Allen says.

"I noticed…" is her reply.

"Don't they have a trigger-response ejection code?"

Korsaume stops for a moment and her eyebrows raise… "You're right."

Allen turns to Lacendu. "Can you use that hand-held to send out a certain signal and code?"

"Yes," she answers.

Korsaume looks at her as Allen peaks back around the corner. "Signal Beta-Beta-Epsilon-Kappa-Beta-Delta… Strength at forty terawatts… Code D – L – 7 – 7 – 4 – 9 – 1."

As Korsaume speaks, Lacendu punches in the information and begins to form the signal. "I'm ready when you two are," Lacendu says once complete.

Korsaume peaks back out to see the six members of the other group coming up with weapons aimed. They pass right next to the window. Allen turns to Lacendu and whispers loudly, "NOW!"

She presses the button to send the signal and Allen and Korsaume both step out with weapons aimed at the window at an angle. The weapons discharge and hit the window shattering it. Pieces of the window fly in all directions, some hitting the group sneaking up on them. With the sapphire shields down, the pieces of glass have nothing to stop them and four of them are cut up bad. Two of them get shots off, and though Allen and Korsaume keep moving when they step out, Korsaume is hit in her left side and she spins around a few times before falling to the ground, her gun hitting the ground and the back hitting her in the upper chest at an angle. She rolls over on her back holding her side and breast.

She yells out in pain.

The group moves out while Maneesha and Flynn; the only two not injured; hide behind walls to keep out of the line of fire.

Mathew picks Korsaume up from the floor, Shivranikka picks up the weapon, and the group moves down the hallway as fast as they can. When they are nearing a turn out of sight, a shot is heard through the hallway that hits the wall next to them.

They round the corner and stop for a few moments.

"That was a warning shot," Allen says. "We've succeeded in angering them."

"Good," Mathew says. "Now they know how we feel... Lacendu, lead us to a medical room. Korsaume needs some patching up..."

"No problem," says Lacendu. "There's one nearby, and I was thinking the same thing already. Let's go..."

The group moves on down this corridor, through a few different turns, and finally to a double-door which is the easiest to open they've found so far. They move in and find one male inside, taking him captive without fanfare, and when they close the doors, Allen uses his weapon to weld the door shut together and to the floor and doorway.

Vaskette begins working on Korsaume immediately. "You like this, don't you..." Vaskette asks.

"Oh, shut up, Doctor."

"No, I'm serious. You really enjoy getting attention like this. You thrill to running out into the danger..." At this, Vaskette rips the shirt away from the open wound. Korsaume doesn't feel any additional pain. Lacendu is watching from the right, and winces at the sight, making a face. She swallows hard, but is strangely glued to the procedure.

"That blast cauterized the wound," Vaskette says. "You're pretty lucky. It caught your kidney..."

"Are you for real," Korsaume asks, leaning her head up to look.

Vaskette puts her left hand up to the woman's head and pushes lightly. "Lie down. I'm working, here..."

"You enjoy this, don't you," Korsaume asks, mocking the doctor.

"Of course. I live for this stuff..." She says it with a smile, taking a device from a tray nearby and holding it to her patient's side, working away.

"That's really gross," Lacendu says. "Excuse me for a moment." She walks over to the sink and throws up.

"That's our Lacy," Korsaume says with a grin. Then she coughs and winces at the pain as Vaskette moves a device across the wound to help heal it.

Mathew walks over to Allen, Shivranikka, and Rosetta who stand around close together. "What do you all think we should do next?"

Shivranikka; the blonde woman with the broad smile, her face almost ten years older now that she is no longer filled with organic technology; says, "While we were walking here, and walking through the corridors on our way to the cells yesterday, I noticed a few things about the technology being utilized throughout this massive facility. Oddly enough, it's some of the cheapest and most efficient energy technology ever created. It's electric/heat hybrid technology. The planet beneath us is 'Saigor Moore,' a planet known in my time as a very dangerous planet not far from my home planet of Mount Ligmon-Ardreptipol about forty light-years from here. The upper atmosphere of Saigor Moore; or 'Praimarre,' or whatever they're calling it now; gives off a radical form of heat nigh equivalent to that of a star, but without the furnace-like effect. Basically, this entire station's energy is being drawn from the emanations of that planet below. I think we have lots of options..."

Allen looks like he's thinking for a moment, and then says, "She's right. We have several options."

"We could try what you folks did to my ships...I believe Lacendu called it a 'shadow-shutdown...'" Shivranikka seems composed as she says this, but it's evident she's holding her feelings back. "This place was built quickly and with the latest technology, even if the structure is completely hodge-podge."

"It makes sense, though," Allen says. "If you're going to build something this massive as fast as they did, the best thing to do is to use equipment old and new and just piece it all together until it fits. Much of the station I've seen so far seems to be consistent with some older model ribbon stations and positioning satellites which Chrinsole would have had access to as a Committee member. He would have been able to re-proportion everything to this location and have some workers piece it all together."

"What about those ships?" Mathew asks. "Those were all brand new ships. I've flown vessels like that only a year ago, according to my records."

Allen thinks for a few moments. "Alright…I don't have an answer for that one."

"What about Chrinsole," Rosetta asks. "He's definitely keeping an eye on us…"

"I don't suppose we could threaten him," Agoparn says, walking up from behind Mathew.

"Doubtful," Allen replies. "His wife is dead, his people are decimated, and he has nothing left to give up. The only way to stop him is directly."

"I have to agree with Allen," Mathew adds. "Any man willing to stoop to the measures he has doesn't have much else left to live for but his own purposes. We're going to have to get creative with our approaches. If Maneesha and her crew aren't already looking for us, they will be soon, and we're going to have to deal with them and him in some semblance of simultaneous…"

About this same moment, there is a knock on the entry door. Allen moves quickly, pushing his crewmates away from it, and he's just in time because the door is blown open by a projectile weapon.

While the crew is getting down behind medical tables and beds, they hear Maneesha say rather loudly, "I've been really nice, so far. You're all officially on my bad list!"

They watch from behind their respective places as she and some of her crewmates walk in.

"I don't suppose we could talk about this," Mathew says standing up to protect Vaskette and Korsaume, who are at the bed where the doctor is still at work.

"Oh, we could," Maneesha replies, "but we're not going to." Her gun is now aimed directly at him. "You're more than welcome to try while I blow your brains out."

"That won't be necessary," says a voice behind the other crew. They turn to see Chrinsole with several bodyguards coming forward.

"Oh, shut up," Maneesha says, a little louder than necessary, looking back at Mathew with her gun at the ready. "I'm not taking orders from you any more. You're so stinkin' blind! These people are doing everything in their power to stop you, and off you go saying, 'I just want to win them over so they'll be on my side,'" the last sentence she says mocking him. Then, "You just really don't get it!"

"That's where you're wrong, Neesh," Chrinsole says, using her nick-name like talking to an old friend. "They've been watched since they stepped aboard this station. I've known right where they were at all times, and I've had security following them since they escaped their little prisons…"

Chrinsole walks right into the infirmary and stands between Maneesha and Mathew with seemingly no regard for his own safety.

Vaskette, at this point, completes her work on Korsaume's side and whispers, "Get off the bed." Korsaume does as she's told and hides behind the bed. Vaskette ducks down behind Mathew.

Maneesha moves the gun over Chrinsole's shoulder. "Move," she says. "That crew behind you and mine have unfinished business."

"Your creed," Chrinsole says with fury. "Any fight you can walk away from isn't finished?"

"That's the one," she replies. "They've walked all over your plans for them, and you want to turn them into your best friends."

Chrinsole nods. "That's right. I do want to turn them into my best friends. I definitely don't want them to fight me on this. They'll win."

"They'll win if you don't kill them now while you have the chance!" she yells.

"NO!" Chrinsole yells back at her.

Mathew turns to Allen, points at his gun, and then points at the wall next to Chrinsole. Allen nods his understanding, and the rest of the crew seems to fall right in line, hiding behind whatever they can.

Shivranikka seems to realize what's going on and sneaks to the other side. Mathew keeps an eye on her, and when he sees that both Shivranikka and Allen are looking at him, he ducks down behind the table as both of them turn and shoot the walls right next to the other group. Chaos ensues and Chrinsole and the other crew duck behind the walls outside in the hallway.

"What's that about," Chrinsole yells after ducking down, suddenly surrounded by his guards.

"It's about us getting out of here," Mathew yells over the table. "We're leaving, and we're taking this place down with us…"

"Not likely," Flynn says back. "You're all in for a real wake-up call."

"Let's talk about this," Chrinsole says. "Come out from behind there and let's deal with this like mature adults…"

Korsaume moves around to Shivranikka and takes the gun from her. Shivranikka then moves over to get near Lacendu.

Mathew looks over at them. "What are you two thinking?"

"Can we try what you and Agoparn did to my ships to this station?" the blonde witch asks.

Lacendu smiles, "Not from here. I need a main-line terminal…"

"If we get you to one, will you do it," Korsaume whispers over.

"Sure," Agoparn replies. Lacendu says, "Yeah…of course."

Mathew looks at Allen. "We need a distraction that will get us out of this room."

Allen smiles, turns his gun off, and unplugs a cord, re-plugging it into a different section which he plugs into the first. Then he turns the gun back on. Power begins building up. Korsaume sees what he's doing and whispers, "You're all going to want to cover your ears for this one."

The whole group gets down carefully and holds their ears with both hands.

"What's going on over there," Maneesha yells. "We've been hearing whispers. What have you decided?"

Allen waits until the gun's overload switch is tripped and the power build-up goes into the red. "We've decided we would like to leave peacefully."

"Wise choice," Chrinsole replies.

"The problem is," Allen continues, "You're not going to let us do that, so…" At this, he tosses the gun out toward the doorway.

It explodes on impact with the floor. The other group, with Chrinsole and his security officers, realize what is happening too little, too late. They're all blown back away and many of them are injured again from the explosion; the ones closest have slight burns on the fronts of their bodies.

"Let's go," Mathew says loudly as he and his crewmates jump to their feet and run out the door, over their enemies, and down the hallway.

"Nice work," Lacendu says, huffing from running so hard.

Allen seems happy as he pulls Lacendu forward to lead the way. "Thanks…"

The group runs quickly through the halls following Lacendu's pointing and statements through her difficult breaths.

Suddenly, she begins slowing down and stops fast, the rest of the group almost knocking each other over. They look ahead down the hall to see more security coming their way.

"Any more bright ideas," Korsaume asks Allen, standing behind him on his left, her gun aimed forward.

"You're holding it," he replies.

She grins. "I'd love to, Allen, but I don't think I stand a chance alone."

"We need more weapons," Allen says.

"Not really," Shivranikka says. She grabs Lacendu's hand-held and punches a few buttons.

"Surrender," says one of the security officers as the group of guards get closer.

"You first," Shivranikka yells back. At this, she punches another button and the lights in the hallway go out.

Allen pulls his crewmates down to the floor as Korsaume opens fire on the opposite side of the hallway from where she was…the blasts bounce off the guards' sapphire shields sending blue lights flickering through the hallway in the darkness.

"Great," Korsaume says to them after hitting to the floor. "What now?"

"Aim for the ceiling above them," Allen suggests. "You should be able to drop some debris on their heads with the right shot…"

She aims a little higher, making a guess at where the guards are and fires a few rounds. In moments, she has the right shot and they hear pieces of ceiling tiles falling on the men, their shouts and complaints making it evident Korsaume hit her target.

"Let's move," Lacendu says. "Now that we've got them down, there's another way around we can take."

The group gets up, and with the help of the light from the hand-held devices they make their way around a few corners, backtracking only a few hundred feet before the lights kick back on.

"That light trick won't work again," Lacendu says.

"That was pretty smart," Mathew says as they run. "Thanks for thinking of it."

Shivranikka says, "Don't mention it. We can't all be gods and goddesses…"

The group makes their way quickly through the hallways and suddenly Lacendu stops. Everyone begins looking around for more guards.

"What's it this time," Mathew asks, almost upset.

Lacendu points to her left. "You'll want some of the items in there."

"What is it," asks Agoparn.

"It's a weapons locker…"

Allen and Korsaume smile at each other.

Shivranikka walks right up to it, picks the lock with a small metal piece from her pocket and enters.

"How'd she do that…?" Allen says with an awkward look to his crewmates.

Korsaume passes everyone and follows the blonde woman into the room. "Shivranikka, why didn't you tell us you could do that?"

Shivranikka turns for only a moment, smiles, and turns back to pick up weapons. “I’m sick of this whole thing. I want to get out of here. Let’s take what we need, end this, and get out…”

“I couldn’t agree with you more,” Allen says.

The crew finds a few weapons they might like to use, leaves quickly, and makes their way on down the hall. They soon arrive at the room Lacendu talked about and they get in with little trouble. A main-line computer is in the center of the room.

Lacendu, Agoparn, and Shivranikka walk over to it.

Mathew turns to the rest of them. “What do you all think? Can we hold off the enemy till they get done?”

There’s a moment of silence before Allen says, “Holding the enemy off isn’t in question, Captain. It’s the part about making sure they can get their work done that’s concerning me. They’ve had time to get someone to another terminal and they’re going to try to block access any way they can for our three.”

“Good point,” Korsaume says. “Maybe we need a new strategy…”

“Like what,” Mathew asks.

She replies, “One of us should go hunting for the other group. The rest of us can stay here and protect them.”

“Great idea,” Mathew exclaims. “Allen, if anyone can do that, it’d be you. I’m putting you in charge of that.”

Allen smiles at Mathew. “I appreciate your faith in me, Captain. I’ll do my best.”

Allen exits the room and makes his way around the corner before they lose sight of him.

Lacendu hacks the main-line computer and is soon looking through the data. She finds an open port and tells Agoparn where to find it. He opens the control panel and sees the wire he needs. He then connects it to his neck and begins searching with Lacendu. Together they come across the files they need and begin working on the equations they need in order to perform the shadow shutdown. They are deep into the system when the battle starts, and Mathew, Rosetta, Korsaume, and Vaskette begin firing.

*****

Allen comes around a corner he is quite familiar with, and he realizes he's not far from the giant room with all the vessels. So far, he hasn't come across any guards, though a worker crossed his path at one point and Allen stole the man's access card, pushed the man into a room and welded the door shut. Now, he begins trying to trace the other crew with the few clues he has, and soon comes around another corner into a corridor where he sees far down at the end the group he's looking for... They're moving quickly and he has an idea which direction they're headed.

He makes his way down the corridor as fast as possible without a sound and follows them to a small room similar to the one he left his crewmates in. Chrinsole is with them, and he gets as close as possible and opens a door to a room right next to the other.

The lights are off inside, and he uses the light on his gun to shine around the room. It's a machine shop, and nearby on a desk is a steam welder. He uses it to drill a hole in the wall between him and the other team.

It is very silent, and he's glad he knows how to use it. Soon, he has access to the last portion of the wall and he grabs a small device he knows is used for sound reinforcement. He disconnects the power cell and reconnects it to a small laser which he uses to noiselessly cut a seamless circle. Finally, he puts a plug to suction the small round piece of wall and pulls on it slightly to allow sound from the room to filter around the piece. Putting his ear up to the cord still connected to the welder and allowing the vibrations to reverberate through the small hole he created, he can hear them talking.

"Can you stop them," Chrinsole asks.

"Of course I can," says Shayley. "They're quick, though. Not to mention the fact that Agoparn has a data-port connected to his brain, so he's going at the speed of thought. I can only go as fast as my fingers will let me."

"We need to change the codes," Chrinsole says. "If I give you my passwords, can you do it?"

"It won't help," Shayley says, rather upset. "They're below the encryption. They're at the programming level. They can bypass passwords with little or no problem at all…"

Chrinsole sounds angry. "Then you'd better come up with something quick. If they shut this place down, it's all over…"

Suddenly, the power goes out in the room, and he can tell Shayley has quit typing.

"What happened?!" Chrinsole is furious.

It's Shayley's voice replying, "They did it. They performed a shadow shutdown."

"You sound as if you're proud of them," Maneesha says.

"Well, it was pretty impressive to watch."

As Allen is listening, he doesn't notice the door to his room opening, and then he feels the air in the hole he made rushing around and realizes they caught on to him.

"Hello," comes a voice through the hole as he hears footsteps enter the door.

Flynn, Reed, and Tex are there at the door, lights on their guns on and aimed at him, and his heart sinks…

Episode 21
To Prevent the Ghost of Future Stars

OPENING:

The debris of the ship was scattered everywhere, and what I saw there was a ghost. It's the ghost of a future not yet born. I've seen this before in dreams, a vessel destroyed by a surrounding force. No one should have to live through that. I would give myself for it, my own life to keep it from happening, but its birth is long over, so I'm stuck here in the present, unable to prevent the ghost of future stars. - Parlin Gray, Captain of the Hemm Freely upon seeing the destruction of a ship he was sent to protect

"We can't hold them off too much longer," Rosetta says. "They've got us on all sides…"

"Makes me wish Allen were here," Korsaume says, sounding just on the edge between upset and sarcastic. "Unfortunately for us, someone sent him off down the hall."

The station's power goes out without warning, the firing stops from both groups, and Rosetta is quick to pull her friends away from the door and close it.

"Great work, you three," Mathew half-whispers; "I take it the shadow shutdown was successful."

Agoparn's voice is heard. "That's correct, Captain," he says.

"What now? They're not going to like us too much." Rosetta sounds pouty.

Korsaume turns the light on her gun on and walks to the back wall. "Let's get out of here." She turns the gun to a lower setting and uses it as a torch to cut a large hole in the wall big enough for everyone to exit through it. When she's done, she kicks the wall and watches it fall back into another room.

"Let's move," Mathew says, and the crew runs out through the hole into a massive room, also without lights. Their footsteps and voices reverberate through the room.

"Where are we," Agoparn asks turning to Lacendu.

"We're in one of the fighter prep rooms…" she responds.

Everyone with a weapon has just turned on the lights on their guns and they are aiming them around the room at numerous fighters. What they soon realize is that there are people in the room as well.

"Um, gang," Vaskette says, putting her arm up on Mathew's shoulder, "Perhaps we should move out of this room…"

"I couldn't agree with you more," Mathew says.

They all take off on a dead run to the right and soon come across stairs up. They take the stairs and keep looking down as the emergency lights suddenly come on and they can see this room looks just like the one they saw a half hour ago through a window.

They reach the top of the stairs, open the door and run down the hall.

"That was great thinking," Agoparn says, drenched with sarcasm. "Let's cut a hole in the back wall…"

"It seemed like a good idea at the time," she responds. "I'm not Allen."

"Great excuse," Vaskette jokes.

"Well, what next," Lacendu says. "We did what we really wanted to do. It should take them at least an hour to get the station back up and running."

"Is that all," Korsaume asks? "I was hoping for more time…"

"All they have to do is reinstall the main system and reset the backup drives. An hour was being a little generous..." Lacendu replies. "I'm sorry, but it was the easiest option we could manage."

"Getting back to what we need to do next," Mathew says, "we need to find Allen. When we find him, we need to come up with some ideas for stopping all those ships they're prepping."

"Then, off we go," says Korsaume. She looks at Lacendu. "Lead the way."

*****

Allen sits strapped to a chair in the middle of a room. The emergency lighting is on, but it doesn't make quite enough light for him to see very well through his blackened eye where Flynn punched him in the face.

Allen had been beaten pretty badly by the other group as punishment for what his friends did. They demanded to know what his and his crew's plans were, but regardless of the pain he was going through as they continued to punch and kick him, he remained silent. Now that he's feeling the full effects of what's been done to him, he's not so sure that was a very good idea.

Chrinsole had to step in and keep them from killing him, and then he had Garmy repair the more sever wounds, but the doctor refused to correct the black eye, or give him anything for the pain.

Now, Allen is staring into the darkened face of Chrinsole as the man makes grand gestures, and he knows he's talking, but he's completely ignoring his captor. His mind is on what he can do next once he gets out of here, and he's making plans for just that…

Suddenly, though, he catches something Chrinsole says, "…we've got your friends cornered, and we're taking them into custody right now…"

"Oh, you are, are you?" Allen asks.

Chrinsole nods.

"Come on, Chrinsole," he says. "I can't hear your head rattle."

The man looks upset, but replies, “Yes, we have your friends cornered and we’re taking them into custody.”

“Why don’t I believe you,” Allen asks.

“It’s true,” Maneesha says. “I just got a call from the guards. Your crewmates were spotted in one of the corridors, and the guards are converging on their location at this very moment.”

Allen tilts his head to the right to look at the floor. “So, what do you want from me?”

“The shadow shut-down your friends performed,” Chrinsole says, “won’t keep us from completing our plans for the Solar Union. The emergency lighting is on and the ship engineers are still working to get ready for the war. In fact, seventy percent of those vessels will be ready within the hour.”

“Did you miss the point where I asked you a question…? What do you want from me?” Allen feels angry.

“I want you to tell me how to defeat your friends. You’re a…”

Allen cracks up laughing; spitting and sputtering and coughing from the pain, but laughing; and says, “You… You…” *cough* “want me to…” More laughter…

“You’re a strategist,” Chrinsole says above the laughter. “I just want some advice on how to deal with them right now so we can end this little charade. I’ll send you and your crewmates away from the station unharmed. I’m tired of you being on my station trying to undermine my plans, and…”

“Is that the best option,” Maneesha asks? “You’re just going to send them away? Why not just invite them to dinner, while you’re at it. Oh, and maybe you could give them the control codes to the station, and…”

“What other option is there, Maneesha,” Chrinsole asks.

“You could kill them…”

Chrinsole screams, “I WON’T DO THAT! I won’t be a party to murder.”

“Yet you’re killing an entire race and trying to destroy the leaders of the Solar Union,” Allen adds.

Chrinsole turns quickly back to Allen with a finger pointed at him and says, "That's different! The Solar Union brought this on themselves! If they'd have done what they promised, we wouldn't even be here now. There wouldn't be an issue."

"That's where you're wrong, Chrinsole," Allen says. "If it wasn't the Agrauves, it'd be someone else. People are always going to find a way to buck the system. It may not have happened at the same time, but someone would have found a reason to try and destroy the Solar Union eventually, just like they'll eventually find a reason to destroy 'Nation.'"

"Why can't I get through to you and your crew? Is it that hard to understand what I'm doing?" Chrinsole asks.

"No, it's not hard at all," Allen replies. "The problem isn't that we don't understand, but that we do… The issue isn't with your reasons; it's your motive that's in question here, Chrinsole."

Chrinsole turns away, his hands clasped behind his back. "My motives are irrelevant if the cause is just…"

"If that's the way you feel, then I have nothing more to say to you," Allen says.

Chrinsole's hands fall to his side, and he balls them up into fists and clinches his teeth. A few hard breaths, he finally says, "Take him to the meeting room. Get him out of my sight!"

*****

"What did you see," Lacendu asks as Korsaume comes back in the door to the room they're hiding in.

"We're surrounded," the weapons expert admits.

"When we were on the Star Expeditioner, Allen used his gun to carve a hole in the floor for us to escape. Do you think you can do that?" Mathew looks around at his crewmates.

"It's a great idea," Korsaume says, "but I'm a little concerned because we don't know the size of any of the rooms around here. If we cut a hole in the floor, the drop might be two meters or more, and we'd kill ourselves doing that."

"What other options are there," Vaskette asks. "I really want to get off this station."

"All we've succeeded in doing is **slowing** 'Nation' down," says Agoparn with a shake of his head. "We really need to **shut** them down."

Rosetta looks upset. "Chrinsole's too stubborn for that," she states.

Mathew grins. "We need to take this fight to Chrinsole himself."

Korsaume smiles back at him. "Agreed, Captain; how do you propose we do that?"

"Is there any way to get ourselves past one of those blockades and make one of them tell us how to find him…"

Korsaume's smile widens. "We could surrender, Sir."

"Are you serious? We never surrender!" Agoparn says.

Mathew and Korsaume peak out the door and see two sets of guards on either side of them up and down the hallway. Their weapons are not aimed, but each guard has full body-armor and they seem to be communicating with each other. The two pull back and Mathew says, "What do the rest of you think?"

Korsaume looks at the rest of them and then back at Mathew. "I believe we should surrender, Sir. Our goal right now is to get to where Chrinsole is, but right now we're surrounded on all sides, and the easiest way would be to let them take us to him."

While the guards are asking them to step out willingly and surrender, the group walks out with their weapons in their outstretched hands as they leave the room to the left and walk toward the guards.

"Stop! Remain where you are," says one of the guards. "The group behind you will remove your weapons."

Guards walk up behind the team and the group willingly gives up their weapons.

"Where will you take us," Mathew asks while Korsaume and Shivranikka walk behind.

"We're going to take you to Chrinsole…"

Vaskette says just barely audible with sarcasm, "Oh, darn."

*****

After the lead guard uses his communications device to get the whereabouts of his commander, the group soon arrives at a fairly large room with a triple-wide doorway. Inside are Chrinsole, Maneesha and her crew, and Allen who is seated in a chair and tied to it.

"Well, it's about time you folks decided to surrender," Chrinsole says with a smile. "I accept your surrender. You will not be harmed…"

"Who said we're surrendering," Mathew says. "We came to get our strategist and shut you down."

"That won't be necessary," says 'Nation's' leader.

"So, you're just going to hand him over to us…" Korsaume asks.

"Well, of course," Chrinsole tells them. "I don't need him. Actually, I've determined you're all just a nuisance. I thought I could change your minds if I had the opportunity to talk with you, but obviously I was wrong."

"Obviously," Lacendu mutters to herself.

Chrinsole hears it and stomps his foot. "Enough with the sarcasm…the criticism… Children have better judgment than the lot of you!"

Rosetta pulls a small hidden gun from her side and aims it at Chrinsole's head, moving closer to him. This, of course, starts a chain reaction of people pulling guns on each other, and within moments, only Mathew's team are without guns aimed at someone besides Chrinsole.

"I'm a bounty huntress," Rosetta says. "I have plenty of kills on my record, and I'm not afraid to use a gun. I'd much rather just shoot you in the head and end this than to let you continue your rant and rave…"

"I'd be concerned," he says, then pauses and adds, "if it weren't for the fact that none of the weapons anyone in this room holds is working." He pulls from his pocket a small box with a button on it. There is a lit green light on it. "As long as this button is down, no weapons will work in here…"

"I don't need a gun," Rosetta says throwing the weapon to the ground. She steps forward and punches him with a right hook.

Chrinsole falls to the floor.

"Take them into custody," he says, spitting and sputtering and pointing.

The guards and Maneesha's team grab Mathew and his crew and hold them. They are then led away through the corridors.

*****

They soon arrive at another large room about as big as a game stadium. There are seats all around the sides in a circular setup with a platform in the center, and the crew is forced to sit down in the lowest set of chairs closest to the floor.

On the platform sit three women; one of them is Dierdre; and two men, and finally Chrinsole comes up from a hole in the floor with Allen and they walk across the four meters to stand in front of them.

Above them, there is a film over a small section of the roof where the star of the planet below shines through illuminating the stadium.

"Well," Chrinsole says, "You're all quite a handful. It's no wonder you've survived on your own for so long. Very resourceful, quick thinking, and extremely knowledgeable… You folks have been allowed to roam too long. We've been keeping our eyes on you since we put you in cells."

"Figures," Lacendu says in a bit of a huff.

Chrinsole smiles at her. "I just can't believe that the eight of you actually thought you would be allowed to run about without our knowledge."

Mathew harrumphs and says, "We could dream, couldn't we?"

Chrinsole ignores him. “The ships are already off with their payloads and are heading out to their destinations prepared for total annihilation of the Solar Union bases in Quadrants One and Two.”

About half the crew sighs loud enough to be heard and Chrinsole adds, “I take it you weren’t expecting us to win.”

Korsaume is the first to speak. “I admit I was expecting that at least one thing we tried would work, but just because ‘Nation’ might win this fight doesn’t mean you’ll win the war. Baitronoc and the Committee may be stopped or even wiped out, but that doesn’t make you right and it sure as heck doesn’t mean you can’t be stopped.”

Chrinsole sounds a bit facetious as he speaks. “Admittedly, I feel a little bit of a buzz right now, knowing that the Solar Union is about to be completely obliterated. Yes, I’m excited about ‘Nation’ being the new power in the Galaxy; but I have no illusions that ‘Nation’ can’t be taken out in one fell swoop. If anyone can do it, it’s the eight of you. You’re not dead, yet, and I’ve no desire to kill you. I’m not completely evil. I’m just one man trying to fight the horrors of a corrupt government; and that, in and of itself, is worth my being right here, right now,” Chrinsole rambles with a smile.

Shivranikka stands up and turns as if to walk out.

“Where are you going,” Chrinsole asks her as a couple of guards from the forty who brought them here stand in her way.

She turns back with a half-frown, thinks for a moment, and then walks around the front of the seats to stand at the bar between the seats and the floor. She stops at the bar, grabs it with both hands and leans lightly over it. “You know, Mister… I was told I was crazy over four hundred years ago. I thought I was going mad, and I was happy to be in that state. After being told I had Siverchan’s disease, I figured someone made it up so they could keep me pacified until they could figure out a way to get rid of me without killing me. I never accepted any of it. I still have a hard time accepting it, but here I am. I still feel the need to be in control of everything and everyone, and nothing you or anyone here can say will make me feel any different. You, sir, have no excuse. You are a child of children who want terribly to get revenge.

"Is that all this whole thing is about? Revenge is such a wholly unreal emotion, and not entirely fulfilling. I know. I've had my revenge on more than a few people. What's to stop you once you've achieved this goal, hmm? What's to keep you from getting revenge on everyone else who's ever done you wrong? You're such an idiot, and to be quite honest with you, I don't want to hear a single other word out of your mouth. Since I know I'm going to have to hear you if I stay here, I've decided to take my leave of you."

She turns and walks up the stairs through the guards.

"Let her go," Chrinsole says with a wave of his hands at a look from the guards.

The men move out of the way as she makes her way out.

"What can she possibly do that we won't be able to stop her?" he asks, mostly to his self. Then, after she is out of earshot, he says to one of the guards, "Michael, take a man with you and keep an eye on her from the monitor room."

"Yes, Sir," a man says, and turns slapping the man next to him on the shoulder and the two walk up the stairs and out a side door.

Mathew shakes his head with a laugh, partly out of disgust, and says, "It's hard to believe you, Chrinsole. We actually thought for a bit about believing you…about going along with you. In some sense of injustice, your way seems right. However, you and I both know what this whole thing is really about. Shivranikka's right. You only want revenge, and anyone who has revenge as an ulterior motive, regardless of the righteousness of his actions, will only head for disaster. It might seem like you'll win this, and you might. Does that mean that because you'll be the dominating force in the Galaxy for a while that everyone should follow you?"

Chrinsole nods to the Captain. "You're right, Mathew. That's why I've already decided what to do with all of you. I'm sending all of you to a small planet about eleven light years from here. It's called Rayne, and it is perfectly habitable. You'll be going in a pod with no internal controls, and when your pod arrives on Rayne, you'll be notified of a place where there is a ship, which will only respond to your commands. The pod is scheduled to take about twenty-one days to get there, and there will be enough food and water for all of you. It is cramped quarters, but it's all we've got.

"I am sad that you'll not join me to be a great part of 'Nation,' but I guess the old adage, 'If you can't beat them, join them,' doesn't seem to be in your repertoire." Then, this to his guards, "Gentlemen, take them away."

Chrinsole turns around and walks back to the stage, stands in the middle and allows the device to lower him below.

Allen's eyes go wide and his face slightly crumples. "That was entertaining."

The guards move around with their guns aimed and ready, and the crew stands up and moves in the direction the three men in front lead them. Allen is pushed from behind by two guards.

Up the stairs, out one of the doors very carefully, and finally through the corridors, Mathew and his crewmates are moved along at a medium pace. They are strangely silent. Lacendu stuffs one of the handhelds down into her pants. None of the guards notice.

As they arrive at the place where the pod is stationed, the door is opened by one of the guards, and another guard steps up to Lacendu. "I'm going to need those handhelds, Madame."

Lacendu's lips move open for a split moment and then close from right to left as she sighs, exasperated. "Fine," she says, shaking her head once at the man. She removes all of the handhelds from her jacket and hands them to the man. "Happy?"

"Not really, Madame," he replies. "In you go…"

The crew moves to get in. Mathew steps aside to allow the rest to get in first. After the last of them are on, he says to the men, "Tell Chrinsole this isn't over." Then, he steps inside and allows them to shut the door.

Mathew is the last to sit down and he looks out the forward window to see the black of space once again. Everyone straps their restraints on.

"What do you think, Captain," Korsaume asks as Rosetta turns her chair to clasp Mathew's left hand with her right.

His chest heaves with a breath. "I think if Chrinsole thinks we're going to let it go at this, he's got another thing coming."

The rest smile, but Mathew's face is stoic.

Moments later, the pod is released. The thrusters kick on and the vacuum behind them can be heard as the pod is shot forward accelerating to about four hundred kilometers per second.

*****

"YOU'RE JOKING!!!" Maneesha yells at Chrinsole.

She and her crew are seated on the sofas in his office. The star of the planet below is on the other side right now, so the internal lighting has taken over and the room is somewhat dull to look at.

Standing up now she continues, her fists balled, "You let them go…?!"

"I didn't **let** them **go**," Chrinsole says, not even looking up at the woman. "I sent them away. They can't control that pod. It's not designed to be controlled, and the thrusters only go one direction until it hits atmosphere."

"You're blowing air out the wrong hole," she retorts in a fury. "You sent the Galaxy's top engineer with them…"

Chrinsole doesn't bother to answer her.

"You really don't get it, do you, Chrinsole. You had the opportunity to just kill them and get it over with and you sent them away. Not only that, but the lead guard has just said that the Captain told them…"

"I was sitting right here when the lead guard told me, so, yes, I heard what Mathew told the lead guard, and I'm not the least bit concerned. By the time Mathew and his crew get back here this station will be a full-on military complex with the best guards in the Galaxy at their posts. This is the new home of the new 'Union.'" Chrinsole doesn't seem to even be bothered by Maneesha's outburst, or explaining himself to her.

"You're so smug you can't even see what's really at stake, here," she says looking flustered.

"If you feel that way, why are you still here?" Chrinsole's words cut her.

"Maybe I should leave," Maneesha says.

Chrinsole agrees. "Maybe you should."

"Fine." She walks toward the door. "Are the rest of you coming," she asks her crewmates.

They all remain seated.

"Really," she says.

A few of them nod their heads.

Shayley says, "I think it's pretty much a consensus. I'm not leaving with you. I've been offered a fantastic job; a great opportunity. I'm not passing it up."

"Same here," says Flynn.

The rest give similar remarks.

"Alright, then," she says, and storms out of the room.

Chrinsole smiles at them.

Garmy adds, "That's why our group will never beat that group you just jettisoned. They at least are willing to follow their captain to the pit of hell and back."

"I wouldn't want to follow Maneesha if she were leading a conga line…" Tex says. "She's brutish and boring…"

"…Not to mention loud and obnoxious," adds Reed.

Chrinsole stands up. "Alright; let's quit bashing poor Maneesha. She's had it rough, and so have the rest of you. I want to let you all know that you are each the heads of your respective divisions. As of now, we begin preparations to make this station what it was meant to be: the headquarters of 'Nation.' You all know your areas where you'll be working, and I want all of you to take the people under you and begin getting this station ready to wrest control of the Solar Union once it's handed to us. Go."

The five remaining members of the group stand up and walk out the door.

Dierdre is seated on one end of one of the sofas in her usual cross-legged fashion. "Good work, Sir. I'm sure things are going to work out just fine, now."

"Was there ever any doubt, Dierdre?"

*****

"You know, Parn; the longer we sit here, the further away we get from that station, and I really want to go back there," Mathew says.

"It doesn't quite work that way, Captain. This thing's maneuvering thrusters don't kick in until it hits atmosphere. People buy these types of escape pods with the destination and length of travel already in mind so that you don't have folks floundering out in space…" Agoparn seems seriously concerned.

Korsaume speaks up, "Isn't there a way to trick the sensors into thinking we've hit atmosphere?"

"Not really," Agoparn replies.

Mathew looks at Lacendu. "I'm assuming you kept at least one of those handhelds, Mathematist…"

Lacendu smirks at him. "Of course, Captain; though I'm not sure you're going to want to touch it. I stuffed it down my pants while we were walking to the pod."

"I don't want it," Mathew replies. "I want you to see if you can hack the computer system on this thing."

"It won't work that way, Captain," Agoparn answers. "This pod receives direct signal from the station of port. Without that signal variance it would be hit and miss. It could take hours and days to find the right signal."

Allen tries, "Lacy, are you still hacked into the station?"

Lacendu raises her eyebrows at him as she stands up and pulls the handheld from her pants, "Of course. I'm not sure what this thing's range is, but if I can get into the station's escape system, I can tell this thing to do whatever I want it to…"

"You can turn on the maneuvering thrusters," asks Vaskette.

"Theoretically," Lacendu responds with a smile at her friend.

"Won't the station know the escape pod is returning?" Rosetta questions.

"Naturally," Mathew says, "but it's not prepared to alert anyone to an incoming escape pod. Escape pods aren't designed to return, and they're not usually regarded as a threat. Once escape pods are gone, they don't come back…"

"This one's going to," Mathew says. "Go ahead and get to work. The sooner you get hooked up to this thing, the sooner we can get back there and stop this madness. I'll be back in a few minutes."

He stands up and walks a few feet away to the lavatory and closes the door.

"I can't wait until this thing is over," says Vaskette. "I'm so tired of running around and fighting everyone and everything."

"To be sure," Allen says, "it's been an insane amount of fun with you folks. When this whole thing does finally end, I'd still like to be your friend."

"Aren't you sweet," Rosetta says with an innocent laugh.

Korsaume glances at Allen and says, "He sure is…"

Lacendu clears her throat looking up at her crewmates. "Alright, if you're not helping, you're hindering. Look around for any panel we can rip off that might lead to a port connection."

In the cramped quarters of the two-room pod they stand up and begin checking the panels on the walls as Mathew exits the lavatory. "What's going on?" he asks.

"We're looking for port access," Rosetta tells him grabbing his hand. "Help me with this panel."

The two use a small piece of metal from a nearby control box to get under the panel and begin pulling it away from the wall. Underneath are numerous wires and Venotronic cards and boxes.

"What exactly are we looking for," Vaskette asks ripping a strip off one side to get her hands under the panel.

Agoparn answers, "It's a small box-like item about three to four inches wide, and is usually blue with red and green markings, and a black label stating, 'Do not touch.'"

"So, don't touch it if we find it," Vaskette comments.

"That's the general idea," he replies.

"I've got something," Allen says, the last to get one of the panels off the wall. "It looks like what you just said, but it's a little smaller than three inches."

"Let me see," Agoparn says walking over to the other. The two men check over the box and see a small device attached to it. "I don't like this, Lacy."

She stands up, still holding on to the handheld and walks over to look between the two men. "Is that a repositioning lead-way?"

"It looks like one," Agoparn replies. "What do we do, now?"

"What's a 'repositioning lead-way,'" Allen asks.

By now, the others have gathered around to see what's going on.

Rosetta answers the question, "It's designed to pick up signals from a single source and redirect them if anyone tries to hack it."

"They thought of everything," Mathew says with the left side of his mouth pulled back. "Please tell me there's something we can do…"

Everyone is silent.

"Come on," he starts, "give me something…"

Agoparn looks at Lacendu. "Well, it is a signal enhancer. Can we hack the RLW?"

Lacendu's eyes are a little wider and she looks around at no one in particular. "Well…" There is a long pause. "Not exactly… If I had a shafting veno, I probably could, but it would require triangulation, and I can't do that in this confined of a space. Makes me wish Shivranikka was still with us."

"I've got an idea," Allen says. "Space is a vacuum, and there's no air resistance, so if we manually start the maneuvering thrusters from each side, we might be able to turn this thing around ourselves."

"We're no match for the onboard computerized maneuvering systems," Lacendu says. "It would take some fast thinking and difficult calculations."

"Can you make the calculations in your head," Mathew asks.

"Of course, but I'm not going to be available to work the thrusters."

"You let us deal with that. You sit down. Each of the rest of us will work a maneuvering thruster. Give us each a number and when you call out a number and time we'll turn our thruster on for that length of time," Mathew says.

"Great idea, Captain," Allen responds. "I knew we made you the leader for some reason."

Lacendu looks a little concerned but says, "We'll give it a shot, Captain."

The crew sets about wresting manual control of all the atmospheric thrusters and soon has the main back thrusters shut down. Within minutes, they are turning the pod around and restarting the main thrusters.

"Captain, we're getting a transmission from a ship not far away," Lacendu says watching the readout on the main panel in the front of the pod. "They've been trying to reach us for several minutes."

Mathew stops what he's doing and walks over to the front of the pod. "Where is the acceptance button on this thing?"

"What… You've never piloted an escape pod," Vaskette asks with a laugh.

He turns to her with a mean smile and says simply, "No…" He turns his head back to the panel still seeing the blinking of the call light. "Ah…here it is…"

He presses it and the caller comes on. "Are you in need of assistance?"

"You have no idea," he replies. "Who am I speaking with…?"

"My name is Sheldon Reegis, Captain of the Mingh Shaoman Register. I'm about four hundred thousand kilometers from your pod and can be there in about ten minutes. Would you like a pickup?"

"Yes," Mathew says. "We'd appreciate that. What is the Mingh Shaoman Register?"

"A Venture Class Star Expeditioner. We're with the Solar Union armada heading for the station around Praimarre," is the answer.

"Captain Sheldon Reegis, we look forward to meeting with you and your crew. Don't mind us that our thrusters will still be heading that direction, too," Mathew replies.

"Understood, Sir. We'll see you soon."

*****

Flynn enters Chrinsole's office to see Shivranikka seated in a chair with her hands tied behind her back and sitting just a few feet from the front of Chrinsole's desk.

"What do you want," Chrinsole asks, sitting on the edge of the desk, obviously interrupted in his discussion with the blonde.

Flynn responds, "There's a Solar Union armada on their way here. Celestial Class, Fighter Class, and several others are all present. It looks like they're ready for full-on war. What are your orders?"

"How many fighters do we still have on the station," Chrinsole asks.

"About forty thousand, Sir…"

"Prepare those ships. How long until the armada arrives," he asks.

"Within an hour and a half, Chrinsole… We can have the ships prepped in about thirty minutes and out there ready for a fight five minutes after that," is Flynn's answer.

Chrinsole's head is bent at the floor, and his eyes move to meet Flynn's. From under his eyebrows, the white under his irises showing, he says, "Then what were you waiting for…?"

"I just wanted to see if you had any contingency plans for a Solar Union armada coming here…" is the reply.

"I counted it as a slim possibility, which is why there are still fighter pilots on this station. Get them on those ships and out into space, Flynn!"

"Alright…alright…Sorry," Flynn says backing away out the door.

As the door closes, and Dierdre; who is seated across from Srulé; clears her throat, Chrinsole continues, "Now, where were we…?"

Shivranikka looks up at him with some semblance of her former smile, which she could hold incessantly only a few days ago, and retorts, "I think you were at the part where you apologize for taking me into custody and ask…no…beg my forgiveness for putting me out so…"

Chrinsole looks hesitantly at her and a laugh creeps up in him. "For an evil despot bent on galactic domination, I must say you've got a fantastic sense of humor. Actually, I was at the part where I tell you that your friends are going to come back here in a matter of days, and when they do I want you to be forthright with them in explaining that my intentions are indeed harmless toward them; as they are toward you… I want them on my side, and I'll do whatever it takes to get them there."

"If your intentions are so harmless, why don't you let me lead 'Nation?' It's what I've always wanted; to be the leader of the Galaxy. I, of course, will have to proclaim myself 'Goddess of the Galaxy,' but I'll let you clean my shoes with a sponge instead of your tongue… See, I can be a nice goddess."

He's not sure whether to laugh at her or smack her, but he does neither. Instead, he stands up from his desk and walks around to the back side, motioning the guard in the corner over to him. "Have Miss Napercolten taken away to the nearby cellblock and hold her in a larger room than before." At this, he looks directly at her, "I don't want her beating herself up again."

"Yes, Sir," the guard says and walks around behind the chair Shivranikka is in and helps her to her feet. "This way, Madame…"

"You're too kind," she says, and neither of the two men is certain who she meant it toward.

*****

About ten minutes later the Mingh Shaoman Register picks up the pod, and Captain Sheldon Reegis greets the crew personally with a handful of his staff.

"I'm Captain Mathew Arnold; this is Huntress Rosetta Firemark, Weapons Expert Korsaume Felder, Mathematician Lacendu Ruric-Trester, Doctor Vaskette Smith, Engineer Agoparn Schroet, and our Strategist, Allen Pendergras."

"It's a pleasure to meet all of you," the other Captain says after shaking hands with each of them in turn. "Welcome aboard my vessel. I assume this pod comes from the station…?"

"You'd be correct in that assumption," says Allen.

"Well, if you're good enough to get expelled from 'Nation,' you must be doing something right," the Captain says to them. "Although, I think you'd all be better off on another vessel than this one."

"Do you have any runners," Korsaume asks. "We'd be more than happy to take one out of here and do a little more personal damage from the inside."

"Now you're talking," Sheldon grins. "I think I might be able to hook you up with one. I don't have it aboard this ship, but there's an Arcgitic Real-helm behind the main fleet, and she has a few hundred fighters and more than a few runners. I've informed the commander of the fleet about your presence and he sounded like he'd heard of you, Captain Arnold. He was asking if you'd be willing to lead a group out."

"Please…just Mathew," comes the reply. "I was a pilot for the Solar Union military forces, and I can't think of anything more I'd like to do than head a flight-fight, but my place is with my crew, so if you'll just see to it that we get the chance to take down the biggest threat to the Solar Union in existence, I think I can be satisfied with the results from that perspective."

Captain Sheldon Reegis seems taken by this short speech and steps back a moment to ponder with his arms folded. His head bobs up and down … not quite a nod. "I believe the Solar Union would be glad to give you that chance, Captain Mathew."

"That's all I ask," Mathew says.

"That's all any of us could ask," Vaskette adds. "We want to go home, and the best way to do that is to end this."

"I couldn't agree with you more," the other Captain replies. "I'll have our ship on the Magistrate Arcgitic Real-helm in a few minutes." He speaks into his ship communicator and says, "Helm, slow us down and inform the Magistrate we're making a short pit stop."

"Understood," comes the response.

*****

It is only a few short minutes later and the Venture Class Star Expeditioner lands in a bay on the massive Magistrate. A short while later, Mathew and his crew exit the ship and greet the commander of the armada, General Maire Res.

"Captain Mathew Arnold," says the General walking up to the crew and shaking hands with him. "I've heard about you and your crew. It's a pleasure to finally meet all of you."

After introductions all around, the General is more than happy to personally walk them to a bay and give them access to a runner after a brief explanation.

The conversation there is mostly palliative and nothing important seems to be forthcoming from the General. Korsaume is treated especially well as a full-fledged member of the CHE.

In just under an hour, the runner is prepared and the crew is on board ready to get under way.

"What's our designation," Mathew asks sitting in the pilot chair, speaking to anyone who can pull it up first.

"The runner's name is Phi Durrange," says Rosetta.

Mathew continues into the communications channel, "Captain Mathew Arnold of the Runner Phi Durrange, prepared for Magistrate escape, awaiting your approval."

"Captain Mathew Arnold, bay doors are opened, phase alert reclined; you are approved for escape. Good luck," says the man on the other end.

"Thank you," Mathew replies as he takes the ship out the escape bay, and this to his crew, "Let's try this one more time…"

The runner's window, as it turns forward to face the station's position, opens to a firefight already started between the 'Nation' ships and Solar Union fighters.

As it seems the runner is headed right toward it, Lacendu says, "Um, we… **are** …planning on going around that, right, Captain?"

"Lieutenant, full shields; steal from all other reserves except life support and propulsion. Prepare for some twists and turns, folks…" Mathew says fairly loud.

"Er, Captain," Allen begins, "I know it's been a while since you've been in a war, and chances are you don't remember the last one you were in, but," breath, "I'm really not all that keen on running headlong into the fray."

"I realize your concerns, but the reason is pretty simple. We stand a better chance of getting there sooner and in tact running through it than we do trying to go around the edges of it. The more ships there are, the less likely we'll be singled out, and I can dodge most of the laser fire…"

"Most…" Vaskette says with concern in her voice.

"Hang on," Mathew says as the runner enters the central firefight. A smile crosses his face. This is his element. He lives for this, and as things get hectic, he soon realizes he has his memories back.

"Captain, we're receiving a call," Rosetta says above the noise of nearby destruction.

"Deal with it," he yells back, "I'm a little busy right now."

Rosetta yells back "It's Captain Ardelle. They got their ship fixed up and they want to know if they can help."

"Heck, yeah," Mathew replies, "Ask them if they can cover our port. There's a lot of ships there right now, thus more fire."

"Got it," she replies and relays the information over the communications channel to the Star Axis C-72.

"Well, at least your girlfriend's alright," Lacendu says with a grin to Agoparn.

"…And I couldn't be happier," he replies from the back of the command deck.

With shots being fired at random everywhere, the Phi Durrange is knocked around quite a bit as they make their way through the biggest portion of the fight. In minutes, the Star Axis C-72 pulls up alongside the runner. Rosetta presses a button to put the call from Captain Ardelle on the speakers.

"Great job, friends. Are you alright the rest of the way," she asks.

"I believe so," Mathew replies. "We greatly appreciate you and your crew's help."

"Not a problem, Captain. We're heading back to help, and letting you go on your way. Good luck to all of you."

"Thank you, Captain Ardelle. We look forward to seeing all of you safe and sound when this fight is over."

"You will," she answers, and the communications line is cut off.

They see the Star Axis pull away and around to face back at the fight.

Mathew leans back just a bit and feels his body relax. "That was pretty intense," he says. "I wasn't expecting it, but just so you're all aware, I just got my memories back…"

"Yay," Lacendu emotes.

Everyone seems in a generally good mood just as the underside of the ship is hit and the entire vessel is shaken.

"What just happened," Mathew yells, "I lost control…"

"We're hit. Helm control is gone…I'm trying to restore," says Agoparn.

"You've got about twenty seconds," Mathew calls back, "or we're going to crash right through the station in about thirty."

"I'm working…I'm working…" Agoparn replies. He stands up and reaches over to a panel ripping it from the wall and looking over some wires. "Bad news, Captain; the wire control is shorted out."

"I'll get one," Korsaume says running past Agoparn while he rips it out of the wall. She makes her way to the room behind the command deck and finds a small device with the correct label and returns.

While she's there, Mathew looks at Allen and says, "Extend battering rams and prepare for collision." Allen obeys immediately. The rams extend forward from the front of the runner, visible to anyone in the front few feet of the command deck.

"Here," Korsaume says handing the box to Agoparn who quickly places it in the old spot and begins plugging the wires back in.

"I hope you've got something," Mathew says. "It's sixteen seconds and counting."

"Oh, we're going to hit the station, Captain, but you've got control," Agoparn answers, sitting down alongside Korsaume and both strapping themselves to the seats.

Mathew grabs the controls and begins trying to slow down the small vessel. Only moments later the runner hits an outer wall of the station and crashes through it into one of the smaller bays.

The sudden slowing pushes everyone inside forward straining the restraints in the chairs. The runner hits the floor at an angle and the rams break off into the floor forcing the runner to crumple slightly as it flips over its top and slides upside-down into the wall where it comes to a halt.

Mathew releases his straps, feeling the effects of tension on his body and falls to the ceiling. He can hear sirens going off in the bay, and the runner's front window is cracking, but not shattered, yet. He moves to the rest to help them out of their restraints and down to the floor.

"We've got to get out of this room," he tells them. "The front window will blow open any moment and we'll be sucked out in the vacuum."

Lacendu is unconscious as Korsaume and Allen help her out of her chair and drag her to the back. Stepping over the doorway, the group moves to the back and Mathew, the last one out, pushes the button to close the door behind them. He turns to see the crack in the front window growing fast, and just as the door shuts tight he hears the vacuum beginning in the command deck."

"Well, we won't be able to use this thing to get off the station…" says Allen, watching Mathew make his way to the back room.

Agoparn is handing out echo suits to the rest of the crew, and Vaskette and Korsaume help get Lacendu into one.

She awakens moments later. "What's going on…?"

Vaskette fills her in.

As the last of the echo suit helmets are strapped on and weapons are handed out to everyone, Mathew informs them, "We go in fast and clean. I want to get in there, find Shivranikka, and stop Chrinsole. Be working on ideas about how to do that as we move. Let's go."

They exit the ship awkwardly, the door out being about six feet up, and they have to help each other get over the lip of the door frame. The gravity on the station is still firm, so they feel a little awkward in their movements as they see the hole they made in the bay opened to space, the star shining in from the back lighting up the far wall with unusual brilliance.

They aren't able to open the nearby door into the station directly as the security system has all doors to the room in lockdown.

"Any suggestions on how to get in," Mathew asks.

"We need to make an enclosure, or get into an already-enclosed room, and then make our way into the main station corridors. All of these bays are equipped with airtight rooms for controllers. There's one on the back wall over there." Allen points to a smallish room about forty meters from their position.

"Lead the way," Mathew says.

They walk across the bay floor to the stairs which lead up to the room. Using some technical conniving, Lacendu is able to break the lock code, and they move aside as the door is thrust open and everything not connected to the walls, ceiling, or floor is pulled out into the bay. Afterwards, they all make their way in and Lacendu finds a way to lock the door back.

"Now, what," Rosetta asks. "None of these hatches leads directly into the station."

"True," Allen says, "but there are panels beneath us which can get us into a room below."

Korsaume and Allen pull a floor plate up and use their weapons to melt the edges of the ceiling tile below.

Mathew jumps down through the grate and lands on the ceiling tile beneath pretty hard. The tile falls through and the air being sucked into the room above actually keeps him from falling to the floor with injury. Instead, he lands fairly softly and rolls with the motion away from the melted metal around the edges of the ceiling tile. Mathew uses his feet to push the hot metal tile aside and calls for them to jump through while he watches for movement in the corridors.

After everyone is down, he turns to Allen. "Use the handheld to find out our location."

"Can we open our suits," he asks. "The handheld is under the echo suit. I didn't think to take it out before we suited up."

"Make it quick," Korsaume says. "We've got company."

Men and women dressed in their blue 'Nation' uniforms arrive on two ends of the hallway. Lacendu hands Allen her gun as he, Agoparn, Korsaume, Mathew, Rosetta, and Vaskette form a circle around her while laying down cover fire as she begins checking the handheld with the downloaded schematics. "Get out of this hallway," Mathew says loudly into the communicator and the crew steps forward into an adjoining corridor while Lacendu looks over the station's layout.

"I've got something, Captain," Lacendu says as the rest of them use the hallway for cover, taking shots at random intervals to keep their enemies guessing.

"What do you have," he asks in return.

"Shivranikka's in a holding cell. We're about three hundred meters away from her."

"Let's move. Korsaume, set your gun to fire at random. Plug a hole through that wall big enough to stuff that gun through at an angle and leave it here. You can take Lacendu's," Mathew orders.

Korsaume follows the instructions quickly and the crew runs down the hallway.

"It won't take them long to figure that one out, Captain" she says.

"We only need a little bit of a head start. Where do we go, Lacy?"

Lacendu looks at the handheld. "Second turn on the right, straight on for a hundred meters, Sir."

As they near their turn there is a blast that hits the floor behind them.

Rosetta says loudly, "That would be our first clue that they figured out our ruse."

They make the turn just as a shot flies past Agoparn's head. He doesn't notice.

As they round the corner they notice some soldiers in 'Nation' uniforms moving into a position and bending to their knees to fire.

"Allen," Korsaume yells, grabbing Lacendu's gun as everyone stops and all but Allen and Korsaume fall to the floor. The first two move up against the wall.

"Knees!" Allen yells back and the two aim their weapons for the men's knees. The shots are fired from both groups, but Allen's and Korsaume's make contact with their destined targets and the men fall to the ground in pain.

"Let's move," Allen yells, and everyone is back on their feet running like mad, jump over the men on the floor and make another corner to the left per Lacendu's instructions just as more shots are fired from behind.

"We should be coming up on Chrinsole's office pretty soon," Lacendu says between panting breaths. "Nikka's cellblock is not far past that."

"We need to set up a barricade," Allen says. "We can't keep running from those men. They'll catch us eventually if we don't make a stand."

"I agree," Mathew says. "Once we hit the cellblock, we'll make our stand."

They come upon a large office door on the left and the cellblock is just to the right down another corridor. They make the corner and stop. Everyone is short of breath.

"We do this here," Mathew says. "Korsaume, take Vaskette, Rosetta, and Parn with you; get Nikka out of her cell." As the four of them move off down the corridor a little more carefully, he turns to the remaining two and asks, "Ideas…?"

Allen moves over to a door and uses his weapon to cut through the metal. With the edges of it still melted, the three of them move it to the edge of the wall and push it out into the side of the hallway, following Allen's lead. The metal begins slowly cooling on the floor and starts to fuse with it.

"This won't hold them off," Lacendu says backing away from the edge of the wall as Mathew gets up against the other wall across from them to see down the corridor and watch for the ones following them.

"So far, so good," Mathew says. "With a little luck, they'll think we've got a better plan than we do…"

"Every time anyone says something like that, I get the warm-fuzzies all over," she retorts.

"It can't be helped," Mathew says. "Use your handheld to get control of the lighting again."

She opens up her suit, grabs her handheld, and links to her "open-door" access to the computer. "I told you earlier I wouldn't be able to pull that trick off again, but I think I can trigger the weapon alarms in Chrinsole's room…make the sensors believe he's in danger."

"That's a great idea," Mathew says. "The more people out in that hallway, the better our chances of confusing them long enough for us to get out of here."

She follows through, and sure enough in a matter of moments, Chrinsole and several guards exit the office only a few meters away. Mathew watches as they enter the corridor, but ducks back behind the edge of the wall before they turn his way.

"What's going on," Chrinsole yells, his voice echoing off the walls.

"They're down that way, Sir," says one of the women. "It's that crew you sent away in an escape pod earlier."

Chrinsole's voice can be heard yelling, "WHAT…?!"

Allen, Lacendu, and Mathew can't help but smile at this.

Just then, they notice that the other four are moving their way with Shivranikka between them.

The eight of them move away from their post at the edge of the adjoining hallway and quietly make their way down the corridor while listening to a few different ideas on what the door on the ground might mean and how it could be a trap.

"Get us out of here," Mathew says to Lacendu, who is already working on an escape route.

"Wow, Captain… Give me a few moments, please. I'm trying," she responds, sounding playfully hurt.

As soon as they are at a spot where they feel their footsteps won't be heard, they break into another run, following instructions from their resident Mathematician.

"How are you feeling," Allen asks of Shivranikka.

"Not bad," she exclaims. "They treated me so gently while you were all on your merry way out of here. What made you decide to return?"

"It's not over, yet," Mathew says. "We've got to stop Chrinsole. The best way to do that is with your help."

"So, you don't love me for my charm, then," she says, "Only for my brain."

"That was all we ever thought about," says Allen.

Shivranikka looks over at him and smiles. "I figured as much."

"Next turn to the left, Captain," Lacendu says. "I hope you don't mind another escape pod."

"Glad to get it," Mathew says. "What do you have in the way of destroying this thing?"

"Gotcha' covered," says Shivranikka. "I already worked that out on the handheld I still had. They never bothered to take it away from me. Guess they figured I was a non-threat."

"We all knew better than that," Allen says. "Why couldn't they have seen it?"

They soon arrive at the escape pod, and Lacendu has already wrested control of it. "This time, I've already got complete control of this one, so maneuvering won't be an issue."

"Good job," Mathew says. "Everyone aboard…"

As they are climbing into the escape pod, Allen turns to allow Shivranikka to enter first, but doesn't see her. "Um, where did Nikka go?"

"What is that girl doing now," Mathew asks in an annoyed voice.

They all hear over their communicators, "Don't worry about me. Get in. Get going. I've already told you I have a plan."

"I hope it includes your survival…" Vaskette says.

"You don't worry your pretty little head about that," the woman replies.

They move to get in, and Mathew is the last, closing the door behind him.

"You'll have to excuse me," she says, "but they've shut down all escape pods. I've locked the door to your escape pod so you can't stop me. There's a manual release mechanism on the outside that will jettison your pod away from here. I've already begun the countdown sequence for the self-destruction of this station. It will be going up in a blaze of glory in about two minutes. You may want to get on the communications channels and inform the armada. I wish you all well."

"Come on," Vaskette says. "You're not planning on going out into space, are you?"

"I'm already at the door. Once I get out there, I'm going to release your pod."

"You could at least take one of our suits," Korsaume says, a tear forming in her eye.

"I won't need it. Even with it on I'd be dead once the station blows."

Everyone is upset, now. "You don't have to do this," Allen says, heart in his throat. "We care about you."

"He's not kidding," Korsaume says.

"I know, Master... That's why I have to do this. I've lived a long time. Having friends like you made the last few months of my life worthwhile… I won't forget you; any of you; as long as I live, which rightly so won't be very long after right now."

They hear through the channel the whooshing sound of air being sucked into space and Shivranikka breathing out hard as the lever is pressed and the pod is released.

As the pod builds up speed the communication's channel is cut off.

Episode 22
The Trappings of Love

OPENING:

The New Union Official e-zine is abuzz with the news of the destruction of the Solar Union's many bases throughout the first two quadrants. As the Solar Committee's death heralds the new age of 'Nation's' life, we can only pause a moment to decide which is better: drop all hope of everything turning out for the best, or go shopping and think happy thoughts. I'm going with the second idea. - Shanune Rhinclaus, Venotronic newscaster, latest transmission

Mathew, Rosetta, Allen, Korsaume, Vaskette, Allen, and Lacendu all sit quietly in the small room of the Star Axis C-72. Captain Ardelle Zysteck sits in a chair at the head of the table, silently watching them.

Finally, she speaks. "Look, I know this is tough on all of you. Shivranikka chose this destiny for herself. She chose to help all of you."

"That doesn't make it any easier," Korsaume responds.

Vaskette seems to be taking it the hardest. Her tears stream down her face, but she makes no sound.

Mathew's covers his mouth with his left hand and rests his elbow on the table.

Everyone remains silent.

"Captain…" The voice comes over the communications line to Captain Ardelle.

"What is it, Lieutenant," she questions.

"The General is on the line. He wants us to dock with the Magistrate, immediately," is the reply.

Ardelle sits quietly for a long moment. Finally, "Inform the General we'll be there shortly and make it happen." She stands up and pushes her chair back a bit. "I'll leave all of you to stew in your sorrow."

A few of them look up at her with some confusion and annoyance at her remark as she exits the room.

*****

Soon, the Star Axis is attached to the Magistrate Arcgitic Real-helm.

Mathew and his crew exit the ship and enter the corridor, lead by a private of the fleet who takes them to a conference room to be debriefed.

After they wait for several minutes, Captain Sheldon Reegis and General Maire Res arrive and take seats.

The General opens the discussion. "Congratulations on a job well done. I've been updated by the Head Keeper of the Solar Union Committee of your exploits and how you all came to be here. It is nothing less than extraordinary."

"Were you also informed of who really ended this," Mathew asks.

"Shivranikka Napercolten," replies the General. "I've been told she was over four hundred years old. I'm not sure I believe it, but if you tell me she was I have no reason to doubt you."

"By the way," says Captain Reegis, "the CHE is commending you all when we get you to one of the military compounds. Baitronoc and most of the Solar Union bases were destroyed, but it seems a few of the Committee members managed to escape to other bases, thanks to your quick explanations when you were on board my vessel for those few minutes."

"Yes," says the General. "We were able to transmit a message to Baitronoc just a few minutes before those mega-mass bombs were dropped, so several thousand people were able to escape."

"What about the Solar Union," Vaskette asks. "How are they planning on rebuilding?"

The General glances at Captain Reegis before responding. "Well, actually, the Solar Union is still at war with much of the 'Nation' fleet, not to mention remnants of the 'Agrauve' fleet. They expect it to last quite a while. The Head Keeper relayed his wish to have all of you join him; help determine the next best course of action for the Solar Union."

There is silence for a moment as the General and Captain both smile at the somber people before them.

"You're heroes," the General merrily says.

Vaskette's face sours. "We've heard that before…"

Captain Reegis thinks for a moment and decides, "Maybe you should all go to the rooms we've prepared for you and rest. We'll be back near your home worlds in about a day or so."

"Thank you," Mathew says. "I think we'll take you up on that offer."

The group stands up after Mathew and follows him out the door. They make their way to Mathew's room with a guard in the lead, and once the guard explains which rooms belong to whom, the group meets in their Captain's room.

Making themselves comfortable in sofas and chairs in the room, they sit quietly for a few minutes.

Korsaume makes the first move. "Alright… We need to get out of this blue and gray we're in and get on with life."

"That's a little hard to do, right now," Vaskette says. "We all need a chance to think."

"It's over, though," Allen adds, "we're all heading back home. A war is still on, but it will end soon enough."

"The real question is, 'who's going to win,'" Rosetta says.

Vaskette inserts, “With any luck, they’ll blow each other up and we’ll have something new to take their places. I’m tired of the fighting.”

“Were you this way before you lost your memory,” asks Agoparn.

“Of course,” states Vaskette… “Did you think that after I got my memories back that I’d be somehow different?”

Agoparn laughs to himself. “The thought did cross my mind.”

“Well, I have no intention of being who I was before,” Mathew says. “With or without my memories, this is my chance to start a new life.” He looks over at Rosetta, reaches his hand across to hers and squeezes it with a smile on his face.

Agoparn stands up. “Well, it’s time for me to go to bed. I’m very sleepy. It’s been a rough couple of days.”

“I couldn’t agree more,” Allen says. “Good night, everyone… See you all tomorrow.”

The remaining crew members stand up except Mathew and Rosetta, and leave the room. Rosetta moves over close to him as he places his left arm around her shoulders and leans his head on hers. They are asleep in moments.

*****

Lacendu sits down on the edge of her bed with the handheld. She pulls a connecting strip from a slot nearby and inserts one end into the handheld’s input. From there, she uses it to load the information about the destination of their first escape pod and its route and sends a telemetric message across space using the ship’s own communications channel to the planet Rayne. Then, she sets the handheld on the nightstand beside the bed and lays back.

“Computer, lights off, please,” she says, and as the lights dim to black her thoughts fade away in blissful sleep.

*****

Eleven hours pass and Mathew and his friends are all seated around a table enjoying a delicious breakfast, laughing and carrying on about all the things that have happened to them in the past few months when the General walks up to the table.

"It's so good to see all of you in such a good mood," he says.

"We really needed that rest," Agoparn says. "I think everything was just a bit overwhelming. It's hard to believe we're actually going home."

The General smiles at them, "I've got something for the young blonde, here."

He gestures to a man walking toward them and Lacendu immediately knows who it is. "Kalchek," she practically shouts it as she jumps up from her chair and runs over to him. The two embrace tightly, and they can see tears in Kalchek's eyes.

A few moments pass and they finally walk over to the table hand-in-hand. "Everyone, I want you to meet my husband, Kalchek Trester."

He shyly waves to them with a big grin on his face. "It's a pleasure to meet all of you. Cendu said you'd all taken very good care of her."

"If it's anything, it's she who took care of us," Vaskette says, a smile hiding something painful inside.

Lacendu looks at Vaskette and says, "We never did tell any of the rest of the crew."

"No, and it's probably a good thing we didn't," the Doctor replies. "Just so you're all aware, Lacy's been pregnant for going on five months."

The rest of the group looks very surprised.

"She's not even showing," Allen says, giving Lacendu the once-over.

Lacendu laughs and looks down at her tummy. "No. Vaskette says all the running around we did is keeping me from gaining regular weight…"

"But…" Vaskette begins, "it's doing well. The baby's growth is almost to the point where Lacy won't have any choice but to show."

Lacendu juts her belly out a bit and pokes herself just above her navel. "Vaskette says it's a girl." She looks up at Kalchek and says, "I want to name her Shivranikka."

Kalchek looks a little shocked. "That's a horrible name with bad connotation… Do you remember the story of Shivranikka Napercolten?"

"Do I," Lacendu says. "Remind me to tell you a story when we get on our way home. We are going back to Segnar, right?"

"Of course, darling… I've informed the school of your return and they look forward to having you on staff again."

She smiles at him and kisses him on the cheek. "You're so sweet!"

Mathew looks up at the General. "So, what's going to happen, now? We cut off the head, but you and I both know that in this case the body won't die. Are there going to be two different organizations trying to run the Galaxy?"

The General speculates, "I hope they're going to try and work out their differences and, I hope, try to reach an understanding to forward peace. The fighting is still going on, but I have a feeling there will be some changes coming soon."

"I hope so," Allen says. "I wouldn't want any more of the same things that brought us here. No one deserves to go through what we've been through."

"Hey," Rosetta sounds a little harsh, but it comes across as more whole-hearted, "It's not all bad…"

"True," Mathew says. "I got a beautiful bounty-huntress out of the deal."

Vaskette argues, "…Though, not everyone can claim a victory… Perspective, I suppose…"

"…And rightfully so," the General says. "I don't expect all of you to feel the same way about everything. The victory the Solar Union claims today is also the underpinnings of oppression for the 'Agrauves.' Hopefully they'll find their place in reconstructing a new and better Union, whether that be the Solar Union, 'Nation,' or some new idea. Whichever way it goes, know that the seven of you helped to make it happen."

A Corporal behind him tapping him on the shoulder stops the General at this point. The man whispers in his ear.

Afterwards, the General looks at the group at the table. "Will you all excuse me? It seems we've reached our destination and they need me on command. Feel free to prepare yourselves for debarkation. I'm glad we could visit." At this, he turns on his heels in military fashion and walks out of the large cafeteria."

"Well," Lacendu says, still gushing with excitement, "I have a surprise for everyone if you're all ready."

The group throws their food trays and cans in the recycler and follows Lacendu and her husband out and down a few corridors to an exit bay.

"Are you leaving us so soon," Agoparn asks.

"Not right away," she responds. "The surprise is inside…"

The doors open at Lacendu's hand image and the group walks in to see a fairly large vessel.

Mathew recognizes it. "It's a Star Field Class Stellar Cruiser," he remarks.

"Yeah…" the blonde-haired woman responds. "It's the ship from Rayne that Chrinsole gave us. He said it would respond to our voice commands, so last night I set up the handheld with the information about the escape pod's destination and sent orders to the ship to come here and park. I approved it through the military on board through data release. It belongs to whoever wants it. I don't need it…"

"We could sell it and make some money…" Agoparn says. "This thing will fetch a pretty nice price."

"Considering most of us are about ten times wealthier than when we left what would we really need more money for…" Mathew asks. "I was just a fighter pilot in the military. I had almost no money whatsoever… Now, I have a card with more than enough money on it for the next twenty years…"

"Do you want it, Captain," Vaskette asks.

He looks over at his girlfriend.

"It's up to you, honey. If you want it, I have no objection."

He looks at all of them with a smile. "I'd love to have it."

"Mind if I hitch a ride," Agoparn asks. "I'd much rather travel home with you guys than on some transport of people I don't know…"

"Me, too," Vaskette adds, "if you two don't mind."

"Not at all," Rosetta replies.

"Anyone else," Mathew asks.

"As much as I'd love to," Lacendu says, "I'm going home with my husband. We have much to catch up on."

Kalchek has a playfully concerned face. "You're not kidding…"

"Well, then, we'd best be leaving," Lacendu says. "I don't want to keep any of you from your destinations."

Vaskette begins weeping almost immediately.

Lacendu releases her husband and grabs Vaskette and holds on tight, tears welling up in her own eyes. The two embrace for several long moments.

Sniffling and trying to stop the tears as the two women release each other, Vaskette says, "I'm sorry, guys. I didn't realize just how much it was going to hurt, knowing I'd be separated from all of you."

"It's quite alright," Allen comments. "I feel the same way, just without all the crying and stuff…"

Korsaume elbows him.

There are soon hugs all around from Lacendu, and handshakes from her husband.

"Bye," Lacendu says, tears rolling down her face. "I'll miss all of you. Look me up on Segnar and let me know how things are going. Use the regular portal venotronics to send me messages and keep me updated."

"Will do," Mathew says. "I'll definitely miss you as well."

She smiles as Kalchek pulls on her and walks her out the door. They don't look back.

"Are you sure you want that ride, Parn," Mathew asks. "Your girlfriend is still on this ship."

"True," he states, "but I'll inform her of where I'm going and why and let her know to come pick me up. I just want to go home and get everything in order. I wouldn't mind going on runs with her in Quadrant Three."

"If you're all ready, I am," Mathew says.

"Let's go, Captain," says Vaskette. "I'm ready to get home."

Agoparn agrees with her.

"Not me," Korsaume states. "I'm with the CHE again, and they'll give me a ship to go back to headquarters and get started on my next assignment. You coming along, Allen?"

"Of course, I am," he answers. "I wouldn't miss it."

"Meet on board in twenty minutes," Mathew says to Agoparn and Vaskette. "We'll begin making preparations at that time."

*****

Mathew arrives at the office of the General of War and rings the buzzer. The two men met once before, long ago; long ago being about five years ago…not long after he first started in the Solar Union military.

He remembers now why he joined. He wanted to prove to his family and friends that he could do something right.

He's learned a few things, being the captain of a small crew. He's learned that he can't do it all himself. He has finally learned that the universe doesn't revolve around him.

Unlike Vaskette's comments earlier, he has changed. He remembers his past, and he knows now that he can be a better person than he once was.

"Enter."

Mathew walks in at the General's command and stands awaiting orders from the man at the desk. The General sits comfortably reading over some reports on a slim-sheet. Finally he looks up at Mathew, smiles, and says, "What can I do for you, Commander?"

Mathew isn't sure how to put it. "I used to be a part of the military's fighting force. I was asked to go elsewhere for a short time, and then forced to Quadrant Four. As such, I feel I have paid my debt to the military, and would like to request an honorary discharge."

The General stands up at this. "You ask quite a bit, Commander Arnold. Your term was nine years. You're the best pilot our fleet ever had. Your commendations speak for themselves, and you're about to receive another with a full honor guard. There's much you would be leaving."

"Not near as much as I'd be getting in the bargain, General Res."

"I will consider your request, but for now, you are free to exit the Magistrate. I understand you have a ship that was given you by Chrinsole. I see no reason for you not to keep it, and am more than happy to give you some time off for a few days. I'll see you back here in three days for the ceremonies."

"Yes, Sir," Mathew says, standing at attention. He turns and walks out of the room when the General says, "Dismissed."

*****

"Is everything in order, Captain," Agoparn asks as Mathew enters the ship's pilot deck.

"Yes," Mathew replies. "Rosetta, prepare the ship for departure. Vaskette, are you ready?"

"Yes, sir," she replies, strapping on the seat restraints. "...Whenever you're ready, Sir."

It is only a matter of minutes before the ship is underway and Agoparn's home world is the first stop.

The ship arrives at Estenhas in only a matter of hours and Mathew lands the ship per the instructions of the station base on the planet.

"...And according to the records, my son, Venzhin Rin Schroet, lives here. I can't wait to get to know him again," Agoparn says as the four of them walk off the ship.

"You didn't tell us you had a son," Vaskette says. "You sly dog…"

"It was a long time ago," he replies. "I was a young man and the woman was young … and beautiful … and we married and had a son. She got bored with me and divorced me. When he got old enough to make the decision for himself, he chose to come live with me. I informed him I was coming home and he said he'd greet me at the station."

The group heads down the ramp and through the door to the main station. It is not very large, and there are very few people. They walk down a small set of stairs and turn a corner to find a young man, about in his late teens, reddish hair, and a soft jaw. The young man smiles at them. "Hi, dad," he says.

Agoparn grins. "Hello, Venzhin. It's good to see you again."

The two men hug for a brief moment.

Afterwards, "So, are these your crewmates on your three-month journey…?"

"Yes…well, some of them. Venzhin, I'd like for you to meet Captain Mathew, Bounty Huntress Rosetta, and Doctor Vaskette." Agoparn introduces them each in turn and the young man is generous and shakes hands with them.

"Will you join my dad and me for some dinner," the young man asks. "There's a great little restaurant here in the station and they serve classic Earth foods like hamburgers and fries…"

"That would be great," Vaskette says, "but we already ate only a short while ago."

Mathew nods to the young man. "We do greatly appreciate your offer, but we're just here to drop off your old man. We've got a couple other stops to make."

Venzhin tilts his head in what seems to be a customary understanding, and says, "Well, then, thank you all for your hospitality, and bringing my dad home safe."

"It was our pleasure," Rosetta says.

Agoparn turns and hugs Vaskette and Rosetta, and then holds his hand out for Mathew to take. Mathew shakes his head and the two men embrace for a moment.

"Captain, it was a pleasure serving under your command. I hope we can do it again sometime and hopefully under better circumstances…" states Agoparn.

"I'm keeping that promise," Mathew says.

Agoparn only smiles as the three turn and walk back up the stairs to board the ship.

Agoparn puts his left arm over his son's shoulders and the two walk away as the dad begins to tell his son a little of what happened to them.

*****

"Where are we going," Allen asks as Korsaume leads him by the hand to a larger bay.

"We've got an appointment to keep," she says. "I have to meet with my commanding officer of the CHE…"

"You mean, General Engall Fremthar," Allen asks, remembering the first time he met the man.

"That's the guy," Korsaume replies. "According to the note I just received, a CHE vessel just arrived on this ship and they want to see me."

The two of them walk into the hangar bay to see a very small ship.

"That's a CHE vessel?" At a nod from his girlfriend, he continues, "I would have thought they would fly something a little bit bigger than that…"

She turns to him, still holding his hand. "Protocol…"

They walk up to the ship and the door opens for them to enter. No one is standing there. They walk up the small set of steps and after they are inside and sit down in the middle of the small ship, the doors close.

"Please fasten your safety harnesses," says a man from the pilot's chair. "We'll be taking off immediately."

At this, the ship lifts into the air noticeably to both of them and exits the ship flying out into open space.

A full hour passes, and several minutes, before the speeding ship arrives at its destination. Allen and Korsaume look out a side window to see the ship: a vessel of the Sharcuran Knights.

After the vessel lands on the main bay, the pilots stand up and enter the small middle room to help the other two remove their safety harnesses. Then, the two of them are escorted off the small ship and into a massive room filled with men and women at attention. In the center of the group is General Fremthar. Allen recognizes the man immediately.

Suddenly, things slow down for Allen and Korsaume. The pilots move off to join the guards at attention and the two walk up to the General.

"Welcome," says General Fremthar. "I have been informed of all you did, and how you were able to stop 'Nation' from completely carrying out its plan."

"We didn't do much," Allen says, but is quickly hushed by Korsaume, and the General completely ignores him.

The General continues, "Sherise Felder, I am here with the Sharcuran Knights to give you a promotion. You are now a full-ranking Taritian Commander with all the rights and privileges thereof."

"Thank you, General," she says, suddenly feeling at ease.

The General looks at Allen. "Who are you?"

"I'm Allen Pendergras. I was a student at…" but he is interrupted.

"I didn't ask where you went to school, Allen Pendergras. Why are you here?"

Korsaume answers, "I dragged him along, General."

"Boyfriend," the General asks, somewhat quieter so that not everyone can hear him. Some do, and they laugh.

"Yes, Sir," she says with pride.

The General moves to stand directly in front of Allen. "I understand you're the best strategist in the Galaxy."

"I was chosen under that impression, General, by the Solar Union Committee. I can make no verification of it," he answers, trying to sound diplomatic and professional.

There is an awkward silence, and then the General laughs. "You might also be one of the most modest. Would you also like to work beside you girlfriend in the CHE?"

He looks over at Korsaume, she nods, and he turns back to the General. "If it means I can be with her, Sir, I would…"

"Fine," the General says. "You are now a member of the Caste of Hierarchical Electorates. Welcome to the CHE, Allen Pendergras…" He holds out his hand, and Allen takes it.

There is no applause, and there is no more attention. The guards and members all are dismissed and the General walks away.

"See," Korsaume says, grabbing her man's collars and pulling him close to her. "That wasn't so difficult, now, was it?"

He grins. "I had no idea if it would even be difficult at all…"

A man nearby clears his throat, letting them know he's still standing there.

"What do you want," Korsaume asks with a bit of a harsh edge in her voice.

The man sounds a bit nervous. "Taritian Sherise, I was asked to take the two of you into another room. Would you both follow me?"

Korsaume looks into Allen's eyes, and then releases his collars. "Shall we?"

"After you," Allen says and allows the woman to follow the young man, and he takes up the rear.

*****

"Who will be here to meet you," Mathew asks.

"Probably no one," Vaskette replies as the three walk off the ship and across the small bay to a double-door.

"You might be surprised," states Rosetta.

The doors open at their approach and they walk out and into a hallway.

"This is where you live," asks Rosetta, almost in surprise.

"It's not much," Vaskette says in what she thinks is agreement, "but it's enough."

"This is rather amazing," says Mathew. "Is this a government-run facility?"

"Yes," Vaskette replies. "It's the biggest government-sponsored medical facility in existence, now that Baitronoc's been destroyed. I work just down the hall."

The three arrive at a door with a window running almost the full length of the door. The lights inside are off.

She opens the door with her handprint, eye-scan, and voice activation, and finally a full body scan. She informs the system of her two guests.

"Computer, lights," Vaskette says as she walks forward a few feet.

As the lights come on, there are people everywhere, and they yell, "Welcome back, Vaskette!" Then, there is applause and some old friends running forward to greet her.

Her face lights up with a big smile, and tears come to her eyes, but she holds them back.

"Greg, Michael, Shanda, Rewan, Legurshmi," she says in order of the five people who are first in line to shake her hand. Quick hugs all around brings Vaskette to introduce the two people she brought in with her.

"This is Mathew Arnold and Rosetta Firemark."

Rewan looks Mathew up and down with a glance and smile. "Well, I can see why you didn't want to be around us…"

"Actually, he's hers," Vaskette replies. "Mathew was the captain of the ship we were on, and my good friend."

"We wanted to see our doctor safe and sound," says Rosetta.

"Won't you stay and enjoy the party," Legurshmi asks.

"We'd love to," Rosetta says, "but we really should get going. We still have a long trip to Shalokeer Raimoore III."

"Wow, that's definitely going to be a long journey. That's what, four hours away on your ship?" asks Michael. "Seriously, hang out for a little. There's plenty of fun to be had right here."

"Speaking of fun," Greg says rather quietly looking directly at Vaskette, "would you join me for a moment?"

"Sure," Vaskette says with a slight curtsey and shy bow of her head.

The two walk off against a corner.

"Hey," he says.

"Hey," she replies.

He clears his throat. "Look, I know we've had our differences in the past, but we get along really well, and, well…"

"I want to go out with you sometime," Vaskette puts in, licking her lips.

Greg grins. "I want you to go out with me. I was thinking maybe in a week there's a big gathering of physicians and the like. We should…" *ahem* "…leave the planet and go to one of the moons for a nice dinner."

"I'd like that," says Vaskette with a shy nod.

"I was thinking, there's this really great place called 'Marrick's.' I haven't been there, yet, but everyone says it's really good…" Greg adds with nervous tension.

Vaskette grabs his hand and walks him back over to the group.

Rosetta sees their hands clasped and nudges Mathew who looks at his girlfriend, sees where her eyes are going, and then looks at Vaskette and Greg.

"Oh," he says. "Um, I think we should get going. There's still a lot to do."

"Thank you, Captain," Vaskette says, "…for everything." She hugs Mathew. "…And you, Rosetta. It was a pleasure to get to know you. I don't think we ever got the chance to just chat."

"It's quite alright," Rosetta says. "I always felt like a fifth wheel anyway... I guess I intentionally tried to steer clear of lengthy conversations with anyone but Mathew..."

"We still couldn't have done it without you," says Vaskette, and then gives the blonde a big hug. Afterwards, "Thanks again...both of you."

"Thank you, Doctor," Mathew says. He and Rosetta turn and walk out, back down the hall, and into the small hangar bay.

"What do you think," Rosetta asks pulling up close to him with her left arm behind his right, hand clasped to his, and her right hand on his shoulder.

"About what...?"

"I feel like everything is falling apart, but I know inside that really we're just going back to the way things were supposed to be..." she replies.

"If things were the way they were supposed to be, according to your theory, the two of us would never have met..." Mathew responds.

"Well ... you know what I mean..." comments Rosetta.

"Yes, and I think I feel a little empty leaving everyone to go their own way. I would love to keep them all and take off on another adventure, but they've got lives to live, and so do we..."

"True," Rosetta says. "So, off to see your sisters'?"

"Absolutely."

*****

Allen and Korsaume arrive in a small conference room with a long table and chairs all around it, but it is on the right side where they are seated on a sofa with plush, comfortable chairs across from it.

The man leading them walks out.

"What do you think is going on," Allen asks.

"Heck if I know," Korsaume replies. "I'd be..."

She is interrupted as the door opens again and Korsaume turns to see her parents walking in. She turns back around feeling her heart sink fast and her face turn red. She whispers, "Oh, frag…"

Clyburn and Ambeedra Felder sit down in the chairs across from the sofa.

"Hello, Sherise," Ambeedra starts off.

"Hey, Mom. Hi, Dad."

There is a long, silent pause.

Finally, Clyburn clears his throat in gesture and says, "We… We were wrong about you."

"Wow…" Korsaume says, sounding with sarcasm and anger mixed. "Is that … is that an apology I hear from my … gasp … dad?"

Ambeedra looks upset. She glances at her husband.

"I guess I deserve that," Clyburn says. "We've treated you pretty unfairly all your life."

Ambeedra glances off to the wall for a second and returns her gaze to her daughter. "We only ever wanted the best for you, Sherise. When Korsaume died, we didn't know how to treat you anymore. We didn't want your sister's death to overshadow the rest of your life."

"Well, it didn't, Mom," Korsaume says. "You and dad overshadowed my life instead. You forced me to try to erase my life so I could be what you wanted me to be. I'm fine being a member of the CHE. I like being my own person. I don't mind striving to be the best where I am. I don't need to be like the two of you…"

"No," Clyburn says in agreement. "No… You don't. You need to be Sherise Felder; whoever that is now…"

Allen looks uncomfortable. "Maybe I should excuse myself and allow the…"

"Shut up," the three of them say together.

Allen seems shocked and completely nervous now. "Alright." He swallows hard.

"I will be myself, Dad. That's all I ever wanted. You two may like protecting Earth from all the horrors that come against it, but I enjoy going on missions; fighting for peace and prosperity throughout our great Galaxy."

"…And you think this man will help you obtain that goal, Sherise," Ambeedra says with sarcasm.

"It's my choice. He's an amazing strategist, and he's proven himself a hundred times over. Besides, he was chosen as the Galaxy's top strategist when this whole thing got started," Korsaume replies.

"That he was," Clyburn says. He stands up and turns his face to Allen. "What about you? Do you think you can bring something to our daughter's life?"

"I 'can' bring something to your daughter's life, Sir. The real question is, 'will I'?" says Allen. "The answer to that question is undoubtedly yes…"

Clyburn stares Allen down. Finally, "Really?"

"Yes, Sir."

Ambeedra stands up next to her husband and holds out her hand toward Allen. Allen stands up and takes it. Neither Clyburn nor his wife smile… Instead, Ambeedra says simply, "Then you have our blessing. I know my daughter will take good care of you. You had better do the same for her…"

As she releases his hand, Clyburn takes it, not giving Allen a chance to say anything more. "If you don't we'll be hunting you down…"

"You don't have to worry about that, Sir. I will."

After releasing Allen's hand, Clyburn places his left hand on the small of his wife's back and the two walk out.

After they're gone, Allen looks at Korsaume. "What was that all about?"

"Welcome to my life…" she says.

"…And your real name is Sherise, which I knew, but Korsaume was a real person?"

"Yes," Korsaume replies. "'Korsaume was my sister. She died when I was young."

"I see." He ponders this for a moment.

"I've lied for so long. It's going to be hard to learn to tell the truth all the time."

"Except, of course, when you're on a mission," Allen says.

"No, I don't have to lie then, either," she replies. "I can work around the truth, but I don't have to lie anymore. They'll put us on assignments together from here on out, so I'll have you to hold me accountable."

"That won't be a problem," Allen says as a smile creeps up on his face.

She leans over to him and kisses him.

*****

Mathew and Rosetta arrive in the Star Field Class Stellar Cruiser on Falgone's fourth largest moon, Shalokeer Raimoore III.

The entire moon is covered in metal, film, and plastic with only a few spots open to the ground. The cruiser arrives and attaches to an extended loft, which holds the ship about four meters over the buildings.

Mathew and Rosetta exit their ship and board the elevator down to the top floor. Then, they get onto a moving conveyer, which takes them about seven kilometers in just under fifteen minutes.

They exit the conveyer and walk through several corridors. Mathew knows right where he's going.

They arrive at a door and Mathew buzzes the door request. They wait several minutes, and he continues to hit the button.

"Do they know you're coming," Rosetta asks.

"No. Not that I'm aware of."

They soon hear voices coming from inside, faint and indistinguishable.

Finally, the door opens and a brown-haired young woman stands there in shock. Then her eyes widen. Finally, her jaw drops. "Zeger…"

Zeger, the violet-haired one, walks over behind her sister and the two just stare.

"Aiya… Zeger…" Mathew gives them something less than a smile.

"Holy… Freaking… Cow…" Aiya says.

"Are you going to invite me in or just stare at me," Mathew asks.

"Come in," Zeger says pushing Aiya with her right arm over to the side and gesturing with her left. "Come in."

The two girls giggle, and then laugh. "BROTHER!" they both say at the same time and jump on him with huge hugs.

"Oh, my gosh," Zeger says backing away only a few inches. "It is so freaking neat to see you again."

Mathew breathes out a quick laugh and retains a smile as he says, "It's neat to see both of you again, too."

Aiya finally backs away from her hug of Mathew and says, "I recognize your friend here. She's the Bounty Huntress who sent us the message that you were alright…"

"Rosetta…" Mathew says. "Her name's Rosetta…"

The blonde steps forward to shake hands with both the sisters. "It's a pleasure to finally meet both of you."

"So," Aiya says to Mathew, looking directly at Rosetta, "you decided to bring her home with you… That's a first."

Zeger, standing with her arms folded, moves slightly to the right to bump Aiya. "Don't mind my sister," Zeger says. "She was certainly not being facetious. Mathew has never brought a woman home with him."

"No, instead he took them on fighter missions and blew people's heads off as a sign of good faith…" Aiya says with a quick giggle.

"A petition for the brown-haired girl," Zeger retorts, her head down close to Aiya's ear. Then, to the other two in the room, "Can we get you anything to drink?"

"I'd love something to drink," Rosetta says pulling up beside her boyfriend and grabbing his right hand in both of hers. "A twenty would be good, if you have one."

"Don't have it," Aiya says, "but Zeger can make a mean Remnaco."

"Are you old enough to be mixing drinks," Mathew calls after Zeger as she walks off.

Zeger waves him off.

"You're all very mean to each other," Rosetta says.

"The effects of being siblings," Aiya says. "Sit! Sit down and tell us all about your fabulous journey. I definitely want to know the part about how you talked a Bounty Huntress into following you home."

*****

Two days pass, and Mathew, Rosetta, Aiya, and Zeger all arrive on the Magistrate Arcgitic Real-Helm via the Stellar Cruiser. There to meet them are Kalchek and Lacendu Ruric-Trester, Vaskette and Greg, Agoparn, his son, ex-wife, and the crew of the Star Axis C-72.

Kalchek, Lacendu, Vaskette, Greg, Agoparn, and Captain Ardelle are off to themselves when Mathew and Rosetta walk over to them leaving Aiya and Zeger to meet some of the other folks on their own, which isn't a problem for the two girls.

"Where's Allen and Korsaume," Rosetta asks, her voice almost a whisper in the openness of the cavernous meeting hall.

"We're still not sure," Vaskette answers. "We haven't been informed of their whereabouts and the ones who would seem the persons to ask aren't very forthcoming with details…"

"The festivities are set for three hours from now, so the two of them have plenty of time…" Agoparn says.

"You know," Lacendu begins, "I didn't realize until I was away from all of you for a few days, but I'm really going to miss not getting to ride around with my crewmates."

"By the way, Captain," Vaskette adds, "this whole ceremony isn't just for us, we found out. There are over four hundred commendations from the Head Keeper being made today…"

"That's quite a bit… He won't have time for all of that," Mathew says.

"It's supposed to be pretty brief, and then the Head Keeper is going to invite the seven of us into a briefing afterwards," Agoparn says.

*****

An hour and a half passes and finally the groups are led to seats in front of the large stage at one end of the room. Thousands of other seats are prepared around the edges of the room and most of the people present are military. Many of the ones awaiting commendations are already seated, and many others are being led to their chairs.

Mathew, Rosetta, Agoparn, Vaskette, and Lacendu are seated on the front row on the right, and on the far right side their friends and family members are seated and given special treatment.

Nearly thirty minutes after they are seated, Korsaume and Allen show up and take their seats with their ex-crewmates. They are greeted with hugs, and after taking their seats make small talk while the remaining thousands of people make their way to seats.

Right on time, a man steps out and quiets the crowd. "Ladies and gentlemen, please give a warm round of applause for our leader, the Head Keeper of the Solar Union, Phillip Dae'Lurgen…"

There is a massive sound of cheering and screaming from everyone around. The cheering and screaming settles and the Head Keeper walks out and stands at the podium until the sound dies down and stops echoing.

"Thank you," he says with a warm smile on his caring face. "You are too kind.

"For years, the Solar Union has been haunted by the 'Agrauves.' We, the Solar Union Committee, tried hard to make sure our word was kept to them, and all that time they felt we had mistreated them.

"Well, the truth is, they were right. We did some things wrong. We didn't pay them in the way we had originally promised them, and now, most of them are dead.

"There are still several thousand men, women, and children on the 'Agrauve' homeworld who have lost their fathers, mothers, brothers, sisters, and other family members to the war that began only a couple of weeks ago.

"Now, we are making a new treaty; one which will include all people, and the 'Agrauves' will be on that list. They will receive the pay our fathers had previously promised them."

There is a thunderous applause. He waits a moment for the room to settle.

"On this day, we stand at the threshold of a new era. Baitronoc has fallen, and much of the Solar Union's bases have been destroyed, but the heart of what we are doing survives. We will hold fast to our principles and pave the way for a brighter future for all humans the Galaxy over.

"There are four hundred twenty-eight men and women sitting before me who helped to fight the war. These men and women accomplished big things. Everyone in this room was a part of the war in some way, no matter how small, but these four hundred twenty-eight did some extraordinary things … went above and beyond.

"In saying this, though, there are eight very special people who did more than was necessary." At this, he motions to Mathew and the others to stand up and turn to face the audience. "Ladies and gentlemen, I present to you Mathew Arnold, Sherise Felder, Lacendu Ruric-Trester, Vaskette Smith, Allen Pendergras, Rosetta Firemark, and Agoparn Schroet."

As he lists off their names, the applause grows and grows and soon everyone in the building is on their feet cheering and screaming.

After the noise dies down and everyone is seated, the Head Keeper continues. "There is one additional person who was not able to make it to this ceremony. We were informed by these fine people that one woman gave her life to save theirs. Her name was Shivranikka Napercolten. Some of you are probably familiar with the old story, and this woman was named after the one in that story.

"According to Mathew and his friends, this Shivranikka was an excellent person with deep convictions and a wonderful smile. Not enough good can be said about her, and I believe the same holds true for these seven as well. We owe a lot to their hard work, and I have requested the honor of meeting with them after this ceremony to discuss ways to improve the Solar Union.

"Who knows…? In a year or so, it may not even be called the Solar Union any longer, but one thing is certain; these folks have seen the inner workings and problems inherent in our society, and I believe they will have some answers on how best to improve our great society.

"However, you're not here to listen to me make over the heroes, or the ones who did so much during this latest war. No, you're here to see some action. You're here to see these people get what they truly deserve."

At this, several men and women line up in front of the stage with small tables holding medals on them.

"I would like to start with the back row and have all of you come forward in single file line to receive your medals of honor."

The last row of men and women stand up and walk to the front in line starting on the right and, after they get their medals, walk around to the left and sit back down in their seats. This row is followed closely by the second from last and moves forward fairly quickly.

Throughout this, there is clapping and cheering from the crowd.

Lastly, the front row with Mathew and his friends are presented with special medals by the Head Keeper himself. Then, they are asked to turn and face the crowd once more while they receive another standing ovation.

*****

"Follow me," says one of the younger military men inviting Mathew and the others through a door in the back and they walk through a corridor to a small office; the office of the Head Keeper.

The ceremony lasted over an hour, and there was a dinner afterwards with toasts and several guest speakers.

Now, the ex-crewmates are seated in the office waiting patiently for the Head Keeper. He arrives without fanfare and sits down behind his desk.

"There were a lot of promises in your speech, Head Keeper," Mathew says. "What do you plan to do now?"

Phillip smiles at them. "You were the ones that helped me think this through. I took you up on your suggestion and had some of the best people under me feed the 'brain' more accurate data. It came up with some new ideas on how to keep things going."

"Really," Vaskette asks. "I would love to know what those were."

He laughs to himself. "You might be surprised... One of its biggest ideas was to have it destroyed. It stated we've relied too heavily on what it answers, and that without completely accurate data it cannot give accurate suggestions."

Korsaume has a look of concern on her face. "Then, what about the Sharcuran Knights? Their job is to protect Earth and the 'brain.'"

"That's true," the Head Keeper admits. "The Sharcuran Knights are interested in doing a little more to protect the Galaxy, not just Earth. I was personally thinking of having them incorporated into the CHE."

"That should go over pretty well," Allen says with sarcasm.

"I didn't say that the transitions the Committee and I have in mind will be easy, but some changes are necessary. We need to grow and change with the times," Phillip replies.

"I take it you brought us in for a reason," Mathew says. "What was that reason?"

"It's pretty simple," he replies. "You were all chosen because you are the best this Galaxy has to offer in your fields. I want to offer you all jobs on the new Council. You'd have top positions and enjoy some higher pay."

The group looks around at each other.

"Even me," Rosetta asks? "I wasn't brought in with these guys originally."

"No… You were not, and the offer does not extend to you. I apologize… I should have been more specific."

Mathew looks at the floor and responds. "I don't really care to, Sir. With all due respect, I'm trying to get out of my nine year contract with the military. I just want to carry on with my life."

The Head Keeper has a saddened look on his face, but he maintains his momentum, looking around at the rest of the group.

"It's not for me," Vaskette adds. "I finally have something good going, and I like being a physician. I don't want to be anything else."

"Same here," comments Lacendu. "I enjoy my teaching career and want to stick with it. Besides, I'm pregnant. I can't be leaving Segnar every time I'm needed for a decision. I have enough decisions to make at home."

"I think all of us feel the same way," says Mathew. "None of us want that pressure all over again. We did our part to free the Solar Union and stop the war. We just want to go back to our lives. We want to live in the freedom we helped to create."

The Head Keeper looks disappointed. "Are you sure I can't change your minds?"

Everyone randomly shakes their heads 'no.'

"Well," he says, gripping his emotions and smiling in spite of how he feels at the moment, "At least you were offered the choice. I don't know what the future holds for our torn Galaxy, but we sure do have a lot of changes ahead. The war between the Solar Union and the 'Agrauves' has been fought and both sides are seeking a peaceful solution, and you are the ones who helped bring that about…"

He stands up and juts his chest with pride. “Thank you all, from my heart, for all you did for us. You helped me see what was wrong with the way things were. We couldn’t have done it without you.”

“Actually, it’s we who should thank you,” Mathew says. “If the Solar Union hadn’t done what they did, we’d still never know the others existed. We’ve made friends on this journey, and learned a lot about ourselves.” He reaches his hand over the desk, the Head Keeper takes it while the rest of the group stands up, and the two men shake hands.

“One last thing,” Mathew says. “Do you think you could get me out of the military?”

Phillip grins. “Are you sure that isn’t the only thing I can do for you…?”

*****

“This is it,” Allen says.

“It sure is,” Korsaume replies. “There’s no turning back, now.”

“Are you sure you won’t let me pilot this thing?”

Korsaume laughs. “What…? And get us killed? I don’t think so…”

“Hey, now, I’ve flown one of these before,” he replies.

“Yes, but not like I’m about to…”

The small shuttle takes off and Allen is soon gripping the seat as it is maneuvered around the edge of a few buildings and off into space from the small moon.

“Go ahead,” she says to him. “Open it up, and quit acting like I’m a bad pilot.”

He opens the small envelope with a sheet of paper in it and unfolds it.

A moment passes, and Korsaume says, “Out loud, please…”

“Oh, right…” he says, and begins reading, “If you’re looking for a friend, the best place to find one is on Kalik Dors. It’s a little out of the way, but you’ll remember me once you find me. I’ll be there waiting for you at the Milli-

King's Ransom. I hope you like classic Chinese food." He turns to his girlfriend. "...Our first assignment?"

She just smiles.

The shuttle flies up toward the planet, and then vectors off to the right around it.

*****

Vaskette arrives at the small bay a few kilometers from her home. She waits patiently for him to arrive. The letter she received instructed her to be here on time. She is only a minute early.

The door to the bay opens moments later and Greg stands in front of her, dressed in a tuxedo, complete with bowtie. His hair is neatly and professionally done. He looks her up and down. She is wearing a forest green gown which goes amazingly well with her deep red hair, and the gown leaves enough of her legs showing that he can't help but look back down to them and notice the shiny red heels.

"You'll have to forgive me," she says a little awkwardly as she notices where his eyes are focused. "I haven't worn heels in a while. Walking in them is a little difficult."

His smile broadens to show teeth, and her heart melts at his face.

"That's alright," he says. "You look lovely. Shall we go?"

She breathes in quickly and affirms.

He takes her by the arm and leads her into the small ship; his ship. However, the two sit in a small room behind the pilot room as a friend of his pilots the ship out and up to one of the moons for a beautiful evening dinner.

*****

Lacendu arrives back on Segnar with her husband, Kalchek.

After a lengthy ride in the back seat of a taxi, it pulls up to their modest home in the suburbs of Shalingdelle, a quarter kilometer from the school.

He places his arm around his wife and uses his free hand to pat her stomach. "You still want to call her Shivranikka?"

"Of course," Lacendu replies. "I can't think of a better way to honor the woman who saved our lives."

"What if it's a boy," he asks.

"I hadn't given it a lot of thought. I'm pretty sure it will be a girl…"

He places his head against hers and the two share a moment before the driver finally says, "Excuse me… Would you like me to drive you around the block?"

"No," says Lacendu. "We were just leaving."

They exit the vehicle and walk to the house. Kalchek unlocks the door and the two walk into their home and sit on a sofa in the living room relaxing and enjoying a long conversation … something they haven't done in a long time.

*****

Agoparn arrives through the connection port on a small runner.

Captain Ardelle is there to greet him. "I'm glad you decided to come along," she says. "I really need a good engineer."

"This thing's been through a lot," Agoparn says. "What you really need is a builder to redo a lot of it…"

She laughs at him, looking around at the hallway. "Yeah, you're probably right. She's got a few scrapes and bruises, but she's still my ship, and she can still fly."

"That's all that really matters," he replies.

She takes him by the arm and the two walk around the ship as she shows him around. When they arrive on the command deck, the navigator turns and looks at his captain. "Sir," he inquires.

"Go ahead, Micken. Take her out." Captain Ardelle leans her head on Agoparn's shoulder. She half-whispers, "I've been waiting for this chance for a long time."

The Star Axis C-72 moves away from the orbital base toward Quadrant 3; Captain Ardelle's, and now Agoparn's, home.

*****

"Well," Mathew asks. "What do you think?"

"I think it's absolutely beautiful," Rosetta says, her hands around his right forearm. "What did you call this planet again?"

"Bienroehaugh. They say it's the second-most beautiful planet in the Galaxy. There are only a handful of ports, and you have to get special permission to land here," he replies.

"So, you called in another favor from the Head Keeper?"

He looks appalled at her. "Of course not… I had to get an old friend of mine who owns some property here to give me permission…"

She laughs at him and looks up at the sky. "Two suns are going to take some getting used to... How long were we staying here?"

"As long as you want," he says. "Heck, we could even get married here, if you want."

The right side of her mouth curls up. "Why, Mathew… You never asked me to…."

She is cut off as he gets down on one knee in the reddish grass and looks up at her, a ring in his left hand that he lifts up to her. "Rosetta Firemark, will you marry me?"

She tackles him to the ground and kisses him. Lying on top of him, she says, "Absolutely!"

He pushes her left arm back behind her with his right and puts the ring on her finger behind her back. The two of them stand up and walk through the open field toward the large ranch home that belongs to Mathew's friend.

Behind them, one of the suns is setting. The other is just passing above, and the orange and red clouds litter the bright blue sky while they walk hand in hand.

Supplemental material, character sheets, and original art by Jeremy Shorter; all in PDF and JPG format; are available for free download at http://members.cox.net/preiso, or you can e-mail Jeremy Shorter at beyondbook@hotmail.com with "Supplemental" in the subject line.

About the Author

Jeremy Shorter was born in Honolulu, Oahu, Hawaii in 1976, and was raised with his only sibling, Sarah, by their parents; Ralph and Sally Shorter; in Florida, Missouri, and Arkansas.

Jeremy graduated from high school in 1994 and currently resides in Arkansas working as an analyst for a worker's compensation insurance company.

He loves to write, read, draw, work on video and audio editing, and is an accomplished musician, singer, and songwriter. He has four albums out of his own, and two with a band he was with in '04-'05. You can check out his and the band's music on myspace.com/jeremyshorter, and myspace.com/41M.

Beyond

www.ingramcontent.com/pod-product-compliance
Lightning Source LLC
Chambersburg PA
CBHW030823310726
48980CB00006B/616/J
* 9 7 8 0 6 1 5 1 5 3 2 7 8 *